W
A ... UNVEILS
HIS MOST SHATTERING
MEGATHRILLER EVER . . .

THE ICARUS AGENDA

"James Bond in his wildest adventures never took this kind of ride. The action, frenzied and shrill, is all over the joint—from the Oval Office to Mexico to the Middle East, California, and the C.I.A."
—New York *Daily News*

"Perhaps more real than we know . . . Ludlum is atop the intrigue-writing heap for good reason. . . . He can choreograph a story. The Oman rescue is as well-crafted as any you are likely to read. And Ludlum does his homework, placing you in foreign streets, encampments, and even in the minds of diabolical conjurers as well as any other writer. . . . Plausible, tightly interwoven."
—*Chicago Sun-Times*

"An eerie ring of authenticity . . . 677 pages of ornate hand-galloping plot."
—*Detroit News*

"Could have come right out of the headlines."
—*John Barkham Reviews*

"Superb, highly enjoyable . . . fast-paced action."
—*Milwaukee Sentinel*

MORE RAVES
FOR ROBERT LUDLUM
THE MODERN MASTER
OF THE SUPERTHRILLER

"MR. LUDLUM STUFFS MORE SURPRISES INTO HIS NOVELS THAN ANY OTHER SIX-PACK OF THRILLER WRITERS COMBINED."
—*The New York Times*

"DON'T EVER BEGIN A LUDLUM NOVEL IF YOU HAVE TO GO TO WORK THE NEXT DAY."
—*Chicago Sun-Times*

"NOBODY IN THE THRILLER TRADE CAN COME UP WITH A MORE PROMISING IDEA THAN LUDLUM."
—*New York* magazine

"LUDLUM KNOWS HOW TO THRILL ARMCHAIR ADVENTURERS."
—*Associated Press*

EXPLOSIVE ACTION FROM ROBERT LUDLUM'S

THE ICARUS AGENDA

"*Get away!*" she shrieked, repeating words she had obviously heard only moments before. "They want to *kill* you!"

The Congressman raced toward the heavy door, grabbing the woman by the arm and propelling her in front of him as the guards opened fire at the empty metal monster surging crazily out of control, veering now into the side of the house toward the sliding glass doors of the veranda. Inside, Evan crashed his shoulder into the door, slamming it shut. That action and the thick steel-reinforced panel of the door saved their lives.

The explosions came like thunderous successive combustions from some massive furnace, shattering windows and walls, firing curtains and drapes and furniture. Out in front of the house the seven guards from the Central Intelligence Agency fell, pierced by shards of glass and metal sent flying by ninety pounds of dynamite lashed to the undercarriage of the automobile's engine. Four were dead, heads and bodies riddled; two were barely alive, blood streaming out of eyes and chests. One, his left hand no more than a bleeding stump, had summoned rage, his weapon on automatic fire as he lurched across the lawn toward the priestly-collared terrorist, who was laughing insanely, his submachine gun spitting fire.

Bantam Books by Robert Ludlum
Ask your bookseller for the books you have missed

THE APOCALYPSE WATCH
THE AQUITAINE PROGRESSION
THE BOURNE IDENTITY
THE BOURNE SUPREMACY
THE BOURNE ULTIMATUM
THE CHANCELLOR MANUSCRIPT
THE CRY OF THE HALIDON
THE GEMINI CONTENDERS
THE HOLCROFT COVENANT
THE ICARUS AGENDA
THE MATARESE CIRCLE
THE MATARESE COUNTDOWN
THE MATLOCK PAPER
THE OSTERMAN WEEKEND
THE PARSIFAL MOSAIC
THE RHINEMANN EXCHANGE
THE ROAD TO GANDOLFO
THE ROAD TO OMAHA
THE SCARLATTI INHERITANCE
THE SCORPIO ILLUSION
TREVAYNE

THE ICARUS AGENDA

Robert Ludlum

NEW YORK · TORONTO · LONDON · SYDNEY · AUCKLAND

For James Robert Ludium
Welcome, friend
Have a great life

This edition contains the complete text of the original hardcover edition.
NOT ONE WORD HAS BEEN OMITTED.

THE ICARUS AGENDA

A Bantam Book / published by arrangement with the author

PUBLISHING HISTORY

Random House hardcover edition published 1988

Bantam export edition / April 1988

Bantam edition / March 1989

ISBN 0-553-27800-2

Published simultaneously in the United States and Canada

Bantam Books are published by Bantam Books, a division of Bantam Doubleday Dell Publishing Group, Inc. Its trademark, consisting of the words "Bantam Books" and the portrayal of a rooster, is Registered in U.S. Patent and Trademark Office and in other countries. Marca Registrada. Bantam Books, 1540 Broadway, New York, New York 10036.

PRINTED IN THE UNITED STATES OF AMERICA

OPM 27

PREFACE

The silhouetted figure in the doorway rushed into the windowless room. He closed the door and quickly made his way in the dark across the black vinyl floor to the brass table lamp on his left. He switched on the light, the low-wattage bulb creating shadows throughout the confined, paneled study. The room was small and confining but not without ornamentation. The objets d'art, however, were neither from antiquity nor from the progressive stages of historical artistry. Instead, they represented the most contemporary equipment of high technology.

The right wall glistened with the reflection of stainless steel, and the quiet whir of a dust-inhibiting, dust-removing air-conditioning unit ensured pristine cleanliness. The owner and sole occupant of this room crossed to a chair in front of a computer-driven word processor and sat down. He turned on a switch; the screen came alive and he typed in a code. Instantly, the bright green letters responded:

Ultra Maximum Secure
No Existing Intercepts
Proceed

The figure hunched over the keyboard, his anxiety at fever pitch, and proceeded to enter his data.

I start this journal now, for the events that follow I believe will alter the course of a nation. A man has come from seemingly nowhere, like an artless messiah without an inkling of his calling or his destiny. He is marked for things beyond his understanding, and if my projections are accurate, this will be a record of his journey. . . . I can only imagine how it began, but I know it began in chaos.

BOOK ONE

1

Masqat, Oman. Southwest Asia
Tuesday, August 10, 6:30 P.M.

The angry waters of the Oman Gulf were a prelude to the storm racing down through the Strait of Hormuz into the Arabian Sea. It was sundown, marked by the strident prayers nasally intoned by bearded muezzins in the minarets of the port city's mosques. The sky was darkening under the black thunderheads that swirled ominously across the lesser darkness of evening like roving behemoths. Blankets of heat lightning sporadically fired the eastern horizon over the Makran Mountains of Turbat, two hundred miles across the sea in Pakistan. To the north, beyond the borders of Afghanistan, a senseless, brutal war continued. To the west an even more senseless war raged, fought by children led to their deaths by the diseased madman in Iran intent on spreading his malignancy. And to the south there was Lebanon, where men killed without compunction, each faction with religious fervor calling the others terrorists when all—without exception—indulged in barbaric terrorism.

The Middle East, especially Southwest Asia, was on fire, and where the fires had previously been repelled, it was no longer. As the waters of the Gulf of Oman furiously churned this early evening and the skies promised a sweep of ravage, the streets of Masqat, the capital of the Sultanate of Oman, matched the approaching storm. The prayers over, the crowds again converged with flaming torches, streaming out of side streets and alleyways, a column of hysterical protest, the target the floodlit iron gates of the American embassy. The façade of pink stucco beyond was patrolled by scruffy long-haired children awkwardly gripping automatic weapons. The trigger meant death, but in their wild-eyed zealotry they could not make the connection with that finality, for they were told there was no such thing as death, no matter what their eyes might tell them. The rewards of martyrdom were everything, the more painful the sacrifice, the more glorious the martyr—the pain of their enemies meant nothing. Blindness! *Madness!*

It was the twenty-second day of this insanity, twenty-one days since the civilized world had been forced once again to accept the dreary fact of incoherent fury. Masqat's fanatical ground swell had burst from nowhere and now was suddenly everywhere, and no one knew why. No one, except the analysts of the darker arts of brushfire insurrections, those men and women who spent their days and nights probing, dissecting, finally perceiving the roots of orchestrated revolt. For the key was "orchestrated." Who? Why? What do they really want and how do we stop them?

Facts: Two hundred forty-seven Americans had been rounded up under guns and taken hostage. Eleven had been killed, their corpses thrown out of the embassy windows, each body accompanied by shattering glass, each death via a different window. Someone had told these children how to emphasize each execution with a jolting surprise. Wagers were excitedly made beyond the iron gates by shrieking maniacal bettors mesmerized by blood. Which window was next? Would the corpse be a man or a woman? How much is your judgment *worth*? How *much*? *Bet!*

Above on the open roof was the luxurious embassy pool behind an Arabic latticework not meant for protection against bullets. It was around that pool that the hostages knelt in rows as wandering groups of killers aimed machine pistols at their heads. Two hundred thirty-six frightened, exhausted Americans awaiting execution.

Madness!

Decisions: Despite well-intentioned Israeli offers, keep them out! This was not Entebbe, and all their expertise notwithstanding, the blood Israel had shed in Lebanon would, in Arab eyes, label any attempt an abomination: the United States had financed terrorists to fight terrorists. Unacceptable. A rapid deployment strike force? Who could scale four stories or drop down from helicopters to the roof and stop the executions when the executioners were only too willing to die as martyrs? A naval blockade with a battalion of marines prepared for an invasion of Oman? Beyond a show of overpowering might, to what purpose? The sultan and his ruling ministers were the last people on earth who wanted this violence at the embassy. The peacefully oriented Royal Police tried to contain the hysteria, but they were no match for the roving wild bands of agitators. Years of quiescence in the city had not prepared them for such chaos; and to recall the Royal Military from the Yemenite borders could lead to unthinkable problems. The armed forces patrolling that festering sanctuary for international killers were as savage as their enemies. Beyond the inevitable fact that with their return to the capital the borders would collapse in carnage, blood would surely flow through the streets of Masqat and the gutters choke with the innocent and the guilty.

Checkmate.

Solutions: Give in to the stated demands? Impossible, and well understood by those responsible though not by their puppets, the children who believed what they chanted, what they screamed. There was no way governments throughout Europe and the Middle East would release over eight thousand terrorists from such organizations as the Brigate Rosse and the PLO, the Baader-Meinhof and the IRA, and scores of their squabbling, sordid offspring. Continue to tolerate the endless coverage, the probing cameras and reams of copy that riveted the world's attention on the publicity-hungry fanatics? Why not? The constant exposure, no doubt, kept additional hostages from being killed, since the executions had been "temporarily suspended" so that the "oppressor nations" could ponder their choices. To end the news coverage would only inflame the wild-eyed seekers of martyrdom. Silence would create the need for shock. Shock was newsworthy and killing was the ultimate shock.

Who?

What?

How?

Who . . . ? That was the essential question whose answer would lead to a solution—a solution that had to be found within five days. The executions had been suspended for a week, and two days had passed, frantically chewed up as the most knowledgeable leaders of the intelligence services from six nations gathered in London. All had arrived on supersonic aircraft within hours of the decision to pool resources, for each knew its own embassy might be next. Somewhere. They had worked without rest for forty-eight hours. Results: Oman remained an enigma. It had been considered a rock of stability in Southwest Asia, a sultanate with educated, enlightened leadership as close to representative government as a divine family of Islam could permit. The rulers were from a privileged household that apparently respected what Allah had given them—not merely as a birthright, but as a responsibility in the last half of the twentieth century.

Conclusions: The insurrection had been externally programmed. No more than twenty of the two-hundred-odd unkempt, shrieking youngsters had been specifically identified as Omanis. Therefore, covert-operations officers with sources in every extremist faction in the Mediterranean-Arabian axis went instantly to work, pulling in contacts, bribing, threatening.

"Who *are* they, Aziz? There's only a spitful from Oman, and most of those are considered retarded. Come on, Aziz. Live like a sultan. Name an outrageous price. *Try* me!"

"*Six* seconds, Mahmet! Six seconds and your right hand is on the floor without a *wrist*! Next goes your left. We're on countdown, *thief.* Give me the information!" *Six, five, four . . . Blood.*

Nothing. Zero. *Madness.*

And then a breakthrough. It came from an ancient muezzin, a holy man whose words and memory were as shaky as his gaunt frame might be in the winds now racing down from Hormuz.

"Do not look where you would logically expect to look. Search elsewhere."

"*Where?*"

"Where grievances are not born of poverty or abandonment. Where Allah has bestowed favor in this world, although perhaps not in the after one."

"Be clearer, please, most revered muezzin."

"Allah does not will such clarification—His will be done. Perhaps He does not take sides—so be it."

"But surely you must have a *reason* for saying what you're saying!"

"As Allah has given me that reason—His will be done."

"How's that again?"

"Quiet rumors heard in the corners of the mosque. Whispers these old ears were meant to hear. I hear so little I should not have heard them had Allah not willed it so."

"There must be more!"

"The whispers speak of those who will benefit from the bloodshed."

"*Who?*"

"No names are spoken of, no men of consequence mentioned."

"Any group or organization? *Please!* A sect, a country, a *people*? The Shiites, the Saudis . . . Iraqi, Irani . . . the *Soviets*?"

"No. Neither believers nor unbelievers are talked of, only 'they.' "

"*They?*"

"That is what I hear whispered in the dark corners of the

mosque, what Allah wants me to hear—may His will be done. Only the word 'they.' "

"Can you identify any of those you *heard*?"

"I am nearly blind, and there is always very little light when these few among so many worshipers speak. I can identify no one. I only know that I must convey what I hear, for it is the will of Allah."

"Why, *muezzin murderris*? Why is it Allah's will?"

"The bloodshed must stop. The Koran says that when blood is spilled and justified by impassioned youth, the passions must be examined, for youth—"

"*Forget* it! We'll send a couple of men back into the mosque with you. Signal us when you hear something!"

"In a month, *ya Shaikh.* I am about to undertake my final pilgrimage to Mecca. You are merely part of my journey. It is the will of—"

"*Goddamnit!*"

"It is your God, *ya Shaikh.* Not mine. Not ours."

2

Washington, D.C.
Wednesday, August 11, 11:50 A.M.

The noonday sun beat down on the capital's pavement; the midsummer's air was still with the oppressive heat. Pedestrians walked with uncomfortable determination, men's collars open, ties loosened. Briefcases and purses hung like deadweights while their owners stood impassively at intersections waiting for the lights to change. Although scores of men and women—by and large servants of the government and therefore of the people—may have had urgent matters on their minds, urgency was difficult to summon in the streets. A torpid blanket had descended over the city, numbing those who ventured outside beyond air-conditioned rooms and offices and automobiles.

A traffic accident had taken place at the corner of Twenty-third Street and Virginia Avenue. It was not major in terms of damage or injury, but it was far from minor where tempers were concerned. A taxi had collided with a government limousine emerging from an underground parking ramp of the State Department. Both drivers—righteous, hot, and fearing their superiors—stood by their vehicles accusing each other, yelling in the blistering heat while awaiting the police who had been summoned by a passing government employee. Within moments the traffic was congested; horns blared and angry shouts came from reluctantly opened windows.

The passenger in the cab climbed impatiently out of the backseat. He was a tall, slender man in his early forties, and seemed out of place in surroundings that included summer suits and neat print dresses and attaché cases. He wore a pair of rumpled khaki trousers, boots and a soiled cotton safari jacket that took the place of a shirt. The effect was that of a man who did not belong in the city, a professional guide, perhaps, who had strayed out of the higher and wilder mountains. Yet his face belied his clothes. It was clean-shaven, his features sharp and clearly defined, his light blue eyes aware, squinting, darting about and assessing the situation as he made his decision. He put his hand on the argumentative driver's shoulder; the man whipped around and the passenger gave him two twenty-dollar bills.

"I have to leave," said the fare.

"Hey, come *on,* mister! You *saw*! That son of a bitch pulled out with no horn, no *nothin'*!"

"I'm sorry. I wouldn't be able to help you. I didn't see or hear anything until the collision."

"Oh, boy! Big John *Q*! He don't see and he don't hear! Don't get *involved,* huh?"

"I'm involved," replied the passenger quietly, taking a third twenty-dollar bill and shoving it into the driver's top jacket pocket. "But not here."

The oddly dressed man dodged through the gathering crowd and started down the block toward Third Street—toward the imposing glass doors of the State Department. He was the only person running on the pavement.

The designated situation room in the underground complex at the Department of State was labeled *OHIO-Four-Zero.* Translated, it meant "Oman, maximum alert." Beyond the metal door rows of computers clacked incessantly, and every now and then a machine—having instantaneously cross-checked with the central data bank—emitted a short high-pitched signal announcing new or previously unreported information. Intense men and women studied the printouts, trying to evaluate what they read.

Nothing. Zero. *Madness!*

Inside that large, energized room was another metal door, smaller than the entrance and with no access to the corridor. It was the office of the senior official in charge of the Masqat crisis; at arm's length was a telephone console with links to every seat of power and every source of information in Washington. The current proprietor was a middle-aged deputy director of Consular Operations, the State Department's little-known arm of covert activities. His name was Frank Swann, and at the moment—a high noon that held no sunlight for him—his head with its prematurely gray hair lay on his folded arms on the top of the desk. He had not had a night's sleep in nearly a week, making do with only such naps as this one.

The console's sharp hum jarred him awake; his right hand shot out. He punched the lighted button and picked up the phone. "*Yes?* . . . What is it?" Swann shook his head and swallowed air, only partially relieved that the caller was his secretary five stories above. He listened, then spoke wearily. "*Who?* Congressman—a *congressman*? The last thing I need is a congressman. How the hell did he get *my* name? . . . Never mind, spare me. Tell him I'm in conference—with God, if you like—or go one better and say with the secretary."

"I've prepared him for something like that. It's why I'm calling from your office. I told him I could only reach you on this phone."

Swann blinked. "That's going some distance for my Praetorian Guard, Ivy-the-terrible. Why so far, Ivy?"

"It's what he said, Frank. And also what I had to write down because I couldn't understand him."

"Let's have both."

"He said his business concerned the problem you're involved with—"

"Nobody *knows* what I'm— Forget it. What else?"

"I wrote it down phonetically. He asked me to say the following: '*Ma efham zain.*' Does that make any sense to you, Frank?"

Stunned, Deputy Director Swann again shook his head, trying to clear his mind further, but needing no further clearance for the visitor five floors above. The unknown congressman had just implied in Arabic that he might be of help. "Get a guard and send him down here," Swann said.

Seven minutes later the door of the office in the underground complex was opened by a marine sergeant. The visitor walked in, nodding to his escort as the guard closed the door. Swann rose from his desk apprehensively. The "congressman" hardly lived up to the image of any member of the House of Representatives he had ever seen—at least in Washington. He was dressed in boots and khakis and a summer hunting jacket that had taken too much abuse from the spattering of campfire frying pans. Was he an ill-timed joke?

"Congressman—?" said the deputy director, his voice trailing off for want of a name as he extended his hand.

"Evan Kendrick, Mr. Swann," replied the visitor, approaching the desk and shaking hands. "I'm the first-term man from Colorado's Ninth District."

"Yes, of course, Colorado's Ninth. I'm sorry I didn't—"

"No apologies are necessary, except perhaps from me—for the way I look. There's no reason for you to know who I am—"

"Let me add something here," interrupted Swann pointedly. "There's also no reason for you to know who *I* am, Congressman."

"I understand that, but it wasn't very difficult. Even newly arrived representatives have access—at least, the secretary I inherited does. I knew where to look over here; I just needed to refine the prospects. Someone in State's Consular Operations—"

"That's *not* a household name, Mr. Kendrick," interrupted Swann again, again with emphasis.

"In my house it was once—briefly. Regardless, I wasn't just looking for a Middle East hand, but an expert in Southwest Arab affairs, someone who knew the language and a dozen dialects fluently. The man I wanted would *have* to be someone like that. . . . You were there, Mr. Swann."

"You've been busy."

"So have you," said the Congressman, nodding his head at the door and the huge outer office with the banks of computers. "I assume you understood my message or else I wouldn't be here."

"Yes," agreed the deputy director. "You said you might be able to help. Is that true?"

"I don't know. I only knew I had to offer."

"*Offer?* On what basis?"

"May I sit down?"

"Please. I'm not trying to be rude, I'm just tired." Kendrick sat down; Swann did the same, looking strangely at the freshman politician. "Go ahead, Congressman. Time's valuable, every minute, and we've been concerned with this 'problem,' as you described it to my secretary, for a few long, hairy weeks. Now, I don't know what you've got to say or whether it's relevant or not, but if it is, I'd like to know why it's taken you so long to get here."

"I hadn't heard anything about the events over in Oman. About what's happened—what's happening."

"That's damn near impossible to believe. Is the Congressman from Colorado's Ninth District spending the House recess at a Benedictine retreat?"

"Not exactly."

"Or is it possible that a new ambitious congressman who speaks some Arabic," went on Swann rapidly, quietly, unpleasantly, "who elaborates on a few cloakroom rumors about a certain section over here and decides to insert himself for a little political mileage down the road? It wouldn't be the first time."

Kendrick sat motionless in the chair, his face without expression, but not his eyes. They were at once observant and angry. "That's offensive," he said.

"I'm easily offended under the circumstances. Eleven of our people have been *killed,* mister, including three *women.* Two hundred thirty-six others are waiting to get their heads blown off! And I ask you if you can really *help* and you tell me you don't *know,* but you have to *offer*! To me that has the sound of a hissing snake, so I watch my step. You walk in here with a language you probably learned making big bucks with some oil company and figure that entitles you to special consideration—maybe you're a 'consultant'; it has a nice ring to it. A freshman pol is suddenly a consultant to the State Department during a national crisis. Whichever way it goes, you win. That'd lift a few hats in Colorado's Ninth District, wouldn't it?"

"I imagine it would if anyone knew about it."

"What?" Once again the deputy director stared at the Congressman, not so much in irritation now but because of something else. Did he *know* him?

"You're under a lot of stress so I won't add to it. But if what you're thinking is a barrier, let's get over it. If you decide I might be of some value to you, the only way I'd agree is with a written guarantee of anonymity, no other way. No one's to know I've been here. I never talked to you or anyone else."

Nonplussed, Swann leaned back in his chair and brought his hand to his chin. "I *do* know you," he said softly.

"We've never met."

"Say what you want to say, Congressman. Start somewhere."

"I'll start eight hours ago," began Kendrick. "I've been riding the Colorado white water into Arizona for almost a month—that's the Benedictine retreat you conjured up for the congressional recess. I passed through Lava Falls and reached a base camp. There were people there, of course, and it was the first time I'd heard a radio in nearly four weeks."

"Four weeks?" repeated Swann. "You've been out of touch all that time? Do you do this sort of thing often?"

"Pretty much every year," answered Kendrick. "It's become kind of a ritual," he added quietly. "I go alone; it's not pertinent."

"Some politician," said the deputy, absently picking up a pencil. "You can forget the world, Congressman, but you still have a constituency."

"No politician," replied Evan Kendrick, permitting himself a slight smile. "And my constituency's an accident, believe me. Anyway, I heard the news and moved as fast as I could. I hired a river plane to fly me to Flagstaff and tried to charter a jet to Washington. It was too late at night, too late to clear a flight plan, so I flew on to Phoenix and caught the earliest plane here. Those in-flight phones are a marvel. I'm afraid I monopolized one, talking to a very experienced secretary and a number of other people. I apologize for the way I look; the airline provided a razor but I didn't want to take the time to go home and change clothes. I'm here, Mr. Swann, and you're the man I want to see. I may be of absolutely no help to you, and I'm sure you'll tell me if I'm not. But to repeat, I had to offer."

While his visitor spoke the deputy had written the name "Kendrick" on the pad in front of him. Actually, he had written it several times, underlining the name. *Kendrick. Kendrick. Kendrick.* "Offer what?" he asked, frowning and looking up at the odd intruder. "*What,* Congressman?"

"Whatever I know about the area and the various factions operating over there. Oman, the Emirates, Bahrain, Qatar—Masqat, Dubai, Abu Dhabi—up to Kuwait and down to Riyadh. I lived in those places. I worked there. I know them very well."

"You lived—*worked*—all over the Southwest map?"

"Yes. I spent eighteen months in Masqat alone. Under contract to the family."

"The sultan?"

"The late sultan; he died two or three years ago, I think. But yes, under contract to him and his ministers. They were a tough group and good. You had to know your business."

"Then you worked for a company," said Swann, making a statement, not asking a question.

"Yes."

"Which one?"

"Mine," answered the new congressman.

"*Yours?*"

"That's right."

The deputy stared at his visitor, then lowered his eyes to the name he had written repeatedly on the pad in front of him. "Good *Lord,*" he said softly. "The Kendrick Group! That's the *connection,* but I didn't *see* it. I haven't heard your name in four or five years—maybe six."

"You were right the first time. Four, to be exact."

"I knew there was *something.* I said so—"

"Yes, you did, but we never met."

"You people built everything from water systems to bridges—racetracks, housing projects, country clubs, airfields—the whole thing."

"We built what we contracted."

"I remember. It was ten or twelve years ago. You were the American wonder boys in the Emirates—and I *do* mean boys. Dozens of you in your twenties and thirties and filled with high tech, piss and vinegar."

"Not all of us were that young—"

"No," interrupted Swann, frowning in thought. "You had a late-blooming secret weapon, an old Israeli, a whiz of an architect. An *Israeli,* for heaven's sake, who could design things in the Islamic style and broke bread with every rich Arab in the neighborhood."

"His name was Emmanuel Weingrass—is Manny Weingrass—and he's from Garden Street in the Bronx in New York. He went to Israel to avoid legal entanglements with his second or third wife. He's close to eighty now and living in Paris. Pretty well, I gather, from his phone calls."

"That's right," said the deputy director. "You sold out to Bechtel or somebody. For thirty or forty million."

"Not to Bechtel. It was Trans-International, and it wasn't thirty or forty, it was twenty-five. They got a bargain and I got out. Everything was fine."

Swann studied Kendrick's face, especially the light blue eyes that held within them circles of enigmatic reserve the longer one stared at them. "No, it wasn't," he said softly, even gently, his hostility gone. "I *do* remember now. There was an accident at one of your sites outside Riyadh—a cave-in when a faulty gas line exploded—more than seventy people were killed, including your partners, all your employees, and some kids."

"Their kids," added Evan quietly. "All of them, all their wives and children. We were celebrating the completion of the third phase. We were all there. The crew, my partners—everyone's wife and child. The whole shell collapsed while they were inside, and Manny and I were outside—putting on some ridiculous clown costumes."

"But there was an investigation that cleared the Kendrick Group completely. The utility firm that serviced the site had installed inferior conduit falsely labeled as certified."

"Essentially, yes."

"That's when you packed it all in, wasn't it?"

"This isn't pertinent," said the Congressman simply. "We're wasting time. Since you know who I am, or at least who I was, is there anything I can do?"

"Do you mind if I ask you a question? I don't think it's a waste of time and I think it *is* pertinent. Clearances are part of the territory and judgments have to be made. I meant what I said before. A lot of people on the Hill continuously try to make political mileage out of us over here."

"What's the question?"

"Why are you a congressman, Mr. Kendrick? With your money and professional reputation, you don't need it. And I can't imagine how you'd benefit, certainly not compared with what you could do in the private sector."

"Do all people seeking elective office do so solely for personal gain?"

"No, of course not." Swann paused, then shook his head. "Sorry, that's too glib. It's a stock answer to a loaded stock question. . . . Yes, Congressman, in my biased opinion, most ambitious men—*and* women—who run for such offices do so because of the exposure, and, if they win, the clout. Combined, it all makes them very marketable. Sorry again, this is a cynic talking. But then I've been in this city for a long time and I see no reason to alter that judgment. And you confuse me. I know where you come from, and I've never heard of Colorado's Ninth District. It sure as hell isn't Denver."

"It's barely on the map," said Kendrick, his voice noncommittal. "It's at the base of the southwest Rockies, doing pretty much its own thing. That's why I built there. It's off the beaten track."

"But why? Why *politics*? Did the boy wonder of the Arab Emirates find a district he could carve out for his own base, a political launching pad maybe?"

"Nothing could have been further from my mind."

"That's a statement, Congressman. Not an answer."

Evan Kendrick was momentarily silent, returning Swann's gaze. Then he shrugged his shoulders. Swann sensed a certain embarrassment. "All right," he said firmly. "Let's call it an aberration that won't happen again. There was a vacuous, overbearing incumbent who was lining his pockets in a district that wasn't paying attention. I had time on my hands and a big mouth. I also had the money to bury him. I'm not necessarily proud of what I did or how I did it, but he's gone and I'll be out in two years or less. By then I'll have found someone better qualified to take my place."

"*Two* years?" asked Swann. "Come November it'll be a year since your election, correct?"

"That's right."

"And you started serving last January?"

"So?"

"Well, I hate to disabuse you, but your term of *office* is for two years. You've either got one more year or *three,* but not two or less."

"There's no real opposition party in the Ninth, but to make sure the seat doesn't go to the old political machine, I agreed to stand for reelection—then resign."

"That's some agreement."

"It's binding as far as I'm concerned. I want out."

"That's blunt enough, but it doesn't take into account a possible side effect."

"I don't understand you."

"Suppose during the next twenty-odd months you decide you like it here? What happens then?"

"It's not possible and it couldn't happen, Mr. Swann. Let's get back to Masqat. It's a goddamned mess, or do I have sufficient 'clearance' to make that observation?"

"You're cleared because I'm the one who clears." The deputy director shook his gray head. "A goddamned mess, Congressman, and we're convinced it's externally programmed."

"I don't think there's any question about it," agreed Kendrick.

"Do you have any ideas?"

"A few," answered the visitor. "Wholesale destabilization's at the top of the list. Shut the country down and don't let anyone in."

"A takeover?" asked Swann. "A Khomeini-style putsch? . . . It wouldn't work; the situation's different. There's no Peacock, no festering resentments, no SAVAK." Swann paused, adding pensively, "No Shah with an army of thieves and no Ayatollah with an army of fanatics. It's not the same."

"I didn't mean to imply that it was. Oman's only the beginning. Whoever it is doesn't want to take over the country; he—or they—simply want to stop others from taking the money."

"*What?* What money?"

"Billions. Long-range projects that are on drafting boards everywhere in the Persian Gulf, Saudi Arabia, and all of Southwest Asia, the only areas in that part of the world that can be relatively stabilized because even hostile governments demand it. What's happening over in Oman now isn't much different from tying up the transport and the construction trades over here, or shutting down the piers in New York and New Orleans, Los Angeles and San Francisco. Nothing's legitimized by strikes or collective bargaining—there's just terror and the threats of more terror provided by whipped-up fanatics. And everything stops. The people over the drafting boards and those in the field on surveying teams and in equipment compounds just want to get out as fast as they can."

"And once they're out," added Swann quickly, "those behind the terrorists move in and the terror stops. It just goes away. *Christ,* it sounds like a waterfront *Mafia* operation!"

"Arabic style," said Kendrick. "To use your words, it wouldn't be the first time."

"You know that for a fact?"

"Yes. Our company was threatened a number of times, but to quote you again, we had a secret weapon. Emmanuel Weingrass."

"*Weingrass?* What the hell could *he* do?"

"Lie with extraordinary conviction. One moment he was a reserve general in the Israeli army who could call an air strike on any Arab group who harassed us or replaced us, and the next, he was a high-ranking member of the Mossad who would send out death squads eliminating even those who warned us. Like many aging men of genius, Manny was frequently eccentric and almost always theatrical. He enjoyed himself. Unfortunately, his various wives rarely enjoyed *him* for very long. At any rate, no one wanted to tangle with a crazy Israeli. The tactics were too familiar."

"Are you suggesting we recruit him?" asked the deputy director.

"No. Outside of his age, he's winding up his life in Paris with the most beautiful women he can hire and certainly with the most expensive brandy he can find. He couldn't help. . . . But there's something you *can* do."

"What's that?"

"Listen to me." Kendrick leaned forward. "I've been thinking about this for the past eight hours and with every hour I'm more convinced it's a possible explanation. The problem is that there are so few facts—almost none, really—but a pattern's there, and it's consistent with things we heard four years ago."

"What things? What pattern?"

"Only rumors to begin with, then came the threats and they *were* threats. No one was kidding."

"Go on. I'm listening."

"While defusing those threats in his own way, usually with prohibited whisky, Weingrass heard something that made too much sense to be dismissed as drunken babbling. He was told that a consortium was silently being formed—an industrial cartel, if you like. It was quietly gaining control of dozens of different companies with growing resources in personnel, technology and equipment. The objective was obvious then, and if the information's accurate, even more obvious now. They intend to take over the industrial development of Southwest Asia. As far as Weingrass could learn, this underground federation was based in Bahrain—nothing surprising there—but what came as a shocker and amused the hell out of Manny was the fact that among the unknown board of directors was a man who called himself the 'Mahdi'—like the Muslim fanatic who threw the British out of Khartoum a hundred years ago."

"The Mahdi? *Khartoum?*"

"Exactly. The symbol's obvious. Except that this new Mahdi doesn't give a damn about religious Islam, much less its screaming fanatics. He's using them to drive the competition out and keep it out. He wants the contracts and the profits in Arab hands—specifically *his* hands."

"*Wait* a minute," Swann interrupted thoughtfully as he picked up his phone and touched a button on the console. "This ties in with something that came from MI-Six in Masqat last night," he continued quickly, looking at Kendrick. "We couldn't follow it up because there wasn't anything to follow, no trail, but it sure as hell made wild reading. . . . Get me Gerald Bryce, please. . . . Hello, Gerry? Last night—actually around two o'clock this morning—we got a nothing-zero from the Brits in Ohio. I want you to find it and read it to me slowly because I'll be writing down every word." The deputy covered the mouthpiece and spoke to his suddenly alert visitor. "If anything you've said makes any sense at all, it may be the first concrete breakthrough we've had."

"That's why I'm here, Mr. Swann, probably reeking of smoked fish."

The deputy director nodded aimlessly, impatiently, waiting for the man he had called Bryce to return to the phone. "A shower wouldn't hurt, Congressman. . . . *Yes,* Gerry, go ahead! . . . 'Do not look where you would logically expect to look. Search elsewhere.' Yes, I've got that. I remember that. It was right after, I think . . . 'Where grievances are not born of poverty or abandonment.' *That's* it! And something else, right around there . . . 'Where Allah has bestowed favor in this world, although perhaps not in the after one.' . . . *Yes.* Now go down a bit, something about whispers, that's all I remember. . . . *There!* That's it. Give it to me again. . . . 'The whispers speak of those who will benefit from the bloodshed.' Okay, Gerry, that's what I needed. The rest was all negative, if I recall. No names, no organizations, just crap. . . . That's what I thought. . . . I don't know yet. If anything breaks, you'll be the first to know. In the meantime, oil up the equipment and work on a printout of all the construction firms in Bahrain. And if there's a listing for what we call general or industrial contractors, I want that, too. . . . When? Yesterday, for God's sake!" Swann hung up the phone, looked down at the phrases he had written, and then up at Kendrick. "You heard the words, Congressman. Do you want me to repeat them?"

"It's not necessary. They're not *kalam-faregh,* are they?"

"No, Mr. Kendrick, none of it's garbage. It's all very pertinent and I wish to hell I knew what to do."

"Recruit me, Mr. Swann," said the Congressman. "Send me to Masqat on the fastest transport you can find."

"Why?" asked the deputy, studying his visitor. "What can you do that our own experienced men in the field can't? They not only speak fluent Arabic, most of them are Arabs."

"And working for Consular Operations," completed Kendrick.

you imagine what it's like *inside*? Lined up against a wall under floodlights and all around you everything's being blasted with bullets, thinking, *Jesus,* I'm going to be killed any *second*! If we ever get those poor souls out, they'll be on couches for years trying to get rid of the nightmares!"

Kendrick let the emotion of the moment pass. "Those hot-heads don't have an arsenal in there, Mr. Swann. I don't think the people running them would allow it. They're *supplied.* Just as the mimeograph machines are supplied because they don't know how to operate your copiers and word processors for the daily bulletins they print for the television cameras. Please try to understand. Maybe one in twenty of those crazies has a minimum intellect, much less a thought-out ideological position. They're the manipulated dregs of humanity given their own hysterical moments in the sun. Maybe it's our fault, I don't know, but I *do* know they're being programmed, and you know it, too. And behind that programming is a man who wants all of Southwest Asia to himself."

"This *Mahdi*?"

"Whoever he is, yes."

"You think you can find him?"

"I'll need help. Getting out of the airport, Arab clothes; I'll make a list."

The deputy director again leaned back in his chair, his fingers touching his chin. "*Why,* Congressman? Why do you want to do this? Why does Evan Kendrick, multimillionaire-entrepreneur want to put his very rich life on the line? There's nothing left for you over there. *Why?*"

"I suppose the simplest and most honest answer is that I might be able to help. As you've pointed out, I made a lot of money over there. Maybe this is the time to give a little of myself back."

"If it was just money or 'a little' of yourself, I'd have no trouble with that," said Swann. "But if I let you go, you'll be walking into a minefield with no training on how to survive. Has that thought struck you, Congressman? It should have."

"I don't intend to storm the embassy," answered Evan Kendrick.

"You might not have to. Just ask the wrong person the wrong question and the results could be the same."

"I could also be in a cab at Twenty-third Street and Virginia Avenue at noontime today and be in an accident."

"I presume that means you were."

"The point is I wasn't driving. I was in a taxi. I'm careful, Mr. Swann, and in Masqat I know my way around the traffic, which isn't as unpredictable as Washington's."

"Were you ever in the service?"

"No."

"You were the right age for Vietnam, I'd guess. Any explanation?"

"I had a graduate school deferment. It kept me out."

"Have you ever handled a gun?"

"I've had limited experience."

"Which means you know where the trigger is and which end to point."

"I said limited, not imbecilic. During the early days in the Emirates, we kept ourselves armed at our construction sites. Sometimes later also."

"Ever had to fire one?" pressed the deputy director.

"Certainly," replied Kendrick, his voice calm, not rising to the bait. "So I could learn where the trigger was and which end to point."

"Very funny, but what I meant was did you ever have to fire a gun at another human being?"

"Is this necessary?"

"Yes, it is. I have to make a judgment."

"All right, then yes, I did."

"When was that?"

"When were they," corrected the Congressman. "Among my partners and our American crew was a geologist, an equipment-logistics man and several refugees from the Army Corps of Engineers—foreman types. We made frequent trips to potential sites for soil and shale testings and to set up fenced compounds for machinery. We drove a camper, and on several occasions we were attacked by bandits—wandering nomad gangs looking for strays. They've been a problem for years, and the authorities warn everyone heading into the interior to protect themselves. Not much different from any large city over here. I used a gun then."

"To frighten or to kill, Mr. Kendrick?"

"By and large to frighten, Mr. Swann. However, there were times when we had to kill. They wanted to kill us. We reported all such incidents to the authorities."

"I see," said the deputy director of Consular Operations. "What kind of shape are you in?"

The visitor shook his head in exasperation. "I smoke an occasional cigar or a cigarette after a meal, *Doctor,* and I drink moderately. I do not, however, lift weights or run in marathons. However, again, I do ride Class Five white water and backpack in the mountains whenever I can. I also think this is a bunch of bullshit."

"Think what you like, Mr. Kendrick, but we're pressed for time. Simple, direct questions can help us assess a person just as accurately as a convoluted psychiatric report from one of our clinics in Virginia."

"Blame that on the psychiatrists."

"Tell me about it," said Swann, with a hostile chuckle.

"No, you tell *me,* " countered the visitor. "Your show-and-tell games are over. Do I go or don't I, and if not, *why* not?"

Swann looked up. "You go, Congressman. Not because you're an ideal choice but because I don't *have* a choice. I'll try anything, including an arrogant son of a bitch, which, under that cool exterior, I think you probably are."

"You're probably right," said Kendrick. "Can you give me briefing papers on whatever you've got?"

"They'll be delivered to the plane before takeoff at Andrews Air Force Base. But they can't leave that plane, Congressman, and you can't make any notes. Someone will be watching you."

"Understood."

"Are you sure? We'll give you whatever deep-cover help we can under severe restrictions, but you're a private citizen acting on your own, your political position notwithstanding. In short words, if you're taken by hostile elements, we don't know you. We can't help you then. We won't risk the lives of two hundred thirty-six hostages. Is *that* understood?"

"Yes, it is, because it's directly in line with what I made clear when I walked in here. I want a written guarantee of anonymity. I was never here. I never saw you, and I never talked to you. Send a memo up to the Secretary of State. Say you had a phone call from a political ally of mine in Colorado mentioning my name and telling you that with my background you should get in touch with me. You rejected the approach, believing it was just another politician trying to make mileage out of the State Department—that shouldn't be difficult for you." Kendrick pulled out a notepad from his jacket pocket and reached over, picking up Swann's pencil. "Here's the address of my attorney in Washington. Have a copy delivered to him by messenger before I get on the plane at Andrews. When he tells me it's there, I'll get on board."

"Our mutual objective here is so clear and so clean I should be congratulating myself," said Swann. "So why don't I? Why do I keep thinking there's something you're not telling me?"

"Because you're suspicious by nature and profession. You wouldn't be in that chair if you weren't."

"This secrecy you're so insistent on—"

"Apparently so are you," Kendrick broke in.

"I've given you my reason. There are two hundred thirty-six people out there. We're not about to give anyone an excuse to pull a trigger. You, on the other hand, if you don't get killed, have a lot to gain. What's *your* reason for this secrecy?"

"Not much different from yours," said the visitor. "I made a great many friends throughout the whole area. I've kept up with a lot of them; we correspond; they visit me frequently—our associations are no secret. If my name surfaced, some zealots might consider *jaremat thaár.*"

"Penalty for friendship," translated Swann.

"The climate's right for it," added Kendrick.

"I suppose that's good enough," said the deputy director without much conviction. "When do you want to leave?"

"As soon as possible. There's nothing to straighten out here. I'll grab a cab, go home and change clothes—"

"No cabs, Congressman. From here on until you get to Masqat you're listed as a government liaison under an available cover and flying military transport. You're under wraps." Swann reached for his phone. "You'll be escorted down to the ramp where an unmarked car will drive you home and then on to Andrews. For the next twelve hours you're government property, and you'll do what we tell you to do."

Evan Kendrick sat in the backseat of the unmarked State Department car staring out the window at the lush foliage along the Potomac. Soon the driver would veer to the left and enter a long wooded corridor of Virginia greenery five minutes from his house. His isolated house, he reflected, his very lonely house, despite a live-in couple who were old friends and the discreet, though not excessive, procession of graceful women who shared his bed, also friends.

Four years and nothing permanent. Permanency for him was half a world away where nothing was permanent but the constant necessity of moving from one job to the next, finding the best quarters available for everyone, and making sure that tutors were available for his partners' children—children he wished at times were his; specific children, of course. But for him there had never been time for marriage and children; ideas were his wives, projects his offspring. Perhaps this was why he had been the leader; he had no domestic distractions. The women he made love to were mostly driven like himself. Again, like himself, they sought the temporary exhilaration, even the comfort, of brief affairs, but the operative word was 'temporary.' And then in those wonderful years there was the excitement and the laughter, the hours of fear and the moments of elation when a project's results exceeded their expectations. They were building an empire—a small one, to be sure—but it would grow, and in time, as Weingrass insisted, the children of the Kendrick Group would go to the best schools in Switzerland, only a few hours away by air. "They'll become a boardroom of international menschen!" Manny had roared. "All that fine education and all those languages. We're rearing the greatest collection of statesmen and stateswomen since Disraeli and Golda!"

"Uncle Manny, can we go fishing?" a young spokesman would invariably implore, wide-eyed conspirators behind him.

"Of course, David—such a glorious name. The river is only a few kilometers away. We'll all catch *whales,* I *promise* you!"

"Manny, *please,*" one of the mothers would invariably object. "Their homework."

"That work is for *home*—study your syntax. Whales are in the *river*!"

All that was permanence for Evan Kendrick. And suddenly it had all been shattered, a thousand broken mirrors in the sunlight, each fragment of bloody glass reflecting an image of lovely reality and wondrous expectations. All the mirrors had turned black, no reflections anywhere. Death.

"Don't do it!" screamed Emmanuel Weingrass. "I feel the pain as much as you. But don't you see, it's what they want you to do, expect you to do! Don't give them—don't give him*—that gratification! Fight them, fight* him*! I will fight with you. Show me your posture, boy!"*

"For whom, Manny? Against whom?"

"You know as well as I do! We're only the first; others will follow. Other 'accidents,' loved ones killed, projects abandoned. You will allow that?"

"I simply don't care."

"So you let him win?"

"Who?"

"The Mahdi!"

"A drunken rumor, nothing more."

"He did it! He killed them! I know it!"

"There's nothing here for me, old friend, and I can't chase shadows. There's no fun any longer. Forget it, Manny, I'll make you rich."

"I don't want your coward money!"

"You won't take it?"

"Of course I'll take it. I simply don't love you anymore."

Then four years of anxiety, futility and boredom, wondering when the warm wind of love or the cold wind of hate would blow across the smoldering coals inside him. He had told himself over and over again that when the fires suddenly erupted, for whatever reason, the time would be right and he would be ready. He was ready now and no one could stop him. Hate.

The Mahdi.

You took the lives of my closest friends as surely as if you had installed that conduit yourself. I had to identify so many bodies—the broken, twisted, bleeding bodies of the people who meant so much to me. The hatred remains, and it's deep and cold and won't go away and let me live my life until you're dead. I have to go back and pick up the pieces, be my own self again and finish what all of us were building together. Manny was right. I ran away, forgiving myself because of the pain, forgetting the dreams we had. I'll go back and finish now. I'm coming after you, Mahdi, whoever you are, wherever you are. And no one will know I was there.

"Sir? Sir, we're here."

"I beg your pardon?"

"This is your house," said the marine driver. "I guess you were catching a nap, but we have a schedule to keep."

"No nap, Corporal, but, of course, you're right." Kendrick gripped the handle and opened the door. "I'll only be twenty minutes or so. . . . Why don't you come in? The maid'll get you a snack or a cup of coffee while you wait."

"I wouldn't get out of this car, sir."

"Why not?"

"You're with OHIO. I'd probably get shot."

Stunned, and halfway out of the door, Evan Kendrick turned and looked behind him. At the end of the street, the deserted tree-lined street without a house in sight, a lone car was parked at the curb. Inside, two figures sat motionless in the front seat.

For the next twelve hours you're government property, and you'll do what we tell you to do.

* * *

The silhouetted figure walked rapidly into the windowless sterile room, closed the door, and in the darkness continued to the table where there was the small brass lamp. He turned it on and went directly to his equipment that covered the right wall. He sat down in front of the processor, touched the switch that brought the screen to life, and typed in the code.

Ultra Maximum Secure
No Existing Intercepts
Proceed

He continued his journal, his fingers trembling with elation.

Everything is in motion now. The subject is on his way, the journey begun. I cannot, of course, project the obstacles facing him, much less his success or failure; I only know through my highly developed "appliances" that he is uniquely qualified. One day we will be able to factor in more accurately the human quotient, but that day is not yet here. Nevertheless, if he survives, lightning will strike—my projections make that clear from a hundred different successfully factored options. The small circle of need-to-know officials have been alerted through ultra max modem communications. Child's play for my appliances.

3

The estimated flying time from Andrews to the U.S. Air Force base in Sicily was seven hours plus. Arrival was scheduled for 5:00 A.M., Rome time—eight o'clock in the morning in Oman, which was four to five hours away depending on the prevailing Mediterranean winds and whatever secure routes were available. Takeoff into the Atlantic darkness had been swift in the military jet, a converted F-106 Delta with a cabin that included two adjacent seats in the rear with tray tables that served as both miniature desks and surfaces for food and drink. Swiveled lights angled down from the ceiling, permitting those reading to move the sharp beams into the areas of concentration, whether they were manuscript, photographs or maps. Kendrick was fed the pages from OHIO-Four-Zero by the man on his left, one page at a time, each given only after the previous page was returned. In two hours and twelve minutes, Evan had completed the entire file.

He was about to start at the beginning again when the young man on his left, a handsome, dark-eyed member of OHIO-Four-Zero, who had introduced himself simply as a State Department aide, held up his hand.

"Can't we take time out for some food, sir?" he asked.

"Oh? Sure." Kendrick stretched in his seat. "Frankly, there's not a hell of a lot here that's very useful."

"I didn't think there would be," said the clean-cut youngster.

Evan looked at his seat companion, for the first time studying him. "You know, I don't mean this in a derogatory sense—I really don't—but for a highly classified State Department operation, you strike me as being kind of young for the job. You can't be out of your twenties."

"Close to it," replied the aide. "But I'm pretty good at what I do."

"Which is?"

"Sorry, no comment, sir," said the seat companion. "Now, how about that food? It's a long flight."

"How about a drink?"

"We've made special provisions for civilians." The dark-haired, dark-browed young man smiled and signaled the Air Force steward, a corporal in a bulkhead seat facing aft; the attendant rose and came forward. "A glass of white wine and a Canadian on the rocks, please."

"A *Canadian*—"

"That's what you drink, isn't it?"

"You've been busy."

"We never stop." The aide nodded to the corporal, who retreated to the miniature galley. "I'm afraid the food is fixed and standard," continued the young man from OHIO. "It's in line with the Pentagon cutbacks . . . and certain lobbyists from the meat and produce industries. Filet mignon with asparagus hollandaise and boiled potatoes."

"Some cutbacks."

"Some lobbyists," added Evan's seat companion, grinning. "Then there's a dessert of baked Alaska."

"What?"

"You can't overlook the dairy boys." The drinks arrived; the steward returned to a bulkhead phone where a white light flashed, and the aide held up his glass. "Your health."

"Yours, too. Do you have a name?"

"Pick one."

"That's succinct. Will you settle for Joe?"

"Joe it is. Nice to meet you, sir."

"Since you obviously know who I am, you have the advantage. You can use my name."

"Not on this flight."

"Then, who am I?"

"For the record, you're a cryptanalyst named Axelrod who's being flown to the embassy in Jiddah, Saudi Arabia. The name doesn't mean much; it's basically for the pilot's logs. If anyone wants your attention, he'll just say 'sir.' Names are sort of off limits on these trips."

"Dr. *Axelrod*?" The corporal's intrusion made the State Department's aide blanch.

"Doctor?" replied Evan, mildly astonished, looking at "Joe."

"Obviously you're a Ph.D.," said the aide under his breath.

"That's nice," whispered Kendrick, raising his eyes to the steward. "Yes?"

"The pilot would like to speak with you, sir. If you'll follow me to the flight deck, please?"

"Certainly," agreed Evan, pushing up the tray table while handing 'Joe' his drink. "At least you were right about one thing, Junior," he mumbled to the State Department man. "He said 'sir.' "

"And I don't *like* it," rejoined "Joe," quietly, intensely. "All communications involving you are to be funneled through *me.*"

"You want to make a scene?"

"Screw it. It's an ego trip. He wants to get close to the special cargo."

"The *what*?"

"Forget it, Dr. *Axelrod.* Just remember, there are to be no decisions without my approval."

"You're a tough kid."

"The toughest, Congress— Dr. Axelrod. Also, I'm not 'Junior.' Not where you're concerned."

"Shall I convey your feelings to the pilot?"

"You can tell him I'll cut both his wings and his balls off if he pulls this again."

"Since I was the last on board, I didn't meet him, but I gather he's a brigadier general."

"He's brigadier-bullshit to me."

"Good Lord," said Kendrick, chuckling. "Interservice rivalry at forty thousand feet. I'm not sure I approve of that."

"Sir?" The Air Force steward was anxious.

"Coming, Corporal."

The compact flight deck of the F-106 Delta glowed with a profusion of tiny green and red lights, dials and numbers everywhere. The pilot and co-pilot were strapped in front, the navigator on the right, a cushioned earphone clipped to his left ear, his eyes on a gridded computer screen. Evan had to bend down to advance the several feet he could manage in the small enclosure.

"Yes, General?" he inquired. "You wanted to see me?"

"I don't even want to *look* at you, Doctor," answered the pilot, his attention on the panels in front of him. "I'm just going to read you a message from someone named *S.* You know someone named *S*?"

"I think I do," replied Kendrick, assuming the message had been radioed by Swann at the Department of State. "What is it?"

"It's a pain in the butt to this *bird,* is what it is!" cried the brigadier general. "I've never landed there! I don't know the field, and I'm told those fucking *Eyetals* over in that wasteland are better at making spaghetti sauce than they are giving approach instructions!"

"It's our own air base," protested Evan.

"The *hell* it is!" countered the pilot as his co-pilot shook his head in an emphatic negative. "We're changing course to Sardinia! Not Sicily but *Sardinia*! I'll have to blow out my engines to contain us on that strip—if, for Christ's sake, we can *find* it!"

"What's the message, General?" asked Kendrick calmly. "There's usually a reason for most things when plans are changed."

"Then you explain it—no, *don't* explain it. I'm hot and bothered enough. Goddamned spooks!"

"The message, please?"

"Here it is." The angry pilot read from a perforated sheet of paper. " 'Switch necessary. Jiddah out. All M.A. where permitted under eyes—' "

"What does that mean?" interrupted Evan quickly. "The M.A. under eyes."

"What it says."

"In English, please."

"Sorry, I forgot. Whoever you are you're not what's logged. It means all military aircraft in Sicily and Jiddah are under observation, as well as every field we land on. Those Arab bastards expect something and they've got their filthy psychos in place, ready to relay *anything* or *anyone* unusual."

"Not all Arabs are bastards or filthy or psychos, General."

"They are in my book."

"Then it's unprintable."

"What is?"

"Your book. The rest of the message, please."

The pilot made an obscene gesture with his right arm, the perforated paper in his hand. "Read it yourself, Arab lover. But it doesn't leave this deck."

Kendrick took the paper, angled it toward the navigator's light, and read the message. *Switch necessary. Jiddah out. All M.A. where permitted under eyes. Transfer to civilian subsidiary on south island. Routed through Cyprus, Riyadh, to target. Arrangements cleared. ETA is close to Second Pillar el Maghreb best timing possible. Sorry. S.* Evan reached out, holding the message over the brigadier general's shoulder and dropped it. "I assume that 'south island' is Sardinia."

"You got it."

"Then, I gather, I'm to spend roughly ten more hours on a plane, or planes, through Cyprus, Saudi Arabia and finally to Masqat."

"I'll tell you one thing, Arab lover," continued the pilot. "I'm glad it's you flying on those Minnie Mouse aircraft and not me. A word of advice: Grab a seat near an emergency exit, and if you can buy a chute, spend the money. Also a gas mask. I'm told those planes stink."

"I'll try to remember your generous advice."

"Now you tell *me* something," said the general. "What the hell is that 'Second Pillar' Arab stuff?"

"Do you go to church?" asked Evan.

"You're damned right I do. When I'm home I make the whole damn family go—no welching on that, by Christ. At least once a month, it's a rule."

"So do the Arabs, but not once a month. Five times a day. They believe as strongly as you do, at *least* as strongly, wouldn't you say? The Second Pillar of el Maghreb refers to the Islamic prayers at sundown. Hell of an inconvenience, isn't it? They work their Arab asses off all day long, mostly for nothing, and then it's sundown. No cocktails, just prayers to their God. Maybe it's all they've got. Like the old plantation spirituals."

The pilot turned slowly in his seat. His face in the shadows of the flight deck startled Kendrick. The brigadier general was black. "You set me up," said the pilot flatly.

"I'm sorry. I mean that; I didn't realize. On the other hand, you said it. You called me an Arab lover."

Sundown. Masqat, Oman. The ancient turbojet bounced onto the runway with such force that some of the passengers screamed, their desert instincts alert to the possibility of their fiery oblivion. Then with the realization that they had arrived, that they were safe, and that there were jobs for the having, they began chanting excitedly. Thanks be to Allah for His benevolence! They had been promised rials for servitude the Omanis would not accept. So be it. It was far better than what they had left behind.

The suited businessmen in the front of the aircraft, handkerchiefs held to their noses, rushed to the exit door, gripping their briefcases, all too anxious to swallow the air of Oman. Kendrick stood in the aisle, the last in line, wondering what the State Department's Swann had in mind when he said in his message that "arrangements" had been cleared.

"Come with me!" cried a berobed Arab from the crowd forming outside the terminal for immigration. "We have another exit, Dr. Axelrod."

"My passport doesn't say anything about *Axelrod.*"

"Precisely. That is why you are coming with me."

"What about immigration?"

"Keep your papers in your pocket. No one wants to *see* them. *I* do not want to see them!"

"Then how—"

"Enough, *ya Shaikh.* Give me your luggage and stay ten feet behind me. Come!"

Evan handed his soft carry-on suitcase to the excited contact and followed him. They walked to the right, past the end of the one-story brown-and-white terminal, and headed immediately to the left toward the tall Cyclone fence beyond which the fumes from dozens of taxis, buses and trucks tinted the burning air. The crowds outside the airport fence were racing back and forth amid the congested vehicles, their robes flowing, shrieking admonishments and screeching for attention. Along the fence for perhaps seventy-five to a hundred feet, scores of other Arabs pressed their faces against the metal links, peering into an alien world of smooth asphalt runways and sleek aircraft that was no part of their lives, giving birth to fantasies beyond their understanding. Up ahead, Kendrick could see a metal building the size of ten Quonset huts. It was the airfield warehouse he remembered so well, recalling the hours he and Manny Weingrass had spent inside waiting for long-overdue equipment promised on one flight or another, often furious with the customs officials who frequently could not understand the forms they had to fill out that would release the equipment—if indeed the equipment had arrived.

The gate in front of the warehouse's hangarlike doors was open, accommodating the line of freight containers, their deep wells filled with crates disgorged from the various aircraft. Guards with attack dogs on leashes flanked the customs conveyor belt that carried the freight inside to anxious suppliers and retailers and the ever-present, ever-frustrated foremen of construction teams. The guards' eyes constantly roamed the frenzied activity, repeating machine pistols in their hands. They were there not merely to maintain a semblance of order amid the chaos and to back up the customs officials in the event of violent disputes, but essentially to be on the lookout for weapons and narcotics being smuggled into the sultanate. Each crate and thickly layered box was examined by the snarling, yelping dogs as it was lifted onto the belt.

Evan's contact stopped; he did the same. The Arab turned and nodded at a small side gate with a sign in Arabic above it. *Stop. Authorized Personnel Only. Violators Will Be Shot.* It was an exit for the guards and other officials of the government. The gate also had a large metal plate where a lock would normally be placed. And it *was* a lock, thought Kendrick, a lock electronically released from somewhere inside the warehouse. The contact nodded twice more, indicating that with a signal Evan was to head for the gate where "violators will be shot." Kendrick frowned questioningly, a hollow pain forming in his stomach. With Masqat under a state of siege, it would not take much for someone to start firing. The Arab read the doubt in his eyes and nodded for a fourth time, slowly, reassuringly. The contact turned and looked to his right down the line of freight containers. Almost imperceptibly he raised his right hand.

Suddenly, a fight broke out beside one of the containers. Curses were shrieked as arms swung violently and fists pounded.

"Contraband!"

"Liar!"

"Your mother is a goat, a filthy she-goat!"

"Your father lies with whores! You are a product!"

Dust flew as the grappling bodies fell to the ground, joined by others who took sides. The dogs began barking viciously, straining at their leashes, their handlers carried forward toward the melee—all but one handler, one guard; and the signal was given by Evan's contact. Together they ran to the deserted personnel exit.

"Good fortune, sir," said the lone guard, his attack dog sniffing menacingly at Kendrick's trousers as the man tapped the metal plate in a rapid code with his weapon. A buzzer sounded and the gate swung back. Kendrick and his contact ran through, racing along the metal wall of the warehouse.

In the parking lot beyond stood a broken-down truck, the tires seemingly only half inflated. The engine roared as loud reports came from a worn exhaust pipe. "*Besuraa!*" cried the Arab contact, telling Evan to hurry. "There is your transport."

"I hope," mumbled Kendrick, his voice laced with doubt.

"Welcome to Masqat, *Shaikh*-whoever."

"You *know* who I am," said Evan angrily. "You picked me out in the crowd! How many *others* can do that?"

"Very few, sir. And I do *not* know who you are, I swear by Allah."

"Then I have to believe you, don't I?" asked Kendrick, staring at the man.

"I would not use the name of Allah if it were not so. Please. *Besuraa!*"

"Thanks," said Evan, grabbing his carryon and running toward the truck's cab. Suddenly, the driver was gesturing out the window for him to climb into the back under the canvas that covered the bed of the ancient vehicle. The truck lurched forward as a pair of hands pulled him up inside.

Stretched out on the floorboards, Kendrick raised his eyes to the Arab above him. The man smiled and pointed to the long robes of an *aba* and the ankle-length shirt known as a *thobe* that were suspended on a hanger in the front of the canvas-topped trailer; beside it, hanging on a nail was the *ghotra* headdress and a pair of white balloon trousers, the street clothes of an Arab and the last items Evan had requested of the State Department's Frank Swann. These and one other small but vital catalyst.

The Arab held it up. It was a tube of skin-darkening gel, which when generously applied turned the face and hands of a white Occidental into those of a Mideastern Semite whose skin had been permanently burnished by the hot, blistering, near-equatorial sun. The dyed pigment would stay darkened for a period of ten days before fading. Ten days. A lifetime—for him or for the monster who called himself the Mahdi.

The woman stood inside the airport fence inches from the metal links. She wore slightly flared white slacks and a tapered dark green silk blouse, the blouse creased by the leather strap of her handbag. Long dark hair framed her face; her sharp, attractive features were obscured by a pair of large designer sunglasses, her head covered by a wide-brimmed white sun hat, the crown circled by a ribbon of green silk. At first she seemed to be yet another traveler from wealthy Rome or Paris, London or New York. But a closer look revealed a subtle difference from the stereotype; it was her skin. Its olive tones, neither black nor white, suggested northern Africa. What confirmed the difference was what she held in her hands, and only seconds before had pressed against the fence: a miniature camera, barely two inches long and with a tiny bulging, convex, prismatic lens engineered for telescopic photography, equipment associated with intelligence personnel. The seedy, run-down truck had swerved out of the warehouse parking lot; the camera was no longer necessary. She grabbed the handbag at her side and slipped it out of sight.

"*Khalehla!*" shouted an obese, wide-eyed, baldheaded man running toward her, pronouncing the name as "Ka-*lay*-la." He was awkwardly carrying two suitcases, the sweat drenching his shirt and penetrating the black pin-striped suit styled on Savile Row. "For God's sake, why did you *drift off*?"

"That dreadful line was simply *too* boring, darling," replied the woman, her accent an unfathomable mixture of British and Italian or perhaps Greek. "I thought I'd stroll around."

"Good Christ, Khalehla, you can't *do* that, can't you under*stand*? This place is a veritable *hell* on earth right now!" The Englishman stood before her, his jowled face flushed, dripping with perspiration. "I was the very next in line for that immigration imbecile, and I looked around and you weren't *there*! And when I started rushing about to find you, three lunatics with guns—*guns!*—stopped me and took me into a room and searched our *luggage*!"

"I hope you were clean, Tony."

"The bastards confiscated my *whisky*!"

"Oh, the sacrifices of being such a successful man. Never mind, darling, I'll have it replaced."

The British businessman's eyes roved over the face and figure of Khalehla. "Well, it's past, isn't it? We'll go back now and get it over with." The obese man winked—one eye after the other. "I've got us splendid accommodations. You'll be very pleased, my dear."

"Accommodations? With *you,* darling?"

"Yes, of course."

"Oh, I really couldn't do that."

"*What?* You said—"

"I *said*?" Khalehla broke in, her dark brows arched above her sunglasses.

"Well, you *implied,* rather emphatically, I might add, that if I could get you on that plane we might have a rather sporting time of it in Masqat."

"Sporting, of course. Drinks on the Gulf, perhaps the races, dinner at El Quaman—yes, all of those things. But in your *room*?"

"Well, well . . . well, certain specifics shouldn't have to be—specified."

"Oh, my sweet Tony. How can I apologize for such a misunderstanding? My old English matron at the Cairo University suggested I reach you. She's one of your wife's dearest friends. Oh, no, I couldn't, really."

"*Shit!*" exploded the highly successful businessman named Tony.

"*Miraya!*" shouted Kendrick over the deafening sounds of the dilapidated truck as it bounced over a back road into Masqat.

"You did not request a mirror, *ya Shaikh,*" yelled the Arab in the rear of the trailer, his English heavily accented but understandable enough.

"Rip out one of the side-view mirrors on the doors, then. Tell the driver."

"He cannot hear me, *ya Shaikh.* Like so many others, this is an old vehicle, one that will not be noticed. I cannot reach the driver."

"*Goddamnit!*" exclaimed Evan, the tube of gel in his hand. "Then you be my eyes, *ya sahbee,*" he said, calling the man his friend. "Come closer to me and watch. Tell me when it's right. Open the canvas."

The Arab folded back part of the rear covering, letting the sunlight into the darkened trailer. Cautiously, holding on to the strips, he moved forward until he was barely a foot away from Kendrick. "This is the *iddahwa,* sir?" he asked, referring to the tube.

"*Iwah,*" said Evan, when he saw that the gel was indeed the medicine he needed. He began spreading it first on his hands; both men watched; the waiting time was less than three minutes.

"*Arma!*" shouted the Arab, holding out his right hand; the color of the skin nearly matched his own.

"*Kwiyis,*" agreed Kendrick, trying to approximate the proportion of gel he had applied to his hands so as to equal the amount for his face. There was nothing for it but to do it. He did, and anxiously watched the Arab's eyes.

"*Mahool!*" cried his newest companion, grinning the grin of significant triumph. "*Delwatee anzur!*"

He had done it. His flesh was now the color of a sun-drenched Arab. "Help me into the thobe and the aba, please," Evan asked as he started to disrobe in the violently shaking truck.

"I will, of course," said the Arab, suddenly in much clearer English than he had employed before. "But now we are finished with each other. Forgive me for playing the naïf with you but no one is to be trusted here; not exempted is the American State Department. You are taking risks, *ya Shaikh,* far more than I, as the father of my children would take, but that is your business, not mine. You will be dropped off in the center of Masqat and you will then be on your own."

"Thanks for getting me there," said Evan.

"Thank you for coming, *ya Shaikh.* But do not try to trace those of us who helped you. In truth, we would kill you before the enemy had a chance to schedule your execution. We are quiet, but we are alive."

"Who *are* you?"

"Believers, *ya Shaikh.* That is enough for you to know."

"*Alfshukre,*" said Evan, thanking the clerk and tipping him for the confidentiality he had been guaranteed. He signed the hotel register with a false Arabic name and was given the key to his suite. He did not require a bellboy. Kendrick took the elevator to a wrong floor and waited at the end of a corridor to see if he had been followed. He had not been, so he walked down the staircase to his proper floor and went to his suite.

Time. *Time's valuable, every minute:* Frank Swann, Department of State. The evening prayers of *el Maghreb* were over; darkness descended and the madness at the embassy could be heard in the distance. Evan threw his small carryon into a corner of the living room, took out his billfold from under his robes, and withdrew a folded sheet of paper on which he had written the names and the telephone numbers—numbers that were by now almost five years old—of the people he wanted to contact. He went to the desk and the telephone, sat down and unfolded the paper.

Thirty-five minutes later, after the effusive yet strangely awkward greetings of three friends from the past, the meeting was arranged. He had chosen seven names, each among the most influential men he remembered from his days in Masqat. Two had died; one was out of the country; the fourth told him quite frankly that the climate was not right for an Omani to meet with an American. The three who had agreed to see him, with varying degrees of reluctance, would arrive separately within the hour. Each would go directly to his suite without troubling the front desk.

Thirty-eight minutes passed, during which time Kendrick unpacked the few items of clothing he had brought and ordered specific brands of whisky from room service. The abstinence demanded by Islamic tradition was more honored in the breach, and beside each name was the libation each guest favored; it was a lesson Evan had learned from the irascible Emmanuel Weingrass. *An industrial lubricant, my son. You remember the name of a man's wife, he's pleased. You remember the brand of whisky he drinks, now that's something else. Now you care!*

The soft knocking at the door broke the silence of the room like cracks of lightning. Kendrick took several deep breaths, walked across the room, and admitted his first visitor.

"It is *you,* Evan? My God, you haven't *converted,* have you?"

"Come in, Mustapha. It's good to see you again."

"But am I seeing *you*?" said the man named Mustapha who was dressed in a dark brown business suit. "And your skin! You are as dark as I am if not darker."

"I want you to understand everything." Kendrick closed the door, gesturing for his friend from the past to choose a place to sit. "I've got your brand of Scotch. Care for a drink?"

"Oh, that Manny Weingrass is never far away, is he?" said Mustapha, walking to the long brocade sofa and sitting down. "The old thief."

"Hey, come on, Musty," protested Evan, laughing and heading for the hotel's dry bar. "He never shortchanged you."

"No, he didn't. Neither he nor you nor your other partners ever shortchanged any of us. . . . How has it been with you without them, my friend? Many of us talk about it even after these four years."

"Sometimes not easy," said Kendrick honestly, pouring drinks. "But you accept it. You cope." He brought Mustapha his Scotch and sat down in one of the three chairs opposite the sofa. "The best, Musty." He raised his glass.

"No, old friend, it is the worst—the worst of times, as the English Dickens wrote."

"Let's wait till the others get here."

"They're not coming." Mustapha drank his Scotch.

"*What?*"

"We talked. I am, as is said in so many business conferences, the representative of certain interests. Also, as the only minister of the sultan's cabinet, it was felt that I could convey the government's consensus."

"About what? You're jumping way the hell ahead of me."

"You jumped ahead of us, Evan, by simply coming here and calling us. One of us; two, perhaps; even in the extreme, three—but *seven.* No, that was reckless of you, old friend, and dangerous for everyone."

"Why?"

"Did you think for a minute," continued the Arab, overriding Kendrick, "that even three recognizable men of standing—say nothing of *seven*—could converge on a hotel within minutes of each other to meet with a stranger without the management hearing about it? *Ridiculous.*"

Evan studied Mustapha before speaking, their eyes locked. "What is it, Musty? What are you trying to tell me? This isn't the embassy, and that obscene mess over there hasn't anything to do with the businessmen or the government of Oman."

"No, it obviously does not," agreed the Arab firmly. "But what I'm trying to tell you is that things have changed here—in ways many of us do not understand."

"That's also obvious," interrupted Kendrick. "You're not terrorists."

"No, we're not, but would you care to hear what people—*responsible* people—are saying?"

"Go ahead."

" 'It will pass,' they say. " 'Don't interfere; it would only inflame them further.' "

"Don't *interfere*?" repeated Evan incredulously.

"And 'Let the politicians settle it.' "

"The politicians *can't* settle it!"

"Oh, there's more, Evan. 'There's a certain basis for their anger,' they say. 'Not the killing, of course, but within the context of certain events,' et cetera, et cetera. I've heard that, too."

"Context of certain events? *What* events?"

"Current history, old friend. 'They're reacting to a very uneven Middle East policy on the part of the United States.' That's the catchphrase, Evan. 'The Israelis get everything and they get nothing,' people say. 'They are driven from their lands and their homes and forced to live in crowded, filthy refugee camps, while in the West Bank the Jews spit on them.' These are the things I hear."

"That's *bullshit*!" exploded Kendrick. "Beyond the fact that there's another, equally painful side to that bigoted coin, it has nothing to do with those two hundred thirty-six hostages or the eleven who've already been butchered! They don't *make policy*, uneven or otherwise. They're innocent human beings, brutalized and terrified and driven to exhaustion by goddamned *animals*! How the hell can *responsible* people say those things? That's not the President's cabinet over there, or hawks from the Knesset. They're civil service employees and tourists and construction families. I repeat—*bullshit*!"

The man named Mustapha sat rigidly on the sofa, his eyes still leveled at Evan. "I know that and you know that," he said quietly. "And *they* know that, my friend."

"Then *why*?"

"The truth, then," continued the Arab, his voice no louder than before. "Two incidents that forged a dreadful consensus, if I may use the word somewhat differently from before. . . . The reason these things are said is that none of us cares to create targets of our own flesh."

"Targets? Your . . . flesh?"

"Two men, one I shall call Mahmoud, the other Abdul—not their real names, of course, for it's better that you not know them. Mahmoud's daughter . . . raped, her face slashed. Abdul's son, his throat slit in an alley below his father's office on the piers. 'Criminals, rapists, murderers!' the authorities say. But we all know better. It was Abdul and Mahmoud who tried to rally an opposition. '*Guns!*' they cried. 'Storm the embassy ourselves,' they insisted. 'Do not let Masqat become another Teheran!' . . . But it was not they who suffered. It was those close to them, their most precious possessions. . . . These are the warnings, Evan. Forgive me, but if you had a wife and children, would you subject them to such risks? I think not. The most precious jewels are not made of stone, but of flesh. Our families. A true hero will overcome his fear and risk his life for what he believes, but he will balk when the price is the lives of his loved ones. Is it not so, old friend?"

"My *God,*" whispered Evan. "You won't help—you *can't.*"

"There is someone, however, who will see you and hear what you have to say. But the meeting must take place with extraordinary caution, miles away in the desert before the mountains of Jabal Sham."

"Who is it?"

"The sultan."

Kendrick was silent. He looked at his glass. After a prolonged moment he raised his eyes to Mustapha. "I'm not to have any official linkage," he said, "and the sultan's pretty official. I don't speak for my government, that's got to be clear."

"You mean you don't care to meet with him?"

"On the contrary, I care to very much. I just want my position clear. I have nothing to do with the intelligence community, the State Department or the White House—God knows not the White House."

"I think that's patently clear; your robes and the color of your skin confirm it. And the sultan wants no connection with you, as emphatically as Washington wants no connection."

"I'm rusty," said Evan, drinking. "The old man died a year or so after I left, didn't he? I'm afraid I didn't keep up with things over here—a natural aversion, I think."

"Certainly understandable. Our current sultan is his son; he's nearer your age than mine, even younger than you. After school in England, he completed his studies in your country. Dartmouth and Harvard, to be exact."

"His name's Ahmat," broke in Kendrick, remembering. "I met him a couple of times." Evan frowned. "Economics and international relations," he added.

"What?"

"Those were the degrees he was after. Graduate and postgraduate."

"He's educated and bright, but he's young. Very young for the tasks facing him."

"When can I see him?"

"Tonight. Before others become aware of your presence here." Mustapha looked at his watch. "In thirty minutes, leave the hotel and walk four blocks north. A military vehicle will be at the corner. Get in and it will take you to the sands of Jabal Sham."

* * *

The slender Arab in the soiled aba ducked into the shadows of the darkened storefront across the street from the hotel. He stood silently next to the woman called Khalehla, now dressed in a tailored black suit, the kind favored by women executives and indistinct in the dim light. She was awkwardly securing a lens into the mount of her small camera. Suddenly, two sharp, high-pitched beeps filled the storefront.

"Hurry," said the Arab. "He's on his way. He's reached the lobby."

"As fast as I can," replied the woman, swearing under her breath as she manipulated the lens. "I ask little of my superiors, but decent, *functioning* equipment is one of them. . . . *There.* It's on."

"Here he comes!"

Khalehla raised her camera with the telescopic infrared lens for night photographs. She rapidly snapped three pictures of the robed Evan Kendrick. "I wonder how long they'll let him live," she said. "I have to reach a telephone."

Ultra Maximum Secure
No Existing Intercepts
Proceed

The journal was continued.

Reports out of Masqat are astonishing. The subject has transformed himself into an Omani, complete with Arab dress and darkened skin. He moves about the city like a native, apparently reaching old friends and contacts from his previous life. The reports, however, are also sketchy, as the subject's shadow routes everything through Langley and as yet I haven't been able to invade the CIA access codes from the Gulf nations. Who knows what Langley conceals? I've instructed my appliances to work harder! The State Department, naturally, is duck soup. And why not?

4

The vast, arid desert appeared endless in the night, the sporadic moonlight outlining the mountains of Jabal Sham in the distance—an unreachable, menacing border towering on the dark horizon. Everywhere the flat surface seemed to be a dry mixture of earth and sand, the windless plain devoid of those swelling, impermanent hills of windblown dunes one conjures up with images of the great Sahara. The hard, winding road beneath was barely passable; the brown military sedan lurched and skidded around the sandy curves on its way to the royal meeting ground. Kendrick, as instructed, sat beside the armed, uniformed driver; in the back was a second man, an officer and also armed. Security started at the pickup; a perceived wrong move on Evan's part and he was flanked. Beyond polite greetings neither soldier spoke.

"This is desert country," said Kendrick in Arabic. "Why are there so many turns?"

"There are many offshoot roads, sir," answered the officer from the backseat. "A straight lane in these sands would mark them too clearly."

Royal security, thought Evan without comment.

They took an "offshoot road" after twenty-five minutes of speeding due west. Several miles beyond, a campfire glowed on the right. As they drew near, Kendrick saw a platoon of uniformed guards circling the fire, facing out, all points of the compass covered; the dark silhouettes of two military trucks loomed in the distance. The car stopped; the officer leaped out and opened the door for the American.

"Precede me, sir," he said in English.

"Certainly," replied Evan, trying to spot the young sultan in the light of the fire. There was no sign of him, nor of anyone not in uniform. Evan tried to recall the face of the boy-man he had met over four years ago, the student who had come home to Oman during a Christmas or a spring break, he could not remember which—he recalled only that the son of the sultan was an amiable young man, as knowledgeable as he was enthusiastic about American sports. But that was all: no face came to him, only the name, Ahmat, which Mustapha had confirmed. Three soldiers in front of him gave way; they walked through the protective ring.

"You will permit me, sir?" said a second officer, suddenly standing in front of Kendrick.

"Permit you what?"

"It is customary under these circumstances to search all visitors."

"Go ahead."

The soldier swiftly and efficiently probed the robes of the aba, raising the right sleeve above the area where Evan had spread the skin-darkening gel. Seeing the white flesh, the officer held the cloth in place and stared at Kendrick. "You have papers with you, *ya Shaikh*?"

"No papers. No identification."

"I see." The soldier dropped the sleeve. "You have no weapons, either."

"Of course not."

"That is for you to claim and for us to determine, sir." The officer snapped out from his belt a thin black device no larger than a pack of cigarettes. He pressed what looked like a red or orange button. "You will wait here, please."

"I'm not going anywhere," said Evan, glancing at the guards, their rifles poised.

"No, you are not, *ya Shaikh,*" agreed the soldier, striding back toward the fire.

Kendrick looked at the English-speaking officer who had accompanied him in the backseat from Masqat. "They take no chances, do they?" he said aimlessly.

"The will of almighty Allah, sir," replied the soldier. "The sultan is our light, our sun. You are *Aurobbi,* a white man. Would you not protect your lineage to the heavens?"

"If I thought he could guarantee my admittance, I certainly would."

"He is a good man, *ya Shaikh.* Young, perhaps, but wise in many ways. We have come to learn that."

"He *is* coming here, then?"

"He has arrived, sir."

The bass-toned roar of a powerful limousine broke the crackling intrusion of the campfire. The vehicle with tinted windows swerved in front of the ring of guards and came to an abrupt stop. Before the driver could emerge, the rear door opened and the sultan stepped out. He was in the robes of his royal office, but with the door still open he proceeded to remove them, throwing his aba into the car, the ghotra headdress remaining on his head. He walked through the circle of his Royal Guard, a slender, muscular man of medium height and broad shoulders. Except for the ghotra, his clothes were Western. His slacks were a tan gabardine, and over his chest was a T-shirt with a cartoon figure wearing a three-cornered American revolutionary hat bursting out of an American football. Underneath, the legend read: *New England Patriots.*

"It's been a long time, Evan Kendrick, *ya Shaikh,*" said the young man in a slightly British accent, smiling and extending his hand. "I like your costume, but it's not exactly Brooks Brothers, is it?"

"Neither is yours unless the Brothers Brooks are into T-shirts." They shook hands. Kendrick could feel the sultan's strength. "Thank you for seeing me, Ahmat. . . . Forgive me—I should say Your Royal Highness. My apologies."

"You knew me as Ahmat, and I knew you as *Shaikh, sir.* Must I still call you 'sir'?"

"That'd be inappropriate, I think."

"Good. We understand each other."

"You look different from what I remember," said Evan.

"I was forced to grow up swiftly—not by choice. From student to teacher, without the proper qualifications, I'm afraid."

"You're respected, I've heard that."

"The office does it, not the man. I must learn to fill the office. Come on, let's talk—away from here." The sultan, Ahmat, took Kendrick's arm and started through his circle of guards only to be stopped by the officer who had searched Evan.

"Your Highness!" cried the soldier. "Your safety is our lives! Please remain within the cordon."

"And be a target by the light of the fire?"

"We *surround* you, sir, and the men will continuously side-step around the circle. The ground is flat."

"Instead, point your weapons beyond the shadows, *ya sahbee,*" said Ahmat, calling the soldier his friend. "We'll only be a few meters away."

"With pain in our hearts, Your Highness."

"It will pass." Ahmat ushered Kendrick through the cordon. "My countrymen are frequently given to trivial melodramatics."

"It's not so trivial if they're willing to make a moving ring and take a bullet meant for you."

"It's nothing special, Evan, and, frankly, I don't know all the men in those bodies. What we *may* have to say to each other could be for our ears only."

"I didn't realize . . ." Kendrick looked at the young sultan of Oman as they walked into the darkness. "Your own *guards*?"

"Anything's possible during this madness. You can study the eyes of a professional soldier but you can't see the resentments or the temptations behind them. Here, this is far enough." Both men stopped in the sand.

"The madness," said Evan flatly in the dim light of the fire and the intermittent moonlight. "Let's talk about it."

"That's why you're here, of course."

"That's why I'm here," Kendrick said.

"What the hell do you want me to *do*?" cried Ahmat in a harsh whisper. "Whatever move I make, another hostage could get shot and one more bullet-riddled body is thrown out a window!" The young sultan shook his head. "Now, I know you and my father worked well together—you and I discussed a few projects at a couple of dinner parties, but I don't expect you to remember."

"I remember," broke in Kendrick. "You were home from Harvard, your second year in graduate school, I think. You were always on your father's left, the position of inheritance."

"Thanks a bunch, Evan. I could have had a terrific job at E. F. Hutton."

"You have a terrific job here."

"I *know* that," said Ahmat, his whispered voice again rising. "And that's why I have to make goddamned sure I do it right. Certainly I can call back the army from the Yemeni border and take the embassy by blowing it apart—and in *doing* so I guarantee the deaths of two hundred thirty-six Americans. I can see your headlines now: 'Arab Sultan Kills,' et cetera, et cetera. *Arab.* The Knesset in Jerusalem has a field day! No *way,* pal. I'm no hair-trigger cowboy who risks innocent lives and somehow in the confusion gets labeled in your press as anti-Semitic. Good *Christ*! Washington and Israel seem to have forgotten that we're *all* Semites, and *not* all Arabs are Palestinians and not *all* Palestinians are terrorists! And I won't give those pontificating, arrogant Israeli bastards another reason to send their *American* F-14s to kill *more* Arabs just as innocent as your hostages! Do you read me, Evan *Shaikh*?"

"I read you," said Kendrick. "Now, will you cool off and listen to me?"

The agitated young sultan exhaled audibly, nodding his head.

"Of course I'll listen to you, but listening isn't agreeing to a damn thing."

"All right." Evan paused, his eyes intense, wanting to be understood despite the strange, obscure information he was about to impart. "You've heard of the Mahdi?"

"Khartoum, the 1880s."

"No. Bahrain, the 1980s."

"*What?*"

Kendrick repeated the story he had told Frank Swann at the State Department. The story of an unknown, obsessed financier who called himself the Mahdi, and whose purpose was to drive out the Westerner from the Middle East and Southwest Asia, keeping the immense wealth of industrial expansion in Arab hands—specifically *his* hands. How this same man who had spread his gospel of Islamic purity throughout the fanatic fringes had formed a network, a silent cartel of scores, perhaps hundreds, of hidden companies and corporations all linked together under the umbrella of his own concealed organization. Evan then described how his old Israeli architect, Emmanuel Weingrass, had perceived the outlines of this extraordinary economic conspiracy, initially by way of threats leveled against the Kendrick Group—threats he had countered with his own outrageous warnings of retribution—and how the more Manny learned, the more he was convinced that the conspiracy was real and growing and had to be exposed.

"Looking back, I'm not proud of what I did," continued Evan in the dim light of the campfire and the flitting desert moon. "But I rationalized it because of what had happened. I just had to get out of this part of the world, and so I walked away from the business, walked away from the fight Manny said we had to confront. I told him his imagination was working overtime, that he was giving credence to irresponsible—and often drunken—goons. I remember so clearly what he said to me. 'Could my wildest imaginings,' he said, 'or even less conceivably *theirs,* come up with a *Mahdi*? Those killers did it to us—*he* did it!' Manny was right then and he's right now. The embassy is stormed, homicidal lunatics kill innocent people, and the ultimate statement is made. 'Stay away, Western Boy. You come over here, you'll be another corpse thrown out a window.' Can't you *see,* Ahmat? There *is* a Mahdi and he's systematically squeezing everyone else out through sheer, manipulative terror."

"I can see that you're convinced," replied the young sultan skeptically.

"So are others here in Masqat. They just don't understand. They can't find a pattern, or an explanation, but they're so frightened they refused to meet with me. *Me,* an old friend going back years, a man they worked with and trusted."

"Terror breeds anxiety. What would you expect? Also, there's something else. You're an American disguised as an Arab. That in itself has to frighten them."

"They didn't know what I was wearing or what I looked like. I was a voice over the telephone."

"An *American* voice. Even more frightening."

"A Western boy?"

"There are many Westerners here. But the United States government, understandably, has ordered all Americans out, and prohibited all incoming American commercial flights. Your friends ask themselves how you got here. And why. With lunatics roaming the streets, perhaps they, also understandably, don't care to involve themselves in the embassy crisis."

"They don't. Because children have been killed—the children of men who *did* want to involve themselves."

Ahmat stood rigidly in place, his dark eyes bewildered, angry again. "There's been crime, yes, and the police do what they can, but I've heard nothing about this—about children being killed."

"It's true. A daughter was raped, her face disfigured; a son was murdered, his throat slit."

"God*damn* you, if you're lying! I may be helpless where the embassy is concerned but not *outside*! Who were they? Give me *names*!"

"None were given to me, not the real ones. I wasn't to be told."

"But Mustapha had to do the telling. There was no one else."

"Yes."

"He'll tell *me,* you can bet your ass on that!"

"Then you see now, *don't* you?" Kendrick was close to pleading. "The pattern, I mean. It's there, Ahmat. An underground network *is* being formed. This Mahdi and his people are using terrorists to drive out all current and potential competition. They want total control; they want all the money funneled to *them.*"

The young sultan delayed his reply, then shook his head. "I'm sorry, Evan, I can't accept that because they wouldn't dare try it."

"Why not?"

"Because the computers would pick up a pattern of payments

to a central hub of the network, that's why. How do you think Cornfeld and Vesco got caught? Somewhere there has to be linkage, a convergence."

"You're way ahead of me."

"Because you're way behind in computer analyses," retorted Ahmat. "You can have a hundred thousand dispersals for twenty thousand separate projects, and where before it would take months, even years, to find the hidden linkages between, say, five hundred corporations, dummy and otherwise, those disks can do it in a couple of hours."

"Very enlightening," said Kendrick, "but you're forgetting something."

"What?"

"Finding those linkages would take place after the fact, after all those 'dispersals' were made. By then the network's in place, and the fox has got one hell of a lot of chickens. If you'll excuse a couple of mixed metaphors, not too many people will be interested in setting traps or sending out hounds under the circumstances. Who could care? The trains are running on time and no one's blowing them up. Of course, there's also a new kind of government around now that has its own set of rules, and if you and your ministers don't happen to like them, you might just be replaced. But again, who cares? The sun comes up every morning and people have jobs to go to."

"You make it sound almost attractive."

"Oh, it always is in the beginning. Mussolini did get those damned trains on schedule, and the Third Reich certainly revitalized industry."

"I see your point, except you're saying that it's the reverse here. An industrial monopoly could move into a void and take over my government because it represents stability and growth."

"Two points for the sultan," agreed Evan. "He gets another jewel for his harem."

"Tell my wife about it. She's a Presbyterian from New Bedford, Massachusetts."

"How did you get away with that?"

"My father died and she's got a hell of a sense of humor."

"Again, I can't follow you."

"Some other time. Let's suppose you're right, and this is a shakedown cruise to see if their tactics can take the weather. Washington wants us to keep talking while you people come up with a plan that obviously combines some kind of penetration followed by a Delta Force. But let's face it, America and its allies are hoping for a diplomatic breakthrough because any strategy that depends on force could be disastrous. They've called in every nut leader in the Middle East and short of making Arafat mayor of New York City they'll deal with anyone, holier-than-thou statements notwithstanding. What's *your* idea?"

"The same as what you say those computers of yours could do in a couple of years from now when it'd be too late. Trace the source of what's being sent into the embassy. Not food or medical supplies, but ammunition and weapons . . . and somewhere among those items the instructions that someone's sending inside. In other words, find this manipulator who calls himself the Mahdi and rip him out."

The T-shirted sultan looked at Evan in the flickering light. "You're aware that much of the Western press have speculated that I, myself, might be behind this. That I somehow resent the Western influence spreading throughout the country. 'Otherwise,' they say, 'why doesn't he do something?' "

"I'm aware of it, but like the State Department, I think it's nonsense. No one with half a brain gives any credence to those speculations."

"Your State Department," said Ahmat reflectively, his eyes still on Kendrick. "You know, they came to me in 1979, when Teheran blew up. I was a student then, and I don't know what those two guys expected to find, but whatever it was, it wasn't me. Probably some Bedouin in a long flowing aba, sitting cross-legged and smoking a hashish water pipe. Maybe if I'd dressed the part, they would have taken me seriously."

"You've lost me again."

"Oh, sorry. You see, once they realized that neither my father nor the family could do anything, that we had no real connections with the fundamentalist movements,. they were exasperated. One of them almost begged me, saying that I appeared to be a reasonable *Arab*—meaning that my English was fluent, if tainted by early British schooling—and what would *I* do if I were running things in Washington. What they meant here was what advice would I offer, if my advice was sought. . . . *God-damnit,* I was *right*!"

"What did you tell them?"

"I remember exactly. I said . . . 'What you should have done in the beginning. It could be too late now, but you might still pull it off.' I told them to put together the most efficient insurgency force they could mount and send it *not* to Teheran but to *Qum,* Khomeini's backwoods headquarters in the north. Send ex-SAVAK agents in first; those bastards would figure out a way to do it if the firepower and compensation were guaranteed. 'Take Khomeini in Qum,' I told them. 'Take the illiterate mullahs around him and get them all out alive, then parade them on world television.' He'd be the ultimate bargaining chip, and those hairy fanatics that are his court would serve to point up how ridiculous they *all* are. A deal could have been made."

Evan studied the angry young man. "It might have worked," he said softly, "but what if Khomeini had decided to stand fast as a martyr?"

"He wouldn't have, believe me. He would have settled; there would have been a compromise, offered by others, of course, but designed by him. He has no desire to go so quickly to that heaven he extols, or to opt for that martyrdom he uses to send twelve-year-old kids into minefields."

"Why are you so sure?" asked Kendrick, himself unsure.

"I met that half-wit in Paris—that's not to justify Pahlevi or his SAVAK or his plundering relatives, I couldn't do that—but Khomeini's a senile zealot who wants to believe in his own immortality and will do anything to further it. I heard him tell a group of fawning imbeciles that instead of two or three, he had twenty, perhaps thirty, even forty sons. 'I have spread my seed and I will continue to spread it,' he claimed. 'It is Allah's will that my seed reach far and wide.' *Bullshit!* He's a dribbling, dirty old man and a classic case for a funny farm. Can you imagine? Populating this sick world with little Ayatollahs? I told your people that once they had him, to catch him on videotape with his guard down, sermonizing to his hick high priests—one-way mirror stuff, that kind of thing. His holy persona would have collapsed in a global wave of laughter."

"You're drawing some kind of parallel between Khomeini and this Mahdi I've described, aren't you?"

"I don't know, I guess so, if your Mahdi exists, which I doubt. But if you're right and he does exist, he's coming from the opposite pole, a very practical, nonreligious pole. Still, anybody who feels he has to spread the specter of the Mahdi in these times has a few dangerous screws loose. . . . I'm still not convinced, Evan, but you're persuasive, and I'll do everything I can to help you, help all of us. But it's got to be from a distance, an untraceable distance. I'll give you a telephone number to call; it's buried—nonexistent, in fact—and only two other people have it. You'll be able to reach me, but *only* me. You see, *Shaikh* Kendrick, I can't afford to know you."

"I'm very popular. Washington doesn't want to know me, either."

"Of course not. Neither of us wants the blood of American hostages on our hands."

"I'll need papers for myself and probably lists of air and sea shippers from areas I'll pinpoint."

"Spoken, nothing written down, except for the papers. A name and an address will be delivered to you; pick up the papers from that man."

"Thank you. Incidentally, the State Department said the same thing. Nothing they gave me could be written down."

"For the same reasons."

"Don't worry about it. Everything coincides with what I've got in mind. You see, Ahmat, I don't want to know you either."

"Really?"

"That's the deal I've cut with State. I'm a nonperson in their books and I want to be the same in yours."

The young sultan frowned pensively, his eyes locked with Evan's. "I accept what you say but I can't pretend to understand. You lose your life, that's one thing, but if you have any measure of success, that's another. Why? I'm told you're a politician now. A congressman."

"Because I'm getting out of politics and coming back here, Ahmat. I'm picking up the pieces and going back to work where I worked best, but I don't want any excess baggage with me that might make me a target. Or anyone with me a target."

"All right, I'll accept that, gratefully on both counts. My father claimed that you and your people were the best. I remember, he once said to me, 'Those retarded camels never have a cost overrun.' He meant it kindly, of course."

"And, of course, we usually got the next project, so we weren't so retarded, were we? Our idea was to work on reasonable margins, and we were pretty good at controlling costs. . . . *Ahmat,* we have only four days left before the executions start again. I had to know that if I needed help I could go to you, and now I do know it. I accept your conditions and you accept mine. Now, please, I haven't an hour to waste. What's the number where I can reach you?"

"It can't be written down."

"Understood."

The sultan gave Kendrick the number. Instead of the usual Masqat prefix of 745, it was 555, followed by three zeros and a fourth five. "Can you remember that?"

"It's not difficult," answered Kendrick. "Is it routed through a palace switchboard?"

"No. It's a direct line to two telephones, both locked in steel drawers, one in my office, the other in the bedroom. Instead of ringing, small red lights flash on; in the office the light is built into the right rear leg of my desk, and in the bedroom it's recessed in the bedside table. Both phones become answering machines after the tenth ring."

"The tenth?"

"To give me the time to get rid of people and talk privately. When I travel outside the palace, I carry a beeper that tells me when that phone has been called. At an appropriate time I use the remote and hear the message—over a scrambler, of course."

"You mentioned that only two other people had the number. Should I know who they are or isn't it any of my business?"

"It doesn't matter," replied Ahmat, his dark brown eyes riveted on the American. "One is my minister of security, and the other is my wife."

"Thanks for that kind of trust."

His gaze still rigid on Kendrick, the young sultan continued. "A terrible thing happened to you here in our part of the world, Evan. So many dead, so many close friends, a horrible senseless tragedy, far more so for the greed that was behind it. I must ask you. Has this madness in Masqat dredged up such painful memories that you delude yourself, reaching for implausible theories if only to strike out at phantoms?"

"No phantoms, Ahmat. I hope to prove that to you."

"Perhaps you will—if you live."

"I'll tell you what I told the State Department. I have no intention of mounting a one-man assault on the embassy."

"If you did something like that, you could be considered enough of a lunatic to be spared. Lunacy recognizes its own."

"Now you're the one being implausible."

"Undoubtedly," agreed the sultan of Oman, his eyes still leveled at the congressman from Colorado. "Have you considered what might happen *not* if you're discovered and taken by the terrorists—you wouldn't live long enough to speculate—but if the very people you say you wanted to meet with actually confronted you and demanded to know your purpose here? What would you tell them?"

"Essentially the truth—as close to it as possible. I'm acting on my own, as a private citizen, with no connection to my government, which can be substantiated. I made a great deal of money over here and I'm coming back. If I can help in any way, it's in my own best interests."

"So the bottom line is self-serving. You intend to return here and if this insane killing can be stopped, it will be infinitely more profitable for you. Also, if it isn't stopped, you have no business to return to."

"That's about it."

"Be careful, Evan. Few people will believe you, and if the fear you spoke of is as pervasive among your friends as you say, it may not be the enemy who tries to kill you."

"I've already been warned," said Kendrick.

"What?"

"A man in a truck, a *sahbee* who helped me."

Kendrick lay on the bed, his eyes wide, his thoughts churning, turning from one possibility to another, one vaguely remembered name to another, a face, another face, an office, a street . . . the harbor, the waterfront. He kept going back to the waterfront, to the docks—from Masqat south to Al Qurayyat and Ra's al Hadd. *Why?*

Then his memory was jogged and he knew why. How many times had he and Manny Weingrass made arrangements for equipment to be brought in by purchasable surplus space on freighters from Bahrain and the Emirates in the north? So many they were uncountable. That hundred-mile stretch of coastline south of Masqat and its sister port of Matrah was open territory, even more so beyond Ra's al Hadd. But from there until one reached the short Strait of Masirah, the roads were worse than primitive, and travelers heading into the interior risked being attacked by *haramaya* on horseback—mounted thieves looking for prey, usually other thieves transporting contraband. Still, considering the numbers and depth of the combined intelligence efforts of at least six Western nations concentrating on Masqat, the southern coastline of Oman was a logical area to examine intensively. This was not to say that the Americans, British, French, Italians, West Germans and whoever else were cooperating in the effort to analyze and resolve the hostage crisis in Masqat had overlooked that stretch of Oman's coast, but the reality was that few American patrol boats, those swift, penetrating bullets on the water, were in the Gulf. The others who were there would not shirk their duties, but neither did they possess that certain fury that grips men in the heat of the search when they know their own are being slaughtered. There might even be a degree of reluctance to engage terrorists for fear of being held responsible for additional executions of innocent people—not of their own. The southern coast of Oman could bear some scrutiny.

The sound erupted as harshly as if a siren's warning had split the hot, dry air of the hotel room. The telephone screamed; he picked it up. "Yes?"

"Get out of your hotel," said the quiet, strained voice on the line.

"*Ahmat?*" Evan swung his legs onto the floor.

"Yes! We're on a direct scrambler. If you're bugged, all they'll hear me say is gibberish."

"I just said your name."

"There are thousands like it."

"What's happened?"

"Mustapha. Because of the *children* you spoke of, I called him and ordered him to come immediately to the palace. Unfortunately, in my anger I mentioned my concerns. He must have phoned someone, said something to someone else."

"Why do you say that?"

"On his way here he was gunned down in his car."

"My *God*!"

"If I'm wrong, the only other reason for killing him was his meeting with you."

"Oh, Christ—"

"Leave the hotel right away but don't leave any identification behind. It could be dangerous to you. You'll see two policemen; they'll follow you, protect you, and somewhere in the street one of them will give you the name of the man who will provide you with papers."

"I'm on my way," said Kendrick, getting to his feet, focusing his mind on removing such items as his passport, money belt, airline tickets and whatever articles of clothing might be traced to an American on a plane from Riyadh.

"Evan *Shaikh,*" Ahmat's voice over the line was low, firm. "I'm convinced now. Your Mahdi exists. His people exist. Go after them. Go after *him.*"

5

"*Hasib!*" The warning came from behind telling him to *watch out*! He spun around only to be pressed into the wall of a building in the crowded narrow street by one of the two policemen following him. His face against the stone, the ghotra protecting his flesh, he turned his head to see two bearded, disheveled youths in paramilitary fatigues striding through the bazaarlike thoroughfare, waving heavy, ugly black repeating weapons in their hands, kicking out at merchants' stalls and rubbing their heavy boots on the surfaces of the squatting curb-sellers' woven rugs.

"Look, sir!" whispered the policeman in English, his voice harsh, angry, yet somehow elated. "They do not *see* us!"

"I don't understand." The arrogant young terrorists approached.

"Stay against the wall!" commanded the Arab, now hammering Kendrick back into the shadows, shielding the American's body with his own.

"Why—" The armed hoodlums passed, thrusting the barrels of their guns menacingly into the robed figures in front of them.

"Be still, sir! They are drunk either with the forbidden spirits or on the blood they have shed. But thanks be to Allah, they are *outside* the embassy."

"What do you mean?"

"Those of us in uniform are not permitted within sight of the embassy, but if *they* come *outside,* it is another matter. Our hands are untied."

"What happens?" Up ahead, one of the terrorists smashed the butt of his weapon into the head of an offending Omani; his companion swung his rifle around at the crowd, warning it.

"Either they face the wrath of the Allah they spit on," replied the policeman, whispering, his eyes filled with rage at the scene, "or they join the other reckless, filthy pigs! Stay here, *ya Shaikh,* sir! Stay in this small bazaar. I will be back, I have a name to give you."

"The *other— What* other filthy pigs?" Evan's words were lost; the sultan's police officer sprang away from the wall, joining his partner, now surging through the shadowed, turbulent sea of abas. Kendrick pulled the ghotra around his face and ran after them.

What followed was as baffling and as swift to the untrained eye as a surgeon's scalpel plunging into a hemorrhaging organ. The second policeman glanced back at his companion. They nodded to each other; both sprang forward, closing in on the two swaggering terrorists. There was an intersecting alleyway up ahead on the right, and as if an unheard signal had pierced the narrow bazaar, the crowds of sellers and buyers dispersed in various directions. Almost instantly the alleyway was empty, a dark, deserted tunnel.

The policemen's two knives were suddenly plunged into the upper right arms of the two arrogant killers. Screams, covered by the intense, growing babble of the moving crowds, followed the involuntary release of weapons as blood spewed out of torn flesh and arrogance turned into infuriated weakness, death perhaps preferable to disgrace, eyes bulging in disbelief.

The terrorists were rushed into the dark alley by Ahmat's two trusted police; unseen hands threw the huge lethal weapons after them. Kendrick parted the bodies in front of him and raced into the deserted tunnel. Twenty feet inside, the youthful, wild-eyed killers were supine on the stone pavement, the policemen's knives above their throats.

"*La!*" shouted Evan's protector, telling him *No!* "Turn away!" he continued in English, for fear Kendrick might misunderstand. "Hide your face and say *nothing*!"

"I *must ask* you!" cried Kendrick, turning, but disobeying the second command. "They probably don't speak English, anyway—"

"They probably do, *ya Shaikh,* sir," broke in the other policeman. "Whatever you have to say, say *later*! As spokesman, my instructions are to be obeyed without question. Is that understood, *sir*?"

"Understood." Evan nodded quickly and walked back toward the arched entrance to the bazaar.

"I will come back, *ya Shaikh,*" said Kendrick's protector, hovering over his prisoner. "We will take these pigs out the other end and I will be back for you—"

The man's words were interrupted by a violent, shattering scream of defiance. Without thinking, Evan whipped his head around, suddenly wishing he hadn't, wondering instantly if the image would ever leave him. The terrorist on the left had grabbed the policeman's long-bladed knife above and yanked it down, slicing it into his own throat. The sight turned Kendrick's stomach; he thought he would vomit.

"*Fool!*" roared the second policeman, not so much in rage as in anguish. "Child! *Pig!* Why do you do this to yourself? Why to *me*?" The protest was in vain; the terrorist was dead, blood covering his bearded young face. Somehow, thought Evan, he had witnessed a microcosm of the violence, the pain, and the futility that was the world of the Middle East and Southwest Asia.

"All is changed," said the first officer, his knife held up, rising above his open-mouthed, incredulous prisoner, and touching his comrade's shoulder. The latter shook his head as if trying to rid his eyes and his mind of the youthful, bloody corpse beneath him, then nodded rapidly, telling his companion he understood. The first officer approached Kendrick. "There will be a delay now. This incident must not reach the other streets, so we must move quickly. The man you seek, the man who is waiting for you is known as El-Baz. You will find him in the market beyond the old south fortress in the harbor. There is a bakery selling orange baklava. Ask inside."

"The south fortress . . . in the harbor?"

"There are two stone fortresses built by the Portuguese many centuries ago. The Mirani and the Jalili—"

"I remember, of course," interrupted Evan, rambling, finding part of his sanity, his eyes avoiding the death wound of the mutilated body on the floor of the dark alleyway. "Two forts built to protect the harbor from raiding pirates. They're ruins now—a bakery selling orange baklava."

"There is no *time,* sir. *Go!* Run out the other side. You cannot be seen here any longer. *Quickly!*"

"First answer my question," shot back Kendrick, angering the police officer by not moving. "Or I stay here and you can answer to your sultan."

"What *question*? Leave!"

"You said these two might join 'other reckless . . . pigs'—those were your words. What other pigs? Where?"

"There is no time!"

"*Answer* me!"

The policeman inhaled deeply through his nostrils, trembling with frustration. "Very well. Incidents like tonight have happened before. We have taken a number of prisoners who are questioned by many people. Nothing must be said—"

"How many?"

"Thirty, forty, perhaps fifty by now. They disappear from the embassy and others, always *others,* take their places!"

"Where?"

The officer stared at Evan and shook his head. "No, *ya Shaikh,* sir, that I will not tell you. *Go!*"

"I understand. Thanks." The congressman from Colorado gripped the cloth of his aba and raced down the alley toward the exit, turning his face away as he ran past the dead terrorist, whose streaming blood now filled the crevices between the cobblestones.

He emerged on the street, looked up at the sky and determined his direction. To the sea, to the ruins of the ancient fortress on the south shore of the harbor. He would find the man named El-Baz and arrange for the proper papers, but his mind was not on that negotiation. Instead, he was consumed by information he had heard only moments ago: *thirty, forty, perhaps fifty by now.* Between thirty and fifty terrorists were being held in some isolated compound in or outside the city, being interrogated with varying degrees of force by the combined intelligence units. Yet if his theory was correct, that these child butchers were the maniacal dregs of Islam, manipulated by an overlord of financial crime in Bahrain, all the interrogation techniques from the pharaohs to the Inquisition to the camps in Hoa Binh would be useless. Unless—*unless*—a name that conjured up a zealot's most fanatical passions was delivered to one of the prisoners, persuading him to divulge what he would normally take his own life before revealing. It would mean finding a very special fanatic, of course, but it *was* possible. Evan had said to Frank Swann that perhaps one in twenty of the terrorists might be intelligent enough to fit this description—one out of twenty, roughly ten or twelve in the entire contingent of killers at the embassy—if he was right. Could one of them be among the thirty to fifty prisoners in that isolated, secret compound? The odds were slim, but a few hours inside, at most a night, would tell him. The time was worth spending if he could be allowed to spend it. To begin his hunt he needed a few words—a name, a place, a location on the coastline, an access code that led back to Bahrain. *Something!* He had to get inside that compound tonight. The executions were to be resumed three days from tomorrow at ten o'clock in the morning.

First the papers from a man called El-Baz.

The ruins of the old Portuguese fortress rose eerily into the dark sky, a jagged silhouette that bespoke the strength and resolve of seagoing adventurers of centuries past. Evan walked rapidly through the area of the city known as Harat Waljat toward the market of Sabat Aynub, the name translated freely as the basket of grapes, a marketplace far more structured than a bazaar, with well-kept shops lining the square, the architecture bewildering, for it was an amalgam of early Arabic, Persian, Indian and the most modern of Western influences. All these, thought Kendrick, would fade one day, an Omani presence be restored, once again confirming the impermanence of conquerors—military, political or terrorist. It was the last that concerned him now. The *Mahdi.*

He entered the large square. A Roman fountain was sending sprays of water above a dark circular pool in whose center stood a statue of some Italian sculptor's concept of a desert sheikh striding forward, robes flowing, going nowhere. But it was the crowds that stole Evan's attention. Most were male Arabs, merchants catering to the rich and foolhardy Europeans, tourists indifferent to the chaos at the embassy, marked by their Western clothes and profusion of gold bracelets and chains, glistening symbols of defiance in a city gone mad. The Omanis, however, were like animated robots, forcing themselves to concentrate on the inconsequential, their ears blocking out the constant gunfire from the American embassy less than a half mile away. Everywhere, their eyes blinked and squinted incessantly, brows frowning in disbelief and disassociation. What was happening in their peaceful Masqat was beyond their understanding; they were no part of the madness, no part at *all,* so they did their best to shut it out.

He saw it. *Balawa bohrtooan.* "Orange baklava," the specialty of the bakery. The Turkish-styled small brown shop with a succession of minarets painted above the glass of the storefront was sandwiched between a large, brightly lighted jewelry store and an equally fashionable boutique devoted to leather goods, the name *Paris* scattered in black and gold signs beyond the glass in front of ascending blocks of luggage and accessories. Kendrick walked diagonally across the square, past the fountain, and approached the door of the bakery.

"Your people were right," said the dark-haired woman in the tailored black suit walking out of the shadows of the Harat Waljat, the miniature camera in her hand. She raised it and pressed the shutter release; the automatic advance took successive photographs as Evan Kendrick entered the bakery shop in the market of Sabat Aynub. "Was he noticed in the bazaar?" she asked, replacing the camera in her purse, addressing the short, robed middle-aged Arab who cautiously stood behind her.

"There was talk about a man running into the alley after the police," said the informant, his eyes on the bakery. "It was contradicted, convincingly, I believe."

"How? He was seen."

"But in the excitement he was *not* seen rushing out, clasping his billfold, which was presumably taken by the pigs. That was the information emphatically exclaimed by our man to the onlookers. Naturally, others emphatically agreed, for hysterical people will always leap on new information unknown to a crowd of strangers. It elevates them."

"You're very good," said the woman, laughing softly. "So are your people."

"We had better be, *ya anisa* Khalehla," responded the Arab, using the Omani title of respect. "If we are less than that, we face alternatives we'd rather not consider."

"Why the bakery?" asked Khaleh. "Any ideas?"

"None whatsoever. I detest baklava. The honey doesn't drip, it pours. The Jews like it, you know."

"So do I."

"Then you both forget what the Turks did to you—both."

"I don't think our subject went into that bakery for either baklava or a historical treatise on the Turks versus the tribes of Egypt and Israel."

"A daughter of Cleopatra speaks?" The informant smiled.

"This daughter of Cleopatra doesn't know what the hell you're talking about. I'm just trying to learn things."

"Then start with the military sedan that picked up your subject several blocks north of his hotel after the prayers of *el Maghreb.* It has considerable significance."

"He must have friends in the army."

"There is only the sultan's garrison in Masqat."

"So?"

"The officers are rotated bimonthly between the city and the posts at Jiddah and Marmul, as well as a dozen or so garrisons along the borders of South Yemen."

"What's your point?"

"I present you with two points, Khalehla. The first is that I find it unbelievably coincidental that the subject, after four years, would so conveniently know a certain friend in the relatively small rotating officer corps stationed this specific fortnight in Masqat in an officer corps that changes with the years—"

"Unusually coincidental, I agree, but certainly possible. What's your second point?"

"Actually, it negates my mentioning the first. These days no vehicle from the Masqat garrison would pick up a foreigner in the manner he was picked up, in the guise he was picked up, without supreme authority."

"The *sultan*?"

"Who else?"

"He wouldn't dare! He's boxed. A wrong move and he'd be held responsible for whatever executions take place. If that happens, the Americans would level Masqat to the ground. He knows that!"

"Perhaps he also knows that he is held responsible both for what he *does* do as well as for what he does *not* do. In such a situation it's better to know what others are doing, if only to offer guidance—or to abort some unproductive activity with one more execution."

Khalehla looked hard at the informant in the dim light of the square's periphery. "If that military car took the subject to a meeting with the sultan, it also brought him back."

"Yes, it did," agreed the middle-aged man, his voice flat, as if he understood the implication.

"Which means that whatever the subject proposed was not rejected out of hand."

"It would appear so, *ya anisa* Khalehla."

"And *we* have to know what was proposed, don't we?"

"It would be dangerous in the extreme for all of us *not* to know," said the Arab, nodding. "We are dealing with more than the deaths of two hundred thirty-six Americans. We are dealing with the destiny of a nation. *My* nation, I should add, and I shall do my best to see that it remains *ours.* Do you understand me, my dear Khalehla?"

"I do, *ya sahib el Aumer.*"

"Better a dead cipher than a catastrophic shock."

"I understand."

"Do you really? You had far more advantages in your Mediterranean than we ever had in our obscure Gulf. It is our time now. We won't let anyone stop us."

"I want you to have your time, dear friend. *We* want you to have it."

"Then do what you must do, *ya sahbitee* Khalehla."

"I will." The well-tailored woman reached into her purse and took out a short-barreled automatic. Holding it in her left hand, she again searched her purse and removed a clip of bullets; with a pronounced click she jammed it into the base of the handle and snapped back the loading chamber. The weapon was ready to fire. "Go now, *adeem sahbee,*" she said, securing the strap of her purse over her shoulder, her hand inside, gripping the automatic. "We understand each other and you must be somewhere else, someplace where others can see you, not here."

"*Salaam aleikum,* Khalehla. Go with Allah."

"I'll send *him* to Allah to plead his case. . . . *Quickly.* He's coming out of the bakery! I'll follow him and do what has to be done. You have perhaps ten to fifteen minutes to be with others away from here."

"At the last, you protect us, don't you? You are a treasure. Be careful, dear Khalehla."

"Tell *him* to be careful. He intrudes."

"I'll go to the Zawadi mosque and talk with the elder mullahs and muezzins. Holy eyes are not questioned. It is a short distance, five minutes at most."

"*Aleikum salaam,*" said the woman, starting across the square to her left, her gaze riveted on the American in Arab robes who had passed beyond the fountain and was walking rapidly toward the dark, narrow streets to the east, beyond the market of Sabat Aynub. *What is that damn fool doing?* she thought as she removed her hat, crushing it with her left hand and shoving it into her purse next to the weapon that she gripped feverishly in her right. *He's heading into the el Shari el Mishkwiyis,* she concluded, mixing her thoughts in Arabic and English, referring to what is called in the West the roughest section of town, an area outsiders avoid. *They were right. He's an amateur and I can't go in there dressed like this! But I have to. My God, he'll get us both killed!*

Evan Kendrick hurried down the uneven layers of stone that was the narrow street, past low, run-down, congested buildings and half-buildings—crumbling structures with canvas and animal skins covering blown-out windows; those that remained intact were protected by slatted shutters, more broken than not. Bare wires sagged everywhere, municipal junction boxes having been spliced, electricity stolen, dangerous. The pungent smells of Arabic cooking intermingled with stronger odors, unmistakable odors—hashish, burning coca leaves smuggled into unpatrolled coves in the Gulf, and pockets of human waste. The inhabitants of this stretch of ghetto moved slowly, cautiously, suspiciously through the dimly lit caverns of their world, at home with its degradation, comfortable with its insulated dangers, at ease with their collective status as outcasts—the ease confirmed by sudden bursts of laughter behind shuttered windows. The dress code of this el Shari el Mishkwiyis was anything but consistent. Abas and ghotras coexisted with torn blue jeans, forbidden miniskirts, and the uniforms of sailors and soldiers from a dozen different nations—soiled uniforms exclusively from the ranks of enlisted personnel, although it was said that many an officer borrowed a subordinate's clothes to venture inside and taste the prohibited pleasures of the neighborhood.

Men huddled in doorways, to Evan's annoyance, for they obscured the barely legible numbers on the sandstone walls. He was further annoyed by the filthy intersecting alleys that unaccountably caused the numbers to skip from one section of the street to the next. *El-Baz. Number 77 Shari el Balah*—the street of dates. Where *was* it?

There it was. A deeply recessed heavy door with thick iron bars across a closed slot that was built into the upper panel at eye level. However, a man in disheveled robes squatting diagonally against the stone blocked the door on the right side of the tunnellike entrance.

"*Esmahlee?*" said Kendrick, excusing himself and stepping forward.

"*Lay?*" replied the haunched figure, asking why.

"I have an appointment," continued Evan in Arabic. "I'm expected."

"Who sends you?" said the man without moving.

"That's not your concern."

"I am not here to receive such an answer." The Arab raised his back, angling it against the door; the robes of his aba parted slightly, revealing the handle of a pistol tucked into an undersash. "Again, who sends you?"

Evan wondered if the sultan's police officer had forgotten to give him a name or a code or a password that would gain him entrance. He had so little time! He did not need this obstruction; he reached for an answer. "I visited a bakery in the Sabat Aynub," he said rapidly. "I spoke—"

"A bakery?" broke in the squatting man, his brows arched beneath his headdress. "There are at least three bakeries in the Sabat Aynub."

"Goddamnit, *baklava*!" spat out Kendrick, his frustration mounting, his eyes on the handle of the gun. "Some asinine orange—"

"Enough," said the guard, abruptly rising to his feet and pulling his robes together. "It was a simple reply to a simple question, sir. A *baker* sent you, you see?"

"All right. *Fine!* May I go inside, please?"

"First we must determine whom you visit. Whom do you visit, sir?"

"For God's sake, the man who lives here . . . works here."

"He is a man without a name?"

"Are you entitled to know it?" Evan's intense whisper carried over the street noises beyond.

"A fair question, sir," said the Arab, nodding pensively. "However, since I was aware of a baker in the Sabat Aynub—"

"Christ on a raft!" exploded Kendrick. "All right. His name is El-Baz! Now will you let me *in*? I'm in a hurry!"

"It will be my pleasure to alert the resident, sir. *He* will let you in if it is *his* pleasure. Certainly you can understand the necessity for—"

It was as far as the ponderous guard got before snapping his head toward the pavement outside. The undercurrent of noises from the dark street had suddenly erupted. A man screamed; others roared, their strident voices echoing off the surrounding stone.

"Elhahoonai!"

"Udam!"

And then piercing the chorus of outrage was a woman's voice. *"Siboni fihalee!"* she cried frantically, demanding to be left alone. Then came in perfect English, "You *bastards*!"

Evan and the guard rushed to the edge of the stone as two gunshots shattered the human cacophony, escalating it into frenzy, the ominous rings of ricocheting bullets receding in the cavernous distance. The Arab guard spun around, hurling himself to the hard stone floor of the entranceway. Kendrick crouched; he had to *know*! Three robed figures accompanied by a young man and woman dressed in slovenly Western clothes raced past, the male in torn khaki trousers clutching his bleeding arm. Evan stood up and cautiously peered around the edge of the stone corner. What he saw astonished him.

In the shadows of the confining street stood a bareheaded woman, a short-bladed knife in her left hand, her right gripping an automatic. Slowly, Kendrick stepped out on the uneven layers of stone. Their eyes met and locked. The woman raised her gun; Evan froze, trying desperately to decide what to do and when to do it, knowing that if he moved quickly she would fire. Instead, to his further astonishment, she began stepping backward into the deeper shadows, her weapon still leveled at him. Suddenly, with the approach of excited voices punctuated by the repeated penetrating sounds of a shrill whistle, the woman turned and raced away down the dark narrow street. In seconds she had disappeared. She had followed him! To kill him? *Why?* Who *was* she?

"*Here!*" In a panicked whisper the guard was calling him. Evan whipped his head around; the Arab was gesturing wildly for him to come to the heavy, forbidding door in the recessed entranceway. "*Quickly,* sir! You have gained admittance. *Hurry!* You must not be observed here!"

The door swung open and Evan ran inside, and was instantly pulled to his left by the strong hand of a very small man who shouted to the guard in the entranceway. "Get away from here!" he cried. "*Quickly!*" he added. The diminutive Arab slammed the door shut, slapping in place two iron bolts as Kendrick squinted his eyes in the dim light. They were in some kind of foyer, a wide, run-down hallway with several closed doors set progressively down both sides of the corridor. Numerous small Persian rugs covered the rough wood of the floor—rugs, Kendrick mused, that would bring very decent prices at any Western auction—and on the walls were more rugs, larger rugs that Evan *knew* would bring small fortunes. The man called El-Baz put his profits into intricately woven treasures. Those who knew about such things would be instantly impressed that they were dealing with an important man. The others, which included most of the police and other regulating authorities, would undoubtedly think that this secretive man covered his floors and his walls with tourist cloth to avoid repairing flaws in his residence. The artist called El-Baz knew his marketing procedures.

"I am El-Baz," said the small, slightly bent Arab in English, extending a veined, large hand. "You are whoever you say you are and I am delighted to meet you, preferably not with the name your revered parents gave you. Please come this way, the second door on the right, please. It is our first and most vital procedure. In truth, the rest has been accomplished."

"Accomplished? *What's* been accomplished?" asked Evan.

"The essentials," answered El-Baz. "The papers are prepared according to the information delivered to me."

"What information?"

"Who you may be, what you may be, where you might come from. That is all I needed."

"Who gave this information to you?"

"I have no idea," said the aged Arab, touching Kendrick's arm, insinuating him down the foyer. "An unknown person instructing me over the telephone, from where I know not. However, she used the proper words and I knew I was to obey."

"She?"

"The gender was insignificant, *ya Shaikh.* The words were all-important. Come. Inside." El-Baz opened the door to a small photographic studio; the equipment appeared out of date. Evan's rapid appraisal was not lost on El-Baz. "The camera on the left duplicates the grainy quality of government identifications," he explained, "which, of course, is as much due everywhere to government processing as it is to the eye of the camera. Here. Sit on the stool in front of the screen. It will be painless and swift."

El-Baz worked quickly, and as the film was non-negative instant, he had no difficulty selecting a print. Burning the others, the old man put on a pair of thin surgical gloves, held the single photo, and gestured toward a wide-curtained area beyond the stretched gray fabric that served as a screen. Approaching it, he pulled back the heavy drapery, revealing a blank distressed wall; the appearance was deceiving. Placing his right foot next to a spot on the chipped floor molding, his gloved right hand reaching for another specific location above, he simultaneously pressed both. A jagged crack in the wall slowly separated, the left side disappearing behind the curtain; it stopped, leaving a space roughly two feet wide. The small purveyor of false papers stepped inside, beckoning Kendrick to follow him.

What Evan saw now was as modern as any machine in his Washington office and of even higher quality. There were two large computers, each with its own printer, and four telephones in four different colors, all with communication modems, all situated on a long white table kept spotlessly clean in front of four typist's chairs.

"Here," said El-Baz, pointing to the computer on the left, where the dark screen was alive with bright green letters. "See how privileged you are, *ya Shaikh.* I was told to provide you with complete information and the sources thereof, but not, however, with any written documents other than the papers themselves. Sit. Study yourself."

"Study myself?" asked Kendrick.

"You are a Saudi from Riyadh named Amal Bahrudi. You are a construction engineer and there is some European blood in your veins—a grandfather, I think; it's written on the screen."

"European . . . ?"

"It explains your somewhat irregular features should anyone comment."

"Wait a minute." Evan bent over, looking closer at the computer screen. "This is a real *person*?"

"He was. He died last night in East Berlin—that is the green telephone."

"Died? Last *night*?"

"East German intelligence, controlled, of course, by the Soviets, will keep his death quiet for days, perhaps weeks, while their bureaucrats examine everything with an eye toward KGB advantage, naturally. In the meantime, Mr. Bahrudi's arrival here has been duly entered on our immigration lists—that's the blue telephone—with a visa good for thirty days."

"So if anyone runs a check," added Kendrick, "this Bahrudi is legitimately here and not dead in East Berlin."

"Exactly."

"What happens if I'm caught?"

"That would hardly concern you. You'd be an immediate corpse."

"But the Soviets could make trouble for us here. They'd know I'm not Bahrudi."

"Could they? Would they?" The old Arab shrugged. "Never pass up an opportunity to confuse or embarrass the KGB, *ya Shaikh.*"

Evan paused, frowning. "I think I see what you mean. How did you *get* all this? For God's sake, a dead Saudi in *East Berlin*—covered up—his dossier, even some grandfather, a *European* grandfather. It's unbelievable."

"Believe, my young friend, whom I do not know nor have ever met. Of course, there must be confederates in many places for men like me, but that is not your concern, either. Simply study the salient facts: revered parents' names, schools, universities—two, I believe, one in the United States, so like the Saudis. You won't need any more than that. If you do, it won't matter. You'll be dead."

Kendrick walked out of the underworld city within a city, skirting the grounds of the Waljat Hospital in the northeast section of Masqat. He was less than a hundred fifty yards from the gates of the American embassy. The wide street was now only half filled with die-hard spectators. The torches and the rapid bursts of gunfire from within the grounds of the embassy created the illusion that the crowds were much larger and more hysterical than they actually were. Such witnesses to the terror inside were interested only in entertainment; their ranks thinned as one by one they were overcome by sleepiness. Ahead, less than a quarter of a mile beyond the Harat Waljat, was Alam Palace, the young sultan's seaside mansion. Evan looked at his watch; the hour and his location were an advantage; he had so little *time* and Ahmat had to move quickly. He looked for a street phone, vaguely remembering that there were several near the hospital entrance—again thanks to Manny Weingrass. Twice the reprobate old architect had claimed his brandy was poisoned, and once an Omani woman had bitten his wandering hand so severely that he required seven stitches.

The white plastic shells of three public phones in the distance reflected the light from the streetlamps. Gripping the inside pocket of his robes where he had put his false papers, he broke into a run, then immediately slowed down. Instinct told him not to appear obvious . . . or threatening. He reached the first booth, inserted a larger coin than was necessary, and dialed the strange number indelibly printed on his mind. *555-0005*.

Beads of sweat formed at his hairline as the progressively slower rings reached eight. Two more and an answering machine would replace the human voice! Please!

"*Iwah?*" came the simple greeting saying, Yes?

"English," said Evan.

"So quickly?" replied Ahmat, astonished. "What is it?"

"First things first. . . . A woman followed me. The light was dim, but from what I could see she was of medium height, with long hair, and dressed in what looked like expensive Western clothes. Also, she was fluent in both Arabic and English. Anybody come to mind?"

"If you mean someone who would follow you into El-Baz's neighborhood, absolutely *no one.* Why?"

"I think she meant to kill me."

"*What?*"

"And a woman gave El-Baz the information about me—over a telephone, of course."

"I know that."

"Could there be a connection?"

"How?"

"Someone moving in, someone looking to steal false papers."

"I hope not," said Ahmat firmly. "The woman who spoke to El-Baz was my wife. I would not trust your presence here with anyone else."

"Thank you for that, but someone else knows I'm here."

"You spoke to four men, Evan, and one of them, our mutual friend, Mustapha, was killed. I agree that someone else knows you're here. It's why the other three are under twenty-four-hour surveillance. Perhaps you should stay out of sight, in hiding, for at least a day. I can arrange it, and we might learn something. Also, I have something I must discuss with you. It concerns this Amal Bahrudi. Go in hiding for a day. I think that would be best, don't you?"

"No," answered Kendrick, his voice hollow at what he was about to say. "Out of sight, yes, but not in hiding."

"I don't understand."

"I want to be arrested, seized as a terrorist. I want to be thrown into that compound you've got somewhere. I've got to get in there *tonight*!"

6

The robed figure raced down the middle of the wide avenue known as the Wadi Al Kabir. He had burst out of the darkness from beyond the massive Mathaib Gate several hundred yards from the waterfront west of the ancient Portuguese fortress called the Mirani. His robes were drenched with the oil and flotsam of the harbor, his headdress clinging to the back of his wet hair. To observers—and there were still many in the street at this late hour—the desperately running man was one more dog from the sea, an alien who had leaped from a ship to gain illegal entrance into this once peaceful sultanate, a fugitive, or a terrorist.

Strident eruptions of a two-note siren grew louder as a patrol car careened around the corner from the Wadi Al Uwar into the Al Kabir. The chase was joined; a police informant had betrayed the point of entry, and the authorities were ready. These days they were always ready, ready and eager and frenzied. A blinding light split the dimly lit street, its beam coming from a movable lamp mounted on the patrol car. The powerful light caught the panicked illegal; he spun to his left, facing a series of shops, their dark storefronts protected by iron shutters, protection that had not been thought of barely three weeks ago. The man pivoted, lurching across the Al Kabir to his right. Suddenly he stopped, blocked by a number of late-night strollers who moved together, stood together, their stares not without fear but somehow collectively saying they had had enough. They wanted their city back. A short man in a business suit but in Arab headdress stepped forward—cautiously, to be sure, but with purpose. Two larger men in robes, perhaps more cautiously but with equal purpose, joined him, followed hesitantly by others. Down the Al Kabir to the south a crowd had gathered; tentatively they formed a line, robed men and veiled women creating a human wall across the street, courage reluctantly summoned out of both exasperation and fury. It all had to stop!

"*Get away!* Spread yourselves! He may have *grenades*!" A police officer had jumped out of the patrol car and was racing forward, his automatic weapon leveled at the quarry.

"*Disperse!*" roared a second policeman, sprinting down the left side of the street. "Don't get caught in our *fire*!"

The cautious strollers and the hesitant crowd beyond scattered in all directions, running for the protection of distance and the shelters of doorways. As if on cue, the fugitive grappled with his drenched robes, pulling them apart and menacingly reaching inside the folds of cloth. A staccato burst of gunfire shattered the Al Kabir; the fugitive screamed, calling on the powers of a furious Allah and a vengeful Al Fatah as he gripped his shoulder, arched his neck and dropped to the ground. He seemed to be dead, but in the dim light no one could determine the extent of his wounds. He screamed again, a roar, summoning the furies of all Islam to descend on the hordes of impure unbelievers everywhere. The two police officers fell on him as the patrol car skidded to a stop, its tires screeching; a third policeman leaped from the open rear door shouting orders.

"Disarm him! Search him!" His two subordinates had anticipated both commands. "It could be *he*!" added the superior officer, crouching to examine the fugitive more closely, his voice even louder than before. "*There!*" he continued, still shouting. "Strapped to his thigh. A packet. Give it to me!"

The onlookers slowly rose in the semidarkness, curiosity drawing them back to the furious activity taking place in the middle of the Al Kabir under the dim wash of the streetlights.

"I believe you are right, sir!" yelled the policeman on the prisoner's left. "Here, this mark! It could be what remains of the scar across his neck."

"*Bahrudi!*" roared the ranking police officer in triumph as he studied the papers ripped from the oilcloth packet. "Amal *Bahrudi*! The *trusted* one! He was last in East Berlin and, by Allah, we *have* him!"

"*All* of you!" yelled the policeman, kneeling to the right of the fugitive, addressing the mesmerized crowd. "Leave! Get *away*! This pig may have protectors—he is the infamous *Bahrudi,* the Eastern European terrorist! We have radioed for soldiers from the sultan's garrison—get *away,* don't be killed!"

The witnesses fled, a disjointed stampede racing south on the Al Kabir. They had summoned their courage, but the prospect of a gun battle panicked them. All was uncertainty, punctuated by death; the only thing the crowd was certain of was that a notorious international terrorist named Amal Bahrudi had been captured.

"The word will spread quickly in our small city," said the sergeant-of-police in fluent English, helping the "prisoner" to his feet. "We will help, of course, if it is necessary."

"I've got a question or two—maybe *three*!" Evan untied the headdress, removing it over his head, and stared at the police officer. "What the hell was all that stuff about 'the trusted one,' the 'Islamic leader' of East European whatever-it-was?"

"Apparently the truth, sir."

"I'm way behind you."

"In the car, please. Time is vital. We must leave here."

"I want *answers*!" The two other policemen walked up beside the congressman from Colorado, gripped his arms and escorted him to the back door of the patrol car. "I played that little charade the way I was told to play it," continued Evan, climbing into the green police sedan, "but someone forgot to mention that this real person whose name I'm assuming is some killer who's throwing bombs around Europe!"

"I can only tell you what I've been told to tell you, which, truthfully, is all I know," replied the sergeant, settling his uniformed figure beside Kendrick. "Everything will be explained to you at the laboratory at the compound headquarters."

"I know about the laboratory. I *don't* know about this Bahrudi."

"He exists, sir."

"I know *that* but not the rest of it—"

"Hurry, driver!" said the police officer. "The other two will remain here." The green sedan lurched in reverse, made a U-turn and sped back toward the Wadi Al Uwar.

"All right, he's real, I understand that," pressed Kendrick rapidly, breathlessly. "But I *repeat.* No one said anything about his being a terrorist!"

"At the headquarters laboratory, sir." The sergeant-of-police lit a brown Arabian cigarette, inhaled deeply and exhaled the smoke through his nostrils in relief. His part of the strange assignment was over.

"There was a great deal that El-Baz's computer did not print out for your eyes," said the Omani doctor, studying Evan's bare shoulder. They were alone in the laboratory examining room, Kendrick sitting on the elongated hard-cushioned table, his feet resting on a footstool, his money belt beside him. "As Ahmat's—forgive me—the great sultan's personal physician, which I have been since he was eight years old, I am now your *only* contact to him in the event you cannot for whatever reason reach him yourself. Is that understood?"

"How do I reach *you*?"

"The hospital or my private number, which I will give you when we are finished. You must remove your trousers and undergarment and apply the dye, *ya Shaikh.* Strip searches are a daily, often hourly, occurrence in that compound. You must be all one flesh color, and certainly no canvas belt filled with money."

"You'll hold it for me?"

"Certainly."

"Back to this Bahrudi, please," said Kendrick, applying the skin-darkening gel to his thighs and lower regions, as the Omani physician did the same to his arms, chest and back. "Why didn't El-Baz tell me?"

"Ahmat's instructions. He thought you might object, so he wished to explain it to you himself."

"I spoke to him less than an hour ago. He didn't say anything other than he wanted to talk about this Bahrudi, that's all."

"You were also in a great hurry and he had much to organize in order to bring about your so-called capture. Therefore he left the explanation to me. Lift your arm up higher, please."

"What's the explanation?" asked Evan, less angry now.

"Quite simply, if you were taken by the terrorists you'd have a fall-back position, at least for a while, with luck providing enough time to help you—if help was at all possible."

"What fall-back position?"

"You'd be considered one of them. Until they learned otherwise."

"Bahrudi's dead—"

"His corpse is in the hands of the KGB," added the doctor instantly, overriding Kendrick's words. "The Komitet is notoriously indecisive, afraid of embarrassment."

"El-Baz mentioned something about that."

"If anyone in Masqat would know, it is El-Baz."

"So if Bahrudi is accepted here in Oman, if *I'm* accepted as this Bahrudi, I might have some leverage. *If* the Soviets don't blow the whistle and tell what they know."

"They will exhaustively examine the whistle before bringing it near their lips. They can't be certain; they will fear a trap, a trap of embarrassment, of course, and wait for developments. Your other arm, please. Lift it straight up, please."

"*Question,*" said Evan firmly. "If Amal Bahrudi supposedly went through your immigration, why wasn't he picked up? You've got one hell of a security force out there these days."

"How many John Smiths are there in your country, *ya Shaikh*?"

"So?"

"Bahrudi is a fairly common Arabic name, more so perhaps in Cairo than in Riyadh but nevertheless not unusual. Amal is the equivalent of your 'Joe' or 'Bill' or, of course 'John.' "

"Still, El-Baz entered him in the immigration computers. Flags would leap up—"

"And rapidly return to their recesses," broke in the Omani, "the officials satisfied by observation and harsh, if routine, questioning."

"Because there's no scar on my neck?" asked Evan quickly. "One of the police in the Al Kabir made a point of a scar across my neck—Bahrudi's neck."

"That is information I know nothing about, but I suppose it's possible; you have no such scar. But there are more fundamental reasons."

"Such as?"

"A terrorist does not announce his arrival in a foreign land, much less a troubled one. He uses false papers. That's what the authorities look for, not the coincidence of one John W. Booth, a pharmacist from Philadelphia, who was cursed with the same name as the assassin from Ford's Theater."

"You're pretty well versed in things American, aren't you?"

"Johns Hopkins Medical School, Mr. *Bahrudi.* Courtesy of our sultan's father, who found a Bedouin child eager for more than a wandering tribal existence."

"How did that happen?"

"It is another story. You may lower your arm now."

Evan looked at the doctor. "You're very fond of the sultan, I gather."

The Omani physician returned Kendrick's gaze. "I would kill for the family, *ya Shaikh,*" he said softly. "Of course, the method would be nonviolent. Perhaps poison or a misdiagnosed medical crisis or a reckless scalpel—something to repay my debt in kind—but I would do it."

"I'm sure you would. And by extension, then, you're on my side."

"Obviously. The proof I am to give you and which was previously unknown to me comes numerically. Five, five, five—zero, zero, zero, five."

"That's good enough. What's your name?"

"Faisal. Dr. *Amal* Faisal."

"I see what you mean—'John Smith.' " Kendrick got off the examining table and walked naked to a small sink across the room. He washed his hands, kneading them with strong soap to remove the excess stains from his fingers, and studied his body in the mirror above the basin. The undarkened white flesh was turning brown; in moments it would be dark enough for the terrorist compound. He looked at the doctor reflected in the glass. "How is it in there?" he said.

"It is no place for you."

"That's not what I asked. I want to know what it's like. Are there rites of passage, any rituals they go through with new prisoners? You must have the place wired—you'd be fools if you don't."

"It's wired and we have to assume they know it; they crowd around the door where the main taps are and make a great deal of noise. The ceiling is too high for audible transmission and the remaining taps are in the flushing mechanisms of the toilets—a civilizing reform instituted by Ahmat several years ago, replacing the floor holes. They've been useless, as if the inmates had determined they were placed there—we don't know this, of course. However, what we minimally hear is not pleasant. The prisoners, like all extremists, continuously vie for who is the most zealous, and as there are constant newcomers, many do not know each other. As a result, the questions are severe and pointed, the methods of interrogation often brutal. They're fanatics, but not fools in the accepted sense, *ya Shaikh.* Vigilance is their credo, infiltration a constant threat to them."

"Then it'll be my credo." Kendrick crossed back to the examining table and the neat pile of prison clothes provided for him. "My vigilance," he continued. "As fanatic as anyone's in there." He turned to the Omani. "I need the names of the leaders inside the embassy. I wasn't permitted to make any notes from the briefing papers, but I memorized two because they were repeated several times. One was Abu Nassir; the other, Abbas Zaher. Do you have any more?"

"Nassir hasn't been seen for over a week; they believe he's gone, and Zaher is not considered a leader, merely a show-off. Recently the most prominent appears to be a woman named Zaya Yateem. She's fluent in English and reads the televised bulletins."

"What does she look like?"

"Who can tell? She wears a veil."

"Anyone else?"

"A young man who's usually behind her; he seems to be her companion and carries a Russian weapon—I don't know what kind."

"His name?"

"He is called simply Azra."

"Blue? The color blue?"

"Yes. And speaking of colors, there's another, a man with premature gray streaks in his hair—quite unusual for one of us. He is called Ahbyahd."

"White," said Evan.

"Yes. He's been identified as one of the hijackers of the TWA plane in Beirut. Only by photographs, however; no name was uncovered."

"Nassir, the woman Yateem, Blue, and White. That should be enough."

"For what?" asked the doctor.

"For what I'm going to do."

"Think about what you're doing," said the doctor softly, watching Evan draw up the loose-fitting prison trousers with the elastic waistband. "Ahmat is torn, for we might learn a great deal by your sacrifice—but you must understand, it could well be your sacrifice. He wants you to know that."

"I'm no fool, either." Kendrick put on the gray prison shirt and slipped into the hard leather sandals common to Arab jails. "If I feel threatened, I'll yell for help."

"You do and they'll be on you like crazed animals. You wouldn't survive ten seconds; no one could reach you in time."

"All right, a code." Evan buttoned the coarse shirt while looking around the police laboratory; his eyes fell on several X rays suspended on a string. "If your people monitoring the taps hear me say that films were smuggled out of the embassy, move in and get me out. Understood?"

" 'Films smuggled out of the embassy—' "

"That's it. I won't say it, or shout it, unless I think they're closing in on me. . . . Now, let the word go inside. Tell the guards to taunt the prisoners. Amal Bahrudi, leader of the Islamic terrorists in East Europe, has been captured here in Oman. Your bright young sultan's strategy for my temporary protection can make a big leap forward. It's my passport into their rotten world."

"It was not designed for that."

"But it's damn convenient, isn't it? Almost as though Ahmat had it in mind before I did. Come to think of it, he might have. Why not?"

"That's ridiculous!" protested the doctor, both palms raised toward Evan. "Listen to me. We can all theorize and postulate as much as we like, but we cannot *guarantee.* That compound is guarded by soldiers and we cannot see into the soul of each man. Suppose there are sympathizers? Look at the streets. Crazed animals awaiting the next execution, wagering bets! America is not loved by every citizen in an aba or conscript in uniform; there are too many stories, too much talk of anti-Arab bias over there."

"Ahmat said the same thing about his own garrison here in Masqat. Only, he called it looking into their eyes."

"The eyes hold the secrets of the soul, *ya Shaikh,* and the sultan was right. We live in constant fear of weakness and betrayal here within. These soldiers are young, impressionable, quick to make judgments about real or imagined insults. Suppose, just *suppose,* the KGB decides to send in a message so as to further destabilize the situation: 'Amal Bahrudi is dead, the man claiming to be him is an impostor!' There would be no time for codes or cries for help. And the manner of your death should not be contemplated lightly."

"Ahmat should have thought of that—"

"*Unfair!*" cried Faisal. "You ascribe to him things he never dreamt of! The Bahrudi alias was to be used *only* as a diversionary tactic in the last extremity, not for anything else! The fact that ordinary citizens could publicly state that they witnessed the capture of a terrorist, even to the point of naming him, would create confusion—*that* was the strategy. Confusion, bewilderment, *indecision.* If only to delay your execution for a few hours—whatever time might be used to extricate *you,* a single individual—that was Ahmat's intention. Not *infiltration.*"

Evan leaned against the table, his arms folded, studying the Omani. "Then I don't understand, and I mean that, Doctor. I'm not looking for demons, but I think there's a lapse in your explanation."

"What is it?"

"If finding me the name of a terrorist—an unaccounted-for, dead terrorist—was to be my fall-back position, as you called it—"

"Your temporary protection, as *you* so rightly called it," interrupted Faisal.

"Then suppose—*just* suppose—I hadn't been around to act in that little melodrama on the Al Kabir tonight?"

"You were never meant to," replied the doctor calmly. "You simply moved up the schedule. It was to take place not at midnight but in the early morning hours, just before the prayers, near the mosque of Khor. The word of Bahrudi's capture would have spread through the markets like the news of a shipment of cheap contraband on the waterfront. Another would have posed as the impostor you are. *That* was the plan, nothing else."

"Then, as the lawyers would say, there's a convenient convergence of objectives, rearranged in time and purpose so as to accommodate all parties without conflict. I hear phrases like that in Washington all the time. Very sharp."

"I am a doctor, *ya Shaikh,* not a lawyer."

"To be sure," agreed Evan, smiling faintly. "But I wonder about our young friend in the palace. He wanted to 'discuss' Amal Bahrudi. I wonder where that discussion would have led us."

"He's not a lawyer either."

"He has to be everything to run this place," said Kendrick sharply. "He has to *think.* Especially now. . . . We're wasting time, Doctor. Mess me up a bit. Not the eyes or the mouth, but around the cheeks and the chin. Then cut into my shoulder and bandage it, but don't dry the blood."

"I beg your *pardon*?"

"For Christ's sake, I'm not going to do it myself!"

The heavy steel door sprang back, yanked by two soldiers who instantly placed their arms against the exterior iron plate as if expecting an assault on the exit. A third guard hurled the wounded, still-bleeding prisoner into the huge concrete hall that served as a mass cell; what light there was, was subdued, provided by low-wattage bulbs encased in wire mesh and bolted to the ceiling. A group of inmates instantly converged on the new entry, several gripping the shoulders of the bloody, disfigured man awkwardly trying to rise from his knees. Others huddled around the imposing metal door chattering loudly among themselves—half shrieking, actually—apparently to drown out whatever was being said inside the compound.

"*Khaleebalak!*" roared the newcomer, his right arm lashing upward, freeing itself, then with a tight fist pummeling the face of a young prisoner whose grimace revealed rotted teeth. "By Allah, I'll break the head of any imbecile here who *touches* me!" continued Kendrick, screaming in Arabic and rising to his full height, which was several inches taller than the tallest man around him.

"We are many and you are *one*!" hissed the offended youngster, pinching his nose to stop the bleeding.

"You may be many but you are lovers of *he*-goats! You are *stupid*! Get *away* from me! I must *think*!" With his last explosive remark, Evan slammed his left arm against those holding it, then instantly pulled it back and thrust his elbow into the throat of the nearest prisoner holding him. With his still-clenched right fist, he swung around and hammered his knuckles into the man's unsuspecting eyes.

He could not remember when he had last hit another person, physically attacked another human being. If his flashing memories were correct, it went back to grammar school. A boy named Peter Somebody-or-other had hidden his best friend's lunch box—a tin box with Walt Disney characters on it—and because his friend was small and Peter Somebody-or-other was bigger than his best friend, he had challenged the bully. Unfortunately, in his anger he had beaten the boy named Peter so severely that the principal called his father and both adults told him he was terribly wrong. A young man of his size did not pick fights. It wasn't fair. . . . But, sir! Dad! . . . No appeal. He had to accept twenty demerits. But then his father said if it happens again, son, do it again.

It happened again! Someone grabbed his neck from behind! *Lifesaving procedure.* Why did it come to mind? Pinch the nerve under the elbow! It releases the grip of a drowning man! *Red Cross Senior Lifesaving Certificate. Summer money on the lake.* In panic, he slid his hand down the exposed arm, reached the soft flesh under the elbow and pressed with all the strength that was in him. The terrorist screamed; it was enough. Kendrick hunched his shoulders and threw the man over his back, slamming him down onto the cement floor.

"Do any of you want *more*?" whispered the newest prisoner harshly, crouching, turning, his height still apparent. "You are *fools*! If it weren't for you idiots, I would not have been taken! I despise *all* of you! Now, leave me alone! I told you, I must *think*!"

"Who are you to insult us and give us orders?" screeched a wild-eyed postadolescent, a harelip impeding his diction. It was all a scene out of Kafka—half-crazed prisoners prone to instant violence, yet nervously aware of more brutal punishment from the guards. Whispers became harsh commands, suppressed insults screams of defiance, while those who spoke looked continuously toward the door, making sure the babble beyond covered whatever they said, keeping it from eavesdropping enemy ears.

"I am who I *am*! And that is enough for she-goat fools—"

"The guards told us your name!" stammered another inmate, this one perhaps thirty, with an unkempt beard and filthy long hair; he cupped his lips with his hands as though they would stifle his words. " 'Amal *Bahrudi*!' " he yelled. " 'The *trusted* one from East Berlin and we've caught him!' . . . So what? Who are you to us? I don't even like the way you look. You look very odd to me! What is an Amal Bahrudi? Why should *we* care?"

Kendrick glanced over at the door and the agitated group of prisoners talking excitedly. He took a step forward, again whispering harshly. "Because I was sent by others much higher than anyone here or in the embassy. Much, *much* higher. Now, I'm telling you for the last time, let me *think*! I have to get information *out*—"

"You try and you'll put us all in front of a firing squad!" exclaimed another prisoner through his teeth; he was short and strangely well groomed, except for unaccountable splotches of urine staining his prison trousers.

"That bothers you?" replied Evan, staring at the terrorist, his voice low and filled with loathing. *It was the moment to establish his credo further.* "Tell me, pretty little boy, are you afraid to die?"

"Only because I could no longer serve our cause!" gushed the boy-man defensively, his eyes darting about, seeking justification. A few in the crowd agreed; there were emotional, knee-jerk nods from those close enough to hear him, swept up in his fears. Kendrick wondered how pervasive was this deviation from zealotry.

"Keep your voice down, you fool!" said Evan icily. "Your martyrdom is service enough." He turned and walked through the hesitantly parting bodies to the stone wall of the immense cell where there was an open rectangular window with iron bars embedded in the concrete.

"Not so fast, odd-looking one!" The rough voice, barely heard above the noise, came from the outer fringes of the crowd. A stocky, bearded man stepped forward. Those in front of him gave way as men casually do in the presence of a noncommissioned superior—a sergeant or a foreman, perhaps; not a colonel or a corporate vice president. Was there someone with more authority in that compound? wondered Evan. Someone else watching closely, someone else giving orders?

"What is it?" asked Kendrick quietly, abrasively.

"I also don't like the way you look! I don't like your face. That's enough for me."

"Enough for *what*?" said Evan contemptuously, dismissing the man with a shrug of his head as he leaned into the wall, his hands gripping the iron bars of the small cell window, his gaze on the floodlit grounds outside.

"Turn around!" ordered the surrogate foreman, or sergeant, in a harsh voice directly behind him.

"I'll turn when I care to," said Kendrick, wondering if he was heard.

"Now," rejoined the man in a voice no louder than Evan's—a quiet prelude to his strong hand suddenly crashing down on Kendrick's right shoulder, gripping the flesh around the bleeding wound.

"Don't *touch* me, that's an order!" Evan shouted, holding his ground, his hands vising the iron bars so as not to betray the pain he felt, his antennae alert for what he wanted to learn. . . . It came. The fingers clenching his shoulder spastically separated; the hand fell away on Evan's command, but tentatively returned a moment later. It revealed enough: the noncom gave orders bluntly, yet he received and executed them with alacrity when they were given by an authoritative voice. Enough. He was not the *man* here in the compound. He was high on the totem pole but not high enough. Was there really another? A further test was called for.

Kendrick stood rigid, then without motion or warning swung swiftly around to his right, dislodging the hand as the stocky man was ignominiously thrown off-balance by the clockwise movement. "All right!" he spat out, his sharp whisper not a statement but an accusation. "What is it about me you don't like? I'll convey your *judgment* to others. I'm sure they'll be interested, for they would like to know who's making *judgments* here in Masqat!" Evan again paused, then abruptly continued, his voice rising in a one-on-one challenge. "Those judgments are considered by many to be curdled in ass's milk. What *is* it, imbecile? What don't you like about me?"

"I do not make judgments!" shouted the muscular terrorist as defensively as the boy-man who feared a firing squad. Then just as quickly as his outburst had erupted, the wary sergeant-foreman, momentarily frightened that his words might have been heard above the babble, regained his suspicious composure. "You're free with words," he whispered hoarsely, squinting his eyes, "but they mean nothing to us. How do we know who you are or where you come from? You don't even look like one of us. You look different."

"I move in circles you don't move in—can't move in. I can."

"He has light-colored eyes!" The stifled cry came from the older, bearded prisoner with the long filthy hair peering forward. "He's a spy! He's come to *spy* on us!" Others crowded in, studying the suddenly more menacing stranger.

Kendrick slowly turned his head toward his accuser. "So might you have these eyes if your grandfather was European. If I cared to change them for your grossly stupid benefit, a few drops of fluid would have been sufficient for a week. Naturally, you're not aware of such techniques."

"You have words for everything, don't you?" said the sergeant-foreman. "Liars are free with words, for they cost nothing."

"Except one's life," replied Evan, moving his eyes, staring at individual faces. "Which I have no intention of losing."

"You are afraid to *die,* then?" challenged the well-groomed youngster with the soiled trousers.

"You yourself answered that question for me. I have no fear of death—none of us should have—but I *do* fear not accomplishing what I've been sent here to accomplish. I fear that greatly—for our most holy cause."

"*Words* again!" choked the stocky would-be leader, annoyed that a number of the prisoners were listening to the strange-looking Euro-Arab with the fluid tongue. "What is this thing you are to accomplish here in Masqat? If we are so stupid, why don't you tell us, *enlighten* us!"

"I will speak only to those I was told to find. No one else."

"*I* think you should speak to me," said the sergeant—now more sergeant than foreman—as he took a menacing step toward the rigid American congressman. "We do not know you but you may know us. That gives you an advantage I don't like."

"And I don't like your stupidity," said Kendrick, immediately gesturing with both hands, one pointing to his right ear, the other at the moving, chattering crowd by the door. "Can't you *understand*?" he exclaimed, his whisper a shout into the man's face. "You could be heard! You must admit you *are* stupid."

"Oh, yes, we are that, sir." The sergeant—definitely a sergeant—turned his head, looking at an unseen figure somewhere in the huge concrete cell. Evan tried to follow the man's gaze; with his height he saw a row of open toilets at the end of the hall; several were in use, each occupant's eyes watching the excitement. Other inmates, curious, many frantic, rushed alternately between the loud group by the heavy door and the crowd around the new prisoner. "But then, sir, *great* sir," continued the heavy-set terrorist mockingly, "we have methods to overcome our stupidity. You should give inferior people credit for such things."

"I give credit when it is due—"

"Our account is due *now*!" Suddenly, the muscular fanatic shot up his left arm. It was a cue, and with the signal voices swelled, raised in an Islamic chant, followed instantly by a dozen others, and then more, until the entire compound was filled with the reverberating echoes of fifty-odd zealots shrieking the praises of the obscure stations leading into the arms of Allah. And then it happened. A sacrifice was in the making.

Bodies fell on him; fists crashed into his abdomen and face. He could not scream—his lips were clamped by strong clawlike fingers, the flesh stretched until he thought his mouth would be torn away. The pain was excruciating. And then abruptly, his lips were free, his mouth halfway in place.

"Tell us!" screamed the sergeant-terrorist into Kendrick's ear, his words lost to the wiretaps by the wildly accelerating Islamic chanting. "Who *are* you? What place in hell do you *come* from?"

"I *am* who I *am*!" shouted Evan, grimacing and holding on as long as he could manage, convinced he knew the Arabic mind, believing a moment would come when respect for an enemy's death would induce a few seconds of silence before the blow was administered; it would be enough. Death was revered in Islam, of friend and adversary alike. He needed those seconds! He had to let the guards know! Oh, Christ, he was being killed! A clenched fist hammered down on his testicles—*when,* when would it *stop* for those few, precious *moments*?

A blurred figure was suddenly above him, bending over, studying him. Another fist crashed into his left kidney; the inward scream did not emerge from his mouth. He could not permit it.

"*Stop!*" cried the voice of the blurred outline above. "Tear off his shirt. Let me see his neck. It is said there is a mark he can't wash away."

Evan felt the cloth being ripped from his chest, his breath sinking, knowing the worst was about to be revealed. There was no scar on his neck.

"It *is* Amal Bahrudi," intoned the man above. The barely conscious Kendrick heard the words and was stunned.

"What do you *look* for?" asked the bewildered sergeant-foreman, furious.

"What is not there," said the echoing voice. "Throughout Europe, Amal Bahrudi is marked by the scar on his throat. A photograph was circulated to authorities confirmed to be him, a picture obscuring the face but not the bare neck where the scar of a knife wound was in clear focus. It has been his best cover, an ingenious device of concealment."

"You *confuse* me!" shouted the squatting, stocky man, his words nearly drowned out by the cacophonous chanting. "What concealment? What *scar*?"

"A scar that never was, a mark that never existed. They all look for a lie. This is Bahrudi, the blue-eyed man who can take pain with silence, the trusted one who moves about Western capitals unnoticed because of the genes of a European grandfather. Word must have reached Oman that he was reported to be on his way here, but regardless, he'll be released in the morning, no doubt with great apologies. You see, there is no scar on his throat."

Through the haze and the terrible pain, Evan knew it was the moment to react. He forced a smile across his burning lips, his light blue eyes centering on the blurred figure above. "A sane man," he coughed in agony. "Please, get me up, get them away from me before I see them all in *hell.*"

"Amal Bahrudi speaks?" asked the unknown man, reaching out with his hand. "Let him up."

"*No!*" roared the sergeant-terrorist, plunging down and pinning Kendrick's shoulders. "There's no sense in what you say! He *is* who he says he is because of a scar that does not *exist*? Where's the sense in that, I ask you?"

"I will know if he lies," replied the figure above, slowly coming into focus for Kendrick. The gaunt face was that of a man in his early twenties, with high cheekbones and intense, dark intelligent eyes flanking a sharp, straight nose. The body was slender, bordering on thin, but there was a supple strength in the way he crouched and held his head. The muscles of his neck stood out. "Let him up," repeated the younger terrorist, his voice casual but no less a command for that. "And instruct the others to gradually stop their chanting—gradually, you understand—but then keep talking among themselves. All must appear normal, including the incessant arguing, which you don't have to encourage."

The angry subordinate gave Evan a last shove into the floor, widening the cut in his shoulder so severely that new blood burst out onto the concrete. The surly man got to his feet, turning to the crowd to carry out his orders.

"Thank you," said Evan, breathless, trembling and getting to his knees, wincing at the pain he felt everywhere, conscious of the bruises on his face and body, aware of the hot lacerations where his flesh had been punctured—again seemingly everywhere. "I would have joined Allah in a minute."

"You still may, which is why I won't bother to stem your bleeding." The young Palestinian shoved Kendrick against the wall into a sitting position, his legs stretched out on the floor. "You see, I have no idea whether you're really Amal Bahrudi or not. I acted on instinct. From the descriptions I've heard, you *could* be he, and you speak an educated Arabic, which also fits. In addition, you withstood extreme punishment when a gesture of submission on your part would have meant you were prepared to deliver the information demanded of you. Instead, you reacted with defiance, and you had to know that at any moment you could have been strangled. . . . That is not the way of an infiltrator who values his life here on earth. It is the way of one of us who will not harm the cause, for, as you remarked, it's a holy cause. And it *is.* Most holy."

Good God! thought Kendrick, assuming the cold expression of a dedicated partisan. *How wrong you are! If I had thought—if I'd been able to think. . . . Forget it!* "What will finally convince you? I tell you now I'm not about to reveal things I shouldn't." Evan paused, his hand covering the swallow in his throat. "Even to the point where you may resume the punishment and strangle me, if you like."

"Both are statements I would expect," said the intense, slender terrorist, lowering himself, now crouching in front of Evan. "You can, however, tell me what it is you came here for. Why were you sent to Masqat? Whom were you told to find? Your life depends on your answers, Amal Bahrudi, and I'm the only one who can make that decision."

He had been right. In spite of the odds he had been right! Escape. He had to escape with this young killer in a holy cause.

7

Kendrick stared at the Palestinian as if, indeed, the eyes held the meaning of a man's soul, although Evan's own eyes were too swollen to betray anything other than overwhelming physical pain. . . . *The remaining taps are in the flushing mechanisms of the toilets: Dr. Amal Faisal, contact to the sultan.*

"I was sent here to tell you that among your people in the embassy there are traitors."

"*Traitors?*" The terrorist remained motionless in his crouching position in front of Evan; beyond a slight frown there was no reaction whatsoever. "That's impossible," he said after several moments of intensely studying 'Amal Bahrudi's' face.

"I'm afraid it's not," contradicted Kendrick. "I saw the proof."

"Consisting of what?"

Evan suddenly winced, grabbing his wounded shoulder, his

hand instantly covered with blood. "If you won't stop this bleeding, *I* will!" He started to push himself up against the stone wall.

"Stay put!" commanded the young killer.

"Why? Why *should* I? How do I know you're not part of the treason—making *money* out of our work?"

"Money . . . ? What *money*?"

"You won't know that until *I* know you have the right to be told." Again Evan pressed himself against the wall, his hands on the floor, trying to rise. "You talk like a man but you're a boy."

"I grew up quickly," said the terrorist, shoving his strange prisoner down again. "Most of us have over here."

"Grow up *now.* My bleeding to death will tell neither of us anything." Kendrick ripped the blood-soaked shirt away from his shoulder. "It's filthy," he said, nodding at the wound. "It's filled with dirt and slime, thanks to your animal friends."

"They're not animals and they're not friends. They are my brothers."

"Write poetry on your own time, mine's too valuable. Is there any water in here—*clean* water?"

"The toilets," answered the Palestinian. "There's a sink on the right."

"Help me up."

"*No.* What *proof*? Whom were you sent to find?"

"Fool!" exploded Evan. "All right. . . . Where is Nassir? Everyone asks: Where is Nassir?"

"Dead," replied the young man, his expression without comment.

"*What?*"

"A marine guard jumped him, took his weapon, and shot him. The marine was killed instantly."

"Nothing was said—"

"What could be said that was productive?" countered the terrorist. "Make a martyr out of a single American guard? Show one of our own to have been overcome? We don't parade weakness."

"Nassir?" asked Kendrick, hearing a rueful note in the young killer's voice. "Nassir was weak?"

"He was a theoretician and not suited to this work."

"A theoretician?" Evan arched his brows. "Our student is an analyst?"

"This student can determine those moments when active involvement must replace passive debate, when force takes over from words. Nassir talked too much, justified too much."

"And you don't?"

"I'm not the issue, *you* are. What proof of treason do you have?"

"The woman Yateem," replied Kendrick, answering the first question, not the second one. "Zaya Yateem. I was told she was—"

"Yateem a *traitor*?" cried the terrorist, his eyes furious.

"I didn't say that—"

"What *did* you say?"

"She was reliable—"

"Far more than that, Amal Bahrudi!" The young man grabbed the remaining cloth of Evan's shirt. "She is *devoted* to our cause, a tireless worker who exhausts herself beyond any of us at the embassy!"

"She also speaks English," said Kendrick, hearing still another note in the terrorist's voice.

"So do I!" shot back the angry, self-proclaimed student, releasing his prisoner within their prison.

"I do, too," said Evan quietly, glancing over at the numerous groups of inmates, many of whom were looking at them. "May we speak English now?" he asked, once more studying his bleeding shoulder. "You say you want proof, which, of course, is beyond my providing, but I *can* tell you what I've seen with my own eyes—in Berlin. You yourself can determine whether or not I'm telling you the truth—since you're so adept at determining things. But I don't want any of your brother animals understanding what I say."

"You're an arrogant man under circumstances that do not call for arrogance."

"I am who I am—"

"You've said that." The terrorist nodded. "*English,*" he agreed, switching from Arabic. "You spoke of Yateem. What about her?"

"You assumed I meant she was the traitor."

"Who *dares*—"

"I meant quite the *opposite,*" insisted Kendrick, wincing, and gripping his shoulder with greater force. "She's trusted, even extolled; she's doing her job brilliantly. After Nassir, *she* was the one I was to find." Evan gasped in pain, an all too easy reflex, and coughed out his next words. "If she had been killed . . . I was to look for a man who's called Azra—if he was gone, another with gray streaks in his hair known as Ahbyahd."

"I am *Azra*!" cried the dark-eyed student. "I am the one called Blue!"

Bingo, thought Kendrick, staring hard at the young terrorist, his eyes questioning. "But you're here in this compound, not at the embassy—"

"A decision of our operations council," broke in Azra. "Headed by Yateem."

"I don't understand."

"Word reached us. Prisoners had been taken and held in isolation—tortured, bribed, broken one way or another into revealing information. It was decided that the strongest among us on the council should also be taken—to provide leadership, *resistance*!"

"And they chose you? *She* chose you?"

"Zaya knew whereof she spoke. She is my sister; I, her blood brother. She is as certain of my dedication as I am of hers. We fight together to our deaths, for death is our past."

Jackpot! Evan arched his neck, his head falling against the hard concrete wall, his pained eyes roaming across the ceiling with the naked bulbs encased in wire. "So I meet my vital contact in the most impossible place possible. Allah may have deserted us after all."

"To *hell* with Allah!" exclaimed Azra, astonishing Kendrick. "You'll be released in the morning. There is no scar across your throat. You'll be free."

"Don't be so sure of that," said Evan, wincing again and again grabbing his shoulder. "To put it plainly, that photograph of me was traced to a jihad cell in Rome and the scar is now questioned. They're searching Riyadh and Manamah for my early dental and medical records. If any were overlooked, if any are found, I'll be facing an Israeli hangman. . . . However, that's not your concern, nor mine at the moment, frankly."

"At least your courage matches your arrogance."

"I told you before," snapped Kendrick, "write poems on your own time. . . . If you are Azra, brother of Yateem, you need information. You have to know what I saw in Berlin."

"The evidence of treason?"

"If not treason, utter stupidity, and if not stupidity, unforgivable greed, which is no less than treason." Evan started once more to rise, pressing his back against the wall, his hands against the floor. This time the terrorist did not stop him. "*Damn* you, *help* me!" he cried. "I can't think like this. I have to wash away the blood, clear my eyes."

"Very well," said the man called Azra haltingly, his expression conveying his intense curiosity. "Lean on me," he added without enthusiasm.

"I only meant for you to help me *up,* " said Kendrick, yanking his arm away once he was on his feet. "I'll walk by myself, thank you. I don't need assistance from ignorant children."

"You may need more assistance than I'm prepared to offer—"

"I forgot," interrupted Evan, lurching, making his way awkwardly toward the row of four toilets and the sink. "The student is both judge and jury, as well as the right hand of Allah, whom he sends to the Devil!"

"Understand this, man of faith," said Azra firmly, staying close to the arrogant, insulting stranger. "My war is not for or against Allah, Abraham or Christ. It is a struggle to survive and live like a human being despite those who would destroy me with their bullets and their laws. I speak for many when I say, Enjoy your faith, practice it, but do not burden me with it. I have enough to contend with in just trying to stay alive if only to fight one more day."

Kendrick glanced at the angry young killer as they neared the sink. "I wonder if I should be talking to you," he said, narrowing his swollen eyes. "I wonder if perhaps you are not the Azra I was sent to find."

"Believe it," replied the terrorist. "In this work, accommodations are made between people of many stripes, many different purposes, all taking from each other for very selfish reasons. Together we can accomplish more for our individual causes than we can separately."

"We understand each other," said Kendrick, no comment in his voice.

They reached the rusted iron sink. Evan turned on the single faucet of cold water at full force, then, conscious of the noise, reduced the flow as he plunged his hands and face into the stream. He splashed the water everywhere over his upper body, dousing his head and his chest and repeatedly around the bleeding wound in his shoulder. He prolonged the bathing, sensing Azra's growing impatience as the Palestinian shifted his weight from foot to foot, knowing that the moment would come. *The remaining taps are in the flushing mechanisms of the toilets.* The moment came.

"Enough!" exploded the frustrated terrorist, gripping Kendrick's unharmed shoulder and spinning him away from the sink. "Give me your information, what you saw in Berlin! *Now!*

What is this proof of treason . . . or stupidity . . . or *greed*? What *is* it?"

"There has to be more than one person involved," began Evan, coughing, each cough more pronounced, more violent, his whole body trembling. "As people leave they take them *out*—" Suddenly, Kendrick bent over, clutching his throat, lurching for the first toilet to the left of the filthy sink. "I'm retching!" he cried, grabbing the edges of the bowl with both hands.

"Take *what* out?"

"*Films!*" spat out Evan, his voice directed toward the area around the toilet's handle. "Films smuggled out of the embassy! . . . For sale!"

"Films? *Photographs?*"

"Two rolls. I intercepted them, bought them both! Identities, *methods*—"

Nothing further could be heard in the enormous concrete terrorist cell. Ear-shattering bells erupted; deafening sounds signaling an emergency reverberated off the walls as a group of uniformed guards rushed in, weapons leveled, eyes frantically searching. In seconds they spotted the object of their search; six soldiers bolted forward toward the row of toilets.

"*Never!*" screamed the prisoner known as Amal Bahrudi. "*Kill* me, if you wish, but you will learn *nothing,* for you *are* nothing!"

The first two guards approached. Kendrick lunged at them, hurling his body at the stunned soldiers, who thought they were rescuing an infiltrator about to be killed. He swung his arms and smashed his fists into the confused faces.

Mercifully, a third soldier hammered the stock of his rifle into the skull of Amal Bahrudi.

All was darkness, but he knew he was on the examining table in the prison laboratory. He could feel the cold compresses on his eyes and ice packs over various parts of his body; he reached up and removed the thick, wet compresses. Faces above him came into focus—bewildered faces, angry faces. He had no time for them!

"*Faisal!*" he choked, speaking Arabic. "Where is Faisal, the *doctor*?"

"I am down here by your left foot," answered the Omani physician in English. "I'm sponging out a rather strange puncture wound. Someone bit you, I'm afraid."

"I can see his teeth," said Evan, now also speaking English.

"They were like those of a saw-toothed fish—only yellow."

"Proper diets are lacking in this part of the world."

"Get everyone out, Doctor," interrupted Kendrick. "Now. We've got to talk—*now*!"

"After what you did in there I doubt they'd leave, and I'm not even sure I'd let them. Are you crazy? They came to save your life and you tore into them, fracturing one man's nose and breaking apart another's bridgework."

"I had to be convincing, tell them that—no, *don't.* Not yet. Get them out. Tell them anything you like, but we've got to *talk.* Then you have to reach Ahmat for me. . . . How long have I been here?"

"Nearly an hour—"

"*Christ!* What time is it?"

"Four-fifteen in the morning."

"Hurry! For God's sake, *hurry*!"

Faisal dismissed the soldiers with calming words, reassuring them, explaining that there were things he could not explain. As the last guard went out the door, he paused, removed his automatic from its holster and handed it to the doctor. "Should I aim this at you while we talk?" asked the Omani after the soldier had left.

"Before sunrise," said Kendrick, pushing away the ice packs and sitting up, painfully swinging his legs over the table. "I want a number of guns aimed at me. But not as accurately as they might be."

"What are you saying? You can't be serious."

"Escape. Ahmat has to arrange an escape."

"*What?* You *are* crazy!"

"Never saner, Doctor, and never more serious. Pick two or three of your best men, which means men you completely trust, and set up some kind of transfer—"

"*Transfer?*"

Evan shook his head and blinked his eyes, the swelling still apparent although reduced by the cold compresses. He tried to find the words he needed for the astonished doctor. "Let me put it this way: somebody's decided to move a few prisoners from here to someplace else."

"Who would do that? Why?"

"Nobody! You make it up and do it, don't explain. . . . Do you have photographs of the men inside?"

"Of course. It's normal arrest procedure, although the names are meaningless. When they're given, they're always false."

"Let me have them, all of them. I'll tell you whom to choose."

"Choose for *what*?"

"The transfer. The ones you're moving out of here to someplace else."

"To *where*? Really, you're not making sense."

"You're not listening. Somewhere along the way, a back street or a dark road outside the city, we'll overpower the guards and escape."

"Overpower . . . ? *We?*"

"I'm part of the group, part of the escape. I'm going back in there."

"Complete madness!" exclaimed Faisal.

"Complete sanity," countered Evan. "There's a man inside who can take me where I want to go. Take *us* where we *have* to go! Get me the police photographs and then reach Ahmat on the triple-five number. Tell him what I've told you, he'll understand. . . . Understand, *hell*! It's what that Ivy League juvenile delinquent had in mind from the beginning!"

"I think perhaps you did also, *ya Shaikh ya Amreekánee.*"

"Maybe I did. Maybe I just want to blame it on someone else. I don't fit into this mold."

"Then something inside is propelling you, reshaping the man who was. It happens."

Kendrick looked into the soft brown eyes of the Omani doctor. "It happens," agreed Evan. Suddenly his mind was filled with the outlines of a murky silhouette; the figure of a man emerged from the raging fires of an earthbound hell. Whirlwinds of smoke enveloped the apparition as cascading rubble fell all around it, muting the screams of victims. *The Mahdi.* Killer of women and children, of friends dear to him, partners in a vision—his family, the only family he ever wanted. All gone, all dead, the vision joining the smoke of destruction, disappearing in the rising vapors until nothing was left but the cold and the darkness. *The Mahdi!* "It happens," repeated Kendrick softly, rubbing his forehead. "Get me the photographs and call Ahmat. I want to be back in that compound in twenty minutes, and I want to be taken out ten minutes later. For God's sake, *move*!"

Ahmat, sultan of Oman, still in slacks and his New England Patriots T-shirt, sat in the high-backed chair, the red light of his private, secure telephone glowing below on the right leg of his desk. With the instrument next to his ear, he was listening intensely.

"So it happened, Faisal," he spoke quietly. "Praise be to Allah, it *happened.*"

"He told me you expected it," said the doctor over the line, his tone questioning.

" 'Expected' is too strong, old friend. Hoped is more appropriate."

"I removed your tonsils, great Sultan, and I attended you over the years for minor illnesses, including a great fear you had that proved groundless."

Ahmat laughed, more to himself than into the phone. "A wild week in Los Angeles, Amal. Who knew what I might have contracted?"

"We had a pact. I never told your father."

"Which means you think I'm not telling you something now."

"The thought occurred to me."

"Very well, old friend—" Suddenly, the young sultan snapped his head up as the door of his royal office was opened. Two women entered; the first was obviously pregnant, an Occidental from New Bedford, Massachusetts, blond, and wearing a bathrobe. His wife. Next to appear was an olive-skinned, dark-haired female dressed fashionably in street clothes. She was known to the household simply as Khalehla. "Beyond common sense, good Doctor," continued Ahmat into the phone. "I have certain sources. Our mutual acquaintance needed assistance, and who better to provide it than the ruler of Oman? We leaked information to the animals at the embassy. Prisoners were being held somewhere, subjected to brutal interrogation. *Someone* had to be sent there to maintain discipline, order—and Kendrick found him. . . . Give our American anything he wants, but delay his schedule by fifteen or twenty minutes, until my two police officers arrive."

"The Al Kabir? Your cousins?"

"Two special police will suffice, my friend."

There was a brief silence, a voice searching for words. "The rumors are true, aren't they, Ahmat?"

"I have no idea what you mean. Rumors are gossip and neither interests me."

"They say you are so much wiser than your years—"

"That's sophomoric," broke in the sultan.

"*He* said you had to be to—'run this place,' " he said. "It's difficult for one who treated you for mumps."

"Don't dwell on it, Doctor. Just keep me informed." Ahmat reached into the drawer where the base of the private telephone lay and punched a series of numbers. Within seconds, he spoke. "I'm sorry, my family, I know you're asleep, but I must again bother you. Go to the compound at once. Amal Bahrudi wants to escape. With *fish.*" He hung up.

"What's happened?" asked the young sultan's wife, rapidly walking forward.

"*Please,*" said Ahmat, his eyes on the stomach of his waddling spouse. "You have only six weeks to go, Bobbie. Move slowly."

"He's too much," said Roberta Aldridge Yamenni, turning her head and addressing Khalehla at her side. "This jock of mine came in around two thousand in the Boston Marathon and he's telling me how to carry a baby. Is that too much?"

"The royal seed, Bobbie," replied Khalehla, smiling.

"Royal, my foot! Diapers are one hell of an equalizer. Ask my mother, she had four of us in six years. . . . Really, darling, what happened?"

"Our American congressman made contact in the compound. We're mocking up an escape."

"It worked!" cried Khalehla, approaching the desk.

"It was your idea," said Ahmat.

"Please, forget it. I'm way out of line here."

"*Nothing's* out of line," the youthful sultan said firmly. "Appearances notwithstanding, *risks* notwithstanding, we need all the help we can get, all the advice we can gather. . . . I apologize, Khalehla. I haven't even said hello. As with my cousins, my lowly policemen, I'm sorry to drag you out at this hour, but I knew you'd want to be here."

"Nowhere else."

"How did you manage it? I mean leaving the hotel at four in the morning."

"Thank Bobbie. I add, however, Ahmat, that neither of our reputations has been enhanced."

"Oh?" The sultan looked at his wife.

"Great Lord," intoned Bobbie, her palms together, bowing and speaking in her Boston accent. "This lovely lady is a courtesan from Cairo—nice ring to it, huh? Under the circumstances—" Here the royal wife outlined her swollen stomach with her hands and continued, "The privilege of rank has its goodies. Speaking as one of Radcliffe's stellar history majors, which my former roommate here will attest to, Henry the Eighth of England called it 'riding in the saddle.' It happened when Anne Boleyn was too indisposed to accommodate her monarch."

"For God's sake, Roberta, this isn't *The King and I* and I'm *not* Yul Brynner."

"You are now, pal!" Laughing, Ahmat's wife looked at Khalehla. "Of course, if you touch him, I'll scratch your eyes out."

"Not to fear, my dear," said Khalehla in mock seriousness. "Not after what you've told me."

"All right, you two," Ahmat interrupted. His brief look expressed the gratitude he felt toward both women.

"We have to laugh now and then," said his wife. "Otherwise I think we'd go stark raving mad."

"Raving as in mad," agreed Ahmat quietly, settling his eyes on the woman from Cairo. "How's your British businessman friend?"

"Raving as in drunk," answered Khalehla. "He was last seen half upright in the hotel's American Bar still calling me names."

"It's not the worst thing that could happen to your cover."

"Certainly not. I obviously go to the highest bidder."

"What about our superpatriots, the elder merchant princes who'd just as soon see me flee to the West in frustration as stay here? They still believe you're working with them, don't they?"

"Yes. My 'friend' told me in the Sabat Aynub market that they're convinced you met with Kendrick. His logic was such that I had to go along with him and agree that you were a damn fool; you were asking for the worst kind of trouble. Sorry."

"What logic?"

"They know that a garrison car picked up the American a few blocks away from his hotel. I couldn't argue, I was there."

"Then they were looking for that car. Garrison vehicles are all over Masqat."

"Sorry, again, it was a wrong move, Ahmat. I could have told you that if I'd have been able to reach you. You see, the circle was broken; they knew Kendrick was here—"

"*Mustapha,*" interrupted the young sultan angrily. "I mourn his death but not the closing of his big mouth."

"Perhaps it was he, perhaps not," said Khalehla. "Washington itself could be responsible. Too many people were involved in Kendrick's arrival, I saw that also. As I understand, it was a State Department operation; there are others who do these things better."

"We don't know who the enemy is or where to *look*!" Ahmat clenched his fist, bringing his knuckles to his teeth. "It could be anyone, *anywhere*—right in front of our eyes. Goddamnit, what do we *do*?"

"Do as he's told you," said the woman from Cairo. "Let him go in under deep cover. He's made contact; wait for him to reach you."

"Is that all I can do? *Wait?*"

"No, there's something else," added Khalehla. "Give me the escape route and one of your fast cars. I brought along my courtesan's equipment—it's in a suitcase outside in the hall—and while I change clothes you coordinate the details with your cousins and that doctor you call an old friend."

"Hey, come on!" protested Ahmat. "I know you and Bobbie go back a long time but that doesn't give you the right to order me to endanger your life! No way, José."

"We're not talking about my life," said Khalehla icily, her brown eyes staring at Ahmat. "Or yours, frankly. We're talking about raw terrorism and the survival of Southwest Asia. Nothing may come of tonight, but it's my job to try to find out, and it's your job to permit me. Isn't that what we've both been trained for?"

"And also give her the number where she can reach you," said Roberta Yamenni calmly. "Reach *us.*"

"Go change your clothes," said the young sultan of Oman, shaking his head, his eyes closed.

"Thank you, Ahmat. I'll hurry, but first I have to reach my people. I don't have much to say, so it'll be quick."

The drunken baldheaded man in the disheveled Savile Row pinstripes was escorted out of the elevator by two countrymen. The girth and weight of their inebriated charge were such that each struggled to hold up his part of the body.

"Bloody disgrace, is what he is!" said the man on the left, awkwardly glancing at a hotel key dangling from the fingers of his right hand, which was even more awkwardly shoved up under the drunk's armpit.

"Come now, Dickie," retorted his companion, "we've all swigged our several too many on occasion."

"*Not* in a goddamned country going up in flames fueled by nigger barbarians! He could start a bloody brawl and *we'd* be hanged by our necks from two lampposts! Where's the damned room?"

"Down the hall. Heavy bugger, isn't he?"

"All lard and straight whisky is my guess."

"I don't know about that. He seemed like a pleasant enough chap who got taken by a fast-talking whore. That sort of thing makes anyone pissed, you know. Did you get whom he worked for?"

"Some textile firm in Manchester. Twillingame or Burlingame, something like that."

"Never heard of it," said the man on the right, arching his brows in surprise. "Here, give me the key; there's the door."

"We'll just throw him on the bed, no courtesies beyond that, I tell you."

"Do you think that fellow will keep the bar open for us? I mean, while we're doing our Christian duty the bugger could lock the doors, you know."

"The bastard had better not!" exclaimed the man named Dickie as the three figures lurched into the darkened room, the light from the hallway outlining the bed. "I gave him twenty pounds to keep the place open, if only for us. If you think I'm shutting my eyes for a single second until I'm on that plane tomorrow, you're ready for the twit farm! I'll not have my throat slit by some wog with a messianic complex, I tell you that, too! Come on, *heave*!"

"Good night, fat prince," said the companion. "And may all kinds of black bats carry you to wherever."

The heavy man in the pin-striped suit raised his head from the bed and turned his face toward the door. The footsteps in the hallway receded; inelegantly he rolled his bulk over and got to his feet. In the shadowed light provided by the dull streetlamps below outside the window, he removed his jacket and hung it up carefully in the open closet, smoothing out the wrinkles. He proceeded to undo his regimental tie, slipping it off his neck. He then unbuttoned his soiled shirt reeking of whisky, removed it also and threw it into a wastebasket. He went into the bathroom, turned on both faucets, and sponged his upper torso; satisfied, he picked up a bottle of cologne and splashed it generously over his skin. Drying himself, he walked back into the bedroom to his suitcase on a luggage rack in the corner. He opened it, selected a black silk shirt, and put it on. As he buttoned it and tucked it under the belt around his thick stomach, he walked over to a window, taking out a book of matches from his trousers pocket. He struck a match, let the flame settle, and made three semicircles in front of the large glass pane. He waited ten seconds, then crossed to the desk in the center of the left wall and switched on the lamp. He went to the door, unlatched the automatic lock and returned to the bed, where he meticulously removed the two pillows from under the spread, fluffed both up for a backrest, and lowered his large frame. He looked at his watch and waited.

The scratching at the door made three distinct eruptions, each semicircular on the wood, if one listened. "Come in," said the man on the bed in the black silk shirt.

A dark-skinned Arab entered hesitantly, in apparent awe of his surroundings and the person within those surroundings. His robes were clean, if not brand-new, and his headdress spotless; his was a privileged mission. He spoke in a quiet, reverent voice. "You made the holy sign of the crescent, sir, and I am here."

"Much thanks," said the Englishman. "Come in and close the door, please."

"Of course, *Effendi.*" The man did as he was told, holding his position of distance.

"Did you bring me what I need?"

"Yes, sir. Both the equipment and the information."

"The equipment first, please."

"Indeed." The Arab reached under his robes and withdrew a large pistol, its outsized appearance due to a perforated cylinder attached to the barrel; it was a silencer. With his other hand the messenger pulled out a small gray box; it contained twenty-seven rounds of ammunition. He walked dutifully forward to the bed, extending the handle of the weapon. "The gun is fully loaded, sir. Nine shells. Thirty-six shells in all."

"Thank you," said the obese Englishman, accepting the equipment. The Arab stepped back obsequiously. "Now the information, if you please."

"Yes, sir. But first I should tell you that the woman was recently driven to the palace from her hotel in the next street—"

"*What?*" Astonished, the British businessman bolted upright on the bed, his heavy legs swinging around, pounding the floor. "Are you *certain*?"

"Yes, sir. A royal limousine picked her up."

"When?"

"Roughly ten to twelve minutes ago. Naturally, I was informed immediately. She is there by now."

"But what about the *old men,* the *merchants*?" The fat man's voice was low and strained, as if he were doing his utmost to control himself. "She made *contact,* didn't she?"

"Yes, sir," answered the Arab tremulously, as though he feared a beating if he replied in the negative. "She had coffee with an importer named Hajazzi in the Dakhil, then much later met with him at the Sabat market. She was taking photographs, following someone—"

"Who?"

"I don't know, sir. The Sabat was crowded and she fled. I could not follow her."

"The palace . . . ?" whispered the businessman hoarsely as he slowly stood up. *"Incredible!"*

"It is true, sir. My information is accurate, or I would not deliver it to such an august personage as yourself. . . . In truth, *Effendi,* I shall praise Allah with all my heart in my every prayer for having met a true disciple of the Mahdi!"

The Englishman's eyes snapped up at the figure of the messenger. "Yes, you've been told that, haven't you?" he said softly.

"I was blessed with this gift of knowledge, singled out among my brothers for the privilege."

"Who else knows?"

"On my life, *no one,* sir! Yours is a sacred pilgrimage to be made in silence and invisibly. I shall go to my grave with the secret of your presence in Masqat!"

"Splendid idea," said the large man in shadows as he raised the pistol.

The two gunshots were like rapid, muted coughs but their power belied the sound. Across the room the Arab was blown into the wall, his spotless robes suddenly drenched with blood.

The hotel's American Bar was dark except for the dull glow of fluorescent tubes from under the counter. The aproned bartender slouched in a corner of his domain, every now and then glancing wearily at the two figures sitting in a booth by a front window, the view outside partially blocked by the lowered, half-closed blinds. The Englishmen are fools, thought the bartender. Not that they should disregard their fears—who lived without them in these mad-dog days, foreigner and sane Omani alike? But these two would be safer from a mad-dog assault behind the locked doors of hotel rooms, unnoticed, unseen. . . . Or would they? mused the bartender, reconsidering. He himself had told the management that they insisted on remaining where they were, and the management, not knowing what the foreigners carried on their persons or who else might know and be looking for them, had stationed three armed guards in the lobby near the American Bar's only entrance. . . . Regardless, the bartender concluded, yawning, wise or unwise, dull-witted or very clever, the Englishmen were extremely generous, that was all that mattered. That and the sight of his own weapon covered by a towel under the bar. Ironically, it was a lethal Israeli submachine gun he had bought from an accommodating Jew on the waterfront. *Hah!* Now the Jews were *really* clever. Since the madness began, they were arming half of Masqat.

"Dickie, *look*!" whispered the more tolerant of the two Englishmen, his right hand separating a pair of slats in the lowered blind covering the window.

"What, Jack . . . ?" Dickie jerked his head up, blinking his eyes; he had been dozing.

"Isn't that our squiffed countryman out there?"

"Who? Where . . . ? My God, you're *right*!"

Outside in the deserted, dimly lit street, the heavy man—upright, agitated, pacing the curb while rapidly looking back and forth—suddenly struck several matches, one after another. He appeared to raise and lower the flames, snapping each match angrily down on the pavement before lighting the next. Within ninety seconds a dark sedan appeared racing down the street; as it abruptly stopped the headlights were extinguished. Astonished, Dickie and his companion watched through the slats of the blind as the fat man, with startling agility and purpose, strode around the hood of the automobile. As he approached the passenger door an Arab wearing a headdress but in a dark Western suit leaped out. Instantly, the heavy Britisher began speaking rapidly, repeatedly jabbing his index finger into the face of the man in front of him. Finally he heaved his large torso around, spun his jowled head and pointed at an area in the upper floors of the hotel; the Arab turned and raced across the pavement. Then, in clear view, the obese businessman pulled a large weapon from his belt as he opened the car door further and quickly, again angrily, lowered himself inside.

"My *God,* did you see that?" cried Dickie.

"Yes. He's changed his clothes."

"His *clothes*?"

"Of course. The light's poor but not for the practiced eye. The white shirt's gone and so are the pinstripes. He's wearing a dark shirt now and his jacket and trousers are a dull black, coarse-woven wool, I should think, hardly becoming the climate."

"What are you *talking* about?" exclaimed the astounded Dickie. "I meant the gun!"

"Well, yes, chap. You're in ferrous metals and I'm in textiles."

"Really, chap, you leave me dumbfounded! We both see a twenty-stone bugger who, fifteen minutes ago, was so squiffed we had to carry him upstairs suddenly running around cold sober in the street, issuing orders to some bloke and brandishing a gun while he jumps into a madly driven car he obviously had signaled—and all *you* see are his clothes!"

"Well, actually, there's more to it than that, old boy. I saw the gun, of course, and the jackrabbit Arab, and that car—obviously driven by a maniac—and the contrariness of it all was why the clothes struck me as odd, don't you see?"

"Not a ha'penny's worth!"

"Perhaps 'odd' is the wrong choice of word—"

"Try the right one, Jack."

"All right, I'll try. . . . That fat bugger may or may not have been squiffed but he was a dandy of the first water. Best featherweight worsted stripe, an Angelo shirt from East Bond, the finest foulard tie Harrods has to offer, and Benedictine shoes—leather from the veldt and sewn to order in Italy. He's dressed to kill, I thought to myself, and everything right for the climate."

"*So?*" asked the exasperated Dickie.

"So out there in the street just now, he's in a jacket and trousers of quite ordinary quality, ill-fitting and far too heavy for this blasted weather, and certainly not the sort of outfit that would stand out in a crowd, much less appropriate for a dawn social or an Ascot breakfast. And while I'm at it, there isn't a textile firm in Manchester I'm not familiar with, and there's no Twillingame or Burlingame or any name remotely similar."

"You don't say?"

"I do say."

"That's a wicket, isn't it?"

"I also say we shouldn't take that plane this morning."

"My God, *why*?"

"I think we should go over to our embassy and wake someone up."

"*What . . . ?*"

"Dickie, suppose that bugger *is* dressed to kill?"

Ultra Maximum Secure
No Existing Intercepts
Proceed

The journal continued.

The latest report is troubling, and insofar as my appliances haven't broken Langley's access codes, I don't even know whether data was withheld or not. The subject has made contact. The shadow speaks of a high-risk option that was 'inevitable'—inevitable!—but extremely dangerous.

What is he doing and how is he doing it? What are his methods and who are his contacts? I must have specifics! If he survives, I will need every detail, for it is the details that lend credence to any extraordinary action, and it is the action that will propel the subject into the conscience of the nation.

But will he survive or will he be yet another buried statistic in an unrevealed series of events? My appliances cannot tell me, they can only attest to his potential, which means nothing if he's dead. Then all of my work will have been for nothing.

8

The four terrorist prisoners were shackled, two sitting on the right side of the speeding, violently shaking police van, the other two opposite them on the left. As arranged, Kendrick sat with the young wild-eyed fanatic whose harelip impeded his screeching pronouncements; Azra was across the way with the gruff older killer who had challenged and attacked Evan, the man he thought of as a sergeant-foreman. By the rattling steel door of the van stood a police guard, his left hand gripping a crossbar on the roof, trying to keep himself upright. In his right, held in place by a taut leather shoulder strap, was a MAC-10 machine pistol. A single scattershot burst would turn the four breathing prisoners into bloodied breathless corpses pinned to the walls of the racing van. Yet, also—as arranged—a ring of keys was hooked to the guard's belt, the same keys that had secured the prisoners' shackles. Everything had been a race against time, precious time. Minutes became hours and hours brought about another day.

"You're insane, you know that, don't you?"

"Doctor, we don't have a choice! That man is Azra—color him Blue."

"Wrong, wrong, wrong! Azra has a chin beard and long hair—we've all seen him on television—"

"He shaved off his beard and cut his hair."

"I ask you. Are you Amal Bahrudi?"

"I am now."

"No you're not! Any more than he is Azra! That man was brought in here five hours ago from a bazaar in the Waljat. He's a drunken imbecile, a swaggering clown, nothing more. His fellow pig slashed his own throat with a policeman's knife!"

"I was there, Faisal. He is Azra, brother of Zaya Yateem."

"Because he tells you so?"

"No. Because I talked to him, listened to him. His holy war isn't for or against Allah, Abraham or Christ. It's for survival in this life, on this earth."

"Madness! All around us, madness!"

"What did Ahmat say?"

"To do as you say, but you must wait until his special police arrive. They are two men he trusts completely—your instructions, I believe."

"Tweedledum and Tweedledee? The two uniforms who've been with me from the bazaar to the Al Kabir?"

"They are special. One will drive the police vehicle, the other will act as your guard."

"Good thinking. I'm really playing out Ahmat's scenario, aren't I?"

"You're unfair, Mr. Kendrick."

"He's not too shabby himself. . . . Here are the other two prisoners I want in the transfer, in the truck with Azra and me."

"Why? Who are they?"

"One's a lunatic who'd curse out his own firing squad, but the other . . . the other is Azra's beard. He does whatever color-me-Blue tells him. Take those two away and there's no one to hold the fort together."

"You're being cryptic."

"The rest are breakable, Doctor. They don't really know anything, but they're breakable. I suggest you take three or four out at a time, put them into smaller cells, and then shoot off some rifles into the back wall of this compound. You might find a few fanatics who aren't so crazy about their own executions."

"You are shedding your true skin, Shaikh Kendrick. You're going into a world of which you know nothing."

"I'll learn, Doctor. That's why I'm here."

The sign came! The guard by the van's door steadied himself, briefly lowering his left hand; he shook it to restore circulation and immediately reached up to grip the crossbar again. He would repeat the action in less than a minute and then it would be the moment for Evan to make his move. The choreography had been created quickly in the compound's laboratory; the attack was to be swift and simple. The guard's reaction was the key to its success. Twenty-two seconds later the guard's left hand plummeted down again in a gesture of weariness.

Kendrick sprang off the bench, his body a compact missile hammering into the guard, whose head crashed against the door with such force that the man's suddenly hysterical expression became instantly passive as he collapsed.

"*Quickly!*" commanded Evan, turning to Azra. "Help me! Get his keys!"

The Palestinian leaped forward, followed by the sergeant-foreman. All together, their shackled hands threw the MAC-10 machine pistol out of the way and ripped the keys from the guard's belt.

"I'll kill him *now*!" shrieked the harelipped zealot, grabbing the weapon and lurching forward in the swaying truck, the gun aimed at the guard's head.

"*Stop* him!" ordered Azra.

"*Fool!*" roared the sergeant-foreman, wrestling the weapon away from the young fanatic. "The driver will hear the shots!"

"He is our holy *enemy*!"

"He is our holy way out of here, you miserable idiot!" said Azra, unlocking Kendrick's shackles and handing Evan the key to do the same for him. The congressman from Colorado did so, then turned to the extended wrists of the sergeant-foreman.

"My name is Yosef," said the older man. "It is a Hebrew name, for my mother was Hebrew, but we are not part of the Jews of Israel—and you are a brave man, Amal Bahrudi."

"I don't like firing squads in the desert," said Kendrick, throwing his shackles on the floor and turning to the young terrorist who would have killed the unconscious guard. "I don't know whether to let you free or not."

"*Why?*" shrieked the boy. "Because I will *kill* for our holy war, *die* for our cause?"

"No, young man, because you might kill us and we're more valuable than you."

"Amal!" cried Azra, gripping Evan's arm, as much to steady himself as to compel Kendrick's attention. "I agree he's an idiot but there are special circumstances. Settlers in the West Bank blew up his family's house and his father's clothing store. His father died in the explosion and Israel's Custodial Commission sold both properties to new settlers for next to nothing." Blue lowered his voice, speaking into Kendrick's ear. "He's a mental case, but he had no one to turn to but us. Yosef and I will control him. Let him free."

"On your head, poet," answered Evan gruffly, unlocking the young terrorist's wrist irons.

"Why do you say a desert execution?" asked Yosef.

"Because the road beneath us is half sand, can't you feel it?" said Kendrick, knowing the route they were taking. "We just disappear, burned or buried in the desert."

"Why *us*?" pressed the older terrorist.

"I can explain me better than I can you: they don't know what to do with me, so why not just kill me. If I'm dangerous or influential, both the danger and the influence go with me." Evan paused, then nodded his head. "Come to think of it," he added, "that probably explains Yosef and the boy; they were the loudest prisoners in there and their voices were probably identified—both are easily distinguishable."

"And me?" asked Azra, staring at Kendrick.

"I should think you could answer that without my help," replied Kendrick, returning the Palestinian's look, a degree of contempt in his eyes. "I tried to break away from you when they came after me by the toilets, but you were too slow."

"You mean they saw us together?"

"The student gets a barely passing grade. Not only together but away from everyone else. It was *your* conference, big shot."

"The truck's slowing down!" exclaimed Yosef as the van braked slightly, heading into a descending curve.

"We have to get out," said Evan. "*Now.* If he's going down into a valley, there'll be soldiers. *Quickly!* We want the high ground. We need it; we'd never climb back up."

"The door!" cried Azra. "It must be padlocked on the outside."

"I have no idea," Kendrick lied, following the scenario as it had been rapidly drawn up in the compound's laboratory. Rivets had been removed and loosened in two panels. "I've never been taken prisoner here. But it doesn't matter. It's a sheet-steel alloy with seams. The four of us rushing together can smash out a partition. The center. It's the weakest." Evan grabbed the hare-lipped boy by the shoulder, pulling him to his left. "All right, wild man. Hit it like you're breaking down the Wailing Wall. The four of us! *Now!*"

"*Wait!*" Azra lurched across the van. "The weapon!" he

exclaimed, picking up the MAC-10 machine pistol and looping the strap over his shoulder, the barrel directed downward. "All right," he said, rejoining the others.

"Go!" shouted Kendrick.

The four prisoners crashed into the center panel of the door as the van lurched over the rocks in the downhill curve. The metal partition gave way, bulging at the seams, moonlight protruding through the wide separations.

"Once more!" roared Yosef, his eyes on fire.

"Remember!" commanded the man now accepted as Amal Bahrudi. "If we break through, tuck into your knees when you hit the ground. We don't need anyone hurt."

Again they rushed the half-collapsed panel. The bottom rivets snapped; the metal flew up in the moonlight and the four figures bolted out on the twisting road that led to a desert valley. Inside the van the guard rolled forward with the pitch of the vehicle's descent, his face streaked with perspiration brought about by fear of his own death. He crawled to his knees and hammered repeatedly on the wall of the driver's carriage. A single thud was heard in response. Their assignment for the night was half finished.

The fugitives also rolled, but against the descent, their movements abruptly halted, reversed by gravity, each straining to regain his balance. Azra and Yosef rose first to their feet, swiveling their necks and shaking their heads, instinctively checking their bruises for signs of anything worse. Kendrick followed, his shoulder on fire, his legs in momentary agony and his hands scraped, but all in all, he was grateful for the harsh requirements of backpacking through the mountains and riding the white water; he hurt but he was not hurt. The harelipped Palestinian had fared the worst; he moaned on the stony earth with its pattern of desert grass, writhing in fury as he tried to rise but could not. Yosef ran to him, and as Evan and Azra studied the valley below, the gruff older man made his pronouncement. "This child has broken his leg," he called over to his two superiors.

"Then kill me *now*!" shrieked the youngster. "I go to Allah and you go on to fight!"

"Oh, shut up," said Azra, gripping the MAC-10 weapon in his hand and walking with Kendrick to the injured boy. "Your compulsion to die becomes boring and your grating voice will instead kill us. Tear his shirt in strips, Yosef. Tie his hands and feet and put him in the road. That truck will race back up the minute it reaches the camp below and those fools realize what's happened. They'll find him."

"You deliver me to my *enemies*?" screamed the teenager.

"Be *quiet*!" replied Azra angrily, strapping the machine pistol to his shoulder. "We're delivering you to a hospital where you'll be taken care of. Children aren't executed except by bombs and missiles—all too frequently, but that's neither here nor there."

"I will reveal *nothing*!"

"You don't know anything," said the man called Blue. "Tie him up, Yosef. Make the leg as comfortable as possible." Azra bent over the youngster. "There are better ways to fight than dying needlessly. Let the enemy heal you so you can fight again. . . . Come back to us, my stubborn freedom fighter. We need you. . . . Yosef, *hurry*!"

As the older terrorist carried out his orders Azra and Kendrick walked back to the road hewn from rock. Far below the white sands began, stretching endlessly in the moonlight, a vast alabaster floor, its roof the dark sky above. In the distance, intruding on the blanket of white, was a small pulsating eruption of yellow. It was a desert fire, the rendezvous that was an intrinsic part of the 'escape.' It was too far away for the figures to be seen clearly, but they were there and rightly assumed to be Omani soldiers or police. But they were not the executioners Amal Bahrudi's companions imagined.

"You're much more familiar with the terrain than I am," said Evan in English. "How far do you judge the camp to be?"

"Ten kilometers, perhaps twelve, no more than that. The road straightens out below; they'll be there soon."

"Then let's go." Kendrick turned, watching the older Yosef carrying the injured teenager to the road. He started toward them.

Azra, however, did not move. "Where, Amal Bahrudi?" he called out. "Where should we go?"

Evan snapped his head back. "*Where?*" he repeated contemptuously. "To begin with, away from here. It'll be light soon, and if I know what I'm talking about, which I do, there'll be a dozen helicopters crisscrossing at low altitude looking for us. We can melt in the city, not here."

"Then what do we do? Where do we go?"

Kendrick could not see clearly in the dim moonlight, but felt the intense, questioning stare leveled at him. He was being tested. "We get word to the embassy. To your sister, Yateem, or the one named Ahbyahd. Stop the photographs and kill the ones involved."

"How do we do that? Get word into the embassy? Did your people tell you that, Amal Bahrudi?"

Evan was prepared; it was the inevitable question. "Frankly, they weren't sure where the pipeline was, and they assumed if any of you had any brains it would change daily. I was to pass a note through the gates directed to your operations council to let me through—through the pipeline wherever it was at the moment."

"Many such notes could be passed as a trap. Why would yours be accepted?"

Kendrick paused; when he answered his voice was low and calm and laced with meaning. "Because it was signed by the Mahdi."

Azra's eyes widened. He nodded slowly and held up his hand. "Who *is*?" he asked.

"The envelope was sealed with wax and not to be broken. It was an insult I found hard to accept, but even *I* follow orders from those who pay the freight, if you know what I mean."

"Those who give us the money to do what we do—"

"If there was a code signifying authenticity, it was for one or all of you on the council to know, not I."

"Give me the note," said Azra.

"*Idiot!*" yelled the congressman from Colorado's Ninth District, exasperated. "When I saw the police closing in on me, I tore it to shreds and scattered it through the Al Kabir! Would you have done *otherwise*?"

The Palestinian remained motionless. "No, obviously not," he replied. "At any rate we won't need it. I'll get us into the embassy. The pipeline, as you call it, is well regulated both inside and out."

"It's so well regulated that films are slipped out under the noses of your well-regulated guards. Send word in to your sister. Change them, every one of them, and start a search immediately for the camera. When it's found, kill the owner and anyone who seems to be a friend. Kill them all."

"On such surface observation?" protested Azra. "We risk wasting innocent lives, valuable fighters."

"Let's not be hypocritical," laughed Amal Bahrudi. "We have no such hesitations with the enemy. We're not killing 'valuable fighters,' we're killing innocent people quite properly to make the world listen, a world that's blind and deaf to our struggles, our very survival."

"By your almighty Allah, now *you're* the one who's blind and deaf!" spat out Azra. "You believe the Western press; it's not to be questioned! Of the eleven corpses, four were already dead, including two of the women—one by her own hand, for she was paranoid about rape, *Arabic* rape; the other, a much stronger woman not unlike the marine who attacked Nassir, threw herself on a young imbecile whose only reaction was to fire his weapon. The two men were old and infirm and died of heart failure. It does not absolve us from causing innocent death, but no guns were raised against them. All this was explained by Zaya and no one believed us. They never will!"

"Not that it matters, but what about the others? Seven, I believe."

"Condemned by our council and rightly so. Intelligence officers building networks against us throughout the Gulf and the Mediterranean, members of the infamous Consular Operations—even two *Arabs*—who sold their souls to sell *us* into oblivion, paid by the Zionists and their American puppets. They deserved death, for they would have seen us all die, but not before we were dishonored, were made caricatures of evil when there is no evil in us—only the desire to live in our own lands—"

"That's enough, *poet,*" broke in Kendrick, looking over at Yosef and the boy terrorist who longed for the arms of Allah. "There's no time for your sermons, we have to get out of here."

"To the embassy," agreed Azra. "Through the pipeline."

Kendrick walked back to the Palestinian, approaching him slowly. "To the embassy, yes," he said. "But not through the pipeline, just to the gates. There you'll send in the message to your sister spelling everything out for her. With those orders my job is finished here and so is yours—yours at least for a day or two."

"What are you talking about?" asked the bewildered Blue.

"My instructions are to bring *one* of you to Bahrain as soon as possible, and you're the one. I was captured and escaped and can't take any more chances. Not now!"

"Bahrain?"

"To the Mahdi. It will only be for a few hours, but it's urgent. He has new orders for you, orders he won't trust to anyone but a member of the council. And you're a member and we're both outside, not inside."

"The airport's watched," said Azra firmly. "It's patrolled by guards and attack dogs; no one can get in or out except by passing through interrogation. We'd never make it. It's the same on the waterfront. Every boat is flagged down and searched or blown out of the water if it does not comply."

"None of that has stopped your people from coming and going through the pipeline. I saw the results in Berlin."

"But you said 'urgent,' and the pipeline is a twenty-four- to forty-eight-hour process."

"Why so long?"

"We travel south only at night and in the uniforms of the Yemeni border garrisons. If we're stopped, we say we're patrolling the coastline. We then rendezvous with the fast deepwater boats—supplied by Bahrain, of course."

"Of course." *He had been right, thought Evan. The southern coast as far as Ra's al Hadd and beyond to the Strait of Masirah was open territory, a cruel wasteland of rock-filled shores and inhospitable interiors, heaven-sent for thieves and smugglers and, above all, for terrorists. And what better protection than the uniforms of the border garrisons, those soldiers chosen for both their loyalty and especially their brutality that equaled or bettered that of the international desperadoes given sanctuary in Yemen?* "That's very good," continued Amal Bahrudi, his tone professional. "How in Allah's name did you get hold of the uniforms? I understand they're unusual—a lighter color, different epaulets, boots designed for desert and water—"

"I had them made," interrupted Azra, his eyes on the valley below. "In Bahrain, of course. Each is accounted for and locked up when not in use. . . . You're right, we must go. That truck will reach the camp in less than two minutes. We'll talk along the way. Come!"

Yosef had placed the bound injured young terrorist across the road, calming him and giving him quiet but firm instructions. Azra and Kendrick approached; Evan spoke. "We'll make better time here on the road," he said. "We'll stay on it until we see the headlights coming up from the valley. *Hurry.*"

Final words of encouragement given to their fallen colleague, the three fugitives started running up the curving ascent to the flat ground several hundred feet above. The terrain was a combination of dry, scrubby brush weaving over the mostly arid earth and short, gnarled trees encouraged by the night moisture blown in from the sea only to be dwarfed by the windless, blistering heat of day. For as far as their eyes could see in the moon's dull wash of light, the road was straight. Breathing hard, his barrel chest heaving, Yosef spoke. "Three or four kilometers north there are more trees, taller trees, much more foliage to hide in."

"You know that?" asked Kendrick, unpleasantly surprised, thinking he was the only one who knew where they were.

"Not this exact road, perhaps, although there are only a few," answered the blunt, older terrorist, "but they are the same. From the sands toward the Gulf the earth changes. Everything is greener and there are small hills. Suddenly, one is in Masqat. It happens quickly."

"Yosef was part of the scouting team under Ahbyahd's command," explained Azra. "They came here five days before we captured the embassy."

"I see. I also see that the entire Black Forest couldn't help us when the light comes up, and Oman isn't the Schwarzwald. There'll be troops and police and helicopters combing every inch of ground. There's no place for us to hide except Masqat." Evan directed his next words to the man called Blue. "Certainly you have contacts in the city."

"Numerous."

"What does that mean?"

"Between ten and twenty, several highly placed. Those fly in and out, of course."

"Call them together in Masqat and bring me to them. I'll choose one."

"You'll *choose* one—"

"All I need is one, but it must be the right one. He'll carry a message for me and I'll have you in Bahrain in three hours."

"To the Mahdi?"

"Yes."

"But you said—you implied—that you don't know who he is."

"I don't."

"Still, you know how to reach him?"

"No," answered Kendrick, a sudden hollow pain in his chest. "Another insult but more readily understood. My operations are in Europe, not here. I simply assumed that you knew where to find him in Bahrain."

"Perhaps it was in the note you destroyed in the Al Kabir, a code—"

"There are *always* emergency procedures!" broke in Evan harshly, trying to control his anxiety.

"Yes, there are," said Azra thoughtfully. "But none that ever directly involve the Mahdi. As you must know, his name is spoken in whispers to only a few."

"I *don't* know. I told you, I don't *operate* in this part of the world—which was why I was chosen . . . obviously."

"Yes, obviously," agreed Blue. "You are far away from your base, the unexpected messenger."

"I don't *believe* this!" exploded Kendrick. "You receive instructions—no doubt *daily,* don't you?"

"We do." Azra looked briefly at Yosef. "But like yourself I am a messenger."

"*What?*"

"I am a member of the council, and young and strong, and not a woman. But neither am I a leader; my years do not permit it. Nassir, my sister Zaya, and Ahbyahd—they were appointed the leaders of the council. Until Nassir's death the three of them shared responsibility for the operation. When sealed instructions came, I delivered them but I did not break the seals. Only Zaya and Ahbyahd know how to reach the Mahdi—not personally, of course, but through a series of contacts that lead to him, get word to him."

"Can you make radio contact with your sister—over a secure frequency or perhaps a sterile telephone? She'd give you the information."

"Impossible. The enemy's scanning equipment is too good. We say nothing on the radio or the telephone that we would not say in public; we must assume it's one and the same."

"Your people in Masqat!" continued Evan rapidly, emphatically, feeling the beads of perspiration on his hairline. "Could one of them go inside and bring it out?"

"Information concerning the Mahdi, no matter how remote?" asked Azra. "She'd execute the one who sought it."

"We've got to *have* it! I'm to bring you to Bahrain—to *him*—by tonight, and I won't risk our sources of operating funds in Europe because I'm held responsible for a failure here that isn't mine!"

"There is only one solution," said Azra. "The one I spoke of below. We go to the embassy, *into* the embassy."

"There's no time for such *complications*!" insisted Kendrick desperately. "I know Bahrain. *I'll* choose a location and we'll call one of your people here to get the word inside to your sister. She or Ahbyahd will find a way to reach one of the Mahdi's contacts. There can't be any mention of either of us, of course—we'll have them say an emergency has arisen. That's *it,* an *emergency;* they'll know what it means! I'll fix the meeting ground. A street, a mosque, a section of the piers or the outskirts of the airport. Someone will come. Someone *has* to!"

The lean, muscular young terrorist once more was silent as he studied the face of the man he believed to be his counterpart in far-off Europe. "I ask you, Bahrudi," he said after the better part of ten seconds. "Would you be so free, so undisciplined, with your financial sources in Berlin? Would Moscow, or the Bulgarian banks in Sofia, or the unseen money in Zagreb tolerate such loose communications?"

"In an emergency they would understand."

"If you *allowed* such an emergency, they would slit your throat with a shearing knife and replace you!"

"You take care of *your* sources and I'll take care of mine, Mr. Blue."

"I will take care of *mine.* Here, now. We go to the embassy!"

The winds from the Gulf of Oman swept over the scrubby grass and the gnarled, dwarfed trees, but they could not prohibit the sound of the persistent two-note siren in the distance coming up from the desert valley. *It was the signal.* Conceal yourselves. Kendrick expected it.

"*Run!*" roared Yosef, grabbing Azra's shoulder and propelling his superior forward on the road. "Run, my brothers, as you have never run before in your lives!"

"The embassy!" cried the man called Blue. "Before the light comes up!"

For Evan Kendrick, congressman from the Ninth District of Colorado, the nightmare that would live with him the rest of his life was about to begin.

9

Khalehla gasped. Her eyes had been suddenly drawn to the rearview mirror—a speck of light, an image of black upon darker black, *something.* And then it was there. Far away on the hill above Masqat, a car was following her! There were no headlights, just a dark, moving shadow in the distance. It was rounding a curve on the deserted road that led to the twisting descent into the valley—to the beginning of the sands of Jabal Sham where the "escape" was to take place. There was only one entrance to and one exit from the desert valley, and her strategy had been to drive off the road out of sight and follow Evan Kendrick and his fellow fugitives on foot once they had broken out of the van. That strategy was now void.

Oh, my God, I can't be caught! They'll kill every hostage in the embassy! What have I done? Get out. Get away!

Khalehla spun the wheel; the powerful car swung around on the soft, sandy earth, leaping over ruts on the primitive road, and reversing its direction. She slammed her foot on the accelerator, stabbing it into the floor, and within moments, her headlights on high beam, she passed the sedan now rushing toward her. A figure beside the astonished driver tried to lunge down, concealing his face and body, but it was impossible.

And Khalehla did not believe what she *saw*!

But then she had to. In a sudden moment of utter clarity she saw it was so right, so perfect—so unmistakably perfect. *Tony!* Fumbling, bumbling, inarticulate Anthony MacDonald. The company reject whose position was secure because the firm was owned by his wife's father but who was nevertheless sent to Cairo, where he could do the least damage. A representative without portfolio, other than hosting dinner parties where he and his equally inept and boring wife invariably got drunk. It was as though a company memorandum had been tattooed on their foreheads: *Not permitted in the U.K. except for obligatory family funerals. Return flight tickets mandatory.* How perfectly ingenious! The overweight, overindulged, underbrained fop in sartorial plumage that could not hide his excesses. The Scarlet Pimpernel could not have matched his cover, and it *was* a cover, Khalehla was convinced of it. In building one for herself she had forced a master to expose his own.

She tried to think back, to reconstruct how he had snared her, but the steps were blurred because she had not thought about it at the time. She had no reason whatsoever to doubt that Tony MacDonald, the alcoholic cipher, was beside himself at the thought of traveling to Oman alone without someone knowledgeable with him. He had complained several times, nearly trembling, that his firm had accounts in Masqat and he was expected to service them despite the horrors going on over there. She had replied—several times—with comforting words that it was basically a U.S.-Israeli problem, not a British one, so he would not be harmed. It was as though he had expected her to be sent there, and when the orders came she had remembered his fears and telephoned him, believing he was her perfect escort to Oman. Oh, just *perfect*!

My God, what a network he must have! she thought. A little over an hour ago he was supposedly paralyzed with alcohol, making an ass of himself in a hotel bar, and here he was at five o'clock in the morning following her in a large blacked-out sedan. One assumption was unavoidable: he had put her under twenty-four-hour surveillance and picked her up after she had driven out of the palace gate, which meant that his informers had unearthed her connection to the sultan of Oman. But for *whom* was the profoundly clever MacDonald playing out his charade, a cover that gave him access to an efficient Omani network of informers and drivers of powerful automobiles at any hour of the day and night in this besieged country where every foreigner was put under a microscope? Which side was he on, and if it was the wrong one, for how many years had the ubiquitous Tony MacDonald been playing his murderous game?

Who was behind him? Did this contradictory Englishman's visit to Oman have anything to do with Evan Kendrick? Ahmat had spoken cautiously, abstractly, about the American congressman's covert objective in Masqat but would not elaborate other than to say that no theory should be overlooked no matter how implausible it seemed. He revealed only that the former construction engineer from Southwest Asia believed that the bloody seizure of the embassy *might* be traced to a man and an industrial conspiracy whose origins were perceived four years ago in Saudi Arabia—perceived, not proven. It was far more than she had been told by her own people. Yet an intelligent, successful American did not risk going undercover among terrorists without extraordinary convictions. For Ahmat, sultan of Oman and fan of the New England Patriots, this was enough. Beyond routing him here, Washington would not acknowledge him, would not help him. "But we can, *I* can!" Ahmat had exclaimed. And now Anthony MacDonald was a profoundly disturbing factor in the terrorist equation.

Her professional instincts demanded that she walk away, *race* away, but Khalehla could not do that. Something had happened, *someone* had altered the delicate balances of past and impending violence. She would not call for a small jet to fly her out of an unknown rock-based plateau to Cairo. Not yet. Not *yet.* Not now! There was too much to learn and so little time! She could not stop!

* * *

"Don't stop!" roared the obese MacDonald, clutching the hand strap above his seat as he yanked his heavy body upright in the sedan. "She was driving out here for a reason, certainly not for pleasure at this hour."

"She may have seen you, *Effendi.*"

"Not likely, but if she did I'm merely a buggered-off client tricked by a whore. Keep going and switch on your lights. Someone may be waiting for them and we have to know who it is."

"Whoever it is may be unfriendly, sir."

"In which case I'm just another drunken infidel you've been hired by the firm to protect from his own outrageous behavior. No different from other times, old sport."

"As you wish, *Effendi.*" The driver turned on the headlights.

"What's up ahead?" asked MacDonald.

"Nothing, sir. Only an old road that leads down to the Jabal Sham."

"What the hell is that?"

"The start of the desert. It ends with the far-off mountains that are the Saudi borders."

"Are there other roads?"

"A number of kilometers to the east and less passable, sir, very difficult."

"When you say there's nothing up ahead, exactly what do you mean?"

"Exactly what I said, sir. Only the road to the Jabal Sham."

"But this road, the one we're on," pressed the Englishman. "Where does *it* go?"

"It does not, sir. It turns left into the road down to the—"

"This Jabal-whatever," completed MacDonald, interrupting. "I see. So we're not talking about two roads, but one that happens to head left down to your bloody desert."

"Yes, sir—"

"A *rendezvous,*" broke in the Mahdi's conduit, whispering to himself. "I've changed my mind, old boy," he continued quickly. "Douse the damned headlights. There's enough of a moon for you to see, isn't there?"

"Oh, yes!" replied the driver in minor triumph while turning off the lights. "I know this road very well. I know every road in Masqat and Matrah very, *very* well. Even the unpassable ones to the east and to the south. But I must say, *Effendi,* I do not understand."

"Quite simple, my boy. If our busy little whore didn't head down to whatever and whomever she intended to reach, someone else will come up here—before the light does, I expect, which won't be too long now."

"The sky brightens quickly, sir."

"Quite so." MacDonald placed his pistol on top of the dashboard, reached into his jacket pocket and pulled out a short pair of binoculars with bulging, thickly coated lenses. He brought them to his eyes and scanned the area ahead through the windshield.

"It is still too dark to see, *Effendi,*" said the driver.

"Not for these little dears," explained the Englishman as they approached another curve in the dim moonlight. "Black out the entire sky and I'll count you the number of those stubby trees a thousand meters away." They rounded the sharp curve, the driver squinting and braking the large sedan. The road was now straight and flat, disappearing into the darkness ahead.

"Another two kilometers and we reach the descent into the Jabal Sham, sir. I will have to go very slowly, as there are many turns, many rocks—"

"Good *Christ*!" roared MacDonald, peering through the infrared binoculars. "Get off the road! *Quickly!*"

"What, sir?"

"Do as I say! Cut your engine!"

"Sir?"

"Turn it *off*! Coast as far as you can into the sand grass!"

The driver swung the car to the right, lurching over the hard, rutted ground, gripping the wheel and spinning it repeatedly to avoid the scattered squat trees barely seen in the night light. Seventy-odd feet into the grass the sedan came to a jolting stop; an unseen, gnarled tree close to the ground had been caught in the undercarriage.

"Sir . . . ?"

"Be *quiet*!" whispered the obese Englishman, replacing the binoculars in his pocket and reaching for his weapon above the dashboard. With his free hand he grabbed the door handle, then abruptly stopped. "Do the lights go on when the door is opened?" he asked.

"Yes, sir," answered the driver, pointing to the roof of the car. "The overhead light, sir."

MacDonald smashed the barrel of his pistol into the glass of the ceiling light. "I'm going outside," he said, again whispering. "Stay here, stay still and stay the hell away from the damned horn. If I hear a sound you're a dead man, do you *understand* me?"

"Clearly, sir. In case of an emergency, however, may I ask why?"

"There are men on the road up ahead—I couldn't say whether three or four; they were just specks—but they're coming this way and they're running." Silently the Englishman opened the door and rapidly, uncomfortably, climbed out. Staying as close to the ground as possible, he made his way swiftly across the sand grass to within twenty feet of the road. In his dark suit and black silk shirt, he lowered his bulk beside the stub of a dwarfed tree, put his weapon to the right of the twisted trunk, and took the infrared binoculars out of his pocket. He trained them on the road, in the path of the approaching figures. Suddenly they were there.

Blue! It was *Azra.* Without his beard but unmistakable! The junior member of the council, brother of Zaya Yateem, the only set of brains on that council. And the man on his left . . . MacDonald could not recall the name, but he had studied the photographs as though they were his passage to infinite wealth—which they were—and he knew it was *he.* A Jewish name, an older man, a terrorist for nearly twenty years . . . Yosef? Yes, *Yosef*! Trained in the Libyan forces after fleeing the Golan Heights. . . . But the man on Azra's left was puzzling; because of his appearance the Englishman felt he should know him. Focusing the infrared lenses on the bouncing, rushing face, MacDonald was perplexed. The running man was nearly as old as Yosef, and the few people in the embassy over thirty years of age were basically there for a reason known to Bahrain; the remainder were imbeciles and hotheads—fundamentalist zealots easily manipulated. Then MacDonald noticed what he should have seen at first: the three men were in prison clothes. They were escaped *prisoners.* Nothing made sense! Were these the men the whore, Khalehla, was racing to meet? If so, everything was doubly incomprehensible. The bitch-whore was working for the enemy out of Cairo. The information was confirmed in Bahrain; it was irrefutable! It was why he had cultivated her, repeatedly telling her of his firm's interests in Oman and how frightened he was to go there under the circumstances and how grateful he would be for a knowledgeable companion. She had swallowed the bait, accepting his offer, even to the point of insisting that she could not leave Cairo until a specific day, a specific time, which meant a very specific flight, of which there was only one a day. He had phoned Bahrain and was told to comply. And *watch her,* which he did. There was no meeting with anyone, no hint of eye contact whatsoever. But in the chaos of Masqat's security-conscious immigration she had strayed away. Damn! *Damn!* She had wandered—*wandered*—out to the air-freight warehouse, and when he found her she was alone by her petulant self. Had she made contact with someone there, passed instructions to the enemy? And if she had, did either have anything to do with the escaped prisoners now racing up the road?

That there was a connection would seem to be irrefutable. And totally out of place!

As the three figures passed him a perspiring Anthony MacDonald pushed himself off the ground, grunting as he got to his feet. Reluctantly—*very* reluctantly—understanding that millions upon millions could depend on the next few hours, he reached a conclusion: the sudden enigma that was Khalehla had to be resolved, and the answers he so desperately needed were inside the embassy. Not only could the millions be lost without those answers, but if the bitch-whore was pivotal to some hideous coup and he failed to stop her, it was entirely possible that Bahrain would order his execution. The Mahdi did not suffer failure.

He had to get inside the embassy and all the hell that it stood for.

The Lockheed C-130 Hercules with Israeli insignia cruised at thirty-one thousand feet above the Saudi desert east of Al Ubaylah. The flight plan from Hebron was an evasive one: south across the Negev into the Gulf of Aqaba and the Red Sea, proceeding south again equidistant from the coasts of Egypt, the Sudan and Saudi Arabia. At Hamdanah the course change was north-northeast, splitting the radar grids between the airports in Mecca and Qal Bishah, then due east at Al Khurmah into the Rub al Khali desert in southern Arabia. The plane had refueled in midair out of the Sudan west of Jiddah over the Red Sea; it would do so again on the return flight, without, however, its five passengers.

They sat in the cargo hold, five soldiers in coarse civilian clothes, each a volunteer from the little-known elite Masada Brigade, a strike force specializing in interdiction, rescue, sabotage and assassination. None was over thirty-two years of age, and all were fluent in Hebrew, Yiddish, Arabic and English. They were superb physical specimens, deeply bronzed from their desert training, and imbued with a discipline that demanded split-second decisions based on instantaneous reactions; each had an intelligence quotient in the highest percentile, and all were motivated in the extreme, for all had suffered in the extreme—either they themselves or their immediate families. Although they were capable of laughing, they were better at hating.

They sat, leaning forward, on a bench on the port side of the aircraft absently fingering the straps of their parachutes, which had only recently been mounted on their backs. They talked quietly among themselves—that is to say, four talked, one did not. The silent man was their leader; he was sitting in the forward position and stared blankly across at the opposite bulkhead. He was perhaps in his late twenties with hair and eyebrows bleached a yellowish-white by the unrelenting sun. His eyes were large and dark brown, his cheekbones high, fencing a sharp Semitic nose, his lips thin and firmly set. He was neither the oldest nor the youngest of the five men, but he *was* their leader; it was in his face, in his eyes.

Their assignment in Oman had been ordered by the highest councils of Israel's Defense Ministry. Their chances of success were minimal, the possibility of failure and death far greater, but the attempt had to be made. For among the two hundred thirty-six remaining hostages held inside the American embassy in Masqat was a deep-cover field director of the Mossad, Israel's unparalleled intelligence service. If he was discovered, he would be flown to any one of a dozen "medical clinics" of both friendly and unfriendly governments where intravenous chemicals would be far more effective than torture. A thousand secrets could be learned, secrets that could imperil the state of Israel and emasculate the Mossad in the Middle East. The objective: *Get him out if you can. Kill him if you cannot.*

The leader of this team from the Masada Brigade was named Yaakov. The Mossad agent held hostage in Masqat was his father.

"*Adonim,*" said the voice in Hebrew over the aircraft's loudspeaker—a calm and respectful voice addressing the passengers as Gentlemen. "We are starting our descent," he continued in Hebrew. "The target will be reached in six minutes, thirty-four seconds unless we encounter unexpected head winds over the mountains which will extend our time to six minutes, forty-eight seconds or perhaps fifty-five seconds, but then who's counting?" Four men laughed; Yaakov blinked, his eyes still on the opposite bulkhead. The pilot went on. "We will circle once over the target at eight thousand feet, so if you have to make any adjustments, mental or physical, with respect to those crazy bed sheets you've got on your dorsal fins, do so now. Personally, I do not care to go out and take a walk at eight thousand feet, but then I can read and write." Yaakov smiled; the others laughed louder than before. The voice again interrupted. "The hatch will be opened at eight thousand five hundred by our brother Jonathan Levy, who, like all experienced doormen in Tel Aviv, will expect a generous tip from each of you for his service. IOUs are not acceptable. The flashing red light will mean you must depart this luxurious hotel in the sky; however, the boys in the parking lot below refuse to retrieve your automobiles under the circumstances. They, too, can read and write and have been judged mentally competent, as opposed to certain unnamed tourists on this airborne cruise." The laughter now echoed off the walls of the plane; Yaakov chuckled. The pilot once more broke in, his voice softer, the tone altered. "Our beloved Israel, may she exist through eternity through the courage of her sons and daughters. And may almighty God go with you, my dear, dear friends. Out."

One by one the parachutes cracked open in the night sky above the desert, and one by one the five commandos from the Masada Brigade landed within a hundred fifty yards of the amber light shining up from the sands. Each man held a miniaturized radio that kept him in contact with the others in case of emergencies. Where each touched ground, each dug a hole and buried his chute, inserting the wide-bladed shovel down beside the fabric and the canvas. Then all converged on the light; it was extinguished, replaced by the single flashlight held by a man who had come from Masqat, a senior intelligence officer of the Mossad.

"Let me look at you," he said, turning his beam on each soldier. "Not bad. You look like ruffians from the docks."

"Your instructions, I believe," said Yaakov.

"They're not always followed," replied the agent. "You must be—"

"We have *no* names," interrupted Yaakov sharply.

"I stand rebuked," said the man from the Mossad. "Truthfully, I know only yours, which I think is understandable."

"Put it out of your mind."

"What shall I call all of you?"

"We are colors, only colors. From right to left they are Orange, Gray, Black and Red."

"A privilege to meet you," said the agent, shining his flashlight on each man—from right to left. "And you?" he asked, the beam on Yaakov.

"I am Blue."

"Naturally. The flag."

"No," said the son of the hostage in Masqat. "Blue is the hottest fire, and that is all you have to understand."

"It is also in refraction the coldest ice, young man, but no matter. My vehicle is several hundred meters north. I'm afraid I must ask you to walk after your exhilarating glide in the sky."

"Try me," said Gray, stepping forward. "I hate those terrible jumps. A man could get hurt, you know what I mean?"

The vehicle was a Japanese version of a Land-Rover without the amenities and sufficiently bashed and scraped to be unobtrusive in an Arab country where speed was a relative abstraction and collisions frequent. The hour-plus drive into Masqat, however, was suddenly interrupted. A small amber light flashed repeatedly on the road several miles from the city.

"It's an emergency," said the Mossad agent to Yaakov, who was beside him in the front seat. "I don't like it. There were to be no stops whatsoever when we approached Masqat. The sultan has patrols everywhere. Draw your weapon, young man. One never knows who may have been broken."

"Who's to *break*?" asked Yaakov angrily, his gun instantly out of his jacket holster. "We're in total *security.* Nobody knows about us—my own wife thinks I'm in the Negev on maneuvers!"

"Underground lines of communication have to be kept open, Blue. Sometimes our enemies dig too deeply into the earth. . . . Instruct your comrades. Prepare to fire."

Yaakov did so; weapons were drawn, each man at a window. The aggressive preparation, however, was unnecessary.

"It is Ben-Ami!" cried the man from the Mossad, stopping the van, the tires screeching and hurtling over the crevices in the badly paved road. "Open the door!"

A small, slender man in blue jeans, a loose white cotton shirt and a ghotra over his head leaped inside, squeezing Yaakov into the seat. "Keep driving," he ordered. "Slowly. There are no patrols out here and we have at least ten minutes before we might be stopped. Do you have a torch?" The Mossad driver reached down and brought up his flashlight. The intruder snapped it on, inspecting the human cargo behind him and the one beside him. "Good!" he exclaimed. "You look like scum from the waterfront. If we're stopped, slur your Arabic and shout about your fornications, do you understand?"

"*Amen,*" said three voices. The fourth, Orange, was contrary. "The Talmud insists on the truth," he intoned. "Find me a big-breasted *houri* and I may go along."

"*Shut* up!" cried Yaakov, not amused.

"What has happened to bring you here?" asked the Mossad agent.

"*Insanity,*" answered the newcomer. "One of our people in Washington got through an hour after you left Hebron. His information concerned an American. A *congressman,* no less. He's here and interfering—going *undercover,* can you *believe* it?"

"If it's true," replied the driver, gripping the steering wheel, "then every thought of incompetence I've ever entertained about the American intelligence community has blossomed to full flower. If he's caught, they'll be the pariahs of the civilized world. It is not a risk to be taken."

"They've taken it. He's here."

"*Where?*"

"We don't know."

"What has it to do with *us*?" objected Yaakov. "One American. One fool. What are his credentials?"

"Considerable, I'm sorry to say," answered Ben-Ami. "And we are to give him what leverage we can."

"*What?*" said the young leader from the Masada Brigade. "*Why?*"

"Because, my colleague notwithstanding, Washington is fully aware of the risks, of the potentially tragic consequences, and therefore has cut him off. He's on his own. If he's captured there's no appeal to his government, for it won't acknowledge him, can't acknowledge him. He's acting as a private individual."

"Then I must ask again," insisted Yaakov. "If the Americans won't touch him, why should *we*?"

"Because they never would have let him come here in the first place unless someone very highly placed thought he was on to something extraordinary."

"But why us? We have our own work to do. I repeat, why *us*?"

"Perhaps because we can—and they can't."

"It's politically disastrous!" said the driver emphatically. "Washington sets whatever it is in motion, then walks away covering its collective ass and dumps it on us. That kind of policy decision must have been made by the Arabists in the State Department. We fail—which is to say, *he* fails while we're there with him—and whatever executions take place they blame on the Jews! The Christ killers did it again!"

"Correction," interrupted Ben-Ami. "Washington did not 'dump' this on us because no one in Washington has any idea we know about it. And if we do our jobs correctly, we won't be in evidence; we give only untraceable assistance, if it's needed."

"You will not answer me!" shouted Yaakov. "*Why?*"

"I did, but you weren't listening, young fellow; you have other things on your mind. I said that we do what we do because perhaps we can. Perhaps, no guarantees at all. There are two hundred thirty-six human beings in that horrible place, suffering as we as a people know only too well. Among them is your father, one of the most valuable men in Israel. If this man, this congressman, has even the shadow of a solution, we must do what we can, if only to prove him right or prove him wrong. First, however, we must find him."

"Who is he?" asked the Mossad driver contemptuously. "Does he have a name or did the Americans bury that also?"

"His name is Kendrick—"

The large shabby vehicle swerved, cutting off Ben-Ami's words. The man from the Mossad had reacted so joltingly to the name that he nearly drove off the road. "*Evan* Kendrick?" he said, steadying the wheel, his eyes wide in astonishment.

"Yes."

"The Kendrick Group!"

"The what?" asked Yaakov, watching the driver's face.

"The company he ran over here."

"His dossier is being flown over from Washington tonight," said Ben-Ami. "We'll have it by morning."

"You don't *need* it!" cried the Mossad agent. "We've got a file on him as thick as Moses' tablets. We've also got Emmanuel Weingrass—whom we frequently wish we did *not* have!"

"You're too swift for me."

"Not now, Ben-Ami. It would take several hours and a great deal of wine— Damn Weingrass; he made me say that!"

"Would you be clearer, please?"

"Briefer, my friend, not necessarily clearer. If Kendrick is back, he *is* on to something and he's here for a four-year-old score—an explosion that took the lives of seventy-odd men, women and children. They were his family. You'd have to know him to understand that."

"*You* knew him?" asked Ben-Ami, leaning forward. "You *know* him?"

"Not well, but enough to understand. The one who knew him best—father figure, drinking companion, confessor, counselor, genius, best friend—was Emmanuel Weingrass."

"The man you obviously disapprove of," interjected Yaakov, his eyes still on the driver's face.

"Disapprove wholeheartedly," agreed the Israeli intelligence officer. "But he's not totally without value. I wish he were but he isn't."

"Value to the *Mossad*?" asked Ben-Ami.

It was as if the agent at the wheel felt a sudden rush of embarrassment. He lowered his voice in reply. "We've used him in Paris," he said, swallowing. "He moves in odd circles, has contact with fringe people. Actually—*God,* I hate to admit it—he's been somewhat effective. Through him we tracked down the terrorists who bombed the kosher restaurant on the rue du Bac. We resolved the problem ourselves, but some damn fool allowed him to be in on the kill. Stupid, *stupid*! And to his credit," added the driver grudgingly, gripping the wheel firmly, "he called us in Tel Aviv with information that aborted five other such incidents."

"He saved many lives," said Yaakov. "Jewish lives. And yet you disapprove of him?"

"You don't *know* him! You see, no one pays much attention to a seventy-eight-year-old bon vivant, a boulevardier who struts down the Montaigne with one, if not two, Parisienne 'models' whom he's outfitted in the St.-Honoré with the funds he received from the Kendrick Group."

"Why does that detract from his value?" asked Ben-Ami.

"He *bills* us for dinners at La Tour d'Argent! Three thousand, four thousand shekels! How can we refuse? He *does* deliver and he was a witness at a particularly violent event where we took matters into our own hands. A fact he now and then reminds us of if the payments are late."

"I'd say he's entitled," said Ben-Ami, nodding his head. "He's an agent of the Mossad in a foreign country and must maintain his cover."

"Caught, strangled, our testicles in a vise," whispered the driver softly to himself. "And the worst is yet to come."

"I beg your pardon?" said Yaakov.

"If anyone can find Evan Kendrick in Oman, it's Emmanuel Weingrass. When we get to Masqat, to our headquarters, I'll place a call to Paris. *Damn!*"

* * *

"*Je regrette,*" said the switchboard operator at the Pont Royale Hotel in Paris. "But Monsieur Weingrass is away for a few days. However, he has left a telephone number in Monte Carlo—"

"*Je suis désolée,*" said the operator at L'Hermitage in Monte Carlo. "Monsieur Weingrass is not in his suite. He was to have dinner this evening at the Hôtel de Paris, across from the casino."

"Do you have the number, please?"

"But of course," replied the ebullient woman. "Monsieur Weingrass is a *most* charming man. Only tonight he brought us all flowers; they fill up the office! Such a beautiful person. The number is—"

"*Désolé,*" intoned the male operator at the Hôtel de Paris with unctuous charm. "The dining room is closed, but the most generous Monsieur Weingrass informed us that he would be at Table Eleven at the casino for at least the next two hours. If any calls come for him, he suggested that the party reaching him should phone Armand at the casino. The number is—"

"*Je suis très désolé,*" gurgled Armand, obscure factotum at the Casino de Paris in Monte Carlo. "The delightful Monsieur Weingrass and his lovely lady did not have luck at our roulette this evening, so he decided to go to the Loew's gaming room down by the water—an inferior establishment, of course, but with competent croupiers; the French, naturally, not the Italians. Ask for Luigi, a barely literate Cretan, but he will find Monsieur Weingrass for you. And do send him my affections and tell him I expect him here tomorrow when his luck will change. The number is—"

"*Naturalmente!*" roared the unknown Luigi in triumph. "My dearest friend in all my life! Signor Weingrass. My Hebrew brother who speaks the language of Como and Lago di Garda like a native—not the Boot or even *napoletano;* barbarians, you understand—he is in front of my eyes!"

"Would you please ask him to come to the telephone. *Please.*"

"He is very engrossed, signore. His lady is winning a great deal of money. It is not good *fortuna* to interfere."

"Tell that *bastard* to get on this phone right now or his Hebrew balls will be put in boiling Arabian goat's milk!"

"*Che cosa?*"

"Do as I say! Tell him the name is *Mossad!*"

"*Pazzo!*" said Luigi to no one, placing the telephone on his lectern. "*Instabile!*" he added, cautiously stepping forward toward the screaming craps table.

Emmanuel Weingrass, his perfectly waxed mustache below an aquiline nose that bespoke an aristocratic past and his perfectly groomed white hair that rippled across his sculptured head, stood quietly amid the gyrating bodies of the frenetic players. Dressed in a canary-yellow jacket and a red-checkered bow tie, he glanced around the table more interested in the gamblers than in the game, every now and then aware that an idle player or one of the excited crowd of onlookers was staring at him. He understood, as he understood most things about himself, approving of some, disapproving of many, many more. They were looking at his face, somewhat more compact than it might be, an old man's face that had not lost its childhood configurations, still young no matter the years and aided by his stylish if rather extreme clothing. Those who knew him saw other things. They saw that his eyes were green and alive, even in blank repose, the eyes of a wanderer, both intellectually and geographically, never satisfied, never at peace, constantly roving over landscapes he wanted to explore or create. One knew at first glance that he was eccentric; but one did not know the extent of the eccentricity. He was artist and businessman, mammal and Babel. He was himself, and to his credit he had accepted his architectural genius as part of life's infinitely foolish game, a game that would involuntarily end for him soon, hopefully while he was asleep. But there were things to live, to experience while he was alive; by his account, approaching eighty, he had to be realistic, as much as it annoyed and frightened him. He looked at the garishly voluptuous girl beside him at the table, so vibrant, so vacuous. He would take her to bed, perhaps fondle her breasts—and then go to sleep. *Mea culpa.* What was the point?

"Signore?" whispered the tuxedoed Italian into Weingrass's ear. "There is a telephone call for you, someone I could never in my life have respect for."

"That's a strange remark, Luigi."

"He insulted you, my dear friend and most considerate guest. If you wish, I will dismiss him in the language of barbarians which he so justly deserves."

"Not everyone loves me as you do, Luigi. What did he say?"

"What he said I would not repeat in front of the grossest French croupier here!"

"You're very loyal, my friend. Did he give you his name?"

"Yes, a Signor Mossad. And I tell you he is deranged, *pazzo*!"

"Most of them are," said Weingrass as he walked quickly to the telephone.

10

The early light progressively threatened. Azra looked up at the morning sky, swearing at himself—including the rough-hewn Yosef in his oaths—for taking a wrong turn at the Kabritta Tower and thus wasting precious minutes. The three fugitives had torn off their prison trousers high above the ankles, at mid-calf, and the sleeves away from their shoulders. Without the benefit of sunlight they could pass for laborers brought in from Lebanon or the slums of Abu Dhabi, spending their rials on the only recreation accessible to them: the whores and the whisky available in the el Shari el Mishkwiyis, that landlocked island of the city.

They were in the recessed concrete employees' entrance of the Waljat Hospital less than two hundred yards away from the gates of the American embassy. A narrow street on the right intersected the broad thoroughfare. Angling around the corner was a line of shops, indistinguishable behind their iron shutters. All business was suspended while the madness lasted. In the distance, inside the gates of the embassy, were ragtag squads of lethargic young people walking slowly, the weight of their weapons dragging their arms and shoulders down, doing what they were ordered to do for their jihad, their holy war. The lethargy, however, would vanish with the first rays of the sun, and manic energy would erupt with the first wave of onlookers, especially the radio and television crews—mainly because of those crews. The angry children were about to go onstage within the hour.

Azra studied the large square in front of the gates. Across the way on the north side stood three white two-story office buildings close to one another. The curtained windows were dark, no signs of light anywhere, which was immaterial in any event. If there were men inside watching, they were too far away from the gates to hear what he would say softly through the bars, and the light was still too dim for him to be definitely identified—if indeed word of their escape had reached the post. And even if it had, the enemy would not mount a rash attack on the basis of vague possibilities; the consequences were too deadly. Actually, the square was deserted except for a row of beggars, their clothes in shreds, squatting in front of the embassy's sandstone walls, their alms plates in front, several with their own excrement in evidence. The filthiest of these outcasts were not potential agents of the sultan or of foreign governments, but others might be. He focused his eyes on each of the latter, looking for sudden, abrupt movements that would betray a man not used to a beggar's locked, hunkered stance. Only someone whose muscles were trained to withstand the interminable stress of a beggar's squat could remain immobile for any length of time. None moved, none squeezed a leg; it was not proof but it was all he could ask for. Azra snapped his fingers at Yosef, removing the MAC-10 weapon from under his shirt and thrusting it toward the older terrorist.

"I'm going over," he said in Arabic. "Cover me. If any of those beggars make un unbeggarly move, I expect you to be there."

"Go ahead. I'll swing out behind you in the hospital's shadow and slip from doorway to doorway on the right side. My aim is unequaled, so if there's one unbeggarly move, there is no beggar!"

"Don't anticipate, Yosef. Don't make a mistake and fire when you shouldn't. I *have* to reach one of those imbeciles inside. I'll stumble down as though it wasn't the best morning of my life." The young Palestinian turned to Kendrick, who was crouched in the sparse foliage by the hospital wall. "You, Bahrudi," he whispered in English. "When Yosef reaches the first building over there, come out slowly and follow him, but for God's sake, don't be obvious! Pause now and then to scratch yourself, spit frequently, and remember that your appearance doesn't belong to someone with good posture."

"I know those things!" Evan lied emphatically, impressed with what he was learning about terrorists. "You think I haven't employed such tactics a thousand times more than you have?"

"I don't know what to think," answered Azra simply. "I do know that I didn't like the way you walked past the Zawawi Mosque. The mullahs and the muezzins were congregating. . . . Perhaps you're better in the refined capitals of Europe."

"I assure you I'm adequate," said Kendrick icily, knowing he had to retain the Arabic version of strength, which came with cold understatement. His playacting was quickly deflated, however, as the young terrorist grinned. It was a genuine smile, the first he had observed in the man who called himself Blue.

"I'm assured," said Azra, nodding his head. "I'm here and not a corpse in the desert. Thank you for that, Amal Bahrudi. Now keep your eyes on me. Go where I direct you."

Pivoting swiftly, Blue rose and walked haltingly across the hospital's short stretch of zoysia lawn and into the wide thoroughfare that led to the square proper. Within seconds, Yosef raced out, ninety degrees to the right of his superior, crossing the narrow street twenty feet from the corner, hugging the side of the building in the dim light's darkest shadows. As the lone, isolated figure of Azra came into clear view staggering toward the embassy gates, Yosef spun around the corner; the last object Evan saw was the murderous MAC-10 machine pistol, held low in his left hand by the blunt sergeant-foreman. Kendrick knew it was the moment to move, and a part of him suddenly wished he were back in Colorado, southwest of Telluride at the base of the mountains and at temporary peace with the world. Then the images came again, filling his inner screen: *Thunder.* A series of deafening explosions. *Smoke.* Walls suddenly collapsing everywhere amid the screams of terrified children about to die. *Children!* And women—young *mothers*—shrieking in horror and protest as tons of rubble came cascading down from a hundred feet above the earth. And helpless men—friends, husbands, *fathers*—roaring defiantly against the cascading hell they knew instantly would be their tomb. . . . The *Mahdi*!

Evan got to his feet, breathed deeply, and started out toward the square. He reached the north-side pavement in front of the barricaded shops, his shoulders bent; he paused frequently to scratch himself and spit.

"The woman was *right,*" whispered the dark-skinned Arab in Western clothes peering out through a loose slat in a boarded-up store that only twenty-two days ago had been an attractive café devoted to selling cardamom coffee, cakes and fruit. "The older pig was so close I could have touched him as he passed by! I tell you, I did not breathe."

"*Shhh!*" warned the man at his side in full Arab dress. "Here he comes. The American. His height betrays him."

"Others will betray him also. He will not survive."

"Who *is* he?" asked the robed man, his whispered voice barely audible.

"It's not for us to know. That he risks his life for us is all that matters. We listen to the woman, those are our orders." Outside, the stooped figure in the street passed the store, pausing to scratch his groin while spitting into the curb. Beyond, diagonally across the square, another figure, blurred in the dim light, approached the embassy gates. "It was the woman," continued the Arab in Western clothes, still squinting between the loose boards, "who told us to watch for them on the waterfront, checking the small boats, and on the roads north and south, even here where they were least expected. Well, reach her and tell her the unexpected has happened. Then call the others on the Kalbah and Bustafi Wadis and let them know they needn't watch any longer."

"Of course," said the robed man, starting toward the back of the deserted dark café with its profusion of chairs eerily perched on top of tables as if the management expected unearthly customers who disdained the floor. Then the Arab stopped, quickly returning to his colleague. "Then what do *we* do?"

"The woman will tell you. *Hurry!* The pig by the gates is gesturing for someone inside. That's where they're going. *Inside!*"

Azra gripped the iron bars, his eyes darting up at the sky; the sprays of light were growing brighter by the minute in the east. Soon the dull dark gray of the square would be replaced by the harsh, blinding sun of Masqat; it would happen at any moment, as it did every dawn, an explosion of light that was suddenly total, all-encompassing. *Quickly! Pay attention to me, you idiots, you mongrels! The enemy is everywhere, watching, scanning, waiting for the instant to pounce, and I am now a prize of extraordinary value. One of us must reach Bahrain, reach the Mahdi! For the love of your goddamned Allah, will somebody come over here? I cannot raise my voice!*

Someone did! A youngster in soiled fatigues broke hesitantly away from his five-man squad, squinting in the still-dim but growing light, drawn by the sight of the odd-looking person at the left side of the huge chained double gate. As he drew nearer he walked faster, his expression slowly changing from the quizzical to the astonished.

"*Azra?*" he cried. "Is it *you*?"

"Be *quiet*!" whispered Blue, pressing both palms repeatedly through the bars. The teenager was one of the dozens of recruits he had instructed in the basic use of repeating weapons and, if he remembered correctly, not a prize pupil among so many just like him.

"They said you had gone on a secret mission, an assignment so holy we should thank almighty Allah for your strength!"

"I was captured—"

"Allah be praised!"

"For what?"

"For your having slain the infidels! If you had not, you would be in the blessed arms of Allah."

"I escaped—"

"Without slaying the infidels?" asked the youngster, sadness in his voice.

"They're all dead," replied Blue with exasperated finality. "Now, listen to—"

"Allah be praised!"

"Allah be *quiet—you* be quiet and listen to me! I must get inside, quickly. Go to Yateem or Ahbyahd—run as if your life depended on it—"

"My life is *nothing*!"

"Mine is, *damn* it! Have someone come back here with instructions. *Run!*"

The waiting produced a pounding in Blue's chest and temples as he watched the sky, watched the light in the east about to inflame this infinitesimal part of the earth, knowing that when it did he would be finished, dead, no longer able to fight the *bastards* who had stolen his life, erased his childhood with blood, taken his and Zaya's parents away in a burst of gunfire sanctioned by the killers of Israel.

He remembered it all so clearly, so painfully. His father, a gentle, brilliant man who had been a medical student in Tel Aviv until, in his third year, the authorities deemed he was better suited to the life of a pharmacist so as to make room for an immigrating Jew in the medical college. It was common practice. Erase the Arabs from the esteemed professions, was the Israeli credo. As the years went on, however, the father became the only "doctor" in their village on the West Bank; the government's visiting physicians from Be'er Sheva were incompetents who were forced to make their shekels in the small towns and the camps. One such physician complained, and it was as if the writing were stamped on the Wailing Wall. The pharmacy was shut down.

"We have our unspectacular lives to live; when will they let us *live* them?" the father and husband had screamed.

The answer came for a daughter named Zaya and a son who became Azra the Terrorist. The Israeli Commission of Arab Affairs on the West Bank again made a pronouncement. Their father was a troublemaker. The family was ordered out of the village.

They went north, toward Lebanon, toward anywhere that would accept them, and along the journey of their exodus, they stopped at a refugee camp called Shatila.

While brother and sister watched from behind the low stone wall of a garden, they saw their mother and father slaughtered, as were so many others, their bodies broken by staccato fusillades of bullets, snapping them into the ground, blood spewing from their eyes and their mouths. And up above, in the hills, the sudden thunder of Israeli artillery was to the ears of children the sound of unholy triumph. Someone had very much approved of the operation.

Thus was born Zaya Yateem, from gentle child to ice-cold strategist, and her brother, known to the world as Azra, the newest crown prince of terrorists.

The memories stopped with the sight of a man running inside the gates of the embassy.

"*Blue!*" cried Ahbyahd, the streaks of white in his hair apparent in the growing light, his voice a harsh, astonished whisper as he raced across the courtyard. "In Allah's name, what *happened*? Your sister is beside herself but she understands that she cannot come outside, not as a woman, not at this hour, and especially not with you here. Eyes are everywhere—what *happened* to you?"

"I'll tell you once we're inside. There's no time now. Hurry!"

"*We?*"

"Myself, Yosef and a man named Bahrudi—he comes from the *Mahdi*! Quickly! The light's nearly up. Where do we go?"

"Almighty God . . . the *Mahdi*!"

"*Please,* Ahbyahd!"

"The east wall, about forty meters from the south corner, there's an old sewer line—"

"I know it! We've been working on it. It's clear now?"

"One must crouch low and climb slowly, but yes, it's clear. There is an opening—"

"Beneath the three large rocks on the water," said Azra, nodding rapidly. "Have someone there. We race against the light!"

The terrorist called Blue slipped away from the chained gates and with gathering speed, slowly, subtly discarding his previous posture, quickly rounded the south edge of the wall. He stopped, pressing his back into the stone, his eyes roaming up the line of barricaded shops. Yosef stepped partially out of a boarded-up recessed doorway; he had been watching Azra and wanted the young leader to know it. The older man hissed, and in seconds "Amal Bahrudi" emerged from a narrow alleyway between the buildings; staying in the shadows, he raced up the pavement, joining Yosef in the doorway. Azra gestured to his left, indicating a barely paved road in front of him that paralleled the embassy wall; it was beyond the stretch of shops on the square; across the way there was only a wasteland of rubble and sand grass. In the distance, toward the fiery horizon, was the rock-laden coastline of the Oman Gulf. One after the other the fugitives raced down the road in their torn prison clothes and hard leather sandals, past the walls of the embassy into the sudden, startling glare of the bursting sun. Azra leading, they reached a small promontory above the crashing waves. With surefooted agility, the world's new crown prince of killers started down over the huge boulders, stopping every now and then to gesture behind him, pointing out the areas of green sea moss where a man could lose his life by slipping and plunging down into the jagged rocks below. In less than a minute they reached an oddly shaped indentation at the bottom of the short cliff where the huge stones met the water. It was marked by three boulders forming a strange triangle at the base of which was a cavelike opening no more than three feet wide and continuously assaulted by the pounding surf.

"There it is!" exclaimed Azra, exultation and relief in his voice. "I knew I could find it!"

"What *is* it?" yelled Kendrick, trying to be heard over the crashing waves.

"An old sewer line," roared Blue. "Built hundreds of years ago, a communal toilet continuously washed down by sea water carried up by slaves."

"They bored through *rock*?"

"No, Amal. They creased the surface and angled the rocks above; nature took care of the rest. A reverse aqueduct, if you like. It's a steep climb, but as someone had to build it, there are ridges for feet—slaves' feet, like our Palestinian feet, no?"

"How do we get in there?"

"We walk through water. If the prophet Jesus can walk *on* it, the least we can do is walk *through* it. *Come.* The *embassy*!"

Perspiring heavily, Anthony MacDonald climbed the open waterfront staircase on the side of the old warehouse. The creaking of the steps under his weight joined the sounds of wood and rope that erupted from the piers where hulls and stretched halyards scraped the slips along the docks. The first yellow rays of the sun pulsated over the waters of the harbor, broken by intruding skiffs and aged trawlers heading out for the day's catch, passing observant marine patrols that every now and then signaled a boat to stop for closer inspection.

Tony had ordered his driver to crawl the car back toward Masqat on the deserted road without headlights until they reached a back street in the As Saada that cut across the city to the waterfront. Only when they encountered streetlamps did MacDonald instruct the driver to switch on the lights. He had no idea where the three fugitives were running or where they expected to hide in the daylight with an army of police searching for them, but he assumed it would be with one of the Mahdi's more unlikely agents in the city. He would avoid them; there was too much to learn, too many contradictory things to understand before a chance confrontation with the young ambitious Azra. But there was one place he could go, one man he could see without fear of being seen himself. A hired killer who followed orders blindly for money, a stick of human garbage who made contact with potential clients only in the filthy alleyways of the el Shari el Mishkwiyis. Only those who had to know knew where he lived.

Tony heaved his way up the last flight of steps to the short, thick door at the top that led to the man he had come to see. As he reached the final step he froze, mouth gaping, eyes bulging. Suddenly, without warning, the door whipped open on greased hinges as the half-naked killer lunged out on the short platform, a knife in his left hand, its long, razor-sharp blade glistening in the new sun, while in his right was a small .22 caliber pistol. The blade was poised across MacDonald's throat, the barrel of the gun jammed into his left temple; unable to breathe, the obese Englishman gripped both railings with his hands to keep from falling back down the steps.

"It is *you,* " said the gaunt, hollow-cheeked man, withdrawing the pistol but keeping the knife in place. "You are not to come here. You are never to come here!"

Swallowing air, his immense body rigid, MacDonald spoke hoarsely, feeling the psychopath's blade across his throat. "If it were not an emergency, I would never have done so, that should be perfectly clear."

"What is clear is that I was *cheated*!" replied the man, wiggling the knife. "I killed that importer's son in the same way I could kill you at this moment. I carved up that girl's face and left her in the streets with her skirt above her head and I was *cheated.*"

"No one meant to."

"Someone *did*!"

"I'll make it up to you. We must talk. As I mentioned, it's an emergency."

"Talk here. You don't come inside. *No* one comes inside!"

"Very well. If you'll be so kind as to permit me to stand rather than hanging on for dear life half over this all too ancient staircase—"

"Talk."

Tony steadied himself on the third step from the top, taking out a handkerchief and blotting his perspiring forehead, his gaze on the knife below. "It's imperative I reach the leaders inside the embassy. Since they cannot, of course, come out, I must go in to them."

"It is too dangerous, especially for the one who gets you inside, since he remains outside." The bone-gaunt killer pulled the blade away from MacDonald's throat, only to readjust it with a twist of his wrist, the glistening point now resting at the base of the Englishman's neck. "You can talk to them on the telephone, people do all the time."

"What I have to say—what I must ask them—can't be spoken over the phone. It's vital that only the leaders hear my words and I theirs."

"I can sell you a number that is not published in the listings."

"It's published somewhere and if you have it others do also. I cannot take the risk. Inside. I *must* get inside."

"You are difficult," said the psychopath, his left eyelid flickering, both pupils dilated. "Why are you difficult?"

"Because I am immensely rich and you are not. You need money for your extravagances . . . your habits."

"You *insult* me!" spat out the killer for hire, his voice strident but not loud, the half-crazed man aware of the fishermen and dock laborers trudging to their morning chores three stories below.

"I'm only being realistic. Inside. How much?"

The killer coughed his foul breath in MacDonald's face, pulling the blade back and settling his rheumy stare on his past and present benefactor. "It will cost a great deal of money. More than you have ever paid before."

"I'm prepared for a reasonable increase, not exorbitant, mind you, but reasonable. We'll always have work for you—"

"There's an embassy press conference at ten o'clock this morning," interrupted the partially drugged man. "As usual, the journalists and television people will be selected at the last minute, their names called out at the gates. Be there, and give me a telephone number so I can give you a name within the next two hours."

Tony did so: his hotel and his room. "How much, dear boy?" he added.

The killer lowered the knife and stated the amount in Omani rials; it was equivalent to three thousand English pounds, or roughly five thousand American dollars. "I have expenses," he explained. "Bribes must be paid or the one who bribes is dead."

"It's *outrageous*!" cried MacDonald.

"Forget the whole thing."

"Accepted," said the Englishman.

Khalehla paced her hotel room, and although she had given up cigarettes for the sixth time in her thirty-two years, she smoked one after another, her eyes constantly straying to the telephone. Under no condition could she operate from the palace. That connection had been jeopardized enough. *Damn* that son of a bitch!

Anthony MacDonald—cipher, drunk . . . someone's agent extraordinary—had his efficient network in Masqat, but she was not without resources herself, thanks to a roommate at Radcliffe who was now a sultan's wife—thanks to Khalehla's having introduced a fellow Arab to her best friend a number of years ago in Cambridge, Massachusetts. *God,* how the world moved in smaller, swifter and even more familiar circles! Her mother, a native Californian, had met her father, an exchange student from Port Said, while both were in graduate school at Berkeley, she an Egyptologist, he a doctoral candidate in Western Civilization, both aiming for academic careers. They fell in love and got married. The blond California girl and the olive-skinned Egyptian.

In time, with Khalehla's birth, the stunned racially absolute grandparents on both sides discovered that there was more to children than the purity of strain. The barriers fell in a sudden rush of love. Four elderly individuals, two couples predisposed to abhor each other, had bridged the gaps of culture, skin and belief by finding joy in a child and other mutually shared pleasures. They became inseparable, the banker and his wife from San Diego and the wealthy exporter from Port Said and his only Arab wife.

"*What am I doing?*" cried Khalehla to herself. This was no time to think about the past, the present was *everything*! Then she realized why her mind had wandered—two reasons really. The pressures had become too great; she needed a few minutes to herself, to think about herself and those she loved if only to try to understand the hatred that was everywhere. The latter was the second, the more important reason. The faces and the words spoken at a dinner party long ago had been lurking in the background, especially the words, quietly echoing off the walls of her mind; they had made an impression on an eighteen-year-old girl about to leave for America.

"The monarchs of the past had precious little to their overall credit," her father had said that night in Cairo when the whole family was together, including both sets of grandparents. "But they understood something our present leaders don't consider—can't consider, actually, unless they try to become monarchs, which wouldn't be seemly in these times no matter how hard some *do* try."

"What's that, young man?" asked the California banker. "I haven't entirely given up on a monarchy. Republican, of course."

"Well, starting with our own pharaohs and then through the high priests of Greece, the emperors of Rome, and all the kings and queens of Europe and Russia, they arranged marriages so as to bring the diverse nations into their central families. Once a person knows another under those circumstances—dining, dancing, hunting, even telling jokes—it's difficult to maintain a stereotyped bias, isn't it?"

Everyone around the table had looked at one another, smiles and gentle nods emerging.

"In such circles, however, my son," remarked the exporter from Port Said, "things did not always work out so felicitously.

I'm no scholar, but there were wars, families against their own, ambitions thwarted."

"True, revered Father, but how much worse might it have all been without such arranged marriages? Far, far worse, I'm afraid."

"I refuse to be used as a geopolitical tool!" Khalehla's mother had exclaimed, laughing.

"Actually, my dear, everything between us was arranged by our devious parents here. Have you any idea how they've profited from our alliance?"

"The only profit I've ever seen is the lovely young lady who's my granddaughter," said the banker.

"She's off to America, my friend," said the exporter. "Your profits may dwindle."

"How does it feel, darling? Quite an adventure for you, I'd think."

"It's hardly the first time, Grandmother. We've visited you and Grandfather a lot, and I've been to quite a few cities."

"It will be different now, dear." Khalehla forgot who had said those words, but they were the beginning of one of the strangest chapters of her life. "You'll be living there," added whoever it was.

"I can't wait. Everyone's so friendly, you feel so wanted, so liked."

Once again those around the table looked at one another. It was the banker who had broken the silence. "You may not always feel that way," he said quietly. "There will be times when you're not wanted, not liked, and it will confuse you, certainly hurt you."

"That's hard to believe, Grandfather," said an ebullient young girl Khalehla only vaguely remembered.

The Californian had briefly looked at his son-in-law, his eyes pained. "As I think back, it's hard for me to believe it, too. Don't ever forget, young lady, if problems arise or if things become difficult, pick up the phone and I'll be on the next plane."

"Oh, Grandfather, I can't imagine doing that."

And she hadn't, although there were times when she came close, only pride and what strength she could summon stopping her. *Shvartzeh Arviyah!* . . . "Nigger-Arab!" was her first introduction to one-on-one hatred. Not the blind, irrational hatred of mobs running amok in the streets, brandishing placards and crudely made signs, cursing an unseen enemy far away across distant borders, but of young people like herself, in a pluralistic community of learning, sharing classrooms and cafeterias, where the worth of the individual was paramount, from entrance through constant evaluation to graduation. One contributed to the whole, but as *himself* or *herself,* not as an institutional robot except perhaps on the playing fields, and even there individual performance was recognized, often more so in defeat, touchingly more so.

Yet for so long she had not been an individual; she had lost *herself.* That had been eradicated, transferred to an abstract, insidious racial collective called *Arab.* Dirty Arab, devious Arab, murderous Arab—Arab, Arab, *Arab*—until she couldn't stand it any longer! She stayed by herself in her room, turning down offers from dormitory acquaintances to visit the collegiate drinking halls; twice had been enough.

The first should have been enough. She had gone to the ladies' room only to find it blocked by two male students; they were Jewish students, to be sure, but they were also *American* students.

"Thought you Arabs didn't drink!" shouted the drunken young man on her left.

"It's a choice one makes," she had replied.

"I'm told you *Arviyahh* piss on the floor of your tents!" cried the other, leering.

"You were misinformed. We're quite fastidious. May I please go inside—"

"Not here, Arab. We don't know what you'd leave on the toilet seat and we have a couple of *yehudiyah* with us. Got the message, *Arab*?"

The breaking point, however, came at the end of her second semester. She had done well in a course taught by a renowned Jewish professor, well enough to have been singled out by the sought-after teacher as the student he deemed to have achieved the most. The prize, an annual event in his class, was a personally inscribed copy of one of his works. Many of her classmates, Jews and non-Jews alike, had come around to congratulate her, but when she left the building three others in stocking masks had stopped her on a wooded path back to her dormitory.

"What did you do?" one asked. "Threaten to blow his house up?"

"Maybe knife his kids with a sharp Arab dagger?"

"Hell, no! She'd call in Arafat!"

"We're going to teach you a lesson, *Shvartzeh Arviyah*!"

"If the book means so much to you, *take* it!"

"No, Arab, *you* take it."

She had been raped. "This is for Munich!" "This for the children in the Golan kibbutz!" "This for my cousin on the beaches of Ashdod, where you bastards *killed* him!" There had been no sexual gratification for the attackers, only the fury of inflicting punishment on the *Arab.*

She had half crawled, half stumbled back toward her dormitory when a very important person came into her life. One Roberta Aldridge, the inestimable Bobbie Aldridge, the iconoclastic daughter of the New England Aldridges.

"*Scum!*" she had screamed into the trees of Cambridge, Massachusetts.

"You must never *tell*!" pleaded the young Egyptian girl. "You don't *understand*!"

"Don't you worry about that, honey. In Boston we have a phrase that means the same thing from Southie to Beacon Hill. 'Them that gives *gets*!' And those motherfuckers will *get,* take my word!"

"*No!* They'll come after me—they won't understand, either! I don't hate Jews . . . my dearest friend since childhood is the daughter of a rabbi, one of my father's closest colleagues. I *don't* hate Jews. They'll say I do because to them I'm just a dirty Arab, but I don't! My family's not like that. We don't hate."

"Hold it, kid. I didn't say anything about Jews, you did. I said 'motherfuckers,' which is an all-inclusive term, so to speak."

"It's finished here. I'm finished. I'll leave."

"The hell you will! You're seeing my doctor, who'd better know his marbles, and then you move in with me. *Christ,* I haven't had a cause in almost two years!"

Praise God and Allah, and all those other deities above. I have a friend. And somehow, within the pain and the hatred of those days, an idea was born that grew into a commitment. An eighteen-year-old girl knew what she was going to do with the rest of her life.

The telephone rang. The past was finished, *over,* the present *was* everything! She ran to the bedside phone, yanked it out of its cradle. "*Yes?*"

"He's here."

"*Where?*"

"The embassy."

"Oh, my *God*! What's happening? What's he doing?"

"He's with two others—"

"There are three, not *four*?"

"We have only seen three. One is at the gate among the beggars. He's been talking to the terrorists inside."

"The *American*! Where is *he*?"

"With the third man. The two of them stay in the shadows; only the first man shows himself. He is the one who makes the decisions, not the American."

"What do you mean?"

"We think he's making arrangements for them to go inside."

"*No!*" screamed Khalehla. "They can't—*he* can't, he *mustn't*! Stop them, stop *him*!"

"Such orders should come from the palace, madame—"

"Such orders come from *me*! You've been *told*! The prisoner compound was one thing, but not the embassy, *never* the embassy, not for *him*! Go out and take them, stop them, kill them if you have to! Kill *him*!"

"*Hurry!*" cried the robed Arab running to his colleague in the front of the boarded-up restaurant and cracking the bolt of his machine gun into the firing position. "Our orders are to take them now, stop them, stop the American. Kill him, if we must."

"*Kill* him?" asked the astonished official from the palace.

"Those are the orders. *Kill* him!"

"The orders have come too late. They're gone."

Ultra Maximum Secure
No Existing Intercepts
Proceed

The figure in the dark sterile room touched the letters of the keyboard with angry precision.

I've broken the Langley access codes and it's madness! Not the CIA, for the liaison is withholding nothing. Instead, the insanity is with the subject. He has gone into the embassy! He can't survive. He'll be found out—at the toilet, at a meal with or without utensils, with a single reaction to a phrase. He's been away too long! I've factored in every possibility and my appliances offer little hope. Perhaps my appliances and I were too quick to render judgment. Perhaps our national messiah is no more than a fool, but then all messiahs have been considered fools and idiots until proven otherwise. That is my hope, my prayer.

11

The three escaped prisoners crawled in the darkness up through the ancient, moss-laden sewer line to a gridded opening on the stone floor of the embassy's east courtyard. Struggling, their hands and feet scraped and bloodied, they emerged into the dazzling sunlight only to be met by a scene Evan Kendrick wished with all his being had remained in darkness. Sixty or more hostages had been removed from the roof to the courtyard for their meager morning food and ablutions. A latrine consisted of wooden planks with circular holes above planter boxes, the men separated from the women by a large transparent screen ripped from one of the embassy's windows. The degradation was complete in that the guards, male and female, walked back and forth in front of the hostages, male and female, laughing and making loud jokes about the functional difficulties their captives were experiencing. The toilet paper, tauntingly held out beyond the reach of trembling hands before it was finally delivered, consisted of printouts from the embassy's computers.

Across the way, in full view of the frightened, humiliated people at the planks, the hostages had formed a line leading to three long, narrow tables with rows of metal plates holding dry bread and small wedges of questionable cheese. Spaced between were filthy pitchers filled with a grayish-white liquid, presumably diluted goat's milk, which was poured sparingly into the prisoners' wooden bowls by a group of armed terrorists behind the tables. Every now and then a hostage was refused a plate or a ladleful of milk; pleading was futile; it resulted in a slap or a fist or a ladle in the face when the cries were too loud.

Suddenly, as Kendrick's eyes were still adjusting to the harsh light a young prisoner, a boy of no more than fourteen or fifteen, tears streaming down his face, his features contorted, screamed in defiance. "You lousy *bastard*! My mother's sick! She keeps throwing up from this crap! Give her something decent, you sons of bitches—"

The boy's words were cut short by the barrel of a rifle across his face, tearing his left cheek. Instead of subduing the youngster, the blow infuriated him. He lunged across the table, grabbing the shirt of the man with the rifle, tearing it off his chest, sending metal plates and pitchers crashing down from the table. In seconds, the terrorists were on him, pulling him away from the bearded man he was wrestling to the ground, pummeling him with rifle butts and kicking his writhing body on the courtyard stone. Several other male hostages, their anger and courage aroused by the boy's action, rushed forward shouting with weak, hoarse voices, their arms flailing pathetically against their arrogant, far stronger enemies. What followed was a brutal suppression of the minirevolt. As the hostages fell they were beaten unconscious and kicked like carcasses being thumped and processed in a slaughterhouse.

"*Animals!*" roared an old man, holding his trousers and walking unsteadily forward from the planks, his resolve and dignity intact. "*Arab* animals! Arab *savages*! Have none of you a shred of civilized decency? Does beating to death weak defenseless men make you heroes of *Islam*? If so, take me and issue yourselves more medals, but in the name of God, stop what you're *doing*!"

"Whose *God*?" shouted a terrorist over the body of the unconscious boy. "A Christian Jesus, whose followers arm our enemies so they can massacre our children with bombs and cannons? Or a wandering Messiah, whose people steal our lands and kill our fathers and mothers? Get your Gods straight!"

"*Enough!*" commanded Azra, striding rapidly forward. Kendrick followed, unable to control himself, thinking that moments before he might have grabbed the MAC-10 weapon off Blue's shoulder and fired into the terrorists. Standing above the bloodied youngster, Azra continued, his voice casual. "The lesson's been taught; don't overteach it or you'll numb those you want to instruct. Take these people down to the infirmary, to the hostage doctor . . . and find the boy's mother. Bring her there also and get her a meal."

"*Why,* Azra?" protested the Palestinian. "No such consideration was shown *my* mother! She was—"

"*Nor* to mine," broke in Blue firmly, stopping the man. "And look at us now. Take this child down and let him stay with his mother. Have someone speak to them about overzealousness and pretend to care."

Kendrick watched in revulsion while the limp, bleeding bodies were carried away. "You did the right thing," he said to Azra in English, his words coldly noncommittal, talking like a technician. "One doesn't always care to, but one has to know when to stop."

The new prince of terrorists studied Evan through opaque eyes. "I meant what I said. Look at us now. The death of our own makes us different. One day we're children, the next we are grown up, no matter the years, and we are experts at death, for the memories never leave us."

"I understand."

"No, you don't, Amal Bahrudi. Yours is an ideological war. For you death is a political act. You are a passionate believer, I have no doubt—but still what you believe is politics. That's not my war. I have no ideology but survival, so that I can extract death for death—and still survive."

"For what?" asked Kendrick, suddenly terribly interested.

"Oddly enough, to live in peace, which was forbidden to my parents. For all of us to live in our own land, which was stolen from us, delivered to our enemies and paid for by rich nations to assuage their own guilt over crimes against a people that were not our crimes. Now we're the victims; can we do less than fight?"

"If you think that's not politics, I suggest you think again. You remain a poet, Azra."

"With a knife and a gun as well as my thoughts, Bahrudi."

There was another commotion across the courtyard, this one benign. Two figures raced out of a doorway, one a veiled woman, the other a man with streaks of white in his hair. Zaya Yateem and Ahbyahd, the one called White, thought Evan, standing rigid, aloof. The greeting between brother and sister was odd; they formally shook hands, looking at each other, then fell into an embrace. The universal guardianship of an older sister for a younger brother—the latter so often awkward, impulsive in the eyes of the older, wiser sibling—bridged races and ideology. The younger child would inevitably grow stronger, the muscular arms of the household, but the older sister was always there to guide him. Ahbyahd was subsequently less formal, throwing his arms around the youngest, strongest member of the Operations Council, and kissing him on both cheeks. "You have much to tell us," exclaimed the terrorist called White.

"I do," agreed Azra, turning to Evan Kendrick, "because of this man. He is Amal Bahrudi from East Berlin, sent by the Mahdi to us here in Masqat."

Above her veil, Zaya's urgent, even violent eyes searched Evan's face. "Amal Bahrudi," she repeated. "I've heard the name, of course. The Mahdi's strings reach great distances. You are far from your own work."

"Uncomfortably so," said Kendrick, in the cultured dialect of Riyadh. "But others are watched, their every move monitored. It was thought that someone unexpected should come here, and East Berlin is a convenient place from which to travel. People will swear you're still there. When the Mahdi called, I responded. In truth it was I who first made contact with his people about a problem you have here, which your brother will explain to you. We may have different objectives, but we all progress by cooperating with each other, especially when our bills are paid."

"But you," said Ahbyahd, frowning. "The Bahrudi of East Berlin, the one who moves anywhere, everywhere. You were found out?"

"It's true I have a reputation for getting around," answered Evan, permitting himself the hint of a smile. "But it certainly won't be enhanced by what happened to me here."

"You were betrayed, then?" asked Zaya Yateem.

"Yes. I know who it was and I'll find him. His body will drift up in the harbor—"

"Bahrudi broke us out," interrupted Azra. "While I was thinking he was *doing.* He deserves whatever reputation he has."

"We go inside, my dearest brother. We'll talk there."

"My dearest sister," said Blue. "We have traitors here, that's what Amal came to tell us—that and one more thing. They're taking photographs and smuggling them outside, *selling* them! If we live, we'll be hunted for years . . . a record of our activities for all the world to see!"

The sister now studied the brother, her dark eyes above the veil questioning. "Photographs? Taken by concealed cameras with sophisticated features to operate and noticed by no one? Do we have such advanced students of photography among our brothers and sisters here, the majority of whom can barely read?"

"He *saw* the photographs! In East Berlin!"

"We'll talk inside."

The two Englishmen sat in front of the large desk at the British embassy, the weary attaché, still in a bathrobe, doing his best to stay awake. "Yes, chaps," he said, yawning. "They'll be here any moment now, and if you don't mind my saying so, I hope there's substance in what you're telling us. MI-Six is seven ways into a dither here, and they're not too charmed by a couple of our own Brits robbing them of a few precious hours of sleep."

"My friend Dickie, here, was in the Grenadiers!" exclaimed Jack, protectively and otherwise. "If *he* thinks there's something to be told you, I think you should pay attention. After all, what are we here for?"

"To make money for your firms?" offered the attaché.

"Well, of course, that's a minor part of it," said Jack. "But first we're *Englishmen,* and don't you forget it. We'll not see the Empire sink into oblivion. Right, Dickie?"

"It already has," said the attaché, stemming another yawn. "Forty years ago."

"You see," interrupted Dickie. "My friend Jack, here, is in ferrous metals but I'm in textiles, and I tell you the way that bugger was dressed, as opposed to the way he had dressed before—he's up to no good. The cloth not only determines the man but it also suits his activities—been that way since the first flax was woven, probably right here in this part of the world, come to think of it—"

"MI-Six has the information," broke in the attaché with the dulled expression of a man numbed by repetition. "They'll be here soon."

They were. Within five seconds of the attaché's remark, two men in open shirts, both needing a shave and neither looking particularly pleasant, walked into the office. The second man carried a large manila envelope; the first man spoke. "Are you gentlemen the reason we're here?" he asked, addressing Dickie and Jack.

"Richard Harding on my left," said the attaché. "And John Preston on the right. May I leave?"

"Sorry, old boy," replied the second man, approaching the desk and opening the envelope. "We're here because you summoned us. That entitles you to stay."

"You're too kind," said the embassy man unkindly. "However, I did not summon you, I merely relayed information that two British citizens *insisted* I relay. That entitles me to get some sleep insofar as I'm not in your line of endeavor."

"Actually," interrupted Jack Preston, "it was Dickie who insisted, but I've always felt that in times of crisis no stone or instinct should be overlooked, and Dickie Harding—a former Grenadier, you know—has had some fine instincts . . . in the past."

"Damn it, Jack, it's got nothing to do with instincts, it's what he was *wearing.* I mean a chap could swelter in the winter Highlands under that material, and if the sheen on his shirt indicated silk or polyester, he'd positively suffocate. *Cotton.* Pure breathing cotton is the only cloth for this climate. And the tailoring of his ensemble, well, I *told* you—"

"Do you mind, sir?" His eyes briefly straying to the ceiling, the second man removed a pile of photographs from the envelope and thrust them between Preston and Harding, cutting off the dialogue. "Would you look these over and see if there's anyone you recognize?"

Eleven seconds later the task was done. "*That's* him!" cried Dickie.

"Believe it is," agreed Jack.

"And you're both bonkers," said the first man from MI-Six. "His name's MacDonald and he's a swizzling, society-boy drunk from Cairo. His wife's father owns the company he works for—an automobile-parts firm—and he's posted over here because he's a complete ass and the second in command at the Cairo branch runs the show. So much for instincts at this hour of the morning. Should I ask where you two spent the night?"

"Now, Dickie, I *did* say that you might be overreacting on rather superficial grounds—"

"A minute, please," interrupted the second MI-Sixer, picking up the enlarged passport photograph and studying it. "A year or so ago one of our military stationed here contacted us and wanted to set up a meeting regarding an E.E. problem he thought was in the making."

"A what?" asked the attaché.

" 'Equipment evaluation'—that's to be read as espionage. He wouldn't say much on the phone, of course, but he did remark that we'd be astonished at the suspect. 'A bloated sot of an Englishman working in Cairo,' or words to that effect. Could this be the man?"

"*Still,*" continued Jack. "I urged Dickie to follow up, not to hold back!"

"Now, really, chap, you weren't all that enthusiastic. You know, we still might make that plane you were so worried about."

"What happened at the meeting?" asked the attaché, leaning forward, his eyes riveted on the second man from MI-Six.

"It never took place. Our military was killed on the waterfront, his throat slit outside a warehouse. They called it a robbery, as nothing was left in his pockets."

"I *do* think we should catch that plane, Dickie."

* * *

"The *Mahdi*?" exclaimed Zaya Yateem, sitting behind the desk in what three weeks before had been the American ambassador's office. "You are to bring one of us to him in Bahrain? *Tonight?*"

"As I told your brother," said Kendrick, seated in a chair next to Ahbyahd and facing the woman. "The instructions were probably in the letter I was to deliver to you—"

"Yes, yes." Zaya spoke rapidly, impatiently. "He explained it to me during our few moments together. But you're *wrong,* Bahrudi. I have no way of directly reaching the Mahdi—no one knows who he is."

"I assume you reach someone who in turn reaches him."

"Naturally, but it could take a day or possibly two days. The avenues to him are complicated. Five calls are made and ten times five are relayed to unlisted numbers in Bahrain, and only *one* of them can reach the Mahdi."

"What happens in an emergency?"

"They're not permitted," intruded Azra, leaning against the wall by a sunlit cathedral window. "I told you that."

"And *that,* my young friend, is ridiculous. We can't do what we do *effectively* without considering the unexpected."

"Granted." Zaya Yateem nodded her head, then shook it slowly. "However, my brother has a point. We are expected to carry on in any emergency for weeks, if we must. Otherwise, as leaders, we would not be given our assignments."

"Very well," said the congressman from the Ninth District of Colorado, feeling the sweat rolling down his neck despite the cool morning breezes sweeping through the open windows. "Then you explain to the Mahdi why we're not in Bahrain tonight. I've done my part, including, I believe, saving your brother's life."

"He's right about that, Zaya," agreed Azra, pushing himself away from the wall. "I'd be a corpse in the desert by now."

"For which I'm grateful, Bahrudi, but I can't do the impossible."

"I think you'd better try." Kendrick glanced at Ahbyahd beside him, then turned back to the sister. "Your Mahdi went to a great deal of trouble and expense to get me here, which I assume means *he* has an emergency."

"The news of your capture would explain what happened," said Ahbyahd.

"Do you really think Oman's security forces will put out the word that they caught me only to admit I escaped?"

"Of course not," answered Zaya Yateem.

"The Mahdi holds your purse strings," added Kendrick. "And he could influence mine, which I don't like."

"Our supplies are low," broke in Ahbyahd. "We need the fast boats from the Emirates, or everything we've done will be for nothing. Instead of sieging, we *ourselves* will be in a state of siege."

"There may be a way," said Zaya, suddenly getting out of the chair, her hands on the desk, her dark eyes above the veil gazing aimlessly in thought. "We've scheduled a press conference this morning; it will be watched everywhere and certainly by the Mahdi himself. At some point in my talk I'll mention that we are sending out an urgent message to our friends. A message that requires an immediate response."

"What good would that do?" asked Azra. "All communications are monitored, we know that. None of the Mahdi's people will risk getting in touch with us."

"They don't have to," interrupted Evan, sitting forward. "I understand what your sister's saying. The response need not be verbal; no communication is necessary. We're not asking for instructions, we're *giving* them. It's what you and I talked about several hours ago, Azra. I know Bahrain. I'll choose a place where we'll be and let one of your contacts here in Masqat forward it, telling him that this is the urgent message your sister spoke of during the press conference." Kendrick turned to Yateem. "That *is* what you had in mind, isn't it?"

"I hadn't refined it," admitted Zaya, "but it's feasible. My thought was merely to speed up the process of reaching the Mahdi. It *is* plausible."

"It's the solution!" cried Ahbyahd. "Bahrudi has given it to us!"

"Nothing is solved at this juncture," said the veiled woman, again sitting down. "There's the problem of getting my brother and Mr. Bahrudi to Bahrain. How can it be done?"

"It's been taken care of," answered Evan, the pounding in his chest accelerating, astonished at his own control, at his casual voice. *He was closer! Closer to the Mahdi!* "I told Azra I have a telephone number, which I won't give you—can't give you—but with a few words will get us a plane."

"Just like *that*?" exclaimed Ahbyahd.

"Your benefactor here in Oman has methods you haven't dreamt of."

"All phone calls in and out are intercepted," objected Azra.

"What I say may be heard, but not what the person I'm calling says. I was assured of that."

"A scrambling device?" asked Yateem.

"They're part of our kits in Europe. A simple cone pressed over the mouthpiece. The distortion is absolute except on the direct connection."

"Make your call," said Zaya, getting up and walking rapidly around the desk as Kendrick did the same, replacing her in the chair. Holding his hand over the numbers, Evan dialed.

"*Yes?*" Ahmat's voice came on the line before the second ring.

"A plane," said Kendrick. "Two passengers. Where? When?"

"My *God*!" exploded the young sultan of Oman. "Let me think. . . . The airport, of course. There's a turn in the road about a quarter of a mile before the cargo area. Someone will pick you up in a garrison car. Tell them it was stolen to get you past the guards."

"When?"

"It will take time. The security's heavy all over and arrangements have to be made. Can you give me a destination?"

"The twenty-second letter split in two."

"V . . . split—a slanted I—Iran?"

"No. By the numbers."

"Twenty-second . . . two. *B*?"

"Yes."

"Bahrain!"

"Yes."

"That helps. I'll make some calls. How soon do you need it?"

"At the height of the festivities here. We have to get out in the confusion."

"That would be around noon."

"Whatever you say. Incidentally, there's a doctor—he has something I may need for my health."

"The money belt, of course. It will be slipped to you."

"Good."

"The turn before the cargo area. Be there."

"We will." Evan hung up the phone. "We're to be at the airport by twelve noon."

"The *airport*?" shouted Azra. "We'll be picked *up*!"

"On the road before the airport. Someone will steal a garrison car and *they'll* pick us up."

"I'll arrange for one of our contacts here in the city to drive you," said Zaya Yateem. "He'll be the one you will give the location to in Bahrain, the meeting ground. You have at least five hours before you leave."

"We'll need clothes, a shower and some rest," said Azra. "I can't remember when I last slept."

"I'd like to look around your operation," remarked Kendrick, getting out of the chair. "I might learn something."

"Whatever you wish, Amal Bahrudi," said Zaya Yateem, approaching Evan. "You saved my dear brother's life, and for that there are no adequate words to express my thanks."

"Just get me to that airport by noon," replied Kendrick, no warmth in his voice. "Frankly, I want to get back to Germany as soon as possible."

"By noon," agreed the female terrorist.

"Weingrass will be here by *noon*!" exclaimed the Mossad officer to Ben-Ami and the five-man unit from the Masada Brigade. They were in the cellar of a house in the Jabal Sa'ali, minutes from the rows of English graves where scores of privateers were buried centuries ago. The primitive stone basement had been converted into a control center for Israeli intelligence.

"How will he get here?" asked Ben-Ami, who had taken the ghotra off his head, the blue jeans and the loose dark shirt far more natural to him. "His passport was issued in Jerusalem, not the most welcome of documents."

"One does not question Emmanuel Weingrass. He undoubtedly has more passports than there are bagels in Tel Aviv's Jabotinsky Square. He says for us to do nothing until he arrives. 'Absolutely *nothing,*' were his exact words."

"You don't sound so disapproving of him as you did before," said Yaakov, code name Blue, son of a hostage and leader of the Masada unit.

"Because I will not have to sign his expense vouchers! There'll *be* none. All I had to do was mention Kendrick's name and he said he was on his way."

"That hardly means he won't submit his expenses," countered Ben-Ami, chuckling.

"Oh, no, I was very specific. I asked him how much it would cost us for his assistance and he replied unequivocally, 'Up yours, this is on me!' It's an American expression that absolves us from payment."

"We're wasting *time*!" cried Yaakov. "We should be scouting the embassy. We've studied the plans; there are a half-dozen ways we might enter and get out with my father!"

Heads snapped and eyes widened at the young leader called Blue. "We understand," said the Mossad officer.

"I'm sorry. I didn't mean to say that."

"You of all people have every right to say it," said Ben-Ami.

"I shouldn't have. I apologize again. But why should we wait for this *Weingrass*?"

"Because he delivers, my friend, and without him we may not."

"I see! You people in the Mossad turn flip-flops. Now it's the *American* you want to help, not our original objective! Damn it, *yes,* my *father*!"

"The result could be one and the same, Yaakov—"

"I'm *not* Yaakov!" roared the young leader. "To you I am only Blue—the son of a father who watched his own father and mother pulled apart in Auschwitz as they clung to each other before each was driven into the showers of gas. I want my father *out* and *safe* and I can *do* it! How much more can that man suffer? A childhood of horror, watching while children his own age were hanged for stealing garbage to eat, sodomized by Wehrmacht pigs, hiding, *starving* in forests all over Poland until the Allies came. Then later blessed with three sons, only to have two of them killed, my brothers *killed,* butchered in Sidon by filthy pig—terrorist *Arabs*! Now I should care about one American *cowboy,* a *politician* who wants to be a hero so he can act in films and have his picture on cereal boxes?"

"From what I've been told," said Ben-Ami calmly, "none of that is true. This American risks his life without help from his own people, without the prospect of future rewards if he lives. As our friend here tells us, he does what he's doing for a reason not much different from yours. To right a terrible wrong that was done to him, to his family, as it were."

"To *hell* with him! That was a family, not a *people*! I say we go to the embassy!"

"I say you don't," said the officer, placing his pistol slowly on the table. "You are now under the command of the Mossad and you will follow our orders."

"*Pigs!*" screamed Yaakov. "You're pigs, *all* of you!"

"Ever so," said Ben-Ami. "All of us."

10:48 A.M. *Oman time.* The controlled press conference was over. The reporters and television crews were securing their notebooks and equipment, prepared to be ushered out through the embassy halls to the outside gates, patrolled by a hundred young men and veiled women marching back and forth with weapons at ready-fire. Inside the conference hall, however, a fat man broke through the guards with unctuous words and approached the table where Zaya Yateem sat. Rifles at his head, he spoke.

"I come from the Mahdi," he whispered, "who pays every shilling you owe."

"You, *too*? The emergency in Bahrain must be serious, indeed."

"I beg your pardon—"

"He's been searched?" asked Zaya of the guards, who nodded. "Let him go."

"Thank you, madame—*what* emergency in Bahrain?"

"Obviously we don't know. One of our own is going there tonight to be told and will return to us with the news."

MacDonald stared into the eyes above the veil, a sharp, hollow pain forming in his enormous chest. *What was happening? Why was Bahrain going around him? What decisions had been made that excluded him? Why? What had the filthy Arab whore done?* "Madame," continued the Englishman slowly, his words measured. "The emergency in Bahrain is a new development, whereas I am concerned with another question equally serious. Our benefactor would like clarified—immediately clarified—the presence of the woman Khalehla here in Masqat."

"Khalehla? There's no woman named Khalehla among us here, but then names are meaningless, aren't they?"

"Not here, not inside *here,* but outside and in contact with your people—your own brother, in fact."

"My *brother*?"

"Precisely. Three escaped prisoners raced to meet her on the road to the Jabal Sham, to meet with the enemy!"

"What are you *saying*?"

"I'm not saying, madame, I'm demanding. *We* are demanding an explanation. The Mahdi insists on it most emphatically."

"I have no idea what you're talking about! It is true three prisoners escaped, one of them my brother along with Yosef and our benefactor's other emissary, a man named Bahrudi from East Berlin."

"*East*— Madame, you're too quick for me."

"If you're really from the Mahdi, I'm astonished you're not aware of him." Yateem stopped, her penetrating large eyes roaming over MacDonald's face. "On the other hand, you could be from anyone, anywhere."

"While in Masqat I am the Mahdi's *only* voice! Call Bahrain and hear it for yourself, madame."

"You know perfectly well such calls are not permitted." Zaya snapped her fingers for the guards; they rushed to the table. "Take this man and bring him to the council room. Then wake my brother and Yosef and find Amal Bahrudi. Another conference is called for. *Now!*"

The clothes Evan chose for himself were a blend of the terrorist dress code: unpressed khaki trousers, a soiled American-style field jacket and a dark shirt open to mid-chest. Except for his age and his eyes, he was similar in appearance to the majority of the fanatic punks who had captured the embassy. Even the years were obscured by his darkened flesh, and his eyes were shaded by the visor of a cloth cap. To complete the image he wanted, a sheathed knife was attached to his jacket and the bulge of a revolver apparent in the right pocket. The "trusted one" was trusted; he had saved the life of Azra, prince of terrorists, and moved freely about the seized embassy, from one sickening scene to another, one group of frightened, exhausted, hopeless group to another.

Hope. It was all he could give, knowing that in the final analysis it was probably false, but he had to give it, give them *something* to cling to, at least to think about in the darkest, most terrifying hours of the night.

"*I'm an American!*" he whispered to shocked hostages wherever he found three or more together, his eyes constantly glancing around at the roving punks who thought he was insulting their prisoners with sudden, audible bursts of anger. "*Nobody's forgotten you! We're doing all we can! Don't mind my shouting at you. I have to.*"

"Thank *God*!" was the constant initial reply, followed by tears and descriptions of horror, invariably including the public execution of the seven condemned hostages.

"They'll kill us all! They don't care! The filthy animals don't care about *death*—ours or *theirs.*"

"*Do your best to stay calm and I mean that! Try not to show fear, that's very, very important. Don't antagonize, but don't crawl to them. Seeing you afraid is like a narcotic to them. Remember that.*"

At one point Kendrick suddenly stood up and shouted abusively at a group of five Americans. His straying eyes had picked out one of Zaya Yateem's personal guards; the man was walking rapidly toward him.

"You! *Bahrudi!*"

"Yes."

"Zaya must see you right away. Come, the council room!"

Evan followed the guard across the roof and down three flights of stairs into a long corridor. He removed his cap, now soaked with perspiration, and was led to the open door of a large embassy office. He walked inside, and four seconds later his world was shattered by the last words he could ever hope to hear.

"Good Christ! You're *Evan Kendrick*!"

12

"*Meen ir ráh-gill da?*" said Evan, mind and body paralyzed, straining, forcing himself to move casually, as he asked Zaya who the obese man was who had spoken English.

"He says he is from the Mahdi," Azra replied, standing between Yosef and Ahbyahd.

"What did he mean?"

"You heard him. He says you're someone named Kendrick."

"Who's that?" asked Evan in English, addressing Anthony MacDonald, trying desperately to remain composed while adjusting not only to the sight of a man he had not seen in nearly five years, but to his very presence in that room. *MacDonald!* The fatuous society drunk from the British colony in Cairo! "My name is Amal Bahrudi, what is yours?"

"You know damned well who I am!" shouted the Englishman, jabbing his index finger in the air, looking in turn at the four Arab councillors, especially Zaya Yateem. "He's not *Amal*-whatever and he's *not* from the Mahdi! He's an American named Evan Kendrick!"

"I studied at two American universities," said Evan, smiling, "but no one ever called me a Kendrick. Other things, yes, but not Kendrick."

"You're *lying*!"

"On the contrary, I'd have to say you're the liar if you claim to be working for the Mahdi. I was shown the photograph of every European in his—shall we say—confidential employ and you certainly were not among them. I would definitely remember because—shall we again say—you have a very distinctive face and figure."

"Liar! *Impostor!* You work with Khalehla the whore, the *enemy*! Early this morning, before daybreak, she was on her way to meet you!"

"What are you talking about?" Kendrick glanced at Azra and Yosef. "I've never heard of a Khalehla, either as an enemy *or* a whore, and before daybreak my friends and I were running for our lives. We had no time for dalliances, I assure you."

"I tell you he's *lying.* I was there and I saw her! I saw all of you!"

"You saw *us*?" asked Evan, eyebrows arched. "How?"

"I drove off the road—"

"You saw us and you did not *help* us?" broke in Kendrick angrily. "And you say you're from the *Mahdi*?"

"He has a point, Englishman," said Zaya. "Why did you not help them?"

"There were things to learn, that's why! And now I *have* learned them. Khalehla . . . *him*!"

"You have extraordinary fantasies, that's what you have, whatever your name is, which I *don't* know. One, however, we can easily dispose of. We're on our way to Bahrain to meet the Mahdi. We'll take you with us. The great man will undoubtedly be delighted to see you again, since you're so important to him."

"I agree," said Azra firmly.

"*Bahrain?*" roared MacDonald. "How in hell are you going to *get* there?"

"You mean you don't know?" said Kendrick.

Emmanuel Weingrass, his slender chest heaving in pain from the most recent fit of coughing, stepped out of the limousine in front of the cemetery at Jabal Sa'ali. He turned to the driver, who held the door, and spoke reverently in an exaggerated British accent. "I shall pray over my English ancestors—so few do, you know. Come back in an hour."

"Howar?" asked the man, holding up one finger. "*Iss'a?*" he repeated in Arabic, using the word for hour.

"Yes, my Islamic friend. It is a profound pilgrimage I make every year. Can you understand that?"

"Yes, yes! *El sallah. Allahoo Akbar!*" answered the driver, rapidly nodding his head, saying that he understood prayers and that God was great. He also held money in his hand, more money than he had expected, knowing that even more could be his when he returned in an hour.

"Leave me now," said Weingrass. "I wish to be alone—*sibni fihahlee.*"

"Yes, yes!" The man closed the door, ran back to his seat and drove away. Manny permitted himself a brief spasm, one vibrating cough compounding the previous one, and looked around to ascertain his bearings, then started across the cemetery to the stone house that stood in a field several hundred yards away. Ten minutes later he was ushered down to the basement, where Israeli intelligence had set up its command post.

"*Weingrass,*" cried the Mossad officer, "it's good to see you again!"

"No, it's not. You're never happy to see me or hear me on the telephone. You know nothing about the work you do, you're only an accountant—a miserly one at that."

"Now, Manny, let's not start—"

"I say we start right away," interrupted Weingrass, looking over at Ben-Ami and the five members of the Masada unit. "Do any of you misfits have whisky? I know this *zohlah* doesn't," he added, implying that the Mossad man was cheap.

"Not even wine," replied Ben-Ami. "It was not included in our provisions."

"No doubt issued by *this* one. All right, accountant, tell me everything you know. Where is my son, Evan Kendrick?"

"Here, but that's all we know."

"That's standard. You were always three days behind the Sabbath."

"*Manny—*"

"Calm yourself. You'll have cardiac arrest and I don't want Israel to lose its worst accountant. Who can tell me more?"

"*I* can tell you more!" shouted Yaakov, code name Blue. "We should be at this moment—*hours* ago—studying the embassy. We have a job to do that has nothing to do with your *American*!"

"So, besides an accountant you have a hothead," said Weingrass. "Anyone else?"

"Kendrick is here without sanction," replied Ben-Ami. "He was flown over under cover but is now left to his own devices. He's unacknowledged if caught."

"Where did you get that information?"

"One of our men in Washington. I don't know who or from what department or agency."

"You'd need a telephone book. How secure is this phone?" asked Weingrass, sitting down at the table.

"No guarantees," said the Mossad officer. "It was installed in a hurry."

"For as few shekels as possible, I'm sure."

"Manny!"

"Oh, shut up." Weingrass took a notebook out of his pocket, flipped through the pages, and riveted his eyes on a name and a number. He picked up the phone and dialed. Within seconds he spoke.

"Thank you, my dear friend at the palace, for being so courteous. My name is Weingrass, insignificant to you, of course, but not to the great sultan, Ahmat. Naturally, I would not care to disturb his illustrious person, but if you could get word to him that I called, perhaps he might return a great favor. Let me give you a number, may I?" Manny did so, squinting at the digits on the phone. "Thank you, my dear friend, and may I say, in respect, that this is a most urgent matter and the sultan may praise you for your diligence. Thank you, again."

The once renowned architect hung up the telephone and leaned back in the chair, breathing deeply to stem the rattling echo erupting in his chest. "Now we wait," he said, looking at the Mossad officer. "And hope that our sultan has more brains and money than you do. . . . My God, he came back! After four years he heard me and my son has come *back*!"

"Why?" asked Yaakov.

"The Mahdi," said Weingrass quietly, angrily, staring at the floor.

"The *who*?"

"You'll learn, hothead."

"He's not really your son, Manny."

"He's the only son I ever wanted—" The telephone rang; Weingrass grabbed it, pulling it to his ear.

"Yes?"

"Emmanuel?"

"At one time, when we found ourselves in Los Angeles, you were far less formal."

"Allah be praised, I'll never forget. I had myself checked when I got back here."

"Tell me, you young stinker, did you ever get a passing grade for that economics thesis in your third year?"

"Only a *B,* Manny. I should have listened to you. You told

me to make it far more complicated—that they liked complications."

"Can you talk?" asked Weingrass, his voice suddenly serious.

"*I* can, but you may not. From this end everything's static. Do you understand?"

"Yes. Our mutual acquaintance. Where is he?"

"On his way to Bahrain with two other people from the embassy—there was supposed to be only one other, but that was changed at the last minute. I don't know why."

"Because there's a string leading to someone else, probably. Is that everyone?"

Ahmat paused briefly. "No, Manny," he said quietly. "There's one other you must not interfere with or acknowledge in any way. She is a woman and her name is Khalehla. I tell you this because I trust you and you should know that she's there, but no one else must ever know. Her presence here must be kept as quiet as our friend's; her exposure would be a catastrophe."

"That's a mouthful, young fellow. How do I recognize this problem?"

"I hope there'll be no cause for you to. She's hidden in the pilot's cabin, which will remain locked until they reach Bahrain."

"That's all you'll tell me?"

"About her, yes."

"I've got to move. What can you do for me?"

"Send you on another plane. As soon as he can, our friend will call and tell me what's happening. When you get there, reach me; here's how." Ahmat gave his scrambled private telephone number to Weingrass.

"Must be a new exchange," said Manny.

"It's no exchange," said the young sultan. "Will you be at this number?"

"Yes."

"I'll call you back with the arrangements. If there's a commercial flight leaving soon, it would be easier all around to get you on it."

"Sorry, can't do that."

"Why not?"

"Everything has to be blind and deaf. I've got seven peacocks with me."

"Seven . . . ?"

"Yes, and if you think there'd be trouble—like catastrophes—

try those highly *intelligent* birds feathered in blue and white."

Ahmat, sultan of Oman, gasped. "The *Mossad*?" he whispered.

"That's about it."

"Holy *shit*!" exclaimed Ahmat.

The small six-passenger Rockwell jet flew northwest at thirty-four thousand feet over the United Arab Emirates and into the Persian Gulf on its eight-hundred-mile course to the sheikhdom of Bahrain. A disturbingly quiet, confident Anthony MacDonald sat alone in the first row of two seats, Azra and Kendrick in the last row together. The door to the pilot's cabin was shut, and according to the man who had met them in the "stolen" garrison car and ushered them through the cargo area to the far end of Masqat's airfield and the plane, that door would remain shut until the passengers left the aircraft. No one was to see them; they would be met at Bahrain's International Airport in Muharraq by someone who would escort them through immigration.

Evan and Azra had gone over the schedule several times, and as the terrorist had never been to Bahrain, he took notes—primarily locations and their spellings. It was imperative to Kendrick that he and Azra separate, at least for an hour or so. The reason was Anthony MacDonald, the most unlikely of the Mahdi's agents. The Englishman might be a shortcut to the Mahdi, and if he was, Evan would abandon the crown prince of terrorists.

"Remember, we escaped together from the Jabal Sham, and when you consider Interpol, to say nothing of the combined intelligence units from Europe and America, there'll be alerts out for us everywhere and with our photographs. We can't take the chance of being spotted together in daylight. After sundown the risk is less, but even then we must take precautions."

"What precautions?"

"Buy different clothes, to begin with; these have the mark of lower-class roughnecks, all right for the conditions in Masqat but not here. Take a taxi to Manamah, that's the city across the causeway on the big island, and get a room at the Aradous Hotel on the Wadi Al Ahd. There's a men's shop in the lobby; buy yourself a Western business suit and get a haircut at the barber's. Write it all down!"

"I am." Azra wrote faster.

"Register under the name of— Come to think of it, Yateem

is a common name in Bahrain, but let's not take the chance."

"My mother's name, Ishaad?"

"Their computers are too full. Use Farouk, everyone else does. T. Farouk. I'll reach you in an hour or two."

"What will you be doing?"

"What else?" said Kendrick, about to tell the truth. "Stay with the English liar who claims to work for the Mahdi. If by any chance he does and his communications broke down, the meeting tonight will be easily arranged. But, frankly, I don't believe him, and if he's the liar I think, I have to learn who he *is* working for."

Azra looked at the man he knew as Amal Bahrudi and spoke softly. "You live in a more complicated world than I do. We know our enemies; we aim our weapons at them and try to kill them because they would kill us. Yet it appears to me that you cannot be sure, that instead of firing your guns in the heat of battle you must first concern yourselves over who *is* the enemy."

"You've had to infiltrate and consider the possibility of traitors; the precautions aren't that much different."

"Infiltration isn't difficult when thousands dress as we do, talk as we do. It's a matter of attitude; we assume the enemy's. As to traitors, we failed in Masqat, you taught us that."

"Me?"

"The *photographs,* Bahrudi."

"Of course. Sorry. My mind's on other things." *It was, but he could not do that again,* thought Kendrick. *The young terrorist was looking curiously at him. He had to remove any doubts. Quickly!* "But speaking of those photographs, your sister will have to provide proof that she's ripped out the entire treacherous business. I suggest other photographs. Corpses in front of a smashed camera, with taped statements that can be circulated—taped confessions, of course."

"Zaya knows what to do; she's the strongest among us, the most dedicated. She won't rest until she's torn apart every room, searched every brother and sister. Methodically."

"Words, poet!" admonished Evan harshly. "Perhaps you don't understand. What happened in Masqat—what was carelessly *permitted* to happen—could affect our operations everywhere. If it gets out and goes unpunished, agents everywhere will be flocking to infiltrate us, worming their way inside to expose us with cameras and recordings!"

"All right, all right," said Azra, nodding, unwilling to hear further criticism. "My sister will take care of everything. I don't think she was convinced until she understood what you did for us in the Jabal Sham, saw what you could do on the telephone. She will quickly take the actions she must, I assure you."

"Good! Rest now, angry poet. We've got a long afternoon and night ahead of us."

Kendrick leaned far back in the seat as though prepared to doze, his half-closed eyes on the back of Anthony MacDonald's large balding head in the first row. There was so much to think about, so many things to consider that he had not had time to analyze, even try to analyze. Yet above everything, there *was* a Mahdi, *the* Mahdi! Not surrounding and starving out Khartoum and George Gordon in the mid-1800s, but living and manipulating terror a hundred years later in Bahrain! And there *was* a complex chain that led to the monster; it was concealed, buried, professionally fashioned, but it was there! He had found a terrorist appendage, only a tentacle, perhaps, but part of the host body. The killer beside him could lead to the main conduit as each electric cable in a building ultimately leads to the central power source. *Five calls are made, ten times five to unlisted numbers in Bahrain and only one can reach the Mahdi:* Zaya Yateem, who knew whereof she spoke. Fifty calls, fifty telephone numbers—one among fifty unknown men or women who knew where the Mahdi was, *who* he was!

He had created an emergency the way Manny Weingrass had always told him to invent emergencies when dealing with potential clients who would not or could not communicate with each other. *Tell the first bozo that you have to have an answer by Wednesday or we're moving on to Riyadh. Tell the second clown we can't wait beyond Thursday because there's a hell of a job in Abu Dhabi that's ours for the asking.*

This was not the same, of course—only a variation of the technique. The terrorist leaders at the embassy in Masqat were convinced an emergency existed for their benefactor, the Mahdi, since he had arranged for East Berlin's "Amal Bahrudi" to bring one of them to Bahrain. Conversely, the forces of the Mahdi had been told on international television that an "urgent message" had been sent out "to friends" and it required an "immediate response"—*emergency!*

Manny, did I do it right? I have to find him, fight him—kill him for what he did to all of us!

Emmanuel Weingrass, mused Evan, his eyes beginning to close, the dead weight of sleep descending. Yet he could not prevent it; a quiet laugh echoed in his throat. He remembered their first trip to Bahrain.

"Now for Christ's sake, bear in mind that we're dealing with a people who run an archipelago, not a landmass bordering another landmass that both sides conveniently call a country. This is a sheikhdom consisting of over thirty goddamned islands in the Persian Gulf. It's nothing you're going to measure in acreage, and they never want you to—that's their strength."

"What are you driving at, Manny?"

"Try to understand me, you unread mechanic. You appeal to that sense of strength. This is an independent state, a collection of eruptions from the sea that protects the ports from the storms of the Gulf and is conveniently situated between the Qatar peninsula and the Hasa coast of Saudi Arabia, the latter extremely important because of the Saudi leverage."

"What the hell has that got to do with a lousy island golf course? Do you play golf, Manny? I never could afford it."

"Chasing a little white ball over a hundred acres of grass while the arthritis is killing you and your heart is blowing apart in frustration has never been my idea of a civilized pursuit. However, I know what we put into this lousy golf course."

"What?"

"Remembrances of things past. Because it's a constant reminder of their present, a reminder to everyone. Their strength."

"Will you come down from orbit, please?"

"Read the historical chronicles of Assyria, Persia, the Greeks and the Romans. Take a peek through the early drawings of the Portuguese cartographers and the logs of Vasco da Gama. At one time or another all of these people fought for control of the archipelago—the portugués held it for a hundred years—why?"

"I'm sure you'll tell me."

"Because of its geographical location in the Gulf, its strategic importance. For centuries it's been a coveted center for trade and the financial repositories of trade—"

The much younger Evan Kendrick had sat up at that moment, now understanding what the eccentric architect was driving at. "That's what's happening now," he had interrupted, "by leaps and bounds, money pouring in from all over the world."

"As an independent state without fear of being conquered in today's world," clarified Weingrass. "Bahrain services allies and enemies alike. So our magnificent clubhouse on this lousy golf course will reflect its history. We'll do it with murals. A businessman looks up at the paintings above the bar and sees all these

things pictured and thinks, Jesus, this is some place! Everybody wanted it! Look at the money they spent! He's now even more anxious to operate here. It's common knowledge that deals are made on golf courses, you young illiterate. Why do you think they want to build one?"

After they had built the somewhat grotesque clubhouse on the second-rate golf course, the Kendrick Group contracted for three banks and two government buildings. And Manny Weingrass was personally pardoned by one of the highest ministers for disturbing the peace at a café on the Al Zubara Road.

The drone of the jet bored into Evan's brain. His eyes were closed.

"I object to this subsidiary operation and I want the record to show it," said Yaakov, code name Blue, of the Masada Brigade, as the seven men climbed into the jet at the far east end of Masqat's airfield. Emmanuel Weingrass immediately joined the pilot, strapping himself into the adjacent seat, coughing quietly, deeply, as he secured the belt. The Mossad officer had remained behind; he had work to do in Oman; his pistol was in the possession of the slender Ben-Ami, who kept it unholstered until the five-man unit had taken their seats in the aircraft.

"The record will show it, my friend," replied Ben-Ami as the plane sped down the runway. "Please try to understand that there are things we cannot be told for the good of all of us. We are the activists, the soldiers—and those who make the decisions are the high command. They do their job and we do ours, which is to follow orders."

"Then I must object to a loathsome parallel," said the unit member, code name Gray. " 'Following orders' is not a phrase I find very palatable."

"I remind you, Mr. Ben-Ami," added code Orange. "For the past three weeks we've trained for a single assignment, one we all believe we can accomplish despite profound doubts back home. We're ready; we're primed for it, and suddenly it's aborted without explanation and we're on our way to Bahrain hunting a man we don't know with a plan we've never seen."

"If there *is* a plan," said code Black. "And not simply a debt owed by the Mossad to a disagreeable old man who wants to find an *American,* a Gentile 'son' that isn't his."

Weingrass turned around; the plane was climbing rapidly, the engines partially muted by the swift ascent. "Listen to me, *peaheads*!" he shouted. "If that *American* has gone to Bahrain with a demented Arab terrorist, it means he's got a damn good reason. It probably hasn't occurred to you musclebound, intellectual crap shooters, but Masqat wasn't planned by those subhuman yo-yos playing with guns. The brains, if you'll pardon an obscure reference, are in Bahrain, and that's what he's after, *who* he's after!"

"Your explanation, if true," said code White, "does not include a plan, Mr. Weingrass. Or do we shoot craps over that issue?"

"The odds may be worse, smart-ass, but no, we don't. Once we've landed and set up shop, I'll be calling Masqat every fifteen minutes until we have the information we need. *Then* we have a plan."

"*How?*" asked Blue angrily, suspiciously.

"We make it up, hothead."

The huge Englishman stood in rigid disbelief as the terrorist Azra started walking away with the Bahrainian official. The quiet man in uniform had met the Rockwell jet beyond the last maintenance hangar at the airport in Muharraq. "*Wait,*" shouted MacDonald, glancing wildly at Evan Kendrick standing beside him. "*Stop!* You can't leave me with this man. I *told* you, he's not who he says he is! He's not one of us!"

"No, he's not," agreed the Palestinian, stopping and looking over his shoulder. "He's from East Berlin and he saved my life. If you're telling the truth, I assure you he'll save yours."

"You *can't*—"

"I must," broke in Azra, turning to the official and nodding.

The Bahrainian, without comment either in his words or in his expression, addressed Kendrick: "As you can see, my associate is coming out of the hangar. He will escort you through another exit. Welcome to our country."

"*Azra!*" screamed MacDonald, his voice drowned out by the roar of jet engines.

"Easy, Tony," said Evan as the second Bahrainian official approached them. "We're entering illegally and you could get us shot."

"*You!* I *knew* it was you! You *are* Kendrick!"

"Of course I am, and if any of our people here in Bahrain knew you used my name, your lovely, besotted Cecilia—it *is* Cecilia, isn't it?—would be a widow before she could ask for another drink."

"By Christ, I don't *believe* it. You sold your firm and went back to America! I was told you'd become a politician of sorts!"

"With the Mahdi's help I might even become President."

"Oh, my *God*!"

"Smile, Tony. This man doesn't like what he's doing and I wouldn't want him to think we're ungrateful. *Smile,* you fat son of a bitch!"

Khalehla, in tan slacks, a flight jacket and a visored officer's cap, stood by the tail of the Harrier jet watching the proceedings a hundred feet away. The young Palestinian killer called Blue had been ushered out; the American congressman and the incredible MacDonald were leaving with another uniformed man, who conveyed them through a maze of cargo alleyways that eluded immigration. This Kendrick, this apparent conformist with some terrible cause, was better than she thought. Not only had he survived the horrors of the embassy—something she believed impossible nine hours ago and over which she had panicked—but he had now separated terrorist from terrorists' agent. *What was on his mind? What was he doing?*

"Hurry up!" she called to the pilot, who was talking to a mechanic by the starboard wing. "Let's go!"

The pilot nodded, briefly throwing his arms up in despair, and the two of them headed toward the exit reserved for precleared flight personnel. Ahmat, the youthful sultan of Oman, had pushed all the buttons at his considerable command in Masqat. The three passengers on the jet were to be led to a stretch of the airport's lower-level concourse far behind the main terminal's taxi line where temporary taxi signs had been mounted on the pavement, each cab driven by a member of the Bahrainian secret police. None had been given any information, only a single order: Report the destination of each passenger.

Khalehla and the pilot said their brief good-byes and both went their separate ways, he to the Flight Control Center for his return-to-Masqat instructions, she to the designated area of the concourse where she would pick up the American and follow him. It would call for all the skill she had to stay out of sight while she followed Kendrick and MacDonald. Tony would spot her in an instant, and the obviously alert American might look twice and remember a dark, filthy street in the el Shari el Mishkwiyis and a woman who held a gun in her hand. The fact that it had not been pointed at him but, instead, at four people in that street of garbage who had tried to rob her or worse would not be readily believed by a man living on the edge of very real peril.

Purpose and paranoia converged in those infinite reaches of a mind under severe stress. He was armed, and one exploding image could trigger a violent response. Khalehla did not fear for her life; eight years of training, including four years in the violent Middle East, had taught her to anticipate, to kill before she was killed. What saddened her was that this decent man should not have to die for what he was doing but it was entirely possible that she could be his executioner. It was growing more possible by the minute.

She reached the area before the passengers from the Oman jet. The traffic on the *Arrivals* level was horrendous: limousines with tinted-glass windows; taxis; ordinary, nondescript cars; pickup trucks of all descriptions. The noise and the fumes were overpowering, the cacophony deafening, under the low concrete ceiling. Khalehla found a shadowed enclave between two cargo bins and waited.

The first to emerge was the terrorist called Azra, accompanied by a uniformed official. The latter flagged a taxi, which sped up to the coarsely dressed young man at the curb. He stepped inside and read from a piece of paper in his hand, giving the driver instructions.

Several minutes later the strange American and the unbelievable Anthony MacDonald walked out on the pavement. Something was *wrong*! thought Khalehla instantly, without really thinking, merely observing. Tony was behaving like his once and former Cairo self! There was agitation in every movement of his huge body, wasted energy craving attention, his eyes bulging, his constantly changing facial expressions those of a drunk pleading for respect—all in contradiction to the superb control necessary to a deep-cover operator with a network of informers in a world-class volatile situation. It was all *wrong*!

And then it happened! As the taxi sped up to the curb, MacDonald suddenly rammed his enormous torso against the American, sending him out into the covered street in front of the rushing cab. Kendrick bounced off the hood, his body flung in midair into the racing traffic of the tunnellike concourse. Brakes screeched, whistles blew, and the congressman from the Ninth District of Colorado was impaled, curved around the shattered windshield of a small Japanese sedan. *Good God, he's dead!* thought Khalehla, running out on the pavement. And then he moved—both arms *moved* as the American tried to push himself up, collapsing as he did so.

Khalehla raced to the car, surging through a knot of police

and Bahrain's secret police who had converged on the scene, rupturing one immovable man's spleen with a vicious, accurate fist. She threw her body over the spastically moving Kendrick while removing the gun from her flight jacket. She spoke to the nearest uniformed man, the weapon angled at his head.

"My name is Khalehla and that's all you have to know. This man is my property and he goes with me. Pass the word and get us out of here or I'll kill you."

The figure raced into the sterile room so agitated that he slammed the door behind him, nearly tripping in the darkness on his way to his equipment. Hands trembling, he brought his appliance to life.

Ultra Maximum Secure
No Existing Intercepts
Proceed

Something's happened! Breakthrough or breakdown, the hunter or the hunted. The last report speaks of Bahrain but without specifics, only that the subject was in a state of extreme anxiety demanding to be flown there immediately. Of course, that assumes he either escaped from the embassy, was taken out by subterfuge, or never went inside at all. But why Bahrain? Everything is too incomplete, as if the subject's shadow was obscuring events for his own reasons—a not unlikely possibility, considering everything that's happened during the past few years and the subpoena powers of Congress and various special prosecutors.

What has happened? What's happening now? My appliances scream for information, but I can't give them anything! To factor in a name without specific reference only spews forth encyclopedic historical data long since inserted—and updated—by photoscam. Sometimes I think my own talents defeat me, for I see beyond factors and equations and find visions.

Yet he is the man! My appliances tell me that and I trust them.

13

Evan struggled against the constricting tape around his left shoulder and then was aware of a stinging sensation that extended throughout his upper chest accompanied by the sharp smell of rubbing alcohol. He opened his eyes, startled to find that he was sitting up in a bed, pillows supporting his back. He was in a woman's bedroom. A dressing table with a low gold-rimmed chair against the wall stood on his left. A profusion of lotions and perfumes were in small ornate bottles in front of a large three-sided mirror bordered with tiny bulbs. Tall cathedral windows flanked the table, the cascading peach-colored drapes made of a translucent material that virtually shouted—as did the rest of the rococo furniture—a hefty decorator's fee. A satin chaise was in front of the far window, beside it a small telephone table cum magazine rack with a top of rose marble. The wall directly in front of the bed, some twenty feet away, consisted of a long row of mirrored closets. On his right, beyond the bedside table, was an ivory-colored writing desk with another gold-rimmed chair, and then the longest single bureau he had ever seen; it was lacquered peach—*pêche,* as Manny Weingrass would insist upon—and extended the entire length of the wall. The floor was covered with soft, thick white carpeting, the pile of which appeared capable of massaging the bare feet of anyone walking across it if he dared. The only item lacking was a mirror over the bed.

The sculptured door was closed, yet he could hear voices beyond it, a man's and a woman's. He turned his wrist to look at his watch; it was gone. *Where was he? How did he get here? Oh, Christ! The airport concourse . . . He was slammed into a car—two rushing cars—and a crowd had gathered around him until, limping, he was led away. Azra! Azra was waiting for him at the Aradous Hotel! . . . And MacDonald! Gone! Oh, my God, everything's blown apart!* Close to panic, only vaguely aware of the late afternoon sun streaming through the windows, he threw off the sheet and climbed out of bed, unsteady, wincing, gritting his teeth with each move he made, but he *could* move and that was all that mattered. He was also naked and suddenly the door opened.

"I'm glad you could get up," said the olive-skinned woman

as Kendrick lurched back to the bed and the *pêche* sheet while she closed the door. "It confirms the doctor's diagnosis; he just left. He said you were badly banged up but the X rays showed no broken bones."

"*X rays?* Where *are* we and who the hell are *you,* lady?"

"You don't remember me, then?"

"If *this,*" exclaimed Evan angrily, sweeping his hand over the room, "is your modest pied-à-terre in Bahrain, I assure you I've never seen it before. It's not a place one easily forgets."

"It's not mine," said Khalehla, shaking her head with a trace of a smile and walking to the foot of the bed. "It belongs to a member of the royal family, a cousin of the Emir, an elderly man with a young wife—his youngest—both of whom are in London. He's quite ill, which accounts for the medical equipment in the basement, a great deal of equipment. Rank and money have their privileges everywhere, but especially here in Bahrain. Your friend the sultan of Oman made this possible for you."

"But someone had to make it possible for him to know what happened—for *him* to make it possible!"

"That was me, of course—"

"I *do* know you," interrupted Kendrick, frowning. "I just can't remember where or how."

"I wasn't dressed like this, and we saw each other under equally unpleasant circumstances. In Masqat, in a dark, filthy alleyway that serves as a street—"

"*Rot town!*" cried Evan, eyes wide, head rigid. "Slime town. El-Baz. You're the woman with the gun; you tried to *kill* me."

"No, not true. I was protecting myself from four thugs, three men and a girl."

Kendrick briefly closed his eyes. "I remember that. A kid in cut-off khakis holding his arm."

"He wasn't a kid," objected Khaleh. "He was a drug addict as stretched out as his girlfriend, and they both would have killed *me* to pay their Arab suppliers for what they needed. I was following you, nothing more, nothing less. Information, that's my job."

"For *whom*?"

"The people I work for."

"How did you know about me?"

"That I won't answer."

"Whom do you work for?"

"In the broad sense, an organization that seeks to find solutions for the multiple horrors of the Middle East."

"Israeli?"

"No," replied Khalehla calmly. "My roots are Arab."

"That doesn't tell me a damn thing but it sure scares me."

"Why? Is it so impossible for an American to think we Arabs might want to find equitable solutions?"

"I've just come from the embassy in Masqat. What I saw there wasn't pretty—Arab-pretty."

"Nor to us. However, may I quote an American congressman who said on the floor of the House of Representatives that 'a terrorist isn't born, he's made.' "

Astonished, Evan looked hard at the woman. "That was the only comment I ever made for the *Congressional Record.* The *only* one."

"You did so after a particularly vicious speech by a congressman from California who practically called for the wholesale slaughter of all Palestinians living in what he termed Eretz Israel."

"He didn't know *Eretz* from *Biarritz*! He was a WASP grubber who thought he was losing the Jewish vote in Los Angeles. He told me that himself the day before. He mistook me for an ally and that I'd approve—goddamnit, he *winked* at me!"

"Do you still believe what you said?"

"Yes," replied Kendrick hesitantly, as if questioning his own response. "No one who's walked through the squalor of the refugee camps can think anything remotely normal can come out of them. But what I saw in Masqat went too far. Forget about the screaming and the wild chants; there was something ice-cold, a methodical brutality that thrived on itself. Those animals were enjoying themselves."

"The majority of those *young* animals never had a home. Their earliest memories are of wandering through the filth of the camps trying to find enough to eat, or clothes for their younger brothers and sisters. Only a pitiful few have any skills, even basic schooling. These things were not available to them. They were outcasts in their own land."

"Tell that to the children of Auschwitz and Dachau!" said Evan in quiet, cold fury. "These people are *alive.* They're part of the human race."

"Checkmate, Mr. Kendrick. I have no answer, only shame."

"I don't want your shame. I want to get out of here."

"You're in no condition to continue what you were doing. Look at you. You're exhausted, and on top of that you've been severely damaged."

The sheet across his waist, Kendrick supported himself on the edge of the bed. He spoke slowly. "I had a gun, a knife and a watch among several other valuable items. I'd like them back, please."

"I think we should discuss the situation—"

"There's nothing to discuss," said the Congressman. "Absolutely nothing."

"Suppose I were to tell you we've found Tony MacDonald?"

"Tony?"

"I work out of Cairo. I wish I could say we were on to him months ago, perhaps years ago, but it wouldn't be true. The first inkling I had was early this morning, before daybreak, in fact. He followed me in a car with no headlights—"

"On the road above the Jabal Sham?" asked Evan, interrupting.

"Yes."

"Then you're Cawley or something like that. Cawley the—enemy, among other things."

"My name is *Khalehla,* the first two syllables pronounced like the French seaport Calais; and I am indeed his enemy, but not the other things, which I can easily imagine."

"You were following me." A statement.

"Yes."

"Then you knew about the 'escape.' "

"Again, yes."

"Ahmat?"

"He trusts me. We go back a long time."

"Then he must trust the people you work for."

"I can't answer that. I said he trusts *me.*"

"That's a corkscrew statement—two corkscrew statements."

"It's a corkscrew situation."

"Where's *Tony*?"

"Holed up in a room at the Tylos Hotel on Government Road under the name of Strickland."

"How did you find him?"

"Through the taxi company. On the way he stopped at a sporting goods store suspected of selling illegal weapons. He's armed. . . . Let's say the driver was cooperative."

" 'Let's say'?"

"It'll suffice. If MacDonald makes a move, you'll be informed immediately. He's already made eleven phone calls."

"To *whom*?"

"The numbers were unpublished. A man will go over to the

Central Exchange in an hour or so when the calling lets up and get the names. They'll be given to you as soon as he has them and can reach an official or a public phone."

"Thanks. I need those numbers."

Khalehla pulled over the small rococo chair in front of the dressing table and sat down opposite Kendrick. "Tell me what you're doing, Congressman. Let me help."

"Why should I? You won't give me my gun or my knife or my watch—or a certain piece of clothing you've probably sold by now. You won't even tell me whom you work for."

"As to your gun, your knife, your watch, *and* your billfold, *and* a money belt with some fifty thousand American dollars, *and* your gold cigarette lighter, *and* a squashed pack of not-for-export American cigarettes—which was very foolish of you—you may have them all if you'll just convince me that what you're doing won't result in the slaughter of two hundred thirty-six Americans in Masqat. We Arabs can't tolerate that possibility; we're despised enough for the horrible things we can't control. As to whom I work for, why should it matter to you any more than it does to your friend and my friend Ahmat? You trust him, he trusts me. So you can trust me, too. A equals B equals C. A therefore equals C. Incidentally, your clothes have been fumigated, laundered and pressed. They're in the first closet on the left."

Evan, perched awkwardly on the edge of the bed, stared at the intense young woman, his lips slightly parted. "That's a hell of a mouthful, lady. I'll have to think about your alphabetical logic."

"I don't know your schedule, but you can't have much time."

"Between eleven-thirty and midnight tonight," said Kendrick, with no intention of revealing anything but a time span. "A young man was with me on the plane. He's a terrorist from the embassy in Masqat."

"He registered at the Aradous Hotel on the Wadi Al Ahd as 'T. Farouk.' "

"How . . . ?"

"Another cooperative driver," answered Khalehla, permitting herself a broader smile. " 'Let's say,' " she added.

"Whoever you work for has a lot of input in a lot of places."

"Oddly enough, the people I work for have nothing to do with it. They wouldn't go this far."

"But you did."

"I had to. Personal reasons; they're off limits, too."

"You're something, Cawley."

"Khalehla—*Kah-layla.* Why don't you call your friend at the Aradous? He bought clothes at the hotel and also got a haircut. I assume these were your instructions. But call him; relieve his mind."

"You're almost too cooperative—like the drivers."

"Because I'm not your enemy and I want to cooperate. Call Ahmat, if you wish. He'll tell you the same thing. Incidentally, like you, I have the triple-five number."

It was as if an unseen veil had been lifted off the Arab woman's face, a lovely, striking face, thought Evan as he studied the large brown eyes that held such care and curiosity in them. Still, he swore silently at himself for being the amateur, not knowing who was real and who was false! *Between eleven-thirty and midnight.* That was the zero hour, the thirty-minute span when he would catch a link, *the* link to the Mahdi. Could he trust this terribly efficient female who told him only so much and no more? Then again, could he do it himself? She had the triple-five number . . . how did she *get* it? Suddenly, the room started to spin around, the sunlight through the windows became a sprayed burst of orange. Where were the *windows*?

"*No,* Kendrick!" shouted Khalehla. "Not *now*! Don't collapse *now*! Make the call, I'll *help* you! Your friend must know that everything is all *right*! He's a terrorist in *Bahrain*! He has nowhere to go—you *must* make the *call*!"

Evan felt the hard slaps against his face, the harsh, stinging blows that rushed the blood to his head, his head that was suddenly cradled in Khalehla's right arm as her left hand reached for a glass on the bedside table. "Drink this!" she commanded, holding the glass to his lips. He did so. The liquid exploded in his throat.

"*Jesus!*" he roared.

"A hundred-and-twenty-proof vodka and brandy," said Khalehla smiling, still holding him. "It was given to me by a British MI-Sixer named Melvyn. 'Get someone to have three of these and you can sell him a gross of anything on the rack,' that's what Melvyn told me. Can I sell you something, Congressman? Like a phone call?"

"I'm not buying. I don't have any money. You've got it."

"Make that call, please," said Khalehla, releasing her prisoner as she retreated to the gold-rimmed dressing-table chair. "I think it's terribly important."

Kendrick shook his head, trying to focus on the telephone. "I don't know the number."

"I have it here." Khalehla reached into the pocket of her flight jacket and pulled out a piece of paper. "The number is five-nine-five-nine-one."

"Thank you, madame secretary." Evan reached for the phone, feeling a thousand aches in his body as he bent over and picked it up, pulling it to his lap. The exhaustion was spreading through him; he could barely move, barely dial. "*Azra?*" he said, hearing the terrorist's voice. "Have you studied the map of Manamah? Good. I'll pick you up at the hotel at ten o'clock." Kendrick paused, darting his eyes up at Khalehla. "If for any reason I'm delayed, I'll meet you in the street at the north end of the Juma Mosque where it joins the Al Khalifa Road. I'll find you. *Understood?* Good." Kendrick, trembling, hung up the phone.

"You have one more call to make, Congressman."

"Give me a couple of minutes." Kendrick leaned back on the pillows. *God,* he was tired!

"You really should make it now. You must tell Ahmat where you are, what you've done, what is happening. He expects it. He deserves to hear it from you, not me."

"All right, all *right.*" With enormous effort, Evan sat forward and picked up the phone, which was still on the bed. "It's direct dialing here in Bahrain. I forgot. What's the code for Masqat?"

"Nine-six-eight," replied Khalehla. "Dial zero-zero-one first."

"I should reverse the goddamned charges," said Kendrick, dialing, barely able to see the numbers.

"When did you last sleep?" asked Khalehla.

"Two—three days ago."

"When did you eat last?"

"Can't remember. . . . How about you? You've been pretty busy yourself, Madame Not-Such-a-Butterfly."

"I can't remember, either. . . . Oh, yes, I did eat. When I left the el Shari el Mishkwiyis, I stopped at that awful bakery in the square and got some orange baklava. More to find out who was there than anything—"

Evan held up his hand; the sultan's buried private line was ringing.

"*Iwah?*"

"Ahmat, it's Kendrick."

"I'm relieved!"

"I'm pissed off."

"What? What are you talking about?"

"Why didn't you tell me about her?"

"*Her?* Who?"

Evan handed the phone to a startled Khalehla.

"It's me, Ahmat," she said, embarrassed. Eight seconds later, after the voice of the perplexed and angry young sultan could be heard across the room, Khalehla continued. "It was either this or having the press learn that an American congressman armed with fifty thousand dollars on him had flown into Bahrain without going through customs. How long would it be before it was learned that he flew in on a plane ordered by the royal house of Oman? And how soon after that would there be speculation about his mission in Masqat? . . . I used your name with a brother of the Emir I've known for years and he arranged a place for us. . . . Thank you, Ahmat. Here he is."

Kendrick took the phone. "She's a biscuit, my old-young friend, but I suppose I'm better off here than where I might be. Just don't give me any more surprises, okay? . . . Why are you so quiet? . . . Forget it, here's the schedule and, remember, no interference unless I ask for it! I've got our boy from the embassy at the Aradous Hotel; and the MacDonald situation, which I assume you know about—" Khalehla nodded, and Evan continued rapidly, "I gather you do. He's being monitored at the Tylos; we'll be given a list of the calls he's been making when he stops making them. Incidentally, they're both armed." Exhausted, Kendrick then described the specifics of the meeting ground as they had been relayed to the agents of the Mahdi. "We only need one, Ahmat, one man who can lead us to him. I'll personally turn the rack until we get the information because I wouldn't have it any other way."

Kendrick hung up the phone and fell back onto the pillows.

"You need food," said Khalehla.

"Send out for Chinese," said Evan. "You've got the fifty thousand, not me."

"I'll have the kitchen prepare you something."

"*Me?*" His lids half closed, Kendrick looked at the olive-skinned woman in the ridiculously rococo gold-rimmed chair. The whites of her dark brown eyes were bloodshot, the sockets blue from exhaustion, the lines of her striking face far more pronounced than her age called for. "What about you?"

"I don't matter. You do."

"You're about to fall out of that Lilliputian throne of yours, Queen Mother."

"I'll handle it, thank you," said Khalehla, sitting upright, blinking in defiance.

"Since you won't give me my watch, what time is it?"

"Ten minutes past four."

"Everything's in place," said Evan, swinging his legs out onto the floor under the sheet, "and I'm sure this garishly civilized establishment can accommodate a wake-up call. 'Rest is a weapon,' I read that once. Battles have been won and lost more through sleep and the lack of sleep than firepower. . . . If you'll modestly look away, I'll grab a towel from what I assume is the largest bathroom in Bahrain over there, and find myself another bed."

"We can't leave this room except to leave the house."

"Why not?"

"Those are the arrangements. The Emir doesn't care for his cousin's young wife; therefore, the defilement caused by your person is restricted to her quarters. There are guards outside to enforce the order."

"I don't *believe* this!"

"I didn't make up the rules, I simply got you a place to stay."

His eyes closing, Kendrick rolled back on the bed and over to the far side, holding up the sheet to negotiate the distance. "All right, Miss Cairo. Unless you want to keep slipping off that silly-looking chair or fall flat on your face on the floor, here's your siesta pad. Before you relent, two things: Don't snore, and make sure I'm up by eight-thirty."

Twenty agonizing minutes later, unable to keep her eyes open and having fallen off the chair twice, Khalehla crept into the bed.

The incredible happened, incredible because neither expected it, nor was it sought, nor had either remotely considered the possibility. Two frightened, exhausted people felt each other's presence and, more asleep than awake, drew closer, at first touching, then slowly, haltingly, reaching, finally holding, grasping at each other; swollen, parted lips seeking, searching, desperately needing the moist contact that promised release from their fears. They made love in a burst of frenzy—not as strangers imitating animals, but as a man and a woman who had communicated, and somehow knew that there had to be a touch of warmth, of comfort, in a world gone mad.

"I suppose I should say I'm sorry," said Evan, his head on the pillows, his chest heaving as if he were swallowing his last breath of air.

"Please don't," said Khalehla quietly. "I'm not sorry. Sometimes . . . sometimes we all need to be reminded that we're part of the human race. Weren't those your words?"

"In a different context, I think."

"Not really. Not when you really think about it. . . . Go to sleep, Evan Kendrick. I won't say your name again."

"What does that mean?"

"Go to sleep."

Three hours later, nearly to the minute, Khalehla got out of the bed, picked up her clothes from the white carpet and, glancing at the unconscious American, quietly dressed. She wrote a note on a sheet of royal stationery and placed it on the bedside table next to the phone. She then went to the dressing table, opened a drawer and removed Kendrick's possessions, including the gun, the knife, the watch and his money belt. She put everything on the floor by the bed except the half-used pack of American cigarettes, which she crushed and shoved into her pocket. She crossed to the door and silently let herself out.

"*Esmah!*" she whispered to the uniformed Bahrainian guard, telling him in a single word to heed her orders. "He is to be awakened at precisely eight-thirty. I myself will reach this royal house to see that it is done. Do you understand?"

"*Iwah, iwah!*" replied the guard, stiff-necked and nodding his head in obedience.

"There may be a phone call for him, asking for 'the visitor.' It's to be intercepted, the information written down, placed in an envelope, and shoved under the door. I'll clear it with the authorities. They're just names and telephone numbers of people doing business with his firm. *Understood?*"

"*Iwah, iwah!*"

"Good." Khalehla gently, pointedly placed Bahrainian dinars worth fifty American dollars into the guard's pocket. He was hers for a lifetime, or at least for five hours. She walked down the ornate curved staircase to the enormous foyer and the carved front door, which was opened by another guard bowing obsequiously. She went out on the bustling pavement, where robes and dark business suits rushed in both directions, and looked for a public telephone. She saw one on the corner and ran toward it.

"This call will be accepted, I assure you, Operator," said

Khalehla, having given the numbers she had been instructed to give in an extreme emergency.

"*Yes?*" The voice five thousand miles away was harsh, abrupt.

"My name is Khalehla. You're the one I was to reach, I believe."

"No one else. The operator said 'Bahrain.' Do you confirm it?"

"Yes. He's here. I've been with him for several hours."

"What's going down?"

"There's a meeting between eleven-thirty and midnight near the Juma Mosque and the Al Khalifa Road. I should be there, sir. He's not equipped; he can't handle it."

"No *way,* lady!"

"He's a *child* where these people are concerned! I can *help*!"

"You can also *involve* us, which is out of the question and you know it as well as I do! Now, get *out* of there!"

"I thought you'd say that . . . *sir.* But may I please explain what I consider to be the negative odds of the equation in this particular operation?"

"I don't want to hear any of that spook bullshit! Get *out* of there!"

Khalehla winced as Frank Swann slammed down the telephone in Washington, D.C.

"The Aradous and the Tylos, I know them both," said Emmanuel Weingrass into the phone in the small secure office at the airport in Muharraq. "T. Farouk and Strickland—good *God,* I can't *believe* it! That daffodil drunk from *Cairo*? . . . Oh, sorry, Stinker, I forgot. I mean that French lilac from Algiers, that's what I meant to say. Go on." Weingrass wrote down the information from Masqat, given by a young man for whom he was beginning to have enormous respect. He knew men twice Ahmat's age and with three times his experience who would have buckled under the stress the sultan of Oman was enduring, not excluding the outrageous Western press that had no concept of his courage. The courage for risks that could bring about his downfall and his death. "Okay, I've got it all. . . . Hey, Stinker, you're quite a guy. You grew up to be a real mensch. Of course, you probably learned it all from me."

"I learned one thing from you, Manny, a very important truth. That was to face things as they were and not to make excuses. Whether it was for fun or in pain, you said. You told me a person could live with failure but not with the excuses that took away his right to fail. It took me a long time to understand that."

"That's very nice of you, young fellow. Pass it on to the kid I read you're expecting. Call it the Weingrass addendum to the Ten Commandments."

"But, Manny—"

"Yes?"

"Please don't wear one of those yellow or red polka-dotted bow ties in Bahrain. They kind of mark you, you know what I mean?"

"Now you're my *tailor*? . . . I'll be in touch, *mensch.* Wish us all good hunting."

"I do, my friend. Above all, I wish I could be with you."

"I know that. I wouldn't be here if I didn't know it—if our friend didn't know it." Weingrass hung up the phone and turned to the six men behind him. They were perched on tables and chairs, several holding their small secondary side arms, others checking the battery charges in their hand-held radios, all watching and listening intently to the old man. "We split up," he said. "Ben-Ami and Gray will come with me to the Tylos. Blue, you take the others to the Aradous Hotel—" Manny stopped, gripped by a sudden coughing seizure; his face reddened and his slender frame shook violently. Ben-Ami and the members of the Masada unit glanced at one another; none moved, each knowing instinctively that Weingrass would rebuff any assistance. But one thing was clear to all of them. They were looking at a dying man.

"Water?" asked Ben-Ami.

"No," replied Manny curtly, the coughing seizure subsiding. "Lousy chest cold, lousy weather in France. . . . All right, where were we?"

"I was to take the others to the Aradous Hotel," answered Yaakov, code name Blue.

"Get yourselves some decent clothes so you won't get thrown out of the lobby. There are shops here in the airport, clean jackets will be enough."

"These are our working clothes," objected Black.

"Paper-bag 'em," said Weingrass.

"What are we to do at the Aradous?" Blue got off the table he was sitting on.

Manny looked down at his notes, then up at the young leader. "In Room Two-zero-one is a man who's called Azra."

"Arabic for 'blue,' " interrupted code Red, glancing at Yaakov.

"He's on the terrorist council in Masqat," broke in Orange. "They say he led the team that stormed the Teverya kibbutz near the Galilee, killing thirty-two, including nine children."

"He planted bombs in three settlements on the West Bank," added Gray, "and blew up a pharmacy, paint-spraying the name 'Azra' on a wall. After the blast the wall was pieced together like a puzzle, and there it was. The name Azra. I've seen him on television."

"*Pig,*" said Yaakov quietly, adjusting the straps of his weapon under the jacket. "When we get to the Aradous, what do we do? Give him tea and cakes or just a medal for humanitarianism?"

"You stay out of his sight!" replied Weingrass harshly. "But don't let him out of yours. Two of you get rooms near his; watch the door. Don't get a glass of water, don't go to the toilet, just watch his door every minute. The two others take up positions in the street, one in front, the other by the employees' exit. Stay in radio contact with each other. Work out simple codes, one-word codes—in Arabic. If he moves, you move with him, but don't let him suspect for even a moment that you're there. Remember, he's as good as you are; he's had to survive, too."

"Are we silently escorting him to a private dinner party?" asked code Blue sarcastically. "This is a plan without the most rudimentary blueprint!"

"The blueprint will come from Kendrick," said Manny, for once not rising to the insult. "If he really has one," he added softly, concern in his voice.

"*What?*" Ben-Ami rose from his chair, not, however, in anger but in astonishment.

"If everything goes according to schedule, he'll pick up the Arab at ten o'clock. With his Masqat terrorist in tow, he expects to make contact with one of the Mahdi's agents, someone who can lead them either to the Mahdi himself or to someone else who can."

"On what *basis*?" asked the incredulous Ben-Ami from the Mossad.

"Actually, it's not bad. The Mahdi's people think there's an emergency, but they don't know what it is."

"An *amateur*!" roared code Red of the Masada unit. "There'll be backups, and blind drones, and backups for *them.* What the hell are we *doing* here?"

"You're here to take out the backups and the drones *and* the backups behind *them*!" shouted Weingrass in reply. "If I have to tell you what to look for, go back and start all over again with the Boy Scouts in Tel Aviv. You follow; you protect; you take out the *bad guys.* You clear a path for that amateur who's putting his life on the line. This Mahdi's the key, and if you haven't understood that by now, there's nothing I can do about it. One word from him, preferably with a gun to his head, and everything stops in Oman."

"It's not without merit," said Ben-Ami.

"But it's without *sense*!" cried Yaakov. "Say this Kendrick does reach your Mahdi. What does he do, what does he *say*?" Code Blue shifted to a broad caricature of an American accent. "Say, pardner, Ah gotta hell of a deal for you, buddy. You call off your dumb goons and Ah'll give you mah new leather boots. *Ridiculous!* He'll be shot in the head the moment he's asked, 'What's the emergency?' "

"That's not without merit, either," repeated Ben-Ami.

"Lawyers now I've got!" yelled Manny. "You think my son is stupid? He built a construction empire on mishegoss? The minute he has something concrete—a name, a location, a company—he reaches Masqat, and our mutual friend, the sultan, calls the Americans, the British, the French and anyone else he trusts who's set up shop in Oman and *they* go to work. Their people here in Bahrain close in."

"Merit," said Ben-Ami once again, nodding.

"Not totally without," agreed code Black.

"And what will *you* be doing?" asked a somewhat subdued yet still-challenging Yaakov.

"Caging a fat fox who's been devouring a lot of chickens in a coop no one ever knew about," said Weingrass.

Kendrick's eyes snapped open. A sound, a scrape—an intrusion on the silence of the bedroom that had nothing to do with the traffic outside the cathedral windows. It was closer, more personal, somehow intimate. Yet it was not the woman, Khalehla; she was gone. He blinked for a moment at the indented pillows beside him, and despite everything that his mind was putting together, he felt a sudden sadness. For those brief few hours with her he had cared, feeling a warmth between them that was only a part of their frantic lovemaking, which in itself would not have happened without that sense of warmth.

What time was it? He turned his wrist and—his watch was not there. *Goddamnit,* the bitch still *had* it! He rolled over on the bed and swung his legs out on the floor without regard for the sheet covering him. The soles of his feet landed on hard objects;

he looked down at the white polar-bear rug and blinked again. Everything that had been in his pockets was there—everything but the pack of cigarettes, which he very much wanted at the moment. And then his eyes were drawn to a gold-bordered sheet of notepaper on the bedside table; he picked it up.

I think we were both kind to each other when each of us needed some kindness. No regrets other than one. I won't see you again. Good-bye.

No name, no forwarding address, just *Ciao, amico.* So much for two passing ships in the Persian Gulf or two uptight, damaged people on a late afternoon in Bahrain. But it was not afternoon any longer, he realized. He was barely able to read Khalehla's note; only the last orange sprays of sundown now streamed through the windows. He reached for his watch; it was seven-fifty-five; he had slept nearly four hours. He was famished, and his years in the deserts, the mountains and the white water had taught him not to travel hard on an empty stomach. A "guard," she had said. "Outside," she had explained. Evan yanked the sheet off the bed, wrapped it around himself and walked across the room. He stopped; on the floor was an envelope. That was the sound he had heard, an envelope shoved under a door, forced under, sliding back and forth because of the thick rug. He picked it up, tore it open and read it. A list of sixteen names, addresses and telephone numbers. *MacDonald!* The roster of calls he had made in Bahrain. One step closer to the Mahdi!

Evan opened the door; the greetings between himself and the uniformed guard were dispensed with rapidly in Arabic. "You are awake now, sir. You were not to be disturbed until eight-thirty o'clock."

"I'd be most grateful if you would disturb me now with some food. The woman said I might get something to eat from your kitchen."

"Indeed, whatever you wish, sir."

"Whatever you can find. Meat, rice, bread . . . and milk, I'd like some milk. Everything as soon as possible, please."

"Very quick, sir!" The guard turned and rushed down the hallway toward the staircase. Evan closed the door and stood for a moment to find his bearings in the now darkened room. He switched on a lamp at the edge of the endless bureau, then started across the thick-piled rug to another door that led to one of the most opulent bathrooms in Bahrain.

Ten minutes later he emerged, showered and shaved, now

dressed in a short terry-cloth robe. He walked to the closet where Khalehla had said his clothes were—"fumigated, laundered and pressed." He opened the mirrored door and barely recognized the odd assortment of apparel he had collected at the embassy in Masqat; it all looked like a respectable paramilitary uniform. Leaving everything on hangers, he draped the starched outfit over the chaise, walked back to the bed and sat down, gazing at his belongings on the floor. He was tempted to check his money belt to see if any of the large bills were missing, then decided against it. If Khalehla was a thief, he did not want to know it, not at the moment.

The telephone rang, its harsh bell less a ring than a prolonged metallic shriek. For a moment he stared at the instrument wondering . . . *who?* He had MacDonald's list; that was the only call Khalehla said he could expect. *Khalehla?* Had she changed her mind? With a rush of unanticipated feeling he reached for the phone, yanking it to his ear. Eight seconds later he wished to God he had not.

"*Amreekanee,*" said the male voice, its flat monotone conveying hatred. "You leave that royal house before morning and you are a dead man. Tomorrow you go quietly back to where you came from, where you belong."

14

Emmanuel Weingrass pulled code Gray's radio to his lips and spoke. "Go ahead and remember to keep the line open. I've got to hear *everything*!"

"If you'll forgive me, Weingrass," replied Ben-Ami from the shadows across Government Road. "I would feel somewhat more secure if our colleague Gray also heard. You and I are not so adept in these situations as those young men."

"They haven't a brain in their collective head. We have two."

"This is not *shul,* Emmanuel, this is what's called the field and it can be very unpleasant."

"I have every confidence in you, Benny boy, as long as you guarantee these kiddie radios can be heard through steel."

"They're as clear as any electronic bug ever developed, with the added function of direct transmission. One just pushes the right buttons."

"One doesn't," said Weingrass, "*you* do. Go on, we'll follow when we hear what this MacDonald-Strickland says."

"Send code Gray first, please." Out of the shadows near the marquee of the Tylos Hotel, Ben-Ami joined the bustling crowds around the entrance. People came and went, mostly male, mostly in Western dress, along with a smattering of women exclusively in Western dress. Taxis disgorged passengers as others filled them, tipping a harried doorman whose sole job was to open and close doors, and every now and then to blow a strident whistle for a lowly, thobe-clad bellhop to carry luggage. Ben-Ami melted into this melee and went inside. Moments later, through the background noise of the lobby, he could be heard dialing; squinting in irritation, Manny held up the radio between himself and the much taller, muscular code Gray. The first words from Room 202 were obscured, then the Mossad agent spoke.

"*Shaikh Strickland?*"

"*Who's this?*" The Englishman's cautious whisper was now distinct; Ben-Ami had adjusted the radio.

"*I'm downstairs. . . . Anah hénah, littee gáhrah—*"

"*Bloody damn black fool!*" cried MacDonald. "*I don't speak that gibberish! Why are you calling from the lobby?*"

"*I was testing you, Mr. Strickland,*" Ben-Ami broke in quickly. "*A man under stress often gives himself away. You might have asked me where my business trip was taking me, perhaps leading to a subsequent code. Then I would have known you were not the man—*"

"*Yes, yes, I understand! Thank Christ you're here! It's taken you long enough. I expected you a half hour ago. You were to say something to me. Say it!*"

"*Not over the telephone,*" answered the Mossad infiltrator firmly. "*Never over the telephone, you should know that.*"

"*If you think I'm just going to let you into my room—*"

"*I wouldn't if I were you,*" interrupted Ben-Ami once again. "*We know you're armed.*"

"*You do?*"

"*Every weapon sold under a counter is known to us.*"

"*Yes . . . yes, of course.*"

"*Open your door with the latch on. If my words are incorrect, kill me.*"

"*Yes . . . very well. I'm sure it won't be necessary. But understand me, whoever you are, one misplaced syllable and you're a corpse!*"

"I shall practice my English, Shaikh Strickland."

A tiny green light suddenly began blinking on the small radio in Weingrass's hand. "What the hell is *that*?" asked Manny.

"Direct transmission," replied code Gray. "Give it to me." The Masada commando took the instrument and pressed a button. "Go ahead."

"He's alone!" said Ben-Ami's voice. "We have to move quickly, take him now!"

"We don't make *any* moves, you Mossad imbecile!" countered Weingrass, grabbing the radio. "Even those mutants from the State Department's Consular Operations can hear what they've just been *told,* but not the holy *Mossad*! They hear only their *own* voices, and maybe Abraham's if he's got a code ring out of a box of corn flakes!"

"Manny, I don't need this," said Ben-Ami slowly, painfully over the radio.

"You need ears, that's what you need, *ganza macher*! That daffodil expects a contact from the Mahdi any minute—someone who's not to call from the lobby but who's to go directly to his room. He's got the words to get MacDonald to open the door—*that's* when we join the party and take them both! What did you have in mind? Breaking the door down courtesy of the Neanderthal here beside me?"

"Well, yes—"

"I don't need this, either," muttered Gray quietly.

"No wonder you idiots blew it in Washington. You thought *Password* was a Mossad drop and not a television show!"

"Manny!"

"Get your secret ass up to the second floor! We'll be there in two minutes, right, Tinker Bell?"

"Mr. Weingrass," said code Gray, the muscles of his lean, muscular jaw working furiously as he snapped off the radio. "You are probably the most irritatingly vexatious man I have ever met."

"*Oy,* such words! In the Bronx you would have been beaten up for that—if ten or twelve of my Irish or Italian buddies could have handled you. Come *on*!" Manny started across Government Road, followed by Gray, who kept shaking his head, not in disagreement but only to purge the thoughts he was thinking.

The hotel corridor was long, the carpet worn. It was the dinner hour and most of the guests were out. Weingrass stood at one end; he had tried to smoke a Gauloise but had crushed it out, burning a hole in the carpet, as it had started a devastating rumble in his chest. Ben-Ami was by the farthest elevator, the ever-present irritated hotel guest waiting for a conveyance that never came. Code Gray was nearest to Room 202, leaning casually against the wall next to a door fifteen feet diagonally across the hall from "Mr. Strickland's." He was a professional; he assumed the posture of a young man eagerly awaiting a woman he was perhaps not meant to meet, even to the point of seeming to talk through the door.

It happened, and Weingrass was impressed. The uniformed doorman from the Tylos's marqueed entrance suddenly walked out of an elevator, his gold-braided cap in his hand; he approached Room 202. He stopped, knocked, waited for the chained door to be partially opened and spoke. The chain was unlatched. Suddenly, with the aggressive speed and purpose of an Olympic athlete, code Gray spun away from the wall, hurling himself at the two figures in the doorway, somehow managing to withdraw a handgun from some unseen place as he crashed his body, surging up laterally, into his two enemies, his feet and arms, again somehow, pulling them together as one entity and sending them across the floor. Two muted shots erupted from the commando's pistol; the automatic in Anthony MacDonald's hand was blown away, as were two of his fingers.

Weingrass and Ben-Ami converged on the door and rushed inside, slamming it shut behind them.

"My *God, look* at me!" screamed the Englishman on the floor, grabbing his bleeding right hand. "Jesus *Christ*! *I* have no—"

"Get a towel from the bathroom," ordered Gray calmly, addressing Ben-Ami. The Mossad agent did as he was told by the younger man.

"I am only a *messenger*!" yelled the doorman, writhing next to the bed in fear. "I was only to deliver a message!"

"The *hell* you're a messenger," said Emmanuel Weingrass, standing over the man. "You're perfect, you son of a bitch. You see who comes, who goes—you're their goddamned *eyes.* Oh, I want to *talk* to you."

"I have no *hand*!" shrieked the obese MacDonald, the blood rolling in tiny rivers down his arm.

"Here!" said Ben-Ami, kneeling down and wrapping a towel around the Englishman's blown-apart fingers.

"Don't do that," ordered code Gray, grabbing the towel and throwing it aside.

"You told me to get it," protested Ben-Ami, confused.

"I've changed my mind," said Gray, his voice suddenly cold,

holding MacDonald's arm down, the blood now rushing out of his two stumped fingers. "*Blood,*" continued the Masada commando, speaking calmly to the Englishman, "especially blood from the right arm—from the *aorta* expelling it from the heart—will have nowhere else to go but on this floor. Do you read me, *khanzeer*? Do you understand me, *pig*? Tell us what we must know or be drained of life. Where is this Mahdi? Who is he?"

"I don't *know*!" shouted Anthony MacDonald, coughing, tears rolling down his cheeks and jowls. "Like everyone else, I call telephone numbers—someone gets *back* to me! That's all I *know*!"

The commando's head snapped up. He was trained to hear things and sense vibrations others did not hear or sense. "Get *down*!" he whispered harshly to Ben-Ami and Weingrass. "Roll to the walls! Behind chairs, *anything*!"

The hotel door crashed open. Three Arabs in sheer white robes, their faces concealed by cloth, lunged through the open space, their muted machine pistols on open-fire, their targets obvious: MacDonald and the Tylos doorman, whose screaming prostrate bodies thumped like jackhammers under the fusillade of bullets until no sounds came from their bleeding mouths. Suddenly the killers were aware of others in the room; they spun, their weapons slashing the air for new targets, but they were no competition for the lethal code Gray of the Masada Brigade. The commando had raced to the left of the open door, his back pressed into the wall, his Uzi ripped from the Velcro straps under his jacket. With a prolonged burst he cut down the three executioners instantly. There were no death reflexes. Each skull was blown apart.

"*Out!*" shouted Gray, lurching to Weingrass and pulling the old man to his feet. "To the staircase by the elevators!"

"If we're stopped," added Ben-Ami, racing to the door, "we're three people panicked by the gunfire."

Out on Government Road, as they rested in an alley that led to the Shaikh Hamad Boulevard, code Gray suddenly swore under his breath, more at himself than at his companions. "Damn, damn, *damn*! I had to *kill* them!"

"You had no choice," said the Mossad agent. "One of their fingers on a trigger and we might all be dead—certainly one of us."

"But with even one of them alive we could have learned so much," countered the man from the Masada unit.

"We learned something, Tinker Bell," said Weingrass.

"Will you *stop* that!"

"Actually, it's a term of affection, young man—"

"What did we learn, Manny?"

"MacDonald talked too much. In his panic the Englishman said things to people over the telephone he shouldn't have said, so he had to be killed for a loose mouth."

"How does that account for the doorman?" asked code Gray.

"Expendable. He got MacDonald's door open for the Mahdi's firing squad. Your gun made the real noise, *they* didn't. . . . And now that we know about MacDonald's mouth and his execution, we can assume two vital facts—like the stress factors when you're designing an overhanging balcony on a building, one weight perched off center on another off-center gravity pitch."

"What the *hell* are you talking about, Manny?"

"My boy, Kendrick, did a better job than he probably realizes. The Mahdi's frightened. He really doesn't know what's going on, and by killing the big mouth, now nobody can *tell* him. He made a mistake, isn't that something? The *Mahdi* made a mistake."

"If your architectural schematics are as abstruse as you are, Mr. Weingrass," said Gray, "I hope none of your designs will follow for buildings in Israel."

"Oh, the *words* that boy has! You sure you didn't go to the High School of Science in the Bronx? Never mind. Let's check out the scene at the Juma Mosque. . . . Tell me, Tinker Bell, did *you* ever make a mistake?"

"I think I made one coming to Bahrain—"

The answer was lost on Emmanuel Weingrass. The old man was doubled over in a coughing seizure against the wall of the dark alleyway.

Stunned, Kendrick stared at the phone in his hand, then in anger slammed it down—anger and frustration and fear. "*You leave that royal house before morning and you are a dead man. . . . Go quietly back to where you came from, where you belong.*" If he needed any final confirmation that he was closing in on the Mahdi, he had it, for all the good it did him. He was virtually a prisoner; one step outside the elegant town house and he would be shot on sight by men waiting for him to appear. Even his "fumigated, laundered and pressed" clothes would not be mistaken for anything but what they were: cleaned-up terrorist apparel. And the order for him to go back where he came from could hardly be taken seriously. He accepted the fact that there would be reluctance to kill an American congressman, even one whose presence in Bahrain could easily be traced to the horrors in Masqat, where he had once worked. An obliterated, bombed-out Oman increasingly demanded by a large segment of the American people would not be in the Mahdi's interests—but neither could the Mahdi permit that congressman to return to Washington. The absence of hard evidence notwithstanding, he knew too much that others far more experienced in the black arts could put to advantage; the Mahdi's solution was all too obvious. The curious, interfering American would be one more victim of these terrible times—along with others, of course. A massacre at an airport terminal; a plane blown out of the sky; a bomb in a coffee shop—so many possibilities, as long as among those killed was a man who had learned too much.

At the end it was as he had conceived it in the beginning. Himself and the Mahdi. Himself *or* the Mahdi. Now he had lost, as surely as if he were in the shell of a building with a thousand tons of concrete and steel crashing down on him.

There was a sharp tapping at the door. *"Odkhul,"* he said in Arabic, telling the visitor to come in, instinctively picking up his weapon from the white rug. The guard walked in, expertly balancing a large tray in the palm of his left hand. Evan shoved the gun under a pillow and stood up as the soldier carried his food to the white desk.

"All is in readiness, sir!" exclaimed the guard, no little triumph in his voice. "I personally selected each item for its proper deliciousness. My wife tells me I should have been a chef rather than a warrior—"

Kendrick did not actually hear the rest of this warrior's paean to himself. Instead, he was suddenly mesmerized by the sight of the man. He was about six feet tall, give or take an inch, with respectable shoulders and an enviably trim waist. Except for that irritating waist, he was Evan's *size* or close to it. Kendrick glanced over at the clean, starched clothes on the chaise and then back at the colorful red-and-blue uniform of the frustrated chef-warrior. Without really thinking, Evan reached down for the hidden weapon as the soldier, humming like an Italian *cuciniere supremo,* placed the steaming plates on the desk. The only thought that kept racing through Kendrick's mind was that a cleaned-up terrorist's outfit would be a target for a salvo of bullets, but not the uniform of a Bahrainian Royal Guard, especially one walking out of a royal house. Actually, there was no alternative. If he did nothing, he was dead in the morning—

somewhere, somehow. He had to do *something,* so he did it. He walked around the outsized bed, stood behind the guard, and with all his strength smashed the handle of the gun into the soldier's bobbing, humming head.

The guard fell to the floor, unconscious, and again without really thinking, Evan sat down at the desk and ate faster than he had ever eaten in his life. Twelve minutes later, the soldier was bound and gagged on the bed as Kendrick studied himself in front of a closet mirror. The creased red-and-blue uniform might have been improved by the experienced fingers of a tailor, but withal and in the shadows of the evening streets, it was acceptable.

He ransacked the row of closets until he found a plastic shopping bag and stuffed his Masqat clothing into it. He looked at the telephone. He knew he would not use that phone, *could* not use it. If he survived the street outside, he would call Azra from another.

His jacket off, the shoulder holster in place, Azra angrily paced the room at the Aradous Hotel consumed by thoughts of betrayal. Where was *Amal Bahrudi*—the man with blue eyes who *called* himself Bahrudi? Was he in reality someone else, someone the foolish, bloated Englishman called "Kendrick"? Was everything a trap, a trap to capture a member of Masqat's organization council, a trap to take the terrorist known as the Arabic Blue? . . . *Terrorist?* How typical of the Zionist killers from the Irgun Zvai Leumi and the Haganah! How easily they erase the massacres of "Jephthah" and Deir Yasin, to say nothing of their surrogate executioners at Sabra and Shatila! They steal a homeland and sell what is not theirs to sell, and kill a child for carrying the Palestinian flag—"an accident of excess," they call it—and yet *we* are the terrorists! . . . If the Aradous Hotel *was* a trap, he could not remain caged in the room; yet if it was not a trap, he had to be where he could be contacted. The Mahdi was everything, his summons a command, for he gave them the means for hope, for spreading their message of legitimacy. When would the world *understand* them? When would the Mahdis of the world be irrelevant?

The telephone rang and Azra raced to it. "*Yes?*"

"I was delayed but I'm on my way. They found me; I was nearly killed at the airport but I escaped. They may even have traced *you* by now."

"*What?*"

"Leaks in the system. Get out, but don't go through the lobby. There's a staircase designed for a fire exit. It's at the south end of the hallway, I think. North or south, one or the other. Use it and go through the restaurant's kitchen to the employees' exit. You'll come out on the Wadi Al Ahd. Walk across the road; I'll pick you up."

"You *are* you, Amal Bahrudi? I can trust you?"

"Neither one of us has a choice, do we?"

"That is not an answer."

"I'm not your enemy," lied Evan Kendrick. "We'll never be friends but I'm not your enemy. I can't afford it. And you're wasting time, poet, part of which is mine. I'll be there in five minutes. Hurry!"

"I go."

"Be careful."

Azra hung up the phone and went to his weapons, which he had cleaned repeatedly and placed in a neat row on the bureau. He took the small Heckler and Koch P9S automatic, knelt down, pulling up his left trouser leg, and inserted the weapon in the crisscrossing calf straps that rested below the back of his knee. Standing up he removed the larger, more powerful Mauser Parabellum pistol and shoved it into his shoulder holster, this followed by the sheathed hunting knife resting alongside the gun. He walked to a chair where he had thrown the coat of his newly purchased suit, put on the jacket and crossed to the door, rapidly letting himself out into the corridor.

Nothing would have seemed odd to him were it not for his concentration on the whereabouts of the staircase and his desire to save time—time now measured in minutes and segments of minutes. He started to his right, to the south end of the hallway, his eyes only partially aware of a door being closed, not an open door but one barely ajar. Meaningless: a careless guest; a Western woman carrying too many shopping boxes. Then, unable to see an exit sign for a staircase, he turned quickly to check the other end, the north end of the hallway. A second door, this one open no more than two inches, was closed swiftly, silently. The first was now no longer meaningless, for surely the second was not. They had found him! His room was being watched. By *whom*? Who were *they*? Azra continued walking, now to the north end of the corridor, but the instant he passed the second door he pivoted against the wall, reached inside his jacket for the long-bladed hunting knife, and waited. In seconds the door opened; he spun around the frame, instantly facing a man he knew was his enemy, a deeply tanned, muscular man near his own age—desert training was written all over him, an Israeli *commando*! Instead of a weapon the startled Jew held a radio in his hand; he was unarmed!

Azra thrust the knife directly forward toward the Israeli's throat. In a lightning move the blade was deflected; the terrorist then arced it down, slicing into the Hebrew's wrist; the radio fell to the carpeted floor as Azra kicked the door shut; the automatic lock clicked.

Gripping his wrist, the Israeli lashed out his right foot, expertly catching the Palestinian's left kneecap. Azra stumbled; another steel toe caught him in the side of his neck, then still another crashed into his ribs. But the angle was right; the Israeli was off-balance! The terrorist lunged, the knife an extension of his arm as he sent it directly into the commando's stomach. Blood erupted, covering Azra's face, as the Israeli, code name Orange of the Masada Brigade, fell back on the floor.

The Palestinian struggled to get up, sharp bolts of pain surging through his ribs and his knee, the tendons in his neck nearly paralyzed. Suddenly, without a scratch or a footstep, the door crashed open, the hotel lock blown out of its mount. The second commando—younger, his thick bare arms bulging in tension, his furious eyes surveying the scene in front of him—whipped his hand beyond his right hip for a holstered weapon. Azra hurled himself against the Israeli, smashing the commando into the door, slamming it shut. Code Blue's gun spiraled across the floor, freeing his right hand to intercept the Palestinian's arm as it slashed down with the blood-streaked blade of the knife. The Israeli hammered his knee up into the terrorist's rib cage as he swung the gripped arm clockwise, forcing Azra toward the floor. Still the Palestinian would not release the knife! Both men parted, crouching, staring at each other, contempt and hatred in both pairs of eyes.

"You want to kill Jews, try to kill *me,* pig!" cried Yaakov.

"Why *not*?" replied Azra, thrusting his knife forward to draw out the Israeli. "You kill Arabs! You killed my mother and father as if you'd pulled the trigger yourself!"

"You killed my two brothers on the Sidon patrols!"

"I may have! I hope so! I was *there*!"

"You are *Azra*!"

Like two crazed animals, the young men flung themselves at each other with violence incarnate, the taking of life—hated life—their only reason for being on earth. Blood burst out of punctured flesh as ligaments were torn and bones broken amid throated cries of vengeance and loathing. Finally it happened, the ending as volcanic as the initial eruption; sheer, brute strength was the victor.

The knife was lodged in the terrorist's throat, reversed and forced to its mark by the commando from the Masada Brigade.

Exhausted and drenched in blood, Yaakov pushed himself off the body of his enemy. He looked over at his slain comrade, code Orange, and closed his eyes. "*Shalom,*" he whispered. "Find the peace we all seek, my friend."

There was no time for mourning, he thought as his eyes flashed open. The body of his comrade, as well as that of his enemy, had to be moved. He had to be at the source for what came next; he had to reach the others. The killer *Azra* was dead! They could now fly back to Masqat, they *had* to. To his *father*! In pain, Blue limped to the bed and yanked back the spread, revealing his dead comrade's Uzi machine pistol. He picked it up, awkwardly strapped it over his shoulder, and went to the door to check the hallway. His *father*!

In the far shadows of the Wadi Al Ahd, Kendrick knew he could not wait any longer, nor could he risk using a telephone. Conversely, he could not remain in the foliage across from the Aradous and do *nothing*! Time was winding down and the contact from the Mahdi expected to find the puppet Azra, newly crowned prince of terrorists, at the rendezvous. It was so clear now, he realized. He had been found out, either through the events at the airport or through a leak in Masqat—the panicked men from the past he had talked to, men who, unlike Mustapha, refused to see him and may have betrayed him for their own safety, as surely as one of them had killed Musty for the same reason. "*We cannot be involved! It's madness. Our families are dead! Our children raped, disfigured . . . dead!*"

The Mahdi's strategy was obvious. Isolate the American and wait for the terrorist to approach the meeting ground alone. Take the young killer, thus aborting the trap, for there is no trap without the American, only an expendable Palestinian on the loose. Kill him, but first find out what happened in Masqat.

Where was Azra? Thirty-seven minutes had passed since they talked; the Arab called Blue was thirty-two minutes late! Evan looked at his watch for the eleventh time and swore silently, furiously, his unspoken words at once a plea for help and an outburst of anger at the swirling clouds of frustration. He had to *move, do* something! Find out where Azra was, for without the terrorist there was no trap for the Mahdi, either. The Mahdi's contact would not show himself to someone he did not know, someone he did not recognize. So *close*! So *far* in the distance of reality!

Kendrick threw the plastic shopping bag containing his starched clothes from Masqat into the densest interior of the bushes bordering the pavement of the Wadi Al Ahd. He walked across the boulevard toward the employees' entrance, a postured, upright Royal Guard arrogantly on royal business. As he went rapidly down the cobblestone alley toward the service entrance, several of the departing help bowed obsequiously, obviously hoping not to be stopped and searched for small treasures they had stolen from the hotel—namely, soap, toilet paper and plates of food scraped from the dinners of jet-lagged or drunken Westerners too far gone to eat. Standard procedure; Evan had been there; it was why he had chosen the Aradous Hotel. Again Emmanuel Weingrass. He and the unpredictable Manny had fled the Aradous by way of the kitchen because a stepbrother of the Emir had heard that Weingrass had promised a stepsister of that royal brother citizenship in the United States if she would sleep with him--a privilege that Manny in no way could provide.

Kendrick passed through the kitchen, reached the south staircase, and walked cautiously up the steps to the second floor. He withdrew the gun from under his scarlet jacket and opened the door. The corridor was empty, and indeed it was the hour of the evening when the affluent visitors to Bahrain were out in the cafés and in the hidden casinos. He sidestepped down the left wall to Room 202, careful of every footstep on the worn carpet. He listened; there was no sound. He knocked quietly.

"*Odkhúloo,*" said the voice in quiet Arabic, addressing not one, but *more* than one to enter.

Strange—*wrong,* thought Evan as he reached for the doorknob. Why the plural, why *more* than one? He turned the knob, spun back into the wall, and kicked the door open with his right foot.

Silence, as if the room were an empty cave, the eerie voice a disembodied recording. Gripping hard the unfamiliar, unwanted, but necessary weapon, Kendrick slipped around the frame and went inside. . . . Oh, *God*! What he saw made him freeze in horror! Azra was slumped against the wall, a knife embedded in his neck, his eyes wide in death, blood still dripping in rivulets down over his chest.

"Your friend, the pig, is dead," said the quiet voice behind him.

Evan whipped around to face a young man as bloodied as Azra. The wounded killer leaned against the wall, barely able to stand, and in his hands was an Uzi machine pistol. "Who *are* you?" whispered Kendrick. "What the hell have you *done*?" he added, now shouting.

The man limped rapidly to the door and closed it, the weapon remaining on Evan. "I killed a man who would kill my people as swiftly as he could find them, who would have killed me."

"Good Christ, you're *Israeli*!"

"You're the American."

"Why did you *do* it? What are you *doing* here?"

"It's not my choice."

"That's no answer!"

"My orders are to give no answers."

"You had to *kill* him?" cried Kendrick, turning and wincing at the sight of the dead, mutilated Palestinian.

"To use his words, 'Why not?' They slaughter our children in schoolyards, blow up planes and buses filled with our citizens, execute our innocent athletes in Munich, shoot old men in the head simply because all are Jews. They crawl up on beaches and murder our young, our brothers and sisters—*why?* Because we are *Jews* living *finally* on an infinitesimal strip of arid, wild land that we tamed. *We! Not* others."

"He never had the chance—"

"*Spare* me, American! I know what's coming and it fills me with disgust. At the last it's the same as it has always been. Underneath, in whispers, the world still wants to blame the Jew. After everything that's been done to us, we're still the irksome troublemakers. Well, hear this, you interfering amateur, we don't want your comments or your guilt or your pity. We only want what belongs to us! We've marched out of the camps and the ovens and the gas chambers to claim what is ours."

"*Goddamn* you!" roared Evan, gesturing angrily at the bleeding corpse of the terrorist. "You sound like him! Like *him*! When will you all *stop*?"

"What difference does it make to you? Go back to your safe condominium and your fancy country club, American. Leave us alone. Go back where you belong."

Whether it was the repeated words he had heard barely an hour ago over the phone, or the sudden images of cascading blocks of concrete crashing down on seventy-eight screaming, helpless loved ones, or the realization that the hated Mahdi was slipping away from him, he would never know. All he knew at that moment was that he hurled himself at the startled, wounded Israeli, tears of fury rolling down his cheeks. "You arrogant *bastard*!" he screamed, ripping the Uzi out of the young man's grip and throwing it across the room, hammering the weakened commando against the wall. "What *right* do you have telling me what to do or where to go? We watch you people kill each other and blow yourselves and everything else up in the name of blind credos! We spend lives and money, and exhaust brains and energy trying to instill a little reason, but *no,* none of you will move an inch! Maybe we *should* leave you alone and let you massacre each other, let the zealots hack each other to death, just so *somebody's* left who'll make some sense!" Suddenly, Kendrick broke away and raced across the room, picking up the Uzi. He returned to the Israeli, the weapon ominously leveled at the commando. "Who *are* you and why are you here?"

"I am code name Blue. That is my response and I will give no other—"

"Code name *what*?"

"Blue."

"Oh, my *God* . . . " whispered Evan, glancing over at the dead Azra. He turned back to the Israeli and, without comment, handed the Uzi machine pistol to the stunned commando. "Go ahead," he said softly. "Shoot up the fucking world. I don't give a damn." With those words, Kendrick walked to the door and let himself out.

Yaakov stared after the American, at the closed door, and then over at the corpse slumped on the floor against the wall. He angled the weapon down with his left hand and with his right pulled out the powerful miniaturized radio from his belt. He pressed a button.

"*Itklem,*" said the voice of code Black outside the hotel.

"Did you reach the others?"

"Code *R* did. They're here—or I should say I can see them walking up the Al Ahd now. Our elder colleague is with *R; G* is with the eldest, but something's wrong with the latter. *G* is holding him. How about you?"

"I'm no good to you now, maybe later."

"*Orange?*"

"He's gone—"

"*What?*"

"No time. So's the pig. The subject's on his way out; he's in a red-and-blue uniform. Follow him. He's gone over the edge. Call me at my room, I'll be there."

As if in a daze, Evan crossed the Wadi Al Ahd and went directly to the line of shrubbery where he had thrown the plastic shopping bag. Whether it was there or not did not really matter; it was simply that he would feel more comfortable, certainly be able to move more quickly and be less of a target now in the clothes from Masqat. Regardless, he had gone this far; he could not turn back. *Only one man,* he kept repeating to himself. If he could find him within the parameters of the meeting ground—the *Mahdi*! He *had* to find him!

The shopping bag was where he had left it, and the shadows of the shrubbery were adequate for his purpose. Crouching in the deepest bushes, he slowly, article by article, changed clothes. He walked out on the pavement and started west toward the Shaikh Isa Road and the Juma Mosque.

"*Itklem,*" said Yaakov into the radio while lying on the bed in his unsullied room, towels wrapped tightly around his wounds, warm and lukewarm wet washcloths scattered about the spread.

"It's *G,*" said code Gray. "How bad are you?"

"Cuts, mainly. Some loss of blood. I'll make it."

"Then you agree that until you do, I take over?"

"That's the line."

"I wanted to hear it from you."

"You've heard it."

"I've got to hear something else. With the pig eliminated, do you want us to abort and head back to Masqat? I can force it if your answer's yes."

Yaakov stared at the ceiling, the conflicts raging inside him, the scathing words of the American still scalding his ears. "No," he said haltingly. "He came too far, he risks too much. Stay with him."

"About *W.* I'd like to leave him behind. With you, perhaps—"

"He'd never permit it. That's his 'son' out there, remember?"

"You're right, forget it. I might add he's impossible."

"Tell me something I don't know—"

"I will," interrupted code Gray. "The subject dropped the uniform and has just passed us across the street. *W* spotted him. He's walking like a dead man."

"He probably is."

"Out."

Kendrick changed his mind and his route to the Juma. Instinct told him to stay with crowds on his way to the mosque. After he turned north on the wide Bab Al Bahrain, he would head right at the huge Bab Al Square into the Al Khalifa Road. Thoughts bombarded him, but they were scattered, unconnected, unclear. He was walking into a labyrinth, he knew that, but he also knew that within that maze there would be a man or men watching, waiting for the dead Azra to appear. That was his only advantage, but it was considerable. He knew who and what they were looking for, but they did not know him. He would circle the rendezvous like an earthbound hawk until he saw *someone,* the right *kind* of someone, who understood he could lose his life if he failed to bring the crown prince of terrorists to the Mahdi. That man would betray himself, perhaps even stop people to stare into their faces, anxiety growing with each passing minute. Evan would find that someone and isolate him—take him and *break* him. . . . Or was he deluding himself, his obsession blinding him? It did not matter any longer, nothing mattered, only one step after another on the hard pavement, weaving his way through the night crowds of Bahrain.

The crowds. He *sensed* it. Men were crowding around *him.* A hand touched his shoulder! He spun around and lashed out his arm to break the grip. And suddenly he felt the sharp point of a needle entering his flesh somewhere near the base of his spine. Then there was darkness. Complete.

The telephone jarred Yaakov awake; he grabbed it. "*Yes?*"

"They've got the American!" said code Gray. "More to the point, they *exist*!"

"Where did it happen? *How?*"

"That doesn't matter; I don't know the streets anyway. What matters is we know where they've *taken* him!"

"You *what*? *How?* And don't tell me *that* doesn't matter!"

"Weingrass did it. *Damn,* it was Weingrass. He knew he couldn't take it any longer on foot, so he gave a delirious Arab *ten thousand dollars* for his broken-down taxi! That *al harmmee* will be drunk for six months! We piled in and followed the subject and saw the whole thing happen. *Damn,* it was *Weingrass*!"

"Control your homicidal tendencies," ordered Yaakov with an uncontrollable smile that vanished quickly. "Where is the subject—*shit!*—Kendrick being held?"

"In a building called the Sahalhuddin on Tujjar Road—"

"Who owns it?"

"Give us time, Blue. Give *Weingrass* time. He's calling in every debt that's owed him in Bahrain, and I'd hate to think what the Morals Commission in Jerusalem would say if we're tied in with him."

"*Answer* me!"

"Apparently six firms occupy the complex. It's a matter of narrowing them down—"

"Someone come and get me," commanded Yaakov.

"So you've found the Mahdi, Congressman," said the dark-skinned Arab in a pure white robe and a white silk headdress with a cluster of sapphires on the crown. They were in a large room with a domed ceiling covered with mosaic tiles; the windows were high and narrow, the furniture sparse and all in dark, burnished wood, the huge ebony desk more like an altar or a throne than a functional work surface. There was a mosquelike quality to the room, like the chambers of some high priest of a strange but powerful order in a land removed from the rest of the world. "Are you satisfied now?" continued the Mahdi from behind the desk. "Or possibly disappointed to find that I am a man like you—no, not like you or anyone else—but still a man."

"You're a *killer,* you son of a *bitch*!" Evan lurched from the thick straight-backed chair, only to be grabbed by two flanking guards and thrown back. "You *murdered* seventy-eight innocent people—men, women, and children screaming as the building collapsed on them! You're *filth*!"

"It was the start of a war, Kendrick. All wars have casualties not restricted to combatants. I submit that I won that very important battle—you disappeared for four years and during those years I made extraordinary progress, progress I might not have made with you here. Or with that abominable Jew, Weingrass, and his flatulent mouth."

"*Manny . . . ?* He kept talking about you, *warning* us!"

"I *silence* such mouths with a terribly swift sword! You may interpret that as a bullet in their heads. . . . But when I heard about you, I knew you'd come back because of that first battle four years ago. You led me, as they say, a merry chase until nine hours ago, *Amal Bahrudi.*"

"Oh?"

"The Soviets are not without men who prefer to be on additional payrolls. Bahrudi, the Euro-Arab, was killed several days ago in East Berlin. . . . Kendrick's name surfaces; a dead Arab with blue eyes and pronounced Occidental features is suddenly in Masqat—the equation was imaginative in the extreme, almost unbelievable, but it balanced. You must have had help, you're not that experienced in these matters."

Evan stared at the striking face with the high cheekbones and the fired eyes that gazed steadily back at him. "Your eyes," said Kendrick, shaking his head, pushing away the last effects of the drug administered to him in the street. "That flat mask of a face. I've seen you before."

"Of course you have, Evan. *Think.*" The Mahdi slowly removed his ghotra, revealing a head of tightly ringleted black hair salted with eruptions of gray. The high, smooth forehead was now emphasized by the dark arched eyebrows; it was the face of a man easily given to obsession, instantly summoning it for whatever purpose it served. "Do you find me in an Iraqi tent? Or perhaps on a podium in a certain Midwest armory?"

"Jesus *Christ*!" whispered Kendrick, the images coming into focus. "You came to see us in Basrah seven or eight years ago and told us you'd make us rich if we turned down the job. You said there were plans to break Iran, break the Shah, and you didn't want any updated airfields in Iraq."

"It *happened.* A true Islamic society."

"*Bullshit!* You must broker their oil fields by now. And you're as Islamic as my Scots grandfather. You're from Chicago—that's the Midwest armory—and you were thrown *out* of Chicago twenty years ago because even your own black constituency—which you bled dry—couldn't take your screaming, fascist *crap*! You took their millions and came over here to spread your garbage and make millions more. My *God,* Weingrass knew who the hell you were and he told you to *shove* it! He said you were *slime—two-bit* slime, if I remember correctly—and if you didn't get the hell out of that tent in Basrah, he'd *really* lose his temper and throw bleach in your face so he could say he only shot a *white* Nazi!"

"Weingrass is—or was—a Jew," said the Mahdi calmly. "He vilified me because the greatness he expected eluded him, but it had started to flower for me. The Jews hate success in anyone but their own kind. It's why they are the agitators of the world—"

"Who the hell are you kidding? He called you one rotten

Shvartzeh and it had nothing to do with whites or blacks or anything else! You're pus and hate, Al Falfa, or whatever you called yourself, and the color of your skin is irrelevant. . . . After Riyadh—that *very* important battle—how many others did you kill, did you *slaughter*?"

"Only what was called for in our holy war to maintain the purity of race, culture and belief in this part of the world." The lips of the Mahdi from Chicago, Illinois, formed a slow, cold smile.

"You goddamned fucking *hypocrite*!" shouted Kendrick. Unable to control himself, Evan again lunged out of the chair, his hands like two claws flying across the desk toward the robes of the killer-manipulator. Other hands reached him before he could touch the Mahdi; he was hurled to the floor, kicked simultaneously in his stomach and his spine. Coughing, he tried to get up; while on his knees the guard on the left gripped his hair, yanking back his head as the man on the right held a knife laterally across his throat.

"Your gestures are as pathetic as your words," said the Mahdi, rising from behind the desk. "We are well on our way to building a kingdom here and there's nothing the paralyzed West can do about it. We set people against people with forces they cannot control; we divide thoroughly and conquer completely without ourselves firing a shot. And you, Evan Kendrick, have been of great service to us. We have photographs of you taken at the airport when you flew in from Oman; also of your weapons, your false papers and your money belt, the last showing what appears to be hundreds of thousands of dollars. We have documented proof that you, an American congressman using the name of Amal Bahrudi, managed to get inside the embassy in Masqat, where you killed an eloquent gentle leader named Nassir and later a young freedom fighter called Azra—all during the days of precious truce agreed to by everyone. Were you an agent of your brutal government? How could it be otherwise? A wave of revulsion will spread over the so-called democracies—the fumbling warlike giant has done it again without regard for the lives of its own."

"*You—*" Evan leaped up, grabbing the wrist that held the knife, wrenching his head away from the hand that gripped his hair. He was struck in the back of the neck, pummeled again to the floor.

"The executions have been moved up," continued the Mahdi. "They will resume tomorrow morning—provoked by your insidious activities, which will be made public. Chaos and bloodshed will result, because of the rash, contemptible Americans, until a solution is found, our solution—*my* solution. But none of this will concern you, Congressman. You will have vanished from the face of the earth, thanks no doubt to your terribly embarrassed government, which is not above punishing traceable failure while issuing feverish denials. There'll be no *corpus delicti,* no inkling of your whereabouts whatsoever. Tomorrow, with first light, you'll be flown out to sea, a bleeding, skinned pig strapped to your naked body, and dropped into the shark-infested shoals of Qatar."

15

"There's nothing *here*!" shouted Weingrass, standing and poring over the papers on the table in the dining room of a Bahrainian official he had known since the Kendrick Group had built an island country club on the archipelago years before. "After all I did for you, Hassan, all the little and not so little fees I passed your way, *this* is what you give me?"

"More is coming, Emmanuel," replied the nervous Arab, nervous because Weingrass's words were heard by Ben-Ami and the four commandos sitting twenty feet away in the Westernized living room on the outskirts of the city. A doctor had been summoned to suture and bandage Yaakov, who refused to lie down; instead, he sat up in an armchair. The man named Hassan glanced at him, mentioning, if only to change the subject of his past with the old architect: "The boy doesn't look well, Manny."

"He gets in scraps, what can I tell you? Someone tried to steal his roller skates. What's coming and when? These are companies, and the products or services they sell. I have to see names, *people*!"

"That's what's coming. It's not easy to convince the Minister of Industrial Regulations to leave his house at two o'clock in the morning and go down to his office to commit an illegal act."

"Industrial and regulations in Bahrain are mutually exclusive words."

"Those are secret papers!"

"A Bahrainian imperative."

"That's not *true,* Manny!"

"Oh, shut up and get me a whisky."

"You're *incorrigible,* my old friend."

"Tell me about it." The voice of code Gray drifted out from the living room. He had returned from the telephone, which he had been using with permission but without being questioned every fifteen minutes.

"May I get you something, gentlemen?" asked Hassan, walking through the dining room arch.

"The cardamom coffee is more than sufficient," answered the older Ben-Ami. "It's also delicious."

"There are spirits, if you wish—as, of course, you've just gathered from Mr. Weingrass. This is a religious house but we do not impose our beliefs on others."

"Would you put that in writing, sir?" said code Black, chuckling. "I'll deliver it to my wife and tell her you're a mullah. I have to go across the city to have bacon with my eggs."

"Thank you, but no spirits, Mr. Hassan," added Gray, slapping Black's knee. "With luck we'll have work to do tonight."

"With greater luck my hands will not be cut off," said the Arab quietly, heading toward the kitchen. He stopped, interrupted by the sound of the front-door chimes. The high-placed courier had arrived.

Forty-eight minutes later, with computer printouts scattered over the dining room table, Weingrass studied two specific pages, going back and forth from one to the other. "Tell me about this Zareeba, Limited."

"The name comes from the Sudanese language," replied the robed official, who had refused to be introduced to anyone. "Roughly, it translates as a protected encampment surrounded by rock or dense foliage."

"The Sudan . . . ?"

"It's a nation in Africa—"

"I *know* what it is. Khartoum."

"That's the capital—"

"Heavens, I thought it was Buffalo!" interrupted Weingrass curtly. "How come they list so many subsidiaries?"

"It's a holding company; their interests are extensive. If a company wishes government licenses for multiple export and import, they're more easily expedited by the corporate umbrella of a very solid firm."

"Horseshit."

"I beg your pardon?"

"It's Bronx for 'Oh, good gracious.' Who runs it?"

"There's a board of directors—"

"There's always a board of directors. I asked you who runs it."

"No one really knows, frankly. The chief executive officer is an amiable fellow—I've had coffee with him—but he doesn't appear to be a particularly aggressive man, if you know what I mean."

"So there's someone else."

"I wouldn't know—"

"Where's the list of directors?"

"Right in front of you. It's beneath the page on your right."

Weingrass lifted the page and picked up the one underneath. For the first time in two hours he sat down in a chair, his eyes roaming the list of names over and over again. "*Zareeba . . . Khartoum,*" he kept saying quietly, every now and then shutting his eyes tightly, his lined face wrinkled by repeated grimaces, as if he were trying desperately to recall something he had forgotten. Finally, he picked up a pencil and circled a name; then pushed the page across the table to the still-standing, rigid Bahrainian official.

"He's a black man," said the high-placed courier.

"Who's white and who's black over here?"

"One tells by the features usually. Of course, centuries of Afro-Arab intermingling often obscure the issue."

"Is it an issue?"

"To some, not most."

"Where did he come from?"

"If he's an immigrant, his country of origin is listed there."

"It says 'concealed.' "

"That generally means the person has fled from an authoritarian regime, usually Fascist or Communist. We protect such people if they contribute to our society. Obviously, he does."

"*Sahibe al Farrahkhaliffe,*" said Weingrass, emphasizing each part of the name. "What nationality is that?"

"I've no idea. Part African, obviously; part Arab, more obviously. It's consistent."

"*Wrongo,* Buster!" exclaimed Manny, startling everyone in both rooms. "It's pure American alias-*fraud*! If this is who I think he is, he's a black son of a bitch from Chicago who got heaved out by his own *people*! They got crapped on because he'd banked their money—some twenty *million,* incidentally—in accommodating banks on this side of the Atlantic. Some eighteen, twenty years ago he was a steamrolling, fire-and-brimstone fanatic called Al Farrah—his fucking ego wouldn't let him drop that part of his past, the hallelujah-chorus part. We knew the big gloxinia was on the board of directors of some fat corporation but we didn't know which one. Besides, we were looking in the wrong direction. Khartoum? *Hell!* South Side *Chicago*! Here's your *Mahdi.*"

"Are you *certain*?" asked Hassan, standing in the archway. "The accusation is inflammatory!"

"I'm certain," said Weingrass quietly. "I should have shot the bastard in that tent in Basrah."

"I beg your pardon?" The Bahrainian official was visibly shaken.

"Never mind—"

"No one has left the Sahalhuddin building!" said code Gray, walking forward into the archway.

"You're sure?"

"I paid a taxi driver who was very willing to accept a considerable sum of money with a great deal more to come if he did my bidding. I call him every few minutes at a public phone. Their two cars are still there."

"Can you trust him?" asked Yaakov from the chair.

"I have his name and license number."

"Doesn't mean a damn thing!" protested Manny.

"I told him that if he lied, I'd find him and kill him."

"I withdraw the statement, Tinker Bell."

"*Will* you—"

"Shut up. What part of the Sahalhuddin does the Zareeba company occupy?"

"The top two floors, if I'm not mistaken. The lower floors are leased by its subsidiaries. Zareeba owns the building."

"Convenient," said Weingrass. "Can you get us the updated structural plans, including the fire and security systems? I read those things pretty well."

"At *this* hour?" cried the official. "It's after three o'clock in the morning! I wouldn't know *how*—"

"Try a million dollars, American," broke in Manny softly. "I'll send it from Paris. My word."

"*What?*"

"Split it up any way you like. That's my *son* in there. *Get* them."

The small room was dark, the only light the white rays of the moon shining through a window high up on the wall—too high to reach, for there was no furniture except a low-slung cot with ripped canvas. A guard had left him a bottle of *seeber-too ah-byahd,* a numbing local whisky, suggesting that what faced him was better faced in a drunken stupor. He was tempted; he was frightened, the fear consuming him, causing him to sweat to the point where his shirt was drenched, his hair soaking wet. What stopped him from uncorking the bottle and draining it was the remnants of anger—and one last act he would perform. He would fight with all the violence he could summon, hoping, perhaps, in the back of his mind for a bullet that would end everything quickly.

Christ, why did he ever think he could do it? What possessed him to believe that he was qualified to do what far more experienced people thought was suicidal? Of course, the question was the answer: he *was* possessed. The hot winds of hate were burning him up; had he not tried they would have burned him out. And he had not failed entirely; he had lost his life but only because he had achieved a measure of success. He had *proved* the existence of the Mahdi! He had hacked a trail through the dense jungle of deceit and manipulation. Others would follow; there was comfort in that.

He looked at the bottle again, at the white liquid that would put him out of it. Unconsciously, he shook his head slowly back and forth. The Mahdi had said his gestures were as pathetic as his words. Neither would be pathetic on that plane flying over the shoals of Qatar.

Each soldier of the Masada Brigade had understood from the beginning and each checked the plastic tape around his left wrist to make certain the cyanide capsule was in its small exposed bubble. None carried papers or any traces of identification; their "working" clothes down to the shoes on their feet and the cheap shell buttons on their trousers were all purchased by Mossad agents in Benghazi, Libya, the core center of terrorist recruitment. In these days of injected chemicals, the amphetamines and the scopolamines, no member of the Masada unit could permit himself to be captured alive where his actions could be even remotely connected to the events in Oman. Israel could not afford being held responsible for the slaughter of two hundred thirty-six American hostages, and the specter of Israeli interference was to be avoided even at the cost of the unholy suicide of each man sent to Southwest Asia. Each understood; each had held out his wrist at the airfield in Hebron for the doctor to secure the ribbed plastic tape. Each had watched as the doctor swiftly brought his left hand to his mouth where hard teeth and the soft rounded bubble met. A quick puncture brought death.

The Tujjar was deserted, the street and lamps muted by pockets of mist drifting in from the Persian Gulf. The building known as the Sahalhuddin was dark except for several lighted offices on the top floor and, five stories below, the dull wash of the foyer neons beyond the glass entrance doors where a bored man sat at a desk reading a newspaper. A small blue sedan and a black limousine were parked at the curb. Two uniformed private guards stood casually in front of the doors, which meant that there was probably security at the rear of the building as well. There was: a single man. Codes Gray, Black and Red returned to the broken-down taxi two hundred yards west at the corner of Al Mothanna Road. Inside, in the backseat, was the wounded Yaakov; in front, Ben-Ami and Emmanuel Weingrass, the latter still studying under the dashboard lights the structural plans of the building. Code Gray delivered the information through an open window; Yaakov issued their instructions.

"You, Black and Red, take out the guards and get inside. Gray, you follow with Ben-Ami and cut the wires—"

"Hold it, Eagle Scout!" said Weingrass, turning in the front seat. "This Mossad relic sitting beside me doesn't know a damn thing about alarm systems except probably how to set 'em off."

"That's not quite true, Manny," protested Ben-Ami.

"You're going to trace precoded wires where they've been altered on purpose, leading to dummy receptacles just for people like you? You'd start an Italian festival down here! I'm going with them."

"*Mr. Weingrass,*" pressed code Blue from the backseat. "Suppose you begin coughing—have one of the attacks we've all sadly observed."

"I won't," answered the architect simply. "I told you, that's my son in there."

"I believe him," said Gray at the window. "And I'm the one who pays for it if I'm wrong."

"You're coming around, Tinker Bell."

"Will you *please*—"

"Oh, shut up. Let's go."

If there had been a disinterested observer in the Tujjar at that hour, the following minutes would have appeared like the intricate movements of a large clock, each serrated wheel turning another, which, in turn, sent motion back into the frenzied momentum of the mechanism, no cog, however, flying out of sequence or making a false move.

Codes Red and Black removed the two private guards in front before either knew there was a hostile presence within a hundred meters of him. Red took off his jacket, squeezed into the tunic of one of the guards, buttoned it, put on the visored cap, pulled it down, and quickly ran back to the glass doors, where he tapped lightly, holding his backside with his left hand, pleading in the shadows with humorous gestures to be permitted inside to relieve himself. Frustrated bowels are a universal calamity; the man inside laughed, put down the newspaper, and pressed a button on the desk. The buzzer was activated; codes Red and Black raced inside, and before the all-night receptionist understood the mistake he had made, he was unconscious on the marble floor. Code Gray followed, dragging a limp guard through the left door, which he caught before it swung shut, and behind him was Emmanuel Weingrass carrying Red's discarded jacket. On cue, code Black ran outside for the second guard as Weingrass held the door. All inside, codes Red and Gray bound and gagged the three security personnel behind the wide reception desk while Black took a long capped syringe from his pocket; he removed the plastic casing, checked the contents level, and injected each unconscious Arab at the base of the neck. The three commandos then pulled the three immobile employees of the Sahalhuddin to the farthest reaches of the enormous foyer.

"Get out of the *light*!" whispered Red, the command directed at Weingrass. "Go into the hall by the elevators!"

"What . . . ?"

"I hear something outside!"

"You *do*?"

"Two or three people, perhaps. *Quickly!*"

Silence. And beyond the thick glass doors, two obviously drunken Americans weaved down the pavement, the words of a familiar melody more softly spoken than sung. *To the tables down at Mory's, to the place we love so well . . .*

"Son of a bitch, you *heard* them?" asked Weingrass, impressed.

"Go to the rear," said Gray to Black. "Do you know the way?"

"I read the plans—of course I do. I'll wait for your signal and take out the last one. My magic elixir is still half full." Code Black disappeared into a south corridor as Gray raced across the

Sahalhuddin's lobby; Weingrass was now in front of him heading for a steel door that led to the basement of the building.

"*Shit!*" cried Manny. "It's locked!"

"To be expected," said Gray, pulling a small black box from his pocket and opening it. "It's not a problem." The commando removed a puttylike gel from the box, pressed it around the lock and inserted a one-inch string fuse. "Stand back, please. It won't explode, but the heat is intense."

Weingrass watched in amazement as the gel first became bright red upon firing, then the bluest blue he had ever seen. The steel melted before his eyes and the entire lock mechanism fell away. "You're *something,* Tinker—"

"Don't *say* it!"

"Let's go," agreed Manny. They found the security system; it was contained in a huge steel panel at the north end of the Sahalhuddin's underground complex. "It's an upgraded Guardian," pronounced the architect, taking a pair of wire cutters from his left pocket. "There are two false receptacles for every six leads—each lead covering fifteen to twenty thousand square feet of possible entry—which, considering the size of the structure, means probably no more than eighteen wires."

"Eighteen wires," repeated Gray hesitantly. "That means six false receptacles—"

"That's it, Tinker—forget it."

"Thank you."

"We cut one of those, we get a rock-*muchacha* band blaring in the street."

"How can you tell? You said the precoded wires were altered—for amateurs like Ben-Ami. How *can* you tell?"

"Mechanics' courtesy, my friend. The slob Joes who work on this stuff hate like hell to read diagrams, so they make it easier for themselves or others who have to service the systems. On every false wire they make a mark, usually with pincer pliers high up toward the main terminal. That way they call in after fixing the system and say they spent an hour tracing the falsies because the diagrams weren't clear—they never are."

"Suppose you're wrong, Mr. Weingrass? Suppose that here there was an honest 'mechanic'?"

"Impossible. There aren't enough of them around," replied Manny, taking a small flashlight and a chisel out of his right pocket. "Come on, pry off the panel; we've got roughly eighty to ninety seconds to snip off twelve leads. Can you imagine? That cheap bastard, Hassan, said these batteries are weak. Go *on*!"

"I can use *plastique,*" said code Gray.

"And with that heat set off every alarm in the place, including the sprinkler system? *Meshuga!* I'm sending you back to *shul.*"

"You're making me *very* upset, Mr.—"

"Shut up. Do your job, I'll get you a badge." The architect handed code Gray the chisel he had taken from Hassan, knowing from the plans of the Sahalhuddin's security it would be necessary. "Do it quickly; these things are sensitive."

The commando jammed the chisel below the panel's lock and with the strength of three normal men pressed forward, snapping the panel open. "Give me the torch!" said the Israeli. "You find the wires!"

One by anxious one Emmanuel Weingrass moved from right to left, the beam of light on each colored wire. *Eight, nine, ten . . . eleven.* "Where's *twelve*?" yelled Manny. "I caught every false lead! There has to be one *more*! Without it they'll all trigger *off*!"

"*Here.* There's a mark here!" cried code Gray, touching the seventh wire. "It's next to the third false lead. You *missed* it!"

"I *got* it!" Weingrass suddenly collapsed in a fit of coughing; he doubled over on the floor straining beyond his endurance to stop the seizure.

"Go ahead, Mr. Weingrass," said Gray gently, touching the old man's thin shoulder. "Let it out. No one can hear you."

"I promised I *wouldn't*—"

"There are promises beyond our control of keeping, sir."

"Stop being so fucking *polite*!" Manny coughed out his last spasm and awkwardly, painfully got to his feet. The commando purposely did not offer assistance. "Okay, soldier-boy," said Weingrass, breathing deeply. "The place is secure—from our point of view. Let's find my boy."

Code Gray held his place. "Despite your less than generous personality, sir, I respect you," said the Israeli. "And for all our sakes, I can't permit you to accompany us."

"You *what*?"

"We don't know what's on the upper floors—"

"*I* do, you son of a bitch! My *boy's* up there! . . . Give me a gun, Tinker Bell, or I'll send a telegram to Israel's Defense Minister telling him you own a *pig* farm!" Weingrass suddenly kicked the commando in the shins.

"Incorrigible!" muttered code Gray without moving his leg. "*Impossible!*"

"Come on, *bubbelah.* A little gun. I know you've got one."

"Please don't use it unless I tell you to," said the commando, lifting his left trouser leg and reaching down for the small revolver strapped behind his knee.

"Actually, I never told you I was part of the Haganah?"

"The *Haganah*?"

"Sure. Me and Menachem had a lot of rough-and-tumbles—"

"Menachem was never part of the *Haganah*—"

"Must have been some other baldheaded fellow. Come on, let's go!"

Ben-Ami, the Uzi gripped in his hands in the shadows of the Sahalhuddin's entrance, kept in touch by radio. "But why is he *with* you?" asked the Mossad agent.

"Because he's impossible!" replied the irritated voice of code Gray.

"That's *not* an answer!" insisted Ben-Ami.

"I have no other. *Out.* We've reached the sixth floor. I'll contact you when it's feasible."

"Understood."

Two of the commandos flanked the wide double doors on the right of the landing; the third stood at the other end of the hall, outside the only other door with light showing through the crack below. Emmanuel Weingrass reluctantly remained on the marble staircase; his anxiety provoked rumblings in his chest but his resolve suppressed them.

"*Now!*" whispered code Gray, and both men crashed the door open with their shoulders, instantly dropping to the floor as two robed Arabs at each end of the room turned, firing their repeating weapons. They were no match for the Uzis; both fell with two bursts from the Israeli machine pistols. A third and a fourth man started to run, one in white robes from behind the enormous ebony desk, the other from the left side.

"*Stop!*" yelled code Gray. "Or you're both *dead*!"

The dark-skinned man in the robes of a lavish aba stood motionless, his glowering eyes riveted on the Israeli. "Have you any idea what you've *done*?" he asked in a low, threatening voice. "The security in this building is the finest in Bahrain. The authorities will be here in minutes. You will lay down your weapons or you will be *killed.*"

"Hello there, *garbage*!" yelled Emmanuel Weingrass, walking into the room with effort as old men do when their legs do not work as well as they once did, especially after a great deal of excitement. "The system's not that good, not when you've subcontracted five or six hundred."

"You!"

"Who else? I should have blown you away years ago in Basrah. But I knew my boy would come back to find you, you *scum* of the earth. It was just a matter of time. Where *is* he?"

"My life for his."

"You're in no position to bargain—"

"Perhaps I *am,*" broke in the Mahdi. "He's on his way to an unmarked airfield where a plane will fly him out to sea. Destination—the shoals of Qatar."

"The *sharks,*" said Weingrass quietly, in cold fury.

"Ever so. One of nature's conveniences. Now, do we bargain? Only I can stop them."

The old architect, his frail body trembling as he breathed deeply, stared at the tall, robed black man, his voice strained as he replied. "We bargain," he said. "And by almighty God you'd better deliver or I'll hunt you down with an army of mercenaries."

"You were always such a melodramatic Jew, weren't you?" The Mahdi glanced at his watch. "There's time. As is the custom on such flights, there can be no ground-to-air radio contact, no subsequent forensic examinations of a plane. They're scheduled to take off with first light. Once outside I'll place the call; the aircraft will not leave, but you and your little army of whatever-they-are will."

"Don't even think about any tricks, you scumball. . . . We deal."

"No!" Code Gray whipped out his knife and lunged at the Mahdi, gripping his robes and throwing him over the desk. "There are *no* bargains, no *deals,* no negotiations *whatsoever.* There's only your life at this moment!" Gray shoved the point of his blade into the flesh below the Chicagoan's left eye. The Mahdi screamed as the blood rolled down his cheek and into his open mouth. "Make your call *now* or lose first *this* eye, then the *other*! After that it won't matter to you where my knife goes next; you won't see it." The commando reached over, grabbed the phone on the desk and slammed it down beside the bleeding head. "That's your bargain, *scum*! Give me the number. I'll dial it for you—just to make sure it's an airfield and not some private barracks. *Give* it to me!"

"No—no, I *can't*!"

"The blade goes in!"

"No, *stop*! There is no airfield, no plane!"

"Liar!"

"Not *now. Later!*"

"Lose your first eye, *liar*!"

"He's here! My God, *stop*! He's *here*!"

"Where?" roared Manny, rushing up to the desk.

"The west wing . . . there's a staircase in the hall on the right, a small storage area below the roof—"

Emmanuel Weingrass did not hear any more. He raced out of the room, screaming with all the breath that was in him. "Evan! *Evan . . . !*"

He was hallucinating, thought Kendrick; a person dear to him from the past was calling to him, giving him courage. The singular privilege of a condemned man, he considered. He looked up from the cot at the window; the moon was moving away, its light fading. He would not see another moon. Soon there would be nothing but darkness.

"Evan! *Evan!*"

It was so like Manny. He had always been there when his young friend needed him. And here at the end he was there to give comfort. *Oh, Lord, Manny, I hope you learn somehow that I came back! That finally I listened to you. I found him, Manny! Others will, too, I know it! Please be a little proud of me—*

"Goddamnit, Kendrick! Where the hell *are* you?"

That voice was no hallucination! Nor were the pounding footsteps on the narrow staircase! And *other* footsteps! Jesus *Christ,* was he already *dead*? "Manny . . . ? *Manny?*" he screamed.

"Here it is! This is the room! Break it *down,* musclehead!"

The door of the small room crashed open like a deafening crack of thunder.

"Goddamn, boy!" cried Emmanuel Weingrass, seeing Kendrick stagger up from his cell cot. "Is *this* any way for a respectable congressman to behave? I thought I *taught* you better!"

Tears in their eyes, father and son embraced.

They were all in Hassan's Westernized living room on the outskirts of the city. Ben-Ami had monopolized the telephone since Weingrass relinquished it after a lengthy call to Masqat and a spirited conversation with the young sultan, Ahmat. Fifteen feet away, around the large dining room table sat seven officials representing the governments of Bahrain, Oman, France, the

United Kingdom, West Germany, Israel and the Palestine Liberation Organization. As agreed, there was no representative from Washington, but there was nothing to fear in terms of America's clandestine interests where a certain congressman was concerned. Emmanuel Weingrass was at that table, sitting between the Israeli and the man from the PLO.

Evan was next to the wounded Yaakov, both in armchairs beside each other, a courtesy for the two most in pain. Code Blue spoke. "I listened to your words at the Aradous," he said softly. "I've been thinking about them."

"That's all I ask you to do."

"It's hard, Kendrick. We've been through so much, not *me,* of course, but our fathers and mothers, grandfathers and grandmothers—"

"And generations before them," added Evan. "No one with a grain of intelligence or sensitivity denies it. But in a way, so have *they.* The Palestinians weren't responsible for the pogroms or the Holocaust, but because the free world was filled with guilt—as it damn well *should* have been—they became the new victims without knowing why."

"I know." Yaakov nodded his head slowly. "I've heard the zealots in the West Bank and the Gaza. I've listened to the Meir Kahanes and they frighten me so—"

"Frighten you?"

"Of course. They use the words that were used against us for, as you say, generations. . . . Yet still, they *kill*! They killed my two brothers and so many countless others!"

"It's got to stop sometime. It's all such a terrible waste."

"I have to think."

"It's a beginning."

The men around the dining room table abruptly rose from their chairs. They nodded to one another and, one by one, walked through the living room to the front door and out to their staff cars without acknowledging the presence of anyone else in the house. The host, Hassan, came through the archway and addressed his last guests. At first it was difficult to hear his words, as Emmanuel Weingrass was doubled up with a coughing seizure in the dining room. Evan started to rise. Yaakov, shaking his head, gripped Kendrick's arm. Evan understood; he nodded and sat back.

"The American embassy in Masqat will be relieved in three hours, the terrorists granted safe escort to a ship on the waterfront provided by Sahibe al Farrahkhaliffe."

"What happens to *him*?" asked Kendrick angrily.

"In this room, and *only* in this room, will that answer be given. I am instructed by the Royal House to inform you that it is to go no further. Is that understood and accepted?"

All heads nodded.

"Sahibe al Farrahkhaliffe, known to you as the Mahdi, will be executed without trial or sentence, for his crimes against humanity are so outrageous they do not deserve the dignity of jurisprudence. As the Americans say, we'll do it 'our way.' "

"May I speak?" said Ben-Ami.

"Of course," answered Hassan.

"Arrangements have been made for me and my colleagues to be flown back to Israel. Since none of us has passports or papers, a special plane and procedures have been provided by the Emir. We must be at the airport concourse within the hour. Forgive us for our abrupt departure. Come along, gentlemen."

"Forgive *us,*" said Hassan, nodding. "For not having the wherewithal to thank you."

"Have you got any whisky?" asked code Red.

"Anything you wish."

"Anything you can part with. It's a long, terrible trip back and I *hate* flying. It frightens me."

Evan Kendrick and Emmanuel Weingrass sat next to each other in the armchairs in Hassan's living room. They waited for their instructions from a harried, bewildered American ambassador, who was permitted to make contact only by telephone. It was as though the two old friends had never been apart—the ofttimes bewildered student and the strident teacher. Yet the student was the leader, the shaker; and the teacher understood.

"Ahmat must be up in space with relief," said Evan, drinking brandy.

"A couple of things are keeping him grounded."

"Oh?"

"Seems there's a group that wanted to get rid of him, send him back to the States because they thought he was too young and inexperienced to handle things. He called them his arrogant merchant princes. He's bringing them to the palace to straighten them out."

"That's one item. What else?"

"There's another bunch who wanted to take things in their own hands, blow up the embassy if they had to, anything to get their country back. They're machine-gun nuts; they're also the ones who were recruited by Cons Op to get you out of the airport."

"What's he going to do about them?"

"Not a hell of a lot unless you want your name shouted from the minarets. If he calls them in, they'll scream State Department connections and all the crazies in the Middle East will have another cause."

"Ahmat knows better. Let them alone."

"There's a last item, and he's got to do it for himself. He's got to blow that boat out of the water, and kill every one of those filthy bastards."

"*No,* Manny, that's not the way. The killing will just go on and on—"

"Wrong!" shouted Weingrass. "You're *wrong*! Examples must be made over and *over* again until they all learn the price they have to pay!" Suddenly the old architect was seized by a prolonged, echoing, rattling cough that came from the deepest, rawest cavities of his chest. His face reddened and the veins in his neck and forehead were blue and distended.

Evan gripped his old friend's shoulder to steady him. "We'll talk about it later," he said as the coughing subsided. "I want you to come back with me, Manny."

"Because of *this*?" Weingrass shook his head defensively. "It's just a chest cold. Lousy weather in France, that's all."

"I wasn't thinking of that," lied Kendrick, he hoped convincingly. "I need you."

"What for?"

"I may be going into several projects and I want your advice." It was another lie, a weaker one, so he added quickly, "Also my house has to be remodeled completely."

"I thought you just built it."

"I was involved with other things and wasn't paying attention. The design's terrible; I can't see half the things I was supposed to see, the mountains and the lakes."

"You never were any damned good reading exterior schematics."

"I need you. Please."

"I have business in Paris. I've got to send out money, I gave my word."

"Send mine."

"Like a million?"

"Ten, if you like. I'm here and not in some shark's stomach. . . . I'm not going to beg you, Manny, but please, I really *do* need you."

"Well, maybe for a week or two," said the irascible old man. "They need me in Paris, too, you know."

"Grosses will drop all over the city, I know *that,*" replied Evan softly, relieved.

"What?"

Fortunately the telephone rang, preventing Kendrick from having to repeat his statement. Their instructions had arrived.

"I'm the man you never met, never spoke to," said Evan into the pay phone at Andrews Air Force Base in Virginia. "I'm heading out to the white water and the mountains, where I've been for the past five days. Is that understood?"

"Understood," answered Frank Swann, deputy director of the State Department's Consular Operations. "I won't even try to thank you."

"Don't."

"I can't. I don't even know your name."

Ultra Maximum Secure
No Existing Intercepts
Proceed

The figure sat hunched over the keyboard, his eyes alive, his mind alert, though his body was racked with exhaustion. He kept breathing deeply as if each breath would keep his brain functioning. He had not slept for nearly forty-eight hours, waiting for developments out of Bahrain. There had been a blackout, a suspension of communications . . . silence. The small circle of need-to-know personnel at the State Department and the Central Intelligence Agency may now themselves be breathing deeply, he considered, but not before. Instead, they had been holding their collective breath. Bahrain represented the irreversible, hard edge of finality, the ending unclear. Not any longer. It was over, the subject airborne. He had won. The figure proceeded to type.

Our man has done it. My appliances are ecstatic, for although they refused to commit themselves, they indicated that he could succeed. In their inanimate way they saw my vision.

The subject arrived here this morning under deep cover thinking that everything is finished, that his life will return to its abnormal normalcy, but he is wrong. Everything is in place, the record written. The means must be found and they will be found. Lightning will strike and he will be the bolt that changes a nation. For him it is only the beginning.

BOOK TWO

Ultra Maximum Secure
No Existing Intercepts
Proceed

The means have been found! As in the ancient Vedic scriptures, a god of fire has arrived as a messenger to the people. He has made himself known to me and I to him. The Oman file is now completed. Everything! And I have obtained everything through access and penetration and I have given everything to him. He's a remarkable man, as I realistically believe I am, and he has a dedication that matches my own.

With the file completed and entered in its entirety, this journal is finished. Another is about to begin.

16

One year later.
Sunday, August 20, 8:30 P.M.

One by one, like quiet, graceful chariots, the five limousines had deposited their owners in front of the marble steps leading to the pillared entrance of the estate on the banks of Chesapeake Bay. The arrivals were erratically spaced so that no sense of urgency was conveyed to suddenly curious onlookers, either on the highway or through the streets of the wealthy village in Maryland's Eastern Shore. It was merely another subdued social gathering of the immensely rich, a common sight in this enclave of financial power brokers. A prosperous local banker might glance out of his window and see the glistening limousines roll by and wish he were privileged to hear the men talk over their brandy or billiards, but that was the extent of his ruminations.

The immensely rich were generous to their exurban environs and the townspeople were richer for them. Crumbs from their tables provided frequent bonuses: there were the armies of domestic and gardening help whose relatives swelled the payrolls with never a complaint from the owners as long as the estates were shipshape for their return from London, Paris or Gstaad. And for those on the upward scale of professions, there was the occasional stock tip over a friendly drink at the commercially quaint tavern in the center of the town. The bankers, the merchants and the perpetually awed residents were fond of their lairds; they guarded the privacy of these distinguished men and women with quiet firmness. And if guarding their privacy meant bending a few laws now and then, it was a small price to pay, and in a sense even moral when one considered how the gossip peddlers and the scandal sheets twisted everything all out of proportion to sell their newspapers and magazines. The ordinary man in the street could get roaring drunk, or have a bloody fight with his wife or his neighbor, or even be in a car accident, and no one took grotesque photographs of him to splatter all over the tabloids. Why were the rich singled out to provide lurid reading for people without an iota of their talents? The rich *were* different. They provided jobs and gave generously to charity drives and often made life just a little bit easier for those they came in contact with, so why should they be persecuted?

So went the townspeople's logic. It was a small accommodation for the local police to keep the blotters cleaner than they might be; it made for harmonious relations. It also made for a number of well-kept secrets in this privileged enclave where the estate on Chesapeake Bay was located.

But secrecy is relative. One man's secret is another's joke; a certain government file marked "classified" has more often than not appeared in public print; and a prominent cabinet member's sexual appetites are confidential fundamentally in terms of his wife finding out, as are hers regarding him. "Cross my heart and hope to die" is a promise made by children of all ages who fail to keep their word, but where extraordinary death is concerned the circle of secrecy must be impenetrable. As it was this night when the five limousines passed through the village of Cynwid Hollow on their way to Chesapeake Bay.

Inside the immense house, in the wing nearest the water, the high-ceilinged library was ornately masculine. Leather and burnished wood predominated, while cathedral windows overlooked the sculptured grounds outside illuminated by floodlights, and seven-foot-high bookshelves formed an imposing wall of knowledge wherever space allowed. Armchairs of soft brown leather, floor lamps at their sides, flanked the windows; a wide cherrywood desk stood at the far right corner of the room, a high-backed swivel chair of black leather behind it. Completing the typical aspects of such a room was a large circular table in the center, a meeting ground for conferences best held in the security of the countryside.

With these items and this ambience, however, ordinary appearances came to an end, and the unusual, if not the strange, became apparent. On the surface of the table, in front of each place, was a brass lamp, its light directed down on a yellow legal pad that was part of the setting. It was as if the small, sharp circles of light made it easier for those at the table to rivet their concentration on whatever notes they made without the distraction of fully illuminated faces—and eyes—of those next to them or across from them. For there were no other lights on in the room; faces moved in and out of shadows, expressions discernible but not for lengthy examination. At the west end of the library, attached to the upper wall molding above the bookshelves, was a long black tube that, when electrically commanded, shot down a silver screen that descended halfway to the parquet floor, as it was now. It was for the benefit of another unusual piece of equipment, unusual because of its permanence.

Built into the east wall beyond and above the table and electronically pushed forward into view, as it was now, was a console of audiovisual components that included projectors for immediate and taped television, film, photographic slides and voice recordings. Through the technology of a periscoped remote-controlled disk on the roof, the sophisticated unit was capable of picking up satellite and shortwave transmissions from all over the globe. At the moment, a small red light glowed on the fourth lateral; a carousel of slide photographs had been inserted and was ready for operation.

All these accoutrements were certainly unusual for such a library even to the rich, for their inclusion took on another ambience—that of a strategy room far from the White House or the Pentagon or the sterile chambers of the National Security Agency. One pressed button and the world, past and current, was presented for scrutiny, judgments rendered in isolated chiaroscuro.

But at the far right corner of this extraordinary room was a curious anachronism. Standing by itself several feet away from the book-lined wall was an old Franklin stove, its flue rising to the ceiling. Beside it was a metal pail filled with coal. What was especially odd was that the stove was glowing despite the quiet whir of the central air conditioning necessitated by the warm, humid night on Chesapeake Bay.

That stove, however, was intrinsic to the conference about to take place on the shores of Cynwid Hollow. Everything written down was to be burned, the notepads as well, for nothing said among these people could be communicated to the world outside. It was a tradition born of international necessity. Governments could collapse, economies rise and fall on their words; wars could be precipitated or avoided on their decisions. They were the inheritors of the most powerful silent organization in the free world.

They were five.

And they were human.

"The President will be reelected by an overwhelming majority two years from this November," said the white-haired man with an aquiline aristocratic face at the head of the conference table. "We hardly needed our projections to determine this. He has the country in the palm of his hand, and short of catastrophic errors, which his more reasonable advisers will prevent, there's nothing anyone can do about it, ourselves included. Therefore we must prepare for the inevitable and have our man in place."

"A strange term, 'our man,' " commented a slender, balding seventy-odd-year-old with sunken cheeks and wide, gentle eyes, nodding his head. "We'll have to move quickly. And yet again things could change. The President is such a charming person, so attractive, so wanting to be liked—loved, I imagine."

"So shallow," broke in a broad-shouldered, middle-aged black, quietly, with no animosity in his voice, his impeccably tailored clothes signifying taste and wealth. "I have no ill feeling toward him personally, for his instincts are decent; he's a decent man, perhaps a good man. That's what the people see and they're probably right. No, it's not him. It's those mongrels behind him—so far behind he most likely doesn't know they exist except as campaign contributors."

"He doesn't," said the fourth member at the table, a rotund middle-aged man with a cherubic face and the impatient eyes of a scholar below a rumpled thatch of red hair; his elbow-patched tweed jacket labeled him an academic. "And I'll bet ten of my patents that some profound miscalculation will take place before his first term is over."

"You'd lose," said the fifth member at the table, an elderly woman with silver hair and dressed elegantly in a black silk dress with a minimum of jewelry. Her cultured voice was laced with those traces of inflection and cadence often described as Middle Atlantic. "Not because you underestimate him, which you do, but because he and those behind him will consolidate their growing consensus until he's politically invincible. The rhetoric will be slanted, but there won't be any profound decisions until his opposition is rendered damn near voiceless. In other words, they're saving their big guns for the second term."

"Then you agree with Jacob that we have to move quickly," said the white-haired Samuel Winters, nodding at the gaunt-faced Jacob Mandel on his right.

"Of course I do, Sam," replied Margaret Lowell, casually smoothing her hair, then suddenly leaning forward, her elbows firmly on the table, her hands clasped. It was an abruptly masculine movement in a very feminine woman, but none at the table noticed. Her mind was the focal point. "Realistically, I'm not sure we can move quickly enough," she said rapidly, quietly. "We may have to consider a more abrupt approach."

"*No,* Peg," broke in Eric Sundstrom, the red-haired scholar on Lowell's left. "Everything must be perfectly normal, befitting an upbeat administration that turns liabilities into assets. This *must* be our approach. Any deviation from the principle of natural evolution—nature being unpredictable—would send out intolerable alarms. That ill-informed consensus you mentioned would rally round the cause, inflamed by Gid's mongrels. We'd have a police state."

Gideon Logan nodded his large black head in agreement, a smile creasing his lips. "Oh, they'd stomp around the campfires, pulling in all the good-thinking people, and burn the asses off the body politic." He paused, looking at the woman across the table. "There are no shortcuts, Margaret. Eric's right about that."

"I wasn't talking melodrama," insisted Lowell. "No rifle shots in Dallas or deranged kids with hang-ups. I only meant time. Do we *have* the time?"

"If we use it correctly, we do," said Jacob Mandel. "The key factor is the candidate."

"Then let's get to him," interrupted the white-haired Samuel Winters. "As you all know, our colleague Mr. Varak has completed his search and is convinced he's come up with our man. I won't bore you with his many eliminations except to say that if there's not complete unanimity among us, we'll examine them—every one. He's studied our guidelines—the assets we seek and the liabilities we wish to avoid; in essence, the talents we're convinced must be there. In my judgment he's unearthed a brilliant, if totally unexpected, prospect. I won't talk for our friend—he does that very well for himself—but I'd be remiss if I did not state that in our numerous conferences he's shown the same dedication to us that his uncle, Anton Varak, was said to have given to our predecessors fifteen years ago." Winters paused, his penetrating gray eyes leveled in turn at each person around the table. "Perhaps it takes a European deprived of his liberties to understand us, understand the reasons for our being. We are the inheritors of Inver Brass, resurrected in death by those who came before us. We ourselves were to be selected by those men should their attorneys determine that our lives continued in the way they envisaged. When the sealed envelopes were given to each of us, each of us understood. There were no further advantages we sought from the society we live in, no benefits or positions coveted beyond those we already possess. Through whatever abilities we had, aided by luck, or inheritance, or the misfortune of others, we had reached a freedom granted to few in this terribly troubled world. But with this freedom comes a responsibility and we accept it, as did our predecessors years ago. It is to use our resources to make this a better country, and through that process hopefully a better world." Winters leaned back in the armchair, his palms upturned as he shook his head, his voice tentative, even questioning. "Lord knows, no one elected us, no one anointed us in the name of divine grace, and certainly no bolts of lightning struck down from the heavens revealing any Olympian message, but we do what we do because we can do it. And we do it because we *believe* in our collective, dispassionate judgment."

"Don't be defensive, Sam," interrupted Margaret Lowell gently. "We may be privileged, but we're also diverse. We don't represent any single color of the spectrum."

"I'm not sure how to take that, Margaret," said Gideon Logan, his eyebrows arched in mock surprise as the members of Inver Brass laughed.

"Dear Gideon," replied Lowell. "I never noticed. Palm Beach at this time of year? You're positively sunburned."

"Someone had to tend to your gardens, madame."

"If you did, I'm no doubt homeless."

"Conceivably, yes. A consortium of Puerto Rican families has leased the property, madame, a commune, actually." Quiet laughter rippled across the table. "I'm sorry, Samuel, our levity isn't called for."

"On the contrary," Jacob Mandel broke in. "It's a sign of health and perspective. If we ever walk away from laughter, especially over our foibles, we have no business here. . . . If you'll forgive me, the elders in the European pogroms taught that lesson. They called it one of the principles of survival."

"They were right, of course," agreed Sundstrom, still chuckling. "It puts a distance, however brief, between people and their difficulties. But may we get to the candidate? I'm absolutely fascinated. Sam says he's a brilliant choice, but totally *unexpected.* I would have thought otherwise, given—as Peg said—the time factor. I thought he'd be someone in the wings, on the political wings of a Pegasus, if you will."

"I really must read one of his books someday," interrupted Mandel again, again softly. "He sounds like a rabbi but I don't understand him."

"Don't try," said Winters, smiling kindly at Sundstrom.

"The candidate," repeated Sundstrom. "Do I gather that Varak has readied a presentation?"

"With his usual regard for detail," answered Winters, moving his head to his left, indicating the glowing red light on the walled console behind him. "Along the way he's unearthed some rather extraordinary information relative to events that took place a year ago, almost to the day."

"Oman?" asked Sundstrom, squinting above the light of his brass lamp. "Memorial services were held in over a dozen cities last week."

"Let Mr. Varak explain," said the white-haired historian as he pressed an inlaid button on the surface of the table. The low sound of a buzzer filled the room; seconds later the library door opened and a stocky blond man in his mid- to late thirties walked into the shadowed light and stood in the frame. He was dressed in a tan summer suit and a dark red tie; his broad shoulders seemed to stretch the fabric of his jacket. "We're ready, Mr. Varak. Please come in."

"Thank you, sir." Milos Varak closed the door, shutting out the dim light of the hallway beyond, and proceeded to the far end of the room. Standing in front of the lowered silver screen, he nodded courteously, acknowledging the members of Inver Brass. The glare of the brass lamps that reflected off the glistening table washed over his face, heightening the prominent cheekbones and the broad forehead below the full head of neatly combed straight blond hair. His eyelids were vaguely sloped, bespeaking a Slavic ancestry influenced by the tribes of Eastern Europe; the eyes behind them were calm, knowing, and somehow cold. "May I say it is good to see all of you again?" he said, his English precise, in his voice the accent of Prague.

"It's good to see you, Milos," countered Jacob Mandel, saying the name with the proper Czech pronunciation, which was "Meelos." The others followed with brief utterances.

"Varak." Sundstrom leaned back in his chair.

"You look well, Milos." Gideon Logan nodded.

"He looks like a football player." Margaret Lowell smiled. "Don't let the Redskins see you. They need linebackers."

"The game is far too confusing for me, madame."

"For them, too."

"I've told everyone about your progress," said Winters, adding softly, "as you believe your progress to be. Before revealing the identity of the man you're submitting to us, would you care to review the guidelines?"

"I would, sir." Varak's eyes roamed around the table as he collected his thoughts. "To begin with, your man should be physically attractive but not 'pretty' or feminine. Someone who meets the maximum requirements of your image-makers—anything less would present too many obstacles for the time we have. Therefore, a man men identify with the masculine virtues of this society and women find appealing. Nor should he be an ideologue unacceptable to vocal segments of the electorate. Further, he must give the appearance of being what you call 'his own man,' above being bought by special interests and with a background to support that judgment. Naturally, he should have no damaging secrets to hide. Finally, the superficial is a most vital aspect of the search. Our man must have those appealing personal qualities that can help propel him into the political spotlight through accelerated public exposure. A figure of real or projected warmth and quiet humor, with documented acts of courage in his past, but nothing he would exploit to overshadow the President."

"His people wouldn't accept that," said Eric Sundstrom.

"In any event, they won't have a choice, sir," answered Varak, his voice softly convincing. "The manipulation will take place in four stages. Within three months our basically anonymous man will rapidly become visible; within six months he will be relatively well known; and at the end of the year he will have a recognition quotient on a par with the leaders of the Senate and the House, the same demographics targeted. These may be considered phases one through three. The fourth phase, several months before the conventions, will be capped by appearances on the covers of *Time* and *Newsweek* as well as laudatory editorials in the major newspapers and on the networks. With the proper financing in the required areas, all this can be guaranteed." Varak paused, then continued. "Guaranteed, that is, with the proper candidate, and I believe we've found him."

The members of Inver Brass stared at their Czech coordinator in mild astonishment, then cautiously looked at one another.

"If we have," offered Margaret Lowell, "and he comes down off the mountain, I'll marry him."

"So will I," said Gideon Logan. "Mixed marriages be damned."

"Forgive me," interrupted Varak. "I did not mean to romanticize the prospect. He's quite a normal person, the qualities I attributed to him are mostly a result of the confidence born of his wealth, which he earned by extremely hard work and taking risks in the right places at the right times. He's comfortable with himself and others because he seeks nothing from others and knows what he is capable of himself."

"Who is he?" asked Mandel.

"May I show him to you?" said Varak, speaking respectfully without replying as he took a remote control unit from his pocket and stepped away from the screen. "It's possible some of you might recognize him, and I shall have to take back my remark about his anonymity."

A bolt of light shot out from the console and the face of Evan Kendrick filled the screen. The photograph was in color, accentuating Kendrick's deep tan as well as the stubble of a beard and the strands of light brown hair that crept down over his ears and the back of his neck. He was squinting into the sun, looking across water, his expression at once studious and apprehensive.

"He looks like a hippie," said Margaret Lowell.

"The circumstances might explain your reaction," answered Varak. "This was taken last week, the fourth week of an annual journey he makes down the rivers of white water in the Rocky Mountains. He goes alone without company or a guide." The Czechoslovakian proceeded to advance the slides, giving each a beat of several seconds. The photographs showed Kendrick in various scenes of riding the rapids, on several occasions strenuously balancing his PVC craft and careening between the treacherous intrusion of jagged rocks, surrounded by sprays of wild water and foam. The mountain forests in the background served to emphasize the perilous smallness of man and his transport against the unpredictable massiveness of nature.

"*Wait* a minute!" cried Samuel Winters, now peering through tortoiseshell glasses. "Hold that one," he continued, studying the photograph. "You never said anything about this to me. He's rounding the bend heading toward the base camp below the Lava Falls."

"Correct, sir."

"Then he must have passed through the Class Five rapids above."

"Yes, sir."

"Without a *guide*?"

"Yes."

"He's crazy! Several decades ago I rode those waters with *two* guides and I was frightened to death. Why would he do it?"

"He's been doing it for years—whenever he came back to the United States."

"Came back?" Jacob Mandel leaned forward.

"Until five years ago he was a construction engineer and developer. His work was centered in the eastern Mediterranean and the Persian Gulf. That part of the world is as far removed from the mountains and the rivers as one can imagine. I think he simply found a certain relief with the change of scenery. He'd spend a week or so on business, then head out to the Northwest."

"Alone, you say," said Eric Sundstrom.

"Not in those days, sir. He'd frequently bring along a female companion."

"Then he's obviously not a homosexual," observed the only female member of Inver Brass.

"I never meant to imply that he was."

"Neither did you mention anything about a wife or a family, which I'd think would be an important consideration. You simply said he now travels alone on what are obviously holidays."

"He's a bachelor, madame."

"That could be a problem," inserted Sundstrom.

"Not necessarily, sir. We have two years to address the situation, and given the probability factors a marriage during an election year might have a certain appeal."

"With the most popular President in history in attendance, no doubt," said Gideon Logan, chuckling.

"It's not beyond possibility, sir."

"My *God,* you're covering the bases, Milos."

"A moment, please." Mandel adjusted his steel-rimmed glasses. "You say he worked in the Mediterranean five years ago."

"He was in production then. He sold the company and left the Middle East."

"Why was that?"

"A tragic accident occurred that took the lives of nearly all his employees and their entire families. The loss profoundly affected him."

"Was he responsible?" continued the stockbroker.

"Not at all. Another firm was charged with using inferior equipment."

"Did he in any way profit from the tragedy?" asked Mandel, his gentle eyes suddenly hard.

"On the contrary, sir, I checked that out thoroughly. He sold the company for less than half its market value. Even the attorneys for the conglomerate that bought him out were astonished. They were authorized to pay three times the price."

The eyes of Inver Brass returned to the large screen and the photograph of a man and his craft careening around a wild bend in the rapids.

"Who took these?" asked Logan.

"I did, sir," replied Varak. "I tracked him. He never saw me."

The slides continued, and suddenly there was an abrupt change. The "prospect" was no longer seen in the rugged clothes of the white water rapids or in day's-end fatigues and T-shirts around a campfire, cooking alone over the flames. He was now photographed clean-shaven, his hair cut and combed, and dressed in a dark business suit, walking up a familiar street, an attaché case in his hand.

"That's Washington," said Eric Sundstrom.

"Now it's the steps leading up to the Rotunda," added Logan with the next slide.

"He's on the Hill," interjected Mandel.

"I *know* him!" said Sundstrom, the fingers of his right hand pressing into his temples. "I know the *face,* and there's a story behind that face but I don't know what it is."

"Not the story I'm about to tell you, sir."

"All right, Milos." Margaret Lowell's voice was adamant. "Enough's enough. Who the hell is he?"

"His name is Kendrick. Evan Kendrick. He's the representative from the Ninth District of Colorado."

"A *congressman*?" exclaimed Jacob Mandel as the photograph of Kendrick on the Capitol's steps remained on the screen. "I've never heard of him, and I thought I knew just about everyone up there. By name, of course, not personally."

"He's relatively new, sir, and his election was not widely covered. He ran on the President's party line because in that district the opposition is nonexistent—winning the primary is tantamount to election. I mention this because the Congressman does not appear to be philosophically in tune with numerous White House policies. He avoided national issues during the primary."

"Outspokenness aside," said Gideon Logan, "are you suggesting he has the independence of someone like, say, Lowell Weicker?"

"In a very quiet way, yes."

"Quiet and new and with a somewhat less than imposing constituency," said Sundstrom. "From that point of view your anonymity's safe. Too safe, perhaps. There's nothing more dismissable in political prime time than a newly elected, unheard-of congressman from an unknown district. Denver's in the First,

Boulder the Second, and the Springs in the Fifth. Where's the Ninth?"

"Southwest of Telluride, near the Utah border," replied Jacob Mandel, then shrugging as if apologizing for his knowledge. "There were some mining stocks, very speculative, that we looked into several years ago. But that man on the screen is *not* the congressman we met and who tried rather desperately to convince us to underwrite the issues."

"Did you underwrite them, sir?" asked Varak.

"No, we did not," answered Mandel. "Frankly, the speculation went beyond the calculated risks of venture capital."

"What you call in America a possible 'scam'?"

"We had no proof, Milos. We just backed away."

"But the congressional representative from that district did his best to enlist your support?"

"Indeed, he did."

"That is why Evan Kendrick is now the congressman, sir."

"Oh?"

"Eric," interrupted Gideon Logan, shifting his large head to look at the academic inventor of space technology. "You said you knew him, at least knew his face."

"I do, I'm *sure* I do. Now that Varak's told us who he is, I think I met him at one of those interminable cocktail parties in Washington or Georgetown, and I distinctly remember that someone said there was quite a story behind him. . . . That was *it.* I never heard the story; it was simply a statement."

"But Milos said that whatever story you had in mind wasn't the one he was going to tell us," said Margaret Lowell. "Isn't that right?" she added, looking at Varak.

"Yes, madame. The remark made to Professor Sundstrom undoubtedly concerned the nature of Kendrick's election. He literally bought it in anger, burying his opponent under an avalanche of local advertising and a series of expensive rallies that were more public circuses than political assemblies. It was said that when the incumbent complained that the election laws were being violated, Kendrick confronted him with his attorneys—not to discuss the campaign but, instead, his opponent's performance in office. The complaints instantly stopped and Kendrick won handily."

"One could say he puts his money where his indignation is," remarked Winters quietly. "However, you have a far more fascinating bit of information for us, Mr. Varak, and since I've heard it, I'll repeat what I said before. It's extraordinary. Please go on."

"Yes, sir." The Czech pressed the remote control and with a muted slap the next photograph appeared on the screen. Kendrick and the Rotunda steps disappeared, replaced by an overview of hysterical crowds racing down a narrow street flanked by buildings of obviously Islamic character, past shops with signs in Arabic above them.

"Oman," said Eric Sundstrom, glancing at Winters. "A year ago." The historian-spokesman nodded.

The slides followed quickly, one after another, depicting scenes of chaos and carnage. There were bullet-ridden corpses and shell-pocked walls, torn-down embassy gates and rows of kneeling terrified hostages behind a rooftop screen of latticework; there were close-ups of shrieking young people brandishing weapons, their mouths gaping in triumph, their zealous eyes wild. Suddenly the rushing slides stopped and the attention of Inver Brass was abruptly riveted on a slide that seemed to have little relevance. It showed a tall, dark-skinned man in long white robes, his head covered by a ghotra, his face in profile, walking out of a hotel; then the screen was split, a second photograph showing the same man rushing across an Arabic bazaar in front of a fountain. The photographs remained on the screen; the bewildered silence was broken by Milos Varak.

"That man is Evan Kendrick," he said simply.

Bewilderment gave way to astonishment. Except for Samuel Winters, the others leaned forward, beyond the glare of the brass lamps, to study the magnified figure on the screen. Varak continued. "These photographs were taken by a case officer of the CIA with a Four-Zero clearance whose assignment was to keep Kendrick under surveillance wherever possible. She did a remarkable job."

"She?" Margaret Lowell arched her brows in approval.

"A Middle East specialist. Her father's Egyptian, her mother an American from California. She speaks Arabic fluently and is used extensively by the Agency in crisis situations over there."

"Over there?" whispered Mandel, stunned. "What was *he* doing over *there*?"

"Just a minute," said Logan, his dark eyes boring into Varak's. "Stop me if I'm wrong, young man, but if I remember correctly, there was an article in the *Washington Post* last year suggesting that an unknown American had interceded in Masqat at the time. A number of people thought that it might have been the Texan Ross Perot, but the story never appeared again. It was dropped."

"You're not wrong, sir. The American was Evan Kendrick, and with pressure from the White House the story was killed."

"Why? He could have made enormous political mileage out of it—if indeed his contribution led to the settlement."

"His contribution *was* the settlement."

"Then I certainly don't understand," remarked Logan quietly as he looked at Samuel Winters.

"No one does," said the historian. "There's no explanation, just a buried file in the archives that Milos managed to obtain. Other than that document, there's nothing anywhere indicating a connection between Kendrick and the events in Masqat."

"There's even a memo to the Secretary of State disavowing any such connection," interrupted Varak. "It does not reflect well on the Congressman. In essence, it suggests that he was a self-serving opportunist, a politician who wished to further himself by way of the hostage crisis because he had worked in the Arab Emirates, and especially Oman, and was trying to insert himself for publicity purposes. The recommendation was not to touch him for the safety of the hostages."

"But they obviously *did* touch him!" exclaimed Sundstrom. "Touch him and *use* him! He couldn't have gotten in there if they hadn't; all commercial flights were suspended. Good Lord, he must have been flown over under cover."

"And just as obviously he's no self-serving opportunist," added Margaret Lowell. "We see him here in front of our eyes and Milos tells us he was instrumental in bringing the crisis to an end, yet he's never uttered a word about his involvement. We'd all know about it if he had."

"And there's *no* explanation?" asked Gideon Logan, addressing Varak.

"None acceptable, sir, and I've gone to the source."

"The White House?" said Mandel.

"No, the man who had to be aware of his recruitment, the one who ran the nerve center here in Washington. His name is Frank Swann."

"How did you find *him*?"

"I didn't, sir. Kendrick did."

"But how did you find *Kendrick*?" pressed Margaret Lowell.

"Like Mr. Logan, I, too, remembered that story of an American in Masqat that was so abruptly dropped by the media. For reasons I can't really explain I decided to trace it down—probably thinking it might involve someone highly placed, someone we should consider, if there was any credence to the story."

Varak paused, a slight, uncharacteristic smile creasing his lips. "Frequently, the most obvious security measures trip up those wishing to be secure. In this case it was the Department of State's entrance logs. Since the killings several years ago, all visitors without exception must sign in and sign out, passing through metal detectors. Among the thousands who did so during the time of the hostage crisis was the unlikely name of a freshman congressman from Colorado seeing a Mr. Swann. Neither meant anything to me, of course, but our computers were better informed. Mr. Swann was the State Department's foremost expert on Southwest Asia, and the Congressman was a man who had made his wealth in the Emirates, Bahrain and Saudi Arabia. In the panic of the crisis, someone had forgotten to remove Kendrick's name from the logs."

"So you went to see this Swann," said Mandel, removing his steel-rimmed glasses.

"I did, sir."

"What did he tell you?"

"That I was completely mistaken. That they had rejected Kendrick's offer to help because he had nothing to contribute. He added that Kendrick was only one of dozens of people—people who had worked in the Arab Emirates—who had made similar offers."

"But you didn't believe him," broke in Margaret Lowell.

"I had a very good reason not to. Congressman Kendrick never signed out after his visit to the State Department that afternoon. It was Wednesday, August 11, and his name is nowhere in the departure logs. He was obviously taken out by special arrangement, which normally signifies the start of a cover, usually a deep cover."

"Consular Operations," said Sundstrom. "State's covert link to the CIA."

"A reluctant but necessary compromise," added Winters. "Toes get stepped on in the dark. Needless to say, Mr. Varak pursued his inquiries at both State and Langley."

"The hero of Oman revealed," said Gideon Logan softly, staring at the figure on the screen. "My *God,* what a hook!"

"A crusading congressman above reproach," chimed in Mandel. "A proven foe of corruption."

"A man of courage," said Mrs. Lowell, "who risked his life for two hundred Americans he couldn't have known, and sought nothing for himself—"

"When he could have had anything he wanted," completed Sundstrom. "Certainly anything in politics."

"Tell us everything you've learned about Evan Kendrick, if you will, Mr. Varak," said Winters as he and the others reached for their lined yellow pads.

"Before I do so," replied the Czech, a slight hesitancy in his voice, "I must tell you that I flew out to Colorado last week and encountered a situation I can't fully explain at this time. I'd rather say so now. An elderly man is living in Kendrick's house on the outskirts of Mesa Verde. I've learned that his name is Emmanuel Weingrass, an architect with dual citizenship in both Israel and the United States, and that he had major surgery a number of months ago. Since then he has been convalescing as the Congressman's guest."

"What's the significance?" asked Eric Sundstrom.

"I'm not sure there is any, but three facts are worth noting. First, as nearly as I can determine, this Weingrass appeared out of nowhere shortly after Kendrick's return from Oman. Second, there's obviously a close relationship between the two of them, and third—somewhat disturbing—the old man's identity, as well as his presence in Mesa Verde, is a closely guarded but poorly kept secret. Weingrass himself is the offender here; whether through age or by nature he's quite gregarious among the workmen, especially the Hispanics."

"That's not necessarily a negative," said Logan, smiling.

"He could have been part of the Oman operation," offered Margaret Lowell. "And that's not negative, either."

"Hardly," agreed Jacob Mandel.

Sundstrom spoke again. "He must have considerable influence with Kendrick," he said, writing on his pad. "Wouldn't you say, Milos?"

"I would assume so. My only point is that I want you to know when *I* don't know something."

"I'd say he's an asset," stated Samuel Winters. "From any point. Proceed, Mr. Varak."

"Yes, sir. Knowing that nothing must leave this room, I've prepared the Congressman's dossier for slide projection." The Czech pressed the remote control unit and the dual photographs of the disguised Kendrick on the violence-oriented streets in Masqat was supplanted by a typewritten page, the letters large, the lines triple-spaced. "Each slide," continued Varak, "represents approximately one fourth of a normal page; all negatives, naturally, were destroyed in the laboratory downstairs. I've done my best to study the candidate as thoroughly as possible, but I may have omitted specifics that might interest some of you. So do not hesitate to question me on them. I will watch you, and if each in turn will nod his head when you've finished reading and making your notes, I will know when to advance the slide. . . . For the next hour or so, what you will see is the life of Congressman Evan Kendrick—from his birth to last week."

With each slide Eric Sundstrom was the first to nod his head. Margaret Lowell and Jacob Mandel vied for the honor of being last, but then they made nearly as many notes as did Gideon Logan. The spokesman, Samuel Winters, made almost none; he was convinced.

Three hours and four minutes later, Milos Varak snapped off the projector. Two hours and seven minutes after that moment, the questions ended and Varak left the room.

"To paraphrase our friend out of context," said Winters. "A nod from each of you signifies consent. Shake your head if it's negative. We'll start with Jacob."

Slowly, pensively, one by one the members of Inver Brass nodded their consent.

"It is agreed, then," continued Winters. "Congressman Evan Kendrick will be the next Vice President of the United States. He will become President eleven months after the election of the incumbent. The code name is Icarus, to be taken as a warning, a fervent prayer that he will not, like so many of his predecessors have done, try to fly too close to the sun and crash into the sea. And may God have mercy on our souls."

17

Representative Kendrick from Colorado's Ninth Congressional District sat at his office desk watching his stern-faced secretary as she kept chattering away about priority mail, House agendas, pre-floor position papers and social functions he really *must* attend, his chief aide's judgment notwithstanding. Her lips kept opening and closing with the rapidity of machine-gun fire, the nasal sounds emanating not much lower in the decibel count.

"*There,* Congressman, that's the schedule for the week."

"It's really something, Annie. But can't you simply send out a blanket letter to everyone saying I've got a social disease and don't want to infect any of them?"

"Evan, *stop* it," cried Ann Mulcahy O'Reilly, a very determined middle-aged veteran of Washington. "You're being sloughed off around here and I won't have it! You know what they're saying here on the Hill? They say you don't give a damn, that you spent a bundle of money just to meet girls as rich as yourself."

"Do you believe that, Annie?"

"How the hell could I? You never *go* anywhere, never *do* anything. I'd praise the saints if you got caught naked in the Reflecting Pool with the biggest tootsie in Washington! Then I'd know you were *doing* something."

"Maybe I don't want to do anything."

"Damn it, you should! I've typed your positions on a dozen issues and they're light-years better than eighty percent of the clowns here, but nobody pays any attention."

"They're buried because they're not popular, Annie; I'm not popular. They don't want me in either camp. The few who notice me on both sides have pinned so many labels on me they cancel themselves out. They can't pigeonhole me so they bury me, which isn't very difficult because I don't complain."

"God knows *I* don't agree with you a lot of the time, but I know a mind at work when I see it. . . . Forget it, Congressman. What are your replies?"

"Later. Has Manny called?"

"I put him off twice. I wanted to get in my session with you."

Kendrick leaned forward, his light blue eyes cold, bordering on anger. "Don't ever do that again, Annie. There's nothing so important to me as that man in Colorado."

"Yes, sir." O'Reilly lowered her eyes.

"I'm sorry," said Evan quickly, "that wasn't called for. You're trying to do your job and I'm not much help. Sorry, again."

"Don't apologize. I know what you've been through with Mr. Weingrass and what he means to you—how often did I bring your work to the hospital? I had no right to interfere. *On* the other hand, I *am* trying to do my job and you're not always the most cooperative boss on the Hill."

"There are other hills I'd rather be on—"

"I'm aware of that, so we'll cross out the social functions; you'd probably do yourself more harm than good anyway." Ann O'Reilly got out of the chair and placed a file folder on Kendrick's desk. "But I think you should look at a proposal from your senatorial colleague from Colorado. I think he wants to chop off the top of a mountain and put in a reservoir. In this town, that usually means a lake followed by high-rise condominiums."

"That transparent son of a *bitch,*" said Evan, whipping open the folder.

"I'll also get Mr. Weingrass on the phone for you."

"Still *Mr.* Weingrass?" asked Evan, turning over pages. "You won't relent? I've heard him tell you to call him Manny dozens of times."

"Oh, now and then I do, but it's not easy."

"Why? Because he yells?"

"Mother of God, no. You can't take offense at that if you're married to a two-toilet Irish detective."

"Two-toilet—?" Kendrick looked up.

"An old Boston expression, but, no, it's not the yelling."

"What, then?"

"A whimsy of humor he keeps repeating. He keeps saying to me over and over—especially when I call him by his first name. 'Kid,' he says, 'I think we've got a vaudeville act here. We'll call it Manny's Irish Annie, what do you say?' And I say, 'Not a hell of a lot, Manny,' and he says, 'Leave my friend, the animal, and fly away with me. He'll understand my undying passion,' and I say to him that the T.T. cop doesn't understand his own."

"Don't tell your husband," offered Kendrick, chuckling.

"Oh, but I did. All *he* said was that he'd buy the airline tickets. Of course, he and Weingrass got drunk a couple of times—"

"Got drunk? I didn't even know they'd met."

"My fault—to my undying regret. It was when you flew to Denver about eight months ago—"

"I remember. The state conference, and Manny was still in the hospital. I asked you to go see him, take him the Paris *Tribune.*"

"And I brought Paddy with me during the evening visiting hours. I'm no centerfold, but even *I'm* not walking these streets at night, and the T.T. cop's got to be good for something."

"What happened?"

"They got along like a shot and a beer. I had to work late one night that week and Paddy insisted on going to the hospital himself."

Evan shook his head slowly. "I'm sorry, Annie. I never knew. I didn't mean to involve you and your husband in my private life. And Manny never told me."

"Probably the Listerine bottles."

"The what?"

"Same color as light Scotch. I'll get him on the phone."

Emmanuel Weingrass leaned against the formation of rock on top of a hill belonging to Kendrick's thirty-acre spread at the base of the mountains. His short-sleeved checkered shirt was unbuttoned to the waist as he took the sun, breathing the clear air of the southern Rockies. He glanced at his chest, at the scars of the surgery, and wondered for a brief moment whether he should believe in God or in Evan Kendrick. The doctors had told him—months after the operation and numerous post-op checkups—that they had cut out the dirty little cells that were eating his life away. He was clean, they pronounced. Pronounced to a man who, on this day, on this rock, claimed he was eighty years of age with the sun beating down on his frail body. Frail and not so frail, for he moved better, spoke better—coughed practically not at all. Yet he missed his Gauloise cigarettes and the Monte Cristo cigars he enjoyed so much. So what could they do? Stop his life a few weeks or months before a logical ending?

He looked over at his nurse in the shade of a nearby tree next to the ever-present golf cart. She was one of the round-the-clock females who accompanied him everywhere, and he wondered what she would do if he propositioned her while leaning casually against the boulder. Such potential responses had always intrigued him, but generally the reality merely amused him.

"Beautiful day, isn't it?" he called out.

"Simply gorgeous," was the reply.

"What do you say we take all our clothes off and really enjoy it?"

The nurse's expression did not change for an instant. Her response was calm, deliberate, even gentle. "Mr. Weingrass, I'm here to look after you, not give you cardiac arrest."

"Not bad. Not bad at all."

The radio telephone on the golf cart hummed; the woman walked over to it and snapped it out of its recess. After a brief conversation capped with quiet laughter, she turned to Manny. "The Congressman's calling you, Mr. Weingrass."

"You don't laugh like that with a congressman," said Manny, pushing himself away from the rock. "Five'll get you twenty it's Annie Glocamorra telling lies about me."

"She did ask if I'd strangled you yet." The nurse handed the phone to Weingrass.

"Annie, this woman's a *letch*!"

"We try to be of service," said Evan Kendrick.

"Boy, that girl of yours gets off the phone pretty damned quick."

"Forewarned, forearmed, Manny. You called. Is everything all right?"

"I should only call in a crisis?"

"You rarely call, period. That privilege is almost exclusively mine. What is it?"

"You got any money left?"

"I can't spend the interest. Sure. Why?"

"You know the addition we built on the west porch so you got a view?"

"Of course."

"I've been playing with some sketches. I think you should have a terrace on top. Two steel beams would carry the load; maybe a third if you went for a glass-blocked steam bath by the wall."

"Glass-blocked . . . ? Hey, that sounds terrific. Go ahead."

"Good. I've got the plumbers coming out in the morning. But when it's done, *then* I go back to Paris."

"Whatever you say, Manny. However, you said you'd work up some plans for a gazebo down by the streams, where they merge."

"*You* said you didn't want to walk that far."

"I've changed my mind. It'd be a good place for a person to get away and think."

"That excludes the owner of this establishment."

"You're all heart. I'm coming back next week for a few days."

"I can't wait," said Weingrass, raising his voice and looking over at the nurse. "When you get here, you can take these heavy-breathing sex maniacs off my hands!"

It was shortly past 10:00 P.M. when Milos Varak walked down the deserted hallway in the House Office Building. He had been admitted by prearrangement, a late-night visitor of one Congressman Arvin Partridge of Alabama. Varak reached the heavy wooden door with the brass plate centered in the sculptured panel and knocked. Within seconds it was opened by a slender man in his early twenties whose eyes looked out anxiously from behind large tortoiseshell glasses. Whoever he was, he was not the gruff, savvy chairman of the Partridge "Gang," that investigative committee determined to find out why the armed services were getting so little for so much. Not in terms of $1,200 toilet seats and $700 pipe wrenches; those were too blatant to be taken seriously and might even be correctable diversions. What concerned the "Birds"—another sobriquet—were the 500 percent overruns and the restricted degree of competitive bidding in defense contracts. What they had only begun to uncover, of course, was a river of corruption with so many tributaries there weren't enough scouts to pursue them in the canoes available.

"I'm here to see Congressman Partridge," said the blond man, his Czech accent not lost on but conceivably misconstrued by the slender young man at the door.

"Did you . . . ?" began the apparent congressional aide awkwardly. "I mean when you saw the guards downstairs—"

"If you're asking me whether or not I was checked for firearms, of course I was, and you should know it. They called you from Security. The Congressman, please. He's expecting me."

"Certainly, sir. He's in his office. This way, sir." The nervous aide led Milos to a second large door. The younger man knocked. "Congressman—"

"Tell him to come in!" ordered the loud Southern voice from inside. "And you stay out there and take any calls. I don't care if it's the Speaker or the President, I'm not here!"

"Go right in," said the aide, opening the door.

Varak was tempted to tell the agitated young man that he was a friendly liaison from the KGB, but decided against it. The aide was there for a reason; few phone calls came to the House Office Building at this hour. Milos stepped inside the large, ornate room with the profusion of photographs on the desk, walls and tables, all in one way or another attesting to Partridge's influence, patriotism and power. The man himself, standing by a draped window, was not as impressive as he appeared in the photographs. He was short and overweight, with a puffed, angry face and thinning dyed hair.

"Ah don't know what you're sellin', Blondie," said the congressman, walking forward like an enraged pigeon, "but if it's what I think it is, I'll take you down so fast you'll wish you had a parachute."

"I'm not selling anything, sir, I'm giving something away. Something of considerable value, in fact."

"*Muleshit!* You want some kind of fuckin' cover-up and I'm not givin' it!"

"My clients seek no cover-up and certainly I don't. But I submit, Congressman, *you* may."

"*Bull!* I listened to you on the phone—you *heard* something, somebody mentioned drugs and I'd better *listen*—so I made some damn clear inquiries and found out what I had to know, what I knew was the truth! We're clean here, clean as a 'Bama stream! Now, I want to find out who sent *you,* what thief in what larcenous boardroom thought he could scare me with this kind of *crap*?"

"I don't think you'd want this kind of 'crap' made public, sir. The information is devastating."

"*Information?* Words! Innuendo! Rumors, *gossip*! Like that black kid who tried to indict the whole gawdamned *Congress* with his lies!"

"No rumors, no gossip," said Milos Varak, reaching into the breast pocket of his jacket. "Only photographs." The Czech from Inver Brass threw the white envelope on the desk.

"*What?*" Partridge went instantly to the envelope; he sat down and tore it open, pulling the photographs out one by one and holding them under the green-shelled desk lamp. His eyes widened as his face went white, then blood-red in fury. What he saw was beyond anything he might have imagined. There were various couples, trios and quartets of partly and fully naked young people using straws with white powder strewn on tables; hastily taken blurred shots of syringes, pills, and bottles of beer and whisky; finally, clear photographs of several couples making love.

"Cameras come in so many sizes these days," said Varak. "Microtechnology has produced them as small as buttons on a jacket or a shirt—"

"Oh, Jesus *Christ*!" cried Partridge in agony. "That's my house in Arlington! And *that's*—"

"Congressman Bookbinder's home in Silver Springs, as well as the houses of three other members of your committee. Your work takes you out of Washington a great deal of the time."

"Who took these?" asked Partridge, barely audible.

"I won't answer that except to give you my word that the person is thousands of miles away without the negatives and no chance of returning to this country. One could say a university exchange student in political science."

"We've achieved so much and now it's all down the goddamned drain. . . . Oh, *God*!"

"*Why,* Congressman?" inquired Varak sincerely. "These young people aren't the committee. They're not your attorneys or your accountants or even senior aides. They're children who've made terrible mistakes in the headstrong environment of the most powerful capital in the world. Get rid of them; tell them their lives and careers are ruined unless they get help and straighten out, but don't stop your committee."

"Nobody will ever believe us again," said Partridge, staring straight ahead as if speaking to the wall. "We're as rotten as everyone we go after. We're hypocrites."

"Nobody has to know—"

"*Shit*!" exploded the congressman from Alabama, pouncing on the phone and pressing a button, holding it down beyond the point where his call was answered. "Get *in* here!" he screamed. The young aide came through the door as Partridge rose from the desk. "You fancy-school son of a *bitch*! I asked you to tell me the truth! You *lied*!"

"No, I *didn't*!" yelled back the young man, his eyes watering behind the tortoiseshell glasses. "You asked me what's going on—what *is* going on—and I told you *nothing*—nothing *is* going on! A couple of us got busted three, four weeks ago and it scared *all* of us! Okay, we were dumb, *stupid,* we all agreed, but we didn't hurt anyone but ourselves! We quit the whole scene and a hell of a lot *more* than that, but you and your hotshots around here never noticed. Your snotty staff works us eighty hours a week, then calls us dumb kids while they use the stuff we feed 'em to get in front of the cameras. Well, what you never noticed is that you've got a whole new kindergarten class here now. The others all quit and you never even *noticed*! I'm the only one left because I *couldn't* get out."

"You're out now."

"You're gawdamned right, Emperor *Jones*!"

"Who?"

"The allusion would grab you," said the young man, dashing out the door and slamming it behind him.

"Who was *that*?" asked Varak.

"Arvin Partridge, Junior," replied the congressman quietly and sitting down, his eyes on the door. "He's a third-year law student at Virginia. They were all law students and we worked their asses off around the clock for spit and little thanks. But we were giving them something, too, and they betrayed the trust we placed in them by giving it."

"Which was?"

"Experience they'd never get anywhere else, not in the courts or in the law books, nowhere but here. My son split legal and grammatical hairs and he knows it. He lied to me about something that can destroy all of us. I'll never trust him again."

"I'm sorry."

"It's not your problem!" snapped Partridge, his reflective voice suddenly gone. "All right, trash boy," he continued harshly, "what do you want from me to keep this committee together? You said no cover-up, but I suppose there are a couple of dozen ways of saying it without saying it. I'll have to weigh the pluses and the minuses, won't I?"

"There are no negatives for you, sir," said Varak, taking out several folded sheets of paper, then unfolding them and placing them on the desk in front of the congressman. They comprised a résumé, a small identification photograph in the upper right-hand corner of the first page. "My clients want this man on your committee—"

"You've *got* something on him!" broke in Partridge.

"Absolutely nothing compromising; he's above reproach where such matters are concerned. To repeat, my clients seek no cover-ups, no extortion, no committee bills sent out or blocked for passage. This man does not know my clients, nor do they personally know him, and he's completely unaware of our meeting tonight."

"Then why *do* you want him with me?"

"Because my clients believe he will be an excellent addition to your committee."

"One man can't do a damn thing, you know that, don't you?"

"Certainly."

"If he's planted to get information, we're leak-proof." Partridge glanced at the snapshots under the green-shelled lamp; he turned them over and slapped them down on the desk. "At least we were."

Varak leaned over and took the photographs. "Do it, Congressman. Put him on the committee. Or, as you said, so much down the drain. When he's in his chair, these will be returned to you along with the negatives. Do it."

Partridge's eyes were on the snapshots in the blond man's hand. "As it happens, there's a vacancy. Bookbinder resigned yesterday—personal problems."

"I know," said Milos Varak.

The congressman looked up into his visitor's eyes. "Who the hell *are* you?"

"Someone devoted to his adopted country, but I'm not important. *That* man is."

Partridge glanced down at the résumé in front of him. "Evan

Kendrick, Colorado's Ninth," he read. "I've barely heard of him and what I did hear doesn't raise any pimples. He's a nobody, a rich nobody."

"That will change, sir," said Varak, turning and heading for the door.

"Congressman, *Congressman*!" yelled Evan Kendrick's chief aide, racing out of the office and running down the House corridor to catch his employer.

"What is it?" asked Evan, pulling his hand away from the elevator button and looking bemused as the breathless young man skidded to a stop in front of him. "It's not like you to raise your voice above a *very* confidential whisper, Phil. Did Colorado's Ninth get buried by a mud slide?"

"It may have just been dug out of a long-standing one. From your viewpoint, that is."

"Do tell?"

"Congressman *Partridge. Alabama's* Partridge!"

"He's rough but a good man. He takes chances. I like what he does."

"He wants you to do it *with* him."

"Do what?"

"Be on his committee!"

"*What?*"

"It's a tremendous step forward, sir!"

"It's a lousy step backward," disagreed Kendrick. "His committee members are on the nightly news every other week, and they're 'fill' for Sunday mornings when our newest congressional comets aren't available. It's the last thing I want."

"Forgive me, Congressman, but it's the first thing you should take," said the aide, calming down, his eyes locked with Evan's.

"Why?"

The young man named Phil touched Kendrick's arm, moving him away from the elevator's gathering crowd. "You've told me you're going to resign after the election and I accept that. But you've also told me that you want a voice in the appointment of your successor."

"I intend to have." Evan nodded his head, now in agreement. "I fought that lousy machine and I want it kept out. Christ, they'd sell every last mountain in the south Rockies as a uranium mine if they could get *one* government exploration—leaked, naturally."

"You won't have any voice at all if you turn Partridge down."

"Why not?"

"Because he really *wants* you."

"Why?"

"I'm not sure, I'm only sure he doesn't do anything without a reason. Maybe he wants to extend his influence west, build a base for his own personal advancement—who knows? But he controls a hell of a lot of state delegations; and if you insult him by saying 'No, thanks, pal,' he'll consider it arrogance and cut you off, both here and back home. I mean, he is one macho presence on the Hill."

Kendrick sighed, his brow wrinkled. "I can always keep my mouth shut, I guess."

It was the third week after Congressman Evan Kendrick's appointment to the Partridge Committee, a totally unexpected assignment that thrilled no one in Washington except Ann Mulcahy O'Reilly and, by extension, her husband, Patrick Xavier, a transplanted police lieutenant from Boston whose abilities were sought and paid for by the crime-ridden capital's authorities. The reasoning behind the chairman's action was generally assumed to be that the old pro wanted the limelight focused on him, not on the other members of the committee. If that assumption was correct, Partridge could not have made a better choice. The Representative from Colorado's Ninth District rarely said anything during the twice-weekly televised hearings other than the words "I pass, Mr. Chairman" when it was his turn to question witnesses. In fact, the longest statement he made during his brief tenure with the "Birds" was his twenty-three-second response to the chairman's welcome. He had quietly expressed his astonishment at having been honored by his selection, and hoped that he would live up to the chairman's confidence in him. The television cameras had left his face midway through his remarks—in precisely twelve seconds—for the arrival of a uniformed janitor who walked through the chambers emptying ashtrays.

"Ladies and gentlemen," said the hushed voice of the announcer, "even throughout such hearings as these, the government does not overlook basic precautions. . . . What? . . . Oh, yes, Congressman Owen Canbrick has completed his statement."

However, on Tuesday of the fourth week a most abnormal thing happened. It was the morning of that week's first televised hearing, and interest ran higher than usual because the primary witness was the representative of the Pentagon's Office of Procurement. The man was a youngish, balding full colonel who had aggressively made a name for himself in logistics, a totally committed soldier of unshakable convictions. He was bright, fast, and blessed with an acerbic wit; he was Arlington's big gun where the sniveling, penny-pinching civilians were concerned. There were many who could not wait for the clash between Colonel Robert Barrish and the equally bright, equally fast and, certainly, equally acerbic chairman of the Partridge Committee.

What was abnormal that morning, however, was the absence of Congressman Arvin Partridge of Alabama. The chairman did not show up and no amount of phone calls or a platoon of aides rushing all over the capital could unearth him. He had simply disappeared.

But congressional committees do not revolve solely around chairmen, especially not where television is concerned, so the proceedings went forward under the lack of leadership provided by a congressman from North Dakota who was nursing the worst hangover of his life, a most unusual malady, as the man was not known to drink. He was considered a mild, abstemious minister of the Gospel who took to heart the biblical admonition of turning swords into plowshares. He was also raw meat for the lion that was Colonel Robert Barrish.

". . . and to finish my statement before this *civilian* inquisition, I state categorically that I speak for a strong, *free* society in lethal combat with the forces of evil that would rip us to shreds at the first sign of weakness on our part. Are our hands to be shackled over minor academic fiduciary procedures that have only the barest relationship to the *status quo ante* of our enemies?"

"If I understand you," said the bleary-eyed temporary chairman, "let me assure you that no one here is questioning your commitment to our nation's defense."

"I would hope not, sir."

"I don't think—"

"*Hold* it, soldier," said Evan Kendrick, at the far end of the panel.

"I beg your pardon?"

"I said wait a minute, will you please?"

"My rank is colonel in the United States Army, and I expect to be addressed as such," said the officer testily.

Evan looked hard at the witness, momentarily forgetting the microphone. "I'll address you any way I like, you arrogant bastard." Cameras jolted, bleeps filled audios everywhere, but too late for the exclusion. ". . . unless you've personally amended the Constitution, which I doubt you've ever read," continued Kendrick, studying the papers in front of him, chuckling quietly. "Inquisition, my ass."

"I *resent* your attitude—"

"A lot of taxpayers resent yours, too," interrupted Evan, looking at Barrish's service record and remembering Frank Swann's precise words over a year ago. "Let me ask you, *Colonel,* have you ever fired a gun?"

"I'm a *soldier*!"

"We've both established that, haven't we? I know you're a soldier; we inquisitorial civilians are paying your salary—unless you rented the uniform." The congressional chamber rippled with quiet laughter. "What I asked you was whether you had ever fired a gun."

"Countless times. Have you?"

"Several, not countless, and never in uniform."

"Then I think the question is closed."

"Not entirely. Did you ever use a weapon for the purpose of killing another human being whose intention was to kill you?"

The subsequent silence was lost on no one. The soft reply was registered on all. "I was never in combat, if that's what you mean."

"But you just said you were in *lethal* combat, et cetera, et cetera, which conveys to everyone in here and the audience out there that you're some kind of modern-day Davy Crockett holding the fort at the Alamo, or a Sergeant York, or maybe an Indiana Jones blasting away at the bad guys. But that's all wrong, isn't it, Colonel? You're an accountant who's trying to justify the theft of millions—maybe billions—of the taxpayers' money under the red, white and blue flag of superpatriotism."

"You son of a . . . ! How *dare* you—" The jolting cameras and the bleeps again came too late as Colonel Barrish rose from his chair and pounded the table.

"The committee is *adjourned*!" yelled the exhausted chairman. "Adjourned, *goddamnit*!"

In the darkened control room of one of Washington's network stations, a gray-haired newscaster stood in a corner studying the congressional monitor. As most of America had seen him do countless times, he pursed his lips in thought, then turned to the assistant beside him.

"I want that congressman—whoever the hell he is—on my show next Sunday."

The upset woman in Chevy Chase cried into the phone, "I tell you, Mother, I never saw him like that before in my life! I mean it, he was positively *drunk*. Thank *God* for that nice foreigner who brought him home! He said he found him outside a restaurant in Washington barely able to walk—can you imagine? Barely able to *walk*! He recognized him, and, being a good Christian, thought he'd better get him off the streets. What's so insane, Mother, is that I didn't think he ever touched a drop of alcohol. *Well,* obviously I was *wrong.* I wonder how many *other* secrets my devoted minister has! This morning he claimed he couldn't *remember* anything—not a *thing,* he said. . . . Oh, my sweet *Jesus*! *Mother,* he just walked in the front door—*Momma,* he's throwing up all over the *rug*!"

"Where the hell *am* I?" whispered Arvin Partridge, Sr., shaking his head and trying to focus his eyes on the shabby curtained windows of the motel room. "In some rat's nest?"

"That's not far off the mark," said the blond man, approaching the bed. "Except that the rodents who frequent this place usually do so for only an hour or two."

"*You!*" screamed the representative from Alabama, staring at the Czech. "What have you *done* to me?"

"Not to you, sir, but for you," answered Varak. "Fortunately, I was able to extricate you from a potentially embarrassing situation."

"*What?*" Partridge sat up and swung his legs over the bed; although not yet oriented, he realized he was fully clothed. "Where? How?"

"One of my clients was dining at the Carriage House in Georgetown where you met the congressman from North Dakota. When the unpleasantness started, he called me. Again, fortunately, I live in the area and was able to get there in time. Incidentally, you're obviously not registered here."

"*Wait* a minute!" yelled Partridge. "*Muleshit!* That meeting between the holy roller and me was a setup! His office gets a call that *I* want to meet him on urgent committee business and *my* office gets the same. We got that Pentagon prick, Barrish, coming in the morning, so we both figure we'd better see each other. I ask him what's going on and he asks me the *same*!"

"I wouldn't know anything about that, sir."

"*Hogshit!* . . . What unpleasantness?"

"You overindulged."

"*Rabbitshit!* I had one fuckin' martini and the sky padre had lemonade!"

"If that's the truth, you both have odd tolerances. You fell over the table and the minister tried to drink the salt."

The chairman of the Partridge Committee glared at the Czech. "Finns," he said quietly. "You dosed us both with Mickey Finns!"

"Before last night I never set foot inside that restaurant."

"You're also a liar, a hell of an experienced one. . . . Good *Christ,* what time is it?" Partridge whipped his wrist up to look at his watch; Varak interrupted.

"The hearing is over."

"*Shit!*"

"The minister was not terribly effective, but your new appointee made an indelible impression, sir. I'm sure you'll see portions of his performance on the evening news, certain words deleted, of course."

"Oh, my *God,*" whispered the congressman to himself. He looked up at the Czech from Inver Brass. "What did they say about me? About why I wasn't there."

"Your office issued a statement that was perfectly acceptable. You were on a fishing boat in Maryland's Eastern Shore. The engine failed and you had to drop anchor a mile away from the marina. It's been substantiated; there are no problems."

"My office issued a statement like that? On whose authorization?"

"Your son's. He's a remarkably forgiving young man. He's waiting outside in your car."

The red-haired salesman in the Saab showroom fairly glowed in astonishment as he signed the papers and counted out ten hundred-dollar bills. "We'll have the car prepped and ready for you by three o'clock this afternoon."

"That's nice," said the buyer, who had listed his profession on the finance-loan agreement as a bartender, currently employed at the Carriage House in Georgetown.

18

"*Zero* hour, Mr. Kendrick," said Colonel Robert Barrish, smiling pleasantly into the camera, his voice the soul of reason. "We must be prepared for it, and with preemptive escalation we push it further and further away."

"Or, conversely, overstock the arsenals to the point where one miscalculation blows up the planet."

"Oh, please," admonished the army officer condescendingly. "That line of rationalization has long since been rendered modus non operandi. We're the professionals."

"You mean our side?"

"Of course I mean our side."

"What about the enemy? Aren't they professionals, too?"

"If you're attempting to lateralize our enemies' technological commitments with ours, I think you'll find you're as misinformed about that as you are about the cost-control effectiveness of our system."

"I take that to mean they're not as good as we are."

"A sagacious assessment, Congressman. Beyond the superiority of our moral commitment—a commitment to God—the high-tech training of our armed forces is the finest on earth. If you'll forgive me here, I must say as part of a great team that I'm immensely proud of our splendid fellows and girls."

"Golly gee, so am I," said Evan, a minor smile on his lips. "But then *I* must say here, Colonel, that I've lost your line of reasoning, or was it preemptive escalation? I thought your comment about professionalism was in response to my remark about the possibility of miscalculation with all those arsenals so full."

"It was. You see, Mr. Kendrick, what I'm patiently trying to explain to you is that our weapons personnel are locked into manuals of procedures that eliminate miscalculation. We are virtually *fail-safe.*"

"*We* may be," agreed Evan. "But what about the other guy? You said—I *think* you said—that he wasn't so smart, that there was no lateralization, whatever that means. Suppose *he* miscalculates? Then, what?"

"He would never have the opportunity to miscalculate again. With minimum loss to ourselves, we would take out—"

"Hold it, *soldier*!" interrupted Kendrick, his tone suddenly harsh, issuing no less than an order. "Back up. 'With minimum loss to ourselves . . .' What does *that* mean?"

"I'm sure you're aware that I'm not at liberty to discuss such matters."

"I think you damn well better. Does 'minimum loss' mean just Los Angeles, or New York, or maybe Albuquerque or St. Louis? Since we're all paying for this minimum-loss umbrella, why not tell us what the weather's going to be like?"

"If you think I'm going to endanger national security on network television . . . well, Congressman, I'm genuinely sorry to say it, but I don't think you have any right representing the American people."

"The whole bunch of them? Never thought I did. I was told this program was between you and me—that I insulted you on television and that you had the right to reply in the same arena. It's why I'm here. So reply, Colonel. Don't keep throwing Pentagonese slogans at me; I have too much respect for our armed services to allow you to get away with that."

"If by 'slogans' you're criticizing the selfless leaders of our defense establishment—men of loyalty and honor who, above all, want to keep our nation strong—then I pity you."

"Oh, come off it. I haven't been here that long, but among the few friends I've made are some brass over in Arlington who probably wince when you drag out your modus non operandis. What I'm *patiently* trying to explain to you, Colonel, is that you don't have a blank check any more than I do or my neighbor down the street does. We live with realities—"

"Then let me *explain* the realities!" broke in Barrish.

"Let me *finish,*" said Evan, now smiling.

"Gentlemen, *gentlemen,*" said the familiar newscaster.

"I'm not casting any doubts on your *commitments,* Colonel," Kendrick interrupted. "You're doing your job and protecting your turf, I understand that." Evan picked up a piece of paper. "But when you said in the hearing—I wrote this down—'minor academic fiduciary procedures,' I wondered what you meant. Are you really above accountability? If you believe that, tell it to Joe Smith down the street who's trying to balance the family checkbook."

"That same Joe Smith will get on his *knees* to us when it dawns on him that we're ensuring his survival!"

"I think I just heard a lot of groans over in Arlington, Colonel. Joe Smith doesn't have to get on his knees to anyone. Not here."

"You're taking my remarks out of context! You know perfectly *well* what I meant, Congressman Partridge!"

"No, Colonel, he's the other guy. I'm the sub who was sent in at left guard."

"*Left* is certainly right!"

"That's an interesting statement. May I quote you?"

"I *know* about you," said Barrish ominously, threateningly. "Don't talk to me about the guy down the street, pretending you're like everyone else." Barrish paused, then as if he could no longer control himself, shouted, "You're not even *married*!"

"That's the most accurate statement you've made here. No, I'm not, but if you're asking me for a date, I'd better check with my girl."

No contest. The Pentagon's big gun backfired, the powder burns all over his face on national television.

"Who the hell *is* he?" asked Mr. Joseph Smith of 70 Cedar Street in Clinton, New Jersey.

"I don't know," replied Mrs. Smith, in front of the television next to her husband. "He's kind of cute, though, isn't he?"

"I don't know about cute, but he just told off one of those snotty officer types who used to give me a lot of shit in 'Nam. He's my buddy."

"He's good," said Inver Brass's Eric Sundstrom, rising and turning off the set in his flat overlooking New York's Gramercy Park. He drained his glass of Montrachet and looked over at Margaret Lowell and Gideon Logan, both sitting in chairs across the room. "He has a quick mind and stays ice-cold. I know that cobra Barrish; he likes nothing better than drawing blood in the spotlight. Kendrick buried him with his own bullshit."

"Our man's kind of cute, too," added Mrs. Lowell.

"What?"

"Well, he's attractive, Eric. That's hardly a liability."

"He's funny," said Logan. "And that's a decided asset. He has the ability and the presence to shift rapidly from the serious to the amusing and that's no small talent. He did the same thing during the hearing; it's not accidental. Kennedy had the same gift; he saw humorous ironies everywhere. The people like that. . . . Still, I think I see a gray cloud in the distance."

"What's that?" asked Sundstrom.

"A man with such quick perceptions will not be easy to control."

"If he's the right man," said Margaret Lowell, "and we have every reason to believe he is, that won't matter, Gideon."

"Suppose he's not? Suppose there's something we don't know? *We* will have launched him, not the political process."

Far uptown in Manhattan, between Fifth and Madison avenues, in a brownstone town house that rose six stories high, the white-haired Samuel Winters sat across from his friend Jacob Mandel. They were in Winters's large top-floor study. Several exquisite Gobelin tapestries were hung on various wall spaces between the bookshelves, and the furniture was equally breathtaking. Yet the room was comfortable. It was used; it was warm; the masterpieces of the past were there to serve, not merely to be observed. Using the remote control, the aristocratic historian snapped off the television set.

"Well?" asked Winters.

"I want to think for a moment, Samuel." Mandel's eyes strayed around the study. "You've had all this since you were born," said the stockbroker, making a statement. "Yet you've always worked so hard."

"I chose a field where having money made things much easier," replied Winters. "I've occasionally felt rather guilty about that. I could always go where I wanted, gain access to archives others couldn't, study as long as I wished. Whatever contributions I've made have been minor compared with the fun I've had. My wife used to say that." The historian glanced at the portrait of a lovely, dark-haired woman dressed in the style of the forties; it was hung behind the desk between two huge windows overlooking Seventy-third Street. A man working could turn and gaze at it easily.

"You miss her, don't you?"

"Terribly. I come up and talk with her frequently."

"I don't think I could go on without Hannah, yet oddly enough, considering what she went through in Germany, I pray to God she leaves me first. I believe the death of another loved one would be too great a pain for her to bear alone. Does that sound awful of me?"

"It sounds remarkably generous—like everything you say and do, old friend. And also because I know so well what you would face by yourself. You'd do it better than I, Jacob."

"Nonsense."

"It must be your temple—"

"When were you last in church, Samuel?"

"Let's see. My son was married in Paris when I broke my leg and couldn't attend, and my daughter eloped with that charming helium-head who makes far more money than he deserves writing those films I don't understand—so it must have been in '45 when I got back from the war. St. John the Divine, of course. *She* made me go when all I wanted to do was get her undressed."

"Oh, you're outrageous! I don't believe you for a minute."

"You'd be wrong."

"He could be dangerous," said Mandel, suddenly changing the subject and reverting to Evan Kendrick. Winters understood; his old friend had been talking but he had also been thinking.

"In what way? Everything we've learned about him—and I doubt there's much more to know—would seem to negate any obsession for power. Without that, where's the danger?"

"He's fiercely independent."

"All to the good. He might even make a fine President. No ties to the tub-thumpers, the yea-sayers and the sycophants. We've both seen him blow the first category away; the rest are easier."

"Then I'm not being clear," said Mandel. "Because it's not yet clear to me."

"Or I'm being stupid, Jacob. What are you trying to say?"

"Suppose he found out about us? Suppose he learned he was code name Icarus, the product of Inver Brass?"

"That's impossible."

"That's not the question. Leap over the impossibility. Intellectually—and the young man has an intellect—what would be his response? Remember now, he's fiercely independent."

Samuel Winters brought his hand to his chin and stared out the window overlooking the street. And then his gaze shifted to the portrait of his wife. "I see," he said, uncertain images coming into focus from his own past. "He'd be furious. He'd consider himself part of a larger corruption, irrevocably tied to it because he was manipulated. He'd be in a rage."

"And in that rage," pressed Mandel, "what do you think he would do? Incidentally, exposing us in the long run is irrelevant. It would be like the rumors of the Trilateral Commission promoting Jimmy Carter because Henry Luce put an obscure governor of Georgia on the cover of *Time.* There was more truth than not in those rumors, but nobody cared. . . . What *would* Kendrick do?"

Winters looked at his old friend, his eyes widening. "My God," he said quietly. "He'd run in disgust."

"Does that sound familiar, Samuel?"

"It was so many years ago . . . things were different—"

"I don't think they were that different. Far better than now, actually, not different."

"I wasn't in office."

"It was yours for the taking. The brilliant, immensely wealthy dean from Columbia University whose advice was sought by succeeding presidents and whose appearances before the House and Senate committees altered national policies. . . . You were tapped for the governorship of New York, literally being swept into Albany, when you learned only weeks before the convention that a political organization unknown to you had orchestrated your nomination and your inevitable election."

"It was a total shock. I'd never heard of it or them."

"Yet you presumed—rightly or wrongly—that this silent machine expected you to do its bidding and you fled, denouncing the whole charade."

"In disgust. It was against every precept of an open political process I'd ever advocated."

"Fiercely independent," added the stockbroker. "And what followed was a power vacuum; there was political chaos, the party in disarray. The opportunists moved in and took over, and there were six years of draconian laws and corrupt administrations from the lower to the upper Hudson."

"Are you blaming me for all that, Jacob?"

"It's related, Samuel. Thrice Caesar refused the crown and all hell broke loose."

"Are you saying that Kendrick might refuse to assume the office presented to him?"

"You did. You walked away in outrage."

"Because people unknown to me were committing enormous sums of money, propelling me into office. Why? If they were genuinely interested in better government and not private interest, why didn't they come forward?"

"Why don't we, Samuel?"

Winters looked hard at Mandel, his eyes sad. "Because we're playing God, Jacob. We must, for we know what others don't know. We know what will happen if we don't proceed our way. Suddenly the people of a great republic don't have a president but a king, the emperor of all the states of the union. What they don't understand is what's behind the king. Those jackals in the background can only be ripped out by replacing him. No other way."

"I understand. I'm cautious because I'm afraid."

"Then we must be extraordinarily careful and make certain Evan Kendrick never learns about us. It's as simple as that."

"Nothing's simple," objected Mandel. "He's no fool. He's going to wonder why all the attention is raining down on him. Varak will have to be a master scenarist—each sequence logically, unalterably leading to the next."

"I wondered, too," admitted Winters softly, once again glancing at the portrait of his late wife. "Jennie used to say to me, 'It's too easy, Sam. Everyone else is out there busting his britches to get a few lines in the newspapers and you get whole editorials praising you for things we're not even sure you did.' It's why I started asking questions, how I found out what had happened, not who but *how.*"

"And then you walked away."

"Of course."

"Why? I mean really, *why*?"

"You just answered that, Jacob. I was outraged."

"Despite everything you might have contributed?"

"Well, obviously."

"Is it fair, Samuel, to say you were not gripped by the fever to *win* that office?"

"Again, obviously. Whether admirable or not, I've never had to win *anything.* As Averell once said, 'Fortunately or unfortunately, I've not had to depend on my current job to eat.' That sums it up, I guess."

"The fever, Samuel. The fever you never felt, the hunger you never had must somehow grip Kendrick. In the final analysis, he has to want to win, desperately *need* to win."

"The fire in the belly," said the historian. "We all should have thought of it first, but the rest of us simply assumed he'd leap at the opportunity. God, we were *fools*!"

"Not 'the rest of us,' " protested the stockbroker, holding up the palms of his hands. "I didn't think about it until I walked into this room an hour ago. Suddenly the memories came back, memories of you and your—fierce independence. From being the bright hope, an extraordinary asset, you became a morally outraged liability who walked away and made room for all the sleazeballs in and out of town."

"You're hitting home, Jacob. . . . I should have stayed, I've known it for years. My wife in a fit of anger once called me a 'spoiled Goody Two-Shoes.' She claimed, like you, I think, that I could have prevented so much, if I accomplished nothing else."

"Yes, you could have, Samuel. Harry Truman was right, it's the leaders who shape history. There would have been no United States without Thomas Jefferson, no Third Reich without Adolf Hitler. But no man or woman becomes a leader unless he or she wants to. They've got to have a burning need to get there."

"And you think our Kendrick lacks it?"

"I suspect he does. What I saw on that television screen, and what I saw five days ago during the committee hearing, was an incautious man who didn't give a damn whose bones he rattled because he was morally outraged. Brains, yes; courage, certainly; even wit and appeal—all of which we agreed had to be part of the ideal composite we sought. But I also saw a streak of my friend Samuel Winters, a man who could walk away from the system because he didn't have the fever in him to go after the prize."

"Is that so bad, Jacob? Not with regard to me—I was never that important, really—but is it so healthy for all officeseekers to be on fire?"

"You don't turn over the store to part-time management, not if it's your major investment. The people rightly expect a full-time landlord, and they sense it when the call isn't basically there, aggressively there. They want their money's worth."

"Well," said Winters, his tone mildly defensive. "I believe the people were not totally unimpressed with me, and I wasn't burning up with fever. On the other hand, I didn't make too many gaffes."

"Good Lord, you never had the chance to. Your campaign was a television blitzkrieg with some of the best photography I've ever seen, your handsome countenance a decided asset, of course."

"I had three or four debates, you know. . . . Three actually—"

"With warthogs, Samuel. They were buried by congenial class—the people love that. They never stop searching the heavens, now the television screens, for that king or that prince to come along and show them the way with comforting words."

"It's a goddamned shame. Abraham Lincoln would have been considered an awkward hick and stayed in Illinois."

"Or worse," said Jacob Mandel, chuckling. "Abraham the Jew in league with the anti-Christs, sacrificing Gentile infants."

"And when he grew the beard, absolute confirmation," agreed Winters, smiling and getting out of his chair. "A drink?" he asked, knowing his friend's answer and heading for the bar beneath a French tapestry on the right wall.

"Thank you. The usual, please."

"Of course." The historian poured two drinks in silence, one bourbon, one Canadian, both with ice only. He returned to their chairs and handed the bourbon to Mandel. "All right, Jacob. I think I've put it all together."

"I knew you could pour and think at the same time," said Mandel, smiling and raising his glass. "Your health, sir."

"*L'chaim,*" replied the historian.

"So?"

"Somehow, some way, this fever you speak of, this need to win the prize, must be instilled in Evan Kendrick. Without it he's not credible and without *him* Gideon's mongrels—the opportunists and the fanatics—move in."

"I believe that, yes."

Winters sipped his drink, his eyes straying to a Gobelin tapestry. "Philip and the knights at Crécy weren't defeated by the English bowmen and the Welsh long knives alone. They had to contend with what Saint-Simon described three hundred years later as a court bled by the 'vile bourgeois corrupters.' "

"Your erudition is beyond me, Samuel."

"How do we *instill* this fever in Evan Kendrick? It's so terribly important that we do. I see it so clearly now."

"I think we start with Milos Varak."

Annie Mulcahy O'Reilly was beside herself. The standard four telephone lines in the congressional office were usually used for outgoing calls; this particular congressman did not normally receive many incoming ones. Today, however, was not only different, it was *crazy.* In the space of twenty-four hours, the smallest, most underworked staff on the Hill became the most frenzied. Annie had to call her two file clerks, who *never* came in on Monday ("Come on, Annie, it ruins a decent weekend"), to get their bouffant heads down to the office. She then reached Phillip Tobias, the bright if frustrated chief aide, and told him to forget his tennis game and drag his promotional ass downtown or she'd kill him. ("What the hell happened?" "You didn't see the Foxley show yesterday?" "No, I was sailing. Why should I have?" "*He* was on it!" "*What?* That can't *happen* without my *approval*!" "They must have called him at home." "The son of a bitch never *told* me!" "He didn't tell me, either, but I saw his name in the *Post*'s late listings." "*Jesus!* Get me a tape, Annie! *Please!*" "Only if you come down and help us man the phones, dearie." "*Shit!*" "I'm a lady, you prick. Don't talk to me that way." "I'm sorry, I'm *sorry,* Annie! *Please.* The *tape*!")

Finally, and only because she was desperate, and only because her husband, Patrick Xavier O'Reilly, had Mondays off because he worked the high-crime shift on Saturdays, she called the two-toilet Irish detective and told him that if he did not come down to help out she'd file a complaint against him for rape—which was only wishful thinking, she added. The only person she was unable to reach was the congressman from Colorado's Ninth District.

"I am so very, very sorry, Mrs. O'Reilly," said the Arab husband of the couple who took care of Kendrick's house, and who Annie suspected was probably an unemployed surgeon or an ex-university president. "The Congressman said he would be away for a few days. I have no idea where he is."

"That's a lot of *crap,* Mr. *Sahara*—"

"You flatter me with dimensions, madame."

"That, *too*! You reach that horned-toad servant of the public and tell him we're going *ape-shit* down here! And it's all because of his appearance on the Foxley show!"

"He was remarkably effective, was he not?"

"*You* know about it?"

"I saw his name in the *Washington Post*'s late listings, madame. Also in the *Times* of New York and Los Angeles, and the *Chicago Tribune.*"

"*He* gets all those papers?"

"No, madame, I do. But he's perfectly welcome to read them."

"Glory be to God!"

The pandemonium in the outside office had become intolerable. Annie slammed down the phone and ran to her door; she opened it, astonished to see Evan Kendrick and her husband shoving their way through a crowd of reporters, congressional aides and various other people she did not know. "Come in *here*!" she yelled.

Once inside the secretarial office and with the door closed, Mr. O'Reilly spoke. "I'm her Paddy," he said, out of breath. "Nice to meet you, Congressman."

"You're my blocking back, pal," replied Kendrick, shaking hands and quickly studying the large broad-shouldered, red-haired man with a paunch four inches larger than his considerable height should permit, and a vaguely florid face that held a pair of knowing, intelligent green eyes. "I'm grateful we got here at the same time."

"In all honesty, we didn't, sir. My crazy lady called over an hour ago and I was able to get here in maybe twenty, twenty-five minutes. I saw the brouhaha in the corridor and figured you might show up. I waited for ya."

"You might have let *me* know, you lousy mick! We've been going crazy in here!"

"And be slapped with a felony charge, darlin'?"

"He really *is* two-toilet Irish, Congressman—"

"*Hold* it, you two," ordered Evan, glancing at the door. "What the hell are we going to do about this? What's *happened*?"

"*You* went on the Foxley show," said Mrs. O'Reilly. "We didn't."

"I make it a point never to watch those programs," mumbled Kendrick. "If I do, I'm expected to know something."

"Now a lot of people know about you."

"You were *damn* good, Congressman," added the D.C. detective. "A couple of boys in the department called and asked me to tell Annie to thank you—I told you, Annie."

"First, I haven't had the chance, and second, with all this confusion I probably would have forgotten. But I think, Evan, that your only clean way is to go out there and make some kind of statement."

"Wait a minute," interrupted Kendrick, looking at Patrick O'Reilly. "Why would anyone in the police department want to thank me?"

"The way you stood up to Barrish and clobbered him."

"I gathered that, but what's Barrish to them?"

"He's a Pentagon hustler with friends in high places. Also a ball-breaker if you've spent a few sleepless nights on stakeout and instead of being thanked you're dumped on."

"What stakeout? What happened?"

"*Mister* Kendrick," broke in Annie. "That's a *zoo* out there! You've got to show yourself, *say* something."

"No, I want to hear this. Go on, Mr.—may I call you Patrick, or Pat?"

" 'Paddy' fits better." The police officer patted his stomach. "That's what I'm called."

"I'm Evan. Drop the 'Congressman'—I want to drop it completely. Please. Go on. How was Barrish involved with the police?"

"I didn't say that, now. He, himself, is cleaner than an Irish bagpipe, which actually isn't too lovely inside, but he's purer than a bleached sheet in the noonday sun."

"Men in your line of work don't thank people for clobbering clean laundry—"

"Well, it wasn't the biggest thing that ever went down; truth be told, by itself it was minor, but something might have come out of it if we could have followed up. . . . The boys were tracking a mozzarella known to launder cash through Miami and points southeast like the Cayman Islands. On the fourth night of the stakeout at the Mayflower Hotel, they thought they had him. You see, one of those Bally-shoe types went to his room at one o'clock in the morning with a large briefcase. One o'clock in the morning—not exactly the start or the shank of the business day, right?"

"Not exactly."

"Well, it turned out that the Bally shoes had legitimate investments with the mozzarella, and the Pentagon logs showed that he'd been in a procurements conference until almost eleven-thirty and, further, he had to catch a plane to Los Angeles at eight in the morning, so the one o'clock was explained."

"What about the briefcase?"

"We couldn't touch it. Much offense was taken in high dudgeon and lots of national security was thrown around. You see, someone made a phone call."

"But not to a lawyer," said Evan. "Instead, to one Colonel Robert Barrish of the Pentagon."

"Bingo. Our noses were shoved in dirt for impugning the motives of a fine, loyal American who was helping to keep the great U.S. of A. strong. The boys were reamed good."

"But you think otherwise. You think a lot more than legitimate investments happened in that room."

"If it walks like a duck and talks like a duck and looks like a duck, it's usually a duck. But not the pair of Bally shoes; he wasn't a duck, he was a slap-tailed weasel whose name was stricken from our *list* of ducks."

"Thanks, Paddy. . . . All right, Mrs. O'Reilly, what do I say out there?"

"Whatever I suggest our boy Phil Tobias will probably object to, you should know that. He's on his way here."

"You called off his Monday-morning tennis? That's courage beyond the call of duty."

"He's sweet and he's smart, Evan, but I don't think his advice can help you now; you're on your own. Remember, those vultures out there are convinced you've been grandstanding all last week—running a parlay from the committee hearing to the Foxley show. If you had ciphered out, no one would give a damn, but you didn't. You took on a heavyweight and made him look like a fast-talking thug and that makes you news. They want to know where you're going."

"Then what do you suggest? You know where I'm going, Annie. What *do* I say?"

Ann Mulcahy O'Reilly looked into Kendrick's eyes. "Whatever you want to, Congressman. Just mean it."

"The plaint of the swan? My swan song, Annie?"

"Only you'll know that when you get out there."

The uproar in the outer office was compounded by the sudden eruption of strobe flashes and the shifting, blinding floodlights of the television crews swinging their lethal mini-cams in the crowd. Questions were shouted and outshouted. Several of the more prominent newspeople were arrogantly demanding their rights for the closest, most prominent positions, so the congressman from Colorado's Ninth District simply walked to his receptionist's desk, moved the blotter and the telephone console aside, and sat on top. He smiled gamely, held up both hands several times and refused to speak. Gradually the cacophony subsided, broken now and then by a strident voice answered by the silent stare of mocked surprise on the part of the shocked representative. Finally, it was understood: Congressman Evan Kendrick was not going to open his mouth unless and until he could be heard by everyone. Silence descended.

"Thanks very much," said Evan. "I need all the help I can get to figure out what I want to say—before *you* say what you want to say, which is different because you've got it *all* figured out."

"*Congressman* Kendrick," shouted an abrasive television journalist, obviously upset with his status in the second row. "Is it *true*—"

"Oh, come on, *will* you?" broke in Evan firmly. "Give me a break, friend. You're used to this, I'm not."

"That's not the way you came over on television, sir!" replied the erstwhile anchorman.

"That was one on one, as I see it. This is one against the whole

Colosseum wanting a lion's dinner. Let me say something first, okay?"

"Of course, sir."

"I'm glad it wasn't you last week, Stan—I think your name is Stan."

"It is, Congressman."

"You would have had my head along with your brandy."

"You're very kind, sir."

"No kidding? It *is* a compliment, isn't it?"

"Yes, Congressman, it is. That's our job."

"I respect that. I wish to hell you'd do it more often."

"*What?*"

"One of the most respected members of my staff," continued Kendrick quickly, "explained to me that I should make a statement. That's kind of awesome if you've never been asked to make a statement before—"

"You *did* run for office, sir," interrupted another television reporter, very obviously moving her blond hair into her camera's focus. "Certainly statements were required then."

"Not if the incumbent represented our district's version of *Planet of the Apes.* Check it out, I'll stand by that. Now, may I go on or do I simply go out? I'll be quite honest with you. I really don't give a damn."

"Go on, sir," said the gentleman often referred to as Stan-the-man, a broad grin on his telegenic face.

"Okay. . . . My very valued staff member also mentioned that some of you, if not all of you, might be under the impression that I was grandstanding last week. 'Grandstanding.' . . . As I understand the term, it means calling attention to oneself by performing some basically melodramatic act, with or without substance, that rivets the attention of the crowds watching—the grandstands—on the person performing that act. If that definition is accurate, then I must decline the title of grandstander because I'm not looking for anyone's approval. Again, I really don't care."

The momentary shock was dispelled by the Congressman's palms pressing the air in front of him. "I'm quite sincere about that, ladies and gentlemen. I don't expect to be around here very long—"

"Do you have a *health* problem, sir?" shouted a young man from the back of the room.

"Do you want to arm-wrestle? . . . No, I have no such problem that I'm aware of—"

"I was a collegiate boxing champion, sir," added the youthful reporter in the rear, unable to contain himself amid humorous boos from the crowd. "Sorry, sir," he said, embarrassed.

"Don't be, young fella. If I had your talent, I'd probably challenge the head of Pentagon procurements *and* his counterpart in the Kremlin, and we'd solve everything the old-fashioned way. One challenger from each side and save the battalions. But no, I don't have your talent and I also have no problems of health."

"Then what *did* you mean?" asked a respected columnist from the *New York Times.*

"I'm flattered you're here," said Evan, recognizing the man. "I had no idea I was worth your time."

"I think you are, and my time's not that valuable. Where are you coming from, Congressman?"

"I'm not certain, but to answer your first question, I'm not sure I belong here. As to your second question, since I'm not sure I should be here, I'm in the enviable position of saying what I want to say without regard to the consequences—the political consequences, I guess."

"That *is* news," said the acerbic Stan-the-man, writing in his notebook. "Your statement, sir."

"Thanks. I think I'd like to get it over with. Like a lot of people, I don't like what I see. I've been away from this country for many years, and maybe you have to get away to understand what we've got—if only to compare it with what others haven't got. There's not supposed to be an oligarchy running this government and yet it seems to me that one has moved in. I can't put my finger on it, or them, but they're there, I know it. So do you. They want to escalate, always *escalate,* always pointing to an adversary who himself has escalated to the top of his economic and technological ladder. Where the hell do we stop? Where do *they* stop? When do we stop giving our children nightmares because all they hear is the goddamned promise of annihilation? When do *their* kids stop hearing it? . . . Or do we just keep going up in this elevator designed in hell until we can't come down any longer, which won't make much difference anyway because all the streets outside will be in flames. . . . Forgive me, I know it's not fair, but I suddenly don't want any more questions. I'm going back to the mountains." Evan Kendrick got off the desk and walked swiftly through the stunned crowd to his office door. He opened it, quickening his steps, and disappeared into the hallway.

"He's not going to the mountains," whispered Patrick Xavier O'Reilly to his wife. "That lad is staying right here in this town."

"Oh, *shussh*!" cried Annie, tears in her eyes. "He's just cut himself off from the entire *Hill*!"

"Maybe the Hill, lass, but not from us. He's put his not-too-delicate finger on it. They all make the money and we're scared shitless. Watch him, Annie, care for him. He's a voice we want to hear."

19

Kendrick wandered the hot, torpid streets of Washington, his shirt open, his jacket slung over his shoulder, not having any idea where he was going, trying only to clear his head by putting one foot ahead of the other in aimless sequence. More often than he cared to count, he had been stopped by strangers whose comments were pretty equally divided but slightly weighted in his favor, a fact he was not sure he liked.

"Hell of a job you did on that double-talking prick, Senator!"

"I'm not a senator, I'm a congressman. Thank you, I guess."

"Who do you think you *are,* Congressman Whatever-your-name-is? Trying to trip up a fine, loyal American like Colonel Barrish. Goddamned left-wing bachelor-fairy!"

"Can I sell you some perfume? The colonel bought some."

"*Disgusting!*"

"*Hey,* man, I dig your MTV! You move good and you sing in a high register. That mother would send all the brothers back to 'Nam for raw meat!"

"I don't think he would, soldier. There's no discrimination in him. We're all raw meat."

"Because you're clever doesn't make you right, sir! And because he was tricked—admittedly by his own words—doesn't make him wrong. He's a man committed to the strength of our nation, and you obviously are not!"

"I think I'm committed to reason, *sir.* That doesn't exclude our country's strength, at least I would hope not."

"I saw no evidence of that!"

"Sorry. It's there."

"Thank you, Congressman, for saying what so many of us are thinking."

"Why don't *you* say it?"

"I'm not sure. Everywhere you turn, someone's shouting at us to stand tough. I was a kid at Bastogne, in the Bulge, and nobody had to tell me to be tough. I *was* tough—and damned scared, too. It just happened; I wanted to live. But things are different now. It's not men against men, or even guns and planes. It's machines flying through the air punching big holes in the earth. You can't aim at them, you can't stop them. All you can do is wait."

"I wish you'd been at the hearing. You just said it better than I ever could with far more impressive credentials."

He really did not want to talk any more; he was talked out and strangers in the streets were not helping him find the solitude he needed. He had to think, sort things out for himself, decide what to do and decide quickly if only to put the decision behind him. He had accepted the Partridge Committee assignment for a specific reason: he wanted a voice in his district's selection of the man who would succeed him, and his aide, Phil Tobias, had convinced him that accepting Partridge's summons would guarantee him a voice. But what Evan wondered was did he really give a damn?

To a degree he had to admit that he did, but not because of any territorial claim. He had walked into a minor political arena an angry man with his eyes open. Could he simply close up shop and take-a-hike because he was irritated over a brief flurry of public exposure? He did not wear a badge of morality on his lapel, but there was something inherently distasteful to him about someone who gave a commitment and walked away from it because of personal inconvenience. On the other hand, in the words of another era, he had thrown out the rascals who had been taking the Colorado's Ninth District to the cleaners. He had done what he wanted to do. What more could the voters of his constituency want from him? He had awakened them; at least he thought he had and had spared neither words nor money in trying to do so.

Think. He really had to think. He would probably keep the Colorado property for some future time as yet unconsidered; he was forty-one; in nineteen years he would be sixty. What the hell did *that* matter? . . . It did matter. He was heading back to Southwest Asia, to the jobs and the people he knew best how to work with, but, like Manny, he was not going to live out his last years, or with luck a decade or two, in those same surroundings. . . . Manny. Emmanuel Weingrass, genius, brilliance personified, autocrat, renegade, totally impossible human being—yet the only father he had ever known. He never really knew his own father; that faraway man had died building a bridge in Nepal when he was barely eight years old, leaving a humorously cynical wife who claimed that having married an outrageously young captain in the Army Corps of Engineers during the Second World War, she had fewer episodes of connubial bliss than Catherine of Aragon.

"*Hey!*" yelled a rotund man who had just walked out of the small canopied door of a bar on Sixteenth Street. "I just seen you! You were on TV sittin' on a desk! It was that all-day news program. *Boring!* I don't know what the hell you said but some bums clapped and some other bums gave you raspberries. It was *you*!"

"You must be mistaken," said Kendrick, hurrying down the pavement. Good Lord, he thought, the Cable News people had rushed to air the impromptu press conference in short order. He had left his office barely an hour and a half ago; someone was in a hurry. He knew that Cable needed constant fill, but with all the news floating around Washington, why *him*? In truth, what bothered him was an observation made by young Tobias during Evan's early days on the Hill. "Cable's an incubating process, Congressman, and we can capitalize on it. The networks may not consider you important enough to cover, but they scan Cable's snippets all the time for what's offbeat, the unusual—their own fill. We can create situations where the C-boys will take the bait, and in my opinion, Mr. Kendrick, your looks and your somewhat oblique observations—"

"Then let's never make the mistake, Mr. Tobias, of ever calling the C-boys, okay?" The interruption had deflated the aide, who was only partially mollified by Evan's promise that the next inhabitant of his office would be far more cooperative. He had meant it; he meant it now, but he worried that it might be too late.

He headed back to the Madison Hotel, only a block or so away, where he had spent Sunday night—spent it there because he had had the presence of mind to call his house in Virginia to learn if his appearance on the Foxley show had created any interruptions at home.

"Only if one wishes to make a telephone call, Evan," Dr. Sabri Hassan had replied in Arabic, the language they both spoke for convenience as well as for other reasons. "It never stops ringing."

"Then I'll stay in town. I don't know where yet, but I'll let you know."

"Why bother?" Sabri had asked. "You probably won't be able to get through anyway. I'm surprised that you did now."

"Well, in case Manny calls—"

"Why not call him yourself and tell him where you are so I will not have to lie. The journalists in this city cannot wait for an Arab to lie; they pounce upon us. The Israelis can say that white is black, or sweet is sour, and their lobby convinces Congress it's for your own good. It is not so with us."

"Cut it out, Sabri—"

"We must leave you, Evan. We're no good to you, we *will* be no good to you."

"What the hell are you talking about?"

"Kashi and I watched the program this morning. You were most effective, my friend."

"We'll talk about it later." He had spent the afternoon watching baseball and drinking whisky. At six-thirty he had turned on the news, one network after another, only to see himself in brief segments from the Foxley show. In disgust, he had switched to an arts channel that showed a film depicting the mating habits of whales off the coast of Tierra del Fuego. He was amazed; he fell asleep.

Today, instinct told him to keep his room key, so he rushed through the Madison's lobby to the elevators. Once inside the room he removed his clothes down to his shorts and lay on the bed. And whether it was a symptom of a repressed ego or sheer curiosity, he turned on the remote control unit and switched the channel to Cable News. Seven minutes later he saw himself walking out of his office.

"Ladies and gentlemen, you have just seen one of the most unusual press conferences this reporter has ever attended. Not only unusual, but unusually one-sided. This first-term representative from Colorado has raised issues of obvious national importance but refuses to be questioned as to his conclusions. He simply walks away. On his behalf it should be said that he denies 'grandstanding' because he apparently is not sure he intends to remain

in Washington—which we assume means government. Nevertheless, his statements were provocative, to say the least."

The videotape suddenly stopped, replaced by the live face of an anchorwoman. "We switch now to the Department of Defense, where we understand that an under secretary in charge of Strategic Deterence has a prepared statement. It's yours, Steve."

Another face, this a dark-haired, blivet-featured reporter with too many teeth who peered into a camera and whispered. "Under Secretary Jasper Hefflefinger, who manages to be hauled out whenever someone attacks the Pentagon, has rushed into the breach opened by Congressman—*who?*—Henryk, of Wyoming—*what?*—Colorado! Here is Under Secretary Hefflefinger."

Another face. A jowled but handsome man, a strong face with a shock of silver hair that demanded attention. And with a voice that would be envied by the most prominent radio announcers of the late thirties and forties. "I *say* to the congressman that we *welcome* his comments. We want the same *thing,* sir! The avoidance of catastrophe, the pursuit of liberty and freedom—".

The asshole went on and on saying everything but also saying nothing, never once addressing the issues of escalation and containment.

Why *me*? shouted Kendrick to himself. *Why me?* To *hell* with it! With *everything*! He shut off the television set, reached for the phone and called Colorado. "Hi, Manny," he said, hearing Weingrass's abrupt hello.

"*Boy,* are you *something*!" yelled the old man into the phone. "I brought you up right, after all!"

"Stow it, Manny, I want out of this shit."

"You want *what*? Did you see yourself on *TV*?"

"That's why I want out. Forget the glassed-in steam bath and the gazebo down by the streams. We'll do it later. Let's you and I head back to the Emirates—by way of Paris, naturally—maybe a couple of months in Paris, if you like. Okay?"

"*Not* okay, you *meshugenah* clown! You got something to say, you *say* it! I taught you always—whether we lost a contract or not—to say what you believed was right. . . . Okay, okay, maybe we fudged a little on time, but we *delivered*! And we *never* charged for extensions even when we had to pay!"

"Manny, that has nothing to do with what's going on here—"

"It's got *everything*! You're building something. . . . And speaking of building, guess what, my goy boy?"

"What?"

"I've started the terrace steam bath and I've given the plans for the gazebo down by the streams. *Nobody* interrupts Emmanuel Weingrass until his designs are completed to his satisfaction!"

"Manny, you're *impossible*!"

"I may have heard that before."

Milos Varak walked down a graveled path in Rock Creek Park toward a bench that overlooked a ravine where offshoot waters of the Potomac rushed below. It was a remote, peaceful area, away from the concrete pavements above, favored by the summer tourists wishing to get away from the heat and hustle of the streets. As the Czech expected, the Speaker of the House of Representatives was already there, sitting on the bench, his thatch of white hair concealed by an Irish walking cap, the visor half over his face, his long, painfully thin frame covered by an unnecessary raincoat in the sweltering humidity of an August afternoon in Washington. The Speaker wanted no one to notice him; it was not his normal proclivity. Varak approached and spoke.

"Mr. Speaker, I'm honored to meet you, sir."

"Son of a bitch, you *are* a foreigner!" The gaunt face with the dark eyes and arched white brows was an angry face, angry and yet defensive, the latter trait obviously repulsive to him. "If you're some fucking Communist errand boy, you can pack it in right now, *Ivan*! I'm not running for another term. I'm out, finished, kaput come January, and what happened thirty or forty years ago doesn't mean doodlely shit! You read me, *Boris*?"

"You've had an outstanding career and have been a positive force for your country, sir—also my country now. As to my being a Russian or an agent from the Eastern bloc, I've fought both for the past ten years, as a number of people in this government know."

The granite-eyed politician studied Varak. "You wouldn't have the guts or the stupidity to say that to me unless you could back it up," he intoned in the pungent accent of a northern New Englander. "Still, you *threatened* me!"

"Only to get your attention, to convince you to see me. May I sit down?"

"Sit," said the Speaker, as if addressing a dog he expected to obey him. Varak did so, maintaining ample space between them. "What do you know about the events that may or may not have taken place sometime back in the fifties?"

"It was the seventeenth of March, 1951, to be exact," replied the Czech. "On that day a male child was born in Belfast's Lady of Mercy Hospital to a young woman who had emigrated to America several years previously. She had returned to Ireland, her explanation indeed a sad one. Her husband had died and in her bereavement she wanted to have their child at home, among her family."

His gaze cold and unflinching, the Speaker said, "So?"

"I think you know, sir. There was no husband over here, but there was a man who must have loved her very much. A rising young politician trapped in an unhappy marriage from which he could not escape because of the laws of the Church and his constituents' blind adherence to them. For years this man, who was also an attorney, sent money to the woman and visited her and the child in Ireland as often as he could . . . as an American uncle, of course—"

"You can prove who these people were?" interrupted the aging Speaker curtly. "Not hearsay or rumor or questionable eyewitness identification, but written proof?"

"I can."

"With what? How?"

"Letters were exchanged."

"*Liar!*" snapped the septuagenarian. "She burned every damned one before she died!"

"I'm afraid she burned all but one," said Varak softly. "I believe she had every intention of destroying it, too, but death came earlier than she expected. Her husband found it buried under several articles in her bedside table. Of course, he doesn't know who *E* is, nor does he care to know. He's only grateful that his wife declined your offer and stayed with him these past twenty years."

The old man turned away, the hint of tears welling in his eyes, sniffed away in self-discipline. "My wife had left me then," he said, barely audible. "Our daughter and son were in college and there was no reason to keep up the rotten pretense any longer. Things had changed, outlooks changed, and I was as secure as a Kennedy in Boston. Even the la-di-das in the archdiocese kept their mouths shut—of course, I let a few of those sanctimonious bastards know that if there was any Church interference during the election, I'd encourage the black radicals and the Jews to raise hell in the House over their holy tax-exempt status. The bishop damn near threw up in apoplexy, screaming all kinds of damnation at me for setting a hellfire public example but I settled his hash. I told him my departing wife had probably slept with him, too." The white-haired Speaker with the deeply lined face fell silent. "Mother of *God,*" he cried to himself, the tears now apparent. "I wanted that girl back!"

"I'm sure you're not referring to your wife."

"You know exactly whom I mean, Mr. No-name! But she couldn't do it. A decent man had given her a home and our son a name for nearly fifteen years. She couldn't leave him—even for me. I'll tell you the truth, I kept her last letter, too. Both letters were our last to each other. 'We'll be joined in the hereafter heaven,' she wrote me. 'But no further on this earth, my darling.' What kind of *crap* was *that*? We could have had a *life,* a goddamned *good* part of life!"

"If I may, sir, I think it was the expression of a loving woman who had as much respect for you as she did for herself and her son. You had children of your own, and explanations from the past can destroy the future. You had a future, Mr. Speaker."

"I would have chucked it all in—"

"She couldn't let you do that, any more than she could destroy the man who had given her and the child a home and a name."

The old man pulled out a handkerchief and wiped his eyes, his voice suddenly reverting to its harsh delivery. "How the hell do you know about all this?"

"It wasn't difficult. You're the leader of the House of Representatives, the second in line for the presidency, and I wanted to know more about you. Forgive me, but older people speak more freely than younger ones do—much of it is due to their unrecognized sense of importance where so-called secrets are concerned—and, of course, I knew that you and your wife, both Catholics, had divorced. Considering your political stature at the time and the power of your Church, that had to be a momentous decision."

"Hell, I can't fault you there. So you looked for the older people who were around at the time."

"I found them. I learned that your wife, the daughter of a wealthy real estate developer who wanted political influence and literally financed your early campaigns, had a less than enviable reputation."

"Before and after, Mr. No-name. Only, I was the last to find out."

"But you did find out," said Varak firmly. "And in your anger and embarrassment you sought other companionship. At the time you were convinced you couldn't do anything about your marriage, so you looked for surrogate comfort."

"Is that what it's called? I looked for someone who could be mine."

"And you found her in a hospital where you went to give blood during a campaign. She was a certified nurse from Ireland who was studying for her registry in the United States."

"How the *hell—*"

"Old people talk."

"Pee Wee Mangecavallo," whispered the Speaker, his eyes suddenly bright, as if the memory brought back a rush of happiness. "He had a little Italian place, a bar with good Sicilian food, about four blocks from the hospital. No one ever bothered me there—I don't think they knew who I was. That guinea bastard, he *remembered.*"

"Mr. Mangecavallo is over ninety now, but he does indeed remember. You would take your lovely nurse there and he would close up his bar at one o'clock in the morning and leave you both inside, asking only that you kept the tarantellas on the jukebox at the lowest levels."

"A beautiful person."

"With an extraordinary memory for one of his age but without, I'm afraid, the control he had as a younger man. He reminisces at length—rambles, actually—saying things over his Chianti that perhaps he would never have said even a few years ago."

"At his age he's entitled—"

"And you *did* confide in him, Mr. Speaker," interrupted Varak.

"No, not really," disagreed the old politician. "But Pee Wee put things together; it wasn't hard. After she left for Ireland, I used to go back there, for a couple of years quite frequently. I'd drink more than I usually did because nobody, like I said, knew me or gave a damn and Pee Wee always got me home without incident, as they say. I guess maybe I talked too much."

"You went back to Mr. Mangecavallo's establishment when she married—"

"*Oh,* yes, that I did! I remember it as if it were yesterday—remember going inside, no memory at all of coming out."

"Mr. Mangecavallo is quite lucid about that day. Names, a country, a city . . . a date—of severance, you called it. I went to Ireland."

The Speaker snapped his head toward Varak, his unblinking

eyes angry and questioning. "What do you want from me? It's all over, all in the past, and you can't hurt me. What *do* you want?"

"Nothing that you would ever regret or be ashamed of, sir. The most stringent background examination could be made and you could only applaud my clients' recommendation."

"Your . . . *clients*? Recommendation . . . ? Some kind of House assignment?"

"Yes, sir."

"The horseshit aside, why would I agree to whatever the hell you're talking about?"

"Because of a detail in Ireland you are not aware of."

"What's that?"

"You've heard of the killer who calls himself Tam O'Shanter, the provisional 'wing commander' of the Irish Republican Army?"

"A *pig*! A blot on every Irish clan's escutcheon!"

"He's your son."

A week had passed and for Kendrick it was further proof of the quick passage of fame in Washington. The Partridge Committee's televised hearings were suspended at the request of the Pentagon, who issued dual statements that it was revising certain financial "in-depth" records, as well as the fact that Colonel Robert Barrish had been promoted to brigadier general and posted to the island of Guam to oversee that most vital outpost of freedom.

One Joseph Smith of 70 Cedar Street in Clinton, New Jersey, whose father had been with the 27th in Guam, roared with laughter as he poked his wife's left breast in front of the television screen. "He's been *hosed,* babe! And that what's-his-face *did* it! He's my *buddy*!"

But as all brief periods of euphoria must come to an abrupt end, so did the temporary relief felt by the representative of the Ninth Congressional District of Colorado.

"Jesus *Christ*!" yelled Phil Tobias, chief aide to the Congressman, as he held his hand over the telephone. "It's the Speaker of the House *himself*! No aide, no secretary, but *him*!"

"Maybe you should let the other 'himself' know about it," said Annie O'Reilly. "He called on your line, not mine. Don't talk, sweetie. Just push the button and announce. It's out of your league."

"But it isn't *right*! His people should have called *me*—"

"*Do* it!"

Tobias did it.

"*Kendrick?*"

"Yes, Mr. Speaker?"

"You got a few minutes to spare?" asked the New Englander, the word "spare" emerging as "spay-yah."

"Well, of course, Mr. Speaker, if you think it's important."

"I don't call a shithead freshman direct if I didn't think it was important."

"Then I can only hope that a shithead Speaker has a vital issue to discuss," replied Kendrick. "If he doesn't, I'll charge my hourly consultation rate to *his* state. Is that understood, Mr. Speaker?"

"I like your style, boy. We're on different sides but I like your style."

"You may not when I'm in your office."

"I like that even better."

Astonished, Kendrick stood in front of the desk staring in silence at the evasive eyes of the gaunt-faced, white-haired Speaker of the House. The old Irishman had just made an extraordinary statement, which should have been, at the very least, a proposal but was, instead, a bombshell in Evan's path of retreat from Washington, D.C. "The Subcommittee on Oversight and Evaluation?" said Kendrick in quiet anger. "Of *Intelligence*?"

"That's it," answered the Speaker, glancing down at his papers.

"How dare you? You can't *do* that!"

"It's done. Your appointment's announced."

"Without my *consent*?"

"I don't need it. I don't say you had the clearest sailing with your own party leaders—you're not the most popular fella on your side of the fence—but with a little convincing, they agreed. You're kind of a symbol of independent bipartisanship."

"Symbol? *What* symbol? I'm no symbol!"

"You got a tape of the Foxley show?"

"It's nonhistory. It's forgotten!"

"Or that little rhubarb you pulled in your office the next morning? That fella from the *New York Times* did a hell of a column on you, made you out like some kind of—what was it? I reread it yesterday—'a reasoned voice among the babel of mad crows.' "

"All that was weeks ago and nobody's mentioned anything of substance since then. I've faded."

"You just sprang back to full flower."

"I refuse the appointment! I don't care to be burdened by secrets involving national security. I'm not staying in government and I consider it an untenable position to be placed in—a dangerous situation, to put it bluntly."

"You publicly refuse and your party will wash you out of its hair—publicly. They'll call you a few names, like a rich mistake and irresponsible, and revive that jackass you buried with your money. He and his little machine are missed around here." The Speaker paused, chuckling. "They gophered for everybody with nice little perks like private jets and fancy suites from Hawaii to the South of France owned by the mining boys. Didn't make a damn bit of difference what party you were with, they just wanted a few addenda on legislation—couldn't care less where they came from. Hell, Congressman, you refuse, you could be doing all of us a favor."

"You really are a shithead, Mr. Speaker."

"I'm pragmatic, son."

"But you've done so many decent things—"

"They came from being practical," interrupted the old pol. "They don't get done with buckets of vinegar, they go down easier with pitchers of warm syrup, like sweet Vermont syrup, get my drift?"

"Do you realize that with one statement you just condoned political corruption?"

"The *hell* I did! I just condoned the acceptance of minor greed as part of the human condition in exchange for major legislation that helps the people who really need it! I got those things through, shithead, by blinking my eyes to incidental indulgences when those who got 'em knew my eyes weren't closed. You rich son of a bitch, you wouldn't understand. Sure, we got a few millionaires around here, but most aren't. They live on yearly salaries that you'd piss away in a month. They *leave* office because they can't put their two or three kids through college on what they make, *forget* vacations. So you're goddamned right, I blink."

"All *right*!" shouted Kendrick. "I can understand that, but what I can't understand is your appointing me to Oversight! There's nothing in my background that qualifies me for such an assignment. I could name you thirty or forty others who know a lot more than I do—which isn't hard because I don't know anything. They follow these things, they love being on the inside of that dumb business—I repeat, I think it's a *dumb business*! Call on one of them. They're all salivating at the chance."

"That kind of appetite isn't what we're lookin' for, son," said the Speaker in his now heavily pronounced down-home, Down East accent that belied decades of sophisticated political negotiations in the nation's capital. "Good healthy skepticism, like what you showed that double-talking colonel on the Foxley show, that's the ticket. You'll make a real contribution."

"You're wrong, Mr. Speaker, because I have nothing to contribute, not even the slightest interest. Barrish was using and abusing generalities, arrogantly refusing to talk straight, only talking down. It was entirely different. I repeat, I have no interest in Oversight."

"Well, now, my young friend, interests change with conditions, like in the banks. Somethin' happens and the rates go up or down accordingly. And some of us are more familiar than others with certain *troubled* areas of the world—you certainly qualify in that regard. As that beautiful book says, talents buried in the ground don't do anybody a cow dung's worth of good, but if they're brought up into the light, they can flourish. Like your new flowering."

"If you're referring to the time I spent in the Arab Emirates, please remember I was a construction engineer whose only concerns were jobs and profits."

"Is that so?"

"The average tourist knew more about the politics and cultures of those countries than I did. All of us in construction stayed pretty much to ourselves; we had our own circles and rarely stepped outside them."

"I find that hard to believe—damn near impossible, in fact. I got the congressional background report on you, young fella, and I tell ya it blew my good New England socks off. Here you are right here in Washington and you built airfields and government buildings for the Arabs, which certainly means you had to have a hell of a lot of conversations with the high muck-a-mucks over there. I mean *airfields;* that's military intelligence, son! Then I learn you speak several Arab languages, not one but several!"

"It's one language, the rest are simply dialects—"

"I tell you you're invaluable, and it's no less than your patriotic duty to serve your country by sharing what you know with other experts."

"I'm *not* an expert!"

"Besides," broke in the Speaker, leaning back in his chair, his expression pensive, "under the circumstances, what with your background and all, if you refused the appointment it'd look like you had somethin' to hide, somethin' maybe we ought to look into. You got somethin' to hide, Congressman?" The Speaker's eyes were suddenly leveled at Evan.

Something to hide? He had everything to hide! Why did the Speaker look at him like that? No one knew about Oman, about Masqat and Bahrain. No one would ever know! That was the agreement.

"There's not a damn thing to hide, but there's everything to let hang out," said Kendrick firmly. "You'd be doing the subcommittee a disservice based on a misplaced appraisal of my credentials. Do yourself a favor. Call one of the others."

"The beautiful book, that most holy of books, has so many answers, doesn't it?" asked the Speaker aimlessly, his eyes once again straying. "Many might be called, but few are chosen, isn't that right?"

"Oh, for *God's* sake—"

"That might well be the case, young fella," broke in the old Irishman, nodding his head. "Only time will tell, won't it? Meanwhile, the congressional leadership of your party has decided that you're chosen. So you're chosen—unless you've got something to hide, something we ought to look into. . . . Now, skedaddle. I've got work to do."

"Skedaddle?"

"Get the fuck out of here, Kendrick."

20

The two bodies of Congress, the Senate and the House, have several committees of matching purpose with similar or nearly similar names. There is Senate Appropriations and House Appropriations, the Senate Foreign Relations and the House Foreign Affairs, the Senate Select Committee on Intelligence and the House Permanent Select Committee on Intelligence, this last with a powerful Subcommittee on Oversight and Evaluation. This counterpartism is one more example of the republic's effective system of checks and balances. The legislative branch of government, actively reflecting the current views of a far wider spectrum of the body politic than either an entrenched executive branch or the life-tenured judiciary, must negotiate within itself and reach a consensus on each of the hundredfold issues presented to its two deliberative arms. The process is patently frustrating, patently exasperating, and generally fair. If compromise is the art of governance within a pluralistic society, no one does it better, or with more aggravation, than the legislative branch of the United States government with its innumerable, often insufferable, and frequently ridiculous committees. This assessment is accurate; a pluralistic society is, indeed, numerous, usually insufferable to would-be tyrants, and almost always ridiculous in the eyes of those who would impose their will on the citizenry. One man's morality should never by way of ideology become another's legality, as many in the executive and the judiciary would have it. More often than not these quasi zealots grudgingly retreat in the face of the uproars emanating from those lower-class, troublesome committees on the Hill. Despite infrequent and unforgivable aberrations, the vox populi is usually heard and the land is better for it.

But there are some committees on Capitol Hill where voices are muted by logic and necessity. These are the small, restricted councils that concentrate on the strategies formed by the various intelligence agencies within the government. And perhaps because the voices are essentially quiet and the members of these committees are examined in depth by stringent security procedures, a certain aura descends over those *selected* to the select committees. They know things others are not privileged to know; they are different, conceivably a better breed of men and women. There also exists a tacit understanding between the Congress and the media for the latter to restrain themselves in areas concerning these committees; a senator or a congressman is appointed, but his or her appointment does not become a cause célèbre. Yet neither is there secrecy; the appointment is made and a basic reason given, both the act and reason stated simply, without embellishment. In the case of the representative from the Ninth District of Colorado, one Congressmcn Evan Kendrick, it was put forth that he was a construction engineer with extensive experience in the Middle East, especially the Persian Gulf. Since few knew little or anything about the area, and it was accepted that the Congressman had been an executive employed somewhere in the Mediterranean years ago, the appointment was considered reasonable and nothing unusual was made of it.

However, editors, commentators and politicians are keenly aware of the nuances of growing recognition, for recognition accompanies power in the District of Columbia. There are committees and then again there are *committees.* A person appointed to Indian Affairs is not in the same league with another sent to Ways and Means—the first does the minimum to look after a discarded, basically disfranchised people; the latter explores the methods and procedures to pay for the entire government to stay in business. Nor is Environment on a par with Armed Services—the former's budgets are continuously, abusively reduced, while the expenditures for weaponry reach beyond all horizons. The allocation of monies is the mother's milk of influence. Yet, simply put, few committees on the Hill can match the nimbus, the quiet mystique, that hovers over those associated with the clandestine world of intelligence. When sudden appointments are made to these *select* councils, eyes watch, colleagues whisper in cloakrooms, and the media is poised at the ready in front of word processors, microphones and cameras. Usually nothing comes of these preparations and the names fade into comfortable or uncomfortable oblivion. But not always, and had Evan Kendrick been aware of the subtleties, he might have risked telling the crafty Speaker of the House to go to hell.

However, he was not aware, and it would not have made any difference if he had been; the progress of Inver Brass was not to be denied.

It was six-thirty in the morning, a Monday morning; the early sun about to break over the Virginia hills, as Kendrick, naked, plunged into his pool, trusting that ten or twenty laps in the cold October water would remove the cobwebs obscuring his vision and painfully spreading through his temples. Ten hours ago he had been drinking far too many brandies with Emmanuel Weingrass in Colorado while sitting in a ridiculously opulent gazebo, both laughing at the visible streams rushing below the glass floor.

"Soon you will see *whales*!" Manny had exclaimed.

"Like you promised the kids in that half dried-up river wherever it was."

"We had lousy bait. I should have used one of the mothers. That black girl. She was *gorgeous*!"

"Her husband was a major, a *big* major, in the Army Engineers. He might have objected."

"Their daughter was a beautiful child. . . . She was killed with all the others."

"Oh, *Christ,* Manny. *Why?*"

"It's time for you to go."

"I don't want to go."

"You must! You have a meeting in the morning, already two hours ahead of us."

"I can skip it. I've skipped one or two others."

"*One,* and at great harm to my well-being. Your jet is waiting at the airfield in Mesa Verde. You'll be in Washington in four hours."

As he swam through the water, each length faster than the last, he thought of Oversight's upcoming morning conference, admitting to himself that he was glad Manny insisted he return to the capital. The subcommittee's meetings had fascinated him—fascinated him, angered him, astonished him, appalled him, but, most of all, fascinated him. There were so many *things* going on in the world that he knew nothing about, both for and against the interests of the United States. But it wasn't until his third meeting that he understood a recurring error in his colleagues' approach to the witnesses from the various intelligence branches. The mistake was that they would look for flaws in the witnesses' strategies for carrying out certain operations when what they should have been questioning were the operations themselves.

It was understandable, for the men who were paraded in front of Oversight to plead their cases—exclusively men, which should have been a clue—were soft-spoken professionals from a violent clandestine world who downplayed the melodramatics associated with that world. They delivered their esoteric jargon quietly, swelling the heads of those listening. It was heady stuff to be a part of that global underground, even in a consulting capacity; it fed the adolescent fantasies of mature adults. There were no Colonel Robert Barrishes among these witnesses; instead, they were a stream of attractive, well-dressed, consistently modest and moderate men who appeared before the subcommittee to explain in coldly professional terms what they could accomplish if monies were provided, and why it was imperative for the nation's security that it be done. More often than not the question was: *Can you do it?* Not whether it was right, or even if it made sense.

These lapses of judgment occurred often enough to disturb the congressman from Colorado, who had briefly been part of that savage, violent world the witnesses dealt with. He could not romanticize it; he loathed it. The terrible, breathless fear that was part of the terrifying game of taking and losing human life in shadows belonged to some dark age where life itself was measured solely by survival. One did not live in that kind of world; one endured it with sweat and with hollow pains in his stomach, as Evan had endured his abrupt exposure to it. Yet he knew that world went on; inhabitants of it had saved him from the sharks of Qatar. Nevertheless, during the coming sessions he probed, asking harsher and harsher questions. He understood that his name was being quietly, electrically, emphatically bounced around the halls of Congress, the Central Intelligence Agency, and even the White House. Who *was* this agitator, this troublemaker? He did not give a damn; they were legitimate questions and he would ask them. Who the hell was sacrosanct? Who was beyond the laws?

There was a commotion above him, wild gestures and shouts he dimly perceived through the water rushing past his face in the pool. He stopped at mid-length and shook his head while treading. The intruder was Sabri, but it was a Sabri Hassan he rarely saw. The ever-calm middle-aged Ph.D. from Dubai was beside himself, fiercely trying to control his actions and his words, but only barely succeeding.

"You must *leave*!" he shouted as Evan cleared his ears of water.

"What . . . *what*?"

"Oman! *Masqat!* The story is on all the channels, all the stations! There are even photographs of you dressed as one of *us*—in *Masqat*! Both the radio and the television keep interrupting programs to report the latest developments! It was just released within the past few minutes; newspapers are holding up their late morning editions for further details—"

"*Jesus Christ!*" roared Kendrick, leaping out of the pool as Sabri threw a towel around him.

"The reporters and the rest of those people will undoubtedly be here in a matter of minutes," said the Arab. "I took the phone off the hook and Kashi is loading our car—forgive me, the car you most generously provided us—"

"Forget that stuff!" yelled Evan, starting toward the house. "What's your wife doing with the car?"

"Putting in your clothes, enough for several days if necessary. Your own automobile might be recognized; ours is always in the garage. I assumed you wanted some time to think."

"Some time to plan a couple of murders!" agreed Evan, dashing through the patio door and up the back staircase, Dr.

Hassan following closely. "How the *hell* did it *happen*? *Goddamnit!*"

"I fear it's only the beginning, my friend."

"*What?*" asked Kendrick, racing into the huge master bedroom, which overlooked the pool, and going to his bureau, where he hurriedly opened drawers, whipping out socks, underwear and a shirt.

"The stations are calling all manner of people for their comments. They're most laudatory, of course."

"What else could they *say*?" said Evan, putting on his socks and shorts while Sabri unfolded his laundered shirt and handed it to him. "That they were all rooting for their terrorist buddies in Palestine?" Kendrick put on the shirt and ran to his closet, yanking out a pair of trousers. Sabri's wife, Kashi, walked through the door.

"*Anahasfa!*" she exclaimed, asking to be pardoned and turning away.

"No time for *eltakaled,* Kashi," cried the congressman, telling her to forget her traditions. "How are you doing with the clothes?"

"They might not be your choices, dear Evan, but they will cover you," replied the sweet-faced anxious wife. "It also occurred to me that you could call us from wherever you are and I can bring things to you. Many people on the newspapers know my husband but none know me. I am never in evidence."

"Your choice, not mine," said Kendrick, putting on a jacket and returning to the bureau for his wallet, money clip and lighter. "We may be closing up this place, Kashi, and heading out to Colorado. Out there you can be my official hostess."

"Oh, that's foolish, dear Evan," giggled Mrs. Hassan. "It's not proper."

"You're the professor, Sabri," added Kendrick, rapidly running a comb through his hair. "When are you going to teach her?"

"When will she listen? Our women must have advantages we men know nothing about."

"Let's *go*!"

"The keys are in the car, dear Evan—"

"Thanks, Kashi," said Kendrick, going out the door and down the staircase with Sabri. "Tell me," continued Evan as both men crossed through the portico into the large garage that housed his Mercedes convertible and Hassan's Cadillac Cimarron. "How much of the story do they have?"

"I can only compare what I've heard with what Emmanuel told me, for you have said literally nothing."

"It's not that I wanted to keep anything from you—"

"Please, Evan," interrupted the professor. "How long have I known you? You are uncomfortable praising yourself, even indirectly."

"Praise, *hell*!" exclaimed Kendrick, opening the garage door. "I *blew* it! I was a dead man with a bleeding pig strapped to my back about to be dropped over the shoals of Qatar! Others did it, not *me.* They saved my overachieving ass."

"Without you they could have done nothing—"

"Forget it," said Evan, standing by the door of the Cadillac. "How much have they learned?"

"In my opinion, very little. Not an iota of what Emmanuel told me, even discounting his natural exaggerations. The journalists are scratching for details, and apparently those details are not forthcoming."

"That doesn't tell me much. Why did you say it was only 'the beginning' when we left the pool?"

"Because of a man who was interviewed—roused willingly out of his house, obviously—a colleague of yours on the House Intelligence Subcommittee, a congressman named Mason."

"*Mason . . . ?*" said Kendrick, frowning. "He's got a big profile in Tulsa or Phoenix—I forget which—but he's a zero. A few weeks ago there was a quiet movement to get him off the committee."

"That's hardly the way he was presented, Evan."

"I'm sure it wasn't. What did he say?"

"That you were the most astute member of the committee. You were the brilliant one whom everyone looked up to and listened to."

"*Bullshit!* I talked some and asked a few questions but never that much, and in the second place I don't think Mason and I ever said more than 'hello' to each other! It's *bullshit*!"

"It's also all over the country—"

The sound of one, then two automobiles screeching to a stop in front of the house broke through the silence of the enclosed garage.

"Good *Christ*!" whispered Evan. "I'm cornered!"

"Not yet," said Dr. Hassan. "Kashi knows what to do. She will admit the early arrivals, speaking Hebrew, incidentally, and usher them into the solarium. She will pretend not to understand them and thus will stall them—for only a few minutes, of course.

Go, Evan, take the pasture road south until you reach the highway. In an hour I'll replace the phone. Call us. Kashi will bring you whatever you need."

Kendrick kept dialing repeatedly, punching the button down with each repeated busy signal until finally, to his relief, he heard the sound of a ring.

"Congressman Kendrick's residence—"

"It's me, Sabri."

"Now I am *truly* astonished you got through. I'm also delighted, for I can once again take the telephone off the hook."

"How are things going?"

"Calamitously, my friend. Also at your office and at your home in Colorado. All are under siege."

"How do you know?"

"Here no one will leave, and, like you, Emmanuel finally reached us—with a great deal of profanity. He claimed to have been trying for nearly half an hour—"

"I've got ten minutes on him. What did he say?"

"The house is surrounded, crowds everywhere. Apparently the newspaper and television people all flew into Mesa Verde, where most were stranded, as three taxis could hardly accommodate such numbers."

"All this must blow Manny's mind."

"What blows his mind, as you phrase it, is the lack of sanitary facilities."

"What?"

"He refused to offer them and then observed acts of necessity on all sides of the house that caused him to rush to your shotgun rack."

"Oh, my God, they're pissing all over the lawn—his *landscaping*!"

"I've heard Emmanuel's tirades many times in the past, but never anything like this. During his outburst, however, he did manage to tell me to call Mrs. O'Reilly at your office, as she was *not* able to get through here."

"What did Annie say?"

"For you to stay out of sight for a while but—in her words—'for God's sake,' call her."

"I don't think so," said Evan thoughtfully. "The less she knows, the better at this point."

"Where are you?" asked the professor.

"At a motel outside of Woodbridge off Route Ninety-five. It's called the Three Bears and I'm in Cabin Twenty-three. It's the last one on the left nearest the woods."

"By which description I assume you need things. Food, no doubt; you cannot go outside and be seen, and there can't be room service at a motel with cabins—"

"No, not food. I stopped at a diner on the way down."

"No one recognized you?"

"There were cartoons on the television set."

"Then, what do you need?"

"Wait until the late editions of the morning papers come out and send Jim, the gardener, into Washington to pick up as many different ones as he can lay his hands on. Especially the majors; they'll have their best people on the story and they'll reach other people."

"I'll make out a list for him. Then Kashi will bring them to you."

It was not until one-thirty in the afternoon that Sabri's wife arrived at the motel in Woodbridge, Virginia. Evan opened the door of Cabin 23, grateful to see that she had driven the gardener's pickup truck. He had not thought of the diversion, but his two friends from Dubai had known better than to drive his Mercedes past the crowds around his house. While Kendrick held the door, Kashi made rapid second and third trips back to the vehicle, for along with the pile of newspapers from all over the country she brought food. There were sandwiches encased in plastic wrap, two quarts of milk in an ice bucket, four hot plates equally divided between Western and Arab dishes, and a bottle of Canadian whisky.

"Kashi, I'm *not* going to be here for a week," said Kendrick.

"This is for today and tonight, dear Evan. You are under a great deal of stress and must eat. The box on the table has silverware and metal stands under which you place the Sterno for heat. There are also place mats and linen, but if I may, if you must leave here abruptly, please call so I may retrieve the silverware and the linens."

"Why? Will the quartermaster throw us in the brig?"

"*I* am the quartermaster, dear Evan."

"Thanks, Kashi."

"You look tired, *yasahbee.* You have not rested?"

"No, I've been watching that damned television, and the more

I watch, the angrier I get. Rest's hard to come by when you're furious."

"As my husband says and I agree with him, you are very effective on television. He also says we must leave you."

"*Why?* He said that to me several weeks ago and I don't know *why*!"

"Of course you do. We are Arabs and you are in a city that distrusts us; you are in a political arena now that does not tolerate us. And we will not bring harm to you."

"Kashi, this *isn't* my arena! I'm getting out, I'm *sick* of it! You say this is a city that doesn't trust you? Why should you be any different? This town doesn't trust *anybody*! It's a city of liars and shills and phonies, men and women who'll climb over any back with their cleats on to get a little closer to the honey. They're messing around with a damn good system, sucking the blood out of every vein they can tap, proclaiming the patriotic holiness of their causes while the country sits by and applauds what it doesn't know it's *paying* for! That's not for me, Kashi, I'm *out*!"

"You're upset—"

"Tell me about it!" Kendrick rushed to the bed and the pile of newspapers.

"*Dear* Evan," broke in the Arab wife, as firmly as Kendrick had ever heard her speak. He turned, several papers in his hands. "Those articles will offend you," she continued, her dark eyes leveled at his, "and to speak truthfully there were parts that offended Sabri and myself."

"I see," said Kendrick quietly, studying her. "All Arabs are terrorists. I'm sure it's here in very bold print."

"Very pointedly, yes."

"But that's not *your* point."

"No. I said you would be offended, but the word is not strong enough. You will be incensed, but before you do anything you cannot take back, please listen to me."

"For God's sake, what *is* it, Kashi?"

"Thanks to you, my husband and I have attended numerous sessions of your Senate and your House of Representatives. Also, because of you, we've been privileged to witness legal arguments before the justices of your Supreme Court."

"They're not all exclusively mine. So?"

"What we saw and heard was remarkable. Issues of state, even laws, openly debated, not by simple petitioners but by learned men. . . . You see the bad side, the evil side, and no doubt what you say has truth, but isn't there another truth? We've watched many impassioned men and women stand up for what they believe without fear of being shunned or silenced—"

"Shunned they can be, not silenced. Ever."

"Still, they *do* take risks for their causes, often profound risks?"

"Hell, yes. They go public."

"For their beliefs?"

"Yes . . ." Kendrick let the word evaporate into the air. Kashi Hassan's point was clear; it was also a warning to him in his moment of self-consuming fury.

"Then there are *good* people in what you called 'a pretty damn good system.' Please remember that, Evan. Please do not diminish them."

"Don't *what*?"

"I express myself poorly. Forgive me. I must go." Kashi walked rapidly to the door, then turned. "I beg you, *yasahbee,* if in your anger you feel you must do something drastic, in the name of Allah, call my husband first, or if you wish, Emmanuel. . . . However, without prejudice, for I love our Jewish brother as I love you, but my husband might be somewhat more composed."

"You can count on it."

Kashi went out the door, and Kendrick literally pounced on the newspapers, turning each over on the bed, their front pages in succeeding rows, the headlines visible.

If a primal scream could have lessened the pain, his voice would have shattered the glass of the suffocating cabin's windows.

The New York Times
New York, Tuesday, October 12

CONGRESSMAN EVAN KENDRICK OF COLORADO SAID TO HAVE BEEN INSTRUMENTAL IN OMAN CRISIS

OUTWITTED ARAB TERRORISTS, SECRET MEMORANDUM INDICATES

The Washington Post
Washington, D.C., Tuesday, October 12

KENDRICK OF COLORADO REVEALED AS U.S. SECRET WEAPON IN OMAN

TRACKED DOWN ARAB TERRORISTS $ CONNECTION

Los Angeles Times
Los Angeles, Tuesday, October 12

DECLASSIFIED RECORDS SHOW KENDRICK, COLORADO REP., KEY TO OMAN SOLUTION
PALESTINIAN TERRORISTS HAD ARAB BACKING—STILL CLASSIFIED

Chicago Tribune
Chicago, Tuesday, October 12

CAPITALIST KENDRICK CUT SHACKLES OFF HOSTAGES HELD BY COMMUNIST TERRORISTS
KILLER ARABS EVERYWHERE IN DISARRAY OVER REVELATIONS

New York Post
New York, Tuesday, October 12

EVAN, THE MENSCH OF OMAN, STUCK IT TO THE ARABS!
MOVE IN JERUSALEM TO MAKE HIM HONORARY CITIZEN OF ISRAEL! NEW YORK DEMANDS A PARADE!

USA Today
Wednesday, October 13

"COMMANDO" KENDRICK DID IT!
ARAB TERRORISTS WANT HIS HEAD! WE WANT A STATUE!

Kendrick stood over the bed, his downcast eyes shifting rapidly from one black-lettered headline to another, his mind drained of all thought but a single question. *Why?* And as the answer eluded him, another question gradually came into focus. *Who?*

21

If there was an answer to either question, neither would be found in the newspapers. They were fraught with "authoritative" and "highly placed" and even "confidential" sources, most countered by "No comment" and "We have nothing to say at this time" and "The events in question are being analyzed," all of which were evasive statements of confirmation.

What had started the furor was a maximum-classified inter-division memorandum under the letterhead of the Department of State. It had surfaced, unsigned, from buried files and was presumably leaked by an employee or employees who felt a great injustice had been done to a man under the unreasonable strictures of national security, the paranoid fear of terrorist reprisals undoubtedly heading the list. Copies of the memorandum had been sent out in concert to the newspapers, wire services and the networks, all arriving between 5:00 and 6:00 A.M., eastern daylight time. Accompanying each memorandum were three different photographs of the Congressman in Masqat. Deniability denied.

It was planned, thought Evan. The timing was chosen to startle the nation as it woke up across the country, bulletins mandatory throughout the day.

Why?

What was remarkable were the facts revealed—as remarkable for what they omitted as for those they paraded. They were astonishingly accurate, down to such points as his having been flown to Oman under deep cover and spirited out of the airport in Masqat by intelligence agents who had provided him with Arab garments and even the skin-darkening gel that made his features compatible with the "area of operations." *Christ! Area of operations!*

There were sketchy, often hypothesized details of contacts he made with men he had known in the past, the names scissored out—black spaces in the memorandum for obvious reasons. There was a paragraph dealing with his voluntary internment in a terrorist compound, where he nearly lost his life, but where he learned the names he had to know in order to trace the men behind the Palestinian fanatics at the embassy, specifically one name—name scissored out, a black space in the copy. He had tracked down that man—scissored out, a black space—and forced him to dismantle the terrorist cadre occupying the embassy in Masqat. That pivotal man was shot—details scissored out, a black *paragraph*—and Evan Kendrick, representative from the Ninth District of Colorado, was returned under protective cover to the United States.

Experts had been summoned to examine the photographs. Each print was subjected to spectrographic analysis for authenticity with respect to the age of the negatives and the possibility of laboratory alterations. Everything was confirmed, even down to the day and the date extracted from 20*X* magnification of a newspaper carried by a pedestrian in the streets of Masqat. The more responsible papers noted the lack of alternative sources that might or might not lend credibility to the facts as they were sketchily presented, but none could question the photographs or the identity of the man in them. And that man, Congressman Evan Kendrick, was nowhere to be found to confirm or deny the incredible story. The *New York Times* and the *Washington Post* unearthed what few friends and neighbors they could find in the capital as well as in Virginia and Colorado. None could recall having seen or heard from the Congressman during the period in question a year ago—not that they would necessarily have expected to, which in itself meant that they probably would have remembered if he had been in touch with them.

The *Los Angeles Times* went further and, without revealing its sources, ran a telephone check on Mr. Kendrick. Except for calls to various local shops and a certain James Olsen, a gardener, only five possibly relevant calls were made from the Congressman's residence in Virginia over a four-week period. Three were to the Arabian Studies departments at Georgetown and Princeton universities; one to the diplomat from the Arab Emirate of Dubai, who had returned home seven months ago; and the fifth to an attorney in Washington, who refused to talk to the press. Relevance be damned; the bird dogs were pointing even though the quarry had disappeared.

The less responsible papers, which meant most of those without the resources to finance extensive investigations, and all of the tabloids, which did not care a whit about verification, if they could spell it, had a pseudo-journalistic field day. They took the exposed maximum-classified memorandum and used it as a springboard for the wild waters of heroic speculation, knowing their issues would be grabbed up by their unskeptical readership. Words in print are more often than not words of truth to the uninformed—a patronizing judgment, to be sure, but all too true.

What was missing in every one of the stories, however, were truths, deep truths, that went beyond the astonishingly accurate revelations. There was no mention of a brave young sultan of Oman, who had risked his life and lineage to help him. Or of the Omanis who had guarded him both at the airport and in the back streets of Masqat. Or of a strange and strikingly professional woman who had rescued him in a congested concourse of another airport in Bahrain after he had been nearly killed, who had found him sanctuary and a doctor who ministered to his wounds. Above all, there was not a word about the Israeli unit, led by a Mossad officer, who had saved him from a death that still made him shiver in horror. Or even of another American, an elderly architect from the Bronx, without whom he would have been dead a year ago, his remains expunged by the sharks of Qatar.

Instead, a common theme ran through all the articles: everything *Arab* was tainted with the brush of inhuman brutality and terrorism. The very word *Arab* was synonymous with ruthlessness and barbarism, not a vestige of decency allowed to a whole people. The longer Evan studied the newspapers, the angrier he became. Suddenly in a burst of fury, he swept them all off the bed.

Why?

Who?

And then he felt a hollow, terrible pain in his chest. *Ahmat!* Oh, my God, what had he *done*? Would the young sultan understand, *could* he understand? By omission—by silence—the American media had condemned the entire country of Oman, leaving to insidious speculation its *Arab* impotence in the face of terrorists, or worse, its *Arab complicity* in the wanton, savage killing of American citizens.

He had to call his young friend, reach him and tell him that he had no control over what had happened. Kendrick sat on the edge of the bed; he grabbed the telephone while reaching into his trousers pocket for his wallet, balancing the phone under his chin as he extracted his credit card. Not remembering the sequence of numbers to reach Masqat, he dialed *O* for an operator. Suddenly the dial tone disappeared and for a moment he panicked, his eyes wide, glancing around at the windows.

"Yeah, twenty-three?" came the hoarse male voice over the line.

"I was trying to call the operator."

"You dial even an area code you get the board here."

"I . . . I have to make an overseas call," stammered Evan, bewildered.

"Not on this phone you don't."

"On a *credit* card. How do I get an operator—I'm charging it to my *credit* card number."

"I'll listen in till I hear you give the number and it's accepted for real, understand?"

He did *not* understand! Was it a *trap*? Had he been traced to a run-down motel in Woodbridge, Virginia? "I don't really think that's acceptable," he said haltingly. "It's a private communication."

"Fancy that," replied the voice derisively. "Then go find yourself a pay phone. There's one at the diner about five miles down the road. Ta-ta, asshole, I've been stuck enough—"

"*Wait* a minute! All *right,* stay on the line. But when the operator clears it, I want to hear you click off, okay?"

"Well, actually, I was gonna call Louella Parsons."

"Who?"

"Forget it, asshole. I'm dialing. People who stay all day are either sex freaks or shooting up."

Somewhere in the far reaches of the Persian Gulf an English-speaking, Arabic-accented operator volunteered that there was no exchange in Masqat, Oman, with the prefix 555. "Dial it, please!" insisted Evan, adding a more plaintive "*Please.*"

Eight rings passed until he heard Ahmat's harried voice. "*Iwah?*"

"It's Evan, Ahmat," said Kendrick in English. "I have to talk to you—"

"*Talk* to me?" exploded the young sultan. "You've got the balls to *call* me, you *bastard*?"

"You know, then? About—what they're saying about me."

"*Know?* One of the nicer things about being a rich kid is that I've got dishes on the roof that pick up whatever I want *from* wherever I want! I've even got an edge on you, *ya Shaikh.* Have you seen the reports from over here and the Middle East? From Bahrain and Riyadh, from *Jerusalem* and *Tel Aviv*?"

"Obviously not. I've only seen these—"

"They're all the same garbage, a nice pile for you to sit on! Do well in Washington, just don't come back here."

"But I *want* to come back. I *am* coming back!"

"Don't, not to this part of the world. We can read and we can hear and we watch television. You did it all by *yourself*! You *stuck* it to the *Arabs*! Get out of my *memory,* you son of a bitch!"

"Ahmat!"

"*Out,* Evan! I would never have believed it of you. Do you become powerful in Washington by calling us all animals and terrorists? Is that the only way?"

"I never did that, I never *said* it!"

"Your world did! The way it keeps saying it again and again and *again,* until it's pretty fucking obvious you want us all in chains! And the latest goddamned scenario is *yours*!"

"*No!*" protested Kendrick, shouting. "Not *mine*!"

"Read your press. Watch it!"

"That's the press, not you and me!"

"You *are* you—one more arrogant bastard out of your blind, holier-than-thou Judeo-Christian hypocrisies—and I am *me,* an Islamic Arab. And you won't spit on me any longer!"

"I never would, never *could*—"

"Nor on my brothers, whose lands you decreed should be stolen from them, forcing whole villages to abandon their homes and their jobs and their insignificantly small businesses—small and insignificant but theirs for generations!"

"For Christ's sake, Ahmat, you're sounding like one of *them*!"

"No kidding?" said the young sultan, both anger and sarcasm in his words. "By 'them' I assume you mean like a kid from one of those thousands upon thousands of families marched under guns into camps fit for pigs. For *pigs,* not families! Not for mothers and fathers and children! . . . Good gracious, Mr. all-knowing, eminently fair *American.* If I sound like one of them, gosh, I'm sorry! And I'll tell you what else I'm sorry about: I got here so late. I understand so much more today than I did yesterday."

"What the hell does *that* mean."

"I repeat. Read your press, watch your television, listen to your radio. Are you superior people getting ready to nuke all the dirty Arabs so you won't have to contend with us anymore? Or are you going to leave it to your cool pals in Israel who tell you what to do anyway? You'll simply give them the bombs."

"Now, just *hold* it!" cried Kendrick. "Those Israelis saved my life!"

"You're damned right they did, but you were incidental! You were just a bridge to what they really flew in here for."

"What are you talking about?"

"I might as well tell you because no one else will, nobody's going to print *that.* They didn't give a shit about you, Mr. Hero. That unit came here to get *one* man out of the embassy, a Mossad agent, a high-ranking strategist posing as a naturalized American under contract to the State Department."

"Oh, my *God,*" whispered Evan. "Did Weingrass know?"

"If he did he kept his mouth shut. He forced them to go after you in Bahrain. *That's* how they saved your life. It wasn't planned. They don't give a good goddamn about anyone or anything but themselves. The *Jews*! Just like you, Mr. *Hero.*"

"Damn it, *listen* to me, Ahmat! I'm not responsible for what's happened here, for what's been printed in the papers or what's on television. It's the last thing I wanted—"

"*Bullshit!*" broke in the young Harvard alumnus and sultan of Oman. "None of it could have been reported without you. I learned things I had no idea about. Who *are* these intelligence agents of yours running around my country? Who are all those contacts you reached?"

"Mustapha, for one!"

"*Killed.* Who flew you in under cover without apprising *me*? I run the goddamn place; who has the *right*? Am I a fucking 'aggie' in a game of marbles?"

"*Ahmat,* I don't know about these things. I only knew I had to *get* there."

"And I'm *incidental*? Wasn't I to be trusted? . . . Of course not, I'm an *Arab*!"

"Now *that's* bullshit. You were being protected."

"From what? An American-Israeli cover-up?"

"Oh, for Christ's sake, *stop* it! I didn't know anything about a Mossad agent at the embassy until you just told me. If I did I would have told *you*! And while we're at it, my sudden young fanatic, I had nothing to do with the refugee camps or marching families into them under guns—"

"You *all* did!" shouted the sultan of Oman. "One genocide for another, but *we* had nothing to do with the other! *Out!*"

The line went dead. A good man and a good friend who had been instrumental in saving his life was gone from his life. As were his plans to return to a part of the world he dearly loved.

Before he showed himself in public, he had to find out what had happened and who had made it happen and *why*! He had to start somewhere and that somewhere was the State Department and a man named Frank Swann. A frontal assault on State was, of course, out of the question. The minute he identified himself alarms would go off, and insofar as his face was seen repeatedly, ad nauseam, on television and half of Washington was searching for him, his every move had to be carefully thought out. First things first: how to reach Swann without Swann or his office knowing it. His office? Evan remembered. A year ago he had walked into Swann's office and spoken to a secretary, giving her several words in Arabic so as to convey the urgency of his visit. She had disappeared into another office and ten minutes later he and Swann were talking in the underground computer complex.

That secretary was not only efficient but also exceedingly protective, as apparently were most secretaries in serpentine Washington. And since that protective secretary was very much aware of one Congressman Kendrick, whom she had spoken to a year ago, she just might be receptive to another voice also protective of her boss. It was worth a try; it was also the only thing he could think of. He picked up the phone, dialed the 202 area code for Washington, and waited for the hoarse manager of the Three Bears motel to come on the line.

"Consular Operations, Director Swann's office," said the secretary.

"Hi, this is Ralph over in ID," began Kendrick. "I've got some news for Frank."

"*Who's* this?"

"It's okay, I'm a friend of Frank's. I just want to tell him that there may be an interdivision meeting called for later this afternoon—"

"*Another* one? He doesn't need that."

"How's his schedule?"

"Overworked! He's in conference until four o'clock."

"Well, if he doesn't want to be put on the grill again, maybe he should have a short day and drive home early."

"Drive? *Him?* He'll parachute into the jungles of Nicaragua, but he won't take chances in Washington traffic."

"You know what I mean. Things are a little jumpy around here. He could be put on the spit."

"He's been on it since six this morning."

"Just trying to help out a buddy."

"Actually, he's got a doctor's appointment," said the secretary suddenly.

"He does?"

"He does now. Thanks, Ralph."

"I never called you."

"Of course not, sweetie. Someone in ID was just checking schedules."

Evan stood in the crowd waiting for a bus at the corner of Twenty-first Street within clear sight of the entrance to the Department of State. After speaking to Swann's secretary, he had left the cabin and driven rapidly up to Washington, stopping briefly at a shopping mall in Alexandria where he bought dark glasses, a wide-brimmed canvas fishing hat and a soft cloth jacket. It was 3:48 in the afternoon; if the secretary had pursued her protective inclinations, Frank Swann, deputy director of Consular Operations, would be coming out of the huge glass doors within the next fifteen or twenty minutes.

He did. At 4:03 and in a hurry, turning left on the pavement away from the bus stop. Kendrick rushed out of the crowd and started after the man from the State Department, staying thirty feet behind him, wondering what means of transportation the nondriving Swann would take. If he intended to walk, Kendrick would stop him in front of a vest-pocket park, or someplace else where they could talk undisturbed.

He was not going to walk; he was about to take a bus heading east on Virginia Avenue. Swann joined several others waiting for the same vehicle now lumbering down the street toward the stop. Evan hurried to the corner; he could not allow the Cons Op director to get on that bus. He approached Swann and touched his shoulder. "Hello, Frank," said Kendrick pleasantly, taking off the dark glasses.

"*You!*" shouted the astonished Swann, startling the other passengers as the doors of the bus cracked open.

"Me," admitted Evan quietly. "I think we'd better talk."

"Good *Christ*! You've got to be out of your mind!"

"If I am, you've driven me there, even if you don't drive—"

It was as far as their brief conversation got, for suddenly an odd voice filled the street, echoing off the side of the bus. "It's *him*!" roared a strange-looking, disheveled man with wide, popping eyes and long, wild hair that fell over his ears and his forehead. "See! *Look!* It's him! *Commando Kendrick!* I seen him all day long on the television—I got seven televisions in my apartment! Nothin' goes on I don't know about! It's *him*!"

Before Evan could react the man grabbed the fishing hat off his head. "*Hey!*" shouted Kendrick.

"See! Look! *Him!*"

"Let's get out of here!" cried Swann.

They started running up the street, the odd-looking man in pursuit, his baggy trousers flopping in the wind he created, Evan's hat in his hand, his arms flailing.

"He's following us!" said the Cons Op director, looking back.

"He's got my hat!" said Kendrick.

Two blocks later, a doddering blue-haired lady with a cane was climbing out of a cab. "*There!*" yelled Swann. "The taxi!" Dodging traffic, they raced across the wide avenue. Evan climbed in the near door as the man from the State Department ran around the trunk to the far side; he helped the elderly passenger out and inadvertently kicked the cane with his foot. It fell to the pavement; so did the blue-haired lady. "Sorry, dear," said Swann, jumping into the backseat.

"Let's go!" yelled Kendrick. "Hurry up! Get out of here!"

"You clowns hold up a bank or somethin'," said the driver, shifting into gear.

"You'll be richer for it if you'll just hurry," added Evan.

"I'm hurryin', I'm hurryin'. I ain't got no pilot's license. I gotta stay earthbound, y'know what I mean?"

As one, Kendrick and Swann whipped around to look out the rear window. Back at the corner the odd-looking man with the wild hair and baggy trousers was writing something down on a newspaper, Evan's hat now on his head. "The name of the company and the cab's number," said the Cons Op director quietly. "Wherever we're going, we'll have to switch vehicles at least a block behind this one."

"Why? Not the switch but the block away?"

"So our driver doesn't see which cab we get into."

"You even sound like you know what you're doing."

"I hope you do," replied Swann breathlessly, taking out a handkerchief and wiping his sweat-drenched face.

Twenty-eight minutes and a second taxi later, the Congressman and the man from the Department of State walked rapidly down the street in a run-down section of Washington. They looked up at a red neon sign with three letters missing. It was a seedy bar that belonged in its environs. They nodded to each other and walked inside, somewhat startled by the intensely dark interior, if only in contrast to the bright October day out in the street. The single glaring, blaring source of light was a television set bolted into the wall above the shabby distressed bar. Several hunched-over, disheveled, bleary-eyed patrons confirmed the status of the establishment. Both squinting in the receding dim wash of light, Kendrick and Swann moved toward the darker regions to the right of the bar; they found a frayed booth and slid in opposite each other.

"You really insist we talk?" asked the gray-haired Swann, breathing deeply, his face flushed and still perspiring.

"I insist to the point of making you the newest candidate for the morgue."

"*Watch* it, I'm a black belt."

"In what?"

Swann frowned. "I was never quite sure, but it always works

in the movies when they show us doing our thing. I need a drink."

"You signal a waiter," said Kendrick. "I'll stay in the shadows."

"Shadows?" questioned Swann, raising his hand cautiously for a heavy black waitress with flaming red hair. "Where's any light in here?"

"When did you last do three push-ups in succession, Mr. Karate Kid?"

"Sometime in the sixties. Early, I think."

"That's when they replaced the light bulbs in this place. . . . Now about me. How the hell *could* you, you *liar*?"

"How the *hell* could you think I *would*?" cried the man from State, suddenly silent as the grotesque waitress stood by the table, arms akimbo. "What'll you have?" he asked Evan.

"Nothing."

"That's not nice here. Or healthy, I suspect. Two ryes, double, thank you. Canadian, if you have it."

"Forget it," said the waitress.

"Forgotten," agreed Swann as the waitress left, his eyes again on Kendrick. "You're funny, Mr. Congressman, I mean really *hilarious.* Consular Operations wants my *head*! The Secretary of State has put out a directive that makes it clear he doesn't know who I *am,* that vacillating, academic fleabag! And the *Israelis* are screaming because they think their precious Mossad may be compromised by anyone digging, and the *Arabs* on our payroll are bitching because they're not getting any credit! And at three-thirty this afternoon the President—the goddamned *President*—is chewing me out for 'dereliction of duty.' Let me tell you, he intoned that phrase just like he knew what the hell he was talking about, which meant *I* knew there were at least two other people on the line. . . . *You're* running? *I'm* running! Damn near thirty years in this dumb business—"

"That's what I called it," interrupted Evan quickly, quietly. "Sorry."

"You *should* be," said Swann without missing a beat. "Because who's going to do this shit except us bastards dumber than the system? You need us, Charlie, and don't you forget it. The problem is we don't have much to show for it. I mean I don't have to rush home to make sure the pool in my backyard has been treated for algae because of the heat. . . . Mainly because I don't have a pool, and my wife got the house in the divorce settlement because she was sick and tired of my going out for a loaf of bread and coming back three months later with the dirt of Afghanistan still in my ears! Oh, no, Mr. Undercover Congressman, I didn't blow the whistle on you. Instead, I did my best to *stop* the blowing. I haven't got much left, but I want to stay clean and get out with what I can."

"You tried to stop the blowing? The whistle?"

"Low-key, very offhand, very professional. I even showed him a copy of the memo I sent upstairs rejecting you."

"Him?"

Swann looked forlornly at Kendrick as the waitress brought their drinks and stood there, tapping the tabletop while the man from State reached into his pocket, glanced at the bill and paid it. The woman shrugged at the tip and walked away.

"*Him?*" repeated Evan.

"Go ahead," said Swann, his voice flat, drinking a large portion of his whisky. "Drive another nail in, what difference does it make? There's not that much blood left."

"I assume that means you don't know who he is. Who *him* is."

"Oh, I've got a name and a position and even a first-rate recommendation."

"Well?"

"He doesn't exist."

"*What?*"

"You heard me."

"He doesn't *exist*?" pressed a frustrated Kendrick.

"Well, one of them does, but not the man who came to see me." Swann finished his first drink.

"I don't believe this—"

"Neither did Ivy, that's my secretary. Ivy the terrible."

"*What* are you talking about?" asked Kendrick plaintively.

"Ivy got a call from Senator Allison's office, from a guy she used to date a couple of years ago. He's one of the Senator's top aides now. He asked her to set up an appointment for a staffer doing some confidential work for Allison, so she did. Well, he turns out to be a blond spook with an accent I placed somewhere in middle Europe, but he's for real, he had you down cold. If you've got a scar that only your mother knows about, believe me, he has a close-up of it."

"That's crazy," broke in Evan softly. "I wonder *why*?"

"So did I. I mean the questions he asked were loaded with PD—"

"I beg your pardon?"

"Prior data on you. He was giving almost as much as he could get from me. He was so pro I was ready to offer him a Euro-job on the spot."

"But why *me*?"

"As I said, I wondered, too. So I asked Ivy to check with Allison's office. To begin with, why would a laid-back senator have that kind of SS—"

"*What?*"

"Not what you think. 'Super-spook.' Come to think of it, I suppose there's a connection."

"Will you *please* stick to the point!"

"Sure," said Swann, drinking his second whisky. "Ivy calls her old boyfriend, and he doesn't know what she's *talking* about. He never made any call to her and he never *heard* of any staffer named—whatever his name was."

"But she had to know who she was talking to, for God's sake! His voice—the small talk, what they said to each other."

"Her old beau was thick from Georgia and had laryngitis when he phoned her, that's what Ivy claimed. But the cracker who *really* called her knew the places they went—even down to a couple of motels in Maryland that Ivy would rather not have her husband know about."

"Christ, it's an *operation.*" Kendrick reached over and took Swann's drink. "*Why?*"

"Why did you just take my whisky? I don't have a swimming pool, remember? Or even a house."

Suddenly the blaring television set above the bar burst forth with the sharply consonated name of "Kendrick!"

Both men snapped their heads over to the source, their eyes wide, unbelieving.

"*Newsbreak! The story of the hour, perhaps the decade!*" yelled a TV journalist among a crowd of leering faces peering into the camera. "*For the last twelve hours all Washington has been trying to find Congressman Evan Kendrick of Colorado, the hero of Oman, but to no avail. The worst fears, of course, center around the possibility of Arab retaliation. We're told the government has directed the police, the hospitals and the morgues to be on the alert. Yet only minutes ago he was seen on this very street corner, specifically identified by one Kasimer Bola—Bola . . . slawski. Where are you from, sir?*"

"*Jersey City,*" replied the wild-eyed man with Kendrick's hat on his head, "*but my roots are in Warsaw! God's holy Warsaw!*"

"*You were born in Poland, then.*"

"Not exactly. In Newark."

"But you saw Congressman Kendrick?"

"Positively. He was talking to a gray-haired man a couple blocks back outside a bus. Then when I shouted 'Commando Kendrick, it's him,' they started running! I know! I got television sets in every room, including the toilet. I never miss anything!"

"When you say a couple of blocks back, sir, you're actually referring to a corner two and a half streets from the Department of State, are you not?"

"You betcha!"

"We're certain," added the sincerely confidential newscaster looking into the camera, *"that the authorities are checking State to see if any such person as our witness has described could be a part of this extraordinary rendezvous."*

"I chased them!" yelled the witness in baggy pants, removing Evan's hat. *"I got his hat! See, it's the commando's own hat!"*

"But what did you hear, Mr. Bolaslawski? Back by the bus?"

"I tell you, things are not always what they seem! You can't be too careful. Before they ran away, the man with gray hair gave Commando Kendrick an order. I think he had a Russian accent, maybe Jewish! The Commies and the Jews—you can't trust 'em, you know what I mean? They never seen the inside of a church! They don't know what the Holy Mass is—"

The television channel abruptly switched to a commercial extolling the virtues of an underarm deodorant.

"I surrender," said Swan, forcibly taking his drink back from Evan and swallowing it whole. "Now I'm a mole. A Russian Jew from the KGB who doesn't know what Mass is. Anything else you want to do for me?"

"No, because I believe you. But you can do something for me, and it's in both our interests. I've got to find out who's doing this to me, who's done what you're being blamed for, and why."

"And if you do find out," interrupted Swann, leaning forward, "you'll tell me? *That's* in my interest, my only interest right now. I've got to get off this hook and put someone else on it."

"You'll be the first to know."

"What do you want?"

"A list of everyone who knew I went to Masqat."

"That's not a list, it's a tight little circle." Swann shook his head, not so much to be negative as to explain. "There wouldn't have been that if you hadn't said you might need us if it came down to something you couldn't handle. I made it clear. We couldn't afford to acknowledge you because of the hostages."

"How tight is the circle?"

"Everything was verbal, you understand."

"Understood. How tight?"

"Nonoperational was restricted to that unmitigated prick, Herbert Dennison, the ball-breaking White House chief of staff, then to the secretaries of State and Defense, and the chairman of the Joint Chiefs. I was the liaison to all four, and you can rule them out. They all had too much to lose and nothing to gain by your surfacing." Swann leaned back in the booth, frowning. "The operational section was on a strict need-to-know basis. There was Lester Crawford at Langley. Les is the CIA's analyst for covert activities in the area, and at the end his station chief in Bahrain was something-or-other Grayson—*James* Grayson, that's it. He was kicking up a fuss about letting you and Weingrass out of his area, thinking the Company had gone nuts and was plowing right into one of those caught-in-the-act situations. Caught-In-the-Act, CIA, get it?"

"I'd rather not."

"Then there were four or five on-scene Arabs, the best we and the Company have, each of whom studied your photograph but weren't given your identity. They couldn't tell what they didn't know. The last two did know who you were; one was on the scene, the other here at OHIO-Four-Zero running the computers."

"The computers?" asked Kendrick. "*Printouts?*"

"You were programmed only on his; you were zapped from the central unit. His name's Gerald Bryce and if he's the whistle-blower, I'll turn myself in to the FBI as Mr. Bolaslawski's Jewish mole for the Soviets. He's bright and quick and a whiz with the equipment, no one better. He'll run Cons Op someday if the girls leave him alone long enough to punch a clock."

"A playboy?"

"Land sakes, *Reverend,* shall we go to vespers? The kid's twenty-six and better-looking than he has a right to be. He's also unmarried, and one hell of a cocksman—others talk about it; he never does. I think that's why I like him. There aren't too many gentlemen left in this world."

"I like him already. Who was the last person, the one on the scene who knew me?"

Frank Swann leaned forward, fingering his empty glass, staring at it before raising his eyes to Kendrick. "I thought you might have figured that out for yourself."

"What? Why?"

"Adrienne Rashad."

"Doesn't mean a thing."

"She used a cover—"

"Adrienne . . . ? A *woman*?" Swann nodded. Evan frowned, then suddenly opened his eyes wide, his brows arched. "*Khalehla?*" he whispered. The man from the State Department nodded again. "She was one of *you*?"

"Well, not one of mine, but one of us."

"*Christ,* she got me out of the airport in Bahrain! That big son of a bitch MacDonald slammed me into the concourse traffic—I was damn near killed and didn't know where I was. *She* got me out of there—how the hell she did it I don't *know*!"

"I do," said Swann. "She threatened to blow the heads off a few Bahrainian police unless they passed her code name up the line and got clearance to take you out. She not only got clearance but also a car from the royal garage."

"You say she was one of us, but not one of you. What does that mean?"

"She's Agency but she's also special, a real untouchable. She has contacts all over the Gulf and the Mediterranean; the CIA doesn't allow anyone to mess with her."

"Without her my cover might have been blown at the airport."

"Without her you would have been a target for every terrorist walking around Bahrain, including the Mahdi's soldiers."

Kendrick was briefly silent, his eyes wandering, his lips parted, a memory. "Did she tell you where she hid me?"

"She refused."

"She could do that?"

"I told you, she's special."

"I see," said Evan softly.

"I think I do, too," said Swann.

"What do you mean by that?"

"Nothing. She got you out of the airport and roughly six hours later made contact."

"Is that unusual?"

"Under the circumstances, you could say it was extraordinary. Her job was to keep you under surveillance and to immediately report any drastic moves on your part directly to Crawford at Langley, who was to reach me for instructions. She didn't do that, and in her official debriefing, she omitted any reference to those six hours."

"She had to protect the place where we were hiding."

"Of course. It had to be royal, and nobody screws around with the Emir or his family."

"Of course." Kendrick again was silent and again he looked into the dark regions of the decrepit bar. "She was a nice person," he said slowly, hesitantly. "We talked. She understood so many things. I admired her."

"Hey, come on, Congressman." Swann leaned over his empty glass. "You think it's the first time?"

"What?"

"Two people in a hairy situation, a man and a woman, neither one knowing whether he or she'll see another day or another week. So they get together, it's natural. So what?"

"That's offensive as hell, Frank. She *meant* something to me."

"All right, I'll be blunt. I don't think you meant anything to her. She's a professional who's gone through a few black wars in her AOO."

"Her *what*? Will you please speak English, or Arabic, if you like, but something that makes sense."

"Area of Operations—"

"They used that in the newspapers."

"Not my fault. If it was up to me, I'd neutralize every bastard who wrote those articles."

"Please don't tell me what 'neutralize' means."

"I won't. I'm only telling you that in the field we all slip now and then when we're exhausted, or just plain scared. We take a few hours of secure pleasure and write it off as a long-overdue bonus. Would you believe we even have lectures on the subject for people we send out?"

"I believe it now. To be honest with you—the circumstances crossed my mind at the time."

"Good. Write her off. She's strictly Mediterranean and hasn't anything to do with the local scene. For starters, you'd probably have to fly to North Africa to find her."

"So all I've got is a man named Crawford in Langley and a station chief in Bahrain."

"No. You've got a blond man with a Middle European accent operating here in Washington. Operating very deep. He got information somewhere and not from me, not from OHIO-Four-Zero. Find him."

Swann gave Evan the standard private numbers at both his office and his apartment and rushed out of the dark, seedy bar as if he needed air. Kendrick ordered a rye from the heavy black waitress with the flaming red hair, and asked her where the pay telephone was, if it existed. She told him.

"If you slam it twice on the lower left corner, you'll get your quarter back." offered the woman.

"If I do, I'll give it to you, okay?" said Evan.

"Give it to your friend," replied the woman. "Crumbs in suits never leave no tips, white or black, makes no difference."

Kendrick got up from the booth and walked cautiously to the dark wall and the phone. It was time to call his office. He could not put any more pressure on Mrs. Ann Mulcahy O'Reilly. Squinting, he inserted the coin and dialed.

"Congressman Kendrick's—"

"It's me, Annie," broke in Evan.

"My God, where *are* you? It's after five and this place is still a madhouse!"

"That's why I'm not there."

"Before I *forget*!" cried Mrs. O'Reilly breathlessly. "Manny called a while ago and was very emphatic but not loud—which I think means he's as serious as he can be."

"What did he say?"

"That you're not to reach him on the Colorado line."

"*What?*"

"He told me to say *'allcott massghoul,'* whatever the hell that is."

"It's very clear, Annie." Weingrass had said *alkhatt mashghool,* Arabic for 'the line is engaged,' a simple euphemism for tampered with, or tapped. If Manny was right, a trace could be lasered out and the origin of any incoming call identified in a matter of moments. "I won't make any calls to Colorado," added Evan.

"He said to tell you that when things calm down, he'll drive to Mesa Verde and call me here and give me a number where you can reach him."

"I'll check back with you."

"Now then, Mr. Superman, is it true what everyone's saying? Did you really do all those things in Oman or wherever it is?"

"Only a few of them. They left out a lot of people who should have been included. Someone's trying to make me out to be something I'm not. How are you handling things?"

"The standard 'No comment,' and 'Our boss is out of town,' " answered O'Reilly.

"Good. Glad to hear it."

"No, Congressman, it's not good because some things can't

be handled standardwise. We can control the loonies and the press and even your peers, but we can't control Sixteen Hundred."

"The *White House*?"

"The obnoxious chief of staff himself. We can't say 'No comment' to the President's mouthpiece."

"What did he say?"

"He gave me a telephone number you're to call. It's his private line, and he made sure I understood that less than ten people in Washington had it—"

"I wonder if the President's one of them," interrupted Kendrick only half facetiously.

"He claimed he is, and in point of fact he said it's a direct presidential order that you call *his* chief of staff immediately."

"A direct *what*?"

"Presidential order."

"Will somebody please read those clowns the Constitution. The legislative branch of this government does not take direct orders from the executive, presidential or otherwise."

"His choice of words was stupid, I grant you," went on Ann O'Reilly quickly, "but if you'll let me finish telling you what he said, you might be more amenable."

"Go on."

"He said they understood why you were keeping out of sight, and that they'd arrange an unmarked pickup for you wherever you say. . . . Now, may I speak as your elder here in Funny Town, *sir*?"

"Please."

"You can't keep on running, Evan. Sooner or later you'll have to show up, and it's better that you know what's on their minds over there before you do. Like it or not, they're on your case. Why not find out how they're coming down? It could avoid a disaster."

"What's the number?"

22

Herbert Dennison, White House chief of staff, closed the door of his private bathroom and reached for the bottle of Maalox, which he kept in the right-hand corner of the marble counter.

In precise sequence, he ingested four swallows of the chalklike liquid, knowing from experience that it would eliminate the hot flashes in his upper chest. Years ago in New York, when the attacks had begun, he had been so frightened that he could barely eat or sleep, so convinced was he that after surviving the hell of Korea he was going to die in the street of cardiac arrest. His then wife—the first of three—had also been beside herself, unable to decide whether to get him first to a hospital or to their insurance agent for an expanded policy. Without his knowing about it she accomplished the latter, and a week later Herbert bit the bullet and admitted himself to the Cornell Medical Center for a thorough examination.

Relief came when the doctors pronounced his heart as strong as a young bull's, explaining to him that the sporadic fits of discomfort were brought about by periodic spasms of excess acid produced, no doubt, by stress. From that day forward, in bedrooms, offices, automobiles and briefcases, bottles of the white pacifying liquid were always available to him. Tension was a part of his life.

The doctors' diagnosis had been so accurate that over the years he could reasonably predict when, give or take an hour or two, the acid attacks would grip him. During his days on Wall Street they invariably came with wild fluctuations in the bond market or when he fought with his peers, who were continually trying to thwart him in his drive for both wealth and position. They were all pukey shits, thought Dennison. Fancy boys from fancy fraternities who belonged to fancy clubs that wouldn't spit on him, much less consider him for membership. Who gave a nun's fart? Those same clubs let in yids and niggers and even spics these days! All they had to do was speak like fairy actors and buy their clothes from Paul Stuart or from some French faggot. Well, he had spat on *them*! He *broke* them! He had the gut instincts of a street fighter in the market and he had cornered so much, *made* so much that the fucking firm *had* to make him president or he would have walked out, taking millions with him. And he had shaped up that corporation until it was the sharpest, most aggressive firm on the Street. He had done so by getting rid of the whining deadwood and that stupid corps of so-called trainees who ate up money and wasted everybody's time. He had two maxims that became corporate holy writ. The first was: *Beat last year's figures or beat feet out of here.* The second was equally succinct: *You don't get trained here, you get here trained.*

Herb Dennison never gave a damn whether he was liked or disliked; the theory that the end justified the means suited him splendidly, thank you. He had learned in Korea that soft-nosed officers were often rewarded with GI caskets for their lack of harsh discipline and harsher authority in the field. He had been aware that his troops hated his proverbial guts to the point where he never dropped his guard against being fragged by a U.S. grenade, and regardless of the losses, he was convinced they would have been far greater had the loosey-goosies been in charge.

Like the crybabies on Wall Street: "We want to build trust, Herb, continuity . . ." Or: "The youngster of today is the corporate officer of tomorrow—a loyal one." *Crap!* You didn't make profits on trust or continuity or loyalty. You made profits by making other people money, that was all the trust and continuity and loyalty they looked for! And he had been proved right, swelling the client lists until the computers were ready to burst, pirating talent from other firms, making damn sure he got what he paid for or the new boys, too, were out on their asses.

Sure, he was tough, perhaps even ruthless, as many called him both to his face and in print, and, yes, he had lost a few good people along the way, but the main thing was that on the percentages he was *right.* He had proved it in both military and civilian life . . . and yet in the end, in both, the pukeys had dumped on him. In Korea the regimental CO had damned near *promised* him the rank of full colonel upon discharge; it never happened. In New York—*Christ,* if possible it was worse!—his name had been floated around as the newest member of the Board of Directors for Wellington-Midlantic Industries, the most prestigious board in international finance. It never happened. In both cases the old-school-tie fraternities had shot him down at the moment of escalation. So he took his millions and said *Screw all of you!*

Again, he had been right, for he found a man who needed both his money and his considerable talents: a senator from Idaho who had begun to raise his startlingly sonorous, impassioned voice, saying things Herb Dennison fervently believed in, yet a politician who could laugh and amuse his growing audiences while at the same time instructing them.

The man from Idaho was tall and attractive, with a smile that had not been seen since Eisenhower and Shirley Temple, full of anecdotes and homilies that espoused the old values of strength, courage, self-reliance and, above all—for Dennison—freedom of choice. Herb had flown down to Washington and a pact was made with that senator. For three years Dennison threw all his energies and several million—plus additional millions from numerous anonymous men for whom he had made fortunes—until they had a war chest that could buy the papacy if it were more obviously on the market.

Herb Dennison belched; the chalky-white liquid pacifier was working, but not rapidly enough; he had to be ready for the man who would walk into his office in a matter of minutes. He took two more swallows and looked at himself in the mirror, unhappy at the sight of his continuously thinning gray hair that he combed straight back on both sides, the sharply defined part on the left, the top of his head consistent with his no-nonsense image. Peering into the glass, he wished his gray-green eyes were larger; he opened them as wide as he could; they were still too narrow. And the slight wattle under his chin reinforced the hint of jowls, reminding him that he must get some exercise or eat less, neither of which appealed to him. And why, with all the goddamned money he paid for his suits, didn't he look more like the men in the ads his British tailors sent him. Still, there was about him an imposing air of strength, emphasized by his rigid posture and the thrust of his jaw, both of which he had perfected over the years.

He belched again and swallowed another mouthful of his personal elixir. *Goddamn Kendrick son of a bitch!* he swore to himself. That nobody-suddenly-somebody was the cause of his anger and discomfort. . . . Well, if he were to be honest with himself, and he *always* tried to be honest with himself, if not always with others, it was not the nobody/somebody by himself, it was the bastard's effect on Langford Jennings, President of the United States. *Shit, piss, and vinegar!* What did Langford have in mind? (In his thoughts Herb had actually pulled himself short, substituting "the President" for "Langford," and that made him angrier still; it was part of the tension, part of the distance that White House authority demanded and Dennison hated it. . . . After the inauguration and three years of calling him by his first name, Jennings had spoken quietly to his chief of staff during one of the inaugural balls, spoken to him in that soft, jocular voice that dripped with self-deprecation and good humor. "You know I don't give a damn, Herb, but I think the office—not me, but the *office*—sort of calls for you to address me as 'Mr. President,' don't you think so, too?" *Damn!* That had been that!)

What *did* Jennings have in mind? Regarding this Kendrick freak, the President had casually agreed with everything Herb had proposed, but the responses had been *too* casual, bordering on disinterest, and that bothered the chief of staff. Jennings's mellifluous voice sounded unconcerned, but his eyes did not convey any lack of concern at all. Every now and then Langford Jennings surprised the whole goddamned bunch of them at the White House. Dennison hoped this was not one of those frequently awkward times.

The bathroom telephone rang, its proximity causing the chief of staff to spill Maalox over his Savile Row suit coat. Awkwardly he grabbed the phone off the wall with his right hand while turning on the hot water faucet with his left and dousing a washcloth under the stream. As he answered he frantically rubbed the wet cloth over the white spots, grateful that they disappeared into the dark fabric.

"*Yes?*"

"Congressman Kendrick has arrived at the East Gate, sir. The strip search is in progress."

"The *what*?"

"They're checking him for weapons and explosives—"

"*Jesus,* I never said he was a *terrorist*! He's in a government car with two Secret Service personnel!"

"Sir, you did indicate a strong degree of apprehension and displeasure—"

"Send him up here at once!"

"He may have to get dressed, sir."

"*Shit!*"

Six minutes later a quietly furious Evan Kendrick was ushered through the door by an apprehensive secretary. Rather than thanking the woman, Evan's expression conveyed another message, more like *Get out of here, lady, I want this man to myself.* She left quickly as the chief of staff approached, his hand extended. Kendrick ignored it. "I've heard about your fun and games over here, Dennison," said Evan, his voice a low, ice-like monotone, "but when you presume to search a member of the House who's here at your invitation—that's what it had better be, you fucker; you don't give orders to me—you've gone too far."

"A complete foul-up of instructions, Congressman! My God, how can you think anything else?"

"With you, very easily. Too many of my colleagues have had too many run-ins with you. The horror stories are rampant, including the one in which you threw a punch at the member from Kansas who, I understand, flattened you out on the floor."

"That's a *lie*! He disregarded White House procedures, for which *I'm* responsible. I may have touched him, merely to keep him in place, but that's all. And that's when he took me by surprise."

"I don't think so. I heard he called you a 'two-bit major' and you went up."

"Distortion. *Complete* distortion!" Dennison winced; the acid was erupting. "Look, I apologize for strip search—"

"Don't. It didn't happen. I accepted removing the jacket, figuring it was standard, but when the guard mentioned my shirt and trousers, my far brighter escorts moved in."

"Then what the hell are you so *uptight* about?"

"That you even considered it, and if you didn't, that you've created a mentality here that would."

"I could defend that accusation, but I won't bother. Now we're going into the Oval Office and, for Christ's sake, don't confuse the man with all that Arab bullshit. Remember, he doesn't know what happened and it won't do any good trying to explain positions. I'll clarify everything for him later."

"How do I know you're capable of that?"

"What?"

"You heard me. How do I know you're either capable or reliable?"

"What are you talking about?"

"I think you'd clarify whatever you want to clarify, telling him whatever you want him to hear."

"Who the hell are you to talk to me this way?"

"Someone probably as rich as you are. Also someone who's getting out of this town, as I'm sure Swann told you, so your political benediction is meaningless to me—I wouldn't accept it in any event. You know something, Dennison? I think you're a bona fide rat. Not the cute Mickey Mouse variety, but the original animal. An ugly, scavenging, long-tailed rodent who spreads a lousy disease. It's called nonaccountability."

"You don't spare words, do you, Congressman?"

"I don't have to. I'm leaving."

"But *he isn't*! And I want him strong, persuasive. He's taking us into a new era. We're standing *tall* again and it's about time. We're telling the crumbs of this world to shit or get off the pot!"

"Your expressions are as banal as you are."

"What are *you*? Some fucking Ivy Leaguer with a degree in

English? Get with it, Congressman. We're playing hardball here; this is *it*! People in this administration move their bowels or they're out. *Got* that?"

"I'll try to remember."

"While you're at it, remember he doesn't like dissent. Everything's cool, got that? No waves at all; everybody's happy, got that?"

"You repeat yourself, don't you?"

"I get things done, Kendrick. That's the name of the hardball game."

"You're a lean, mean machine, you are."

"So we don't like each other. So what? It's no big deal—"

"I've got *that,*" agreed Evan.

"Let's go."

"Not so fast," said Kendrick firmly, turning away from Dennison and walking to a window as if the office were his, not that of the President's man. "What's the scenario? That *is* the term, isn't it?"

"What do you mean?"

"What do you want from me?" asked Kendrick, looking out at the White House lawn. "Since you're doing the thinking, why am I here?"

"Because ignoring you would be counterproductive."

"Really?" Kendrick turned again to face the White House's chief of staff. "Counterproductive?"

"You've got to be acknowledged, is that clear enough? He can't sit on his ass and pretend you don't exist, *right*?"

"Oh, I see. Say that during one of his entertaining although not terribly enlightening press conferences someone brings up my name, which is inevitable now. He can't very well say that he's not sure whether I play for the Jets or the Giants, can he?"

"You got it. Let's go. I'll shape the conversation."

"You mean control it, don't you?"

"Call it what you like, Congressman. He's the greatest President of the twentieth century, and don't you forget it. My job is to maintain the status quo."

"It's not *my* job."

"The hell it isn't! It's all our jobs. I was in combat, young fella, and I watched men die defending our freedoms, our way of life. I tell you, it was a goddamned holy thing to see! And this *man,* this *President,* has brought those values back, those sacrifices we prize so much. He's *moved* this country in the right direction by the sheer force of his will, his *personality,* if you like. He's the best!"

"But not necessarily the brightest," interrupted Kendrick.

"That doesn't mean shit. Galileo would have made a lousy Pope and a worse Caesar."

"I suppose you've got a point."

"I certainly do. Now the scenario—the *explanation* is simple and all too damned familiar. Some son of a bitch leaked the Oman story and you want it forgotten as soon as possible."

"I do?"

Dennison paused, studying Evan's face as if it were decidedly unattractive. "That's based directly on what that jerk Swann told the chairman of the Joint Chiefs—"

"Why is Swann a jerk? He didn't leak the story. He tried to throw off the man who came to see him."

"He let it happen. He was the CO of that operation and he let it happen and I'll see him hung."

"Wrong past tense."

"What?"

"Never mind. But just to make sure we're both using the same scenario, why do I want everything forgotten as soon as possible?"

"Because there could be reprisals against your lousy Arab friends over there. That's what you told Swann and that's what he told his superiors. You want to change it?"

"No, of course not," said Kendrick softly. "The scenario's the same."

"Good. We'll schedule a short ceremony showing him thanking you on behalf of the whole damn country. No questions, just a restricted photo session and then you fade." Dennison gestured toward the door; both men started toward it. "You know something, Congressman?" remarked the chief of staff, his hand on the knob. "Your showing up like this has ruined one of the best whispering campaigns any administration could ask for—public-relations-wise, that is."

"A whispering campaign?"

"Yeah. The longer we kept quiet, deflecting questions on the basis of national security, the more people thought the President forced the Oman settlement all by himself."

"He certainly conveyed that," said Evan, smiling, not unkindly, as if he admired a talent he did not necessarily approve of.

"I tell you he may not be an Einstein, but he's still a fucking genius." Dennison opened the door.

Evan did not move. "May I remind you that eleven men and women were murdered in Masqat? That two hundred others will have nightmares for the rest of their lives?"

"That's right!" replied Dennison. "And *he* said it—with goddamned *tears* in his eyes! He said they were true American heroes, as brave as those who fought at Verdun, Omaha Beach, Panmunjom and Danang! The man *said* it, Congressman, and he *meant* it, and we stood *tall*!"

"He said it as he narrowed the options, making his message clear," agreed Kendrick. "If any one person was responsible for saving those two hundred thirty-six hostages, it must have been him."

"So?"

"Never mind. Let's get this over with."

"You're a fruitcake, Congressman. And you're right, you don't belong in this town."

Evan Kendrick had met the President of the United States only once. The meeting lasted for approximately five, perhaps six, seconds, during a White House reception for the freshmen congressmen of the chief executive's party. It had been mandatory for him to attend, according to Ann Mulcahy O'Reilly, who practically threatened to blow up the office if Evan refused to go to the affair. It was not that Kendrick disliked the man, he kept telling Annie; it was just that he did not agree with a lot of things Langford Jennings espoused—perhaps more than a lot, maybe most. And in answer to Mrs. O'Reilly's question as to why he had run on the ticket, he could only reply that in an election the other party did not stand a chance of being elected.

The predominant impression Evan had while briefly shaking hands with Langford Jennings in that reception line was more in the abstract than in the immediate, yet not totally so. The *office* was both intimidating and overwhelming. That a single human being could be entrusted with such awesome global power stretched any thinking man's mind to its limits. A miscue during some horrible miscalculation could blow up the planet. Yet . . . yet . . . despite Kendrick's personal evaluation of the man himself, which included a less than brilliant intellect and a proclivity for oversimplification as well as tolerance for such zealous clowns as Herbert Dennison, there was about Langford Jennings a striking image that was larger than life, an image that the ordinary citizen of the republic desperately longed for in the presidency. Evan had tried to understand the gossamer veil that shielded the man from closer scrutiny and had finally come to the conclusion that scrutiny itself was irrelevant compared with his impact. So were the impacts of Nero, Caligula, any number of mad, authoritarian popes and emperors, and the ultimate villains of the twentieth century, Mussolini, Stalin and Hitler. Yet this man displayed none of the evil inherent in those others; instead, he conveyed a strong, pervasive trustworthiness that seemed to radiate from his inner self. Jennings was also blessed with a large, attractive physique, and a much larger belief, and the purity of his belief was everything to him. He was also one of the most charming, ingratiating men Kendrick had ever observed.

"*Damn,* it's good to meet you, Evan! May I call you Evan, Mr. Congressman?"

"Of course, Mr. President."

Jennings came around the desk in the Oval Office to shake hands, gripping Kendrick's left arm as their hands clasped. "I've just finished reading all that secret stuff about what you did, and I tell you, I'm so *proud—*"

"There were a lot of others involved, sir. Without them I'd have been killed."

"I understand that. Sit down, Evan, sit, *sit*!" The President returned to his chair; Herbert Dennison remained standing. "What you did, Evan, as a single *individual,* will be a textbook lesson for generations of young people in America. You took the whip in your hands and made the damn thing snap."

"Not by myself, sir. There's a long list of people who risked their lives to help me—and several lost their lives. As I said, I'd be dead if it weren't for them. There were at least a dozen Omanis, from the young sultan down, and an Israeli commando unit that reached me when I literally had only a few hours to live. My execution was already scheduled—"

"Yes, I understand all that, Evan," interrupted Langford Jennings, nodding and frowning compassionately. "I also understand that our friends in Israel insist that there be no hint of their involvement, and our intelligence community here in Washington refuses to risk exposing our personnel in the Persian Gulf."

"The Gulf of Oman, Mr. President."

"I'm on your side," said Jennings, grinning his famous self-deprecating grin that had charmed a nation. "I'm not sure I know one from the other but I'll learn tonight. As my hatchet cartoonists would balloon it, my wife won't give me my cookies and milk till I get it all straight."

"That would be unfair, sir. It's a geographically complex part of the world if a person's not familiar with it."

"Yes, well, somehow I think even I might master it with a couple of grammar school maps."

"I never meant to imply—"

"It's okay, Evan, it's my fault. I slip now and then. The main issue here is what do we do with you. What do we do, given the restrictions placed on us for the sake of protecting the lives of agents and subagents who are working for us in an explosive part of the globe?"

"I'd say those necessary restrictions call for keeping everything quiet, classified—"

"It's a little late for that, Evan," broke in Jennings. "National security alibis can only go so far. Beyond a certain point you arouse too much curiosity; that's when things can get sticky—and dangerous."

"Also," added Herbert Dennison, gruffly breaking his silence, "as I mentioned to you, Congressman, the President can't simply ignore you. It wouldn't be the generous or patriotic thing to do. Now, the way I see it—and the President agrees with me—we'll schedule a short photo session here in the Oval Office, where you'll be congratulated by the President, along with a series of shots showing you both in what'll look like confidential conversation. That'll be consistent with the intelligence gray-out required by our counterterrorist services. The country will understand that. You don't tip off your tactics to those Arab scumballs."

"Without a lot of Arabs I wouldn't have gotten anywhere, and you goddamned well know it," said Kendrick, his angry eyes rigid on the chief of staff.

"Oh, we know it, Evan," interrupted Jennings, his own eyes obviously amused by what he observed. "At least *I* know it. By the way, Herb, I had a call from Sam Winters this afternoon and I think he has a hell of an idea that wouldn't violate any of our security concerns, and, as a matter of fact, could explain them."

"Samuel Winters is not necessarily a friend," countered Dennison. "He's withheld a number of policy endorsements we could have used with Congress."

"Then he didn't agree with us. Does that make him an enemy? Hell, if it does, you'd better send half the marine guards up to our family quarters. Come on, Herb, Sam Winters has been an adviser to presidents of both parties for as long as I can remember. Only a damn fool wouldn't accept calls from him."

"He should have been routed through me."

"You see, Evan?" said the President, his head askew, grinning mischievously. "I can play in the sandbox but I can't choose my friends."

"That's hardly what I—"

"It certainly is what you meant, Herb, and that's okay with me. You get things done around here—which you constantly remind me of, and *that's* okay, too."

"What did Mr. Winters—*Professor* Winters—suggest?" asked Dennison, the academic title spoken sarcastically.

"Well, he's a 'professor,' Herb, but he's not your average run-of-the-mill teacher, is he? I mean, if he wanted to, I suppose he could buy a couple of pretty decent universities. Certainly the one I got out of could be his for a check he wouldn't miss."

"What was his idea?" pressed the chief of staff anxiously.

"That I award my friend, Evan, here, the Medal of Freedom." The President turned to Kendrick. "That's the civilian equivalent of the Congressional Medal of Honor, Evan."

"I know that, sir. I don't deserve it, nor do I want it."

"Well, Sam made a couple of things clear to me and I think he's right. To begin with, you *do* deserve it, and whether you want it or not, I'd look like a chintzy bastard not awarding it to you. And *that,* fellas, I will not accept. Is that clear, Herb?"

"Yes, Mr. President," said Dennison, his voice choked. "However, you should know that although Representative Kendrick is standing unopposed for reelection to guarantee you a congressional seat, he intends to resign his office in the near future. There's no point, since he has his own objections, to focus more attention on him."

"The *point,* Herb, is that I *won't* be a chintzy bastard. Anyway, he looks like he could be my younger brother—we could get mileage out of that. Sam Winters brought it to my attention. The image of a go-getting American family, he called it. Not bad, wouldn't you say?"

"It's not *necessary,* Mr. President," rejoined Dennison, now frustrated, his hoarse voice conveying the fact that he could not push much further. "The Congressman's fears are valid. He thinks there could be reprisals against friends of his in the Arab world."

The President leaned back in his chair, his eyes fixed blankly on his chief of staff. "That doesn't wash with me. This is a dangerous world, and we'll only make it more dangerous by knuckling under to such speculative crap. But in that vein I'll explain to the country—from a position of *strength,* not fear—that I won't permit full disclosure of the Oman operation for reasons of counterterrorist strategy. You were right about that part, Herb. Actually, Sam Winters said it to me first. Also, I will *not* look like a *chintzy bastard.* It simply isn't me. Understood, Herb?"

"Yes, sir."

"Evan," said Jennings, his infectious grin again creasing his face. "You're my kind of man. What you did was *terrific*—what I read about it—and this President won't stint! By the way, Sam Winters mentioned that I should say we worked together. What the hell, my *people* worked with you, and that's the gospel truth."

"Mr. President—"

"*Schedule* it, Herb. I looked at my calendar, if that doesn't offend you. Next Tuesday, ten o'clock in the morning. That way we'll hit all the networks' nightly news, and Tuesday's a heavy night."

"But Mr. President—" began a flustered Dennison.

"Also, Herb, I want the Marine Band. In the Blue Room. I'll be damned if I'll be a chintzy bastard! It's not *me*!"

A furious Herbert Dennison walked back to his office with Kendrick in tow for the purpose of carrying out the presidential order: Shake out the specifics for the award ceremony in the Blue Room on the following Tuesday. With the Marine Band. So intense was the chief of staff's anger that his large, firm jaw was locked in silence.

"I'm really on your case, aren't I, Herbie?" said Evan, noting the bull-like quality of Dennison's stride.

"You're on my case and my name isn't Herbie."

"Oh, I don't know. You looked like a Herbie back there. The man cut you down, didn't he?"

"There are times when the President is inclined to listen to the wrong people."

Kendrick looked over at the chief of staff as they marched down the wide hallway. Dennison ignored the tentative greetings of numerous White House personnel heading in the opposite direction, several of whom stared wide-eyed at Evan, obviously recognizing him. "I don't get it," said Kendrick. "Our mutual dislike aside, what's your problem? *I'm* the one being stuck where I don't want to be, not you. Why are you howling?"

"Because you talk too goddamned much. I watched you on the Foxley show and that little display in your office the next morning. You're counterproductive."

"You like that word, don't you?"

"I've got a lot of others I can use."

"I'm sure you do. Then again I may have a surprise for you."

"*Another* one? What the hell is it?"

"Wait till we get to your office."

Dennison ordered his secretary to hold all calls except those on Priority Red. She nodded her head rapidly in obedient acknowledgment, but in a cowed voice explained. "You have more than a dozen messages now, sir. Nearly every one is an urgent callback."

"Are they Priority *Red*?" The woman shook her head. "What did I just *tell* you?" With these courteous words the chief of staff propelled the Congressman into his office and slammed the door shut. "Now, what's this surprise of yours?"

"You know, Herbie, I really must give you some advice," replied Evan, walking casually over to the window where he had stood previously; he turned and looked at Dennison. "You can be rude to the help as much as you like or as long as they'll take it, but don't you ever again put your hand on a member of the House of Representatives and shove him into your office as if you were about to administer a strap."

"I didn't *shove* you!"

"I interpreted it that way and that's all that matters. You have a heavy hand, Herbie. I'm sure my distinguished colleague from Kansas felt the same way when he decked you on your ass."

Unexpectedly, Herbert Dennison paused, then laughed softly. The prolonged deep chuckle was reflective, neither angry nor antagonistic, more the sound of relief than anything else. He loosened his tie and casually sat down in a leather armchair in front of his desk. "Christ, I wish I were ten or twelve years younger, Kendrick, and I'd whip your tail—I could have done it even at that age. At sixty-three, however, you learn that caution is the better part of valor, or whatever it is. I don't care to be decked again; it's a little harder to get up these days."

"Then don't ask for it, don't provoke it. You're a very provocative man."

"Sit down, Congressman—in *my* chair, at *my* desk. Go on, go *ahead.*" Evan did so. "How does it feel? You get a tingling in your spine, a rush of blood to your head?"

"Neither. It's a place to work."

"Yeah, well, I guess we're different. You see, down the hall is the most powerful man on earth, and he relies on me, and to tell you the truth, I'm no genius, either. I just keep the booby hatch running. I oil the machinery so the wheels turn, and the oil I use has a lot of acidity in it, just like me. But it's the only lubricant I've got and it works."

"I suppose there's a point to this," said Kendrick.

"I suppose there is and I don't think you'll be offended. Since I've been here—since *we've* been here—everybody bows like gooks in front of me, saying all kinds of flattering things with big smiles . . . only with eyes that tell me they'd rather put a bullet in my head. I've been through it before; it doesn't bother me. But here you show up and you tell me to go fuck off. Now, that's really *refreshing.* I can deal with that. I mean I *like* your not liking me and my not liking you—does that make sense?"

"In a perverse sort of way, I suppose. But then you're a perverse man."

"Why? Because I'd rather talk straight than in circles? Pointless lip service and ass-kissing drivel only waste time. If I could get rid of both, we'd all accomplish ten times what we do now."

"Did you ever let anyone know that?"

"I've tried, Congressman, so help me God, I've tried. And you know something? Nobody believes me."

"Would you if you were they?"

"Probably not, and maybe if they did the booby hatch would turn into a certifiable looney bin. Think about it, Kendrick. There's more than one side to my perversity."

"I'm not qualified to comment on that, but this conversation makes things easier for me."

"Easier? Oh, that surprise you're going to lay on me?"

"Yes," agreed Evan. "You see, up to a point I'll do what you want me to do—for a price. It's my pact with the Devil."

"You flatter me."

"I don't mean to. I'm not given to ass-kissing drivel, either, because it wastes *my* time. As I read you, I'm 'counterproductive' because I've made some noise about several things I feel pretty strongly about and what you've heard goes against your grain. Am I right, so far?"

"Right on the tiny tin dime, kiddo. You may look different, but to me there's a lot of that stringy, long-haired protest crap in you."

"And you think that if I'm given any kind of platform there

might be more to come, and that *really* frosts your apricots. Right again?"

"Right in the fly's asshole. I don't want anything or anyone to interrupt *his* voice, *his* commitments. He's taken us out of the pansy patch; we're riding a strong Chinook wind and it feels good."

"I won't try to follow that."

"You probably couldn't—"

"But basically you want two things from me," continued Evan rapidly. "The first is for me to say as little as possible and nothing at all that calls into question the wisdom emanating from this booby hatch of yours. Am I close?"

"You couldn't get closer without being arrested."

"And the second is in what you said before. You want me to fade—and fade fast. How am I doing?"

"You've got the brass ring."

"All right, I'll do both—up to a point. After this little ceremony next Tuesday, which neither of us wants but we lose to the man, my office will be flooded with demands from the media. Newspapers, radio, television, the weekly magazines—the whole ball of wax. I'm news and they want to sell their merchandise—"

"You're not telling me anything I don't know or don't like," interrupted Dennison.

"I'll turn everything down," said Kendrick flatly. "I won't grant any interviews. I won't speak publicly on any issue, and I'll fade just as fast as I can."

"I'd kiss you right now except that you mentioned something kind of counterproductive, like 'up to a point.' What the hell does that mean?"

"It means that in the House I'll vote my conscience, and if I'm challenged on the floor I'll give my reasons as dispassionately as I can. But that's in the House; off the Hill I'm not available for comment."

"We get most of our PR flak off the Hill, not on it," said the White House chief of staff reflectively. "The *Congressional Record* and cable's C-Span cameras don't put a dent in the *Daily News* and *Dallas.* Under the circumstances, thanks to that smooth son of a bitch Sam Winters, your offer is so irresistible I wonder what the price is. You have a price, I assume."

"I want to know who blew the whistle on me. Who leaked the Oman story so very, *very* professionally."

"You think *I* don't?" erupted Dennison, bouncing forward.

"I'd have the bastards deep-sixed fifty miles off Newport News in torpedo cans!"

"Then help me find out. That's my price, take it or take me replaying the Foxley show all over the country, calling you and your crowd exactly what I honestly think you are. A bunch of bumbling Neanderthals faced with a complicated world you can't understand."

"*You're* the fucking expert?"

"Hell, no. I just know that *you're* not. I watch and I listen and see you cutting off so many people who could help you because there's a zig or a zag in their stripes that doesn't conform to your preconceived pattern. And I learned something this afternoon; I saw it, heard it. The President of the United States talked to Samuel Winters, a man you disapprove of, but when you explained why you didn't like him, that he withheld endorsements that could help you with Congress, Langford Jennings said something that impressed the hell out of me. He said to you that if this Sam Winters disagreed with some policy or other, it did *not* make him an *enemy.*"

"The President frequently doesn't understand who his enemies are. He spots ideological allies quickly and sticks by them—sometimes too long, frankly—but often he's too generous to detect those who would erode what he stands for."

"That's about the weakest and most presumptuous argument I've ever heard, *Herbie.* What are you shielding your man from? Diverse opinions?"

"Let's go back to your big surprise, Congressman. I like the topic better."

"I'm sure you do."

"What do you know that we don't that can help us find out who leaked the Oman story?"

"Essentially what I learned from Frank Swann. As head of the OHIO-Four-Zero unit, he was the liaison to the secretaries of Defense and State as well as the chairman of the Joint Chiefs, all of whom knew about me. He told me to rule them out as possible leaks, however—"

"*Far* out," interrupted Dennison. "They've got soft-boiled eggs all over their faces. They can't answer the simplest questions, which makes them look like prime idiots. Incidentally, they're not idiots and they've been around long enough to know what maximum-classified is and why it's there. What else?"

"Then outside of you—and frankly I rule you out only because my surfacing is about as 'counterproductive' as your fractured gray cells could conjure—that leaves three other people."

"Who are they?"

"The first is a man named Lester Crawford at the Central Intelligence Agency; the second, the station chief in Bahrain, James Grayson. The last is a woman, Adrienne Rashad, who's apparently special property and operates out of Cairo."

"What about them?"

"According to Swann, they're the only ones who knew my identity when I was flown over to Masqat."

"That's *our* personnel," said Dennison pointedly. "What about your people over there?"

"I can't say it's impossible, but I think it's remote. The few I reached, except for the young sultan, are so removed from any contact with Washington that I'd have to consider them last, if at all. Ahmat, whom I've known for years, certainly wouldn't for a lot of reasons, starting with his throne and, equally important, his ties with this government. Of the four men I spoke to on the telephone, only one responded and he was killed for it—undoubtedly with the consent of the others. They were frightened out of their skins. They didn't want anything to do with me, no acknowledgment of my presence in Oman whatsoever, and that included anyone they knew who did meet with me and who might make them suspect. You'd have to have been there to understand. They all live with the terrorist syndrome, with daggers at their throats—and at the throat of every member of their families. There'd been reprisals, a son killed, a daughter raped and disfigured because cousins or uncles called for action against the Palestinians. I don't believe any of those men would have spoken my name to a deaf dog."

"*Christ,* what kind of a world do those goddamned Arabs live in?"

"One in which the vast majority try to survive and make lives for themselves and their children. And we haven't helped, you bigoted bastard."

Dennison cocked his head and frowned. "I may have deserved that shot, Congressman, I'll have to think about it. Not so long ago it was fashionable not to like Jews, not to trust them, and now that's changed and the Arabs have taken their place in the scheme of our dislikes. Maybe it's *all* bullshit, who knows? . . . But what I want to know now is who sprung you out of the top-secret woodwork. You figure it's someone from our ranks."

"It has to be. Swann was approached—fraudulently approached, as it turns out—by a blond-haired man with a European accent who had in-depth data on me. That information could only have come from government files—my congressional background check probably. He tried to tie me in with the Oman situation, but Swann firmly denied it, saying he had specifically turned me down. However, Frank had the impression that the man wasn't convinced."

"We know about the blond spook," broke in Dennison. "We can't find him."

"But he dug and found someone else, someone who confirmed either intentionally or unintentionally what he was tracking down. If we rule you out, and if we also rule out State, Defense and the Joint Chiefs, it has to be Crawford, Grayson or the Rashad woman."

"Cross out the first two," said the White House chief of staff. "Early this morning I grilled Crawford right here in this office, and he was ready to challenge me to a game of Saigon roulette for even suggesting the possibility. As far as Grayson is concerned, I reached him in Bahrain five hours ago and he damned near had apoplexy thinking we even *considered* him the leak. He read the black-operations book to me as if I were the dumbest kid on the block who should be thrown into solitary for calling him on an unsecured line in foreign territory. Like Crawford, Grayson's an old-line professional. Neither one would risk throwing away his life's work over you, and neither could be tricked into doing it."

Kendrick leaned forward in Dennison's chair, his elbows on the desk. He stared at the far wall of the office, conflicting thoughts racing through his mind. Khalehla, born Adrienne Rashad, had saved his life, but had she saved it only to sell him? She was also a close friend of Ahmat, who could be damaged by his association with her, and Evan had hurt the young sultan enough without adding a turned intelligence agent to the list. Yet Khalehla had understood him when he needed understanding; she was kind when he needed kindness because he was so afraid—both for his life and for his inadequacies. If she had been tricked into revealing him and he exposed her ineptness, she was finished in a job she intensely believed in. . . . Yet if she had not been tricked, if for reasons of her own she had exposed him—then all *he* would expose was her betrayal. Which was the truth? Dupe or liar? Whichever it was, he had to find out for himself without the specter of official scrutiny. Above all, dupe or liar, he had to know *whom* she had reached or *who* had reached her. For only the "who" could answer the "why" he had been exposed as Evan of Oman. And that he had to learn! "Then out of the seven of you, there's only one unaccounted for."

"The woman," agreed Dennison, nodding his head. "I'll put her on a revolving spit over the hottest goddamn fire you ever saw."

"No, you won't," countered Kendrick. "You and your people won't get near her until I give you the word—if I give it. And we're going to go one step further. No one's to know you're flying her back here—under cover, I think is the term. Absolutely *no one.* Is that understood?"

"Who the hell are *you*—"

"We've been through this, Herbie. Remember next Tuesday in the Blue Room? With the Marine Band and all those reporters and television cameras? I'll have a great big platform to climb on if I want to and express a few opinions. Believe me, you'll be among the first targets, decked ass and all."

"*Shit!* May the one being blackmailed be so bold as to ask why this female spook gets preferred treatment?"

"Sure," replied Evan, his gaze settled on the chief of staff. "That woman saved my life and you're not going to ruin hers by letting her own people know you've got her under your well-advertised White House shotgun. You've done enough of that around here."

"All right, all right! But let's get one thing clear. If she's the sieve, you turn her over to me."

"That'll depend," said Kendrick, sitting back.

"On *what,* for Christ's sake?"

"On the how and the why."

"More riddles, Congressman?"

"Not for me," answered Evan, suddenly rising from the chair. "Get me out of here, Dennison. Also, since I can't go home, either to my house in Virginia or even out to Colorado, without being swamped, can someone in this booby hatch rent me a lodge or a cabin in the country under another name? I'll pay for a month or whatever's necessary. I just want a few days to figure things out before I go back to the office."

"It's been taken care of," said the chief of staff abruptly. "Actually, it was Jennings's idea—to put you on ice over the weekend in one of those sterile houses in Maryland."

"What the hell is a sterile house? Please use language I can understand."

"Let's put it this way. You're the guest of the President of the United States in a place no one can find that is reserved for people we don't want found. It dovetailed with my considered opinion that Langford Jennings should make the first public statements about you. You've been seen here, and as sure as rabbits have little rabbits the word'll get out."

"You're the scenario writer. What do we say—what do *you* say, since I'm in isolation?"

"That's easy. Your safety. It's the President's primary concern after conferring with our counterterrorist experts. Don't worry, our writers will come up with something that'll make the women cry into their handkerchiefs and the men want to go out and march in a parade. And since Jennings has the last word in these things, it'll probably include some whacked-up image of a powerful knight of the Round Table looking after a brave younger brother who carried out a joint dangerous mission. *Shit!*"

"And if there's any truth to the reprisal theory," added Kendrick, "it'll make me a target."

"That'd be nice," agreed Dennison, nodding again.

"Call me when you've made arrangements for the Rashad woman."

Evan sat in the leather lounge chair in the study of the impressive sterile house on Maryland's Eastern Shore in the township of Cynwid Hollow. Outside, within the walls of the floodlit grounds, guards moved in and out of the lights as they patrolled every foot of the acreage, their rifles at the ready, their eyes alert.

Kendrick snapped off the third replay he had watched on television of President Langford Jennings's suddenly called press conference regarding one Congressman Evan Kendrick of Colorado. It was more outrageous than Dennison had projected, filled with gut-wrenching pauses accompanied by a constant series of well-rehearsed grins that so obviously conveyed the pride and the agony beneath the surface of the man smiling. The President once again said everything in general terms and nothing specific—except in one area: *Until all proper security measures are in place, I have asked Congressman Kendrick, a man we are all so proud of, to remain in protective seclusion. And with this request, I hereby give dire warning. Should cowardly terrorists anywhere make any attempt on the life of my good friend, my close colleague, someone I look upon no less than I would a younger brother, the full might of the United States will be employed by ground, sea and air against determined enclaves of those responsible.* Determined? Oh, my God!

A telephone rang. Evan looked around trying to find out where it was. It was across the room on a desk; he swung his legs off the lounger and walked to the startlingly intrusive instrument.

"Yes?"

"She's flying over on military transport with a senior attaché from the embassy in Cairo. She's listed as a secretarial aide, the name's unimportant. The ETA is seven o'clock in the morning our time. She'll be in Maryland by ten at the latest."

"What does she know?"

"Nothing."

"You had to say something," insisted Kendrick.

"She was told it was new and urgent instructions from her government, instructions that could be transmitted only in person over here."

"She bought that nonsense?"

"She didn't have a choice. She was picked up at her flat in Cairo and has been in protective custody ever since. Have a lousy night, you bastard."

"Thanks, Herbie." Evan hung up the phone, both relieved and frightened by the prospect of tomorrow morning's confrontation with the woman he had known as Khalehla, a woman he had made love to in a frenzy of fear and exhaustion. That impulsive act and the desperation that led to it had to be forgotten. He had to determine whether he was re-meeting an enemy or a friend. Regardless, there was now a schedule, at least for the next twelve or fifteen hours. It was time to call Ann O'Reilly and, through her, reach Manny. It did not matter who knew where he was; he was the official guest of the President of the United States.

23

Emmanuel Weingrass sat in the red Naugahyde booth with the stocky, mustached owner of the Mesa Verde café. The past two hours had been stressful for Manny, somewhat reminiscent of those crazy days in Paris when he had worked with the Mossad. The current situation was nowhere near as melodramatic and his adversaries were hardly lethal, but still he was an elderly man who had to get from one place to another without being seen or stopped. In Paris he had to run a gauntlet of terrorist scouts without being noticed from Sacré-Coeur to the Boulevard de la Madeleine. Here in Colorado he had to get from Evan's house to the town of Mesa Verde without being stopped and locked up by his team of nurses, all of whom were charging about because of the activity outside.

"How did you do it?" asked Gonzalez-Gonzalez, the café's owner as he poured Weingrass a glass of whisky.

"Civilized man's second oldest need for privacy, Gee-Gee. The toilet. I went to the toilet and climbed out a window. Then I mingled with the crowd taking pictures with one of Evan's cameras, like a real photographer, you know, until I got a taxi here."

"*Hey,* man," interrupted Gonzalez-Gonzalez. "Those cats are making *dineros* today!"

"Thieves, they are! I climbed in and the first thing the *goniff* said to me was 'One hundred dollars to the airport, mister.' So I said to him, taking off my hat, 'The State Taxi Commission will be interested to hear about the new Verde rates,' and he says to me, 'Oh, it's you, Mr. Weingrass, just a joke, Mr. Weingrass,' and then I tell him, 'Charge 'em two hundred and take me to Gee-Gee's!' "

Both men broke into loud laughter as the pay telephone on the wall beyond the booth erupted in a staccato ring. Gonzalez placed his hand on Manny's arm. "Let García get it," he said.

"Why? You said my boy called twice before!"

"García knows what to say. I just told him."

"Tell *me*!"

"He'll give the Congressman the number of my office phone and tell him to call back in two minutes."

"Gee-Gee, what the hell are you *doing*?"

"A couple of minutes after you came in, a *gringo* I don't know arrived."

"So what? You get plenty of people in here you don't know."

"He doesn't belong here, Manny. He ain't got no raincoat or no hat or no camera, but he still don't belong here. He's got on a suit—with a vest." Weingrass started to turn his head. "*Don't,*" ordered Gonzalez, now gripping Weingrass's arm. "Every now and then he looks over here from his table. He's got you on his mind."

"So what do we do?"

"Just wait and get up when I tell you to."

The waiter named García hung up the pay phone, coughed once, and went over to the dark-suited, red-haired man with a vest. He leaned down and said something close to the well-dressed customer's face. The man stared coldly at his unexpected messenger; the waiter shrugged and crossed back to the bar. The man slowly, unobtrusively, put several bills on the table, got up, and walked out the nearby entrance.

"*Now,*" whispered Gonzalez-Gonzalez, rising and gesturing for Manny to follow him. Ten seconds later they were in the owner's disheveled office. "The Congressman will call back in about a minute," said Gee-Gee, indicating the chair behind a desk that had seen better days decades ago.

"You're sure it was Kendrick?" asked Weingrass.

"García's cough told me yes."

"What did José say to the guy at the table?"

"That he believed the message on the telephone must be for him, since no other customer fit his description."

"What was the message?"

"Quite simple, *amigo.* It was important for him to reach his people outside."

"Just *that*?"

"He left, didn't he? That tells us something, doesn't it?"

"Like what?"

"*Uno,* he has people to reach, no? *Dos,* they are either outside this grand establishment or he can talk to them by other means of communication—namely, a fancy telephone in an automobile, yes? *Tres,* he did not come in here in his also-fancy suit to have a Tex-Mex beer that practically chokes him—as my fine sparkling wine often chokes you, no? *Cuatro,* he is no doubt *federale.*"

"Government?" asked Manny, astonished.

"Personally, of course, I have never been involved with illegals crossing the borders from my beloved country to the south, but the stories reach even such innocents as myself. . . . We know what to look for, my friend. *Comprende, hombre?*"

"I always said," said Weingrass, sitting behind the desk. "Find the classiest non-class joints in town and you can learn more about life than in all the sewers of Paris."

"Paris, France, means a great deal to you, doesn't it, Manny?"

"It's fading, *amigo.* I'm not sure why, but it's fading. Something's happening here with my boy and I can't understand it. But it's important."

"He means much to you also, yes?"

"He is my *son.*" The telephone rang, and Weingrass yanked it up to his ear as Gonzalez-Gonzalez went out the door. "*Air-head,* is that *you*?"

"What have you got out there, Manny?" asked Kendrick over the line from the sterile house on Maryland's Eastern Shore. "A Mossad unit covering you?"

"Far more effective," answered the old architect from the Bronx. "There are no accountants, no CPAs counting the shekels over an egg cream. Now, *you.* What the hell *happened*?"

"I don't know, I swear I don't *know*!" Evan recounted his day in detail, from Sabri Hassan's startling news about the Oman revelations while he was in his pool to his hiding out in a cheap motel in Virginia; from his confrontation with Frank Swann of the State Department to his arrival at the White House under escort; from his hostile meeting with the White House chief of staff to his eventual presentation to the President of the United States, who proceeded to louse up everything by scheduling an award ceremony in the Blue Room next Tuesday—with the Marine Band. Finally, to the fact that the woman named Khalehla, who had first saved his life in Bahrain, was in reality a case officer in the Central Intelligence Agency and was being flown over for him to question.

"From what you've told me, she had nothing to do with exposing you."

"Why not?"

"Because you believed her when she said she was an Arab filled with shame, you told me that. In some ways, Air-head, I know you better than you know yourself. You are not easily fooled about such matters. It's what made you so good with the Kendrick Group. . . . For this woman to expose you would only add to her shame and further inflame the crazy world she lives in."

"She's the only one left, Manny. The others wouldn't; they couldn't."

"Then there are others beyond others."

"For God's sake, *who*? These were the only people who knew I was there."

"You just said this Swann told you a blond creep with a foreign accent figured you were in Masqat. Where did *he* get his information?"

"No one can find him, not even the White House."

"Maybe I know people who *can* find him," interrupted Weingrass.

"*No,* Manny," insisted Kendrick firmly. "This isn't Paris and those Israelis are way off limits. I owe them too much, although someday I'd like you to explain to me the interest they had in a certain hostage at the embassy."

"I was never told," said Weingrass. "I knew there was an initial plan the unit had trained for and I assumed it was designed to reach someone inside, but they never discussed it in front of me. Those people know how to keep their mouths shut. . . . What's your next move?"

"Tomorrow morning with the Rashad woman. I told you."

"After that."

"You haven't been watching television."

"I'm at Gee-Gee's. He only allows videotapes, remember? He's got a replay on one of the '82 Series, and most everyone at the bar thinks it's today. What's on television?"

"The President. He announced that I'm in protective seclusion."

"Sounds like jail to me."

"In a way it is, but the prison's tolerable and the warden's given me privileges."

"Do I get a number?"

"I wouldn't know it. There's nothing printed on the phone, only a blank strip, but I'll keep you informed. I'll call you if I move. Nobody could trace this line and it doesn't matter if they did."

"Okay, now let me ask you something. Did you mention me to anyone?"

"Good God, no. You may be in the classified Oman file and I did say that a lot of other people deserved credit besides myself, but I never used your name. Why?"

"I'm being followed."

"What?"

"It's a wrinkle I don't like. Gee-Gee says the clown on my tail is federal and that there are others with him."

"Maybe Dennison picked you out from the file and assigned you protection."

"From what? Even in Paris I'm vault-tight—if I wasn't, I'd have been dead three years ago. And what makes you think I'm in any file? Outside of the unit no one knew my name and *none* of our names were used in that conference the morning we all left. Finally, Air-head, if I'm being protected, it'd be a good idea to let me know about it. Because if I'm dangerous enough to warrant that kind of protection, I might just blow the head off someone I don't know who's protecting me."

"As usual," said Kendrick, "you may have an ounce of logic in your normal pound of implausibility. I'll check on it."

"Do that. I may not have too many years left but I wouldn't want them cut short by a bullet in my head—from either side. Call me tomorrow, because now I've got to get back to the coven before the inhabitants report my departure to the head police warlock."

"Give my regards to Gee-Gee," added Evan. "And tell him that when I'm home he's to stay the hell out of the importing business. Also, thank him, Manny." Kendrick hung up the phone, his hand still on it. He picked it up and dialed *O*.

"Operator," said a somewhat hesitant female voice after more unanswered rings than seemed normal.

"I'm not sure why," began Evan, "but I have an idea that you're not an ordinary run-of-the-mill operator for the Bell Telephone Company."

"*Sir . . . ?*"

"It doesn't matter, miss. My name is Kendrick and I have to reach Mr. Herbert Dennison, the White House chief of staff, as soon as possible—it's urgent. I'm asking you to do your best to find him and have him call me within the next five minutes. If that's impossible, I'll be forced to call my secretary's husband, who's a lieutenant on the Washington police, and tell him I'm being held prisoner at a location I'm fairly certain I can identify accurately."

"Sir, *please*!"

"I think I'm being reasonable and very clear," interrupted Evan. "Mr. Dennison is to reach me within the next five minutes, and the countdown's begun. Thank you, Operator, have a good day." Again Kendrick hung up the phone, but now he removed his hand and walked over to a wall bar, which held an ice bucket and assorted bottles of expensive whisky. He poured himself a drink, looked at his watch, and proceeded toward a large casement window that looked out on the rear floodlit grounds. He was amused at the sight of a croquet course bordered by white wrought-iron furniture; he was less amused by the sight of a marine guard dressed in the casual, unmilitary uniform of the estate's staff. He was pacing a garden path near the stone wall, his uncasual, very military repeating rifle angled in front. Manny was right: he was in jail. Moments later the telephone rang and the congressman from Colorado walked back to it. "Hello, Herbie, how are you?"

"How *am* I, you son of a bitch? I'm in the goddamned shower, that's how I am. *Wet!* What do you want?"

"I want to know why Weingrass is being followed. I want to know why his name ever surfaced anywhere, and you'd better have a damn good explanation, like his personal well-being."

"Back up, ingrate," said the chief of staff curtly. "What the hell is a Weingrass? Something put out by Manischewitz?"

"Emmanuel Weingrass is an architect of international renown. He's also a close friend of mine and he's staying at my house in Colorado, and for reasons that I don't have to give you, his being there is extremely confidential. Where and to whom have you circulated his name?"

"I can't circulate what I've never heard of, you fruitcake."

"You're not lying to me, are you, Herbie? Because if you are, I can make the next few weeks very embarrassing for you."

"If I thought that lying would get you off my back, I'd go to the well, but I haven't got any lies where a Weingrass is concerned. I don't know who he is, so help me."

"You read the debriefing reports on Oman, didn't you?"

"It's one file and buried. Of course I read it."

"Weingrass's name never appeared?"

"No, and I'd remember if it did. It's a funny name."

"Not to Weingrass." Kendrick paused, but not long enough for Dennison to interrupt. "Could anyone in the CIA or NSA or any of those outfits put a guest of mine under surveillance without informing you?"

"No *way*!" shouted the White House suzerain. "Where you and the rutabaga you've laid on us are concerned, no one moves *sideways* for an *inch* without my knowing about it!"

"One last question. In the Oman file, was there any mention of the person flying back with me from Bahrain?"

It was Dennison's turn to pause. "You're a little obvious, Congressman."

"You're a little closer to those soft-boiled eggs over your face. If you think I'm bad news for you and your man now, don't even speculate on the architect's connection. Leave it alone."

"I'll leave it alone," agreed the chief of staff. "With a name like Weingrass I can make another connection and it scares me. Like the Mossad."

"Good. Now, just answer my question. What was in the file about the flight from Bahrain to Andrews?"

"The cargo consisted of you and an old Arab in Western

clothes, a longtime subagent for Cons Op who was being flown over for medical treatment. His name was Ali something-or-other; State cleared him and he vanished. That's straight, Kendrick. No one in this government is aware of a Mr. Weingrass."

"Thanks, Herb."

"Thanks for the 'Herb.' Is there anything I can do?"

Evan stared at the casement window, then at the floodlit grounds and the marine guard outside and everything the scene represented. "I'm going to do you a favor and say no," he said softly. "At least for now. But you can clarify something for me. This phone has a tap on it, doesn't it?"

"Not the usual variety. There's a little black box like those on aircraft. It has to be removed by authorized personnel and the tapes processed under the strictest security measures."

"Can you stop the operation for, say, thirty minutes or so, until I reach someone? You'd want it that way, believe me."

"I'll accept that. . . . Sure, there's an override on the line; our people use it a lot when they're in those houses. Give me five minutes and call Moscow, if you like."

"Five minutes."

"May I go back to my shower now?"

"Try Clorox this time." Kendrick replaced the phone and took out his wallet, slipping his index finger under the flap behind his Colorado driver's license. He removed the scrap of paper with Frank Swann's two private telephone numbers written on it and again looked at his watch. He would wait ten minutes and hope that the deputy director of Consular Operations was at one place or the other. He was. At his apartment, of course. After curt greetings, Evan explained where he was—where he thought he was.

"How's 'protective seclusion'?" asked Swann, sounding weary. "I've been to several of those places when we've interrogated defectors. I hope you've got one with stables or at least two pools, one inside, naturally. They're all alike; I think the government buys them as political payoffs for the rich who get tired of their estates and want to buy new ones gratis. I hope somebody's listening. I don't have a pool anymore."

"There's a croquet course, I've seen that."

"Small time. What have you got to tell me? Am I any closer to getting off the hook?"

"Maybe. At least I've tried to take some heat off you. . . . Frank, I've got to ask you a question and we can both say anything we like, use any names we like. There's no tap on the phone here now."

"Who told you that?"

"Dennison."

"And you *believed* him? Incidentally, I couldn't care less if this transcript's given to him."

"I believe him because he has a clue as to what I'm going to say and wants to put a couple of thousand miles between the administration and what we're going to talk about. He said we're on an 'override.' "

"He's right. He's afraid of some loose cannon hearing your words. What is it?"

"Manny Weingrass, and through him linkage to the Mossad—"

"I told you, that's a no-no," broke in the deputy director. "Okay, we're *really* on override. Go ahead."

"Dennison told me that the Oman file lists the cargo on the plane from Bahrain to Andrews Air Force Base on that last morning as consisting of me and an old Arab in Western clothing who was a subagent for Consular Operations—"

"And who was being brought over here for medical treatment," interrupted Swann. "After years of invaluable cooperation our clandestine services owed Ali Saada and his family that much."

"You're sure that was the wording?"

"Who would know it better? I wrote it."

"*You?* Then you knew it was Weingrass?"

"It wasn't difficult. Your instructions relayed by Grayson were pretty damned clear. You demanded—demanded, mind you—that an unnamed person accompany you on that plane back to the States—"

"I was covering for the Mossad."

"Obviously, and so was I. You see, bringing someone in like that is against the rules—forget the law—unless he's on our books. So I put him on the books as someone else."

"But how did you know it was Manny?"

"That was the easiest part. I spoke to the chief of the Bahrainian Royal Guards, who was assigned as your covert escort. The physical description was probably enough, but when he told me that the old bastard kicked one of his men in the knee because he let you stumble getting into the car to the airport, I knew it was Weingrass. His reputation, as they say, has always preceded him."

"I appreciate your doing that," said Evan softly. "Both for him and for me."

"It was the only way of thanking you that I could think of."

"Then I can assume that no one in Washington intelligence circles knows that Weingrass was involved in Oman."

"Absolutely. Forget Masqat, he's a nonperson. He's just not among the living over here."

"Dennison didn't even know who he was—"

"Of course not."

"He's being followed, Frank. Out in Colorado, he's under someone's surveillance."

"Not ours."

Eight hundred ninety-five feet due north of the sterile house on the waters of Chesapeake Bay was the estate of Dr. Samuel Winters, honored historian and for over forty years friend and adviser to presidents of the United States. In his younger days the immensely wealthy academic was considered an outstanding sportsman; trophies for polo, tennis, skiing and sailing lined the shelves of his private study, attesting to his former skills. Now there remained for the aging educator a more passive game that had been a minor passion with the Winters family for generations, initially making its appearance on the lawn of their mansion in Oyster Bay during the early twenties. The game was croquet, and whenever any member of the family built on new property, among the first considerations was a proper lawn for the very official course that never deviated from the 40- by 75-foot dimensions as prescribed by the National Croquet Association in 1882. So one of the sights that caught the eye of a visitor to Dr. Winters's estate was the croquet "field" to the right of the enormous house above the waters of the Chesapeake. Its charm was enhanced by the many pieces of white wrought-iron furniture that bordered the course, areas of respite for those studying their next moves or having a drink.

The scene was identical with the croquet course at the sterile house 895 feet to the south of Winters's property, and it was only fitting that it should be, for all the land upon which both mansions stood originally belonged to Samuel Winters. Five years ago—with the silent resurrection of Inver Brass—Dr. Winters had quietly donated the south estate to the United States government for use as a "safe," or "sterile," house. In order to deter the amiably curious and divert hostile probes by potential enemies of the United States, the transaction was never revealed.

According to the property records filed in the Town Hall of Cynwid Hollow, the house and grounds still belonged to Samuel and Martha Jennifer Winters (the latter deceased), and for which the family's accountants annually paid the inordinately high shoreline taxes, refunded secretly by a grateful government. If any of the curious, friendly or unfriendly alike, inquired into the activity at this aristocratic compound, they were invariably told that it never stopped, that limousines and caterers carried and cared for the great and the near great of the academic world and industry, all representing the varied interests of Samuel Winters. A squad of strong young gardeners kept the place trim to a fare-thee-well, and served also as staff, seeing to the needs of the constant stream of visitors. The image conveyed was that of a multimillionaire's multipurpose think tank in the countryside—far too open to be anything but what it purported to be.

To maintain the integrity of that image, all bills were sent to Samuel Winters's accountants, who promptly paid them with duplicates of these payments forwarded to the historian's personal lawyer, who, in turn, had them hand-delivered to the Department of State for covert reimbursement. It was a simple arrangement and beneficial to all concerned, as simple and as beneficial as it was for Dr. Winters to suggest to President Langford Jennings that Congressman Evan Kendrick might simply benefit by a few days out of the media limelight at the "safe house" south of his property, since there was no activity there at the time. The President gratefully concurred; he would have Herb Dennison take care of the arrangements.

Milos Varak removed the large anti-impedance earphones from his head and shut down the electronic console on the table in front of him. He swung his chair to the left, snapped a switch on the nearby wall, and instantly heard the quiet gears that lowered the directional dish on the roof. He then got out of the chair and wandered aimlessly around the sophisticated communications equipment in the soundproof studio in the cellars of Samuel Winters's house. He was alarmed. What he had overheard on the telephone intercept from the sterile house was beyond his understanding.

As the State Department's Swann so unequivocally confirmed, no one in the Washington intelligence community was aware of Emmanuel Weingrass. They had no idea that "the old Arab" who had flown back from Bahrain with Evan Kendrick *was* Weingrass. In Swann's words, his "thank you" to Evan

Kendrick for the Congressman's efforts in Oman was to get Weingrass secretly out of Bahrain and with equal secrecy into the United States by using a disguise and a cover. The man and the cover had bureaucratically disappeared; Weingrass was virtually a "nonperson." Too, Swann's deception was mandatory because of Weingrass's Mossad connection, a deception thoroughly understood by Kendrick. In point of fact, the Congressman himself had taken extreme measures to conceal the presence and the identity of his elderly friend. Milos had learned that the old man had been entered into the hospital under the name of Manfred Weinstein, and put in a room in a private wing with its own secluded entrance, and that upon release he had been flown to Colorado in a private jet to Mesa Verde.

Everything was *private;* Weingrass's name was never recorded anywhere. And during the months of his convalescence the irascible architect only infrequently left the house and never to places where the Congressman was known. *Damn!* thought Varak. Except for Kendrick's close personal circle that excluded *everyone* but a trusted secretary, her husband, an Arab couple in Virginia and three overpaid nurses whose generous salaries included total confidentiality, Emmanuel Weingrass did not *exist*!

Varak walked back to the console table, disengaged the Record button, rewound the tape, and found the words he wanted to hear again.

Then I can assume that no one in Washington intelligence circles knows that Weingrass was involved in Oman?

Absolutely. Forget Masqat, he's a nonperson. He's just not among the living over here.

Dennison didn't even know who he was—

Of course not.

He's being followed, Frank. Out in Colorado, he's under someone's surveillance.

Not ours.

"Not ours . . ." *Whose?*

That question was what alarmed Varak. The only people who knew that there *was* an Emmanuel Weingrass, who had been told how much that old man meant to Evan Kendrick, were the five members of Inver Brass. Could one of them—?

Milos did not want to think anymore. At the moment it was too painful for him.

* * *

Adrienne Rashad was snapped awake by the sudden turbulence encountered by the military aircraft. She looked across the aisle in the dimly lit cabin with its less-than-first-class accommodations. The attaché from the embassy in Cairo was obviously upset—afraid, to be precise. Yet the man was experienced enough with such transport to bring along a comforting friend, specifically an outsized leather-bound flask, which he literally ripped out of his briefcase and drank from until he was aware that his "cargo" was looking at him. Sheepishly he held up the flask toward her. She shook her head and spoke over the sound of the jet engines. "Just potholes," she said.

"*Hey,* pals!" cried the voice of the pilot over the intercom. "Sorry about the potholes but I'm afraid this weather's unavoidable for about another thirty minutes or so. We have to stick to our channel and away from commercial routes. You should have flown the friendly skies, buddies. Hang on!"

The attaché drank once again from the flask, this time longer and more fully than before. Adrienne turned away, the Arab in her telling her not to observe a man's fear, the Western woman in her makeup saying that as an experienced military flier she should allay her companion's fear. The synthesis in her won the argument; she smiled reassuringly at the attaché and returned to her thoughts that had been broken off by sleep.

Why had she been so peremptorily ordered back to Washington? If there were new instructions so delicate that they could not be put on scramblers, why hadn't Mitchell Payton called her with at least a clue? It wasn't like "Uncle Mitch" to permit any interference with her work unless he told her something about it. Even with the Oman mess a year ago, and if ever there was a priority situation that was it, Mitch had sent sealed instructions to her by diplomatic courier telling her without explanation to cooperate with the State Department's Consular Operations no matter how offended she might be. She had, and it had offended her, indeed. Now out of the blue she had been ordered back to the States, virtually incommunicado, without a single word from Mitchell Payton.

Congressman Evan Kendrick. For the past eighteen hours his name had rolled across the world like the sound of approaching thunder. One could almost see the frightened faces of those who had been involved with the American, looking up at the sky wondering if they should run for cover, run for their lives, under the threat of the impending storm. There would be vendettas against those who had aided the interfering man from the West. She wondered who had leaked the story—no, "leaked" was too innocuous a word—who had *exploded* the story! The Cairo papers were filled with it, and a quick check confirmed that throughout the Middle East Evan Kendrick was either a holy saint or a hideous sinner. Canonization or an agonizing death was awaiting him depending upon where those judging him were, even within the same country. *Why?* Was it Kendrick himself who had done this? Had this vulnerable man, this improbable politician who had risked his life to avenge a terrible crime decided after a year of humility and self-denial to strike out for a political prize? If so, it was not the man she had known so briefly yet so intimately a year ago. With reservations but not regret she remembered. They had made love—improbably, frenetically, perhaps inevitably under the circumstances—but those transient moments of splendid comfort were to be forgotten. If she had been brought back to Washington because of a suddenly ambitious congressman, they had never existed.

24

Kendrick stood by the windows overlooking the wide circular drive in front of the sterile house. Dennison had called him well over an hour ago with word that the plane from Cairo had landed and the Rashad woman had been taken to a waiting government car; she was on her way to Cynwid Hollow under escort. The chief of staff wanted Evan to know that the CIA case officer had strenuously objected when she was not permitted to make a telephone call from Andrews Air Force Base.

"She kicked up a stink and refused to get in the car," Dennison had complained. "She said she hadn't heard directly from her superiors and the Air Force could go pound sand. Goddamned *bitch*! I was on my way to work and they reached me on the limo phone. You know what she said to *me*? 'Who the hell are *you*?' *That's* what she said to me! Then to twist the knife, she holds the phone away and asks out loud, 'What's a Dennison?' "

"It's that modest low profile you keep, Herb. Did anybody tell her?"

"The bastards *laughed*! That's when *I* told her she was under the President's orders and she either got in that car or she could spend five years in Leavenworth."

"It's a men's prison."

"I *know* that. *Heh!* She'll be there in an hour or so. Remember, if she's the sieve I get her."

"Maybe."

"I'll get a presidential order!"

"And I'll read it on the nightly news. With footnotes."

"Shit!"

Kendrick started to leave the window for another cup of coffee when a nondescript gray sedan appeared at the base of the circular drive. It swept around the curve and stopped in front of the stone steps, where an Air Force major swiftly got out of the far backseat. He walked rapidly around the trunk and opened the curbside door for his official passenger.

The woman Evan had known as Khalehla emerged into the morning sunlight, squinting at the brightness, disturbed and unsure. She was hatless, her dark hair hanging to her shoulders over a white jacket above green slacks and low-heeled shoes. Under her right arm she clenched a large white handbag. As Kendrick watched her the memory of that late afternoon in Bahrain came back to him. He recalled the shock he had felt when she walked through the door of the bizarre royal bedroom bemused that he had raced back for the cover of the bed sheet. And how, despite his panic, bewilderment and pain—or perhaps adding to all three—he had been struck by the cool loveliness of her sharply defined Euro-Arabian face and the glare of intelligence in her eyes.

He had been right; she *was* a striking woman who carried herself erect, almost defiantly, even now as she walked toward the massive door of the sterile house, where inside she would be faced with the unknown. Kendrick observed her dispassionately; there was no rush of remembered warmth in his reaction to her—only cold, intense curiosity. She had lied to him that late afternoon in Bahrain, lied both by what she said and what she did not say. He wondered if she would lie to him again.

The Air Force major opened the door of the enormous living room for Adrienne Rashad. She walked in and stopped, standing motionless, staring at Evan by the window. There was no astonishment in her eyes, just that frigid glare of intellect.

"I'll be going," said the Air Force officer.

"Thank you, Major." The door closed and Kendrick stepped forward. "Hello, Khalehla. It *was* Khalehla, wasn't it?"

"Whatever you say," she replied calmly.

"But then it isn't Khalehla, is it? It's Adrienne—Adrienne Rashad."

"Whatever you say," she repeated.

"That's a little redundant, isn't it?"

"And all this is very stupid, Congressman. Did you have me flown back here to give you another testimonial? Because if you did, I won't do it."

"Testimonial? That's the *last* thing I want."

"Good, I'm glad for you. I'm sure the representative from Colorado has all the endorsements he needs. So there's *no* need for someone whose life and the lives of a great many colleagues depend on anonymity to step forward and add to your swelling cheers."

"That's what you think? I want endorsements, cheers?"

"What *am* I to think? That you took me away from my work, exposed me to the embassy and the Air Force, probably crippled a cover I've developed over the past several years just because I went to bed with you? It happened once, but I assure you it will never happen again."

"Hey, wait a minute, bright lady," protested Evan. "I wasn't looking for any fast action. For Christ's sake, I didn't know where I was or what had happened, or what would happen *next.* I was scared stiff, and knew I had things to do that I didn't think I *could* do."

"You were also exhausted," added Adrienne Rashad. "I was, too. It happens."

"That's what Swann said—"

"That *bastard.*"

"No, hold it. Frank Swann's not a bastard—"

"Shall I use another word? Like pimp? An unconscionable pimp."

"You're wrong. I don't know what your business was with him but he had a job to do."

"Like sacrificing you?"

"Maybe. . . . I admit the thought's not too attractive, but he was pretty well boxed in then."

"Forget it, Congressman. Why am I here?"

"Because I have to learn something, and you're the only one left who can tell me."

"What is it?"

"Who broke the story on me? Who violated the agreement I made? I was told that those who knew I went to Oman—and they were damn few, a tight little circle they called it—*none* of them would have any reason to do it and every reason in the world *not* to. Outside of Swann and his computer chief, whom he swears by, there were only seven other people in the entire government who knew. Six have been checked out, all absolutely negative. You're the seventh, the only one left."

Adrienne Rashad stood motionless, her face passive, her eyes furious. "You ignorant, arrogant *amateur,*" she said slowly, her voice acid.

"You can call me any goddamned names you *like,*" began Evan angrily, "but I'm going to—"

"*May* we go for a walk, Congressman?" broke in the woman from Cairo, crossing to a large bay window on the other side of the room that looked over a dock to the rocky shoreline of the Chesapeake.

"What?"

"The air in here is as oppressive as the company. I'd like to take a *walk,* please." Rashad raised her hand and pointed outside; she then nodded her head twice as if reinforcing a command.

"All right," mumbled Kendrick, bewildered. "There's a side entrance back there."

"I see it," said Adrienne-Khalehla, starting for the door at the rear of the room. They walked outside onto a flagstone patio that joined a manicured lawn and a path leading down to the dock. If there had been boats lashed to the pilings or secured to the empty moorings bouncing on the water beyond, they had been removed for the autumn winds. "Keep up your harangue, Congressman," continued the undercover case officer for the CIA. "You shouldn't be deprived of that."

"Just *hold* it, Miss Rashad or whatever the hell your name is!" Evan stopped on the white concrete path halfway to the shoreline. "If you think what I'm talking about amounts to a 'harangue,' you're sadly mistaken—"

"For God's sake, keep walking! You'll get all the conversation you want, *more* than you want, you damn fool." The bay shore to the right of the dock was a mixture of dark sand and stones so common to the Chesapeake; to the left was the boathouse, also common. What was not common, however, except to the larger estates, was a profusion of tall trees some fifty yards both north and south of the dock and the boathouse. They provided a measure of privacy, more in appearance than in reality, but the sight of them had appealed to the field agent from Cairo. She headed to the right, over the sand and the stones close to the gently lapping waves. They passed the border of trees and kept going until they reached a large rock that rose out of the ground by the water's edge. Above, the immense house could not be seen. "This'll do," said Adrienne Rashad.

"*Do?*" exclaimed Kendrick. "What was that little exercise all *about*? And while we're at it let's get a couple of things straight. I appreciate the fact that you probably saved my life—*probably,* not by any manner of means provable—but I don't take orders from you, and in my considered opinion I'm *not* a damn fool, and regardless of my amateur status you're answering to *me,* I'm not answering to *you*! Check and double check, lady?"

"Are you finished?"

"I haven't even begun."

"Then before you do, let me address the specifics you've just raised. That little exercise was to get us out of there. I presume you know it's a safe house."

"Certainly."

"And that anything you say in every room, including the toilet and the shower, is recorded."

"Well, I knew the telephone was—"

"Thank you, Mr. Amateur."

"I don't have a damn thing to *hide*—"

"Keep your voice down. Talk into the water as I am."

"What? *Why?*"

"Electronic voice surveillance. The trees will distort sound because there's no direct visual beams—"

"What?"

"Lasers have improved the technology—"

"*What?*"

"Shut up! Whisper."

"I repeat, I haven't got a damn thing to hide. Maybe *you* do, but I *don't*!"

"Really?" asked Rashad, leaning against the huge rock and talking down into the small, slowly encroaching waves. "You want to involve Ahmat?"

"I've mentioned him. To the President. He should know how much help that kid was—"

"Oh, Ahmat will appreciate that. And his personal doctor? And his two cousins who helped you and protected you? And El-Baz, and the pilot who flew you to Bahrain? . . . They could all be *killed.*"

"Outside of Ahmat, I never mentioned anyone *specifically*—"

"Names are irrelevant. Functions aren't."

"For Christ's sake, it was the President of the United States!"

"And contrary to rumors, he does communicate beyond a microphone?"

"Of course."

"Do you know *who* he talks to? Do you know them personally? Do you know how reliable they are in terms of maximum security; does *he*? Do you know the men who are on the listening devices up in that house?"

"Of course not."

"What about me? I'm a field officer with an acceptable cover in Cairo. Would you have talked about *me*?"

"I did, but only to Swann."

"I'm not referring to what you did with someone in authority who knew everything because he was the control, I'm talking about up *there.* If you started questioning me up in that *house,* mightn't you have brought up any or all the people I've just mentioned? And to break the bank, Mr. Amateur, isn't it conceivable that you might have mentioned the *Mossad*?"

Evan closed his eyes. "I might have," he said softly, nodding. "If we'd gotten into an argument."

"An argument was unavoidable, which is why I got us out and came down here."

"Everyone up there is on our side!" protested Kendrick.

"I'm sure they are," agreed Adrienne, "but we don't know the strengths or the weaknesses of people we've never met and can't see, do we?"

"You're paranoid."

"It goes with the territory, Congressman. Furthermore, you *are* a damn fool, as I think I've amply demonstrated by your lack of knowledge regarding safe houses. I'll skip the question as to who gives orders to whom because it's irrelevant, and go back to your first point. In all likelihood I did *not* save your life in Bahrain, but, instead, because of that bastard Swann, put you in an untenable position we and certain pilots call the point of no return. You were not expected to survive, Mr. Kendrick, and I *did* object to that."

"Why?"

"Because I cared."

"Because *we*—"

"That, too, is irrelevant. You were a decent man trying to do a decent thing for which you weren't equipped. As it turned out, there were others who helped you far more than I ever could.

I sat in Jimmy Grayson's office and we were both relieved when we got word you were airborne out of Bahrain."

"Grayson? He was one of the seven who knew I was there."

"Not until the last hours, he didn't," said Rashad. "Even I wouldn't tell him. It had to come from Washington."

"In White House language, he was put on the spit yesterday morning."

"For what?"

"To see if he was the one who leaked my name."

"*Jimmy?* That's even more stupid than thinking it was *me.* Grayson wants a directorship so badly he can taste it. Also, he doesn't care to have his throat slit and his body mutilated any more than I do."

"You say those words very easily. They come quickly to you, maybe too quickly."

"About Jimmy?"

"No. About yourself."

"I see." The woman who had called herself Khalehla moved away from the rock. "You think I've rehearsed all this—with myself, of course, because I damn well couldn't reach anyone else. And, of course, I'm half Arab—"

"You walked into the room up there as if you expected to see me. I wasn't any surprise to you."

"I did, and you weren't."

"Why and why not? On both counts?"

"Process of elimination, I suppose—and an arrangement, a man I know who protects me from *real* surprises. For the last day and a half, you've been hot news throughout the Mediterranean, Congressman, and a lot of people are shaking, including myself. Not only *for* myself but for many others I used and misused to keep you in sight. Someone like me builds a network based on trust, and right now that trust, my most vital commodity, has been called into question. So you see, Mr. Kendrick, you've wasted not only my time and my concentration but a great deal of the taxpayers' money to bring me back here for a question any experienced intelligence officer could answer."

"You could have sold me, sold my name for a price."

"For what? My *life*? For the lives of those I used to track you, men who are important to me and the work I do—work I think has real value, which I tried to explain to you in Bahrain? You really *believe* that?"

"Oh, Jesus, I don't know *what* to believe!" admitted Evan, expelling his breath and shaking his head. "Everything I wanted to do, everything I'd planned, has been thrown out in the garbage. Ahmat doesn't want to see me again, I can't go back—there or anywhere else in the Emirates or the gulfs. He'll see to it."

"You *wanted* to go back?"

"More than anything. I wanted to take up my life again where I did my best work. But first I had to find and get rid of a son of a bitch who'd crippled everything, killed for the sake of killing—so many."

"The Mahdi," interrupted Rashad, nodding. "Ahmat told me. You did it. Ahmat's young and he'll change. In time he'll understand what you did for everyone over there and be grateful. . . . But you just answered a question. You see, I thought that you might have blown the story yourself, but you didn't, did you?"

"*Me?* You're out of your *mind*! I'm getting out of here in six months!"

"There's no political ambition, then?"

"Christ, *no*! I'm packing it in, I'm leaving! Only, now I haven't got any place to go. Someone's trying to stop me, making me into something I'm not. What the hell is *happening* to me?"

"Offhand I'd say you were being exhumed."

"Being *what*? By *whom*?"

"By someone who thinks you were slighted. Someone who believes you deserve public acclaim, prominence."

"Which I don't want! And the President isn't helping. He's awarding me the Medal of Freedom next Tuesday in the goddamned Blue Room with the whole Marine Band! I told him I didn't want it, and the son of a bitch said I had to show up because he refused to look like a 'chintzy bastard.' What kind of reasoning is *that*?"

"Very presidential—" Rashad suddenly stopped. "Let's walk," she said quickly as two white-suited members of the staff appeared at the base of the dock. "Don't look around. Be casual. We'll just stroll down this poor excuse for a beach."

"May I talk?" asked Kendrick as he fell in step.

"Not anything germane. Wait till we get around the bend."

"Why? Can they hear us?"

"Possibly. I'm not really sure." They followed the curve of the shoreline until the trees obscured the two men on the dock. "The Japanese have developed directional relays, although I've never seen one," continued Rashad aimlessly. Then she stopped again and looked up at Evan, her intelligent eyes questioning. "You spoke to Ahmat?" she asked.

"Yesterday. He told me to go to hell but not to go back to Oman. Ever."

"You understand that I'll check with him, don't you?"

Evan was suddenly astonished, then angry. *She* was questioning *him,* accusing him, checking up on *him.* "I don't give a damn what you do, my only concern is what you may have *done.* You're convincing, Khalehla—excuse me—Miss Rashad, and you may believe what you say, but the six men who knew about me had everything to lose and not a goddamned thing to gain by saying that I was in Masqat last year."

"And *I* had nothing to lose but my life and the lives of those I've cultivated throughout the sector, some of whom, incidentally, are very dear to me? Get off your plug horse, Congressman, you look ridiculous. You're not only an amateur, you're insufferable."

"You know, it's possible you could have made a *mistake*!" cried Kendrick, exasperated. "I'd almost be willing to give you the benefit of the doubt—I implied as much to Dennison and told him I wouldn't let him hang you for it."

"Oh, you're too kind, sir."

"No, I meant it. You *did* save my life, and if you made a slip and dropped my name—"

"Don't compound your asininity," Rashad broke in. "It's far, *far* more likely that any five of the others might have made a slip like that than either Grayson or myself. We live in the field; we don't make that kind of mistake."

"Let's walk," said Evan—no guards in sight, only his doubts and his confusion forcing him to move. His problem was that he believed her, believed what Manny Weingrass said about her: "*. . . she had nothing to do with exposing you. . . . it would only add to her shame and further inflame the crazy world she lives in.*" And when Kendrick protested that the others couldn't have, Manny had added: "*Then there are others beyond others. . . .*" They came to a dirt path that led up through the trees apparently to the stone wall bordering the estate. "Shall we explore?" asked Evan.

"Why not?" said Adrienne coldly.

"Look," he continued as they climbed the wooded slope side by side, "say I believe you—"

"Thank you so much."

"All right, I *do* believe you! And because I do I'm going to tell you something that only Swann and Dennison know; the others don't, at least I don't think they do."

"Are you sure you should?"

"I need help and they can't help me. Maybe you can; you were *there*—with me—and you know so many things I don't know. How events are kept quiet, how secret information gets passed to those who should have it, procedures like that."

"I know some, not all by any means. I'm based in Cairo, not here. But go ahead."

"Some time ago a man came to see Swann, a blond man with a European accent who had a great deal of information about me—Frank called it PD."

"Prior data," said Rashad, interrupting. "It's also called 'privileged detail,' and usually comes from the vaults."

"Vaults? What vaults?"

"It's the vernacular for classified intelligence files. Go on."

"After impressing Frank, *really* impressing him, he came right out and made his point. He told Swann that he had concluded that I'd been sent to Masqat by the State Department during the hostage crisis."

"*What?*" She exploded, her hand on Kendrick's arm. "Who was he?"

"Nobody knows. No one can find him. The identity he used to get to Frank was false."

"Good *Christ,*" whispered Rashad as she looked up at the ascending path; bright sunlight broke through the wall of trees above. "We'll stay here for a moment," she said quietly, urgently. "Sit down." They both lowered themselves on the dirt path surrounded by thick trunks and foliage. "*And?*" pressed the woman from Cairo.

"Well, Swann tried to throw him off; he even showed him a note to the Secretary of State that we both mocked up rejecting me. Obviously the man didn't believe Frank and kept digging, deeper and deeper until he got it all. What came out yesterday morning was so accurate it could only have come from the Oman file—from the vaults, as you call them."

"I *know* that," whispered Rashad, her anger indelibly mixed with fear. "My God, someone *was* reached!"

"One of the seven—*six*?" he amended quickly.

"Who were they? I don't mean Swann and his OHIO-Four computer man, but outside of Dennison, Grayson and me?"

"The secretaries of State and Defense, and the chairman of the Joint Chiefs."

"None of them could even be approached."

"What *about* the computer man? His name is Bryce, Gerald

Bryce, and he's young. Frank swore by him, but that's only his judgment."

"I doubt it. Frank Swann's a bastard, but I don't think he could be fooled that way. Someone like Bryce is the first person you'd think of, and if he's smart enough to run that kind of operation, he knows it. He also knows he could face thirty years in Leavenworth."

Evan smiled. "I understand Dennison threatened you with five years there."

"I told him it was a men's prison," said Adrienne, responding with a grin.

"So did I," said Kendrick, laughing.

"So then I said if he had any more goodies in store for me, I wouldn't get in Cleopatra's barge, never mind the government car."

"Why *did* you get in?"

"Sheer curiosity. It's the only answer I can give you."

"I accept it. . . . So where are we? The seven are out and a blond European is in."

"I don't know." Suddenly Rashad touched his arm again. "I've got to ask you some questions, Evan—"

"*Evan?* Thank you."

"I'm sorry. Congressman. That *was* a slip."

"Don't be, please. I think we're entitled to first names."

"Now *you* stop—"

"But do you mind if I call you Khalehla? I'm more comfortable with it."

"So am I. The Arab part of me has always resented the deniability of Adrienne."

"Ask your questions—Khalehla."

"All right. When did you decide to come to Masqat? Considering the circumstances and what you were able to do, you were late getting there."

Kendrick took a deep breath. "I'd been riding the rapids in Arizona when I reached a base camp called Lava Falls and heard a radio for the first time in several weeks. I knew I had to get to Washington. . . ." Evan recounted the details of those frantic sixteen hours going from a comparatively primitive campsite in the mountains to the halls of the State Department and finally down to the sophisticated computer complex that was OHIO-Four-Zero. "That's where Swann and I made our agreement and I was off and running."

"Let's go back a minute," said Khalehla, only at that moment taking her eyes off Kendrick's face. "You hired a river plane to take you to Flagstaff, where you tried to charter a jet to D.C., is that right?"

"Yes, but the charter desk said it was too late."

"You were anxious," suggested the field agent. "Probably angry. You must have thrown your weight around a bit. A congressman from the great state of Colorado, et cetera."

"More than a bit—and lots more of the et cetera."

"You reached Phoenix and got the first commercial flight out. How did you pay for your ticket?"

"Credit card."

"Bad form," said Khalehla, "but you had no reason to think so. How did you know whom to reach at the State Department?"

"I didn't, but remember, I'd worked in Oman and the Emirates for years, so I knew the sort of person I wanted to find. And since I had inherited an experienced D.C. secretary who has the instincts of an alley cat, I told *her* what to look for. I made it clear that it would undoubtedly be someone in State's Consular Operations, Middle East, or Southwest Asia sections. Most Americans who've worked over there are familiar with those people—frequently up to their teeth."

"So this secretary with the instincts of an alley cat began calling around asking questions. That must have raised a few eyebrows. Did she keep a list of whom she called?"

"I don't know. I never asked her. Everything was kind of frantic and I kept in touch with her on one of those air-to-ground phones during the flight from Phoenix. By the time I landed she had narrowed the possibilities down to four or five men, but only one was considered an expert on the Emirates and he was also a deputy director of Cons Op. Frank Swann."

"It would be interesting to know if your secretary did keep a list," said Khalehla, arching her neck, thinking.

"I'll phone her."

"Not from here you won't. Besides, I'm not finished. . . . So you went to State to find Swann, which means you checked in with security."

"Naturally."

"Did you check out?"

"Well, no, not actually, not at the lobby desk. Instead, I was taken down to the parking area and driven home in a State Department car."

"To your house?"

"Yes, I was on my way to Oman and had to get some things together—"

"What about the driver?" interrupted Khalehla. "Did he address you by name?"

"No, never. But he did say something that shook me up. I asked him if he wanted to come in for a snack or coffee while I packed, and he said, 'I might get shot if I got out of this car,' or words to that effect. Then he added, 'You're from OHIO-Four-Zero.' "

"Which means *he* wasn't," said Rashad quickly. "And you were in front of your house?"

"Yes. Then I stepped out and saw another car about a hundred feet behind us at the curb. It had to have been following us; there are no other houses on that stretch of road."

"An armed escort." Khalehla nodded. "Swann covered you from minute-one and he was right. He didn't have the time or the resources to trace everything that had happened to you minus-one."

Evan was bewildered. "Would you mind explaining that?"

"Minus-one is before you reached Swann. An angry rich congressman using a chartered plane to Flagstaff makes a lot of noise about getting to Washington. He's turned down, so he flies to Phoenix, where he no doubt insists on the first flight out and pays with a credit card, *and* starts calling his secretary, who has the instincts of an alley cat, telling her to find a man he doesn't know but is sure exists at the Department of State. She makes her calls—frantically, I think you said—reaching a number of people who have to wonder why. She gets you a narrowed-down quorum—which means she's reached *a lot* of her contacts who could give her the information and who also had to wonder why, and you turn up at State demanding to see Frank Swann. Am I right? In your state of mind, did you demand to see him?"

"Yes. I was given a runaround, told he wasn't there, but I knew he was, my secretary had confirmed it. I guess I was pretty adamant. Finally, they let me go up to his office."

"Then after you talked with him he made his decision to send you to Masqat."

"So?"

"That tight little circle you spoke of wasn't very little or very tight, Evan. You did what anyone else would do under the circumstances—under the stress you felt. You left a number of impressions during that agitated journey from Lava Falls to

Washington. You could easily be traced back through Phoenix to Flagstaff, your name and your loud insistence on fast transportation remembered by a lot of people, especially because of the time of night. Then you show up at the State Department, where you made more noises—incidentally, checking in with security but not checking out—until you were permitted to go up to Swann's office."

"Yes, but—"

"Let me finish, please," interrupted Khalehla again. "You'll understand, and I want us both to have the full picture. . . . You and Swann talk, make your agreement of anonymity, and as you said, you're off and running to Masqat. The first leg was made to your house with a driver who was not part of OHIO-Four-Zero any more than the guards in the lobby. The driver was simply assigned by a dispatcher and the guards on duty were merely doing their jobs. They're not in the rarefied circles; nobody up there brings them in on top-secret agendas. But they're human; they go home and talk to their wives and their friends because something *different* happened in their normally dull jobs. They might also answer questions casually put to them by people they thought were government bureaucrats."

"And one way or another they all knew who I was—"

"As did a lot of other people in Phoenix and Flagstaff, and one thing was clear to all of them. This important man's upset; this congressman's in a hell of a hurry; this big shot's got a problem. Do you see the trail you left?"

"Yes, I do, but who would *look* for it?"

"I don't know, and that troubles me more than I can tell you."

"Troubles *you*? Whoever it was has blown my *life* apart! Who would *do* it?"

"Someone who found an opening, a gap that led to the rest of the trail from a remote campsite called Lava Falls to the terrorists in Masqat. Someone who picked up on something that made him want to look further. Perhaps it was the calls your secretary made, or the commotion you caused at the State Department's security desk, or even something as crazy as hearing the rumor that an unknown American had interceded in Oman—it wasn't crazy at all; it was printed and squashed—but it could have started somebody thinking. Then the other things fell in place and you were there."

Evan put his hand over hers. "I have to know who it was, Khalehla, I have to *know.*"

"But we *do* know," she said softly, correcting herself, her voice flat as if seeing something she should have seen before. "A blond man with a European accent."

"*Why?*" Kendrick removed his hand as the word exploded from his throat.

Khalehla looked at him, her gaze compassionate, yet beneath her concern was that cold analytical intelligence in her eyes. "The answer to that has to be your overriding concern, Evan, but I have another problem and it's why I'm frightened."

"I don't understand."

"Whoever the blond man was, whomever he represents, he reached way down deep in our cellars and took out what he should never have been given. I'm stunned, Evan, *petrified,* and those words aren't strong enough for the way I feel. Not only by what's been done to you, but by what's been done to us. We've been compromised, penetrated where such penetration should have been impossible. If they—whoever they are—can dig you up out of the deepest, most secure archives we have, they can learn a lot of other things *no one* should have access to. Where people like me work that can cost a great many lives—very unpleasantly."

Kendrick studied her taut, striking face, seeing the fear in her eyes. "You mean that, don't you? You *are* frightened."

"So would you be if you knew the men and women who help us, who trust us, who risk their lives to bring us information. Every day they wonder if something they did or didn't do will trip them up. A lot of them have committed suicide because they couldn't stand the strain, others have gone mad and disappeared into the deserts preferring to die at peace with their Allah than go on. But most *do* go on because they believe in us, believe that we're fair and really want peace. They deal with gun-wielding lunatics at every turn, and as bad as things are, it's only through them that they're not worse, with a great deal more blood in the streets. . . . Yes, I'm frightened because many of those people are friends—of mine and my father and mother. The thought of them being betrayed, as you were betrayed—and that's what you were, Evan, *betrayed*—makes me want to crawl out on the sands and die like those we've driven mad. Because someone way down deep is opening our most secret files to others outside. All he or she needed in your case was a name, your name, and people are afraid for their lives in Masqat and Bahrain. How many other names can be fed? How many other secrets learned?"

Evan reached over, not covering her hand but now holding it, gripping it. "If you believe that, why don't you help me?"

"Help you?"

"I have to know who's doing this to me, and you have to know who's over there, or down there, making it possible. I'd say our objectives dovetail, wouldn't you? I've got Dennison in a vise he can't squirm out of, and I can get you a quiet White House directive to stay over here. Actually, he'd jump at the chance to find a leak; it's an obsession with him."

Khalehla frowned. "It doesn't work that way. Besides, I'd be out of my class. I'm very good where I am, but out of my element, my *Arab* element, I'm not first-rate."

"Number *one,*" countered Kendrick firmly. "*I* consider you first-rate because you saved my life and I consider my life relatively important. And two, as I mentioned, you have expertise in areas I know nothing about. *Procedures.* 'Covert avenues of referral'—I learned that one as a member of the Select Committee on Intelligence, but I haven't the vaguest idea what it means. Hell, lady, you even know what the 'cellars' are, when I always thought they were the basements of a suburban development, which, thank God, I never had to build. Please, you said in Bahrain that you wanted to help me. Help me *now*! Help yourself."

Adrienne Rashad replied, her dark eyes searching his coldly. "I *could* help, but there might be times when you'd have to do as I tell you. Could you do that?"

"I'm not wild about jumping off bridges or tall buildings—"

"It would be in the area of what you'd say, and to certain people I'd want you to say it. There might also be times when I wouldn't be able to explain things to you. Could you accept that?"

"Yes. Because I've watched you, listened to you, and I trust you."

"Thank you." She squeezed his hand and released it. "I'd have to bring someone with me."

"Why?"

"First of all, it's necessary. I'd need a temporary transfer and he can get it for me without giving an explanation—forget the White House, it's too dangerous, too unstable. Second, he could be helpful in areas way beyond my reach."

"Who is he?"

"Mitchell Payton. He's director of Special Projects—that's a euphemism for 'Don't ask.' "

"Can you trust him? I mean totally, no doubts at all."

"No doubts at all. He processed me into the Agency."

"That's not exactly a reason."

"The fact that I've called him 'Uncle Mitch' since I was six years old in Cairo is, however. He was a young operations officer posing as an instructor at the university. He became a friend of my parents—my father was a professor there and my mother's an American from California; so was Mitch."

"Will he give you a transfer?"

"Yes, of course."

"You're sure of that?"

"He has no choice. I just told you, someone's giving away a part of our soul that's not for sale. It's you this time. Who's it going to be next?"

25

Mitchell Jarvis Payton was a trim sixty-three-year-old academic who had been suckered into the Central Intelligence Agency thirty-four years ago because he fit a description someone had given to the personnel procurement division at the time. That someone had disappeared into other endeavors and no job had been listed for Payton—only the requirements, marked *urgent.* However, by the time his prospective employers realized that they had no specific employment for the prospect it was too late. He had been signed up by the Agency's aggressive recruiters in Los Angeles and sent to CIA headquarters in Langley, Virginia, for indoctrination. It was an embarrassing situation, as Dr. Payton, in a rush of personal and patriotic fervor, had submitted his resignation, effective immediately, to the State Board of Regents. It was an inauspicious beginning for a man whose career would develop so auspiciously.

MJ, as he was called for as long as he could remember, had been a twenty-nine-year-old associate professor with a doctorate in Arabian Studies from the University of California, where he subsequently taught. One bright morning he was visited by two gentlemen from the government who convinced him that his country urgently needed his talents. What the specifics entailed they were not at liberty, *of course,* to disclose, but insofar as they represented the most exciting sphere of government service, they assumed that the position was overseas, in the area of his expertise. The young bachelor had leaped at the opportunity, and when faced with perplexed superiors in Langley, who wondered what to do with him, he adamantly suggested that he had cut his ties in L.A. because he had at least assumed that he would be sent to Egypt. So he had been sent to Cairo *(We can't get enough observers in Egypt who understand the goddamned language).* As an undergraduate he had studied American literature, chosen because Payton did not think there was a hell of a lot of it. It was for this reason that an employment agency in Rome, in reality a CIA subsidiary, had placed him at the Cairo University as an Arabic-speaking instructor of American literature.

There he had met the Rashads, a lovely couple who became an important part of his life. At Payton's first faculty meeting he sat beside the renowned Professor Rashad, and in their preconference small talk he learned that Rashad had not only gone to graduate school in California but had married a classmate of MJ's. A deep friendship blossomed, as did MJ's reputation within the Central Intelligence Agency. Through talents he had no idea he possessed, and which at times actually frightened him, he discovered that he was an exceptionally convincing liar. They were days of turmoil, of rapidly shifting alliances that had to be monitored, the spreading American penetration kept out of sight. He was able, through his fluent Arabic and his understanding that people could be motivated with sympathetic words backed up with money, to organize various groups of opposing factions who reported on each other's movements to him. In return, he provided funds for their causes—minor expenditures for the then sacrosanct CIA but major contributions to the zealots' meager coffers. And through his efforts in Cairo, Washington averted a number of potentially explosive embarrassments. So, typical of the old-school-tie network in D.C.'s intelligence community, if a good fellow did such a fine job where he was, forget the convergence of specific factors that made him good where he was and bring him back to Washington to see what he could do there. M.J. Payton was the exception in a long line of failures. He succeeded James Jesus Angleton, the Gray Fox of clandestine operations, as the director of Special Projects. And he never forgot what his friend Rashad told him when he reached his ascendancy.

"You never could have made it, MJ, if you had married. You have the self-confidence of never having been manipulated."

Perhaps.

Yet a test of manipulation had come full force to him when

the headstrong daughter of his dear friends had arrived in Washington, as adamant as he had ever seen her. A terrible thing had happened in Cambridge, Massachusetts, and she was determined to devote her life—at least a part of her life—to lessening the fires of hatred and violence that were ripping her Mediterranean world apart. She never told "Uncle Mitch" what had happened to her—she did not have to, really—but she would not take no for an answer. She was qualified; she was as fluent in English and French as she was in Arabic, and she was currently learning both Yiddish and Hebrew. He had suggested the Peace Corps and she had slammed her purse down on the floor in front of his desk.

"*No!* I'm not a child, Uncle Mitch, and I don't have those kinds of benevolent impulses. I'm concerned only with where I come from, where I was born. If you won't use me, I'll find others who will!"

"They could be the wrong others, Adrienne."

"Then stop me. Hire me!"

"I'll have to talk to your parents—"

"You *can't*! He's retired—*they're* retired, and they live up north in Baltim-on-the-Sea. They'd only worry about me, and in their worrying cause problems. Find me translating jobs, or a floating consultant's position with exporters—certainly you can do that! Good *God,* Uncle Mitch, you were a small-time instructor at the university and *we* never said anything!"

"You didn't know, my dear—"

"The hell I didn't! The whispers around the house when a *friend* of Uncle Mitch's was coming and how I had to stay in my room, and then one night when suddenly three men came, all wearing *guns* on their belts, which I'd never *seen*—"

"Those were emergencies. Your father understood."

"Then you understand me now, Uncle Mitch. I have to do this!"

"All *right,*" consented M.J. Payton. "But you understand *me,* young lady. You'll be put through a concentrated course in Fairfax, Virginia, in a compound that's not on any map. If you fail, I can't help you."

"Agreed," had said Adrienne Khalehla Rashad, smiling. "Do you want to bet?"

"Not with you, you young tigress. Come on, let's go to lunch. You don't drink, do you?"

"Not really."

"I do and I will, but I won't bet you."

And it was good for Payton's wallet that he did not bet. Candidate No. 1344 finished the excruciating ten-week course in Fairfax, Virginia, at the head of her class. Women's liberation be damned, she was better than twenty-six men. But then, her "Uncle Mitch" thought, she had a motive the others did not have: one half of her was Arab.

All that was more than nine years ago. But now on this Friday afternoon nearly ten years later, Mitchell Jarvis Payton was appalled! Field agent Adrienne Rashad, currently on duty in the West Mediterranean Sector, Cairo Post, had just called him from a pay telephone at the Hilton Hotel here in Washington! What in the name of God was she doing *here*? On whose authority was she removed from her post? All officers attached to Special Projects, especially *this* officer, had to have their orders cleared through *him*. It was incredible! And the fact that she would not come out to Langley but, instead, insisted on meeting him at an out-of-the-way restaurant in Arlington did not calm MJ's nerves. Especially after she said to him, "It's absolutely vital that I don't run into anyone I know, or who might know me, Uncle Mitch." Beyond the ominous tone of her statement, she had not called him Uncle Mitch in years, not since she was in college. His unrelated "niece" was a troubled woman.

Milos Varak got off the plane at Durango, Colorado, and walked across the terminal to the counter of the car rental agency. He produced a false driver's license and a correspondingly false credit card, signed the lease agreement, accepted the keys and was directed to the lot where the car awaited him. In his briefcase was a detailed map of lower southwest Colorado listing such things as the wonders of the Mesa Verde National Park and the descriptions of hotels, motels, and restaurants, the majority of which were found in and around such cities as Cortez, Hesperus, Marvel and, farther east, Durango. The least detailed area was a dot called Mesa Verde itself; the designation of "town" did not apply. It was a geographical location more in people's minds than on the books; a general store, a barbershop, a small outlying private airport and a café called Gee-Gee's constituted its industry. One passed through Mesa Verde, one did not live there. It existed for the convenience of farmers, field hands, and those inveterate travelers who invariably got lost by taking the scenic routes to New Mexico and Arizona. The anomaly of the airport was for the benefit of those dozen or so privileged landowners who had built estates for themselves in the backcountry and simply wanted it. They rarely, if ever, saw the stretch of road with the general store, the barbershop and Gee-Gee's. Their necessities were flown in from Denver, Las Vegas and Beverly Hills—thus the airport. The exception here was Congressman Evan Kendrick, who had surprisingly run for political office. He had made the mistake of thinking that Mesa Verde could produce votes, which it would have done if the election had been held south of the Rio Grande.

Varak, however, very much wanted to see that stretch of road the locals referred to as Mesa Verde, or just plain Verde, as Emmanuel Weingrass called it. He wanted to see how the men dressed, how they walked, what the stresses of field work had done to their bodies, their muscles, their posture. For the next twenty-four or, at most, forty-eight hours he would have to melt in. Milos had a job to do that in one sense saddened him beyond measuring the pain, but it was something he had to do. If there was a traitor to Inver Brass, within Inver Brass, Varak had to find him . . . or her.

After an hour and thirty-five minutes of driving he found the café named Gee-Gee's. He could not go inside dressed as he was, so he parked the car, removed his jacket, and strolled into the general store across the street.

"Ain't seen you before," said the elderly owner, turning his head as he stacked bags of rice on a shelf. "Always nice to see a new face. You headin' for New Mex? I'll put you on the right road, no need to buy anythin'. I keep tellin' people that, but they always feel they got to part with cash when all they want is directions."

"You're most kind, sir," said Milos, "but I'm afraid I must part with cash—not mine, of course, my employer's. It's most coincidental, but I'm to purchase several bags of rice. It was omitted in the delivery from Denver."

"Oh, one of the biggies in the hills. Take what you like, son—for cash, of course. At my age I don't carry out."

"I wouldn't think of it, sir."

"Hey, you're a foreign fella, ain't cha?"

"Scandinavian," replied Varak. "I'm just temporary, filling in while the chauffeur is ill." Milos picked up three bags of rice and carried them to the counter; the owner followed toward the cash register.

"Who you work for?"

"The Kendrick house, but he doesn't know me—"

"Hey, isn't that *somethin'* about young Evan? Our own congressman the *heero* of Oman! I tell ya, makes a man stand tall, like the President says! He come in here a couple a times—three, four maybe. Nicest fella you'd want to meet; real down-to-earth, you know what I mean?"

"I'm afraid I've never met him."

"Yeah, but if you're out there at the house, you know ol' Manny, that's for sure! A real pistol, ain't he? I tell ya, that crazy Jewish fella is somethin' else!"

"He certainly is."

"That'll be six dollars and thirty-one cents, son. Skip the penny if you ain't got it."

"I'm sure I have—" Varak reached into his pocket. "Does Mr. . . . Manny come in here often?"

"Some. Maybe two, three times a month. Drives with one of them nurses of his, then as soon as she turns her back, he splits over to Gee-Gee's. He's some fella. Here's your change, son."

"Thank you." Milos picked up the bags of rice and turned toward the door, but was suddenly stopped by the owner's next words.

"I figure those girls snitched on him, though, 'cause Evan must be gettin' a little stricter lookin' after his ol' pal, but I guess you know that."

"Yes, of course," said Varak, looking back at the man and smiling. "How did you find out?"

"Yesterday," replied the owner. "What with all the fuss out at the house Manny got Jake's cab to bring him down to Gee-Gee's. I saw him, so I went to the door and shouted to him about how great the news was, y'know. He yelled back something like 'My sugar,' or something, and went inside. That's when I saw this other car comin' real slow down the street with a guy talkin' on a *telephone*—you know, one of them *car* telephones. He parked across from Gee-Gee's and just stayed there watchin' the door. Then later he was on that telephone again and a few minutes after that he got out and went into Gonzalez's place. No one else had gone in, so that's when I figured he was keepin' tabs on Manny."

"I'll tell them to be more careful," said Milos, still smiling. "But just to make sure we're talking about the same man, or one of them, what did he look like?"

"Oh, he was city, all right. Fancy duds and slick-down hair."

"Dark hair, then?"

"No, sorta reddish."

"Oh, *him*?" said Varak convincingly. "Approximately my size."

"Nope, I'd say a mite taller, maybe more than a mite."

"Yes, of course," agreed the Czech. "I imagine we often think of ourselves as taller than we are. He's somewhat slender, or perhaps it's his height—"

"*That's* him," broke in the owner. "Not much meat on his bones, not like you, no sirree."

"Then he was driving the brown Lincoln."

"Looked blue to me, and big, but I don't know one car from another these days. All look the same, like unhappy bugs."

"Well, thank you, sir. I'll certainly tell the team to be more discreet. We wouldn't want Manny upset."

"Oh, don't worry about *me* tellin' him. Manny had a big operation, and if young Evan thinks he needs closer watchin', I'm for it. I mean, ol' Manny, he's a pistol—Gee-Gee even waters his whisky when he can get away with it."

"Thank you again. I'll inform the Congressman of your splendid cooperation."

"Thought you didn't know him."

"When I meet him, sir. Good-bye."

Milos Varak started the rented car and drove down the stretch of road leaving behind the general store, the barber shop, and Gee-Gee's café. *A tall, slender man with neatly combed reddish hair and driving a large blue sedan.* The hunt had begun.

"I don't *believe* it!" whispered Mitchell Jarvis Payton.

"Believe, MJ," said Adrienne Rashàd over the red-checkered tablecloth at the rear of the Italian restaurant in Arlington. "What did you really know about Oman?"

"It was a Four-Zero operation out of State and liaisoned by Lester Crawford, who wanted a list of our best people with the widest range of contacts in the southwest basin. That's *all* I knew. There may be others more qualified than you, but not where contacts are concerned."

"You had to assume the operation involved the hostages."

"Of course, we all did, and to tell you the truth I was torn. Your friendship with Ahmat and his wife was no secret to me, and I had to assume that others also knew. You see, I didn't want to submit your name to Les, but your past work with Projects called for it and your ties to the royal family demanded it. Also, I realized that if I left you out for personal reasons and you ever learned about it, you'd have my head."

"I certainly would have."

"I'll confess to a minor sin, however," said Payton, smiling a sad smile. "When it was all over, I walked into Crawford's office and made it clear that I understood the rules but I had to know that you were all right. He looked up at me with those fish eyes of his and said you were back in Cairo. I think it bothered him even to tell me that. . . . And now *you* tell me that the whole damned operation was blown open by one of *us*! A Four-Zero strategy can't be unsealed for years, often decades! There are records going back to World War Two that won't see the light of day until the middle of the next century, if then."

"Who controls those records, MJ, those files?"

"They're carted off to oblivion—stored in warehouses around the country controlled by government custodians with armed guards and alarm systems so high-tech they reach instantly back to Washington, alerting us here, as well as the departments of State and Defense and the White House strategy rooms. Of course, for the past twenty years or so, with the proliferation of sophisticated computers, most are stored in data banks with access codes that have to be coordinated between a minimum of three intelligence services and the Oval Office. Where original documents are considered vital, they're sealed and packed off." Payton shrugged, his palms upturned. "Oblivion, my dear. It's all foolproof, theftproof."

"It obviously isn't," disagreed the field agent from Cairo.

"It is, when those records reach the level of security controls," countered MJ. "So I think you'd better tell me everything you know and everything the Congressman told you. Because if what you say is true, we've got a bastard somewhere between the decision to go maximum and the data banks."

Adrienne Khalehla Rashad leaned back in the chair and began. She withheld nothing from her once and always Uncle Mitch, not even the sexual accident that had occurred in Bahrain. "I can't say I'm sorry, professionally or otherwise, MJ. We were both stretched and scared and, frankly, he's a hell of a decent man—out of his depth, but kind of fine, I guess. I reconfirmed it this morning in Maryland."

"In *bed*?"

"Good Lord, no. In what he said, what he's reaching for. Why he did what he did, why he even became a congressman and now wants out, as I've told you. I'm sure he's got warts all over him, but he's also got a good anger."

"I think I detect certain feelings in my 'niece' that I've wanted to see for a long, long time."

"Oh, they're there, I'd be a hypocrite to deny them, but I

doubt that there's anything permanent. In a way, we're alike. I'm projecting, but I think we're both more consumed with what *we* have to do, as two separate people, than in what the other wants. Yet I like him, MJ, I really do like him. He makes me laugh, and not just at him but with him."

"That's terribly important," said Payton wistfully, his smile and his gentle frown even sadder than before. "I've never found anyone who could genuinely make me laugh . . . not *with* her. Of course, it's a flaw in my own makeup. I'm too damned demanding, and worse off for it."

"You have no flaws, *or* warts," insisted Rashad. "You're my Uncle Mitch and I won't hear of it."

"Your father always made your mother laugh. I envied them at times, despite the problems they faced. He *did* make her laugh."

"It was a defense mechanism. Mother thought he could say 'divorce' three times and she'd have to split."

"Rubbish. He adored her." Then as deftly as if they had not strayed from the Masqat crisis, Payton returned to it. "Why did Kendrick insist on anonymity in the first place? I know you've told me, but run it by me again, will you?"

"You sound suspicious and you shouldn't be. It's a perfectly logical explanation. He intended to go back and take up where he left off five—six years ago. He couldn't do that with the baggage of Oman around his neck. He can't do it *now* because everyone wants his head, from the Palestinian fanatics to Ahmat and all those who helped him and are frightened to death that they'll be exposed. What's happened to him during the past two days proves that he was right. He wants to go back and now he can't. No one will let him."

Again Payton frowned, the sadness gone, replaced by a cold curiosity that bordered on doubt. "Yes, I understand that, my dear, but then you have only his word that he wanted to go back—wants to go back."

"I believe him," said Rashad.

"He may believe it himself," offered the director of Special Projects. "*Now,* as it were, having had second thoughts provoked by thinking things through."

"That's cryptic as hell, MJ. What do you mean?"

"It may be a minor point, but I think it's worth considering. A man who wants to fade from Washington, really fade, and not open a law office or a public relations firm or some other such gratuity for the government service he sought, doesn't usually do battle with Pentagon heavyweights in televised committee hearings, or go on a Sunday network program that reaches the broadest audience in the country, *or* hold a provocative personal press conference guaranteed to get wide exposure. Nor does he continue to be a bête noire on a select subcommittee for intelligence, asking hard questions that may not promote his name in the public eye but certainly circulates it around the capital. Taken collectively, those activities aren't the mark of a man anxious to leave the political arena or the rewards it can offer. There's a certain inconsistency, wouldn't you say?"

Adrienne Rashad nodded. "I asked him about all that, at first accusing him of even wanting another on-the-scene testimonial from me, and having a bad case of political ambition. He blew up, denying any such motives, insisting vehemently that he wanted only to get out of Washington."

"Could these be his second thoughts?" suggested Payton. "I ask it kindly because any sane person would have them. Say this very successful individual—and he's nothing if not an individualist; I've seen that for myself—gets a touch of our Potomac virus and tells himself to go for it, use all the marbles he's got, including what he did in Oman. Then he wakes up and thinks, My God, what have I done? What am I doing here? I don't belong among these people! . . . It wouldn't be the first time, you know. We've lost a great many good men and women in this city who came to that same conclusion—they *didn't* belong here. Most are fiercely independent people who believe in their judgments, generally borne out by success in one field or another. Unless they want power for the sheer sake of a driving ego—which your instincts about Kendrick would seem to dismiss and I *trust* your instincts—these people have no patience with the mazes of endless debate and compromise that are the by-products of our system. Could our congressman be someone like that?"

"Offhand, I'd say it's his profile to a capital *p,* but again it's only instinct."

"So isn't it possible that your attractive young man—"

"Oh, come on, MJ," interrupted Rashad. "That's so *antediluvian.*"

"I substitute it for a term I refuse to use with my niece."

"I accept your version of courtesy."

"Propriety, my dear. But isn't it possible that your friend woke up and said to himself, I've made a terrible mistake making a hero out of myself and now I've got to undo it?"

"It would be if he was a liar, which I don't think he is."

"But you do see the inconsistency of his behavior, don't you? He's acted one way and then claims to be the opposite."

"You're saying that he's protesting too much, and I'm saying that he isn't because he's not lying, either to himself or to me."

"I'm exploring every avenue before we look for a bastard, who—if you're right—was reached by another bastard, a blond-haired one. . . . Did Kendrick tell you why he publicly took on the Pentagon as well as the entire defense industry, to say nothing of his less public but well-circulated criticisms of our own intelligence services?"

"Because he was in a position to say those things and he thought they should be said."

"Just like that? That's his explanation?"

"Yes."

"But he had to seek the positions that gave him the opportunity to speak in the first place. Good Lord, the Partridge Committee, then the Select Subcommittee for Intelligence; they're politically coveted chairs, to say the very least. For every one of those seats there are four hundred congressmen who'd sell their wives for the assignments. They don't just fall into a member's lap, they have to be *worked* for, *fought* for. How does he explain that?"

"He can't. They just fell into his lap. And rather than fighting for them, he fought to stay off them."

"I *beg* your pardon?" exclaimed M. J. Payton, astonished.

"He said that if I didn't believe him I should go talk to his chief aide, who had to strong-arm him into taking the Partridge assignment, and then see the Speaker of the House himself and ask that conniving old Irish leprechaun what Evan told him to do with his subcommittee. He didn't want either job, but it was explained to him that if he didn't take them, he wouldn't have a damn thing to say about his successor in Colorado's Ninth. That's important to him; it's why he ran for office. He got rid of one party sleazeball and didn't want another taking his place."

Payton slowly leaned back in his chair, bringing his hand to his chin, his eyes narrowed. Over the years Adrienne Rashad had learned when to be silent and not interrupt her mentor's thinking. She did both now, prepared for any of several responses but not the one she heard. "This is a different ball game, my dear. If I remember correctly, you told Kendrick that you thought he was being exhumed by someone who believed he deserved acclaim for what he did. It goes far deeper than that, I'm afraid. Our congressman is being programmed."

"Good Lord, for *what*?"

"I don't know, but I think we'd better try to find out. Very quietly, very cautiously. We're dealing with something rather extraordinary."

Varak saw the large dark blue sedan. It was parked off the winding, tree-lined road cut out of a forest several hundred yards west of Kendrick's house and it was empty. He had passed the Congressman's impressive hedge-bound grounds, still under minor siege by a few obstinate, hopeful reporters with a camera crew, and intended to head north to a motel on the outskirts of Cortez. The sight of the blue vehicle, however, changed his mind. The Czech continued around the next bend and drove the car into a cluster of wild brush that fronted the trees. On the seat beside him was his attaché case; he opened it and took out the items he thought he might need, several imperative, several hopeful. He put them in his pockets, got out of the car, closed the door quietly, and walked around the curve and back to the blue sedan. He approached the far door nearest the woods and studied the vehicle for traps—trips that would set off an alarm if someone tampered with the lock, or with pressure on the doors, or even light beams that extended from the front to the rear spoked wheels activated by solid objects breaking the beams.

He found two out of three with one so serious that it told him something: there were secrets in that automobile far more valuable than clothes or jewelry or even confidential business papers. A row of tiny holes had been drilled and painted over along the lower frames of the windows; they were jets that released a nonlethal vapor that would immobilize an intruder for a considerable length of time. They had been conceived and perfected initially for diplomats in troubled countries where it was nearly as important to question assailants as to save lives. They could be set off by chauffeurs during an assault or by alarms when the car was unoccupied. They were now being marketed among the rich throughout the world, and it was said that the suppliers of the mechanisms could not keep up with the demand.

Varak looked around and quickly walked to the rear of the sedan, reached into his pocket and dropped to the ground in the vicinity of the tail pipe. He crawled under the car and instantly went to work; less than ninety seconds later he emerged, stood up and ran into the woods. The hunt had begun and the waiting began.

Forty-one minutes later he saw a tall, slender figure walking down the road. The man was in a dark suit, his coat open, a vest showing; his hair was neatly combed and more red than brown. Someone in charge, thought Milos, should be given a lesson in basic cosmetic tactics. One never permitted an employee to go out in the field with red hair; it was simply foolish. The man proceeded to unlock first the right front door, then rounded the hood and unlocked the driver's side. However, before opening it, he crouched out of sight where there was apparently a third release, stood back up and climbed inside. He started the car.

The powerful engine coughed repeatedly, then suddenly there was a loud rattling from beneath the chassis and an expulsion of fumes followed by the sound of crashing metal. The muffler and the tail pipe had blown apart, accompanied by an explosion of vapor on all sides of the automobile. Varak lowered himself, a handkerchief over his face, and waited for the clouds to disappear, clinging to the trees as they rose to the sky. Slowly he stood up.

The driver, a surgical mask on his face and a gun in his hand, also watched the rising clouds as he spun repeatedly around in the seat checking every direction for an assault. None came, and his confusion was obvious. He picked up the car telephone, then hesitated and Milos understood. If the problem was a simple mechanical failure and he reached his controls, say thirty or three hundred or three thousand miles away, he would be severely criticized. He replaced the phone and put the car into gear; the sound was so thunderous he stopped instantly. One did not call attention to such a vehicle anywhere, anytime; one chose another alternative, like reaching a garage and being towed in for a simple exterior repair. And yet . . . ? So another period of waiting began. It lasted nearly twenty minutes; despite his red hair, the man was a professional. Apparently convinced that no attack was forthcoming, he cautiously got out of the car and walked to the rear. Gun in one hand, a flashlight in the other, he continued to look around in all directions as Varak crept silently forward in the brush. The redheaded surveillant suddenly crouched, throwing the beam of light into the undercarriage. Milos knew he had only seconds to reach the edge of the road before the man discovered the heat-expanding plastic inserted in the tail pipe or noticed the markings on the muffler made by the small, diamond-edged knife-saw. The moment came as Varak briefly parted the foliage eight feet from the crouching, peering man.

"*Christ!*" exploded the slender, well-dressed redhead, leaping back, spinning first to his right, then to his left, his automatic leveled, his back now to Milos. The Czech raised a third item he had taken from his attaché case; it was a Co2-propelled dart gun. Once again he parted the leaves in front of him and quickly fired. The narcotic dart hit its mark, embedding itself in the back of the man's neck. The red-haired surveillant whipped violently around, dropping the flashlight as he desperately tried to reach behind him and rip out the offending needle. The more frenzied his movements were, the more rapidly the blood rushed to his head, rushing also the circulation of the serum. It took eight seconds; the man fell to the ground, struggling against the inevitable effects, finally lying immobile on the country road. Varak walked out of the woods and swiftly pulled the redhead back into them, then returned for the man's gun and flashlight. He proceeded to search the man for undoubtedly false identification cards.

They were not false. The unconscious figure below him was a special agent for the Federal Bureau of Investigation. Among his ID papers was the unit to which he had been assigned two months and ten days ago—one day after the meeting of Inver Brass at Cynwid Hollow, Maryland.

Milos removed the dart, carried the man out to the road, and placed him behind the wheel of the blue sedan. He concealed the flashlight and the gun beneath the seat, closed the door, and walked back to his rented car around the bend. He had to find a telephone and reach a man at the Federal Bureau in Washington.

"There's no information on that unit," said Varak's contact at the FBI. "It came down through administration circles, its origin in California, in San Diego, I think."

"There's no California White House now," objected Milos.

"But there's another 'House,' in case you've forgotten."

"*What?*"

"Before I go on, Checkman, we're going to need some data from you. It concerns an operation out of Prague that's gathering fruit over here. It's minor but irritating. Will you help us?"

"Certainly. I'll find out whatever I can. Now, what is the *house* in San Diego, California, that can cause the Bureau to form a special unit?"

"Simple, Checkman. It belongs to the Vice President of the United States."

It is agreed, then. Congressman Evan Kendrick will be the next Vice President of the United States. He will become President eleven months after the election of the incumbent.

In silence, Varak hung up the phone.

26

It had been five weeks since the calamitous ceremony in the White House's Blue Room, a calamity compounded by Ringmaster Dennison's incessant attempts to focus everyone's attention on the presenter of the Medal of Freedom award and not on the recipient. The conductor of the Marine Band had misread his instructions. Instead of playing a haunting pianissimo of "America the Beautiful" under the President's peroration, he plunged into a fortissimo version of the "Stars and Stripes" march, all but drowning out the chief of state. It was only when Congressman Kendrick stepped up to receive the award and express his thanks that the band struck the chords of the song in a low, swelling pianissimo, adding emotional impact to the recipient's self-effacing words. To the ringmaster's fury, Kendrick had refused to read the brief speech given to him by Dennison ten minutes before the ceremony, thus instead of extolling the President's "secret but extraordinary assistance," he thanked all those he could not mention by name for saving his life and bringing about the solution of the Masqat crisis. This particular moment was embarrassingly punctuated by a loud whispered "*Shit!*" from the ranks of Langford Jennings's aides on the platform.

The final insult to the ringmaster was brought about solely by himself. During the short photo session where no questions were permitted because of antiterrorist strategies, Herbert Dennison absently withdrew a small bottle of Maalox from his pocket and drank from it. Suddenly cameras were aimed at him, strobes exploding, as the President of the United States turned and glared. It was too much for the acid-prone chief of staff. He spilled the chalk-white liquid over his dark suit jacket.

At the end, Langford Jennings, his arm around Evan's shoulders, had walked out of the room and into the carpeted hallway.

"That went *beautifully,* Congressman!" exclaimed the President. "Except for a certain asshole who's supposed to run these things."

"He has a lot of pressures on him, sir. I wouldn't be too harsh."

"On *Herb*?" said Jennings quietly, confidentially. "And have to do what *he* does? No way. . . . I gather he gave you something to read and you wouldn't do it."

"I'm afraid he did and I wouldn't."

"Good. It would have looked like a damned cheap setup. Thanks, Evan, I appreciate it."

"You're welcome," said Kendrick to this large charismatic man who kept surprising him.

The ensuing five weeks had been as Evan thought they would be. The media clamored for his attention. But he kept his word to Herbert Dennison and would continue to keep it. He refused all interviews, claiming simply that to accept one he would feel obligated to accept all, and that would mean he could not adequately serve his constituency, a constituency, incidentally, he continued to hold. The November election in Colorado's Ninth District was merely a ritual; under the circumstances the opposition could not even find a candidate. Yet in terms of the media, some were more succinct than others.

"You big son of a bitch," had teased the acerbic Ernest Foxley of the Foxley program. "I gave you your first break, your first decent exposure."

"I don't think you understand," Kendrick said. "I never wanted any breaks, any exposure."

After a pause the commentator replied. "You know what? I believe you. Why is that?"

"Because I'm telling you the truth and you're good at what you do."

"Thank you, young man. I'll pass the word and try to call off the hounds, but don't give us any more surprises, okay?"

There were no surprises to give *anyone,* thought Kendrick angrily, driving through the Virginia countryside in the early December afternoon. His house in Fairfax had become a virtual base of operations for Khalehla, the property given a large measure of sophistication by way of the Central Intelligence Agency's Mitchell Payton. The director of Special Projects had first ordered the construction of a high brick wall that fronted the grounds, admittance achieved through a wide white wrought-iron gate electronically operated. Surrounding the property an equally tall Cyclone fence was placed deep in the earth, the green metal so thick it would take an explosive, a blowtorch, or a furiously manipulated hacksaw to break through, the invading sounds heard easily by a unit of guards. Payton then had installed a continuously "swept" telephone in Evan's study with extension lights in various other rooms that told whoever saw them to reach that instrument as quickly as possible. A communicating computer had been placed alongside the phone and was hooked up to a modem connecting it solely to the director's private office. When he had information he wanted Khalehla or the Congressman to evaluate, it was immediately transmitted, all printouts to be shredded and burned.

In accord with the President's publicly stated instructions, Special Projects had moved swiftly at the beginning and assumed responsibility for all security measures mounted to protect the hero of Oman from terrorist reprisals. Kendrick was impressed, initially because of the security arrangements. In the space of one hour after a presidential limousine had driven him away from the estate in Maryland, Mitchell Payton had total control of his movements—in a sense, of his life. The communications equipment came later, quite a bit later, the delay due to Khalehla's obstinacy. She had resisted the idea of moving into Kendrick's house, but after eighteen days of hotel living and numerous awkward out-of-the-way meetings with Evan and her Uncle Mitch, the latter had put his foot down.

"Damn it, my dear, there's no way I can justify the cost of a safe house solely for one of my people, nor would I list the reason if I could, and I certainly can't install the equipment we need in a hotel. Also, I've passed the official word from Cairo to D.C. that you've resigned from the Agency. We can't afford you in the sector any longer. So I really don't think you have a choice."

"I've been trying to convince her," Kendrick had interrupted in the private room of a restaurant across the Maryland border. "If she's worried about appearances, I'll put it in the *Congressional Record* that my aunt's in town. How about an older aunt with a face-lift?"

"Oh, you bloody fool. All *right,* I'll do it."

"What equipment?" Evan asked, turning to Payton. "What do you need?"

"Nothing you can buy," answered the CIA director. "And items only we can install."

The next morning a telephone-repair truck had drawn up to

the house. It was waved onto the grounds by the Agency patrols, and men in telephone-company uniforms went to work while over twenty stonemasons were completing the wall and ten others were finishing the impenetrable fence. Linemen climbed successive poles from a junction box, pulling wires from one to another, and sending a separate cable to Kendrick's roof. Still others drove a second truck around the rear drive and into the attached garage where they uncrated the computer console and carried it into the downstairs study. Three hours and twenty minutes later, Mitchell Payton's equipment was in place and functioning. That afternoon Evan had picked up Khalehla in front of her hotel on Nebraska Avenue.

"Hello there, Auntie?"

"I want a dead bolt on the guest room door," she had replied, laughing as she threw her soft nylon bag into the rack behind the seat and climbed in.

"Don't bother, I never mess with older relatives."

"You already have, but not now." She had turned to him, adding with gentle yet firm sincerity. "I mean that, Evan. This isn't Bahrain; we're in business together, not bed. Okay?"

"That's why you wouldn't move in before?"

"Of course."

"You don't know me very well," Kendrick had said after a few moments of silence in the traffic.

"That's part of it."

"Which leads me to a question I've wanted to ask you but I thought you might take it the wrong way."

"Go ahead."

"When you walked into that house in Maryland last month, among the first things you mentioned was Bahrain. Yet later you told me the house was wired, that anything we said would be heard. Why did you say it then?"

"Because I wanted the subject dispensed with as rapidly and as thoroughly as possible."

"Meaning that others—people cleared to read the transcripts—would assume or suspect what happened."

"Yes, and I wanted my position clear, which was not supine. My following statements were consistent."

"Case closed," said Evan, heading into the Beltway toward Virginia.

"Thanks."

"By the way, I've told the Hassans all about you—sorry, not all, of course. They can't wait to meet you."

"They're your couple from Dubai, aren't they?"

"Far more than 'a couple.' Old friends from long ago."

"I didn't mean it in a belittling sense. He's a professor, isn't he?"

"With luck he'll have a post at either Georgetown or Princeton next spring; there was a little matter of papers that we've managed to clear up. Incidentally, 'small world' department, he reveres your father. He met him once in Cairo, so be prepared for a lot of reverence."

"That'll pass quickly," laughed Khalehla. "He'll learn soon enough that I'm neither in his or Dad's league."

"You can use a computer, though, can't you?"

"Well, yes, I can. I frequently have to."

"*I* can't. Sabri's wife, Kashi, can't, and certainly *he* can't, so maybe you're way out of our league."

"Flattery doesn't suit you, Evan. Remember the dead bolt in the door."

They had arrived at the house, where Khalehla was warmly greeted by Kashi Hassan; an instant friendship was formed, as was a tradition among Arabic women.

"Where's Sabri?" Kendrick had asked. "I want him to meet Khalehla."

"He's in your study, dear Evan. He's instructing a gentleman from the Central Intelligence Agency how to operate the computer in case of an emergency."

It had been over three weeks since the Khalehla-Langley axis had been in full operation, and they were no closer to learning anything new than they were since the sterile house in Maryland. Scores of people who even *might* have had the slightest possible access to the Oman file were put under Payton's intelligence microscopes. Every step in the maximum-classified procedure was studied for flaws in personnel; none were found. The file itself was written by the State Department's Frank Swann in tandem with the Agency's Lester Crawford, the mechanics involving a single word processor, the typing done in shifts of a thousand words per typist with all proper names omitted, inserted later solely by Swann and Crawford.

The decision to go to maximum classification was reached by *overview,* a summary without details, but with the highest recommendations of the secretaries of State and Defense and the Joint Chiefs, as well as the Central Intelligence Agency. It was all accomplished without Kendrick's name or the identities or nationalities of other individuals or military units; the basic information had been submitted to the select committees of the Senate and the House for approval at the conclusion of the crisis fifteen months ago. Both congressional approvals were instantly forthcoming; it was also assumed that the *Washington Post* press leak concerning an unknown American in Masqat had come from an indiscreet member of these committees.

Who? How? Why? They were back where they had started from: by all the rules of logic and elimination, the Oman file was beyond reach, yet it had been stolen.

"There's something *not* logical," Payton had pronounced. "A hole in the system and we're missing it."

"No kidding," Kendrick had agreed.

Payton's decision regarding Evan's sudden appointments to both the Partridge Committee and the Select Subcommittee for Intelligence had floored Kendrick. Neither the manipulative Partridge nor the equally manipulating Speaker of the House should be approached directly. Why *not*? Evan had objected. If he was the one being *programmed,* he had every right to confront those who were willing accessories.

"No, Congressman," Payton had said. "If they were blackmailed into appointing you, you can be sure they'll stonewall and send out alarms. Our blond European and whoever he works for will go further underground. We don't stop them; we simply can't find them. I remind you, it's the 'why' that concerns us. Why are *you,* a relatively apolitical freshman representative from an obscure district in Colorado, being pushed into the political center?"

"It's died down a lot—"

"You don't watch television very much," Khalehla had said. "Two cable networks did retrospectives on you last week."

"*What?*"

"I didn't tell you. There was no point. It would only have made you angry."

Kendrick lowered the Mercedes's window and stuck out his arm. The government mobile unit behind him was new and the turn in the country road ahead was halfway around a long wooden curve, the turn itself close to a blind one. He was warning his guards, and he supposed there was a minor irony in that. . . . His thoughts returned to the "lousy enigma," as he and Khalehla had come to call the whole elusive mess that had screwed up his life. Mitch Payton—it was now "Mitch" and "Evan"—had driven over from Langley the other evening.

"We're working on something new," the director of Special Projects had said in the study. "On the assumption that Swann's European had to reach a great many people in order to compile the information he had on you, we're assembling some data ourselves. It may offend you, but we, too, are going back over your life."

"How many years?"

"We picked you up when you were eighteen—the chances of anything before then having relevance is remote."

"*Eighteen?* Christ, isn't *anything* sacred?"

"Do you want it to be? If so, I'll call it off."

"No, of course not. It's just kind of a shock. You can get that sort of information?"

"It's nowhere near as difficult as people think. Credit bureaus, personnel files and routine background checks do it all the time."

"What's the point?"

"Several possibilities—realistically two, I suppose. As I mentioned, the first is our doggedly curious European. If we could put together a list of people he had to reach in order to learn about you, we'd be closer to finding *him,* and I think we all agree, he's the linchpin. . . . The second possibility is something we haven't attempted. In trying to unearth the vanishing blond man and whoever's behind him, we've concentrated on the events in Oman and the file itself. We've restricted our microscopes to government-oriented areas."

"Where else would we look?" Kendrick had asked.

"Your personal life, I'm afraid. There could be something or someone in your own past, an event, or people that you knew, an incident perhaps that galvanized friends or conceivably enemies who wanted to advance your position—or conversely—make you a target. And make no mistake, Congressman, you *are* a potential target, nobody's kidding about that."

"But, MJ," broke in Khalehla. "Even if we found people who either liked him or hated him, they'd have to be Washington-connected. Mr. Jones from Ann Arbor, Michigan—friend *or* enemy—couldn't just go to the max-classified data banks or the archives and say, 'By the way, there's a certain file I'd like to have a copy of so I can mock up a fake memorandum for the newspapers.' I don't understand."

"Neither do I, Adrienne—or should I call you 'Khalehla,' which will take some getting used to."

"There's no reason for you to call me Khalehla—"

"Don't interrupt," said Evan, smiling. "Khalehla's just fine," he added.

"Yes, well, I really *don't* understand," continued Payton. "But as I told you, there's a hole in the system, a gap we've missed, and we have to try everything."

"Then why not go after Partridge and the Speaker of the House?" pressed Kendrick. "If I could do what I did in Masqat, they can't be so tough to break down."

"Not yet, young man. The timing isn't right, and the Speaker's retiring."

"Now *I* don't understand."

"MJ means he's working on both," Khalehla had explained.

Evan braked the Mercedes around the long curve in the Virginia woods and waited until he saw the mobile unit in his rearview mirror; he then turned right into the pasture road that was the back way to his house. The guards would admit him. He wanted to hurry now; it was why he had taken the shortcut. Khalehla had called him at the office and told him Mitchell Payton's list had arrived over the computer printout. His past was about to be presented to him.

Milos Varak walked down the boarded path toward the enormous beach fronting the Hotel del Coronado three miles over the bridge from San Diego. He had worked diligently for weeks to find a crack through which he could penetrate the ranks of the Vice President of the United States. Most of the time was spent in Washington; the administration's Secret Service was not easily invaded. Until he found a man, a dedicated man, with a strong physique and a disciplined mind, but with an unacceptable avocation that if exposed would destroy his assets, as well as his career and undoubtedly his life. He was a well-compensated procurer for various high-ranking members of the government. He had been primed for his work by the elders of his "family," who had spotted his potential and sent him to the finest parochial schools and through a major university—major but not rich, for that image would be incorrect. The elders wanted a well-groomed, fine-looking, upstanding young man placed in a position to dispense favors in return for certain accommodations. And what better favors were there than below a weak man's belt, and how better to reach accommodations than the knowledge thereof. The elders were pleased, had been pleased for a number of years. This man came from the Mafia; he was Mafia; he served the Mafia.

Varak approached the lone figure in a raincoat by the rocks of a jetty several hundred yards from the high, imposing Cyclone fence of the Naval Air Station.

"Thank you so much for seeing me," said Milos pleasantly.

"I thought you had an accent on the phone," said the well-spoken, well-trained, dark-featured man. "Are you a redbird courier? Because if you are, you've reached the wrong swallow."

"A Communist? I'm the furthest thing from it. I'm so American your *consiglieri* could present me to the Vatican."

"That's insulting, to say nothing of being totally inaccurate. . . . You made several very stupid statements, so stupid that you provoked my curiosity, which is why I'm here."

"For whatever reason, I'm grateful that you are."

"The bottom line was pretty clear," interrupted the Secret Service agent. "You threatened me, sir."

"I'm sorry you were offended, I never meant to threaten you. I merely said that I was aware of certain additional services you provided—"

"Stop being so polite—"

"There's no reason to be discourteous," said Varak courteously. "I simply wanted you to understand my position."

"You don't *have* a position," corrected the government man with emphasis. "Our records are unblemished, if you get my point."

The Czech shifted his feet in the sand and waited while the roar of a jet passing over from the Naval Air Station diminished in the sky. "You're saying that there are *no* records and your point is that you won't discuss anything concrete because you think I may be wearing a recording device." Varak unbuttoned his jacket, separating it. "Be my guest, search me. Personally, I wouldn't care to have my voice on the same tape with yours. . . . Please, go ahead. I will, of course, remove my weapon and hold it in my hand, but I won't stop you."

The White House guardian was sullen, hesitant. "You're too accommodating," he said, standing motionless.

"On the other hand," added Milos quickly. "We can dispense with this awkwardness if you'd just read something I've prepared for you." The Czech released his jacket, reached into his pocket and pulled out several sheets of folded paper. He snapped them open and handed them to the Secret Service agent.

As the man read, his eyes narrowed and his lips parted, frozen into the start of a snarl; in seconds a reasonably strong and attractive face became ugly. "You're a dead man," he said quietly.

"That could be shortsighted, don't you think? Because if I am, surely so are you. The capos would descend like a pack of wild dogs while the dons, drinking their fine red wine as if it were your blood, waited to hear of your very unpleasant death. Records? What are *those*? Names, dates, times, locations—and correspondingly, opposite each entry, the results of your sexual merchandise, or rather, blackmailed into *being* results. Bills amended, contracts awarded, government projects voted up or down according to their allocations. I'd say it's *quite* a record. And where does it all lead back to? Let me guess. The most unlikely source one can imagine. . . . An unpublished telephone number listed under a false name and address but located in the apartment of a member of the government's Secret Service."

"Those girls are dead. . . . The boys are dead—"

"Don't blame them. They had no more of a choice than you do now. Believe me, it's better to assist me than to oppose me. I have no interest in your extracurricular activities; you provide a service that if you didn't somebody else would for roughly the same results. All I want from you is information, and in exchange I'll burn every copy of those pages. Of course, you have only my word for it, but as I'm likely to call upon your expertise again, I'd be stupid to release them, and I assure you I'm not stupid."

"Obviously not," agreed the Mafia soldier, his voice barely audible. "Why throw a gun away when you can still use it."

"I'm glad you understand my position."

"What sort of information are you looking for?"

"It's innocuous, nothing that will upset you. Let's start with the FBI unit that's been assigned to the Vice President. Aren't you people doing your job? Do you need a special task force from the Bureau?"

"It hasn't anything to do with us. We're in place for protection. They're investigative."

"You can't protect unless you investigate."

"It's different levels. We come up with something, we turn it over to the Bureau."

"What did you come up with that called for this unit?"

"We didn't," answered the man. "A couple of months ago a series of threats were made against Viper and—"

"Viper?"

"The Vice President."

"It's not a very flattering code name."

"It's not in general use, either. Just among the detail."

"I see. Go on—These threats. Who made them?"

"That's what the unit's all about. They're trying to find out because they're still being made."

"How?"

"Phone calls, telegrams, paste-up letters—they come from different places, which keep the Feds in the air a lot tracing them down."

"Without success?"

"Not yet."

"Then they're a *roving* task force, here one day, somewhere else the next. Are their movements coordinated from Washington?"

"When Viper's there, sure. When he's out here, it's here, and when he's on the road it's wherever he's at. The unit's controlled by his personal staff; otherwise too much time is wasted checking back and forth with D.C."

"You were out here five weeks ago, weren't you?"

"Around then, yes. We just got back ten days ago; he spends a lot of time out here. As he likes to say, the President covers the East and he covers the West, and he's got the better deal because he gets away from Funny Town."

"That's a foolish statement for a Vice President to make."

"That's Viper, but that's not to say he's a fool. He's not."

"Why do you call him Viper?"

"As long as you want it straight I guess we don't like him, or the crowd he pals around with—especially out here. Those bastards treat us like Puerto Rican houseboys. The other afternoon one of them said to me, 'Boy, get me another G and T.' I told him I'd better check with my superiors in the Secret Service to see if I was assigned to him."

"Weren't you afraid the Vice—Viper—might take offense?"

"Christ, he doesn't mess with us. Like the Fed unit, we only answer to his staff chief."

"Who's he?"

"Not he, *she.* We've got another code for her; it's not as good as Viper but it fits. We call her Dragon Bitch—Dame Bountiful in the logs, which she likes."

"Tell me about her," said Varak, the antennae of an adult lifetime picking up a signal.

"Her name's Ardis Vanvlanderen, and she came on board

about a year ago replacing a hell of a good man who was doing a hell of a good job. So good he got a terrific offer from one of Viper's friends. She's in her forties and one of those tough executive ladies who looks like she wants to cut your balls off when you go into her office just because you're a male."

"An unattractive woman, then?"

"I wouldn't say that. She's got a decent enough face and a foxy body, but it'd be hard to work up a letch for her unless you like the type. My guess is she screws by the numbers."

"Is she married?"

"There's a gonzo who comes around saying he's her husband, but nobody pays much attention to him."

"What does he do? What's his business?"

"He's Palm Springs social set. Stocks and bonds when they don't interfere with his golf, that's the way I read him."

"That's significant money."

"He's a heavy contributor and never misses a superbash at the White House. You know the type—wavy white hair and a big gut with lots of shiny teeth in a tuxedo; they always get their pictures taken dancing. If he could read a whole book through in English, they'd probably make him the ambassador to the Court of St. James—I take it back. With his money, half a book."

Varak studied the Secret Service guard. The man was obviously relieved at being asked such innocuous questions. His answers were more complete than they had to be, bordering on the false confidentiality of gossip. "I wonder why someone like that would send his wife out to work, even if it is for the Vice President."

"I don't think he has anything to say about it. You don't send a sharp item like her anywhere she doesn't want to go. Besides, one of the maids told us she was wife number three or four, so maybe Vanvlanderen learned to let 'em hang loose and do their thing."

"And you say she does it well?"

"Like I said, very sharp, very pro. Viper doesn't make a move without her."

"What's *he* like?"

"Viper?" Suddenly another jet took off from the Naval Air Station, the roar of the engines thunderous. "Viper's Viper," said the Mafia plant when the earthshaking noise had vanished. "Orson Bollinger's a party glad-hander with an insider's grasp of every fucking thing that goes on, and nothing goes on that doesn't serve the boys in the back rooms of California because they take care of him."

"You're very astute."

"I observe."

"You do a great deal more than that. Only I'd suggest you be more cautious in the future. If I can find you, others might, too."

"*How?* Goddamn you, *how*?"

"Diligence. And over the weeks watching for a mistake someone had to make. It could have been one of the others in your detail for something else—we're all human; none of us lives in a freezer—but it turned out to be you. You were tired, or perhaps you had that extra drink, or simply felt you were too secure. Regardless, you made a phone call to Brooklyn, New York, obviously not the way you were supposed to make it, not from an untraceable pay telephone."

"*Frangie!*" whispered the *capo supremo.*

"Your cousin, Joseph 'Fingers' Frangiani, second underboss of the Ricci family in Brooklyn, inheritors of the Genovese interests. It was all I needed, *amico.*"

"You foreign low-life son of a *bitch*!"

"Don't waste obscenities on me. . . . One last question, and why not be civil?"

"*What?*" cried the furious man from the Mafia, his black eyebrows arched, his right hand instinctively reaching behind his jacket.

"*Stop!*" roared the Czech. "One inch more and you're dead."

"Where's your *gun*?" choked the agent, without a breath.

"I don't need it," replied Varak, his eyes boring in on his would-be killer. "And I'm sure you know that."

Slowly, the Secret Service man brought his right hand in front of him. "One question, that's all!" he said, his animus reflected in his face. "You've got one last question."

"This Ardis Vanvlanderen. How was her appointment as the Vice President's chief of staff explained to you? Words must have been said, reasons given. After all, you're Bollinger's personal security and you worked well with her predecessor."

"We're his security, not corporate executives. Explanations weren't required."

"Nothing was said? It's an unusual position for a woman."

"Plenty was said so we wouldn't miss the point, but no explanation. Bollinger called everybody together and told us how pleased he was to announce the appointment of one of the most talented executives in the country, someone who was assuming the job at such personal sacrifice that we should all thank the powers that be for her patriotism. The 'her' was the first inkling we had that it was a woman."

"Interesting phrase 'powers that be.' "

"He talks that way."

"And he doesn't make a move without her."

"I don't think he'd dare. She's heavy metal and she keeps the house in order."

"Whose order?"

"What?"

"Never mind. . . . That's all for now, *amico.* Please be so kind as to leave first, will you? I'll call you if I need you."

The mafioso, the hot, ancestral blood of the Mediterranean rushing to his head, jabbed his index finger at the Czech and spoke in a hoarse voice. "You'll stay out of my fucking life if you know what's good for you."

"I hope to stay as far away from you as possible, Signor Mezzano—"

"Don't you call me a pimp!"

"I'll call you anything I like, but as to what's good for me, I'll be the judge of that. Now *fila*! *Capisce?*"

Milos Varak watched his reluctant informer walk over the sand in silent fury until the *mezzano* disappeared into the maze of beach accesses toward the hotel. The Czech let his mind wander. . . . *she came on board about a year ago; he's a heavy contributor; Viper doesn't make a move without her.* It was thirteen months ago when Inver Brass had begun the search for a new Vice President of the United States, the incumbent considered a pawn of the President's unseen contributors—men who intended to run the country.

It was past four o'clock in the morning and Khalehla would not stop. She kept pressing Evan, changing cassettes on the recorder and repeating names over and over again, insisting that wherever he recognized anything at all he describe in detail *everything* he could remember. The computer printout from Mitchell Payton's office at the Central Intelligence Agency included a hundred twenty-seven selected names with corresponding occupations, marriages, divorces and deaths. In each case the individual listed had either spent considerable time with Kendrick or had been present during a period of high activity and could conceivably have been instrumental in his academic or career decisions.

"Where the hell did he *get* these people?" asked Evan, pacing the study. "I swear I don't remember half of them, and most of the other half are blurs except for old friends I'll always remember, and none of them could be remotely connected with what's happening. Christ, I had three roommates in college, two others in graduate school and a sixth shared an apartment with me in Detroit when I worked in a lousy job over here. Later there were at least two dozen others I tried unsuccessfully to raise backing from for the Middle East and some of them are on that list—why I don't know, but I do know all those lives are being lived in the suburbs with green lawns and country clubs and colleges they can barely afford for their kids. They have nothing to do with *now.*"

"Then let's go over the Kendrick Group again—"

"There *is* no Kendrick Group," broke in Evan angrily. "They were killed, blown away, drowned in concrete! . . . Manny and I are all that's left, you know that."

"I'm sorry," said Khalehla gently, sitting on the couch drinking tea. The printout was on the coffee table in front of her. "I meant the dealings you had over here in the States *while* there was the Kendrick Group."

"We've gone over them. There weren't that many—mostly in high-tech equipment."

"Let's go over them again."

"It's a waste of time but go ahead."

" 'Sonar Electronics, Palo Alto, California,' " read Khalehla, her hand on the printout. "The representative was a man named Carew—"

" 'Screw Carew,' " said Kendrick, chuckling. "That was Manny's comment. We bought some sounding devices that didn't work, and they still wanted payment after we sent them back."

" 'Drucker Graphics, Boston,' the representative, a G. R. Shulman. Anything?"

"Gerry Shulman, good man, good service; we worked with them for years. Never a problem."

" 'Morseland Oil, Tulsa.' The rep was someone named Arnold Stanhope."

"I told you about him—them."

"Tell me again."

"We did preliminary surveying for them in the Emirates. They kept wanting more than they were willing to pay for, and since we were growing, we could afford to drop them."

"Was there acrimony?"

"Sure, there always is when chiselers find out they can't do business as usual. But there wasn't anything silence couldn't cure. Besides, they found some other jokers, a Greek outfit who caught on to them and delivered a survey that must have been made on the floor of the Oman Gulf."

"Freebooters; every one of you," said Khalehla, smiling and lowering her hand on the printout. " 'Off Shore Investments, Limited, headquarters Nassau, the Bahamas, contact Ardis Montreaux, New York City.' They funneled a lot of capital to you—"

"Which we never touched because it was a sham," interrupted Evan sharply. "It better damn well say that there."

"It says here, 'Skip it.' "

"What?"

"I wrote it. It's what you said before, 'Skip it.' What's Off Shore Investments, Limited?"

"*Was,*" corrected Kendrick. "It was a high-class boilerplate operation on the international scale—high-class and international but still boilerplate. Build a company up with large Swiss accounts and hot air, then sell off and switch the assets, leaving the buyers with a balloon full of helium."

"*You* got mixed up with something like that?"

"I didn't know it was something like that. I was a lot younger and impressed as hell that they wanted to list us as part of their structure . . . even more impressed with the money they banked for us in Zurich. Impressed, that is, until Manny said 'Let's try to get some, just for the hell of it.' He knew exactly what he was doing; we couldn't pull out two francs. Off Shore's signatures controlled all withdrawals, all assignments."

"A dummy setup and you were the dummies."

"That's it."

"How did you get involved?"

"We were in Riyadh, and Montreaux flew over and conned me. I hadn't learned that there weren't any shortcuts—not that kind."

"Ardis Montreaux. Ardis. . . . That's an odd name for a man."

"Because it's not a man—she's not a man. She's a lot tougher."

"A woman?"

"Believe it."

"With your innate skepticism she must have been very persuasive."

"She had the words. She also wanted our heads when we

pulled out; she claimed we were costing them millions. Weingrass asked her whose millions this time."

"Perhaps we should—"

"Skip it," Evan broke in firmly. "She married an English banker and lives in London. She's faded."

"How do you know?"

Showing minor embarrassment, Kendrick answered quickly and quietly. "She called me a couple of times . . . as a matter of fact to apologize. Skip it."

"Sure." Khalehla went on to the next firm on the printout. As she spoke she wrote two words after Off Shore Investments, Limited. *Check out.*

Ardis Montreaux Frazier-Pyke Vanvlanderen, born Ardisolda Wojak in Pittsburgh, Pennsylvania, walked into the marble foyer of the suite at the Westlake Hotel in San Diego. She threw her sable stole over the back of a velour chair and raised her voice, her speech a cultivated mid-Atlantic, rather more nasal stage British than old-money American, but still afflicted with the harsh tones of Monongahela Slavic in the upper registers.

"*Andy*-boy, I'm home! We've got less than an hour to get up to La Jolla, so *move* it, sweetie!"

Andrew Vanvlanderen, heavyset, with stark white wavy hair and dressed in a tuxedo, walked out of the bedroom, a drink in his hand. "I'm ahead of you, babe."

"I'll be ready in ten minutes," said Ardis, peering into a foyer mirror and fingering the curls of her perfectly coifed frosted brown hair. She was closing in on fifty and of medium height but gave the impression of being younger and taller due to erect posture, a slender figure topped by generous breasts, and a well-coordinated face punctuated by large, penetrating green eyes. "Why not call for the car, sweetie?"

"The car can wait. So can La Jolla. We've got to talk."

"Oh?" The Vice President's chief of staff looked over at her husband. "You sound serious."

"I am. I had a call from your old boyfriend."

"Which one, darling?"

"The only one who counts."

"Good God, he called *here*?"

"I told him to—"

"That was dumb, Andy-boy, just plain *dumb*!" Ardis Vanvlanderen walked rapidly, angrily out of the foyer and down into the sunken living room. She sat in a red silk wing chair and abruptly crossed her legs, her large eyes riveted on her husband. "Take risks with money—on commodities or futures or your stupid horses or any goddamned thing you like, but *not* where I'm concerned! Is that understood, darling?"

"Listen, bitch—*Dragon* Bitch—with what I've paid out, if I want firsthand information I'm going to get it. Is *that* understood?"

"All right, all right. Cool off, Andy."

"You start a rhubarb and then you tell *me* to cool it?"

"I'm sorry." Ardis arched her neck back into the chair, breathing audibly through her open mouth, her eyes briefly closed. In seconds she opened them, leveled her head, and continued. "Really, I'm sorry. It's been a particularly rotten Orson day."

"What's Viper done now?" asked Vanvlanderen, drinking.

"Be careful with those names," said his wife, laughing softly. "We wouldn't want our all-American gorillas to learn they're being bugged."

"What's Bollinger's problem?"

"He's feeling insecure again. He wants a written ironclad guarantee that he'll be on the ticket next July or we settle ten million on him in a Swiss account."

Vanvlanderen coughed a swallow of whisky into his glass. "Ten *million*?" he gasped. "Who the fuck does that comedian think he is?"

"The Vice President of the United States with a few secrets in his skull," replied Ardis. "I told him we wouldn't accept anyone else, but it wasn't good enough. I think he senses that Jennings doesn't consider him a world-beater and would let him go."

"Our beloved telegenic wizard, Langford Jennings, hasn't a goddamned thing to say about it! . . . Is Orson right? *Does* Jennings dislike him?"

"Dislike's too strong. He just dismisses him, that's what I hear from Dennison."

"*That* one's got to go. One of these days Herb's going to get more curious than we want him—"

"Forget him," interrupted Mrs. Vanvlanderen. "Forget Dennison and Bollinger and even your stupid horses. What did my straying, cat-hunting old boyfriend have to say that was so important you had him call here?"

"Relax. He phoned from my Washington attorney's office; we share the same firm there, remember? But first, let's *not* forget

Orson. Give him his guarantee. A simple sentence or two and I'll sign it. It'll make him happy and happy is better."

"Are you *crazy*?" cried Ardis, bouncing forward in the chair.

"Not at all. To begin with, he'll *be* on the ticket or he'll just disappear . . . like former vice presidents usually do."

"Oh, my," said Ardis, drawing out the word *my* in admiration. "You're my kind of fella, Andy-boy. You think so clearly, so succinctly."

"Long years of learning, babe."

"Now, what did mixed-up old Dimples have to say? Who's after his sensitive skin now?"

"Not his, *ours*—"

"Which is his and don't you forget it. It's why I'm here, lover, why he introduced us and brought us together."

"He wants us to know that the little group of deluded super people are moving into high gear. During the next three months their congressman will start getting editorials in progressively stronger papers. The theme will be 'examining his positions' and he'll pass all the exams. The point, of course, is to create a ground swell. Our Cupid is worried, very worried. And to tell you the truth I'm sweating a few bullets myself. Those benevolent lunatics know what they're doing; this whole thing could get out of control. Ardis, we've got *millions* riding on the next five years. I'm *goddamned* worried!"

"Over nothing," said his perfectly coiffed wife, getting out of her chair. She stood for a moment and looked at Vanvlanderen, her wide green eyes only partially amused. "Since you figure to save ten million on Bollinger one way or another—and *my* way is better, certainly safer, than any alternative—I think it's only reasonable that you bank an equal amount for me, don't you, darling?"

"Somehow I fail to see the overpowering reason."

"It could be your undying love for me . . . or perhaps one of the more extraordinary coincidences of my career floating among the rich, the beautiful, the powerful and the politically ambitious, especially in the area of government largess."

"How's that again?"

"I won't recite the litany of why we're all doing what we're doing, or even why I've cast my not inconsiderable talents with you, but I will now let you in on a little secret I've kept all to myself for, lo, these many weeks."

"I'm fascinated," said Vanvlanderen, putting his drink down

on a marble table and closely observing his fourth wife. "What is it?"

"I know Evan Kendrick."

"You *what*?"

"Our brief association goes back a number of years, more than I care to dwell on, frankly, but for a few weeks we had something in common."

"Outside of the obvious, what?"

"Oh, the sex was pleasant enough but immaterial . . . to both of us. We were young people in a hurry with no time for attachments. Do you remember Off Shore Investments?"

"If he was part of that outfit, we can nail him with fraud! Certainly enough to take him out if he climbs on board. *Was* he?"

"He was, but you can't. He pulled out in loud moral indignation, which was the start of that house-of-cards' collapse. And I wouldn't be too anxious to nail Off Shore's principals unless you're tired of me, sweetie."

"You?"

"I was the main missionary. I recruited the components."

"I'll be *damned.*" Vanvlanderen laughed as he picked up his drink and raised the glass to his wife. "Those thieves sure as hell knew whom to hire for the right jobs. . . . *Wait* a minute. You knew Kendrick well enough to sleep with the son of a bitch and you never *said* anything?"

"I had my reasons—"

"They better be damned *good*!" exploded the President's heavy contributor. "Because if they're not, I may just break your ass, you *bitch*! Suppose he saw you, *recognized* you, remembered Off Shore and put two and two together and got *four*! I don't *take* those kinds of chances!"

"It's my turn to say 'Relax,' Andy," countered the contributor's wife. "The people around a vice president aren't news or even newsworthy. When's the last time you can recall the name of any individual on a vice president's staff? They're a gray, amorphous group—*presidents* won't have it any other way. Besides, I don't think my name's even been in the papers except as 'Mr. and *Mrs.* Vanvlanderen, guests at the White House.' Kendrick still thinks I'm Frazier-Pyke, a banker's wife living in London, and if you remember, although both of us were invited to the Medal of Freedom ceremony, you went alone. I begged off."

"Those aren't reasons! Why didn't you *tell* me?"

"Because I knew what your reaction would be—take her out of the picture—when *I* realized I could be far more useful to you in it."

"How, for Christ's sake?"

"*Because* I knew him. I also knew I had to get current on him, but not with some private investigating firm that could end up burning us later, so I took the official high road. The Federal Bureau of Investigation."

"The threats against Bollinger?"

"They'll stop tomorrow. Except for one man who'll continue here on a special basis, the unit will be recalled to Washington. Those mocked-up threats were the paranoid fantasies of a harmless lunatic I invented who supposedly fled the country. You see, sweetie, I found out what I had to know."

"Which is?"

"There's an old Israeli Jew named Weingrass whom Kendrick worships. He's the father Evan never had, and when there was the Kendrick Group he was called the company's 'secret weapon.' "

"*Munitions?*"

"Hardly, darling," laughed Ardis Vanvlanderen. "He was an architect, a damned good one, and did pretty spectacular work for the Arabs."

"What about him?"

"He's supposed to be in Paris, but he's not. He's living in Kendrick's house in Colorado, with no passport entry or any official immigration status."

"So?"

"The soon-to-be-anointed Congressman brought the old man back for an operation that saved his life."

"*So?*"

"Emmanuel Weingrass is going to have a medical relapse that will kill him. Kendrick won't leave his side, and when it's over it'll be too late. I *want* the ten million, Andy-boy."

27

Varak studied the members of Inver Brass, each face around the table reflected in the light of the brass lamp in front of him—and her. The Czech's concentration was strained to the limit because he had to focus on two levels.

The first was the information he delivered; the second was on the immediate reaction each had to certain facts within that information. He had to find one pair of eyes that were suspect and he could not find them. That was to say, there were no momentary flashes of astonishment or fear on the faces of the members as he gradually, logically approached the subject of the current Vice President of the United States and his staff, touching ever so lightly on the "innocuous" details he had learned from a Mafia plant in the Secret Service. There was nothing, only blank riveted stares. So while he spoke with conviction and conveyed roughly 80 percent of the truth, he kept watching their eyes, the second level of his mind recalling the salient facts of the life behind each face reflected in the light.

And as he looked at each face, its features heightened by the chiaroscuro wash from the lamps, he felt, as he always did, that he was in the presence of giants. Yet one was not; one had revealed the existence of Emmanuel Weingrass in Mesa Verde, Colorado, a secret unknown to the most clandestine departments in Washington. One of those shadowed faces in front of him was a traitor to Inver Brass. Who?

Samuel Winters? Old money from an American dynasty going back to the railroad and oil barons of the late-nineteenth century. An honored scholar satisfied with his privileged life; an adviser to presidents regardless of party. A great man at peace with himself. Or was he?

Jacob Mandel? A venerated financial genius who had designed and implemented reforms that revitalized the Securities and Exchange Commission into a viable and far more honorable asset to Wall Street. From Lower East Side Yiddish poverty to the halls of merchant princes, and it was said that no decent man who knew him could call him an enemy. Like Winters, he wore his honors well and there were few he had not attained. Or were there others he strove for secretly?

Margaret Lowell? Again aristocratic old money from the New York–Palm Beach orbit, but with a twist that was virtually unheard of in those circles. She was a brilliant attorney who eschewed the rewards of estate and corporate law for the pursuit of advocacy. She worked feverishly in the legal vineyards on behalf of the oppressed, the dispossessed and the disfranchised. Both theorist and practitioner, she was rumored to be the next woman on the Supreme Court. Or was the advocacy a supreme cover for the championship of opposite causes *under* cover?

Eric Sundstrom? The wunderkind scientist of earth and space technology, holder of over twenty hugely remunerative patents, of which the vast majority of proceeds were given away to engineering and medical institutions for the advancement of those sciences. His was a towering intellect concealed by a cherubic face with tousled red hair, an impish smile and a ready sense of humor—as if he were embarrassed by his gifts, even quick to feign mild offense if they were singled out. Or was it all pretense, the guilelessness a sham?

Gideon Logan? Perhaps the most complex of the quintet, and because he was a black man, again perhaps, understandable. He had made several fortunes in real estate, never forgetting where he came from, hiring and nursing along black firms in his developments. It was said that he quietly did more for civil rights than any single corporation in the country. The current administration, as well as its predecessor, had offered him a variety of cabinet posts, all of which he refused, believing he could achieve more as a respected independent force in the private sector than if he was identified with a political party and its practices. A nonstop worker, he seemingly permitted himself only one indulgence: a luxurious oceanfront estate in the Bahamas where he spent infrequent weekends fishing on his forty-six-foot Bertram with his wife of twelve years. Or was the legend that was Gideon Logan incomplete? The answer was yes. Several years of his whirlwind, meteoric life were simply unknown; it was as if he had not existed.

"Milos?" asked Margaret Lowell, her elbow forward on the table, her head resting on the extended fingers of her hand. "How in heaven's name has the administration managed to keep the threats against Bollinger quiet? Especially with a Bureau unit exclusively assigned to him."

Strike Margaret Lowell? She was opening the obvious can of worms in which was found the Vice President's chief of staff.

"I must assume it's through the direction of Mrs. Vanvlanderen, her executive expertise, as it were." *Watch the eyes. The muscles of their faces—the jaws. . . . Nothing. They reveal nothing! Yet one of them knows! Who?*

"I realize she's Andrew Vanvlanderen's wife," said Gideon Logan, "and 'Andy-boy,' as he's called, is one hell of a fund-raiser, but why was she appointed, to begin with?"

Strike Gideon Logan? He was stirring up the worms.

"Perhaps I can answer that," replied Jacob Mandel. "Before she married Vanvlanderen she was a headhunter's dream. She turned around two companies that I know of from bankruptcy into profitable mergers. I'm told she's distastefully aggressive, but no one can deny her managerial talents. She'd be good in that job; she'd keep the political sycophants at bay."

Strike Jacob Mandel? He had no compunction about praising her.

"I ran across her once," said Eric Sundstrom emphatically, "and in plain words she was a *bitch.* I assigned a patent to Johns Hopkins Medical and she wanted to broker the damn thing."

"What was there to broker?" asked the attorney Lowell.

"Absolutely nothing," answered Sundstrom. "She tried to convince me that such large grants required an overseer to make sure the money went where it was supposed to go and not for new jockstraps."

"She probably had a point," said the lawyer, nodding as if from experience.

"Not for me. Not the way *she* talked and the med school's president's a good friend of mine. She'd have driven him up the wall so often he would have returned the patent. She's a bitch, a real bitch."

Strike Eric Sundstrom? He had no compunction whatsoever about damning her.

"I never met her," interjected Samuel Winters, "but she was married to Emory Frazier-Pyke, a fine-tuned banker in London. You remember Emory, don't you, Jacob?"

"Certainly. He played polo and you introduced me as a silent branch of the Rothschilds—which, unfortunately, I think he believed."

"Someone told me," continued Winters, "that poor Frazier-Pyke lost a considerable amount of money in a venture she was associated with but came away with a wife. It was the Off Shore Investments crowd."

"Some fine-tuning he had," added Mandel. "*Goniffs,* every one of them. He should have checked with his polo ponies or even the silent Rothschild."

"Perhaps he did. She didn't last long and old Emory has always been a stickler for the straight and narrow. She could have been a thief, too."

Strike Samuel Winters? The traitor in Inver Brass would not raise the speculation.

"In one way or another," commented Varak without emphasis, "you are all at least aware of her, then."

"*I* wasn't," said Margaret Lowell, bordering on the defensive, "but after hearing the others I can tell you who else knows her—'aware' is a touch too dull. My ex-husband, the alley cat; it was the Frazier-Pyke that did it."

"*Walter?*" Sundstrom's voice and expression were both humorously questioning.

"My boy made so many business trips to London I thought he was advising the Crown, and he frequently mentioned that this Frazier-Pyke was his banker over there. Then one morning the maid phoned me at the office saying that Casanova had an urgent call from an 'FP' in London, but she didn't know where he was. She gave me the number and I called saying to somebody—I assumed a secretary—that M. Lowell was on the line for 'FP.' I was subsequently greeted by an exuberant voice virtually yelling at me. '*Dahling,* I'll be in New York tomorrow and we can have five full *days* together!' I said 'How nice' and hung up."

"She travels in the right circles for her purposes," said Gideon Logan, chuckling. "Andy-boy Vanvlanderen will keep her in blue chips and sables until he gets bored."

Varak had to change the subject quickly! If he was right about there being a traitor around the table, and he *was* right—whatever was said about Ardis Vanvlanderen would get back to her and he could not permit anything further. "From everyone's reactions," he said pleasantly, aimlessly, "we can assume that there are some opportunists who are immensely capable. However, it's not important." *Watch them. Every face.* "She serves the Vice President well, but that's essentially immaterial to us. . . . Back to our candidate, everything proceeds on schedule. The Midwest newspapers, starting with Chicago, will be the first to speculate on his credentials, both in columns and editorials. They've all been provided with extensive background material on Kendrick as well as tapes of the Partridge Committee, the Foxley program and his own quite remarkable press conference. From this core the word will spread both East and West."

"How were they approached, Milos?" asked the spokesman, Samuel Winters. "The newspapers and the columnists, I mean."

"A legitimate ad hoc committee that we've formed in Denver. The seed, when planted, grew quickly. The Colorado branch of the party was enthusiastic, especially as the money was contributed by donors who insisted on remaining anonymous. The state functionaries see a potentially viable candidate and the wherewithal to launch him, as well as the attention it focuses on Colorado. Win or lose, *they* can't lose."

"That 'wherewithal' could be a legal problem," said Margaret Lowell.

"Nothing significant, madam. It's provided in sequences, no amount over the legal limit as mandated by the election laws—which are quite obscure, if not mystifying, in my opinion."

"If I need a lawyer, I'll call you, Milos," added Lowell, smiling and sitting back in her chair.

"I've furnished each of you with a copy of the names of the newspapers, their editorial writers and the columnists involved in this phase—"

"To be burned in our coal stove," broke in Winters softly.

"Of course," "Naturally," "Most certainly," came the chorus of quiet replies.

Which was the liar?

"Tell me, Varak," said the brilliant cherubic Sundstrom. "According to everything we know, everything you've brought us, our candidate hasn't displayed an iota of that 'fire in the belly' we hear so much about. Isn't it terribly important? Doesn't he have to ultimately *want* the job?"

"He'll want it, sir. As we've learned, he's what might be called a closet activist who runs out of the closet when the conditions call for his abilities."

"Good Lord, Samuel, he's a rabbi, too?"

"Hardly, Mr. Mandel," replied the Czech, permitting himself a tight grin. "What I mean to say, no doubt poorly—"

"The words are lovely, Milos."

"Thank you, sir, you're too kind. But what I'm trying to say is that on two dramatic occasions in his life—one extraordinarily dangerous to him personally—he chose to take the most difficult courses of action because he felt he could effect a change for the better. The first was his decision to replace a corrupt congressman; the second, of course, was Oman. In short words, he must once again be convinced that his person and his abilities are needed—uniquely needed for the good of the country."

"That's a tall order," said Gideon Logan. "He's obviously a man of realistic sensibilities who makes a pretty fair appraisal of his qualifications. His bottom line may be . . . 'I'm not qualified.' How do we overcome that?"

Varak looked around the table, his expression that of a man trying to be understood. "I suggest symbolically, sir."

"How's that?" asked Mandel, removing his steel-rimmed glasses.

"For example, the current Secretary of State, although he is frequently maligned by his colleagues and the White House staff as a stubborn academic, is the most reasoned voice in the administration. I know privately that he has managed to block a number of rash actions recommended by the President's advisers because the President respects him—"

"He damn well *should,*" exclaimed Margaret Lowell.

"I think the European alliance would fall apart without him," offered Winters.

"There wouldn't *be* an alliance without him," agreed Mandel, anger on his normally passive face. "He's a beacon of rationality in a sea of belching Neanderthals."

"If I may, sir? Could your use of the word 'beacon' be construed as a symbol?"

"That's logical," answered Gideon Logan. "Our Secretary of State is by all means a symbol of intelligent moderation. The nation, too, respects him."

"He intends to resign," said Varak simply.

"*What?*" Sundstrom sat forward. "His loyalty to Jennings wouldn't permit it."

"His sense of integrity shouldn't permit him to stay," said Winters with finality.

"Out of loyalty, however," explained Varak, "he's agreed to attend the Middle East NATO conference at the UN mission on Cyprus in three weeks. It's both a show of unity and a way of giving the President's men time to find a replacement who will be acceptable to the Congress. Then he leaves for 'pressing personal reasons,' the main one being his frustration with the National Security Council, which continues to undercut him."

"Has he explained that to the President?" asked Lowell.

"According to my source, he has not," replied Varak. "As Mr. Mandel has pointed out, he's a rational man. He understands that it's easier and far better for the country to replace one person than an entire council of presidential advisers."

"Tragic," said Winters, "yet inevitable, I imagine. But how does the Secretary of State relate to Evan Kendrick? I fail to see the connection."

"It's in the symbol itself," said Eric Sundstrom. "He's got to understand its importance. Am I right, Milos?"

"Yes, sir. If Kendrick's convinced that it's crucial for the country to have a strong vice president who's perceived by our allies and enemies alike as a voice of reason within an imperial presidency—where the benign emperor frequently has no clothes—and that the world will breathe easier for it, then, in my judgment, he'll again make the difficult choice and be available."

"From all we've learned, I suppose he would," agreed Gideon Logan. "But who the hell is going to *convince* him of that?"

"The only man he'll listen to," said Milos Varak, wondering if he was about to sign a death warrant. "Emmanuel Weingrass."

Ann Mulcahy O'Reilly was a Washington secretary not easily disturbed. Over the years since she and Paddy moved down from Boston, she had worked for the bright and the unbright, the would-be good and the would-be thieves; nothing much surprised her anymore. But then she had never worked for anyone like Congressman Evan Kendrick. He was the all-time reluctant resident of Washington, its most persistently unwilling politician, and a perversely demurring hero. He had more ways to elude the ineluctable than a cat with nine lives to the cube, and he could vanish with the agility of the Invisible Man. Yet his proclivity for disappearing notwithstanding, the Congressman always left open lines of communication; he would either call in on a fairly regular basis or leave a number where he could be reached. However, for the past two days there had been no word from Kendrick and no number at which he could be found. Those two facts by themselves would not normally have alarmed Mrs. O'Reilly, but two others did: throughout the day—since nine-twenty that morning—neither the house in Virginia nor the home in Colorado could be reached by telephone. In both cases the operators in Virginia and Colorado reported disruptions of service, and that status was still unchanged at nearly seven o'clock in the evening. *That* disturbed Annie O'Reilly. So quite logically she picked up the phone and dialed her husband at police headquarters.

"O'Reilly," said the gruff voice. "Detective squad."

"Paddy, it's me."

"Hi, tiger. Do I get beef stew?"

"I'm still at the office."

"Good. I've got to talk to Evan. Manny called me a couple of days ago about some cockamamie license plates—"

"That's the point," interrupted Mrs. O'Reilly. "I want to talk to him, too, but it seems I can't." Annie told her husband about the strange coincidence of both the Congressman's phones in Virginia and Colorado being out of order simultaneously and that he had neither checked in with her for the past two days nor left an alternate number where she could reach him. "And that's not like him, Paddy."

"Call Congressional Security," said the detective firmly.

"In a pig's ass I will. You whisper that lad's name to Security all the bells go off, and you know what he thinks about those bells. He'd have my head in a basket if there's even a halfway decent explanation."

"What do you want *me* to do?"

"Can you take a quiet look-see over in Fairfax, darlin'?"

"Sure. I'll call Kearns in Arlington and have him send a radio car out there. What's the address again?"

"No, Paddy," said Mrs. O'Reilly quickly. "I can hear the bells already. That's the police."

"What the hell do you think I do for a living? Ballet?"

"I don't want the police involved, what with reports and all. The Agency's got guards out there and I could get my broadside in a wringer. I meant *you,* lover. You're a friend in the area who just happens to be a cop doing a favor for your wife, who just happens to be Kendrick's secretary."

"That's a lot of just-happens, tiger. . . . What the hell? I like beef stew."

"With extra potatoes, Paddy."

"And onions. Lots more onions."

"The biggest I can find—"

"I'm on my way."

"And, Paddy, if that shrinking violet has had both phones taken off the hook, you tell him I know about his girlfriend from Egypt and I just might leak it if he doesn't call me."

"What girlfriend from—"

"Button it," ordered Mrs. O'Reilly. "Manny let it drop yesterday when he was a mite squiffed and couldn't find his broth of a boy, either. Hurry along now. I'll wait for the call here."

"What about my beef stew?"

"I've got one frozen," lied the lass born Ann Mary Mulcahy.

Thirty-eight minutes later, after taking two wrong turns in the dark Virginia countryside, Detective First Grade O'Reilly found the road that led to Kendrick's house. It was a road he had traveled over exactly four times but never at night. Each trip had been made to see old Weingrass after he got out of the hospital

"Congressman Kendrick's office."

"Annie, let me do the talking," broke in the detective rapidly, softly. "And don't ask questions—"

"I know that tone of voice, Paddy, so I have to ask one. Is he all right?"

"There's no sign of him. His car's gone; he's not here."

"But others are—"

"No more questions, tiger, but I've got one for you, and by the saints you'd better be able to answer it."

"What?"

"Who's Evan's contact at the Agency?"

"He deals directly with the unit."

"*No.* Someone *else.* Higher up. There has to be *somebody*!"

"Wait a minute!" cried Annie, her voice rising. "Of course, there is. He just doesn't talk about him . . . a man named Payton. A month or so ago he told me that if this Payton ever called, I was to put him through immediately, and if Evan wasn't here I was to find him."

"You're sure he's with the CIA?"

"Yes, yes I am," said Mrs. O'Reilly thoughtfully. "One morning he called me from Colorado saying he needed this Payton's number and where I could find it in his desk—in the bottom drawer of his desk under a checkbook. It was a Langley exchange."

"Would it be there now?"

"I'll look. Hold on." The wait of no more than twenty seconds was nearly unbearable for the detective, made worse by the sight of the large brightly lighted house beyond the open gate. It was both an invitation and a target. "Paddy?"

"*Yes!*"

"I've *got* it."

"Give it to me. Quickly!" She did so, and O'Reilly issued an order that was not to be disobeyed. "Stay in the office until I call you or pick you up. *Understood?*"

"Is there a reason?"

"Let's say I don't know how far up, or down, or sideways, this kind of thing reaches, and I happen to like beef stew."

"Oh, my *God,*" whispered Annie.

O'Reilly did not hear his wife; he had disconnected the line and within seconds was dialing the number Annie had given him. After eight agonizing rings a woman's voice came over the phone. "Central Intelligence Agency, Mr. Payton's office."

"Are you his secretary?"

"No, sir, this is the reception desk. Mr. Payton has gone for the day."

"*Listen* to me, please," said the Washington detective with absolute control. "It's urgent that I reach Mr. Payton immediately. Whatever the regulations, they can be broken, can you understand me, girl? It's an emergency."

"Please identify yourself, sir."

"Hell's fire, I don't want to, but I will. I'm Lieutenant Patrick O'Reilly, Detective First Grade, District of Columbia Police Department. You've *got* to find him for me!"

Suddenly, startlingly, a male voice was on the line. "*O'Reilly?*" the man said. "Like in O'Reilly, the secretary of a certain congressman?"

"The same, sir. You don't answer your goddamned *phone*—excuse my language?"

"This is a trunk line to my apartment, Mr. O'Reilly. . . . You may switch systems, Operator."

"Thank you, sir." There was a snap over the phone.

"Yes, Mr. O'Reilly? We're alone now."

"I'm not. I'm in the company of six corpses thirty yards away from my car."

"*What?*"

"Get out here, Mr. Payton. Kendrick's house. And if you don't want headlines, call off any relieving unit that's heading here."

"Secure," said the stunned director of Special Projects. "The relief comes on at midnight; it's covered by the men inside."

"They're dead, too. They're all dead."

Mitchell Payton crouched beside the dead body of the guard nearest the gate, wincing under the beam of O'Reilly's flashlight. "Good *God,* he was so young. They're all so *young*!"

"*Were,* sir," said the detective flatly. "There's no one alive, outside or inside. I've turned off most of the lights, but I'll escort you through, of course."

"I must . . . of course."

"But I won't unless you tell me where Congressman Kendrick is—*if* he is, or whether he was supposed to be here, which would mean he probably *isn't.* I can and obviously should call the Fairfax police. Am I clear, sir?"

"Gaelically clear, Lieutenant. For the time being this *must* remain an Agency problem—a catastrophe, if you like. Am *I* clear?"

"Answer my question or rest assured I'll do my sworn duty and call Fairfax headquarters. *Where* is Congressman Kendrick? His car's not here and I want to know whether I should be relieved by that fact or not."

"If you can find any relief in this situation, you're a very strange man—"

"I mourn these people, these strangers to me, as I've mourned hundreds like 'em in my time, but I *know* Evan Kendrick! Now, if you have the information, I want it this very moment or I go to my vehicle and radio my report to the police in Fairfax."

"For God's sake, *don't* you threaten me, Lieutenant. If you want to know where Kendrick is, ask your wife!"

"My *wife*?"

"The Congressman's secretary, in case it's slipped your mind."

"You fancy *rumbugger*!" exploded Paddy. "Why the hell do you think I'm out here? To pay a two-toilet social call on my old society chum, the millionaire from Colorado? I'm here, Chauncy-boyo, because Annie hasn't heard from Evan in two days, and since nine o'clock this morning both his phone here *and* in Mesa Verde don't ring! Now, that's what you might call a coincidence, *isn't* it!"

"Both his telephones—" Payton snapped his head around, peering above.

"Don't bother," said O'Reilly, following the director's gaze. "One line's been cut and expertly spliced into another; the thick cable to the roof's intact."

"Good *Christ*!"

"In my opinion, you need His immediate help. . . . *Kendrick!* Where the hell *is* he?"

"The Bahamas. Nassau, in the Bahamas."

"Why did you think my wife, his *secretary,* knew that? And you'd better have a good goddamned reason for thinking so, *Dan Fancy,* because if this is some kind of spook shit to involve Annie Mulcahy in one of your fuck-ups, I'll have more blue jackets swarming around here than you got in Eyeran!"

"I thought so because he told me, Lieutenant O'Reilly," said Payton, his voice cold, his eyes straying, his thoughts apparently racing.

"He never told *her*!"

"Obviously," agreed the CIA director, now staring at the house. "However, he was explicit. The day before yesterday he said that on the way to the airport he would stop at his office and leave the information with his secretary, Ann O'Reilly. He stopped; he went up to his office; the mobile unit confirmed it."

"What time was that?"

"Around four-thirty, if I remember the mobile's logs."

"Wednesday?"

"Yes."

"Annie wasn't there. Every Wednesday she leaves at four o'clock in the afternoon and Kendrick knows it. It's her crazy aerobics class!"

"He obviously forgot."

"Not likely. Come with me, sir."

"I beg your pardon?"

"Out to my car."

"We have work to do here, Lieutenant, and I have several calls to make—from *my* car. Alone."

"You're not doing a damn thing until I speak to Congressman Kendrick's secretary." Sixty-five seconds later with Payton standing by the open door, the voice of Patrick O'Reilly's wife came over the cellular phone's speaker.

"Congressman Kendrick's—"

"Annie," interrupted her husband. "After you left the office Wednesday afternoon, who was there?"

"Only Phil Tobias. It's slow these days; the girls left earlier."

"Phil who?"

"Tobias. He's Evan's chief aide and washer of the bottles."

"He never said anything to you, yesterday or today? About seeing Kendrick, I mean."

"He hasn't been here, Paddy. He didn't show up today *or* yesterday. I left half a dozen messages on his answering machine but I haven't heard from him, the high-hog PR brat that he is."

"I'll talk to you later, tiger. Stay where you are. *Understood?*" O'Reilly replaced the phone and turned in the seat, looking up at the man from the Central Intelligence Agency. "You heard, sir. I think that an apology from yours truly is in order. You have it, Mr. Payton."

"I neither seek it nor want it, Lieutenant. We've botched up so damned much in Langley that if someone thinks that his wife may be caught in one of our bungles, I can't fault him for telling us off."

"I'm afraid that was it. . . . Who goes after Tobias? You or me?"

"I can't deputize you, O'Reilly. There's no provision for it in the law and, frankly, there are specific provisions against it, but

I can ask for your help, and I desperately need it. I can cover for tonight on the basis of genuine national security; you're off the hook for not reporting. But where this Tobias is concerned I can only plead."

"For what?" asked the detective, getting out of the car and quietly closing the door.

"To keep me informed."

"You don't have to plead for that—"

"Before any official report is released," added Payton.

"That you've got to plead for," said Paddy, studying the director. "To begin with, I couldn't guarantee it. If he's spotted in Switzerland or floats up in the Potomac, I wouldn't necessarily know about it."

"We're obviously thinking along the same lines. However, you have what's referred to as clout, Lieutenant. Forgive me, but I've had to learn about everyone around Evan Kendrick. The District of Columbia Police Department virtually bribed you to come to Washington twelve years ago from Boston—"

"Grade pay, nothing shady."

"Grade pay nearly equivalent to chief of detectives, a position you turned down four years ago because you didn't want the desk."

"Holy Jesus—"

"I've had to be thorough. . . . And since your wife works for the Congressman, I believe a man in your position could insist on being informed if and when anything relevant to Phillip Tobias comes down, as he also works, or worked, in Kendrick's office."

"I suppose I could, that's my girl. But it leads me to a question or two."

"Go right ahead. Any questions you have may help me."

"Why is Evan in the Bahamas?"

"I sent them there."

"Them? The Egyptian woman? . . . Old Weingrass told my wife."

"She works for us; she was part of Oman. There's a man in Nassau who fronted a company that Kendrick was briefly associated with years ago. He's not terribly reputable and neither was the firm, but we felt he was worth checking out."

"For what purpose?"

The director of Special Projects looked over the roof of the car at Evan Kendrick's house, at the now dimly lit windows and what they held beyond the glass. "All that will come later,

O'Reilly. I won't hold anything back, I promise you. But from what you've described to me I have work to do. I have to reach the shroud squad and that can only be done at my car."

"The *shroud* squad? What the hell is that?"

"A group of men neither of us would care to be a part of. They pick up corpses they can never testify about, forensically examine evidence they've been sworn not to reveal. They're necessary and I respect every one of them, but I wouldn't *be* one of them."

Suddenly, the staccato, grating ring of the detective's cellular telephone erupted. It had been tripped to *Emergency,* the sound echoing throughout the still, cold night, bouncing off the brick wall, each echo receding into the woods beyond. O'Reilly yanked open the door and grabbed the phone, pulling it to his ear. "*Yes?*"

"Oh, *Jesus,* Paddy!" screamed Ann Mulcahy O'Reilly, her voice amplified over the speaker. "They *found* him! They found *Phil*! He was down under the boilers in the basement. Good *Christ,* Paddy! They say his *throat* was cut! Jesus, Mary, and Joseph, he's *dead,* Paddy!"

"When you say 'they,' *exactly* who do you mean, tiger?"

"Harry and Sam from night maintenance—they just reached me, scared out of their skins, and told me to call the police!"

"You just *did,* Annie. Tell them to stay where they are. They're not to touch anything or say anything until I get there! Understood?"

"Not *say* anything . . . ?"

"It's a quarantine, I'll explain later. Now call C-Security and have five men armed with shotguns posted outside the office. Say your husband's a police officer and *he* made the request because of personal threats against *him. Understood?*"

"Yes, Paddy," replied Mrs. O'Reilly, in tears. "Oh, holy Jesus, he's *dead*!"

The detective spun around in the seat. The CIA director was running to his car.

28

It was four-seventeen in the afternoon, Colorado time, and Emmanuel Weingrass's patience had run out. It had been close to eleven o'clock in the morning when he personally discovered that the phone was not working, subsequently learning that two of the nurses had known it several hours earlier when they tried to place calls. One of the girls had driven into Mesa Verde to use the grocery store phone and report the disruption of service to the telephone company; she returned with the assurance that the problem would be repaired as soon as possible. "Possible" had now dragged out over five hours, and that was unacceptable to Manny. A renowned congressman—to say nothing of the national hero that he was—demanded far better treatment; it was an affront Weingrass had no intention of tolerating. And although he said nothing to his coven of witches, he had bad thoughts—disturbing thoughts.

"Hear this, you prognosticators for the Thane of Cawdor!" he shouted at the top of his lungs on the glass-enclosed veranda at the two nurses playing gin rummy.

"What in heaven's name are you talking about, Manny?" asked the third from a chair by the arch in the living room, lowering her newspaper.

"Macbeth, you illiterate. I'm laying down the law!"

"The law's the only thing you could handle in that department, Methuselah. . . . *Gin!*"

"So little you know about the Bible, Miss Erudite. . . . I will not remain beyond reach of the outside world any longer. One of you will either drive me into town, where I can call the president of this meshugenah telephone company or I will urinate all over the kitchen."

"You'll be in a straitjacket first," said one of the girls playing cards.

"Wait a minute," countered her partner. "He can call the Congressman and *he* could put on some pressure. I *really* have to reach Frank. He's flying out tomorrow—I told you—and I haven't been able to make a reservation at the motel in Cortez."

"I'm for it," said the nurse in the living room. "He can call from Abe Hawkins's grocery store."

"Knowing you dears, sex will out," said Manny. "But we call from the phone in Gee-Gee's office. I don't trust anyone named Abraham. He probably sold weapons to the Ayatollah and forgot to make a profit. . . . I'll just get a sweater and my jacket."

"I'll drive," offered the nurse in the living room, dropping the newspaper beside the chair and rising. "Put on your overcoat, Manny. It's cold and there's a strong wind from the mountains."

Weingrass muttered a minor epithet as he passed the woman and headed for his bedroom in the south wing of the first floor.

Once out of sight in the stone hallway, he hastened his pace; he had more to retrieve than a sweater. Inside his large room, redesigned by him to include sliding glass doors across the south wall opening onto a flagstone terrace, he walked rapidly to the highboy, grabbing and dragging a chair from his desk to the tall dresser. Cautiously, holding on to the knobs, he climbed on the chair, reached over the curlicued top of the imposing piece of furniture and removed a shoe box. He lowered himself back to the floor, carried the box to the bed and opened it, revealing a .38 caliber automatic and three clips of shells.

The concealment was necessary. Evan had given orders that his shotgun case be locked and all ammunition removed, and that no handguns be permitted in the house. The reason had been too painful for either man to bring up: Kendrick believed with more logic than less that if his old friend thought the cancer had returned, he would take his own life. But for Emmanuel Weingrass, after the life he had led, to be without a weapon was anathema to him. Gee-Gee Gonzalez had remedied the situation, and Manny had only once smashed open the shotgun case and that was when the media had descended on them pissing all over the grounds.

He slapped in one clip, put the other two in his pockets, and carried the chair back to the desk. He went to his closet, took a long, heavy-knit sweater from the shelf and slipped it on; it covered the protrusions effectively. He then did something he had not done since the redesigned room had been built, not even when the reporters and the television crews had assaulted them. He inspected the locks on the sliding doors, crossed to a red switch hidden behind the drapes, and turned on the alarm. He walked out of the bedroom, closing the door, and joined the nurse in the front hall; she was holding his overcoat for him.

"That's a handsome sweater, Manny."

"I got it on sale in a Monte Carlo *après-ski* shop."

"Do you always have to have a flip answer?"

"No kidding, it's true."

"Here, put on your coat."

"I look like a Hasid in that thing."

"A what?"

"Heidi in the edelweiss."

"Oh, no, I think it's very masculine—"

"Oy, let's get out of here." Weingrass started for the door, then stopped. *"Girls!"* he shouted, his voice carrying to the veranda.

"Yes, Manny?"

"*What?*"

"Please listen to me, ladies, I'm serious. I'd feel much more comfortable, what with the phone being out, if you would please turn on the main alarm. Humor me, my lovelies. I'm a foolish old man to you, I realize that, but I really would feel better if you did this for me."

"How sweet of him—"

"Of course we will, Manny."

That humble crap always works, thought Weingrass, continuing toward the door. "Come on, hurry up," he said to the nurse behind him who was struggling with her parka. "I want to get to Gee-Gee's before that phone company closes up for the month."

The winds from the mountains *were* strong; the trek from the massive front door to Kendrick's Saab Turbo halfway down the circular drive was made by leaning into the gusts. Manny shielded his face with his left hand, his head turned to the right, when suddenly the wind and his discomfort became irrelevant. At first he thought that the swirling leaves and erratic pockets of dust were distorting his still-viable eyesight—and then he knew it was not so. There was movement, *human* movement, beyond the tall hedges that fronted the road. A figure had rushed to the right, lurching to the ground behind a particularly thick area of the foliage. . . . Then another! This one following the first and going farther.

"You okay, Manny?" shouted the nurse as they approached the car.

"This stuff is kindergarten compared with the passes in the Maritime Alps!" yelled back Weingrass. "Get in. *Hurry up.*"

"Oh, I'd love to see the Alps someday!"

"So would I," mumbled Weingrass, climbing into the Saab, his right hand unobtrusively slipping under the overcoat and the sweater to reach his automatic. He pulled it out and lowered it between the seat and the door as the nurse inserted the key and started the engine. "When you get to the road, turn left," he said.

"No, Manny, you're wrong. The quickest way to Mesa Verde is to the right."

"I know that, lovely thing, but I still want you to turn left."

"Manny, if you're trying to *pull* something at your age I'm going to be furious!"

"Just turn left, drive around the curve, and stop."

"*Mister* Weingrass, if you think for an *instant*—"

"I'm getting out," broke in the old architect quietly. "I don't want to alarm you, and I'll explain everything later, but right now you're going to do exactly as I tell you. . . . *Please.* Drive." The astonished nurse did not understand Manny's soft-spoken words but she understood the look in his eyes. There were no theatrics, no bombast; he was simply giving her an order. "Thank you," he continued, as she drove out between the wall of tall hedges and swung left. "I want you to take the Mancos road back into Verde—"

"That'll add at least ten minutes—"

"I know, but it's what I want you to do. Go directly to Gee-Gee's as fast as you can and tell him to call the police—"

"*Manny!*" cried the nurse, interrupting as she tightly gripped the wheel.

"I'm sure it's nothing at all," said Weingrass quickly, reassuringly. "Probably just someone whose car broke down or a hiker who's lost. Nevertheless, it's better to check these things out, don't you think?"

"I don't know *what* to think, but I'm certainly not letting you out of this car!"

"Yes, you will," disagreed Manny, casually raising the automatic as if studying the trigger housing, no threat at all in his action.

"Good *God*!" yelled the nurse.

"I'm perfectly safe, my dear, because I'm a cautious man to the point of cowardice. . . . Stop here, please." The near-panicked woman did as she was told, her frightened eyes shifting rapidly back and forth between the weapon and the old man's face. "Thank you," said Weingrass, opening the door, the sound of the wind sudden, powerful. "I'll probably find our harmless visitor inside having coffee with the girls," he added, stepping out and closing the door by pressing it shut. Wheels spinning, the Saab raced away. No matter, thought Manny, the gusts of wind covered the sound.

As it also covered whatever sounds he made heading back toward the house, unavoidable sounds, as he stayed out of sight on the border of the road, his feet cracking the fallen branches at the edge of the woods. He was as grateful for the racing dark clouds above in the sky as he was for the dark overcoat; both kept his being seen to a minimum. Five minutes later and several yards deeper into the woods, he stood by a thick tree at midpoint opposite the wall of hedges. He again shielded his face from the wind and, squinting, peered across the road.

They were there! And they were not lost. His disturbing thoughts had been valid. And rather than being lost the intruders were waiting—for something or someone. Both men wore leather jackets and were crouched in front of the hedges talking rapidly to each other, the man on the right constantly, impatiently glancing at his wristwatch. Weingrass did not have to be told what that meant; they were waiting for someone or *more* than someone. Awkwardly, feeling his age physically but not in his imagination, Manny lowered himself to the ground and began prowling around on his hands and knees, not sure what he was looking for but knowing he had to find it, whatever it was.

It was a thick, heavy limb newly blown down by the wind, sap still oozing from the shards where it had been snapped from a larger source in the trunk. It was about forty inches long; it was swingable. Slowly, more awkwardly and painfully, the old man rose to his feet and made his way back to the tree where he had been standing, diagonally across the road from the two intruders no more than fifty feet away.

It was a gamble, but then so was what was left of his life, and the odds were infinitely better than they were at roulette or chemin de fer. The results, too, would be known more quickly, and the gambler in Emmanuel Weingrass was willing to place a decent bet that one of the intruders would stay where he was out of basic common sense. The aged architect moved back in the woods, selecting his position as carefully as if he were refining a final blueprint for the most important client of his life. He was; the client was himself. *Make total use of the natural surroundings* had been axiomatic with him all his professional life; he did not veer from that rule now.

There were two poplars, both wide and about seven feet apart forming an abstract forest gate. He concealed himself behind the trunk on the right, gripped the heavy limb and raised it until it leaned against the bark above his head. The wind careened through the trees, and through the multiple sounds of the forest he opened his mouth and roared a short singsong chant, one-third human, two-thirds animal. He craned his neck and watched.

Between the trunks and the lower foliage, he could see the startled figures across the road. Both men spun around in their crouching positions, the man on the right gripping his companion's shoulder, apparently—*hopefully,* prayed Manny—issuing orders. He *had.* The man on the left got to his feet, pulled a gun from inside his jacket, and started for the forest across the road to Mesa Verde.

Everything was timing now. Timing and direction, the brief, seductive sounds leading the quarry into the fatal sea of green as surely as the sirens lured Ulysses. Twice more Weingrass emitted the eerie calls, and then a third that was so pronounced that the intruder rushed forward, slapping branches in front of him, his weapon leveled, his feet digging into the soft earth—toward and finally into the forest gate.

Manny pulled back on the thick, heavy limb and swung it with all his strength down and across into the head of the racing man. The face was shattered, blood spurting out of every feature, the skull a mass of broken bone and cartilage. The man was dead. Breathlessly, Weingrass walked out from behind the trunk and knelt down.

The man was an Arab.

The winds from the mountains continued their assault. Manny pulled the gun from the corpse's still-warm hand and, even more awkwardly, far more painfully, edged his way back toward the road. The dead intruder's companion was a wild core of misdirected energy; he kept spinning his head toward the woods, toward the road from Mesa Verde and down at his watch. The only thing he had not done was display a weapon, and that told Weingrass something else. The terrorist—and he *was* a terrorist; *both* were terrorists—was either a rank amateur or a thorough professional, nothing in between.

Feeling the pounding echo in his frail chest, Manny permitted himself a few moments to breathe, but only moments. The opportunity might not come again. He moved north, from tree trunk to tree trunk, until he was sixty feet above the anxious man, who kept glancing south. Again timing; Weingrass walked as fast as he could across the road and stood motionless, watching. The would-be killer was now close to apoplectic; twice he started into the road toward the woods, both times returning to the hedges and crouching, staring at his watch. Manny moved forward, his automatic gripped in his veined right hand. When he was within ten feet of the terrorist, he shouted.

"*Jezzar!*" he roared, calling the man a butcher in Arabic. "If you move, you're dead! *Fahem?*"

The dark-skinned man spun around, clawing the earth as he rolled into the hedges, loose dirt flying up into the old architect's face. Through the hurling debris, Weingrass understood why the terrorist had not displayed a weapon; it was on the ground beside him, inches from his hand. Manny fell to his left on the road as the man grabbed the gun, now lunging backward, enmeshing himself in prickly green web, and fired twice; the reports were barely heard! They were two eerily muted spits in the wind; a silencer was attached to the terrorist's pistol. The bullets, however, were not silent; one shrieked through the air above Weingrass, the second ricocheted off the cement near his head. Manny raised his automatic and pulled the trigger, the calm of experience, despite the years, steadying his hand. The terrorist screamed through the rushing wind and collapsed forward in the hedges, his eyes wide, a rivulet of blood trickling from the base of his throat.

Hurry up, you decrepit bastard! cried Weingrass to himself, struggling to his feet. *They were waiting for someone! You want to be a senile ugly duck in a gallery? Your meshugenah head blown off would serve you right. Shush! Every bone is boiling in pain!* Manny lurched toward the body wedged in the hedges. He bent down, pulled the corpse forward, then gripped the man's feet, and, grimacing, using every iota of strength that was in him, dragged the body across the road and into the woods.

He wanted only to lie on the ground and rest, to let the hammering in his chest subside and swallow air, but he knew he could not do that. He had to keep going; he had to be ready; above all, he had to take someone alive. These people were after his *son*! Information had to be learned . . . all manner of death to follow.

He heard the sound of an engine in the distance . . . and then the sound disappeared. Bewildered, he sidestepped slowly, cautiously, between the trees to the edge of the woods and peered out. A car was coming up the road from Mesa Verde, but it was either idling or coasting, or the wind was too strong. It was *coasting,* for now only the rolling tires could be heard as it approached the wall of tall hedges, barely moving, finally stopping before the first entrance to the circular drive. Two men were inside; the driver, a stocky man, not young but not much over forty, got out first and looked around, obviously expecting to be met or signaled. He squinted in the dark afternoon light and, seeing no one, crossed the road to the wooded side and started walking forward. Weingrass shoved his automatic into his belt and bent down for the second killer's pistol with the perforated silencer attached to the barrel. It was too large for a pocket, so, like the Arab, he placed it at his feet. He stood up and stepped farther back into the overgrowth; he checked the weapon's cylinder. There were four bullets left. The man approached; he was now directly in front of Manny.

"*Yosef!*" The name was suddenly carried on the wind, half shouted by the driver's companion, who had left the car and was racing down the road, his quickening steps impeded by a pronounced limp. Manny was perplexed; Yosef was a Hebrew name, yet these killers were not Israelis.

"Be *quiet,* boy!" commanded the older man gruffly in Arabic as his partner stopped breathlessly in front of him. "You raise your voice like that again—*anywhere*—I'll ship you back to the Baaka in a coffin!"

Weingrass watched and listened to the two men no more than twenty feet away on the edge of the road. He was mildly astonished, but now understood the use of the Arabic word, *walad,* or "boy." The driver's companion *was* a boy, a youngster barely sixteen or seventeen, if that.

"You'll send me nowhere!" answered the young man angrily, a speech impediment obvious, undoubtedly a harelip. "I'll never walk properly again because of that pig! I could have become a great martyr of our holy cause but for *him*!"

"Very well, very well," said the older Arab with a Hebrew name, not without a degree of compassion. "Throw cool water on your neck or your head will explode. Now, what is it?"

"The American radio! I just heard it and I understand enough to—understand!"

"Our people at the other *house*?"

"No, nothing like that. The *Jews*! They executed old Khouri. They *hanged* him!"

"What did you expect, Aman? Forty years ago he was still working with the German Nazis left in northern Africa. He killed Jews; he blew up kibbutzim, even a hotel in Haifa."

"Then we must kill the murderer, Begin, and all the old men of the Irgun and the Stern! Khouri was a symbol of greatness for us—"

"Oh, be quiet, boy. Those old men fought the British more than they did us. They, *or* old Khouri, have nothing to do with what we must do today. We must teach a lesson to a filthy politician who pretended to be one of us. He hid in our clothes and used our tongue and betrayed the friendship we offered him. *Now,* boy! Concentrate on *now.*"

"Where are the others? They were to come out on the road."

"I don't know. They may have learned something or seen something and gone inside the house. Lights are being turned on now; you can see through those high bushes. Each of us will crawl up from either side of the half-circle entrance. Go through the grass to the windows. We will probably learn that our comrades are having coffee with whoever is there before slicing their throats."

Emmanuel Weingrass raised the silenced pistol, firming it against the trunk of a tree, moving it back and forth between the two terrorists. He wanted both *alive*! The words in Arabic referring to the "other house" so shocked him that in fury he might well blow both their heads away. They wanted to kill his *son*! If they *had* they would pay dearly, in agony—misguided youth or age irrelevant. Terrible pain would be the only consequence. He leveled the weapon at the pelvic region of both killers, back and forth, back and forth. . . .

He fired just as a sudden gust of wind swirled along the road, two rounds into the older man, one into the boy. It was as if neither could possibly comprehend. The child collapsed screaming, writhing on the ground; his elder companion was made of stronger—*much* stronger—stuff. He staggered to his feet, turning to the source of fire, and lurched forward, the stocky hulk a furious monster in pain.

"Don't come any closer, *Yosef*!" yelled Manny, exhausted almost beyond endurance and holding on to the tree. "I don't want to kill you, but I will! *You* of the Hebrew name who kills *Jews*!"

"My *mother*!" screamed the approaching giant of a man. "She renounced *all* of you! You are killers of my *people*! You take everything that is ours and *spit* on us! I am half Jew, but who are the *Jews* to kill my father and shave the head of my mother because she loved an *Arab*? I will take you to *hell*!"

Weingrass held on to the trunk of the tree, his fingernails bleeding as he dug into the bark, his long black overcoat billowing in the wind. The broad, dark figure lunged out of the forest darkness, his enormous hands gripping the old man's throat.

"*Don't!*" screamed Manny, knowing instantly that there was no choice. He fired the last shell, the bullet penetrating the wrinkled forehead above him. Yosef fell away, his final gesture one of defiance. Trembling and gasping for breath, Weingrass leaned against the tree, staring down at the ground, at the body of a man who had been in torment over an insignificant territorial arrangement that forced humans to kill each other. In that moment, Emmanuel Weingrass came to a conclusion that had eluded him from the moment he was capable of thinking; he knew the answer now. The arrogance of blind belief led all the mendacities of human thought. It pitted man viciously against man in the pursuit of the ultimate unknowable. Who had the *right*?

"Yosef . . . *Yosef,*" cried the boy, rolling over in the underbrush by the edge of the road. "Where are you? I'm hit, I'm *hit*!"

The child did not know, thought Weingrass. From where the wounded boy lay writhing he could not see, and the wind from the mountains further muffled the muted gunshot. The maniacal young terrorist did not realize that his comrade Yosef was dead, that he alone had survived. And his survival was uppermost in Manny's mind; there could be no new martyr for a holy cause brought on by self-inflicted death. Not here, not now; there were facts to be learned, facts that could save the life of Evan Kendrick. *Especially* now!

Weingrass shoved his bleeding fingers into his overcoat pocket and dropped the silenced weapon on the ground. Summoning what strength he had left, he pushed himself away from the tree and made his way as quickly as he could south through the woods, stumbling again and again, his frail arms pushing the branches from his face and body. He veered toward the road; he reached it and saw the killer's car in the darkening distance. He had gone far enough. He turned and started back on the mercifully smooth surface—*faster . . . faster! Move your goddamned spindly legs! That boy must not move, he must not crawl, he must not see!* Manny felt the blood rushing to his head, the pounding in his rib cage deafening. *There* was the young Arab! He *had* moved—was moving, crawling into the woods. In moments he would see his dead companion! It could not happen!

"*Aman!*" shouted Weingrass breathlessly, remembering the name used by the half-Jew, Yosef, as if it were his own. "*Ayn ent? Kaif el-ahwal?*" he continued in Arabic, urgently asking the boy where he was and how he was. "*Itkallem!*" he roared against the wind, ordering the young terrorist to respond.

"Here, in here!" yelled the teenage Arab in his own language. "I've been shot! In the hip. I can't find Yosef!" The young man rolled over on his back to greet an expected comrade. "*Who are you?*" he screamed, struggling to reach under his field jacket for a gun as Manny approached. "I don't *know* you!"

Weingrass smashed his foot against the boy's elbow, and as the empty hand whipped out from under the cloth he stepped on it, pinning it to the young Arab's chest. "No more of that, you fool of a child!" said Manny, his Arabic that of a Saudi officer reprimanding a lowly recruit. "We haven't covered you to have you cause even *more* trouble. Of course you were shot, and I trust you realize that you were merely wounded, not killed, which could have been easily managed!"

"What are you *saying*?"

"What were you *doing*?" shouted Manny in reply. "Running in the road, raising your voice, crawling around our objective like a thief in the night! Yosef was right, you should be shipped back to the Baaka."

"*Yosef?* . . . Where *is* Yosef?"

"Up in the house with the others. Come, I'll help you. Join them." Afraid of falling over, Weingrass held on to the branch of a sapling as the terrorist pulled himself up, gripping Manny's hand. "First, give me your weapon!"

"*What?*"

"They think you're stupid enough. They don't want you armed."

"I don't *understand—*"

"You don't have to." Weingrass slapped the bewildered young fanatic across the face and simultaneously shoved his right hand between the buttoned fold of the boy's jacket to pull out the would-be killer's gun. It was appropriate; it was a .22 caliber pistol. "You can shoot gnats with this," said Manny, grabbing the teenager's arm. "Come along. Hop on one foot if it's easier. We'll paste you up."

What remained of the late afternoon sun was obscured by the swirling dark clouds of a gathering storm surging out of the mountains. The drained, exhausted old man and the wounded youngster were halfway across the road when suddenly the roar of an engine was heard and headlights of a racing automobile caught them in the beams. The car was bearing down on them, thundering up from the south out of Mesa Verde. Tires shrieking, the powerful vehicle side-slipped into a skid and pounded to a stop only yards away from Weingrass and his captive, who were lunging toward the hedges, Manny's grip tightening on the Arab's field jacket. A man leaped from the large black sedan as Weingrass—lurching, stumbling—reached into his overcoat pocket for his own .38 automatic. The figure rushing toward him was a blur in the old architect's eyes; he raised his gun to fire.

"*Manny!*" yelled Gee-Gee Gonzalez.

Weingrass fell to the ground, his hand still gripping the wounded terrorist. "*Grab* him!" he ordered Gee-Gee with what seemed like the last breath in his lungs. "Don't let him go—hold his *arms*. They sometimes carry cyanide!"

* * *

The young Arab was given a needle by one of the two nurses; he would be unconscious until morning. His bullet wound was bloody, not serious, the bullet itself having passed through the flesh; it was cleansed, the openings butterflied with heavy tape and the bleeding stopped. He was then carried by Gonzalez to a guest room, his arms and legs strapped to the four corners of the bed, where the nurses covered his naked body with two blankets to help prevent conceivable trauma.

"He's so terribly young," said the nurse placing the pillow under the teenage Arab's head.

"He's a killer," responded Weingrass icily, staring at the terrorist's face. "He'd kill you without thinking for an instant about the life he was taking—the way he wants to kill Jews. The way he *will* kill us if we let him live."

"That's revolting, Mr. Weingrass," said the other nurse. "He's a child."

"Tell that to the parents of God knows how many Jewish children who were never permitted his years." Manny left the room to rejoin Gonzalez, who had hastily gone outside to drive his all too recognizable car into a garage; he had returned and was pouring himself a large glass of whisky at the bar on the veranda.

"Help yourself," said the architect, walking into the enclosed porch and heading for his leather armchair. "I'll put it on your bill like you do with me."

"You crazy old man!" spat out Gee-Gee. "*Loco!* You plain *loco;* you know that? You coulda been killed! *Muerto!* You *comprende*? *Muerto, muerto*—dead, dead, *dead,* you old fool! Maybe that I could live with, but not when you give me a heart attack! I don't live so good with a heart attack when it's fatal, you *comprende,* you know what I mean?"

"Okay, okay. So you can have that drink on the house—"

"*Loco!*" shouted Gonzalez again, drinking the whisky in what appeared to be a single swallow.

"You've made your point," agreed Manny. "Have another. I won't start charging until the third."

"I don't know whether to go or whether to stay!" said Gee-Gee, once more pouring a drink.

"The police?"

"Like I told you, who had time for the *police*? And if *I* called them, they'd come around in a month! . . . Your girl, the *ama de cría*—the nurse—she's calling them. I only hope she found one of those *payasos.* Sometimes you gotta call Durango to get someone out here."

The phone on the bar rang—it *rang,* but it was not the ring of a telephone; instead it was a steady whir-toned sound. Weingrass was so startled that he nearly fell to the floor pushing himself out of the chair.

"You want me to get it?" asked Gonzalez.

"No!" roared Manny, walking rapidly, unsteadily, toward the bar.

"Don't bite off my *cabeza.*"

"Hello?" said the old man into the phone, forcing control on himself.

"Mr. Weingrass?"

"Perhaps yes, perhaps no. Who are you?"

"We're on a laser patch into your telephone line. My name is Mitchell Payton—"

"I know all about you," interrupted Manny. "Is my boy all *right*?"

"Yes, he is. I've just spoken to him in the Bahamas. A military aircraft has been dispatched from Homestead Air Force Base to pick him up. He'll be in Washington in a few hours."

"*Keep* him there! Surround him with guards! Don't let anyone *near* him!"

"Then it's happened out there? . . . I feel so useless, so incompetent. I should have posted guards. . . . How many were killed?"

"Three," said Manny.

"Oh, my *God.* . . . How much do the police know?"

"They don't. They haven't got here yet."

"They *haven't.* . . . Listen to me, Mr. Weingrass. What I'm about to say will appear strange if not insane to you, but I know what I'm talking about. For the time being, this tragic event *must* be contained. We'll have a far greater chance to catch the bastards by avoiding panic and letting our own experts go to work. *Can* you understand that, Mr. Weingrass?"

"Understood and arranged," answered an old man who had worked with the Mossad, a certain impatient condescension creeping into his voice. "The police will be met outside and told it was a false alarm—a neighbor whose car had broken down and couldn't reach us on the phone, that's all."

"I forgot," said the director of Special Project quietly. "You've been here before."

"I've been here," agreed Manny, without comment.

"Wait a minute!" exclaimed Payton. "You said three were dead, but you're talking to me, you're *all right.*"

"The three were *them,* not us, Mr. CIA Incompetent."

"*What?* . . . Jesus *Christ*!"

"He wasn't much help. Try Abraham."

"Please be *clearer,* Mr. Weingrass."

"I had to kill them. But the fourth's alive and under sedation. Get your experts out here before I kill him, too."

29

The CIA station chief in the Bahamas, a short, deeply tanned man with broad features, maneuvered quickly from his office at the embassy on Queen Street. An armed escort was sent by the Nassau police to the Cable Beach Hotel, on the shores of Bay Road, where four uniformed officers rapidly accompanied a tall man with light brown hair and a striking olive-skinned woman from their suite on the seventh floor to a waiting vehicle in the efficiently emptied drive outside the imposing marble lobby. The hotel's director of operations, an alert Scotsman named McLeod, had mapped out a route through the service corridors, where his most trusted security guards stood watch, to the brightly lighted entrance fronted by two enormous fountains sending floodlit sprays up into the dark sky. McLeod's two assistants—an immense good-humored man with a booming laugh and the improbable name of Vernal, accompanied by an attractive young hostess—courteously explained to arrivals and departures that their delays would be brief. They persuasively explained while the five-man motorcycle unit swept the dramatically shadowed grounds. The station chief had personalized everything; favors were done for him. He knew by name everyone there was to know in the Bahamas. And they knew him. In silence.

Evan and Khalehla, shielded by the wall of police, climbed into the government vehicle, the CIA man in the front seat. Kendrick was beyond talking; Khalehla could only grip his hand, knowing only too well what he was experiencing. Clarity of thought eluded him; burning sorrow and a furious anger had replaced it. Tears had welled in his eyes over the deaths of Kashi and Sabri Hassan; he did not have to be told of the mutilations, he could easily, horribly imagine what they were. Yet those tears had been quickly, impulsively wiped away by a clenched fist. A reckoning was coming—that, too, was in his eyes, in the cores of his pupils. *Fury.*

"As you can understand, Congressman," said the station chief, turning partially around in the seat beside the driver. "I don't know what's going on, but I can tell you that a plane from Holmstead Air Force Base in Florida is on its way to take you back to Washington. It should arrive about five or ten minutes after we get to the airport."

"We know that," said Khalehla pleasantly.

"It would have been here by now, but they said there's rotten weather out of Miami and several commercial flights are on the same route. That probably means they wanted to stock up the aircraft properly for you, sir—I mean the two of you, of course."

"That's most kind of them," said the field agent from Cairo, squeezing Evan's hand, conveying the fact that he did not have to speak.

"If there's anything you think you might have left behind at the hotel, we'll gladly take care of it—"

"There's *nothing,*" exclaimed Kendrick, whispering harshly.

"He means we've taken care of everything, thank you," said Khalehla, pulling Evan's hand against her leg and grasping it even more firmly. "This is obviously an emergency, and the Congressman has a great deal on his mind. May I assume we've been cleared through customs?"

"This parade is driving straight through the cargo gates," replied the government man, glancing briefly, closely at Kendrick, then turning away as if he had unwittingly invaded another's privacy. The rest of the trip was made in silence until the high steel gates of the cargo terminal swung open and the procession drove through over the tarmac to the end of the first runway. "The F-106 from Homestead should be landing soon," said the station chief.

"I'm getting out." Evan reached for the handle of the door and yanked it back. It was locked.

"I'd rather you didn't, Congressman Kendrick."

"Let me out of this car."

"Evan, it's his job." Khalehla gently but firmly held Kendrick's arm. "He has to go by the rules."

"Do they include suffocating me?"

"I'm breathing fine—"

"You're not *me*!"

"I know, darling. No one can be you right now." Rashad angled her head and looked out the rear window, scanning the terminal's buildings and the grounds. "Our status is as clean as it could be," she said, turning back to the intelligence officer. "Let him walk. I'll stay with him and so can the men."

"A 'clean status'? You're one of us?"

"Yes, but you've already forgotten me, *please.* . . . The flight to Washington's going to be rough enough."

"Sure. We're okay. The guy who made up this rule isn't here. He just said, 'Don't let him out of that vehicle,' in a very loud voice."

"MJ can be extreme."

"MJ . . . ? Come on, let's get some air. Release the doors, please, driver."

"Thank you," said Evan quietly to Khalehla. "And I'm *sorry—*"

"You don't have a damn thing to be sorry about. Just don't make a liar out of me and get shot. It could ruin my day. . . . Now, *I'm* sorry. It's no time for dumb wisecracks."

"Wait a minute." Kendrick began to open the door then stopped, his face inches from hers in the shadows. "A few moments ago you said that no one could be me right now and I agree. But that said, I'm awfully glad you're you. Right now."

They walked in a brief Bahamian drizzle, talking quietly, the CIA officer a polite distance behind, the guards flanking them with ominously drawn side arms. Suddenly, from out of the cargo area a small dark sedan came racing across the field, its high-pitched engine screaming. The guards converged on Evan and Khalehla, shoving them to the ground, the CIA officer throwing himself over Kendrick and pulling the Rashad woman into his side. As quickly as the panic started, it stopped. There were rapid blasts of a two-note siren; the car was an airport vehicle. The leader of the motorcycle escort holstered his weapon and approached the uniformed man who climbed out of the small sedan. They talked quietly and the police officer returned to the stunned Americans, who were getting to their feet.

"There is an emergency telephone call for your friend, sir," he said to the station chief.

"Patch it out here."

"We have no such equipment."

"I want something better than that."

"I was told to repeat the letters 'MJ.' "

"That's better enough," said Khalehla. "I'll go with him."

"Hey, come on," countered the CIA man. "There are other rules, too, and you know them as well as I do. It's a lot easier securing a single than a double. *I'll* go and take four men. You stay here with the others and cover for me, okay? This is the meeting ground and you could have a nervous pilot on your hands looking for some special luggage, mainly you."

The telephone was on the wall of a deserted warehouse. The call was transferred and the first words Kendrick heard from Mitchell Payton caused every muscle in his body to lock, his mind on fire.

"You've got to hear the worst. There was an assault on Mesa Verde—"

"Christ, *no*!"

"Emmanuel Weingrass is all right! He's all *right,* Evan."

"Is he *hurt*? *Wounded?*"

"No. In fact *he* did the wounding—the killing. One of the terrorists is still alive—"

"I *want* him!" shouted Kendrick.

"So do we. Our people are on the way out there."

"Mesa Verde was the terrorists' backup for Fairfax, wasn't it?"

"Unquestionably. But right now it's also our only hope in tracking down the others. Whatever that survivor knows, he'll tell us."

"Keep him alive."

"Your friend Weingrass has seen to it."

"Strip him for cyanide."

"It's been done."

"He can't be left alone for a minute!"

"We know that."

"Of course you do," said Evan, closing his eyes, his face drenched with sweat and rain. "I'm not thinking, I can't think. How's Manny taking it?"

"With considerable arrogance, to be truthful."

"That's the first decent news I've heard."

"You're entitled to it. He was truly remarkable for a man of his age."

"He was always remarkable . . . at any age. I've got to get out there. Forget Washington. Fly me directly to Colorado."

"I assumed you would make that request—"

"It's not a request, Mitch, it's a demand!"

"Of course. It's also the reason why your plane is delayed. The

Air Force has punched up the fueling for Denver and points west and is clearing a flight plan above the commercial routes. The aircraft has a maximum speed of Mach two point three. You'll be home in less than three hours, and remember, say nothing to anyone about Fairfax. Weingrass has already contained Mesa Verde."

"*How?*"

"Let him tell you."

"Do you really think you can keep everything quiet?"

"I will if I have to go to the President myself, and at this point I don't think there's any alternative."

"How will you get past the palace guard?"

"I'm working on that. There's a man I studied with years ago in my early life as a would-be historian. We've kept in touch in a casual way and he has a great deal of influence. I think you know the name. It's Winters, Samuel Winters—"

"*Winters?* He's the one who told Jennings to give me the Freedom Medal in that crazy ceremony."

"I remembered. It's why I thought of him. Have a good flight, and my love to my niece."

Kendrick walked to the warehouse door where his police escort stood, two inside, two outside, their weapons leveled in front of them. Even the CIA's station chief, who in the dim light looked as though he might be Bahamian himself, held a small revolver in his hand. "You people always carry those things?" asked Evan without much interest.

"Ask your friend who knew that the 'status was clean,' " replied the intelligence officer, waving Kendrick through the door.

"You're joking. *She* has one?"

"Ask her."

"How did she get on the plane in the States? The metal detectors, then customs over here?"

"One of our little secrets, which isn't so secret. A luggage or customs supervisor just happens to show up when we're passing through and the detector is shut down for a couple of seconds, and with customs an immigration inspector is alerted as to what not to find."

"That's pretty loose," said Kendrick, climbing into the official airport car.

"Not in nearby places like this. The supervisors not only work for us but they're monitored. Farther away our equipment is waiting for us inside." The station chief sat beside Evan in the backseat of the small sedan and the driver sped out to the runway.

The huge, sleek military jet known as the F-106 Delta Dart had arrived, its engines idling in a bass roar as Khalehla stood by a ramp of metal steps talking with an Air Force officer. It was only as he approached the two of them that Kendrick recognized the type of aircraft he was about to enter; it was not a calming recognition. The jet was similar to the one that had flown him to Sardinia over a year ago, the first leg on his journey to Masqat. He turned to the intelligence officer walking beside him and extended his hand.

"Thanks for everything," he said. "I'm sorry I haven't been more pleasant company."

"You could have spit in my face and I'd still have been proud to meet you, Congressman."

"I wish I could say I appreciate that . . . what *is* your name?"

"Call me Joe, sir."

"Call me Joe." A young man on the same type of aircraft a year ago had been called Joe. Was another Oman, another Bahrain in his future?

"Thank you, Joe."

"We're not quite finished, Mr. Kendrick. One of those AF boys with the rank of colonel or above has to sign a paper."

The signer in question was not a colonel, he was a brigadier general and he was black. "Hello again, Dr. Axelrod," said the pilot of the F-106. "It seems I'm your personal chauffeur." The large man held out his hand. "That's the way the powers that be like it."

"Hello, General."

"Let's get one thing straight, Congressman. I was out of line last time and you handed it to me and you were right. But I'll tell you now that if they transfer me to Colorado, I'll vote for you in spades—don't take that idiomatically."

"Thanks, General," said Evan, attempting to smile. "However, I won't be needing any more votes."

"That'd be a damn shame. I've been watching you, listening to you. I like the sweep of your wing and that's something I know about."

"I think you're supposed to sign a paper."

"I never got one in Sardinia," said the general officer, accepting a letter of release from the CIA station chief. "You sure you're gonna accept this li'l old document from an uppity goin'-on-fifty nigger in a general's suit, Mr. Old School Tie?"

"Shut your mouth, *boy,* I'm half Paiute Indian. You think you've got problems?"

"Sorry, son." The Air Force officer signed and his special cargo got on board.

"What happened?" asked Khalehla when they reached their seats. "Why did MJ call?"

His hands shaking, his voice trembling at the sudden enormity of it all, at the violence and the near death of Emmanuel Weingrass, he told her. There was a pained helplessness both in his eyes and in his halting, frightened spurts of explanation. "*Christ,* it's got to *stop*! If it doesn't, I'll kill everyone I care for!" She could only grip his hand again and let him know that she was there. She could not fight the lightning in his mind. It was too personal, too soul-racking.

Thirty minutes into the flight, Evan convulsed and leaped out of his seat, racing up the aisle to the toilet. He retched, throwing up everything he had eaten in the last twelve hours. Khalehla ran behind him, forcing the narrow door open and grabbing his forehead, holding him, telling him to let it all out.

"*Please,*" coughed Kendrick. "Please, get *out* of here!"

"Why? Because you're so different from the rest of us? You hurt but you won't cry? You bottle it up until something's got to give?"

"I'm not wild about pity—"

"You're not getting it, either. You're a grown man who's gone through a terrible loss and nearly suffered a greater one—for you the greatest one. I hope I'm your friend, Evan, and as a friend I don't pity you—I respect you too much for that—but I *do* feel for you."

Kendrick stood up, grabbing paper towels from the dispenser, pale and visibly shaken. "You know how to make a guy feel terrific," he said guiltily.

"Wash your face and comb your hair. You're a mess." Rashad walked out of the small enclosure past two uniformed and startled flight crew. "The damn fool ate some bad fish," she explained without looking at either man. "Will one of you close the door, please?"

An hour passed; drinks were served by the Air Force attendants, followed by a microwaved dinner eaten heartily by the intelligence agent from Cairo but barely picked at by the Congressman. "You need food, friend," said Khalehla. "This beats the hell out of any commercial menu."

"Enjoy."

"How about you? You move it around but you don't eat."

"I'll have another drink."

Their heads snapped up with the piercing sound of a buzzer heard easily over the outside roar of the engines. For Evan it was déjà vu; a buzzer had sounded a year ago and he had been summoned to the flight deck. Now, however, the corporal who answered the intercom on the bulkhead walked back and spoke to Khalehla. "There's a radio transmission for you, miss."

"Thank you," said Rashad, turning and seeing the alarm in Kendrick's expression. "If it was anything important, they'd ask for you. Relax." She made her way up the aisle, gripping the few well-separated seats for balance in the mild turbulence, and sat in the seat in front of the bulkhead. The crewman handed her the phone; the spiraling cord was more than adequate for the reach. She crossed her legs and answered. "This is Pencil Two, Bahamas. Who are you?"

"One of these days we've got to get rid of that garbage," said Mitchell Payton.

"It works, MJ. If I'd used 'Banana Two,' how would you have responded?"

"I'd have called your father and told him you were a naughty girl."

"We don't count. We know each other. . . . What is it?"

"I don't want to talk to Evan, he's too upset to think clearly. You have to."

"I'll try. What's the query?"

"I want your evaluation. The information you got from that fellow you went to see from the old Off Shore Investment crowd in Nassau—you're convinced he's reliable, aren't you?"

"His information is, he isn't, but he can't hide if he lied for money. The man's a floating drunk who lives off what's left of his wits, which may have been more acute before his brain was soaked in gin. Evan showed him two thousand in cash and, believe me, he would have given away the secrets of the drug trade for it."

"Do you recall exactly what he said about the woman Ardis Montreaux?"

"Certainly. He said that he kept track of the money whore, as he called her, because she owed him and one day he was going to collect."

"I mean her marital status."

"Of course I remember, but Evan told you over the phone, I heard him."

"Tell me yourself. No mistakes can be made."

"All right. She divorced the banker Frazier-Pyke, and married a wealthy Californian from San Francisco named Von Lindemann."

"He was specific about San Francisco?"

"Not actually. He said, 'San Francisco or Los Angeles,' I think. But he was very specific about California, that was the point. Her new husband was a Californian and terribly rich."

"And the name—try to recall precisely. You're certain it was *Von Lindemann*?"

"Well . . . yes. We met him in a booth at the Junkanoo and there was a steel band, but *yes,* that was the name. Or if it isn't exact, it's certainly close enough."

"*Banco!*" cried Payton. "*Close* enough, my dear. She married a man named Van*vlanderen,* Andrew *Vanvlanderen,* from Palm Springs."

"So blame a mouth drowned in gin."

"We're beyond gin, Field Agent Rashad. Andrew Vanvlanderen is one of Langford Jennings's most distinguished contributors—read that as a mother lode for the presidential coffers."

"That's interesting."

"Oh, we're even beyond interest. Ardisolda Wojak Montreaux Frazier-Pyke Vanvlanderen, an admittedly gifted and obviously talented administrator, is currently Vice President Orson Bollinger's chief of staff."

"That's *fascinating.*"

"I think the situation calls for an informal but nonetheless quite official visit from one of our Middle East specialists—you'll be in southwest Colorado, barely an hour away. I choose you."

"Good God, MJ, on what *basis*?"

"Threats were supposedly made against Bollinger and an FBI unit was assigned to him. They kept it quiet—too quiet in my judgment—and now the unit's suddenly recalled, the emergency declared over."

"Coinciding with the attacks on *Fairfax* and *Mesa Verde*?" suggested Khalehla, sharply interrupting.

"It sounds crazy, I know, but it's there. Call it the twitching of an old professional's nostrils, but I detect an odor of amateurish offal drifting out of San Diego."

"Implicating the *Bureau*?" asked Rashad, astonished.

"No. . . . Using it. I'm working on an interagency interrogation. I intend to interview every member of that unit."

"You still haven't answered me. What's the reason for my going to San Diego? We're not domestic."

"The same as mine for questioning the unit. With regard to those threats against Bollinger, we're looking into the possibility of terrorist involvement. The good Lord knows that if we're pressed to reveal tonight's events, we have every justification. . . . I don't know where it is, my dear, but somewhere in this madness there's a connection—and a blond man with a European accent."

Khalehla glanced around the cabin as she spoke. The two attendants were talking quietly in their seats and Evan was staring blankly out the window. "I'll do it, of course, but you're not making my life any easier. It's obvious that my boy had an affair with this Vanvlanderen woman—not that it bothers me but it bothers him."

"Why? That strikes me as an odd sort of morality. It was a long time ago."

"You're missing the point, MJ. Sex isn't the morality. He was conned, seduced into almost becoming an international crook, and he can't forget it or forgive himself maybe."

"Then I'll relieve your concerns for the time being. Kendrick must not be told anything about San Diego at this juncture. In his state of mind God knows what he'd do if he even had an inkling of such a connection, and we don't need any loose cannons. Make up something about an emergency business trip and be convincing. I want you to interrogate that very odd lady from left field. I'll prepare a scenario for you by morning."

"I'll handle it."

"I trust you brought your hat-switch papers out of Cairo."

"Of course."

"You may want to use them. We're on extremely thin ice. Incidentally, none of our people know you, nor do you know them. If I come up with something, I'll somehow relay it through Weingrass in Colorado. . . . *Very* thin ice."

"Even Evan realizes that."

"May I ask how things are going with you two? I warn you, I'm inordinately fond of him."

"Let's put it this way. We had a lovely two-bedroom suite at Cable Beach and last night I could hear him pacing the living room outside my door until all hours of the morning. I damn near walked out and ordered him inside."

"Why didn't you?"

"Because everything's so confusing for us, so consuming for

him—and now tonight, so horrible. I don't think either of us could handle personal complications."

"Thank heaven we're on scrambler. Follow your instincts, Field Agent Rashad. They've served us well in Special Projects. . . . I'll call you in the morning with instructions. Good hunting, dear niece."

Khalehla returned to her seat and Evan's anxious stare. "Other worlds go on and they're just as deadly, I'm afraid," she said, buckling her seat belt. "That was the station chief in Cairo. Two of our contacts disappeared in the Sidi Barrani district—it's a Libyan connection. I told him what to look for and whom to go after. . . . How are you feeling?"

"All right," he answered, studying her face.

"Our distinguished passengers and our not too shabby crew," came the general's deep loud voice over the intercom from the flight deck. *"It seems we're destined to repeat ourselves, Dr. Axelrod. Remember that 'southern island'?"* The pilot went on to explain that in order to avoid the excitement—and publicity—of an "AF bird" dropping in at the airports of Durango or Cortez, they were instructed to head directly into the one at Mesa Verde. The runway was deemed officially adequate *"but our touchdown could be a mite rocky, so when I give the word, belt 'em up tight. We're starting our descent from the satellites; arrival estimated in forty-five minutes—if I can find the damn place. . . . Remember, Doctor?"*

As the general had predicted with considerable understatement, the landing shook the aircraft with a series of massive vibrations, the blasting eruptions of the braking jets filling the fuselage. Outside on the ground, thanks were expressed, goodbyes said, and the brigadier delivered his special cargo to a field officer of the Central Intelligence Agency. Khalehla and Evan were ushered quickly to an armor-plated sedan flown down from Denver, their motorcycle escort an armed six-man contingent from the State Police, oblivious as to why the governor's office had ordered them to the backcountry "millionaires' airport" near the Mesa Verde National Park.

"Let me get you current, Congressman," said the CIA man, sitting, as had his colleague in the Bahamas, in the front seat beside the driver. "There are five of us here, but two will fly back to Virginia with the prisoner and the three dead bodies. . . . I'm spelling things out because I was told I can speak in front of the lady, that you were official, miss."

"Thank you for your confidence," said the unrecognized agent for Special Projects.

"Yes, ma'am. . . . We've contracted a half-dozen forest rangers from the park for the night, each backgrounded, each a combat veteran, to guard your house and grounds. Tomorrow a unit from Langley will arrive to take up their posts."

"Christ, what if there's another *Fairfax*?" whispered Evan.

Khalehla pressed her elbow into Kendrick's side, coughing as she did so.

"I beg your pardon?"

"Nothing. Sorry. Go ahead."

"A couple of points—and I don't mind telling you that old Jewish guy should be put in someone's hall of fame, if somebody else doesn't put him in a padded cell—but you both have to know the facts, the cover. Weingrass worked it out before we got there—*wow,* he's a pistol!"

"Noted and accepted," said Kendrick. "What are the facts?"

"The nurses know very little; they think there was only one terrorist, a hallucinating fanatic at that. The three bodies were hidden in the woods until the police left, then carried by your Mexican friend Gonzalez back to the garage without the nurses seeing him. They were on the other side of the house, on the porch with Manny—Jesus, how did he get me to call him 'Manny'? Anyway, Gonzalez locked the doors to the garage and drove back to his restaurant. Mr. Weingrass guarantees us he'll keep quiet."

"Mr. Weingrass is right," confirmed Evan.

"We don't like the arrangement, but I guess you three go back a long time."

"We go back a long time," said Kendrick.

"So the Congressman shouldn't make any references to the magnitude of the assault," broke in Khalehla. "Is that what you're saying?"

"That's exactly what I'm saying. Everything's *containment,* Mr. Kendrick, that's the order from on-high in Langley. As far as anyone here is concerned, we're just government personnel, no Agency, no Bureau, no identifications offered and none asked for. They're all too frightened to look for complications, which is usually the case in these situations. A plane will fly in around three o'clock this morning. The prisoner and his dead friends will be taken back to Virginia. He will be sent to an interrogations clinic, the others to the forensic labs. Manny said—Excuse me, *Mr. Weingrass* said I should make all this clear to you."

"It's clear."

"Thank you, sir. Boy, that Manny! Do you know he punched me in the stomach when I told him I was taking over. I mean, he threw a fist into my gut!"

"Standard," said Kendrick, peering out the tinted window at the road. They were only ten minutes from the house. From Manny.

They embraced in the doorway, Evan holding the old man far more firmly than the other held him. Then Weingrass gently boxed Kendrick's ears and spoke. "You never got manners from your parents? Behind you is a lady I want very much to meet."

"Oh, sorry," said Evan, backing away. "Manny, this is Khalehla . . . Khalehla Rashad."

Old Weingrass stepped forward, taking Khalehla's hand in his. "We come from a troubled land, you and I. You are an Arab and I am a Jew, but there are no such distinctions in this house, no preconceptions, and I must tell you that I love you very much for giving such joy to my son."

"My God, you *are* a marvel."

"Yes," agreed Manny, nodding twice.

"I love you, too, for all that you mean to Evan." Khalehla placed her arms around the frail architect, her face pressed against his. "I feel as if I've known you all my life."

"I sometimes have that effect on people. Also sometimes the opposite, as if their lives had taken a sudden turn for the worse."

"Mine hasn't," said Khalehla, releasing Manny but holding his shoulders. "I've met the legend and he turns out to be a terrific person," she added, smiling warmly.

"Don't spread such disinformation, Miss Secret Agent. You'll ruin my reputation. . . . To business before I bring you in to the others." Weingrass turned in the hallway and peered around the stone archway. "Good. The girls are on the veranda giving us a few minutes to ourselves."

"That fellow from the CIA filled us in," said Kendrick. "The one who came down to the airport to meet us."

"Oh, you mean Joe."

"Joe?"

"They're all Joe, John, Jim—you notice, no Irvings or Miltons—forget it. . . . Payton told me you know about the Hassans."

"He knows," interrupted Khalehla, absently reaching for

Evan's hand and gripping it; the gesture was not lost on Manny and it obviously touched him. "It was horrible—"

"It's all horrible, my lovely child. *Animals* who kill their *own!* Kashi and Sabri, they spoke so lovingly of you, Adrienne Khalehla Rashad, and I don't have to tell you what they thought of my son. . . . So we will mourn privately, each to himself and herself, remembering what they meant to us. But that must be later, not now."

"Manny," broke in Kendrick. "I have to make arrangements—"

"I've made them. There'll be a private Islamic service, and their remains will be flown back to Dubai for burial in Ash Sharigah. The coffins will be sealed, of course."

"Mr. Weingrass—"

"*That* business should have come first. If you call me 'mister,' I won't love you so much."

"All right . . . Manny. MJ wasn't clear. MJ—that's Payton."

"I know, I know," interrupted Weingrass. "I told him that if he got the phone fixed we could be more cordial, so I think he had somebody killed and now it's working. We're Emmanuel and Mitchell now, and he calls too much. I'm sorry, you had a question?"

"What's my cover here? I feel like an idiot, but I simply don't know. The field agent in the car said I was official, but official *what*? Who am I to these people?"

"Mitchell suggested that you say you're a representative from the State Department accompanying the Congressman."

"*State?*"

"Maybe he wants to blame somebody if things don't work out. I understand it's a popular pastime in Washington."

"No, he isn't like that. . . . Oh, I *do* see. If I have to give instructions, I'm in a position to do it."

"Wouldn't you have to show a State Department ID if someone asked for it?" said Evan.

"Well . . . yes."

"You mean you've got one?"

"Well, sort of."

"That's illegal—"

"We wear different hats at different times, Evan."

"You also have a gun. That Paiute Indian station chief in the Bahamas told me."

"He shouldn't have."

"You wouldn't also happen to work for the Mossad, would you," said Weingrass, grinning.

"No, but you do—you have. And some of my closest friends do."

"You're in good hands, *bubbelah.* . . . More business. Mitchell wants Evan to look at the merchandise here—the one in the bedroom and the bodies; they're under sheets in the garage and they're leaving by air express during the night."

"And the nurses have no idea they're *out* there?" said Kendrick, his tone disbelieving.

"Your friend Payton was adamant—'fanatic' is more like it. 'Containment, containment,' he kept saying over and over again."

"How are you going to get them past that group of park rangers outside?"

"They've rented a van from Durango. It'll be left at the airport, where someone will pick it up and drive it out here. Then it'll be backed into the garage out of sight, the whole operation supervised by Payton's men. They seem to know what they're doing."

"They do," said Khalehla softly. "Has anyone spoken to the girls about what they're to say, or, rather, what they shouldn't say?"

"I did, and for once they took me seriously, but I don't know how long it'll last. They're still shook up and they don't know a quarter of what happened."

"I'll get them together while you and Evan make your grisly rounds and back you up—very officially. MJ's right. I'll play State Department."

"Why?" asked Evan. "Just curious."

"To keep the Agency out of it. We have no jurisdiction domestically, and someone might just remember it and let her imagination run rampant. Simpler is better."

"Very pro," said Weingrass approvingly. "So how do I introduce you?"

"I'm simply a Miss Adrienne from the Department of State. Do you mind lying?"

"Let me think," said Manny, frowning. "I once told a lie—I believe it was in July 1937. . . . Let's go." Grabbing Evan's arm and Khalehla's hand, Weingrass ushered them through the stone arch into the living room, shouting to the three nurses on the enclosed porch beyond. "*Herewith,* my coven of uglies, is the true *warlock*! Pay homage to the man who pays for your sexual indulgences and your excessive cases of muscatel!"

"*Manny!*"

"They love me," said Weingrass quietly, while striding across the floor. "They throw dice for my bed."

"For *God's* sake—"

"Be quiet, darling. He *is* a marvel."

"He broke his leg jumping out of the truck with us above the Jabal Sham," said Kendrick, staring down at the unconscious young man strapped to the bed. "He's only a kid."

"But your ID's positive?" asked the CIA officer standing beside Emmanuel Weingrass. "He was with you in Oman, there's no doubt about it."

"None at all. I'll never forget him. There was a fire in him you're not likely to find in many teenagers over here . . . except maybe in the urban rot."

"Let's go out the back door and into the garage."

"That's Yosef," said Evan, closing his eyes. "His mother was a Jew—and for a few hours he was my friend. He protected me . . . oh, *Christ.*"

"*Stop* it!" shouted Manny. "He came here to *kill* you!"

"Of course he did. Why not? I pretended to be one of them in their goddamned holy cause. . . . They shaved his mother's head, can you imagine that?"

"He shouted that at me when he tried to kill me," said Weingrass simply. "If it makes you feel better, I didn't want to kill him. I wanted to take anyone I could alive."

"Knowing Yosef, you didn't have a choice."

"I didn't."

"These other two," interrupted the impatient CIA officer, lifting up the sheets. "Do you recognize them?"

"Yes. They were both in the compound, but I never knew their names. The one on the right had soiled trousers; the other, long ragged hair and stared like he had some kind of messianic complex—I figured he was psychotic. That's all I can tell you."

"You've already told us what we have to know. All these men that you've identified were with you in Oman."

"Yes, I knew each one. . . . They wanted their revenge, and if I were them, I'm not sure I'd feel so differently."

"You're not a terrorist, Congressman."

"What separates a terrorist from a 'freedom fighter'?"

"For starters, *sir,* terrorists make it a point to kill innocent people. Ordinary men and women who just happened to be there, kids with backpacks, employees—young and old alike—simply doing their jobs. Where's your case, *sir*?"

Kendrick studied the field agent, suddenly jolted, remembering Fairfax and the Hassans. "I apologize for a stupid and fatuous remark. I regret it deeply."

"What the hell," said the CIA man, shrugging off his momentary anger. "We're all stretched and too damned many labels are thrown around anyway."

They returned to the house, where Khalehla was speaking to the nurses on the porch. Whatever she was saying she had the rapt attention of the three women; they sat motionless in their chairs, their intelligent eyes riveted on "the representative from the State Department." Evan and Manny walked in and crossed quietly to the bar while the CIA officer went to the guest room to check on a colleague and the prisoner.

"I've explained everything, Congressman Kendrick," said Khalehla, her voice official, "as far as I'm permitted to, of course, and these ladies have agreed to cooperate. One had a visitor arriving tomorrow, but she'll call and tell him there's a medical emergency and not to come."

"Thanks a lot," muttered Weingrass, pouring himself a drink under Kendrick's watchful gaze. "Now I'm a corpse."

"Thank *you,* Manny," remarked the nurse in question dryly.

"I want to thank all of you," said Evan quickly. "Washington's convinced this is an isolated incident, a young lunatic on the loose—"

"So was Sirhan-Sirhan," broke in the nurse who had driven into Mesa Verde to reach Gonzalez, "and the description didn't change the results."

"I've told them the prisoner is being transferred back East under cover tonight and not to be concerned if they hear noises on the grounds or in the garage."

"*Very* pro," mumbled Weingrass.

"I only have one question," said the third nurse, looking at Khalehla. "You mentioned that the quarantine was temporary. . . . Well, not that I'm about to be invited to the Grand Prix in Monte Carlo, but how long is temporary?"

"Too many crowds during the Grand Prix," interjected Manny, drinking. "You can't cross the streets and the Bains de Mer go crazy."

"No more than a few days," answered Kendrick, again speaking quickly. "They just want to run the usual checks. . . . And if you get that invitation, Manny will personally accompany you."

"Congressman, try Daffy Duck."

"Meshugah."

There was a sudden, startling commotion outside. Shouts were heard and a horn blared. "Get away from the *windows*!" shouted the CIA agent, racing through the living room. "On the floor! *Everyone on the floor!*"

Evan lunged toward Khalehla, astonished to realize she had dropped between the throw rugs and was rolling over and over to the base of a sliding door, an automatic in her hand.

"It's okay, it's *okay*!" yelled a voice from the front lawn.

"That's one of us," said the man from the Central Intelligence Agency, on his knees, his weapon also in his hand. "What the *hell*—?" He got to his feet and ran into the living room with Kendrick following him. The massive front door opened and a startled well-dressed figure walked haltingly inside escorted by a park ranger. He carried a black medicine bag; it was open; it had been searched.

"I never expected such a reception," said the doctor. "I know we're not always welcome, but this is a bit much. . . . *Congressman,* it's such an *honor.*" They shook hands, the CIA agent watching, bewildered.

"I'm afraid we haven't met, have we?" asked Evan, equally confused.

"No, we haven't, but we're neighbors, if approximately seven more miles into the hills is a neighbor. My name's Lyons."

"I'm sorry about your reception. You'll have to blame it on an overprotective President. What is it, Dr. Lyons? Why are you here?"

"Because *he* wasn't *there,*" replied the intruder, smiling gamely. "I'm Mr. Weingrass's new doctor. If you'll check his schedule, he was to be in my office in Cortez at four o'clock this afternoon. He never arrived and we couldn't reach him on the telephone, so as this house is on the way to mine I thought I'd drop in and see if there was a problem." The physician stopped and reached into his pocket, taking out an envelope. "Incidentally, in line with those overprotective measures, here's my clearance from the Walter Reed Hospital, countersigned by the proper officials in the administration. I'm to show this to Mr. Weingrass and his nurses, or at least the one who accompanied him to my office. He's all right, isn't he?"

"*Manny!*" yelled Kendrick irritably.

Weingrass appeared in the veranda archway, a drink in his hand. "Why are you screaming at me?"

"Weren't you supposed to be at the doctor's office this afternoon?"

"Oh, yeah, somebody called last week—"

"It was my receptionist, Mr. Weingrass," explained Dr. Lyons. "She said you wrote it down and agreed to be there."

"Yeah, well, I do that now and then, but I feel fine, so why trouble you. Also, you're not my doctor."

"Mr. *Weingrass,* your doctor passed away several weeks ago from a cardiac seizure. It was in the papers and I know you received an announcement of the funeral."

"Yeah, well I don't go to those, either. Mine's overdue."

"Nevertheless, as long as I'm here, why don't we have a look?"

"What are we looking for?"

"A little tub-thumping and a short blood sample for the lab."

"I feel fine."

"I'm sure you are fine," agreed Lyons, nodding. "It's just routine and won't take more than a couple of minutes. . . . It really is an honor to meet you, Congressman."

"Thanks very much. . . . Go on, Manny. Do you want one of the nurses to assist you, Doctor?"

"It doesn't really matter—"

"So she can wax lascivious over my naked chest?" protested Weingrass, interrupting. "Come on, Doc. You tap around my ribs and go out and buy yourself a Cadillac."

"At least a Ferrari," countered Lyons, smiling at Kendrick.

Emmanuel Weingrass and his new doctor walked down the stone hallway toward the bedroom.

30

It was ten minutes past one in the morning, and exhaustion hung like circles of dead heavy mist throughout the house in Mesa Verde. The CIA field agent, his eyes dark with fatigue, walked onto the enclosed porch, where Evan and Khalehla sat on the leather couch diagonally across from Manny in his recliner. The three nurses had left, each to her own room, each having been dismissed from duty for the rest of the night; the presence of armed guards patrolling the grounds outside had stretched their nerves. The patient would survive sleep without being looked in on every half hour. Dr. Lyons had guaranteed it.

"Washington's anxious," announced the weary intelligence officer. "The schedule's been moved up, so I'm going down to the airport for the van now. The plane should be here in about an hour, which means we don't have much time. They want that bird to come in and get out."

"The tower down there doesn't operate all night unless by prearrangement," said Kendrick. "Have you thought about that?"

"Hours ago, in time for your flight from the Bahamas. The Air Force flew over a team of controllers from Colorado Springs. The cover's an AF training maneuver cleared through your office. Nobody objects and no one questions."

"How come?"

"Because you're you, sir."

"Is there anything we can do here?" asked Khalehla quickly, before Evan could make a comment.

"Yes, there is," answered the field agent. "If you wouldn't mind, I'd rather not have anyone up when I get back. We've got this thing worked out by the numbers, and I mean fractions, so the fewer distractions the better."

"How are you going to handle those cowboys from the park outside?" said Weingrass, grimacing but obviously not from the question he asked. "I put my head out the door a couple of times before these two got here and they rushed up to me like I was a runaway bear."

"They've been told a foreign VIP is arriving to see the Congressman—in fact, *that's* the reason they're here. And since the meeting is highly confidential—and in deference to the visitor who wants to keep it that way, all patrols will remain out of sight. They'll be on the sides of the house and down at the gazebo."

"They bought that nonsense?" interjected Weingrass.

"They have no reason to question it."

"Because he's *him,*" agreed Manny, nodding.

"And because they're being paid three hundred dollars apiece for losing a night's sleep."

"Very pro, Mr. Containment. You're better than I thought."

"I have to be. . . . Well, if I don't see you again, it's been a real pleasure meeting you, Congressman. Someday I'll be able to tell my kids about it. . . . No, please don't get up, sir, I've got to run. You, too, Miss Official, as Mr. Weingrass would say. . . . And you, Manny, I tell you, it's been an experience. I *think* I'm glad you're on our side."

"You should be, you need all the help you can get. . . . *Ciao,* young man. Have a good track-down and if the odds are only five to one against you, you'll win."

"Thanks, Manny, I intend to." The intelligence officer turned briefly to Evan and Khalehla on the couch. "I mean that," he added quietly. "I heard the reference to Fairfax in the car and let it pass, but it wasn't easy. You see, I'm the only one here who knows what happened; it's why I insisted on leading this team. My older sister's son, my nephew—I brought him into the Agency—he was part of that unit. I *intend* to have a damned good track-down." The CIA man left quickly.

For starters, sir, terrorists make it a point to kill innocent people. Ordinary men and women who just happened to be there, kids with backpacks, and employees—young and old alike—simply doing their jobs. Where's your case, sir?

"How terrible for him," said Khalehla. "He must feel such hurt, such guilt."

"Which of us doesn't?" asked Kendrick, his voice floating, then stopped abruptly with a sudden, forced intake of air.

"You can't blame yourself for what's happened," insisted Khalehla.

"*Happening,*" exclaimed Kendrick. "It's *happening*! How the hell did these people get into the country? Who *let* them in? Where are our so-called *brilliant* security measures that can catch fifth-rate Soviet agents we exchange for set-up reporters in Moscow because it's good *PR,* but we can't stop a dozen killers who come in to *kill*? Who makes it *possible*?"

"We're trying to find out."

"You're a little late, aren't you?"

"*Stop* it!" ordered Weingrass, leaning forward, punching the space in front of him with his forefinger. "This girl has nothing to do with what you're talking about and I won't have it!"

"I *know* that!" said Kendrick, reaching for Khalehla's hand, "and she knows I know it. It's just that everything's so insane—I feel so helpless, so frightened. *Goddamnit,* how many others have to be killed? We can't stop these people! They're maniacs and they're running loose and we'll never *find* them!" Evan lowered his voice, his eyes filled with pain, leveled at the field agent from

Cairo. "Any more than we've found the bastards who stole that 'theft-proof' Oman file and splattered me all over the world. How long has it been—eight, ten weeks? We're no closer than when we began. At least now we know why they did it. It wasn't to make me a hero, or to promote my so-called career as a political contender for Christ knows what . . . it was to set me up for the kill! A 'vengeance death' I believe is the literal Arabic translation. The point is we're not *getting* anywhere!"

"Listen to me," said Khalehla softly. "I'm going to say something I probably shouldn't, but sometimes we break a rule because hope is important, too. . . . Other things have happened that you don't know about—*are* happening, as you say—and each new piece of information brings us a step closer to the truth about this whole horrible mess."

"That's pretty cryptic, young lady."

"Manny, try to understand. Evan does because we have an agreement. He knows that there are times when I can't explain things."

"May an old man who's been a resident in your territory once or twice before ask why?"

"If you mean your work with Mossad, you shouldn't have to—forgive my being blunt. . . . The basis is an imperative need-to-know, because what you don't know you can't reveal."

"The Amytals and the Pentothals?" asked Weingrass. "In the old days, scopolamine? Come on, my lovely girl, we're not in the back streets of Marrakech or the partisan mountains of Ashot Yaaqov. Who would use chemicals on us here?"

"I'm sure that young prisoner Evan identified, the one who's on his way to a clinic in Virginia, probably felt the same way. Within twenty-four hours his entire life will be on tape."

"Not applicable," insisted Weingrass.

"Perhaps not, but something else is. As of six hours ago we have a trace—a *possible* trace—that may take us higher up in this government than any of us wishes. If we're wrong, Congressman Kendrick of Colorado can't be a part of it; quite simply, he can't *know* anything. He has total deniability. As a result, neither can you, Manny."

"That radio transmission on the plane," said Evan, looking hard at Khalehla. "There was no station chief in Cairo, was there?" Khalehla shrugged, releasing his hand and reaching for her drink on the coffee table in front of the couch. "All right, no specifics," continued Kendrick, "but let's talk about the truth—forget deniability, which I don't give a damn about.

What kind of truth are you after? Give me an *overview*—I've heard that word ad nauseam in Washington. What kind of people are doing what to *whom*? Whoever they are, they've killed my friends—*our* friends. I have a right to *know.*"

"Yes, you do," said Khalehla slowly, sitting rigid on the couch, looking alternately at Evan and Emmanuel Weingrass, finally settling on Kendrick. "You said it yourself, questioned it yourself—part of the truth, anyway. Someone *did* let these killers in and made it possible for them to kill. Passports were provided without restrictions, and as I can easily picture their general appearances because I'm one of them, those false papers had to be terribly good to get past the antiterrorist experts we and our allies have at every immigration point here and abroad, including the Soviets, I might add. Beyond those papers are the logistics, the lines of supply without which terrorists can't operate. Weapons, ammunition, money, driver's licenses, and pre-rented vehicles; locations where they can hide and prepare themselves, even down to the most up-to-date clothing made in this country in case they're arrested and interrogated. Then there are such items as train and airline reservations, all made in advance, the tickets delivered before they walk into a terminal, except when they're on a platform or in a flight lounge at the last minute. You see, nothing is inconsequential to these people; everything is vital down to the last detail for the success of any given mission." Khalehla paused, shifting her gaze between both men. "Someone's made all of these things available to them, and whoever it is, or whoever they are, they shouldn't *be* where they are in this government or have the accesses they have. It's more important than I can ever explain that they be found."

"You said that about those who stole the Oman file."

"And you believe they're the same people."

"*Aren't* they? It's pretty obvious to me."

"Not to me."

"The setup. It's the explanation for a revenge kill. *Me.*"

"Suppose they're *separate,*" insisted Khalehla. "One giving birth to the other? It's been ten weeks, remember? The impetus for killing you in the heat of vengeance that is intrinsic to *jaremat thaár* has passed."

"You just pointed out all the details that had to be put in place. That takes time."

"If they have the resources to do what they've done in ten weeks, they could do it in ten days, Evan."

Emmanuel Weingrass held up his hand, palm forward; it was

a command for quiet and he expected to be obeyed. "You are now telling us that instead of one enemy my son has two? The Arabs from the Baaka Valley and someone else over here who works with them or *against* them? Are you making sense, my lovely child?"

"Two *forces,* both elusive, one a deadly enemy, certainly . . . the other I just don't know. I only know what I sense, and I'm not being evasive. When MJ doesn't have the answers, he keeps blaming it on what he calls 'gaps.' I guess that's what I'm falling back on. There are too many gaps."

Weingrass grimaced again, a silent belch filling his gaunt cheeks. "I accept your perceptions," he said. "If Mitchell ever throws you out, I'll find you reasonable employment with the Mossad, avoiding a certain accountant who would let you starve." The old architect suddenly breathed deeply and leaned back in his chair.

"Manny, what *is* it?" said Khalehla, her question causing Kendrick to turn his head, alarmed.

"Are you all right?" asked Evan.

"I'm ready for the Olympics," replied Weingrass. "Except that one minute I'm cold, the next minute I'm hot. It was all that running around in the woods like a kid. Lyons told me my systolic was a little high, or maybe it was the other one, and that I had a few bruises where I shouldn't have. . . . I told him I was wrestling bulls on the south forty. I've got to rest these bones, children." The old man got out of his chair. "Would you believe, Khalehla, that I'm not a kid?"

"I think you're not only very young, but also remarkable."

"Extraordinary is more appropriate, actually," offered Manny. "But right now I feel the effects of my virtuosity. I'm going to bed."

"I'll get one of the nurses," said Kendrick, starting to rise.

"For *what*? So she can take advantage of me, *ravage* me? I want rest, boy! . . . And let *them* rest, Evan. They've been through a lot and they don't even know what they've been through. I'm fine, just tired. Try running in the Olympics when *you're* sixty."

"Sixty?"

"Shut up, son. I can still give you a run for your money for that lovely girl."

"Could it have been something the doctor gave you?" asked Khalehla, smiling warmly at the compliment.

"So what did he give? Nothing. He just took a little blood for his meshugenah laboratory and offered me some pills, which I told him I'd throw down the toilet. They were probably samples he got for nothing and then charges enough for a new wing on his fancy house. . . . *Ciao,* young things."

The two of them watched as the old man walked through the archway into the living room, each step firmly planted ahead of the other as if he were summoning strength he did not feel. "Do you think he's okay?" asked Evan when Weingrass was out of sight.

"I think he's exhausted," said Khalehla. "You try doing what he did tonight—forget sixty *or* eighty—try tomorrow."

"I'll look in on him every now and then."

"We'll take turns. That way we'll both feel better without waking the nurses."

"Which is another way of saying they'll stay put and away from the windows."

"I guess it is," admitted Rashad. "But we'd still feel better, even if it's on both counts."

"Do you want another drink?"

"No, thanks—"

"I do." Kendrick got up from the couch.

"I haven't finished."

"What?" Evan turned as Khalehla rose and stood in front of him.

"I don't want a drink . . . but I do want you."

In silence, Kendrick looked down at her, his eyes roving over her face, finally settling, staring into her eyes. "Is this pity? Be merciful to the confused man in pain?"

"You'll get no pity from me, I told you that. I respect you too much, I told you that, too. As for the poor, confused man in pain, who's pitying whom?"

"I didn't mean it that way—"

"I know you didn't. I'm just not sure how you meant it."

"I told you before. I'm not looking for any fast action, not with you. If it's all I can have, I'll take it, but it's not what I'm looking for."

"You talk too goddamned much, Evan."

"You evade too much. You told Manny that you weren't evasive, but you are. For at least six weeks I've tried to get near you, tried to get you to talk about *us,* tried to break down that glass wall you've erected, but 'No *dice,*' says the bright lady."

"Because I'm scared, damn you!"

"Of what?"

"Of *both* of us!"

"Now you're the one who's talking too much."

"Well, you certainly didn't talk last *night.* You think I didn't hear you? Pacing up and down like an ape in a cage outside my door?"

"Why didn't you open it?"

"Why didn't you break it down?" They both laughed quietly, their arms encircling each other. "Do you want a drink?"

"No. . . . I want you."

There was not the frenzy of Bahrain. There was urgency, of course, but it was the urgency of lovers, not of two desperate strangers grasping for release in a world gone crazy. Their world was not sane—they were all too aware of that—yet they had found a semblance of order between themselves, and the discovery was splendid and warm and suddenly filled with promise, where before there was only a void filled with uncertainty . . . each about the other.

It was as if both were insatiable. Climax was followed by quiet talk, and one or the other looked in on Emmanuel Weingrass, then more talk, bodies together, rushing once again for the fulfillment both craved. Neither could stop holding the other, pulling, weaving, rolling, until the sweet juices were exhausted . . . and still they could not let each other go until sleep came.

The earliest morning sun broke open the Colorado day. Drained but strangely at peace within the warm, temporary cave they had found for themselves, Evan reached for Khalehla. She was not there; he opened his eyes. She was *not* there. He elbowed himself up on the pillow; her clothes were draped on a chair and he breathed again. He saw that the doors to both his bathroom and the clothes closet were open, and then he remembered and laughed quietly, ruefully, to himself. The hero of Oman and the experienced intelligence agent from Cairo had gone to the Bahamas with one carry-on bag apiece, and in the rush of events had promptly left both either in a Nassau police car or on an Air Force F-106. Neither had noticed until after their first stampeded race for the bed, after which Khalehla had stated dreamingly.

"I bought an outrageous nightgown for this trip—more in hope than in realistic expectation—but I think I'll put it on." Then they had looked at each other, mouths gaped, eyes widened. "Oh, my *God*!" she cried. "Where the hell did we leave it? I mean *them,* the *two* of them!"

"Did you have anything incriminating in yours?"

"Only the nightie—it wasn't right for Rebecca of Sunnybrook Farm. . . . Oh, good Lord! A couple of real pros *we* are!"

"I never claimed to be one—"

"Did *you* have—"

"Dirty socks and a sex manual—more in hope than in realistic expectation." They had fallen back into each other's arms, the humor of the situation telling them something else about themselves. "You'd wear that nightgown for roughly five seconds before I tore it off and then you'd have to charge the government for the loss of personal property. I just saved the taxpayers at least six dollars. . . . Come here."

One of them had checked on Manny; neither could remember which.

Kendrick got out of bed and went to his closet. He owned two bathrobes; one was missing so he went into his bathroom to make himself feel and look reasonably presentable. After a shower and a shave he applied too much cologne, but then, he reflected, it had not hurt him nearly twenty years ago in college with an air-head cheerleader. Had it been *that* long ago since impressions mattered to him? He put on his second bathrobe, walked out of the room and down the stone hallway to the arch. Khalehla was sitting at the heavy pine table with the black leather top in the living room, talking quietly into the telephone. She saw him and smiled briefly, concentrating on the person at the other end of the line.

"It's all clear," she said as Evan approached. "I'll be in touch. Good-bye." Khalehla got up from the table, the outsized bathrobe draped strikingly, revealingly around her body. She pulled the folds of fabric together and came to him, suddenly reaching out and placing her hands on his shoulders. "Kiss me, Kendrick," she ordered gently.

"Aren't I supposed to say that?"

They kissed until Khalehla understood that in another moment they would be heading back to the bedroom. "Okay, okay, Kong, I've got things to tell you."

"Kong?"

"I wanted you to break down a door, remember? . . . Good heavens, you forget things."

"I may be incompetent but I hope not inadequate."

"You're probably right about the first, but you're definitely not inadequate, my darling."

"Do you know how much I love to hear you say that?"

"What?"

" 'My darling'—"

"It's an expression, Evan."

"At this moment I think I'd kill if I thought you used it with anyone but me."

"Please."

"Have you? *Do* you?"

"You're asking me if I just like to sleep around occasionally, aren't you?" said Khalehla calmly, removing her arms from him.

"That's pretty rough. No, of course not."

"Since we're talking and I've been doing a lot of thinking, let's tackle this. I've had attachments, as you've had, and I've called several 'darling,' even 'dearest,' I suppose, but if you want to know the truth, you insufferable egotist, I've never called anyone '*my* darling.' Does that answer your question, you rat."

"It'll do," said Evan, grinning and reaching for her.

"No, please, Evan. Talking is safer."

"I thought you just gave me an order to kiss you. What changed?"

"You had to talk and I had to start thinking again. . . . And I don't think I'm ready for you."

"Why not?"

"Because I'm a professional and I have work to do and if I'm screwed up with you—figuratively and literally—I can't do it."

"Again, why not?"

"Because, you idiot, I'm very close to being in love with you."

"That's all I'm asking for. Because I do love you."

"Oh, those words are so easy, so facile. But not in my business, not in the world I live in. The word comes down: Have so-and-so killed, or let him be killed—whichever it is, it solves a multitude of problems. . . . And what happens if it turns out to be you . . . my darling. Could *you* do it if you were me?"

"Could it really ever come down to that?"

"It has; it might. It's called third-party omission, as in what do *I* know, but *they* know what I'll permit. You see, you're one human being—terrific or despicable, depending on the point of view—and by giving you away we might save two hundred or four hundred people on a plane because '*they*' couldn't get *you* unless we gave you away before a flight. . . . Oh, my little world is filled with benignly neglected morality because all we deal with is malignant immorality."

"Why stay in it? Why not get out?"

Khalehla paused, looking at him, her eyes unwavering. "Because we save lives," she answered finally. "And every now and then something happens that reduces the malignancy, showing it for what it is, and peace is just a little closer. More often than not we've been a part of that process."

"You've got to have a life beyond that, a life of your own."

"Oh, I will one day, because one day I won't be useful anymore, at least not where I want to be. I'll be a known commodity—first you're suspected, then you're exposed and then you're useless, and that's when you'd better get out of town. My superiors will try to convince me I can be valuable in other posts; they'll dangle the bait of a pension in front of me and a nice choice of sectors, but I don't think I'll bite."

"According to that scenario, what will you do?"

"Good Lord, I speak six languages fluently and read and write four. Coupled with my background, I'd say my qualifications are ample for any number of jobs."

"That sounds reasonable except for one thing. There's a missing ingredient."

"What are you talking about."

"Me. . . . That's what I'm talking about."

"Oh, come on, Evan."

"No," said Kendrick, shaking his head. "No more 'Oh, come on' or 'Please, Evan.' I won't settle for that. I know what I feel and I think I know what you feel and to disregard those feelings is both stupid and a waste."

"I told you, I'm not ready—"

"I never thought I'd *ever* be ready," interrupted Kendrick, his voice soft and flat. "You see, I've done some thinking, too, and I've been pretty harsh on myself. I've been selfish most of my life. I've always loved the freedom I have, to go and do what I've wanted to do—badly or well, it didn't make much difference as long as I could do it. Self-sufficient, I guess is the term—self, self, *self.* Then you come along and blow the whole damn thing to pieces. You show me what I *don't* have, and by showing me you make me feel like an idiot. . . . I have no one to share anything with, it's as simple as that. No one I care for enough to run to and say 'Look, I did it,' or even 'Sorry, I didn't do it.' . . . Sure, Manny's there, *when* he's there, but his own opinion notwithstanding, he's not immortal. You said last night that you were scared . . . well, I'm the one who's scared now, frightened beyond any fear I thought I'd ever experience. That's the fear of losing you. I'm not much good at begging or groveling, but I'll beg and grovel or do anything you like, but please, *please,* don't leave me."

"Oh, my *God,*" said Khalehla, closing her eyes, the tears rolling separately, slowly, down her cheeks. "You son of a bitch."

"It's a start."

"I *do* love you!" She rushed into his arms. "I shouldn't, I *shouldn't*!"

"You can always change your mind in twenty or thirty years."

"You've loused up my life—"

"You haven't made mine any easier."

"*Very* nice!" came the sonorous voice from the stone archway.

"*Manny!*" cried Khalehla, releasing Evan, pushing him away and looking over his shoulder.

"How long have you *been* there?" asked Kendrick harshly, snapping his head around.

"I came in on the begging and the groveling," replied Weingrass in a scarlet bathrobe. "It always works, boy. The strong-man-on-his-knees bit. Never fails."

"You're *impossible*!" shouted Evan.

"He's adorable."

"I'm both, but keep your voices down, you'll wake up the coven. . . . What the hell are you doing out here at this hour?"

"This hour is eight o'clock in Washington," said Khalehla. "How are you feeling?"

"*Ahnnh,*" answered the old man, flicking the palm of his right hand as he walked into the living room. "I slept but I didn't sleep, you know what I mean? And you clowns didn't help, opening the door every five minutes, you also know what I mean?"

"It was hardly every five minutes," said Khalehla.

"You've got your wristwatch, I've got mine. . . . So what did my friend Mitchell say? That's the eight o'clock in Washington, if I'm not mistaken."

"You're not," agreed the intelligence officer from Cairo. "I was about to explain—"

"Some explanation. The violins were in full *vibrato.*"

"Manny!"

"Shut up. Let her talk."

"I have to leave—for a day, perhaps two."

"Where are you going?" asked Kendrick.

"I can't tell you that . . . my darling."

31

Welcome to Stapleton Airport in Denver, ladies and gentlemen. If you need information regarding connecting flights, our personnel will gladly assist you inside the terminal. The time here in Colorado is five minutes past three in the afternoon.

Among the disembarking passengers spilling out of the exit ramp were five priests whose features were Caucasian but whose skin was darker than that of most Occidentals. They moved together and talked quietly among themselves, their English stilted, yet understandable. They might have been from a diocese in southern mainland Greece or from the Aegean islands, or possibly Sicily or Egypt. They might have been, but they were not. They were Palestinians and they were not priests. Instead, they were killers from the most radical branch of the Islamic jihad. Each held a small carry-on bag of soft black cloth; together they walked into the terminal heading for a newsstand.

"*La!*" exclaimed one of the younger Arabs under his breath as he picked up a newspaper and scanned the headlines. "*Laish!*"

"*Iskut!*" whispered an older companion, pulling the young man away and telling him to be quiet. "If you speak, speak English."

"There is nothing! They still report *nothing*! Something is wrong."

"We know something is wrong, you fool," said the leader known throughout the terrorist world as Ahbyahd, the name meaning "the white-haired one" despite the fact that his close-cropped prematurely gray head was more salt-and-pepper than white. "That's why we're here. . . . Carry my bag and take the others to Gate Number Twelve. I'll meet you there shortly. Remember, if anyone stops you, *you* do the talking. Explain that the others do not speak English, but don't elaborate."

"I shall give them a Christian blessing with the blood of Allah all over their throats."

"Keep your tongue and your knife to yourself. No more Washingtons!" Ahbyahd continued across the terminal, glancing around as he walked. He saw what he had to find and approached a Travelers Aid courtesy desk. A middle-aged woman looked up at him, smiling pleasantly at his obviously bewildered expression.

"May I help you, Father?"

"I believe this is where I was instructed to be," replied the terrorist humbly. "We have no such fine accommodations on the island of Lyndos."

"We try to be of service."

"Perhaps you have a . . . a notice for me—further instructions, I'm afraid. The name is Demopolis."

"Oh, yes," said the woman, opening the top right-hand drawer of the desk. "Father Demopolis. You're certainly a long way from home."

"The Franciscan retreat, an opportunity of a lifetime to visit your splendid country."

"Here we are." The woman pulled out a white envelope and handed it to the Arab. "It was delivered to us around noontime by a charming man who made a most generous contribution to Travelers Aid."

"Perhaps I may add my gratitude," said Ahbyahd, feeling the small hard, flat object in the center of the envelope as he reached for his billfold.

"Oh, no, I wouldn't hear of it. We've been paid handsomely for such a little thing as holding a letter for a man of the cloth."

"You are very kind, madam. May the Lord of Hosts bless you."

"Thank you, Father. I appreciate that."

Ahbyahd walked away, quickening his steps, veering to a crowded corner of the airport terminal. He tore open the envelope. Taped to the blank card inside was a key to a storage locker in Cortez, Colorado. Their weapons and explosives had been delivered on schedule, as well as money, articles of clothing, an untraceable rented automobile, alternate passports of Israeli origin for nine Maronite priests, and airline tickets to Riohacha, Colombia, where arrangements had been made to fly them to Baracoa, Cuba, and points east. Their rendezvous for the trip home—home yet not home, not the Baaka; that was *not* home!—was a highway motel near the airport in Cortez; a flight the next morning would take them to Los Angeles, where nine holy men would be "assistance pre-cleared" on Avianca for Riohacha. Everything had gone according to schedule—*schedules* worked out once the amazing offer had reached the Baaka Valley in Lebanon: *Find him. Kill him. Bring honor to your cause. We'll give you everything you need, but never our identities.* Yet had those so precise schedules, those so precious gifts, borne fruit? Ahbyahd did not know; he could not know and it was why he had called a relay telephone number in Vancouver, Canada, demanding that new and lethal supplies be included in the Cortez delivery. It had been nearly twenty-four hours since the attack on the house in Fairfax, Virginia, and close to eighteen hours after the storming of the hated enemy's home in Colorado. Their mission had been conceived as a combined assault that would stun the Western world with blood and death, avenging the brothers who had been killed, proving that the ultimate security ordered by the President of the United States for a single man was no match for the skills and the commitments of a dispossessed people. Operation Azra demanded the life of an ordained American hero, an impostor who had claimed to be one of them, who had broken bread and sorrow with them, and who finally had betrayed them. That man had to die, along with all who surrounded him, protected him. A lesson had to be *taught*!

That most loathsome of enemies had not been found in Fairfax; it was presumed that Yosef's unit would find him and kill him at his house in the western mountains. Yet there was nothing, *nothing*! The five of them from Command One had waited in their adjoining hotel rooms—waiting, *waiting* for the telephone to ring and hear the words spoken: *Operation Azra is now complete. The hated pig is dead!* . . . Nothing. And most strange of all, there were no screaming headlines in the newspapers, no shocked, anguished men or women on television revealing yet another triumph for the holy cause. What had *happened*?

Ahbyahd had gone over every step of the mission and could fault none. Every conceivable problem but one had been anticipated and solutions found in advance, either through the byways of official corruption in Washington or with sophisticated technology and bribed or blackmailed telephone technicians in Virginia and Colorado. The one unforeseen and unforeseeable problem was a suddenly suspicious aide to the despicable politician who quite simply had to be killed quickly. Ahbyahd had sent the one "priest" of their small brigade who had not been in Oman to Kendrick's office late Wednesday afternoon before the attack on Fairfax. The purpose was merely to cross-check the latest intelligence that confirmed the American congressman's presence in the capital. The "priest's" cover was immaculate; his papers—religious and official—were in order and he brought with him "greetings" from numerous "old friends," each of them a living person from Kendrick's past.

The "priest" had been caught reading a secretary's desk calendar while waiting for the aide to come out into the deserted office. The aide had promptly gone back inside; the "priest" had quietly opened the door and heard the young man on the telephone asking for Congressional Security. He had to die. Quickly, efficiently, taken under a gun to the bowels of the massive Capitol and dispatched swiftly. Yet even that death had not been made public.

What had *happened*? What *was* happening? The martyrs of the holy mission would not, *could* not, return to the Baaka Valley without the trophy of vengeance they so desperately sought and so richly deserved. It was unthinkable! If there was no rendezvous in Cortez, blood would flow over blood at a place called Mesa Verde. The terrorist put the key in his pocket, threw the blank card and the envelope on the terminal floor, and started toward Gate 12.

"Sweetie!" shouted Ardis Vanvlanderen, walking into the living room from the office she had built for herself out of a guest room in San Diego's Westlake Hotel.

"What is it, babe?" asked her husband, sitting in a velour armchair in front of a television set.

"Your problems are over. Those zillions of millions are safe for the next five years! Keep building your missiles and super-duper sonics until the cows shit uranium. . . . I mean it, lover, your worries are *over*!"

"I know that, babe," said Andrew Vanvlanderen without moving, his eyes fixed on the screen. "I'll see it and hear it anytime now."

"What are you talking about?" She stopped and stood motionless, staring down at her husband.

"They've got to release it soon. They can't keep it quiet much longer. . . . *Jesus,* it's been damn near twenty-four *hours*!"

"I have no idea what that muddled mind of yours is conjuring, but I can tell you that Emmanuel Weingrass is on his way out. There was a certain doctor for hire. He's been injected—"

"He's out now. So's Kendrick."

"What?"

"I couldn't wait for you, lover—none of us could. There were better ways, more logical ways—*expected* ways."

"What the hell have you done?"

"Given an aggrieved people the opportunity to avenge themselves on someone who screwed them to hell and back. I found the survivors. I knew where to look."

"Andy-boy," said Ardis, sitting down across from her husband, her large green eyes fixed on his distracted face. "I repeat," she added quietly, "what have you done?"

"Removed an obstacle that would have weakened the military strength of this country to an unacceptable degree—turning the most powerful giant of the free world into a pitiful dwarf. And doing so cost me personally in the neighborhood of eight hundred million dollars—and cost our group *billions.*"

"Oh, my *God*. . . . You couldn't wait—you couldn't *wait.* You reached the *Arabs*!"

"Mr. President, I *need* these few days," pleaded Mitchell Payton, sitting forward on a straight-backed chair in the upstairs living quarters of the White House. It was one-fifty-five in the morning. Langford Jennings sat in the corner of the couch dressed in pajamas and a bathrobe, his legs crossed, a slipper dangling from one foot, his steady questioning gaze never leaving the CIA director's face. "I realize that by coming directly to you I've broken several hundred valid restrictions, but I'm as alarmed as I've ever been in my professional life. Years ago a young man said to his commander in chief that there was a cancer growing on the presidency. This is a far older man saying essentially the same thing, except that in this case any knowledge of the disease—if it exists, as I believe it does—has been kept from you."

"You're here, Dr. Payton," said Jennings, his resonant voice flat, the fear unmistakable. "Yes, *Dr.* Payton—I've had to learn a few things quickly—because Sam Winters made it clear to me that if you said you were alarmed, most other men would be in shock. From what you've told me I understand what he means. I'm in shock."

"I'm grateful for an old acquaintance's intercession. I knew he'd remember me; I wasn't sure he'd take me seriously."

"He took you seriously. . . . You're sure you've told me everything? The whole rotten mess?"

"Everything I know, sir, everything we've pieced together, admitting, of course, that I have no 'smoking gun.' "

"That's not the most favorite phrase around these premises."

"In all candor, Mr. President, if I thought those words had

any application whatsoever to these premises, I wouldn't be here."

"I appreciate your honesty." Jennings lowered his head and blinked, then raised it, frowning, and spoke pensively. "You're right, there's no application, but why are you so sure? My opponents ascribe all manner of deceits to me. Aren't you infected? Because looking at you and knowing what I know about you, I can't imagine that you're an ardent supporter of mine."

"I don't have to agree with everything a man believes to think decently of him."

"Which means I'm okay but you wouldn't vote for me, right?"

"Again, may I speak in candor, sir? The secret ballot is sacred, after all."

"In all candor, *sir,*" said the President, a slow smile creasing his lips.

"No, I wouldn't vote for you," answered Payton, returning the smile.

"IQ problems?"

"Good God, no! History shows us that an overly involved mind in the Oval Office can be consumed by an infinity of details. Above a certain level, an immensity of intellect is irrelevant and frequently dangerous. A man whose head is bursting with facts and opposing facts, theories and countertheories, has a tendency to endlessly debate with himself beyond the point where decisions are demanded. . . . No, sir, I have no problem with your IQ, which is far more than sufficient unto the day."

"Is it my philosophy, then?"

"Candor?"

"Candor. You see, I have to know right now whether I'm going to vote for *you,* and it hasn't a damn thing to do with quid pro quo."

"I think I understand that," said Payton, nodding. "All right, I suppose your rhetoric does bother me at times. It strikes me that you reduce some very complicated issues to . . . to—"

"Simplistics?" offered Jennings quietly.

"Today's world is as complicated and tumultuous as the act of Creation itself, however it came about," replied Payton. "Wrong moves by only a few and we're back where we started, a lifeless ball of fire racing through the galaxy. There are no easy answers any longer, Mr. President. . . . You asked for candor."

"I sure as hell got it." Jennings laughed softly as he uncrossed his legs and sat forward, his elbows on his knees. "But let me tell you something, Doctor. You try expounding on those complicated, tumultuous problems during an election campaign, you'll never be in a position to look for the complex solutions. You end up bellyaching from the bleachers, but you're not part of the team—you're not even in the game."

"I'd like to believe otherwise, sir."

"So would I but I can't. I've seen too many brilliant, erudite men go down because they described the world as they knew it to be to electorates who didn't want to hear it."

"I would suggest they were the wrong men, Mr. President. Erudition and political appeal aren't mutually exclusive. Someday a new breed of politician will face a different electorate, one that will accept the realities, those harsh descriptions you mentioned."

"*Bravo,*" said Jennings quietly as he leaned back on the couch. "You've just described the reason for my being who I am—why I do what I do, what I've done. . . . All governing, Dr. Payton, since the first tribal councils worked out languages over fires in their caves has been a process of transition—even the Marxists agree with that. There's no *Utopia;* in the back of his mind Thomas More knew that, because nothing is as it was—last week, last year, last century. It's why he used the word 'Utopia'—a place that doesn't exist. . . . I'm right for my time, my moment in the change of things, and I hope to Christ it's the change you envision. If I'm the bridge that brings us out alive to that crossing, I'll go to my grave a damned happy man and my critics can go to hell."

Silence.

The once and former Professor Mitchell Jarvis Payton observed the most powerful man in the world, his eyes betraying mild astonishment. "That's an extremely scholarly statement," he said.

"Don't let the word get out, my mandate would disappear and I need those critics. . . . Forget it. You pass, MJ, I'm voting for you."

"MJ?"

"I told you, I had to do some fast gathering and faster reading."

"Why do I 'pass,' Mr. President? It's a personal as well as a professional question, if I may ask it."

"Because you didn't flinch."

"I beg your pardon?"

"You haven't been talking to Lang Jennings, a farmer from Iowa whose family made a few bucks because his daddy happened to buy forty-eight thousand acres in the mountains that developers sold their souls for. You've been talking to the head honcho of the Western world, the man who could take this planet right back to that ball of fire. If I were you, I'd be frightened confronting that fellow. Frightened and cautious."

"I'm trying not to be both, and I didn't even know about the forty-eight thousand acres."

"You think a relatively poor man could ever be president?"

"Probably not."

"Probably never. Power is to the rich, or the damn-near broke who haven't a thing to lose and a lot of clout and exposure to gain. . . . Regardless, *Dr.* Payton, you come here through a back door making an outrageous request, asking me to sanction the covert domestic activities of an agency prohibited by law from operating domestically. Further, and in the process, you want me to permit you to suppress extraordinary information involving a national tragedy, a terrorist massacre meant to kill a man the country owes a great deal to. In essence, you're asking me to violate any number of rules vital and intrinsic to my oath of office. Am I right so far?"

"I've given you my reasons, Mr. President. There's a web of circumstances that spreads from Oman to California, and it's so clear that it has to be more than coincidence. These fanatics, these terrorists, kill for one purpose that overrides all other motivations. They want to focus attention on themselves, they demand headlines to the point of suicide. Our only hope of catching them and the people here behind them is to withhold those headlines. . . . By sowing confusion and frustration someone may make a mistake in the heat of anger, reach someone else they shouldn't reach, breaking the chain of secrecy, and there *has* to be a chain, sir. Those killers got *in* here, which took powerful connections to begin with. They're moving around from one end of the country to the other with weapons; that's no simple feat, considering our security procedures. . . . I have a field agent from Cairo going to San Diego and the best man we have in Beirut heading for the Baaka Valley. They both know what to look for."

"*Jesus!*" cried Jennings, leaping up from the couch and pacing, the slipper falling off his foot. "I can't believe Orson is any *part* of this! He's not my favorite bedfellow but he's not insane—he's also not suicidal."

"He may *not* be a part of it, sir. Power, even a vice president's power, attracts the would-be powerful—or the would-be more powerful."

"God*damn* it!" shouted the President, walking over to a Queen Anne desk on which there were scattered papers. "No, wait a minute," said Jennings, turning. "In your own words you have this web of circumstances that somehow extends from the Oman crisis all the way across the world to San Diego. You say it has to be more than coincidence but that's all you've got. You don't have that well-advertised smoking gun, just a couple of people who knew each other years ago in the Middle East and one who suddenly shows up where you don't expect her."

"The woman in question has a history of borderline financial manipulations for very high stakes. She would hardly be enticed by an obscure political position that's light-years away from her normal compensation. . . . Unless there were other considerations."

"Andy-boy," said the President, as if to himself. "Gladhander Andy. . . . I never knew that about Ardis, of course. I thought she was a bank executive or something he met in England. Why would Vanvlanderen want her to work for Orson in the first place?"

"In my judgment, sir, it's all part of the web, the chain." Payton stood up. "I need your answer, Mr. President."

" 'Mr. President,' " repeated Jennings, shaking his head as if he could not quite accept the title. "I wonder if that word sticks in your throat."

"I beg your pardon?"

"You know what I mean, Doctor. You arrive here at one o'clock in the morning with this paranoid scenario asking me to commit impeachable offenses. Then when I ask you a few questions you proceed to tell me: *A,* You wouldn't vote for me. *B,* I'm simplistic. *C,* At best, I'm a predecessor of better men. *D,* I can't differentiate between coincidence and valid circumstantial evidence—"

"I never said *that,* Mr. President."

"You implied it."

"You asked for candor, sir. If I thought—"

"Oh, come on, get off it," said Jennings, turning toward the antique desk with the papers strewn across the top. "Are you aware that there's not a single person in the entire White House staff of over a thousand who would say those things to me? That doesn't include my wife and daughter, but then they're not official staff and they're both tougher than you are, incidentally."

"If I offended you, I apologize—"

"Don't, *please.* I told you that you passed and I wouldn't want to rescind the grade. I also wouldn't permit anyone else but someone like you to ask me to do what you've asked me to do. Quite simply, I wouldn't trust them. . . . You've got a green light, Doctor. Go wherever the hell the train takes you, just keep me informed. I'll give you a sacrosanct number that only my family has."

"I need a presidential finding of nondisclosure. I've prepared one."

"To cover your ass?"

"Certainly not, sir. I'll countersign it, assuming full responsibility for the request."

"Then why?"

"To protect those below me who are involved but who have no idea why." Payton reached into his jacket pocket and withdrew a folded page of paper. "This makes it clear that your staff has not been consulted."

"Thanks a bunch. So we both hang."

"No, Mr. President. Only myself. Nondisclosure is built into the statutes of the 1947 Act of Congress institutionalizing the CIA. It permits extraordinary action on the part of the Agency in times of national crisis."

"Any such finding would have to have a time limit."

"It does, sir. It's for a period of five days."

"I'll sign it," said Jennings, taking the paper and reaching for another on the Queen Anne desk. "And while I do I want you to read this—actually, you don't have to. Like most computerized printouts from the press office, it takes too long. It came to me this afternoon."

"What is it?"

"It's an analysis of a campaign to push Congressman Evan Kendrick onto the party's ticket next June." The President paused. "As the vice presidential candidate," he added softly.

"May I see that, please?" asked Payton, stepping forward, his hand outstretched.

"I thought you might want to," said Jennings, handing the elongated page to the director of Special Projects. "I wondered if you'd take it as seriously as Sam Winters took you."

"I do, sir," answered Payton, now rapidly, carefully scanning the eye-irritating computer print.

"If there's any substance to that paranoia of yours, you may find a basis there," said the President, watching his unexpected visitor closely. "My press people say it could fly . . . fly fast and high. As of next week, seven respectable newspapers in the Midwest will do more than raise Kendrick's name, they'll damn near editorially endorse him. Three of those papers own radio and television stations in concentrated areas north and south, and, speaking of coincidences, audio and visual tapes of the Congressman's television appearances were supplied to all of them."

"By whom? I can't find it here."

"You won't. There's only a half-assed ad hoc committee in Denver no one's ever heard of and they don't know anything. Everything's fed to Chicago."

"It's incredible!"

"Not really," disagreed Jennings. "The Congressman could prove to be an attractive candidate. There's a quiet electricity about him. He projects confidence and strength. He could catch on—fast and high, as my people say. Orson Bollinger's crowd, which I suppose is my crowd, could be having a collective case of the trots."

"That's not the incredibility I'm talking about, Mr. President. When I'm presented with such an obvious connection, even I have to back off. It's too simple, *too* obvious. I can't believe Bollinger's crowd could be that stupid. It's too incriminating, entirely too dangerous."

"You're losing me, Doctor. I thought you'd say something like 'Aha, my dear Watson, here's the proof!' But you're not, are you?"

"No, sir."

"If I'm going to sign this goddamned impeachable piece of paper, I think I'm entitled to know why."

"Because it really *is* too obvious. Bollinger's people learn that Evan Kendrick is about to be launched in a nationwide campaign to replace their Vice President, so they hire Palestinian terrorists to *kill* him? Only a maniac could invent that scenario. One flaw among a hundred-odd arrangements, one killer taken alive—which we *have*—and they could be traced . . . will be traced, if you'll sign that paper."

"Who will you find, then? What will you find?"

"I don't know, sir. We may have to start with that ad hoc committee in Denver. For months Kendrick has been maneuvered into a political limelight he never sought—has run from, actually. Now, on the eve of the real push there's the obscenity of Fairfax and the aborted assault on Mesa Verde, aborted by an old man who apparently doesn't let his age interfere with his actions. He *killed* three terrorists."

"I want to meet him, by the way," interrupted Jennings.

"I'll arrange it, but you may regret it."

"What's your point?"

"There are two factions, two camps, and neither is unsophisticated. Yet, on the surface, one may have committed an extraordinary blunder, which doesn't make sense."

"You're losing me again—"

"I'm lost myself, Mr. President. . . . Will you sign that paper? Will you give me five days?"

"I will, Dr. Payton, but why do I have the feeling that I'm about to face a guillotine?"

"Wrong projection, sir. The public would never allow your head to be chopped off."

"The public can be terribly wrong," said the President of the United States, bending over the Queen Anne desk and signing the document. "That's also part of history, Professor."

The streetlamps along Chicago's Lake Shore Drive flickered in the falling snow, creating tiny bursts of light on the ceiling of the room at the Drake Hotel. It was shortly past two in the morning and the muscular blond man was asleep in the bed, his breathing deep and steady, as if his self-control never left him. Suddenly his breathing stopped as the sharp, harsh bell of the telephone erupted. He bolted up to a sitting position, swinging his legs out from under the loose covers to the floor, and yanked the phone out of its cradle. "Yes?" said Milos Varak, no sleep in his voice.

"We have a problem," said Samuel Winters from his study in Cynwid Hollow, Maryland.

"Can you discuss it, sir?"

"I don't see why not, at least briefly and with abbreviations. This line is clean and I can't imagine anyone plugging into yours."

"Abbreviations, please."

"Roughly seven hours ago something horrible happened at a house in the Virginia suburbs—"

"A *storm*?" broke in the Czech.

"If I understand you, yes, a terrible storm with enormous loss."

"*Icarus?*" Varak nearly shouted.

"He wasn't there. Neither was he in the mountains, where a similar attempt was made but thwarted."

"Emmanuel Weingrass!" whispered the Czech under his breath. "He was the target. I knew it would happen!"

"It wouldn't appear so, but why do you say that?"

"Later, sir. . . . I drove down from Evanston around twelve-thirty—"

"I knew you were out, I started calling you hours ago but didn't leave word, of course. Is everything on schedule?"

"Ahead of it, but that's not what I mean. There was nothing on the radio about either event, and that's astonishing, isn't it?"

"If things go as I expect," answered Winters, "there'll *be* nothing for at least several days, if then."

"That's even more astonishing. How do you know that, sir?"

"Because I believe I've arranged it. A man I trust has gone privately to Sixteen Hundred through my intervention. He's there now. If there's any hope of catching those responsible, he needs the blackout."

With enormous relief, Milos Varak instantly understood that Samuel Winters was not the traitor within Inver Brass. Whoever the informer was, he would never prolong the hunt for killers if they were sent out by San Diego. Beyond that truth, that relief, the Czech coordinator had someone to confide in.

"Sir, please listen to me carefully. It's imperative—I repeat, imperative—that you call a meeting tomorrow as early as possible. It must be *during* the day, sir, *not* at night. Every hour will count in each of the time zones."

"That's a startling request."

"Call it an emergency. It *is* an emergency, sir. . . . And somehow, some *way,* I must find another emergency. I must force someone to make a move."

"Without specifics, can you give me a reason?"

"Yes. The one thing we never thought could happen within the group has happened. There's someone who shouldn't be there."

"Good *God*! . . . You're *certain*?"

"I'm certain. Seconds ago I eliminated you as a possibility."

It was four twenty-five in the morning, California time; seven twenty-five in the eastern United States. Andrew Vanvlanderen sat in his overstuffed velour chair, his eyes glazed, his heavy body weaving, his white wavy hair disheveled. In a burst of frenzy he suddenly threw a thick-based glass of whisky across the space into the television set; it glanced off the mahogany cabinet and dropped ineffectually on the white rug. In fury he picked up a marble ashtray and heaved it into the screen of the twenty-four-hour All News program. The convex glass picture shattered and the set imploded with a loud, sharp report as black smoke rushed out of the electronic entrails. Vanvlanderen roared incoherently at nothing and everything, his quivering lips trying to form words he could not find. In seconds his wife ran out of the bedroom.

"What are you *doing*?" she screamed.

"There's—*augh!*—nothing, not a goddamned *thing*!" he shrieked, his speech garbled, his neck and face flushed, the veins in his throat and forehead distended. "Not a fucking *thing*! What's *happened*? What's going *on*? They can't *do* this! I paid them a straight *two million*!" And then, without warning or the slightest indication of anything other than being in the grip of rage, Vanvlanderen lurched out of the chair, his arms trembling, his hands shaking violently, pressing a wall of air he could not see through his bulging eyes, and fell forward on the floor. As his face crashed into the rug a furious guttural cry was the last sound from his throat.

His fourth wife, Ardis Wojak Montreaux Frazier-Pyke Vanvlanderen, took several steps forward, her face white, her skin stretched to the parchment of a mask, her large eyes staring down at her dead husband. "You son of a *bitch*!" she whispered. "How could you leave me with this mess, whatever it *is*? Whatever the *hell* you've *done*!"

32

Ahbyahd called his four "priests" together in the motel room he shared with the young member of the mission who spoke fluent English and who had never been in Oman. It was 5:43 A.M., Colorado time, and the long vigil was over. There would be no rendezvous. Command Two had not made contact, which meant that Yosef and his men were dead; there was no other explanation. The hardened veteran who was half Jew but with a consummate hatred of all things Western and Israeli would never permit a single member of his team to be taken alive. It was why he had demanded that the crippled, harelipped boy who would not be denied should be at his side at all times.

At the first sign of even conceivable capture, I will put a bullet in your head, child. Do you understand?

I will do it first, old man. I seek my glorious death far more than my miserable life.

I believe you, you young fool. But please remember the words of Azra. Alive you can fight, dead you cannot.

The martyred Azra was right, thought Ahbyahd. However, Azra had not defined the ultimate sacrifice sought by all who truly believed. It was to die *while* fighting. That was why the jihad was impervious to traps, even to death. And the thunderous silence that resulted from the attack on the house in Virginia and the absence of Yosef and his men could only *be* a trap. It was the Western way of thinking: Deny the accomplishment, acknowledge nothing; force the hunters to search further and lead them into a trap. It was so *meaningless.* If the trap meant killing the enemy, in this instance the possibility of killing a great enemy, what did death matter? In their martyrdom they would find an exhilaration of happiness unknown in the life they led here on earth. There was no greater glory for the believer than to walk into the gentle clouds of Allah's heavens with the blood of their enemies on his hands in a just war.

It was this reasoning that confused Ahbyahd. Did not the Christians incessantly talk about walking into the arms of Christ for the causes of Christ, calling for wars in his name? Did not the Jews exalt their chosen status under Abraham's God to the exclusion of all others, fighting for deliverance as the Maccabees did, dying for their beliefs atop the Masada? Was Allah to be deemed unworthy in this company? Who decreed it? The Christians and the Jews? Ahbyahd was no scholar, barely a student of such difficult subjects, if the truth be known, but these were things taught by the elders, men steeped in the holy Koran. The lessons were clear: their enemies were quick to invent and fight for their own grievances but quicker still to deny the pain of others. The Christians and the Jews were very free in calling upon their Almighties in any conflict that threatened *them,* and they would certainly continue to deny the just cause of the lowly Palestinian, but they could not deny him his martyrdom. They *would* not in a distant place called Mesa Verde, thousands of kilometers from Mecca.

"My brothers," began the white-haired one, facing the four men of his command in the small, dingy motel room. "Our time has come and we approach it with rapture, knowing that a far better world lies before us, a heaven where we will be free, neither slaves nor pawns to others here on earth. If through the grace of Allah we survive to fight again, we will bring home to our brothers and sisters the holy kill of vengeance that so justly belongs to us. And the world will know that we have done it, know that five men of valor penetrated and destroyed all within two fortresses built by the great enemy to stop us. . . . Now we must prepare. First with prayers, and then with the more practical applications of our cause. Depending on what we learn, we strike when they will least expect an attack—not with the cover of night but in sunlight. By sundown we will either be with the holy hour of Salat el Maghreb or in the arms of Allah."

It was shortly past noon when Khalehla walked off the plane and into the lounge at San Diego's international airport. She was instantly aware of being watched mainly because her observer made no pretense of not doing so. The nondescript overweight man in an unpressed, ill-fitting gabardine suit was eating popcorn from a white cardboard container. He nodded his head once, turned, and started walking down the wide, crowded corridor toward the terminal. It was a signal. In moments Rashad caught up with him, slowing her pace to his at his side.

"I gather you weren't waiting to pick me up," she said without looking at him.

"If I was, you'd be on your knees begging me to take you home, which I'll probably have to do."

"Your modesty is as irresistible as you are."

"That's what my wife says, except she adds 'beauty.' "

"What is it?"

"Call Langley. I have a feeling that all hell's broken loose, but call from one of these phones, not my place, if it's going to be my place. I'll wait up ahead; if we're a team, just nod and follow me . . . at a respectful distance, naturally."

"I think I'd like a name. Something."

"Try Shapoff."

"*Gingerbread?*" said Khalehla, briefly shifting her eyes to glance at the field officer so highly regarded that he was practically a legend at the Agency. "East Berlin? Prague? Vienna—"

"Actually," interrupted the man in the disheveled gabardine suit. "I'm a left-handed periodontist from Cleveland."

"I guess I had a different picture of you."

"That's why I'm 'Gingerbread' . . . stupid goddamned name. Make your call."

Rashad peeled off at the next pay telephone. Anxious and not familiar with the latest phone procedures, she pushed the Operator button and, while feigning a bewildered French accent, placed a collect call to a number she had long since committed to memory.

"Yes?" said Mitchell Payton at the other end of the line.

"MJ, it's me. What's happened?"

"Andrew Vanvlanderen died early this morning."

"Killed?"

"No, it was a stroke; we've established that. There was a fair amount of alcohol in his blood and he was a mess—unshaven, eyes bloodshot, reeking of body sweat and worse—but it was a stroke."

"Damn . . . *damn*!"

"There was also an interesting set of circumstances—always circumstances, nothing clean. He'd been sitting in front of a television set for hours on end and obviously smashed it with a marble ashtray."

"Touchy, touchy," said the agent from Cairo. "What does his wife say?"

"Between excessive tears and pleas for seclusion, the stoic widow claims he was depressed over heavy losses in the market and other investments. Which, of course, she insists she knows nothing about, which of course she does. That marriage had to be consummated above a financial statement under the mattress."

"Did you check on her information?"

"Naturally. His portfolio could support several small nations. Two of his horses even won the daily double at Santa Anita last week and, along with a few others, are galloping toward millions in stud fees."

"So she was lying."

"She was lying," agreed Payton.

"But not necessarily about the depression."

"Let's try substituting another word. Rage, perhaps. Manic rage coupled with hysterical fear."

"Something didn't happen?" suggested Khalehla.

"Something was not made public as *having* happened. Perhaps it did, perhaps it didn't . . . perhaps it was botched. Perhaps, and this could be the trigger, *perhaps* several of the killers were taken alive, as, indeed, one was in Mesa Verde."

"And captured people can be made to talk volumes without knowing it."

"Precisely. All that's needed is one source who can describe one location, a method of travel, a drop. We have such a source, such a person. There are too many complications to hide everything. Whoever's behind these killings has to realize that, at least suspect it. That may have been on Andrew Vanvlanderen's mind."

"How are things going with the prisoner?"

"He's under now, or, as the doctors say, he's being taken up. He's a maniac. He's tried everything from self-asphyxiation to swallowing his tongue. As a result, they had to inject tranquilizers before they could give him the serums, slowing things a bit. The doctors tell me that we should have the first reports within an hour or so."

"What do *I* do now, MJ? I can't very well barge in on the grieving widow—"

"On the contrary, my dear," interrupted Payton. "That's exactly what you're going to do. We're going to turn this damned circumstantial liability into an asset. When a person like Mrs. Vanvlanderen accepts a position involving close ties with the potential successor to the President of the United States, personal considerations become secondary. . . . You'll apologize profusely, of course, but then stay with the scenario as we've outlined it."

"When you think about it," said Khalehla, "given the circumstances, the timing couldn't be better. I'm the last person she'll expect. It'll shake her up."

"I'm glad you agree. Remember, you may show compassion, but the cold business of national security comes first."

"What about Shapoff? Are we a team?"

"Only if you need him. We've lent him to naval intelligence, consultant status, and I'm glad he's there, but I'd rather you start solo. Work out contact arrangements."

"I gather he hasn't been briefed."

"No, only to give you whatever assistance you may ask for."

"I understand."

"Adrienne," said the director of Special Projects, drawing out the name. "There's something else you should also know. We may be a step closer to our blond-haired European and, equally important, what he's all about."

"Who is he? What did you find out?"

"We don't know *who* he is, but I'd say he's working for people who want to see Evan in the White House . . . or at least closer to it."

"My God! He'd never consider it in a thousand *years*! Who *are* these people?"

"Very rich and very resourceful, I'd guess." Payton briefly told her about the impending nationwide campaign to launch Kendrick into the vice presidency. "Jennings said his people are convinced it could fly—'fast and high' were his words. And in my opinion he wouldn't have the slightest objection."

"Right down to the President's own reaction," said Khalehla, her voice quiet, floating into the pay phone. "Every step, every move that was made was thought out and analyzed. All but one."

"What do you mean?"

"Evan's response, MJ. He'd never take it."

"Perhaps that's the shoe that hasn't dropped."

"It would have to be an iron boot the size of the Sphinx's foot. . . . Then there *are* two groups, one pushing our hero congressman onto the national ticket, the other doing its damnedest to keep him off."

"I came to the same conclusion and told the President as much. Go to work, Officer Rashad. Call me when you're settled in your hotel. I may have news from our doctors by then."

"I don't suppose I could get in touch with my grandparents, could I? They live near here, you know."

"Am I speaking with a *twelve*-year-old? Absolutely *not*!"

"Understood."

It was three o'clock in the winter afternoon, Eastern standard time, and the limousines were parked in the drive at the estate in Cynwid Hollow. The chauffeurs smoked cigarettes, talking quietly among themselves. Inside, the conference had begun.

"This will be a brief meeting," said Milos Varak, addressing the members of Inver Brass sitting in their chairs, the glare of the lamps illuminating their faces in the large, dimly lit study. "But the information was so vital, I appealed to Dr. Winters. I felt it was imperative that you be apprised."

"That's obvious," said Eric Sundstrom testily. "I've left an entire laboratory not knowing what to do next."

"You dragged me out of court, Milos," added Margaret Lowell. "I assume you're right, as you usually are."

"I flew back from Nassau," said Gideon Logan, laughing softly, "but then I wasn't doing anything but fishing until that damned ship's phone jingled. Also, I wasn't catching anything."

"I wish I could say I was even that productive, but I can't," offered Jacob Mandel. "I was at a Knicks' game when the beeper went off. I nearly didn't hear it, in fact."

"I think we should proceed," said Samuel Winters, an edge to his voice, part impatience and part something else, conceivably anger. "The information is devastating."

Margaret Lowell glanced over at the white-haired historian. "Of course we will, Sam. We're just catching our breath."

"I may have spoken of fishing," said Gideon Logan, "but my mind wasn't on fishing, Samuel."

The spokesman of Inver Brass nodded, his tentative smile unsuccessful. "Forgive me if I appear irritable. The truth is that I'm frightened, and so will you be."

"Then there's nothing in my laboratories as important to me as right now," said Sundstrom gently, as if rightly rebuked. "Please, go ahead, Milos."

Watch every face, every pair of eyes. Study the muscles of their jaws and around their lids and their hairlines. Look for involuntary swallows and pronounced veins on their necks. One of these four nearest me here knows the truth. One is the traitor.

"Palestinian terrorists have struck Congressman Kendrick's houses both in Virginia and Colorado. There was a considerable loss of life."

A kind of controlled pandemonium broke out in that extraordinary room inside the estate on Chesapeake Bay. Its occupants fell back into chairs or sat forward over the table in shock; throated cries came from stretched lips, eyes wide in horror or narrowed in disbelief, and the questions rapidly assaulted Varak like the sharp reports of repeated rifle fire.

"Was Kendrick *killed*?"

"When did it *happen*?"

"I've heard nothing *about* it!"

"Was anyone taken *alive*?" This last question, the questioner instantly examined by Milos Varak, was Gideon Logan, his dark face set in fury—or was it frenzy . . . or fear?

"I'll answer everything I can," said the Czech coordinator of Inver Brass, "but I must tell you that I'm not fully informed. The word is that Kendrick survived and is in protective custody. The attacks took place late yesterday afternoon or possibly in the early evening—"

"*Possibly?*" shouted Margaret Lowell. "*Yesterday?* Why don't you *know*—why don't we *all* know, why doesn't the *country* know?"

"There's a total blackout, apparently requested by the intelligence services and granted by the President."

"Obviously designed to go after the Arabs," said Mandel. "They kill for publicity, and if they don't get it they go crazier than they already are. Crazy people stand out—"

"And if they're alive they have to get *out* of the country," added Sundstrom. "Can they get out, Varak?"

"It would depend on the sophistication of their arrangements, sir. On who made it possible for them to get in."

"Were any of the Palestinians *taken* alive?" persisted Gideon Logan.

"I can only speculate," answered the Czech, his eyes neutral but beneath that neutrality searching intensely. "I was fortunate to learn what I did before the blackout was made total; the loss of life was not broken down at that point."

"What are your speculations?" asked Sundstrom.

"At best, there is only a ten to fifteen percent chance that any of the assailants was captured—alive. The figure is based on Mideast statistics. It's customary for terrorist teams to carry cyanide capsules sewn into their lapels, concealed razor blades and syringes taped to various parts of their bodies, anything that facilitates taking their own lives rather than revealing information through torture or drugs. Remember, except for the inability to kill their enemies, death is no sacrifice for these people. Instead, it's a rite of passage to an afterlife of joy, not in overabundance for them here."

"Then it's possible that one or two or more might have been captured alive," pressed Logan, making a statement.

"It's possible, depending upon how many were involved. It's a priority, if it can be accomplished."

"Why is it so important, Gideon?" asked Samuel Winters.

"Because we're all aware of the extraordinary measures taken to protect Kendrick," replied the black entrepreneur, studying Varak's face, "and I think it's imperative to know how these unschooled fanatics penetrated such security. Any word on that, Milos?"

"Yes, sir. Mine, and hardly official, but it's only a matter of days before the federal units make the connection I made."

"What the *hell* is it?" cried Margaret Lowell, her voice loud and sharp.

"I assume you're all aware of Andrew Vanvlanderen—"

"No," broke in Lowell.

"What about him?" asked Gideon Logan.

"Should we be?" chimed in Mandel.

"He died," said Eric Sundstrom, sitting back in his chair.

"What?" The word shot out three times in succession.

"It happened early this morning in California, too late for the Eastern papers," explained Winters. "The cause of death was listed as a heart attack. I heard it on the radio."

"So did I," added Sundstrom.

"I haven't listened to a radio." Margaret Lowell.

"I was on a boat and then a plane." Gideon Logan.

"I was at a basketball game." Jacob Mandel, guiltily.

"It's not the biggest news story of the day," continued Sundstrom, sitting forward. "The late editions of the *Post* had it on page four or five, I think, and Vanvlanderen was at least known in this town. Outside of here and Palm Springs, not too many people have ever heard his name."

"What's the connection to the Palestinians?" asked Logan, his dark eyes riveted on Varak.

"The alleged heart attack is open to question, sir."

Each face around the table was like granite—hard, immobile. Slowly, each looked at the others, the enormity of the implication rolling over them like an immense powerful wave.

"That's an extraordinary statement, Mr. Varak," said Winters quietly. "Would you explain, as you did to me, please?"

"The men around Vice President Bollinger, by and large the heaviest contributors to the party with interests to protect, are fighting among themselves. I've learned that there are different factions. One wants to replace the Vice President with a specific candidate, another wants to retain him, and still another insists on waiting until the political landscape is clearer."

"So?" intoned Jacob Mandel, removing his silver-rimmed glasses.

"The one person obviously *unacceptable* to everyone is Evan Kendrick."

"And, Milos?" said Margaret Lowell.

"Everything we do entails a degree of risk, Counselor," replied Varak. "I've never tried to minimize that despite the fact that I've guaranteed your anonymity. Nevertheless, to initiate the campaign for Congressman Kendrick, we had to create a political committee through which to funnel materials and considerable funds with yourselves nowhere in evidence. It took several weeks, and it's possible that the news reached San Diego. . . . It's not difficult to imagine the reactions of Bollinger's people, especially the faction most disposed toward him. Kendrick is a legitimate American hero, a viable candidate who could be swept onto the ticket in a wave of popularity just as we have proposed he should be. Those people might panic and look for quick, final solutions. . . . Among them would have to be the Vanvlanderens; and Mrs. Vanvlanderen, the Vice President's chief of staff, has extensive ties in Europe and the Middle East."

"Good *Christ*!" exclaimed Sundstrom. "Are you suggesting that Vice President Bollinger is responsible for these terrorist attacks, these *killings*?"

"Not directly, no, sir. It could be more on the order of King Henry's remarks within the royal court regarding Thomas Becket. 'Will no one rid me of this turbulent priest?' The King gave no order, no instructions, he simply asked a pointed question, probably while laughing, but his knights didn't miss the point. And the point here is that powerful people were instrumental in getting those killers into the country and supplied once they were here."

"It's *incredible*!" said Mandel, gripping his glasses, his voice a whisper.

"Just a minute," interrupted Gideon Logan, his large head at an angle, his eyes still riveted on the Czech. "You've also suggested that Vanvlanderen's stroke might have been something else. What makes you suspect that, and if you're right, how is it related to the Palestinians?"

"My initial suspicions about his stroke came when I learned that within an hour of the body's arrival at the mortuary Mrs. Vanvlanderen gave the order for immediate cremation, claiming that they had a mutual pact for the procedure."

"Said procedure eliminating any chance for an autopsy." Attorney Lowell nodded her head, clarifying the obvious. "What's the Palestinian connection, Milos?"

"To begin with, the timing. A healthy sportsman with no history of hypertension is suddenly dead less than twenty-four hours after the attacks on Kendrick's homes. Then, of course, learning further about Mrs. Vanvlanderen's extensive Middle East contacts—that was prompted by our brief discussion about her during the last meeting. These are things the federal investigators will piece together within a matter of days, and, if valid, find probable cause to relate them to the massacres."

"But if Vanvlanderen *was* dealing with the terrorists, why was he killed?" asked a bewildered Sundstrom. "He was the one holding the strings."

"I'll answer that, Eric," said Margaret Lowell. "The best way to put evidence out of reach is to destroy it. The courier is killed, not the one who sends the message. That way the instigator can't be traced."

"Too much, too *much*!" cried Jacob Mandel. "Such high levels of our government can be such *garbage*?"

"We know they can be, my friend," answered Samuel Winters. "Otherwise we ourselves would not be doing what we're doing."

"The tragedy of it," said the financier, shaking his head in sorrow. "A nation of such promise so racked from within. They'll change all the rules, all the laws. For *what*?"

"For themselves," replied Gideon Logan quietly.

"What do you think will happen, Milos?" asked Margaret Lowell.

"If there's any substance to my speculations and the blackout runs its course, I believe a cover story will be created completely omitting any reference to government officials making contact with terrorists. Scapegoats, dead ones, will be found. Washington can't afford to do otherwise; foreign policy would be in shambles."

"And Bollinger?" Once again Sundstrom sat back in his chair.

"Officially, if the scapegoats are sufficiently convincing, he could be taken, as you say here, off the hook. . . . That's officially, not where we are concerned."

"That's an interesting statement, if not an illuminating one, Mr. Varak," said Winters. "Would you mind clarifying?"

"Not at all, sir. Although I must return to Chicago, I've made arrangements with certain personnel at the telephone company in San Diego to provide me with records of every call placed to Bollinger's residence, his office and each member of his staff. They will state all initiating numbers and times, including pay phones and their locations. Unless I'm mistaken, we'll have enough ammunition, if only circumstantial, to persuade the Vice President to gracefully remove himself from the ticket."

The last limousine sped out of the drive as Samuel Winters hung up the telephone in the ornate, tapestried living room and joined Varak at the large front window.

"Which one *is* it?" said the Czech, staring out at the disappearing vehicle.

"I think you'll know before it's morning in California. . . . The helicopter will be here in a few minutes. The jet's cleared for takeoff at four-thirty in Easton."

"Thank you, sir. I trust we haven't made all these arrangements for nothing."

"Your case was very strong, Milos. Whoever it is won't dare place a call. He *or* she will have to appear in person. Is everything set at the hotel?"

"Yes. My driver at the airport in San Diego will have the keys to the service entrance and the suite. I'll use the freight elevator."

"Tell me," said the aristocratic white-haired historian. "Is it possible the scenario you presented to us this afternoon could be right? *Could* Andrew Vanvlanderen actually have made contact with the Palestinians?"

"No, sir, it's *not* possible. His wife would never permit it. She'd have killed him herself if he tried. Those kinds of complicated arrangements could be traced, with difficulty, of course, but she'd never take the chance. She's too professional."

In the distance, over the waters of Chesapeake Bay, the chopping sounds of a helicopter's rotors could be heard. They grew louder.

Khalehla dropped her purse on the floor, threw the two boxes and the three shopping bags on the bed and followed them, shoving the bags aside as her head hit the bulge of the pillows. She had asked "Gingerbread" Shapoff to drop her off at a department store so she could buy some clothes, since those she owned were in Cairo or Fairfax or in a Bahamian police car or on a U.S. Air Force jet.

"Fiddle-dee-dee," she said in a weary imitation of Scarlet O'Hara as she stared at the ceiling. "I'd like to think about *everything* tomorrow," she continued to herself out loud, "but, goddamnit, I can't." She sat up and reached for the hotel telephone, and dialed the appropriate numbers to reach Payton in Langley, Virginia.

"Yes?"

"MJ, don't you ever go home?"

"Are *you* home, my dear?"

"I don't know where it is any longer, but I'll let you in on a secret, Uncle Mitch."

"Uncle . . . ? Good heavens, you must want a pony ride. What is it?"

"Home may end up being with a certain mutual friend of ours."

"My, you *have* made progress."

"No, he did. He even talked about twenty or thirty years."

"Of what?"

"I don't know. A real home and babies and things like that, I guess."

"Then let's bring him out alive, Adrienne."

Khalehla shook her head, not in the negative but to bring herself back to the reality at hand. "The 'Adrienne' did it, MJ. Sorry."

"Don't be. We're entitled to our glimpses of happiness, and you know I want it all for you."

"It never happened for you, though, did it?"

"It was my choice, Field Officer Rashad."

"Gotcha, pal, or should I *sir*?"

"Say whatever you like, but listen to me. The first report is in from the clinic—the prisoner. They're apparently traveling as priests, Maronite priests on Israeli passports. That boy doesn't know very much; he's an also-ran who was somehow permitted to be part of the team because of Kendrick. He was crippled while he was with our congressman in Oman."

"I know, Evan told me. They were in a police truck heading down to the Jabal Sham. To their executions, they thought."

"Things get fuzzy here . . . that youngster was told very little and rightly so, he's completely unstable. From what our chemists can piece together, however, the two teams were to make contact near an airport—'Command One' joining 'Command Two,' which presumably means the Fairfax crowd was to hook up with the Colorado unit out *there.*"

"That's a lot of arranging, MJ, a lot of mileage. They've got savvy travel agents working on their itineraries."

"Very savvy and very hidden. One might almost say bureaucratically obscured."

"Speaking of which, I'm two floors above the grieving widow."

"Her office has been alerted. She's been told to expect your call."

"Then I'll straighten up and go to work. Incidentally, I had to buy a few things to dress the part, but I'll be damned if I'll pay for them. Let's say they're not me; they're a little on the severe side."

"I thought, considering Mrs. Vanvlanderen's past associations, you might be somewhat more chic."

"Well, they're not *that* severe."

"I didn't think so. Call me when it's over."

Khalehla hung up the phone, looked at it for a moment, then reached down for her purse on the floor. She opened it and took out a sheet of notepaper on which she had written Evan's telephone number in Mesa Verde. Seconds later she dialed.

"The Kendrick residence," said a woman's voice Khalehla recognized as belonging to one of the nurses.

"May I speak with the Congressman, please? This is Miss Adrienne of the State Department."

"Sure, hon, but you'll have to hang on while I get him. He's outside saying good-bye to that nice young Greek."

"Who?"

"I think he's Greek. He knows a lot of people the Congressman knew over in Arabia or wherever he was."

"What are you talking about?"

"The priest. He's a young priest from—"

"Get Evan away!" screamed Khalehla, lurching to her feet. "Yell for the guards! The *others* are *out* there! They want to *kill* him!"

33

It had been so simple, thought Ahbyahd, watching from the woods across from the despised enemy's huge house. A sincere and pleasant young priest whose papers were in order and, of course, who had no weapons on him, bearing greetings from friends of the great man. Who could refuse him a brief audience, this innocent religious from a distant land unaware of the formalities attached to calling upon great men? His initial rejection had been countermanded by the enemy himself; the rest was up to a highly inventive believer. What remained was up to all of them. They would not fail.

Their young comrade was walking out of the house! He was shaking hands with the loathsome "Amal Bahrudi" under the watchful eyes of the guards in business suits and carrying automatic weapons. The believers could only estimate the size of the guard force; it was a minimum of twelve men, conceivably more inside. With the love of Allah the first assault would remove a large block of them, killing most and severely wounding the rest beyond functioning.

Their comrade was being escorted down the circular drive to

the automobile, courteously parked on the road beyond the tall hedges. Only moments now. And the beloved Allah looked favorably upon them! Three more guards appeared, bringing the total in front of the house to seven. Do your work, our brother! Drive *accurately*!

The comrade reached the automobile; he bowed his head politely, making the sign of the cross, and once again shook hands, now with his single escort concealed from the others by the hedges. He then opened the door and briefly coughed, supporting himself on the back of the seat as his right arm reached down over the fabric. Suddenly, with the swiftness and assurance of a true believer, he spun around gripping a double-edged blade in his hand and plunging it into the guard's throat before the government man could see what was happening. Blood erupting, the guard fell as the terrorist grabbed the weapon and the body simultaneously, dragging the corpse across the road and into the overgrowth at the edge of the woods. He looked over in Ahbyahd's direction, nodded, and raced back to the car. Ahbyahd, in turn, snapped his fingers and signaled the brothers behind him hidden among the trees. The three men crept forward, dressed, as the white-haired one, in paramilitary clothing and gripping light-framed submachine guns, grenades clipped to their field jackets.

The English-speaking killer behind the wheel started the engine, shifted the car into gear, and drove slowly, casually, toward the left entrance of the circular drive. Then abruptly, with the motor suddenly roaring at its highest pitch, he swung the vehicle sharply to the right and into the entrance while he reached below the dashboard and flipped a switch. Opening the door, he aimed the car over the large front lawn toward the milling guards talking with the Congressman and leaped out of the racing automobile onto the gravel. As he hit the ground he heard a woman's screams through the cacophony of the thundering engine and the roars of the government patrols. One of the nurses had come running out the front door yelling incoherently; at the sight of the driverless onrushing automobile, she turned and screamed again, now at Kendrick, who was nearest the stone entrance.

"*Get away!*" she shrieked, repeating words she had obviously heard only moments before. "They want to *kill* you!"

The Congressman raced toward the heavy door, grabbing the woman by the arm and propelling her in front of him as the guards opened fire at the empty metal monster surging crazily out of control, veering now into the side of the house toward the sliding glass doors of the veranda. Inside, Evan crashed his shoulder into the door, slamming it shut. That action and the thick steel-reinforced panel of the door saved their lives.

The explosions came like thunderous successive combustions from some massive furnace, shattering windows and walls, firing curtains and drapes and furniture. Out in front of the house the seven guards from the Central Intelligence Agency fell, pierced by shards of glass and metal sent flying by ninety pounds of dynamite lashed to the undercarriage of the automobile's engine. Four were dead, heads and bodies riddled; two were barely alive, blood streaming out of eyes and chests. One, his left hand no more than a bleeding stump, had summoned rage, his weapon on automatic fire as he lurched across the lawn toward the priestly-collared terrorist, who was laughing insanely, his submachine gun spitting fire. Both men killed each other in the chill of the brisk Colorado day under the blinding Colorado sunlight.

Kendrick lunged up against the stone wall in the hallway, pressing himself into the bulging rock design. He looked down at the nurse. "Stay where you are!" he ordered as he inched his way toward the corner of the living room. Smoke was billowing everywhere, carried by the breezes through the shattered windows. He heard the shouts outside; the guards from their flanking positions around the house were converging, professionals covering one another as they moved into new positions. Then there were four detonations one after the other—*grenades*! These were followed by other voices screaming in Arabic. "*Death to our enemies! Death to a great enemy! Blood will be answered by blood!*" Repeated bursts from automatic weapons broke out from different directions. Two other grenades exploded, one thrown through the smashed windows directly into the living room, blowing apart the far wall. Evan spun around for the protection of the stone, then as the debris settled, he shouted.

"Manny! *Manny?* Where *are* you? *Answer* me!"

There was no reply, only the seemingly perverted, steady ringing of the telephone. The gunfire outside escalated to deafening proportions, burst upon burst, bullets ricocheting off rock, thumping into wood, screeching wildly through the air. Manny had been on the porch, the porch with glass doors! Kendrick had to get out there. He *had* to! He rushed into the smoke and fire of the living room, shielding his eyes and his nostrils, when suddenly a figure flew into the shattered front windows, crashing through the fragments of glass. The man rolled on the floor and sprang to his feet.

"*Ahbyahd!*" screamed Evan, paralyzed.

"*You!*" roared the Palestinian, his weapon leveled. "My life has glory! *Glory!* Beloved Allah be *praised*! You bring me *great* happiness!"

"Am I *worth* it to you? So many killed? So many butchered? Am I really *worth* it? Does your Allah demand so much death?"

"You can speak of *death*?" shrieked the terrorist. "Azra dead! Yaakov dead! Zaya killed by Jews from the skies over the Baaka! All the others . . . hundreds, thousands—*dead*! Now, *Amal Bahrudi,* such a clever traitor, I take you to *hell*!"

"Not *yet*!" came the voice, half whispered, half shouted from the archway leading to the porch. The words were accompanied by two loud, reverberating gunshots that momentarily drowned out the rapid fire outside. Ahbyahd, the white-haired one, arched back under the impact of the powerful weapon, a portion of his skull blown away. Emmanuel Weingrass, his face and shirt drenched with blood, his left shoulder pressed into the interior of the arch, slid to the floor.

"*Manny!*" yelled Kendrick, racing over to the old architect, kneeling down and lifting his upper body off the hard floor. "Where are you hit?"

"Where wasn't I?" replied Weingrass throatily, with difficulty. "Check the two girls! When . . . everything started they went to the windows. . . . I tried to stop them. Check them, *goddamn* you!"

Evan looked over at the two bodies on the porch. Beyond them, the sliding doors were no more than frames bordering sharp, pointed fragments of thick glass. The car bomb had done its work; there was little left of two human beings but shredded skin and blood. "There's nothing to check, Manny. I'm sorry."

"Oh, you call yourself a *God* in your fucking *heaven*!" screamed Weingrass, tears welling in his eyes. "What more do you want, you *fraud*!" The old man collapsed into unconsciousness.

Outside, the gunfire stopped. Kendrick prepared for the worst, wrenching the .357 Magnum out of Manny's hand, wondering briefly who had given it to him, instantly knowing it was Gee-Gee Gonzalez. He gently lowered Weingrass and stood up. He walked cautiously into the smoldering living room, and was suddenly assaulted by the stench of wet smoke—water was showering out of the ceiling sprinklers.

A *gunshot*! He dropped to the floor, his eyes darting in all directions, followed by his weapon.

"*Four!*" shouted a voice from beyond the shattered windows. "I count four!"

"One went inside!" yelled another. "Approach and fire at any goddamn thing that moves! *Christ,* I don't want our body count! And I also don't want one of these motherfuckers to walk out *alive*! Do you *understand* me?"

"Understood."

"He's dead!" yelled Evan with what voice he had left. "But there's another, a wounded man in here. He's alive and he's severely wounded and he's one of us."

"*Congressman?* Is that you, Mr. Kendrick?"

"It's me, and I never want to hear that title again." Once more the telephone started ringing. Evan got to his feet and headed wearily toward the charred pine desk, drenched by the separated sprays from the sprinklers. Suddenly, he saw the nurse who had saved his life walk hesitantly around the stone arch of the hallway. "Stay out of here," he said. "I don't want you to go out there."

"I heard you say there was someone wounded, sir. That's what I'm trained for."

The telephone kept ringing.

"*Him,* yes. Not the others. I don't want you to see the others!"

"I'm no spring chicken, Congressman. I did three tours of duty in 'Nam."

"But these were your *friends*!"

"So were countless others," said the nurse, no comment in her voice. "Is it Manny?"

"Yes."

The telephone kept ringing.

"After your call, please reach Dr. Lyons, sir."

Kendrick picked up the phone. "Yes?"

"Evan, thank *Christ*! It's MJ! I just heard from Adrienne—"

"Fuck off," said Kendrick, disconnecting the line and dialing Information.

At first the room spun around, then faraway thunder grew louder and bolts of lightning crashed into his mind. "Would you please repeat that, Operator, so I'm absolutely clear about what you've just said."

"Certainly, sir. There's no listing for a Dr. Lyons in Cortez or the Mesa Verde district. In fact, there's no one named Lyons—L-y-o-n-s—in the area."

"That was his *name*! I saw it on the clearance from the State Department!"

"I beg your pardon?"

"Nothing. . . . *Nothing!*" Evan slammed down the phone, and no sooner had he done so than it started ringing again. "*Yes?*"

"My darling! Are you all *right*?"

"Your fucking MJ *blew* it! I don't know how many are dead and Manny's shot up like a slaughtered pig! He's not only half gone but he doesn't even have a doctor!"

"Call Lyons."

"He doesn't *exist*! . . . How did you know about here?"

"I spoke to the nurse. She said a priest was there and, darling, *listen* to me! We found out only minutes ago that they were traveling as priests! I reached MJ and he's beside himself. He's got half of Colorado moving in, all federals and sworn to secrecy!"

"I just told him to take a hike."

"He's not your enemy, Evan."

"Who the hell *is*?"

"For God's sake, we're trying to find *out*!"

"You're a little slow."

"And they're very fast. What can I tell you?"

Kendrick, his hair drenched and his body soaked from the sprinklers, looked over at the nurse, who was ministering to Weingrass. Her eyes were filled with tears, her throat holding back her hysteria from the sight of her friends on the veranda. Evan spoke softly. "Tell me you're coming back to me. Tell me it's all going to end. Tell me I'm not going mad."

"I can tell you all of those things, but you have to believe them. You're alive and that's all that matters to me right now."

"What about the others who aren't alive? What about Manny? Don't they count?"

"Manny said something last night that impressed me very much. We were talking about the Hassans, Sabri and Kashi. He said we will each remember them and mourn for them in our own ways . . . but it must come later. To some that may sound cold, but not to me. He's been where I've been, my darling, and I know where he's coming from. None are forgotten, but for the moment we must forget them and do what we have to do. Does that make sense to you . . . my darling?"

"I'm trying to make sense out of it. When are you coming back?"

"I'll know in a couple of hours. I'll call you."

Evan hung up the phone as the multiple sounds of sirens and approaching helicopters grew louder, all centering on an infinitesimal spot of the earth erroneously called Mesa Verde, in Colorado.

"It's a perfectly lovely apartment," said Khalehla softly, walking through the marble foyer toward the sunken living room of the Vanvlanderen suite.

"It's convenient," offered the new widow, a handkerchief gripped in her hand as she closed the door and joined the intelligence officer from Cairo. "The Vice President can be quite demanding, and it was either this or having to run another house when he's in California. Two houses are a bit much—his *and* mine. Do sit down."

"Are they all like this?" asked Khalehla, sitting in the armchair designated by Ardis Vanvlanderen. It was across from the large, imposing brocade sofa; the lady of the house was quick to establish the pecking order of the seating arrangements.

"No, actually, my husband had it remodeled to our taste." The widow brought the handkerchief briefly to her face. "I suppose I should get used to saying 'my late husband,' " she added, lowering herself sadly on the couch.

"I'm *so* sorry, and to repeat what I said, I apologize for intruding at such a time. It's unconscionable, and I made that clear to my superiors, but they insisted."

"They were right. Affairs of state must go on, Miss Rashad. I understand."

"I'm not sure I do. This interview could have taken place at least tomorrow morning, in my opinion. But, again, others think otherwise."

"That's what fascinates me," said Ardis, smoothing the black silk of her Balenciaga dress. "What can be so vitally important?"

"To begin with," replied Khalehla, crossing her legs and removing a wrinkle from her dark gray suit, acquired by way of San Diego's Robinson's. "What we talk about must remain between ourselves. We don't want Vice President Bollinger unduly alarmed." The agent from Cairo took out a notebook from her black purse and smoothed her dark hair, which was pulled back and knotted in a severe bun. "As I know you've been told, I'm posted overseas and was flown back for this assignment."

"I was told that you're an expert in Middle East affairs."

"That's a euphemism for terrorist activities. I'm half Arab."

"I can see that. You're quite beautiful."

"You're *very* beautiful, Mrs. Vanvlanderen."

"I get by as long as I don't dwell upon the years."

"I'm sure we're close in age."

"Let's not dwell on that, either. . . . What *is* this problem? Why was it so urgent that you see me?"

"Our personnel who work the Baaka Valley in Lebanon have uncovered startling and disturbing information. Do you know what a 'hit team' is, Mrs. Vanvlanderen?"

"Who doesn't?" answered the widow, reaching for a pack of cigarettes on the coffee table. She extracted one and picked up a white marble lighter. "It's a group of men—usually men—sent out to assassinate someone." She lit the cigarette; her right hand almost imperceptibly trembled. "So much for definitions. Why does it concern the Vice President?"

"Because of the threats that were made against him. The reason for the unit you requested from the Federal Bureau of Investigation."

"That's all over," said Ardis, inhaling deeply. "It turned out to be some kind of psychotic crank who probably didn't even own a gun. But when those filthy letters and the obscene phone calls started coming in, I felt we couldn't take chances. It's all in the report; we chased him through a dozen cities until he got on a plane in Toronto. For Cuba, I understand, and it serves him right."

"He may not have been a crank, Mrs. Vanvlanderen."

"What do you mean?"

"Well, you never found him, did you?"

"The FBI worked up a very complete profile, Miss Rashad. He was determined to be mentally deranged, some kind of classic case of schizophrenia with overtones of a Captain Avenger complex or something equally ridiculous. He was essentially harmless. It's a closed book."

"We'd like to reopen it."

"Why?"

"Word from the Baaka Valley is that two or more hit teams have been dispatched over here conceivably to assassinate Vice President Bollinger. Your crank may have been the point, wittingly or unwittingly, but nevertheless, the point."

"The 'point'? What are you talking about? I can't even understand your language except that it sounds preposterous."

"Not at all," said Khalehla calmly. "Terrorists operate on the principle of maximum exposure. They will frequently announce an objective, a target, well in advance of execution. They do this in many ways, many variations."

"Why would terrorists want to kill Orson—Vice President Bollinger?"

"Why did you think the threats against him should be taken seriously?"

"Because they were *there.* I could do no less."

"And you were right," agreed the intelligence officer, watching the widow crushing out her cigarette and reaching for another, which she promptly lighted. "But to answer your question, should the Vice President be assassinated, there's not only a void on a political ticket assured of reelection, but considerable destabilization."

"For what purpose?"

"Maximum exposure. It would be a spectacular kill, wouldn't it? Even more so, as the record would show that the FBI had been alerted and then withdrawn, outsmarted by superior strategy."

"*Strategy?*" exclaimed Ardis Vanvlanderen. "*What* strategy?"

"A psychotic crank who wasn't a crank at all but a strategic diversion. Pivot attention on a harmless crank, then close the book while the real killers move into place."

"That's *crazy*!"

"It's been repeated over and over again. In the Arabic mind, everything progresses geometrically in stages. One step leads to another, the first not necessarily related to the third, but the connection is there if you look for it. Talking of classic cases, this diversion fits the bill."

"It *wasn't* a 'diversion'! There were the phone calls and the numbers were traced to different cities, the pasted-up letters with the filthy language!"

"Classic," repeated Khalehla softly, writing.

"What are you doing?"

"Reopening the book . . . and noting your convictions. May I ask you a question?"

"Certainly," replied the widow, her voice controlled but tight.

"Among Vice President Bollinger's many supporters—many friends, I should say—here in California, can you think of any who might not be either?"

"*What?*"

"It's no secret that the Vice President moves in wealthy circles. Is there anyone with whom he's had differences, or more than one, a particular group, perhaps? Over policy or procurements or government allocations."

"Good God, what are you *saying*?"

"We've reached the bottom line, Mrs. Vanvlanderen, the reason I'm here. Are there people in California who would rather have another candidate on the ticket? Frankly, another Vice President?"

"I can't believe I'm *hearing* this! How *dare* you?"

"I'm not the one who's daring, Mrs. Vanvlanderen. Someone else is. International communications, no matter how obscured, can ultimately be traced. Perhaps not at first to a specific individual or individuals, but to a sector, a location. . . . There's a third party, or parties, involved in this terrible thing, and they're here in southern California. Our people in the Baaka have zeroed in on initial cablegrams routed through Beirut from Zurich, Switzerland, original dateline . . . San Diego."

"San Diego . . . ? *Zurich?*"

"Money. A convergence of interests. One party wants a spectacular kill with maximum exposure, while the other wants the spectacular target removed but must stay as far away from the kill as possible. Both objectives take a great deal of money. 'Follow the money' is a maxim in our work. We're tracing it now."

"Tracing it?"

"It will only be a matter of days. The Swiss banks are cooperative where drugs and terrorism are concerned. And our agents in the Baaka are forwarding descriptions of the teams. We've stopped them before and we'll stop them now. We'll find the San Diego connection. We simply thought you might have some ideas."

"*Ideas?*" cried the stunned widow, crushing out the cigarette. "I can't even think, it's all so incredible! Are you certain that some enormous, *extraordinary* error hasn't been made?"

"We don't make errors in these matters."

"Well, *I* think that's pretty shit-kicking egotistical," said Ardis, the speech of Monongahela overriding her cultivated British. "I mean, Miss Rashad, you're not *infallible.*"

"In some cases we have to be; we can't afford not to be."

"Now, *that's* asinine! . . . I mean—I mean *if* there are these hit teams, and *if* there are communications to Zurich and Beirut from . . . from the San Diego *area,* anyone could have sent them, giving any names they wanted to! I mean they could have used *my* name, for Christ's sake!"

"We'd instantly discount anything like that." Khalehla answered the unasked what-if question as she closed her notebook and replaced it in her purse. "It would be a setup, and far too obvious to be taken seriously."

"Yes, that's what I mean, a setup! Someone could be *setting up* one of Orson's friends, isn't that possible?"

"For the purpose of assassinating the Vice President?"

"Maybe the—what did you call it?—the *target* is somebody else, isn't *that* possible?"

"Somebody else?" asked the field agent, nearly wincing as the intense widow grabbed another cigarette.

"*Yes.* And by sending cablegrams from the San Diego area implicating an innocent Bollinger supporter! That *is* possible, Miss Rashad."

"It's very interesting, Mrs. Vanvlanderen. I'll convey your thoughts to my superiors. We'll have to consider the possibility. A double omission with a false insert."

"*What?*" The widow's scratching voice was right out of a long-gone Pittsburgh saloon.

"Shop talk," said Khalehla, rising from the chair. "It simply means disguise the target, omit the source, and provide a false identity."

"You people talk goddamned funny."

"It serves a purpose. . . . We'll stay in constant touch with you, and we have the Vice President's schedule. Our own people, all counterterrorist experts, will quietly supplement Mr. Bollinger's security forces at every location."

"Yeah—awright." Mrs. Vanvlanderen, the cigarette in her hand, the handkerchief forgotten on the brocade sofa, escorted Rashad out of the living room and up to the door.

"Oh, about the double omission–insert theory," said the intelligence officer in the marble foyer. "It's interesting, and we'll use it to press the Swiss banks for quick action, but I don't think it really holds water."

"*What?*"

"All numbered Swiss accounts have sealed—and therefore unsealable—codes leading to points of origin. They are often labyrinthine, but they can be traced. Even the greediest Mafia overlord or Saudi arms merchant knows he's mortal. He's not going to leave millions to the gnomes of Zurich. . . . Good night, and, again, my deepest sympathies."

Khalehla walked back to the closed door of the Vanvlanderen suite. She could hear a muted scream of panic wrapped in obscenities from within; the sole resident of the tailored-to-taste apartment was going over the edge. The scenario had *worked.* MJ was right! The negative circumstances of Andrew Vanvlanderen's death had been reversed. What had been a liability was now an asset. The contributor's widow was breaking.

Milos Varak stood in a dark storefront thirty yards to the left of the entrance to the Westlake Hotel, ten yards from the corner where the service entrance was located on the intersecting street. It was 7:35 P.M., California time; he had outraced every commercial flight across the country from Washington, D.C., Maryland and Virginia. He was in place for the moment of revelation, and equally important, everything was arranged upstairs in the hotel. The cleaning staff of the management—a management genuinely concerned with the grieving widow's sorrow—included a new member, experienced and instructed by the Czech. Frequency-designed intercepts had been placed in every room; no conversation could take place without being recorded by Varak's voice-activated tapes in the adjoining suite.

Taxis drove up to the hotel on the average of one every three minutes and Milos studied each departing fare. He had seen twenty to thirty, losing count but not his concentration. Suddenly he was aware of the unusual: a cab stopped on his *left,* across the intersecting street at least a hundred feet away. A man got out and Varak moved farther back into the unlighted store recess.

"I heard it on the radio."

"So did I."

"She's a bitch!"

"And if they're alive, they have to get out of the country. Can they get out . . . ?"

"What are your speculations?"

"It's not the biggest news story of the day."

"And Bollinger?"

The man in the topcoat, the lapels pulled up, covering his face, walked rapidly across the street toward the hotel's entrance. He passed within ten feet of Inver Brass's coordinator. The traitor was Eric Sundstrom, and he was a man in panic.

34

Ardis Vanvlanderen gasped. "Good *Christ,* what are *you* doing here?" she cried, literally yanking the rotund Sundstrom through the door and slamming it shut. "Are you out of your *mind*?"

"I'm very much in it, but yours is out to lunch. . . . Stupid, stupid, *stupid*! What did you and that horse's ass of a husband of yours think you were *doing*?"

"The Arabs? The hit teams?"

"Yes! Goddamned fools—"

"It's all *preposterous*!" screamed the widow. "It's a horrendous mix-up. Why would we—why would *Andy* want to have Bollinger killed?"

"Bollinger . . . ? It's *Kendrick,* you bitch! Palestinian terrorists attacked his houses in Virginia and Colorado. There's a blackout on the news, but a lot of people were killed—not, however, the golden boy himself."

"*Kendrick?*" whispered Ardis, panic in her large green eyes. "Oh, my God . . . and they think the killers are coming out here to assassinate Bollinger. They've got it all *backwards*!"

"They?" Sundstrom froze, his face ashen. "What are you talking about?"

"We'd both better sit down." Mrs. Vanvlanderen walked out of the foyer and down into the living room, to the couch and her cigarettes. The pale scientist followed, then veered to a dry bar, where there were bottles, decanters, glasses and an ice bucket. Without glancing at the labels, he picked up a bottle at random and poured himself a drink.

"Who is *they*?" he asked quietly, intensely, as he turned and watched Ardis on the couch lighting a cigarette.

"She left about an hour and a half ago—"

"She? *Who?*"

"A woman named Rashad, a counterterrorist expert. She's with a cross-over unit, CIA joining up with State. She never *mentioned* Kendrick!"

"*Jesus,* they've put it together. Varak said they would and they *did*!"

"Who's Varak?"

"We call him our coordinator. He said they'd find out about your Middle East interests."

"My *what?*" shouted the widow, her face contorted, her mouth gaping.

"That Off Shore company—"

"Off Shore Investments," completed Ardis, again stunned. "It was eight months out of my life but that's *all* it was!"

"And how you have contacts throughout the whole area—"

"I have *no* contacts!" screamed Mrs. Vanvlanderen. "I left over ten years ago and never went back! The only Arabs I know are a few high rollers I met in London and Divonne."

"Rollers in bed or at the tables?"

"*Both,* if you want to know, lover boy! . . . Why would they *think* that?"

"Because you gave them a damn good reason to start looking when you had that son of a bitch cremated this morning!"

"*Andy?*"

"Was there someone else hanging around here who happened to drop dead? Or perhaps was *poisoned*? In a cover-up!"

"What the hell are you talking about?"

"Your fourth or fifth husband's body, that's what I'm talking about. No sooner does it reach the damned mortuary than you're on the phone ordering his immediate cremation. You think that's not going to start people wondering—people who are paid to wonder about things like that? No autopsy, ashes somewhere over the Pacific."

"I never *made* such a call!" roared Ardis, leaping up from the couch. "I never gave such an *order*!"

"You *did*!" yelled Sundstrom. "You said you and Andrew had a pact."

"I didn't say it and *we* didn't have one!"

"Varak doesn't bring us wrong information," stated the high-tech scientist firmly.

"Then someone lied to him." The widow suddenly lowered her voice. "Or he was lying."

"Why would he? He's never lied before."

"I don't know," said Ardis, sitting down and stabbing out her cigarette. "Eric," she continued, looking up at Inver Brass's traitor. "Why did you come all the way out here to tell me this? Why didn't you just call? You have our private numbers."

"Varak again. Nobody really knows how he can do what he

does—still, he does it. He's in Chicago, but he's made arrangements to be given the telephone number of every incoming call to Bollinger's office and residence, as well as the office and residence of each member of his staff. Under those conditions I don't make phone calls."

"In your case it might be hard to explain to that council of senile lunatics you belong to. And the only calls I've gotten were from the office and friends with condolences. Also the Rashad woman; none of those would interest Mr. Varak or your benevolent society of rich misfits."

"The Rashad woman. You say she didn't mention the attacks on Kendrick's houses. Assuming Varak's wrong and the investigating units haven't put certain facts together and come up with you and perhaps a few others out here, why *didn't* she? She had to know about them."

Ardis Vanvlanderen reached for a cigarette, her eyes now betraying an unfamiliar helplessness. "There could be several reasons," she said without much conviction as she snapped up the flame of the lighter. "To begin with, the Vice President is frequently overlooked where clearances are concerned regarding security blackouts—Truman had never heard of the Manhattan Project. Then there's the matter of avoiding panic, *if* these attacks took place—and I'm not ready to concede that they did. Your Varak's been caught in one lie; he's capable of another. Regardless, if the full extent of the damage in Virginia and Colorado was known, we might lose staff control. No one likes to think he might be killed by suicidal terrorists. . . . Finally, I go back to the attacks themselves. I don't believe they ever happened."

Sundstrom stood motionless, gripping the glass in both hands, as he stared down at his former lover. "He did it, didn't he, Ardis?" he said softly. "That financial megalomaniac couldn't stand the possibility that a small group of 'benevolent misfits' might replace his man with another who could cut off his pipeline to millions and probably would."

The widow collapsed back into the couch, her long neck arched, her eyes closed. "Eight hundred million," she whispered. "That's what he said. Eight hundred million for him alone, billions for all the rest of you."

"He never told you what he was doing, what he had done?"

"Good *Christ,* no! I'd have put a bullet in his head and called one of you to deep-six him in Mexico."

"I believe you."

"Will the *others*?" Ardis sat up, her eyes pleading.

"Oh, I think so. They know you."

"I swear to you, Eric, I didn't know a *thing*!"

"I said I believed you."

"The Rashad woman told me they were tracing the money he sent through Zurich. Can they *do* that?"

"If I knew Andrew, it would take them months. His coded pay-in sources ranged from South Africa to the Baltic. Months, a year, perhaps."

"Will the others know that?"

"We'll see what they say."

"What? . . . *Eric!*"

"I called Grinell from the airport in Baltimore. He's no part of Bollinger's staff and God knows he stays in the background, but if we have a chairman of the board, I think we'd all agree he's the fellow."

"Eric, what are you telling me?" asked Mrs. Vanvlanderen, her voice flat.

"He'll be here in a few minutes. We agreed we should have a talk. I wanted a little time with you alone, but he should be here shortly." Sundstrom glanced at his watch.

"You've got that glassy look in your eyes, lover boy," said Ardis, slowly getting up from the couch.

"Oh, yes," agreed the scientist. "The one you always laughed at when I couldn't . . . shall we say, perform."

"Your mind was so often on other things. You're such a brilliant man."

"Yes, I know. You once said that you always knew when I was solving a problem. I went limp."

"I loved your mind. I still love it."

"How could you? You don't really have one yourself, so how would you know."

"Eric, Grinell *frightens* me."

"He doesn't frighten me. He has a mind."

The chimes of the front door filled the Vanvlanderen suite.

Kendrick sat in a small canvas chair by the cot in the cabin of the jet that was flying them to Denver. Emmanuel Weingrass, his wounds prevented from further bleeding by the surviving nurse in Mesa Verde, kept blinking his dark eyes, made darker by the lined white flesh surrounding them.

"I've been thinking," said Manny with difficulty, half coughing the words.

"Don't talk," broke in Evan. "Conserve your strength. Please?"

"Oh, get off it," replied the old man. "What have I got? Twenty more years and I don't get laid?"

"Will you *stop* it?"

"No, I won't stop it. Five years I don't see you, so we get back together and what happens? You get too attached—to *me.* What are you, a *feygele* with a hang-up for old guys? . . . Don't answer that, Khalehla will do it for you. You two must have busted your parts last night."

"Why don't you ever talk like a normal person?"

"Because normalcy bores me, just like you're beginning to bore me. . . . Don't you know what all this shit is about? I brought up a dummy? You can't figure?"

"No, I can't figure, all *right*?"

"That lovely girl was on the button. Someone wants to make you very important in this country, and someone else is having bowel movements over the prospect. You can't *see* that?"

"I'm beginning to, and I hope the other guys win. I don't want to be important."

"Maybe you should be. Maybe it's where you belong."

"Who the hell says so? Who thinks so?"

"The people who don't *want* you—you think about that. Khalehla told us that these garbage maniacs who came over here to kill you didn't just hop on a plane from Paris or walk off a cruise ship. They had help, influential help. How did she put it? . . . Passports, weapons, money—even driver's licenses and clothes and hideouts. Those things, especially the paperwork, you don't pick up at Walgreen's. They take contacts with power in high places, and the people who can pull those kinds of strings are the bastards who want you dead. . . . Why? Does the outspoken Congressman pose a threat to them?"

"How can I be a threat? I'm getting out."

"They don't know that. All they see is a mensch politician who, when he opens his mouth, everybody in Washington shuts up and listens to him."

"I don't talk that much, so the listening's minor, practically nonexistent."

"The point is that when you do talk, they don't. You got what I call listening credentials. Like I do, frankly." Weingrass coughed, bringing a trembling hand to his throat. Evan bent over him, concerned.

"Take it easy, Manny."

"Be quiet," ordered the old man. "You hear what I've got to say. . . . Those bastards see a real American hero who's awarded a big medal by the President and put on important committees in the Congress—"

"The committees came before the medal—"

"Don't interrupt. After a couple of months the sequence of things blurs—anyway, you just made it stronger. This hero takes on the Pentagon brass over national television *before* he's a hero and damn near indicts the whole damned bunch of them as well as all those big industrial complexes who supply the machine. Then what does he do? He *demands* accountability. Terrific word, 'accountability'—the bastards all hate it. They've got to start sweating, kid. They've got to figure that maybe this joker-hero will get more powerful, maybe chair one of those committees, or even get elected to the Senate, where he could do some real damage."

"You're exaggerating."

"Your girlfriend wasn't!" countered Weingrass loudly, staring into Kendrick's eyes. "She told us that her elite group may have tapped into a nerve center higher up in the government than they want to think about. . . . Doesn't all this present a blueprint to you, although I admit you were never the hottest shot with a blueprint I ever knew?"

"Of course it does," answered Evan, nodding slowly. "There's no nation in the world that doesn't have its degrees of corruption, and I doubt there ever will be."

"Oh, *corruption*?" intoned Manny, eyes rolling, as if the word were part of a Talmudic chant. "Like in one guy stealing a buck's worth of paper clips from the office and another taking a million with a cost overrun, is that what you mean?"

"Basically, yes. Or ten million, if you like."

"Insignificant *peanuts*!" shouted Weingrass. "Such people do not deal with Palestinian terrorists thousands of miles away for the sole purpose of positively removing themselves from a *kill*. They wouldn't know *how*! Also, you didn't look into that lovely girl's eyes, or maybe you don't know what to look for. You've never been there."

"She says she knows where you're coming from because you *have* been there. All right, I haven't, so what are you talking about?"

"When you're there, you're scared," said the old man. "You're walking toward a black drape that you're going to pull down. You're excited; the curiosity's killing you and so is the fear. All of those things. You try like hell to suppress them, even hide some from yourself, and that's part of it because you can't afford to lose an ounce of control. But it's all there. Because once that drape is yanked away you know you'll be looking at something so *nuts* you wonder if anyone will believe it."

"You saw all that in her eyes?"

"Enough, yes."

"Why?"

"She's getting near the edge, kid."

"*Why?*"

"Because we're not dealing—she's not dealing—with simple corruption, even terrific corruption. What's behind that black curtain is a government within the government, a bunch of servants running the master's house." The old architect suddenly went into a spasm of coughing, his whole body trembling, his eyes shut tight. Kendrick grabbed his arms; in moments the convulsion was over and Manny blinked again, breathing deeply. "Listen to me, my dumb son," he whispered. "Help her, really help her, and help Payton. Find the bastards and rip them *out*!"

"Of course I will, you know that."

"I *hate* them! That youngster under chemicals, that Ahbyahd you knew in Masqat—we might have been friends in another time. But that time won't ever come as long as there are bastards who pit ourselves against ourselves because they make billions out of hatred."

"It's not that simple, Manny—"

"It's a larger part of it than you *think*! I've *seen* it! . . . 'They have more than you do, so we'll sell you more than *they* have'—that's one of the come-ons. Or 'They'll kill you unless you kill them first, so here's the firepower—for a price.' It goes right up the goddamned ladder: 'They spent twenty million on a missile, we'll spend *forty* million!' Do we really want to blow up the fucking planet? Or is everyone listening to lunatics who listen to men who sell hatred and peddle fear?"

"On that level, it's that simple," said Evan, smiling. "I may even have mentioned it myself."

"Keep mentioning it, kid. Don't walk away from that platform we talked about—mainly regarding a certain Herbert Dennison we also talked about who you scared the shit out of. Remember, you got listening credentials like me. Use 'em."

"I'll have to think about it, Manny."

"Well, while you're thinking," coughed Weingrass, his right

hand on his chest, "why don't you think about why you had to lie to me? You and the doctors, that is."

"What?"

"It's back, Evan. It's back and it's worse because it never went away."

"What's back?"

" 'Big casino,' I think is the gentle phrase. The cancer's running rampant."

"No, it *isn't.* We ran you through a dozen tests. They got it—you're clean."

"Tell that to these little suckers who are choking off my air."

"I'm no doctor, Manny, but I don't think that's a symptom. During the last thirty-six hours you've been through a couple of wars. It's a wonder you can breathe at all."

"Yeah, but while they're patching me up at the hospital you have them run one of those little checks, and don't lie to me. There are some people in Paris I've got to take care of, some things I've got locked away they should have. So don't lie to me, understand?"

"I won't lie to you," said Kendrick as the aircraft started its descent into Denver.

Crayton Grinell was a slender man of medium height and a perpetually gray face made prominent by sharp prominent features. When greeting someone, for the first time or the fiftieth, whether a waiter or a board chairman, the forty-eight-year-old attorney who specialized in international law greeted that person with a shy smile that conveyed warmth. The warmth and the modesty were accepted readily until one looked into Grinell's eyes. It was not that they were cold, for they were not, yet neither were they particularly friendly; they were expressionless, neutral, the eyes of a cautiously curious cat.

"Ardis, my *dear* Ardis," said the lawyer, walking into the foyer and holding the widow, gently patting her shoulder as one might console a faintly disagreeable aunt who had lost a far more agreeable husband. "What can I say? What can anyone say? Such a loss for us all, but how much more so for you."

"It was sudden, Cray. Too sudden."

"Of course it was, but we must all look for something positive in our sorrows, mustn't we? You and he were spared a prolonged and agonizing illness. Since the end must come, it's better if it's quick, isn't it?"

"I suppose you're right. Thank you for reminding me."

"Not at all." Disengaging himself, Grinell looked over at Sundstrom, who was standing in the large sunken living room. "Eric, how good to see you," he said solemnly, walking across the foyer and down the marble steps to shake hands with the scientist. "Somehow it's right that we both should be with Ardis at a time like this. Incidentally, my men are outside in the hallway."

"Fucking bitch!" Sundstrom muttered the words, his breath a whisper as the grieving Mrs. Vanvlanderen closed the door, the sound of the closing and the noise of her heels on the marble covering the mumble uttered by her former lover.

"Would you care for a drink, Cray?"

"Oh, no thank you."

"I think I will," said Ardis, heading for the dry bar.

"I think you should," agreed the attorney.

"Is there anything I can do? At the legal end here, or with arrangements, anything at all?"

"I imagine you'll be doing it, the legal things, I mean. Andy-boy had lawyers all over the place, but I gathered you were his main man."

"Yes, I was, and we've all been in touch during the day. New York, Washington, London, Paris, Marseilles, Oslo, Stockholm, Bern, Zurich, West Berlin—I'm handling everything personally, of course."

The widow stood motionless, a decanter halfway to her glass, staring at Grinell. "When I said 'all over the place,' I didn't think *that* far all over the place."

"His interests were extensive."

"Zurich . . . ?" said Ardis, as if the name of the city had slipped out unintentionally.

"It's in *Switzerland*!" broke in Sundstrom harshly. "And let's cut the crap."

"Eric, really—"

"Don't 'Eric, really' *me,* Cray. That bullheaded horse's ass did it. He contracted the Palestinians and paid them out of Zurich. . . . Remember Zurich, *sweetie*? . . . I told you in Baltimore, Cray. He *did* it!"

"I couldn't get a confirmation on the assaults in Fairfax or Colorado," said Grinell calmly.

"Because they never *happened*!" yelled the widow, her right hand trembling as she poured a drink from the heavy crystal decanter.

"I didn't say that, Ardis," objected the attorney softly. "I merely said I couldn't get a confirmation. However, I did get a later call, no doubt placed by a well-paid drunk who was handed a phone after the number was dialed, thus eliminating the identity of the source. The words he obviously repeated are all too familiar. 'They're following the money,' he said."

"Oh, *Jesus*!" exclaimed Mrs. Vanvlanderen.

"So now we have two crises," continued Grinell, walking to a white marble telephone on a red-lined marble table against the wall. "Our weak, ubiquitous Secretary of State is on his way to Cyprus to sign an agreement that could cripple the defense industry, and one of our own is linked to Palestinian terrorists. . . . In a way, I wish to heaven I knew how Andrew did it. We may be far clumsier." He dialed as the widow and the scientist watched. "The switch from Design Six to Design Twelve, Mediterranean, is confirmed," said the attorney into the phone. "And prepare the medical unit, if you will, please."

35

Varak raced around the corner to the service entrance and took the freight elevator up to his floor. He then walked rapidly to his rooms, unlocked the door and rushed to the sophisticated vertical recording equipment against the wall, somewhat startled to see that so much tape had been used. He ascribed it to various telephone calls received by Ardis Vanvlanderen. He flipped the switch that allowed dual transmission, tape and direct audio, put on the earphones and sat down to listen.

She left about an hour and a half ago.

She? Who?

A woman named Rashad, a counterterrorist expert. She's with a cross-over unit. . . .

The Czech glanced at the spool of exposed tape. There were at least twenty-five minutes of recorded conversation on it! What was the former operations officer from Egypt doing in *San Diego*? It made no sense to Milos. She had resigned from the Agency; he had *confirmed* it. The quiet but official word out of Cairo and Washington was that she had been "open to compromise." He assumed it was the Oman operation and thoroughly accepted her vanishing. She *had* to fade—but she had *not*! He listened further to the conversation taking place in the Vanvlanderen suite. Sundstrom was speaking.

He did it, didn't he, Ardis? That financial megalomaniac couldn't stand the possibility that a small group of 'benevolent misfits' might replace his man with another who could cut off his pipeline to millions and probably would.

Then Ardis Vanvlanderen:

Eight hundred million, that's what he said. Eight hundred million for him alone, billions for all the rest of you. . . . I didn't know a thing!

Varak was stunned. He had made *two* enormous errors! The first concerned the covert activities of Adrienne Khalehla Rashad, and as difficult as it was for him to accept this error, he could do so, for she was an experienced intelligence officer. The second he could *not* accept! The false scenario he had presented to Inver Brass had been *true*! It had never occurred to him that Andrew Vanvlanderen would act independently of his wife. How *could* he? Theirs was a La Rochefoucauld marriage, one of convenience, of mutual benefit, certainly not of affection, to say nothing of love. Andy-boy had broken the rules. A bull in financial heat had crashed open the gates of his corral and raced into the slaughterhouse. Varak listened.

Another voice, another name. A man named Crayton Grinell. The tape rolled as the Czech concentrated on the words being spoken. Finally:

So now we have two crises. Our weak, ubiquitous Secretary of State is on his way to Cyprus to sign an agreement that could cripple the defense industry. . . . The switch from Design Six to Design Twelve, Mediterranean, is confirmed.

Varak tore off the earphones. Whatever remained to be heard in the Vanvlanderen suite would be recorded. He had to move quickly. He got out of the chair and rushed across the room to the telephone. He picked it up and pressed the numbers for Cynwid Hollow, Maryland.

"Yes?"

"Sir, it's Varak."

"What is it, Milos? What have you learned?"

"It's Sundstrom—"

"*What?*"

"That can wait, Dr. Winters, something else cannot. The Secretary of State is flying to Cyprus. Can you find out *when*?"

"I don't have to find out, I know. So does everyone else who watches television or listens to the radio. It's quite a breakthrough—"

"*When,* sir?"

"He left London about an hour ago. There was the usual statement about bringing the world closer to peace and that sort of thing—"

"In the *Mediterranean*!" interrupted Varak, controlling his voice. "It will happen in the Mediterranean."

"What will?"

"I don't know. A strategy called Design Twelve, that's all I heard. It will happen on the ground or in the air. They want to stop him."

"*Who* does?"

"The contributors. A man named Grinell, Crayton Grinell. If I tried to break in and find out, they might take me. There are men outside the door and I cannot jeopardize the group. I certainly would never willingly disclose information, but there are drugs—"

"Yes, I know."

"Reach Frank Swann at the State Department. Tell the switchboard to raise him wherever he is and use the phrase 'crisis containment.'"

"Why Swann?"

"He's a specialist, sir. He ran the Oman operation for State."

"Yes, I know that, but I might have to tell him more than I care to. . . . There may be a better way, Milos. Stay on the line, I'm going to put you on hold." Each ten seconds that went by seemed like minutes to Varak, then they *were* minutes! What was Winters *doing*? They did not have minutes to waste. Finally the spokesman for Inver Brass was back on the phone. "I'm going to switch us to a conference call, Milos. Another will be joining us, but it's understood that neither of you is required to identify yourself. I trust this man completely and he accepts the condition. He's also in what you term 'crisis containment' and has far greater resources than Swann." There were two clicks over the line and Winters continued. "Go ahead, gentlemen. Mr. A, this is Mr. B."

"I understand you have something to tell me, Mr. A."

"Yes, I do," replied Varak. "The circumstances are not relevant but the information is verified. The Secretary of State is in imminent danger. There are people who do not want him to attend the conference on Cyprus and they intend to stop him. They're employing a plan or a tactic called 'Design Twelve, Mediterranean.' The individual who gave the order is named Grinell, a Crayton Grinell of San Diego. I know nothing about him."

"I see. . . . Let me phrase this as delicately as I can, Mr. A. Are you in a position to tell us the current whereabouts of this Grinell?"

"I have no choice, Mr. B. The Westlake Hotel. Suite Three C. I have no idea how long he'll be there. Hurry, and send firepower. He's guarded."

"Will you do me the courtesy, Mr. A, of remaining on the line for a moment or two?"

"So you can trace this leg of the call?"

"I wouldn't do that. I've given my word."

"He'll keep it," interrupted Samuel Winters.

"It's difficult for me," said the Czech.

"I'll be quick."

A single click was heard and Winters spoke. "You really didn't have a choice, Milos. The Secretary is the sanest man in the administration."

"I'm aware of that, sir."

"I can't get over Sundstrom! *Why?*"

"No doubt a combination of reasons, not the least of which are his patents in space technology. Others may build the hardware but the government is the primary buyer. Space is now synonymous with defense."

"He can't want more money! He gives most of it *away.*"

"But if the market slows down, so does production and therefore the experimentation—the last is a passion with him."

Another click. "I'm back, Mr. A," said the third party. "Everyone's alerted over in the Mediterranean, and arrangements have been made to pick up Grinell in San Diego as quietly as possible, of course."

"Why was it necessary for me to remain on the phone?"

"Because, quite frankly, if I hadn't been able to make the arrangements in San Diego," said Mitchell Payton, "I was going to appeal to your patriotism for further assistance. You're obviously an experienced man."

"What kind of assistance?"

"Nothing that would compromise our understanding with regard to this call. Only to follow Grinell should he leave the hotel and call our go-between with the information."

"What made you think I'm in a position to do that?"

"I didn't. I could only hope, and there were several things to do quickly, mainly the Mediterranean."

"For your information, I'm not in such a position," lied Varak. "I'm nowhere near the hotel."

"Then I may have made two mistakes. I mentioned, 'patriotism,' but by the way you speak, this may not be your country."

"It is my country now," said the Czech.

"Then it owes you a great deal."

"I must go." Varak hung up the phone and walked rapidly back to the tape machine. He sat down and clamped the earphones over his head, his eyes straying to the reel of tape. It had *stopped.* He listened. Nothing. Silence! In desperation he snapped a succession of switches up and down and left and right. There was no response with any of them . . . no sound. The voice-activated recorder was not functioning because the Vanvlanderen suite was empty! He had to *move*! Above everything, he had to find Sundstrom! For the sake of Inver Brass, the traitor had to be killed.

Khalehla walked down the wide corridor toward the elevators. She had called MJ and, after discussing the horror of Mesa Verde, played him the entire conversation with Ardis Vanvlanderen that she had recorded on the miniaturized equipment concealed in her black notebook. Both were satisfied; the grieving widow had left her grief behind in a sea of hysteria. It was apparent to both of them that Mrs. Vanvlanderen had known nothing about her dead husband's contact with the terrorists, but had learned about it after the fact. The sudden appearance of an intelligence officer from Cairo with the upside-down information she carried had been enough to send Ardis the manipulator right through the roof of her skull. Uncle Mitch had been true to form.

"Take five, Field Officer Rashad."

"I'd like to take a shower and have a quiet meal. I don't think I've eaten since the Bahamas."

"Order room service. We'll stand for one of your outrageous bills. You've earned it."

"I *hate* room service. All those waiters who deliver food for a single female preen as though they're the answer to her sexual fantasies. If I can't have one of my grandmother's meals—"

"You *can't.*"

"Okay. Then I know a few good restaurants—"

"Go ahead. By midnight I'll have a list of every telephone number our distraught widow has called. Eat well, my dear. Get energy. You may be working all night."

"You're too generous. May I call Evan, who with any luck could be my intended?"

"You may but you won't get him. Colorado Springs sent a jet to take him and Emmanuel to the hospital in Denver. They're airborne."

"Thanks again."

"You're welcome, Rashad."

"You're too kind, *sir.*"

Khalehla pressed the button for the elevator, hearing the rumble in her stomach. She had *not* eaten since the meal on the Air Force jet, and that had been somewhat destroyed by the nervous enzymes produced by Evan's condition—the vomiting and all it signified. . . . Dear Evan, brilliant Evan, dumb Evan. The risk-taker with more morals than suited his approach to life; she wondered briefly if he would have that same integrity if he had failed. It was an open question; he was a compulsively competitive man who looked somewhat arrogantly down from his perch of *not* having failed. And it was not hard to understand how he had fallen under the spell, or shell, of Ardis Montreaux in Saudi Arabia ten or twelve years ago. That girl must have been something, a flashy lady on a fast track with a face and a body to go with the course. Yet he had fled from the spider—that was *her* Evan.

She heard the ping of the bell and the elevator doors parted. Happily, it was empty; she stepped inside and pressed the button for the lobby. The panels closed and the machine started its descent, only to slow down immediately. She looked up at the lighted numbers over the doors; the elevator was stopping at the third floor. It was simply a coincidence, she thought. MJ was sure that Ardis Vanvlanderen, proprietor of Suite 3C, would not dare leave the hotel.

The doors opened, and while her eyes remained disinterestedly straight ahead, Khalehla was relieved to peripherally see that the passenger was a lone man with light-colored hair and what appeared to be immense shoulders that filled out his jacket to the point of almost stretching the fabric. Yet there was something strange about him, she thought. As one can when one is alone with a single human being in a small enclosure, she could sense a high level of energy emanating from her unknown companion. There was an atmosphere of anger or anxiety that seemed to permeate the elevator. Then she could feel him looking at her, not the way men usually appraised her—furtively, with glances; she was used to that—but staring at her, the unseen eyes steady, intense, unwavering.

The doors closed as she casually grimaced to herself; it was the expression of someone who may have forgotten something. Again casually, she opened her purse as if to check for the possibly missing item. She exhaled audibly, her face relaxed; the item was there. It was. Her gun. The elevator began its descent as she glanced at the stranger.

She *froze*! His eyes were two orbs of controlled white heat, and the short, neatly combed hair was light blond. He could be no one *else*! The blond European . . . he was one of *them*! Khalehla lurched for the panel as she yanked out her automatic, dropping her purse and pressing the emergency button. Beyond the doors, the alarm sounded as the elevator jerked to a stop and the blond man stepped forward.

Khalehla fired, the explosion deafening in the tight enclosure, the bullet passing over the intense stranger's head as it was meant to.

"Stop where you are!" she commanded. "If you know anything about me, you know my next shot will go right into your forehead."

"You are the Rashad woman," said the blond man, his speech accented, his voice strained.

"I don't know who you are, but I know *what* you are. Scum-rotten, that's what you are! Evan was right. All these months, all the stories about him, the congressional committees, the coverage over the world. It was to set him up for a Palestinian kill! It was as simple as *that*!"

"No, you are wrong, *wrong,*" protested the European as the alarm bell outside kept up its abrasive ringing. "And you must *not* stop me now! A terrible thing is about to happen and I've been in touch with your people in Washington."

"*Who?* Who in Washington?"

"We don't give names—"

"Bullshit!"

"*Please,* Miss Rashad! A man is getting *away.*"

"Not you, Blondie—"

Where the blows came from and how they were delivered with such speed Khalehla would never know. For an instant there had been a blurring motion on her left, then a surging hand, as fast as any human hand she had ever seen, stung her right arm, followed by a counterclockwise twist of her right wrist, wrenching the weapon away. Where she might have expected her wrist to be broken it merely burned, as if briefly scalded by a splash of boiling water. The European stood in front of her holding the gun. "I did not mean to harm you," he said.

"You're very good, Scum-rotten, I'll give you that."

"We are not enemies, Miss Rashad."

"Somehow I find that hard to believe." The elevator telephone rang from the box below the panel, its bell echoing off the four walls of the small enclosure. "You're not getting out of here," added Khalehla.

"*Wait,*" said the blond man as the ringing persisted. "You saw Mrs. Vanvlanderen."

"She told you that. So what?"

"She couldn't have," broke in the European. "I've never met her but I *have* taped her. She had visitors later. They talked about you—she and two other men, one named Grinell."

"I never heard of him."

"They're both traitors, enemies of your government, of your country, to be precise, as your country was conceived." The telephone kept up its insistent ringing.

"Fast words, Mr. No Name."

"No more *words*!" cried the blond man, reaching under his jacket and withdrawing a thin large black automatic. He flipped both weapons around, gripping the barrels, the handles extended toward Khalehla. "Here. Take them. Give me a *chance,* Miss Rashad!"

Astonished, Khalehla held the guns and looked into the eyes of the European. She had seen that plea in too many eyes before. It was not the look of a man afraid to die for a cause, but furious about the prospect of not living to pursue it. "All right," she said slowly. "I may or I may not. Turn *around,* your arms against the wall! Farther back, your weight on your hands!" The telephone was now a steady, deafening ring as the field officer from Cairo expertly ran her fingers over the body of the blond man, concentrating on the armpits, the indented shell of his waist, and his ankles. There were no weapons on him. "Stay there," she ordered as she reached down and pulled out the telephone from the box. "We couldn't open the panel for the phone!" she exclaimed.

"Our engineer is on his way, madam. He was on his dinner break but we've just located him. We apologize profusely. However, our indicators show no fire or—"

"I think we're the ones to apologize," interrupted Khalehla. "It was all a mistake—my mistake. I pushed the wrong button. If you'll just tell me how to make it work again, we'll be fine."

"Oh? Yes, yes, of course," said the male voice, suppressing his irritation. "In the telephone box there's a switch. . . ."

The lobby doors opened and the European immediately spoke to the formally dressed manager, who was waiting for them. "There is a business associate I was to meet here quite some time ago. I'm afraid I overslept—a long, trying flight from Paris. His name is Grinell, have you seen him?"

"Mr. Grinell and the distraught Mrs. Vanvlanderen left a few minutes ago with their guests, sir. I assume it was a memorial service for her husband, a fine, fine gentleman."

"Yes, he, too, was an associate. We were to be at the service but we never got the address. Do you know it?"

"Oh, no, sir."

"Would *anybody*? Would the doorman have heard any instructions to a taxi?"

"Mr. Grinell has his own limousine—limousines, actually."

"Let's go," said Khalehla quietly, taking the blond man's arm. "You're becoming a little obvious," she continued as they walked toward the front entrance.

"I may have failed, which is far more important."

"What's your name?"

"Milos. Just call me Milos."

"I want more than that. I've got the fire, remember?"

"If we can reach an acceptable accommodation, I'll tell you more."

"You're going to tell me one *hell* of a lot more, Mr. Milos, and there won't be any more of those fast maneuvers of yours. Your gun is in my purse, and mine is under my coat aimed at your chest."

"What do we do now, Miss Supposedly Retired Central Intelligence Officer from Egypt?"

"We eat, you nosy bastard. I'm starved, but I'll pick up every morsel of food with my left hand. If you make a wrong move across the table, you'll never be able to have children, and not just because you're dead. Am I clear?"

"You must be very good."

"Good enough, Mr. Milos, good enough. I'm half Arab and don't you forget it."

They sat across from each other in a large circular booth selected by Khalehla in an Italian restaurant two blocks north of the hotel. Varak had detailed everything he had heard over the earphones from the Vanvlanderen suite. "I was shocked. I never thought for an instant that Andrew Vanvlanderen would act unilaterally."

"You mean without his wife putting 'a bullet in his head' and calling one of the others to 'deep-six' him in Mexico?"

"Exactly. She would have done it, you know. He was stupid."

"I disagree, he was very bright, considering his purpose. Everything that was done to and for Evan Kendrick led to a logical *jaremat tháar,* Arabic for a vengeance kill. You provided that, Mr. Milos, starting with the first moment you met Frank Swann at the State Department."

"Never with that intention, I assure you. I never thought it was remotely possible."

"You were wrong."

"I was wrong."

"Let's go back to that first moment—in fact, let's go back over the whole damn thing!"

"There's nothing to go back over. I've said nothing of substance."

"But we know far more than you think. We just had to unravel the string, as my superior put it. . . . A reluctant freshman congressman is manipulated onto important congressional committees, positions that others would sell their daughters for. Then because of mysteriously absentee chairmen, he's on national television, which leads to more exposure, topped by the explosive, worldwide story about his covert actions in Oman, and ending up with the President awarding him the highest medal a civilian can get. The agenda is pretty clear, isn't it?"

"It was organized quite well, in my opinion."

"And now there's about to be launched a national campaign to place him on the party ticket, in effect making him the next Vice President of the United States."

"You know about that?"

"Yes, and it's hardly a spontaneous act on the part of the body politic."

"I trust it will appear so."

"Where are you *coming* from?" asked Khalehla, leaning over, picking at her veal dish with the left hand, her right out of sight under the table.

"I must tell you, Miss Rashad, that it pains me to watch you eating so awkwardly. I'm not a threat to you and I won't run."

"How can I be sure of either? That you're not a threat and that you won't run?"

"Because in certain areas our interests are the same, and I am willing to work with you on a limited basis."

"My God, what arrogance! Would Your Eminence be so kind

as to describe these areas and the limits of your generous assistance?"

"Certainly. To begin with, the safety of the Secretary of State and exposing those who would have him killed as well as knowing why, although I think we can assume the reason. Then the capture of the terrorists who attacked Congressman Kendrick's houses with considerable loss of life, and confirming the Vanvlanderen connection—"

"*You* know about Fairfax and Mesa Verde?" Varak nodded. "The blackout's total."

"Which brings us to the limits of my participation. I must remain far in the background and will not discuss my activities except in the most general terms. I will, however, if it's necessary, refer you by code name to certain individuals in the government who will attest to my dependability in security matters here and abroad."

"You don't think much of yourself, do you?"

Milos smiled cautiously. "I really don't have an opinion. However, I come from a country whose government was stolen from the people, and made up my mind years ago what I would do with my life. I have confidence in the methods I've developed. If that's arrogance, so be it, and I apologize, but I don't think of it that way."

Khalehla slowly pulled her right hand out from under the table and with her left picked up the purse at her side. She shoved her automatic into it and leaned back, shaking her hand to restore circulation. "I think we can dispense with the hardware, and you're right, it's terribly awkward trying to cut meat with a left-handed fork while your other wrist is paralyzed."

"I was going to suggest that you order something simpler, perhaps an antipasto, or a dish you might eat with your fingers, but I didn't feel it was my place."

"Do I detect a sense of humor behind that severe expression?"

"An attempt, perhaps, but I don't feel very humorous at the moment. I won't until I know the Secretary of State has arrived safely on Cyprus."

"You alerted the proper people; there's nothing more you can do. They'll take care of him."

"I'm counting on it."

"Then to business, Mr. Milos," said Khalehla, returning to her meal, again slowly, her eyes on Varak. "Why Kendrick? Why did you do it? Above all, *how* did you do it? You tapped into sources that were supposedly untappable! You went in where no one should be able to go and ripped out secrets, stole a theft-proof file. Whoever gave you those should be taken out and put in the field so he'd know what it's like to have no protection, to be naked without weapons in the dark streets of a hostile city."

"Whatever assistance was given to me was rendered by a source who trusted me, who knew where I was coming from, as you phrased it."

"But *why*?"

"I'll give you a limited response, Miss Rashad, and speak only in general terms."

"Hooray for you. So give."

"This country imperatively needs changes in an administration that will undoubtedly be reelected."

"Who says so other than the voters?"

"Off limits, except again, in general terms . . . although I shouldn't have to use even them. You've seen for yourself."

Khalehla put down her fork and looked at the European. "San Diego? Vanvlanderen? Grinell?"

"San Diego, Vanvlanderen and Grinell," repeated the Czech quietly. "To clarify further: monies obviously sent through Zurich and Beirut to the Baaka Valley for the purpose of eliminating a political contender—namely, Congressman Kendrick. And now an apparent attempt to stop a brilliant Secretary of State from attending a disarmament conference whose purpose is to reduce the proliferation—the production—of space and nuclear weapons."

"San Diego," said Khalehla, leaving her food on the plate. "Orson Bollinger?"

"An enigma," replied Varak. "What does he know? What doesn't he know? Regardless, he's the rallying point, the funnel into an unbeatable administration. He has to be replaced, thus eliminating the people around him who order him to march to their drums."

"But why Evan *Kendrick*?"

"Because he is now an unbeatable contender."

"He'll never accept it; he'll tell you to go to hell. You don't know him, I *do.*"

"A man doesn't necessarily want to do what he must do, Miss Rashad. But he will do it if the reasons are made clear to him why he should."

"You think that's *enough*?"

"I don't know Mr. Kendrick personally, of course, but I

don't think there's another human being I've studied so closely. He's a remarkable man, yet so realistically modest about his achievements. He made a great deal of money out of an exploding Middle East economy, then walked away from millions more because he was morally offended and emotionally distraught. He then entered the political arena for no other reason than to replace a—what did you call me?—a scum-rotten, who was lining his pockets in Colorado. Finally, he went to Oman knowing he might not come back, for he believed he could help in a crisis. That's not a man you take lightly. *He* may but you don't."

"Oh, good Lord," said Khalehla. "I'm hearing a variation of my own words."

"In support of his political advancement?"

"No, to explain why he wasn't a liar. But I should tell you there's another reason why he went back to Oman. It falls under the not too benevolent heading of a kill. He was convinced he knew who was behind the terrorists in Masqat: the same monster who'd been responsible for killing all seventy-eight people who made up the Kendrick Group, including wives and children. He was right; the man was executed according to Arabic law."

"That's hardly a negative, Miss Rashad."

"No, it isn't, but it somewhat alters the circumstances."

"I'd prefer to think it adds a dimension of properly sought justice, which further confirms our choice of him."

"Our?"

"Off limits."

"I repeat, he'll turn it down."

"He will if he learns how he was manipulated. He may not if he's convinced he is needed."

Khalehla again leaned back in the booth, studying the Czech. "If I'm hearing correctly, you're suggesting something that's deeply offensive to me."

"It shouldn't be." Varak sat forward. "No one can force a man to accept elective office, Miss Rashad; he has to seek it. Conversely, no one can force a political party's leading senators and congressmen to accept a *new* candidate; they must want him. . . . It's true that circumstances were created to bring out the man, but we could not create the man; he was there to begin with."

"You're asking me not to tell him about this conversation, not to tell him about you. . . . Have you any idea how many weeks we've been *looking* for you?"

"Have you any idea how many months we looked for Evan Kendrick?"

"I don't *give* a damn! He *was* manipulated and he knows it. You can't hide, I won't let you. You've put him through too much. Dear friends killed, now possibly an old man who's been a father to him for fifteen years. All his plans shot to hell—*too* much!"

"I can't change what's happened, I can only grieve for my errors of judgment and no one will grieve more, but I ask you to think of your country, my country now. If we've helped to produce a political force, it was only because the force existed in his own right, with his own instincts. Without him, any number of perfectly decent men will be acceptable to the party leadership because they're familiar and comfortable, but they will not be a *force*. . . . Do I make myself clear?"

"According to history, a Vice President once said that the office wasn't worth a 'bucket of warm spit.' "

"Not these days, and certainly not in the hands of Evan Kendrick. You were obviously in Cairo when he appeared on television here—"

"I was in Cairo," interrupted Khalehla, "but we have an American channel—tapes, of course. I saw him and I've seen him here subsequently and repeatedly, thanks no doubt to your . . . agenda. He was very good, very intelligent and appealing."

"Miss Rashad, he's unique. He's unbuyable and he speaks his mind and the country is taken with him."

"Because of you."

"No, because of *him*. He's done the things he's done, they weren't invented; he's said the things he's said, the words weren't provided. What can I tell you? I analyzed over four hundred possibilities, using the most advanced computers, and one man stood out. Evan Kendrick."

"You want nothing from him?"

"You say you know him. If we did, what do you think he'd do?"

"Turn you over to some anticorruption committee and make damn sure you spent time in prison."

"Exactly."

Khalehla shook her head, her eyes closed. "I'd like a glass of wine, Mr. Milos. I've got a few things to think about."

Varak signaled a waiter and ordered two glasses of chilled Chablis, leaving the choice to the waiter's discretion. "Among my many deficiencies," said the Czech, "is a lack of knowledge of wines beyond those of my country."

"I don't believe that for an instant. You're probably a certified sommelier."

"Hardly. I hear friends order specific vineyards and vintages and I marvel at them."

"Do you really have friends? I think of you as rather an éminence grise."

"*Je comprends,* but you're wrong. I live quite a normal life. My friends think I'm a translator, free-lance, naturally, at home."

"*Bien,*" said the agent from Cairo. "That's how I began."

"There's no office to contact, only an answering machine, which I can reach from wherever I am."

"Me, too."

The wine arrived and, after sipping, Khalehla spoke. "He can't go back," she said, as if speaking to herself, then partially including Varak. "At least not for a few years, if then. Once the blackout's lifted there'll be a lot of hot blood running in the Baaka Valley."

"I assume you're talking about the Congressman?"

"Yes. The terrorists were caught, in a manner of speaking. . . . There was a third and final attack several hours ago. It took place in Mesa Verde and was every bit as devastating as Fairfax."

"Several *hours* . . . ? Was Kendrick there?"

"Yes."

"*And?*"

"He's alive, I'm told, by seconds. But like Virginia, many of our personnel were killed."

"I'm sorry. . . . Weingrass was severely hurt, I gather. That's whom you were referring to when you mentioned an old man, wasn't it?"

"Yes. They're flying him to a hospital in Denver. Evan's with him."

"The terrorists, *please,*" said Varak, his eyes boring into hers.

"All together there were nine of them. Eight are dead; one survived, the youngest."

"And when the blackout's lifted, as you say, there will be hot blood in the Baaka. It's why Kendrick can't go back to that part of the world."

"He wouldn't live forty-eight hours. There's no way to protect him from the crazies."

"There is here and none better than the government's Secret Service. In these matters nothing is perfect, there is only the best."

"I know." Khalehla drank from her glass of wine.

"You understand what I'm saying, don't you, Miss Rashad?"

"I think so."

"Let events run their natural course. There's a legitimate political action committee dedicated to supporting Congressman Kendrick for higher office. Let them work unencumbered and let the country respond—one way or another. And if we're both right about the Vanvlanderens and the Grinells and the people they represent, let Evan Kendrick make up his own mind. Because even if we expose them and stop them, there are hundreds more who will take their places. . . . A force *is* needed, a *voice* is needed."

Khalehla raised her eyes from the wine. She nodded twice.

36

Kendrick walked along Denver's Seventeenth Street toward the Brown Palace Hotel barely aware of the light snow that was floating down from the night sky. He had told the cabdriver to let him off several blocks away; he wanted to walk; he had to clear his mind.

The doctors at the Denver General had patched Manny up, relieving Evan by explaining that the wounds, although messy, consisted mainly of embedded fragments of glass and metal. The loss of blood was considerable for a man of his age but not critical; it would be replaced. The bewilderment started when Kendrick took one of the doctors aside and told him about Weingrass's concerns that the cancer had returned. Within twenty minutes all of Manny's tests had been electronically transmitted from Washington, and the chief oncologist had spoken to the D.C. surgeon who had operated on the old architect. Then about two hours into his four-hour stay at the hospital, a technician had arrived from some laboratory or other and conferred quietly with another doctor. There had been a mild flurry of activity and Evan was asked to leave the room while various samples were taken from Manny's body. An hour after that the chief of pathology, a thin man with inquisitive eyes, approached Kendrick in the waiting room.

"Congressman, has Mr. Weingrass been out of the country recently?"

"Not within the past year, no."

"Where was that?"

"France . . . Southwest Asia."

The doctor's eyebrows had arched. "My geography's not very good. Where is Southwest Asia?"

"Is this necessary?"

"Yes, it is."

"Oman and Bahrain."

"He was *with* you? . . . Excuse me, but your exploits are common knowledge."

"He was with me," answered Evan. "He's one of the people I couldn't thank publicly because it wouldn't be in his interest."

"I understand. We have no press office here."

"Thank you. Why do you ask?"

"Unless I'm mistaken, and I could be, he's infected with a—let's say a virus—that to the best of my knowledge is indigenous to central Africa."

"That *couldn't* be."

"Then perhaps I'm wrong. Our equipment is among the finest in the West, but there's better. I'm having lung tissue and blood samples sent to the CDC in Atlanta."

"The what?"

"Centers for Disease Control."

"*Disease?*"

"It's just a precaution, Mr. Kendrick."

"Have them flown there tonight, Doctor. There'll be a jet waiting at Stapleton Airport within the hour. Tell Atlanta to go to work the minute your findings arrive—I'll pay whatever the cost even if they have to stay there around the clock."

"I'll do what I can—"

"If it would help," said Evan, not sure whether he was bluffing or not, "I'll have the White House call them."

"I don't think that will be necessary," said the pathologist.

As he left the hospital, having said good night to a heavily sedated Manny, he remembered the vanished Dr. Lyons of Mesa Verde, the physician without an address or a telephone but with full government clearance to be presented to a congressman and/or his staff. *What* clearance? Why was *clearance* necessary?

. . . Or was it simply a very impressive document, a device for slipping into the private world of one Evan Kendrick? He decided to say nothing to anyone. Khalehla would know better what to do.

He approached the Brown Palace and was suddenly aware through the falling snow of the colored lights on the Christmas decorations extending across the wide avenue from the old classic structure to the new south tower. Then he heard the strains of a carol filling the street. *Deck the halls with boughs of holly, fa-la-la-la-la . . . la-la-la-la.* Merry Christmas from the legacy of Masqat, he thought.

"Where the hell have you *been*?" shouted M.J. Payton, causing Khalehla to hold the telephone away from her ear.

"Having dinner."

"He's *there*! Our blond European is in the *hotel*!"

"I know. I had dinner with him."

"You *what*?"

"As a matter of fact, he's here in my room now. We're going over what we know. He's not what we thought."

"*Damn* you, Adrienne! Tell that son of a bitch Mr. *B* would like to talk to Mr. *A*!"

"Good God, *you* were the one?"

"Cap it, Rashad! Put him on the line."

"I'm not sure he'll agree." The agent from Cairo again had to pull the phone away. She turned to Varak. "A Mr. *B* would like to talk to Mr. *A.*"

"I should have known," said the Czech, getting out of the chair. He walked to the bedside telephone as Khalehla relinquished it and moved away. "Greetings again, Mr. *B.* Nothing has changed, you understand. No names, no identities."

"What does my niece call you? Mind you, she's my niece."

"She calls me by the erroneous name of Milos."

"*Meelos?* Slavic?"

"American, sir."

"I forgot, you made that clear."

"The Secretary of State, *please*?"

"He's arrived in Cyprus."

"I'm relieved."

"We all are, if, indeed, there was cause for alarm to begin with."

"The information was accurate."

"Unfortunately, we haven't been able to confirm it at our end.

Grinell wasn't at the hotel and he hasn't shown up at his residence."

"He's with the Vanvlanderen woman."

"Yes, we know. According to a desk clerk, there were several others with them both. Any ideas?"

"Grinell's guards, according to the information I received. I mentioned to you that there were men with him, that you should be prepared."

"Yes, you did. . . . Do we work together?"

"From a distance."

"What have you got to offer?"

"Proof of certain things I've told Miss Rashad," replied Varak, thinking of the edited tapes and transcripts he would provide the intelligence officer—edited so that Eric Sundstrom would remain an anonymous conspirator; a dead man did not need an identity. "Perhaps nothing more, but it's the core of what you need."

"It will be gratefully accepted."

"However, there's a price, Mr. *B.*"

"I don't make payments—"

"Of course you do," broke in the Czech. "You do so all the time."

"What is it?"

"As long as my demands require a complicated explanation, I'll let Miss Rashad tell you in her own words. I'll reach her tomorrow and we'll communicate through her. If your answer is positive, I will arrange for the delivery of my material to you."

"And if it's not?"

"Then I'd advise you to weigh the consequences, Mr. *B.*"

"Let me speak to my niece, if you please."

"As you wish." Varak turned to Khalehla and handed her the telephone as he headed back to his chair.

"I'm here," said Rashad.

"Just answer yes or no, and if you can't answer, stay silent for a second or two. All right?"

"Yes."

"Are you safe?"

"Yes."

"Would his material help us?"

"Yes—emphatically."

"Just 'yes' is sufficient, Agent Rashad. . . . He's obviously staying at the hotel—do you think he'll remain there?"

"No."

"Has he given you any information as to how he got the Oman file?"

"No."

"Lastly, can we live with his demands?"

"We're going to— Sorry to break the rules."

"I see," said the astonished director of Special Projects. "You will explain that extraordinary and extraordinarily insubordinate statement to me, won't you?"

"We'll talk later." Khalehla hung up the phone and turned to Varak. "My superior's upset."

"With you or with me? It wasn't difficult to imagine the gist of his questions."

"With both of us."

"Is he really your uncle?"

"I've known him for over twenty years and that's enough about him. Let's talk about you for a moment. It wasn't difficult to imagine a couple of his questions to you, either."

"Only a moment, please," insisted the Czech. "I really must leave."

"You told him that Grinell was with the Vanvlanderen woman and that the others were Grinell's guards."

"I did."

"Yet you told me that there were *two* men in the Vanvlanderen suite and that the guards were outside."

"That's true."

"Who was that other man, and why are you protecting him?"

"*Protecting?* . . . I believe I also told you that they were both traitors. You'll hear that on the tapes, read it in the transcripts I'll deliver to you if your superior agrees to my conditions, as you have agreed."

"I'll convince him."

"Then you'll hear for yourself."

"But you *know* him! Who *is* he?"

Varak got out of the chair, his hands pressed in front of him. "Again, we are off limits, Miss Rashad. But I'll tell you this much. He's the reason I must leave. He's human filth, whatever words you care to use . . . and he's mine. I'll scour this city all night until I find him, and if I don't, I know where I *can* find him, tomorrow or the next day. I repeat, he's *mine.*"

"A *jaremat thaár,* Mr. Milos?"

"I do not speak Arabic, Miss Rashad."

"But you know what it means, I've told you."

"Good night," said the Czech, going to the door.

"My *uncle* wants to know how you got the Oman file. I don't think he'll stop hunting you down until he finds out."

"We all have our priorities," said Varak, turning, his hand on the knob. "Right now his and yours are in San Diego and mine are elsewhere. Tell him that he has nothing to fear from my source. He would go to his grave before endangering one of your people, one of our people."

"Goddamn you, he already *has*! *Evan Kendrick!*" The telephone rang; they both whipped their heads around, staring at it. Khalehla picked it up. "Yes?"

"It *happened*!" cried Payton in Langley, Virginia. "Oh, my God, they *did* it!"

"What is it?"

"The Larnaca Hotel on Cyprus! The west wing was blown up; there's nothing left, just debris. The Secretary of State's dead, they're *all* dead!"

"The hotel on Cyprus," repeated Khalehla, looking at the Czech, her voice a frightened monotone. "It was blown up, the Secretary's dead, they're all dead. . . ."

"Give me that phone!" roared Varak, rushing across the room and grabbing it. "Did no one check the cellars, the air-conditioning ducts, the structural *underpinnings*?"

"The Cypriot security forces claimed they checked everything—"

"Cypriot *security*?" yelled the furious Czech. "It's riddled with a dozen hostile elements! Fools, fools, *fools*!"

"Do you want my job, Mr. *A*?"

"I wouldn't take it," said Varak, controlling his anger, lowering his voice. "I do not work with amateurs," he added contemptuously, hanging up and going to the door. He turned and spoke to Khalehla. "What was needed here today were the brains of Kendrick of Oman. He would have been the first to tell all of you what to do, what to look for. And you probably would not have listened to him." The Czech opened the door, let himself out and slammed it shut.

The telephone rang. "He's gone," said Rashad, picking it up, knowing instinctively who was on the line.

"I offered him my job, but he made it clear that he didn't work with amateurs. . . . Strange, isn't it? A man without any credentials that we know about alerts us, and we blow it. And a year ago we send Kendrick to Oman and he does what five hundred professionals from at least six countries couldn't do. It makes you wonder, doesn't it. . . . I'm getting old."

"No *way,* MJ!" cried the agent from Cairo. "They happen to be bright guys and they hit jackpots, that's all. You've done more than they'll *ever* do!"

"I'd like to believe that, but tonight's pretty horrible for whatever ego I've got left."

"Which should be a bunch! . . . But it's also a good moment for me to explain that insubordinate remark I made to you a few minutes ago."

"Please do. I'm receptive. I'm not even sure I have a hell of a lot of breath left."

"Whomever Milos works for, they want nothing from Evan. When I pressed him, he pointed out the obvious. If they made any demands on him, he'd throw them to the wolves, and he's right, Evan would."

"I also agree. So what does he want?"

"To back off and let events take their course. They want us to let the race go on."

"Evan won't run—"

"He may when he learns about the black knights who are running things in California. Say we stop them; there are hundreds more waiting to take their places. Milos is right, a voice *is* needed."

"But what do *you* say, niece?"

"I want him alive, not dead. He can't go back to the Emirates—he may convince himself that he can, but he'd be killed the moment he got off the plane. And he can't vegetate in Mesa Verde, not with his energy and imagination—that's a form of death, too, you know. . . . The country could do worse, MJ."

"Fools, *fools*!" whispered Varak to himself as he dialed while studying a diagram of the Vanvlanderen suite in his hand; there were small red Xs marked in each room. Seconds later a voice was on the other end of the line.

"Yes?"

"Sound Man?"

"Prague?"

"I need you."

"I can always use your money. You roll high."

"Pick me up in thirty minutes, the service entrance. I'll explain what I want you to do on the way to your studio. . . . There are no changes in the diagram?"

"No. You found the key?"

"Thank you for both."

"You paid. Thirty minutes."

The Czech hung up the phone and looked at the packed recording equipment in front of the door. He had listened to Rashad's interview with Ardis Vanvlanderen, and despite his anger over the tragedy of the Secretary of State's death, he had smiled—grimly, to be sure—at the bold strategy employed by the field agent from Cairo and her superior. Based on what they had learned, they had gambled on the presumed truth of Andrew Vanvlanderen's actions and turned it into an irresistible lie: Palestinian hit teams, the target *Bollinger,* Kendrick never even mentioned! *Brilliant!* The appearance of Eric Sundstrom within two hours after Rashad's astonishing, convoluted information—an appearance designed to trap a traitor of Inver Brass and not based on any presumption of Vanvlanderen's guilt—had been the combined detonations that blew apart the cemented structure of deceit in San Diego. One took things where one could find them.

Varak went to the door, opened it cautiously and slipped out into the corridor. He walked rapidly to the Vanvlanderen suite down the hall and, with the key provided by the Sound Man, let himself inside, the diagram still in his hand. With swift catlike strides he went from room to room removing the tiny electronic intercepts from their recesses—under tables and chairs, secreted beneath the deep cushions of the sofa, behind mirrors in the four bedrooms, under the medicine cabinets in the various bathrooms, and inside two burners in the kitchen. He left the widow's office for last, counting the red Xs, satisfied that he had collected every tap so far. The office was dark; he found the desk lamp and switched it on. Ten seconds later he pocketed the four intercepts, three from the office itself, one from the small attached bathroom, and concentrated on the desk. He looked at his watch; the dismantling operation had taken nine minutes, leaving him at least fifteen to examine Mrs. Vanvlanderen's domestic inner sanctum.

He started with the desk drawers, pulling one out after another, riffling through meaningless papers devoted to vice presidential trivia—schedules, letters from individuals and institutions deemed worthy of answering someday, position papers from the White House, State, Defense and various other administrative agencies that had to be studied so they could be explained to Orson Bollinger. There was nothing of value, nothing at all related to the subterranean manipulations taking place in southern California.

He looked around the large paneled office, at the bookshelves, the graceful furniture and at the framed photographs on the walls . . . photographs. There were over twenty of them scattered about the dark paneling in crisscrossing patterns. He walked over and began examining them, snapping on a table lamp for better light. They were the usual collection of self-aggrandizing pictures showing Mr. and Mrs. Andrew Vanvlanderen in the company of political heavyweights, from the President on down through the upper ranks of the administration and Congress. Then on the adjacent wall were photographs of the widow herself without her late husband. Judging from appearances, these were obviously from Ardis Vanvlanderen's past, a personal testimonial that made clear her past was not inconsequential. Expensive cars, yachts, ski slopes and luxurious furs predominated.

Varak was about to abandon the panoply of conceit when his eyes fell on an enlarged candid shot obviously taken in Lausanne, Switzerland, Lake Geneva's northern Leman Marina in the background. Milos studied the face of the dark-skinned man standing beside the effervescent center of attraction. He knew that face but he could not place it. Then, as if following a scent, the Czech's eyes roamed down to the lower right, to another enlarged snapshot also taken in Lausanne, this in the gardens of the Beau-Rivage Palace. There was the same man again—who *was* he? And next to it yet another, now in Amsterdam, in the Rozengracht, the same two subjects. Who *was* that man? *Concentrate!* Images came, fragments of elusive impressions but no name. Riyadh . . . Medina, Saudi Arabia. A shocked and furious Saudi family . . . a scheduled execution, then an escape. Millions upon millions had been involved . . . eight to ten years ago. Who *was* he? Varak considered taking one of the photographs, then instinctively knew he should not. Whoever the man was, he represented another telling aspect of the machine built around Orson Bollinger. A missing photograph of that face might send out alarms.

Milos turned off the table lamp and started back toward the desk. It was time to leave, to get his equipment and meet the Sound Man down in the street outside the service entrance. He reached for the dome-shaped lamp on the desk when suddenly he heard the door opening in the foyer. Swiftly he turned off the light and moved to the office door, partially closing it so he could slip behind and watch through the space of the hinged panel.

The tall figure came into view, a lone man walking confidently into familiar surroundings. Varak frowned for an instant; he had not thought about the intruder for weeks. It was the red-haired FBI agent from Mesa Verde, a member of the unit assigned to the Vice President at the request of Ardis Vanvlanderen—the man who had led him to San Diego. Milos was momentarily bewildered, but only momentarily. The unit had been recalled to Washington, yet one player had remained behind. . . . More accurately, one had been bought before Varak had found him in Mesa Verde.

The Czech watched as the redheaded man walked around the living room as if looking for something. He picked up a glass from beneath an ivory-shelled lamp on a table to the left of the couch, then went through a door leading to the kitchen. He returned moments later with a spray can in one hand, a dish-towel in the other. He crossed to the dry bar, where he picked up each bottle separately, spraying each and wiping it clean. He next sprayed the copper rim of the bar top and rubbed it thoroughly with the cloth. From the bar he proceeded to go to every solid piece of furniture in the sunken living room and repeated the cleaning process as if he were purifying the premises. What he was doing was apparent to Varak: the agent was eliminating the forensic presence of Eric Sundstrom, removing the scientist's fingerprints from the area.

The man put down the spray can and the towel on the coffee table, then casually started across the room . . . toward the office! The Czech spun silently out from behind the partially closed door and raced into the small bathroom, closing its door, now more than partially, leaving barely an inch between the edge and the frame. As Milos had done, the FBI agent turned on the desk lamp, sat down in the chair and opened the lower right-hand drawer. However, he did something that Varak had not done: he pressed an unseen button. Instantly, the vertical molding of the desk shot out.

"Jesus *Christ*!" said the red-haired man to himself, his stunned cry a whisper as he peered into an obviously empty recess. Without wasting motion, he reached for the telephone on the desk, virtually ripping it out and dialing. Within seconds he spoke. "It's not here!" he cried. "No, I'm *certain*!" he added after a pause. "There's *nothing*! . . . What do you want from me? I followed your instructions and I'm telling you there's not a goddamned *thing*! . . . *What?* Down the street from your house? All right, I'll get on it and call you back." The agent depressed the telephone plate, released it and dialed eleven digits: long distance. "Base Five, this is Blackbird, special assignment San

Diego, code six-six-zero. Confirm, please. . . . Thank you. Do we have vehicles in La Jolla I don't know about? . . . We don't. . . . No, nothing urgent, probably the press. They must have found out the VP is going to an art-show soirée—you got that, soirée—with the fruitcake crowd. He wouldn't know a Rembrandt from Al Capp, but he's got to fake it. I'll check it out, forget it." Again the lanky red-haired man hung up and redialed. "There's nothing from our side," he said quietly, almost immediately. "No, there's no law that says we have to be told. . . . CIA? We'd be the last to know. . . . Okay, I'll call the airport. Do you want me to reach your pilot? . . . Whatever you say, then I'm getting out of here. The Agency and the Bureau don't mix, we never have." The FBI man hung up as Varak stepped out of the dark bathroom, his thin black automatic in his hand.

"You're not getting out of here that fast," said the coordinator of Inver Brass.

"*Christ!*" screamed the redheaded agent, lunging out of the chair and hurling himself at Varak in the doorway, gripping the Czech's right wrist with the strength of a panicked animal, propelling Milos back into the wall above the toilet, crashing Varak's head into the tastefully papered Sheetrock. The Czech straddled the commode in the dark bathroom, whipping his left leg around the man's torso and vising it while yanking his right hand and gun straight up, half tearing the agent's left arm out of its socket. It was over; the man collapsed on the floor, gripping his damaged arm as if it were broken.

"Get up," said Varak, the weapon at his side, not bothering to level it at his prisoner. The red-haired man struggled, wincing while he pulled himself up by the rim of the marble washbasin. "Go back in there and sit down," ordered Milos, shoving the agent through the door to the desk.

"Who the hell *are* you?" asked the man breathlessly, plummeting into the chair, still holding his arm.

"We've met, but you wouldn't know about it. A country road in Mesa Verde, west of a certain congressman's house."

"That was *you*?" The agent shot forward, only to be pushed back by Varak.

"When did you sell out, federal man?"

The agent studied Milos in the wash of the desk lamp. "If you're some kind of naturalized spook from a cross-over unit, you'd better get one thing straight. I'm here on special assignment to the Vice President."

"A 'cross-over' unit? I see you've been talking to some very excitable people. . . . There is no cross-over unit and those vehicles around Grinell's house were dispatched from Washington—"

"They weren't! I just *checked*!"

"Perhaps the Bureau wasn't informed, or perhaps you were lied to, it doesn't matter. Like all privileged soldiers from elite organizations, I'm sure you can claim that you were merely following orders, as in removing fingerprints and searching for hidden documents of which you know nothing."

"I don't!"

"But you did sell out and that's all that matters to me. You were prepared to accept money and privileges for services rendered under your official status. Are you also prepared to lose your life for these people?"

"*What?*"

"Now, you get this straight," said Varak quietly, raising his automatic and suddenly pressing it into the agent's forehead. "Whether you live or die means absolutely nothing to me, but there's a man I must find. Tonight."

"You don't know Grinell—"

"Grinell is immaterial to me, leave him to others. The man I want is the one whose fingerprints you so carefully removed from this apartment. You'll tell me where he is right now or your brains will be all over this desk, and I will not bother to clean them up. The scene will add a further convincing nuance of evil consistent with everything that's taking place out here. . . . Where *is* he?"

His entire body trembling, his breath short, the red-haired man spat out the words rapidly. "I don't know and I'm not *lying*! I was ordered to meet them on a side street near the beach in Coronado. I swear I don't know where they were going."

"You just called."

"It's a cellular phone. He's mobile."

"Who was in Coronado?"

"Just Grinell and this other guy, who told me where he walked and everything he touched here in Vanvlanderen's place."

"Where was *she*?"

"I don't know. Maybe she was sick or had an accident. There was an ambulance across from Grinell's limo."

"But you *do* know where they're going. You were about to call the airport. What were your instructions?"

"To have maintenance get the plane ready for takeoff in an hour."

"Where is the plane?"

"San Diego International. The private strip south of the main runways."

"What's the destination?"

"That's between Grinell and his pilot. He never tells anyone."

"You offered to call the pilot. What's his number?"

"Christ, I don't *know*! If Grinell wanted me to call him, he would have told me. He didn't."

"Give me the cellular number." The agent did and the Czech committed it to memory. "You're certain it's accurate?"

"Go ahead and try it."

Varak pulled the gun away and replaced it in his shoulder holster. "I heard a term tonight that fits you, federal man. Scum-rotten, that's what you are. But as I said, you're of no consequence to me, so I'm going to let you go. Perhaps you can start building your defenses as the obedient soldier betrayed by his superiors, or perhaps you'd be better off heading to Mexico and points south. I don't know and I don't care. But if you call that mobile phone, you're a dead man. Do you understand that?"

"I just want to get out of here," said the agent, bolting out of the chair and running into the sunken living room toward the marble steps and the foyer door.

"So do I," whispered Milos to himself. He looked at his watch; he was late for the Sound Man downstairs. No matter, he thought, the man was quick and would quickly grasp what he wanted from the tapes and the transcripts. Then he would borrow the Sound Man's car and park it in the lot at San Diego's international airport. There in a private strip south of the main runways he would find the traitor of Inver Brass. He would find him and kill him.

The telephone rang, jarring Kendrick out of a fitful sleep. Disoriented, his eyes centered on a hotel window and the heavy snow whirling in circles in the winds beyond the glass. The phone rang again; blinking, he found the source, turned on the bedside lamp, and picked it up, glancing at his watch as he did so. It was five-twenty in the morning. *Khalehla?*

"Yes, hello?"

"Atlanta stayed up all night," said the hospital's chief of pathology. "They just called me and I thought you'd want to know."

"Thank you, Doctor."

"You may not care to. All the tests are positive, I'm afraid."

"Cancer?" asked Evan, swallowing.

"No. I could give you the medical term, but it wouldn't mean anything to you. You could call it a form of salmonella, a strain of virus that attacks the lungs, clotting the blood until it closes off the oxygen. I can understand why, on the surface, Mr. Weingrass thought it was the cancer. It's not, but that's no gift."

"The *cure*?" said Kendrick, gripping the phone.

After a brief silence the pathologist replied quietly, "None known. It's irreversible. In the African Kasai districts they slaughter the cattle and burn them, raze whole villages and burn them, too."

"I don't give a *goddamn* about cattle and African villages! . . . I'm sorry, I don't mean to yell at you."

"It's perfectly all right, it goes with the job. I looked on the map; he must have eaten in an Omani restaurant that served central African food for imported laborers perhaps. Unclean dishes, that sort of thing. It's the way it's transmitted."

"You don't know Emmanuel Weingrass; those are the last places he'd eat at. . . . No, Doctor, it wasn't transmitted, it was planted."

"I beg your pardon?"

"Nothing. How long has he got?"

"The CDC says it can vary. A month to three, perhaps four. No more than six."

"May I tell him it could stretch to a couple of years."

"You can tell him anything you like, but he may tell you otherwise. His breathing isn't going to get any easier. Oxygen will have to be readily available."

"It will be. Thank you, Doctor."

"I'm sorry, Mr. Kendrick."

Evan got out of the bed and paced about the room in growing anger. A phantom doctor unknown in Mesa Verde but not unknown to certain officials in the United States government. A pleasant doctor who only wished to take a little blood . . . and then disappeared. Suddenly Evan shouted, his cry hoarse, the tears rolling down his face. "*Lyons,* where *are* you? I'll *find* you!"

In frenzy he smashed his fist through the window nearest him, shattering the glass, so that the wind and the snow careened through the room.

37

Varak approached the last of the maintenance hangars in the private area of San Diego's international airport. Police and armed customs personnel in electric carts and motorbikes drove continuously through the exposed narrow streets of the huge flat complex, voices and static erupting sporadically from the vehicles' radios. The individual rich and the highly profitable corporations who were the area's clients might avoid the irritations of normal air travel, but they could not avoid the scrutiny of federal and municipal agencies patrolling the sector. Each plane prepped for departure underwent not only the usual flight plan and route clearances but thorough inspections of the aircraft itself. Furthermore, each person boarding was subject to the possibility of being searched on probable cause, almost as if he or she were a member of the unwashed. Certain of the questionable rich did not really have it that good.

The Czech had casually gone into the comfortable preflight lounge where the elite passengers waited in luxury before take-off. He inquired about the Grinell plane, and the attractive clerk behind the counter was far more cooperative than he had expected.

"Are you on the flight, sir?" she had asked, about to type his name into her computer.

"No, I'm only here to deliver some legal papers."

"Oh, then I suggest you go down to Hangar Seven. Mr. Grinell rarely stops in here, he goes straight to preclearance and then to the aircraft when it's rolled out for inspection."

"If you could direct me . . . ?"

"We'll have one of our carts drive you down."

"I'd prefer to walk, if you don't mind. I'd like to stretch my legs."

"Suit yourself, but stay in the street. Security here is touchy and there are all kinds of alarms."

"I'll run from streetlight to streetlight," Milos said, smiling. "Okay?"

"Not a bad idea," the girl replied. "Last week a Beverly Hills hotshot got juiced in here and wanted to walk, too. He took a wrong turn and ended up in the San Diego jail."

"For simply walking?"

"Well, he had some funny pills on him—"

"I don't even have aspirin."

"Go outside, turn right to the first street, and right again. It's the last hangar on the edge of the strip. Mr. Grinell has the best location. I wish he'd come in here more often."

"He's a very private person."

"He's invisible, that's what he is."

Varak kept glancing around while nodding his head at the drivers of carts and low-slung motor scooters who approached him from both directions, some slowing down, others rushing past. He saw what he wanted to see. There were trip lights between the row of hangars on the right, connecting beams from opposing short poles in the ground designed to look like demarcations—of what? wondered the Czech. Lawns between suburban houses of the future where neighbor feared neighbor? On the left side of the street there was nothing but a vacant expanse of tall grass that bordered an auxiliary runway. It would be his way out of the private field once his business was concluded.

The clerk at the preflight lounge had been accurate, Milos mused, as he neared the immense open doors of the final hangar. Grinell's plane *was* in the best location. Once cleared, the aircraft could move out to the field through the opposite door, takeoff imminent as controlled by the tower—no minutes wasted during slow hours. Certain of the rich had it better than he thought.

Two uniformed guards stood inside the hangar at the edge of the drive where the blacktop met the concrete floor of the interior. Beyond them a Rockwell jet with men crawling over its silver wings stood immobile, a metal bird soon to soar into the night sky. Milos studied the guards' uniforms; they were neither federal nor municipal; they were from a private security firm. The realization gave birth to another thought as he noted that one of the men was quite large and very full in the waist and shoulders. Nothing was lost in trying; he had reached his post for the kill, but how much more satisfying it would be to execute a traitor at close range, making certain of the execution.

Varak walked casually down the asphalt toward the imposing entrance of the hangar. Both guards stepped forward, one crushing out a cigarette under his foot.

"What's your business here?" asked the large man on the Czech's right.

"Business, I think," answered Varak pleasantly. "Rather confidential business, I believe."

"What does that mean?" said the shorter guard on the left.

"You'll have to ask Mr. Grinell, I'm afraid. I'm merely a messenger, and I was told to speak to only one person, who should convey the information to Mr. Grinell when he arrives."

"More of that bullshit," added the shorter patrol to his companion. "If you got papers or cash, you gotta get 'em precleared. They find somethin' on the plane they don't know about, it don't head out, and Mr. Grinell will explode, you get me?"

"Loud and clear, my friend. I have only words that must be repeated accurately. Do *you* get *me*?"

"So talk."

"One person," said Varak. "And I choose *him,*" continued Milos, pointing at the large man.

"He's dumb. Take me."

"I was told whom to choose."

"Shit!"

"Please come with me," said the Czech, gesturing to the right behind the trip lights. "I'm to record our conversation but without anyone in earshot."

"Why don't you tell the boss *himself*?" objected the overlooked guard on the left. "He'll be here in a couple of minutes."

"Because we're never to meet face-to-face—anywhere. Would you care to ask him about it?"

"More bullshit."

Once around the corner of the hangar, Varak raised his cupped left hand. "Would you please speak directly into this?" he said, again pleasantly.

"Sure, mister."

They were the last words the guard would remember. The Czech sent the hard flat base of his right hand into the man's shoulder blade, following the blow with three chops to his throat and a final two-knuckled assault on his upper eyelids. The guard collapsed, and Varak swiftly began to remove his clothes. A minute and twenty seconds later he was overdressed in the large man's private security uniform; he cuffed the trouser legs and shoved up his sleeves, pulling the uniform over his wrists. He was ready.

Forty seconds later a black limousine drove down the street and stopped at the base of the asphalt entrance to the hangar.

The Czech moved out of the shadows and walked slowly into the chiaroscuro light. A man emerged from the huge car, and although Milos had never seen him, he knew that man was Crayton Grinell.

"Hi, boss!" yelled the guard at the left of the hangar as the overcoated gray-faced figure walked quickly, angrily across the blacktop. "We got your message, Benny's recording something—"

"Why isn't the goddamned plane out on the *strip*?" roared Grinell. "Everything's cleared, you idiots!"

"*Benny* talked to them, boss, *I* didn't! Five, ten minutes, they told him. It would have been different if *I* was on the phone! *Shit,* I don't put up with no shit, you know what I mean? You should'a told that guy to speak to me, that Benny—"

"Shut up! Get my driver and tell him to move this son of a bitch out! If they can't fly it, *he* can!"

"Sure, boss. Anything you say, boss! . . . They're starting the jets now!"

As the guard started shouting to the driver of the limousine the Czech joined the rush of activity and began running toward the outsized automobile.

"*Thanks!*" cried the passing chauffeur, seeing Varak's uniform. "*He* goes on at the last minute!"

Milos raced around the trunk of the car to the street side, yanked open the backseat, and leaped inside to a jump seat. He sat rigid, staring at the puffed face of an astonished Eric Sundstrom. "Hello, Professor," he said softly.

"It was a trap—you set a *trap* for me!" screamed the scientist in the dark shadows of the seat as the roar of jet engines filled the night outside. "But you don't know what you're *doing,* Varak! We're on the edge of a breakthrough in *space*! So many wondrous things to learn! We were *wrong*—Inver Brass is *wrong*! We must go *on*!"

"Even if we blow up half the planet?"

"Don't be an ass!" cried Sundstrom, pleading. "Nobody's going to blow up anything! We're a civilized people on both sides, civilized and frightened. The more we build, the more fear we instill—that's the world's ultimate protection, don't you *see*?"

"You call that civilized?"

"I call it progress. *Scientific* progress! You wouldn't understand, but the more we build, the more we *learn.*"

"Through weapons of destruction?"

"*Weapons . . . ?* You're pitifully naive! 'Weapons' is merely a *label.* Like 'fish' or 'vegetables.' It's the excuse we employ to fund scientific advancement on a scale that would be otherwise prohibitive! The 'bigger bang for the buck' theory is obsolete—we have all the bang we'll ever need. It's in the delivery systems—orbital guidance and hookups, directional lasers that can be refracted in space to pinpoint a manhole cover from thousands of miles above."

"And deliver a bomb?"

"Only if someone tries to *stop* us," answered the scientist, his voice strained, as if the mere prospect was enough to summon his fury. Then that fury broke. His cherubic features suddenly turned into the grotesque components of some monstrous gargoyle. "Research, research, *research*!" he cried, his strident speech like the squeals of a furious pig. "Let no one *dare* stop us! We're moving into a new world where science will rule all civilization! You're meddling with a political faction that *understands* our needs! You can't be *tolerated*! Kendrick is *dangerous*! You've seen him, heard him . . . he'd hold hearings, ask stupid questions, obstruct our *progress*!"

"That's what I thought you'd say." Varak slowly reached beneath the uniform to the fold of his jacket. "Do you know the universal penalty for treason, Professor?"

"What are you talking about?" His hands trembling, his heavy body shaking as the sweat rolled down his face, Sundstrom edged toward the door. "I've betrayed no one . . . I'm trying to stop a terrible *wrong,* a horrible mistake committed by misguided lunatics! You've got to be *stopped,* all of you! You cannot interfere with the greatest scientific machine the world has ever known!"

In the shadows Varak withdrew his automatic; a reflection of light beamed up from the barrel into Sundstrom's eyes. "You've had months to say those things; instead you were silent while the others trusted you. Through your betrayal lives were lost, bodies mutilated . . . you're filth, Professor."

"*No!*" screamed Sundstrom, crashing into the door, his trembling fingers hitting the handle as the door swung out, the scientist's rotund body following in frenzied panic. Milos fired; the bullet seared into Sundstrom's lower spine as the traitor fell to the asphalt shrieking. "*Help* me, *help* me! He's trying to *kill* me! Oh, *my God,* he *shot* me! . . . Kill him, *kill* him!" Varak fired again, his aim now steady, the bullet accurate. The back of the scientist's skull blew apart.

In seconds, amid screams of confusion, gunfire was returned from the hangar. The Czech was hit in the chest and left shoulder. He sprang out of the street-side door, rolling on the ground, over and over again directly behind the limousine until he reached the opposite curb. In pain he crawled above it, scrambling on his hands and knees into the darkness of the tall grass that was the border of an auxiliary airstrip. He almost did not make it; from all directions there were the sounds of sirens and racing engines. The entire security force was converging on Hangar Seven, as across the street the guard and Grinell's chauffeur closed in on the limousine, firing repeatedly into the vehicle. Varak was hit again. An aimless ricochet, a wild shot, burned its way into his stomach. He had to get away! His business was *not* concluded!

He turned and started running through the tall grass, ripping first the uniformed jacket off, then stopping briefly to remove the trousers. Blood was spreading through his shirt, and his legs grew unsteady. He had to conserve his strength! He had to get across the field and reach a road, find a telephone. He *had* to!

Searchlights. From a tower behind him! He was back in Czechoslovakia, in prison, racing across the compound to a fence and freedom. A beam swung close, and as he had done in that prison outside Prague, he lurched to the ground and lay motionless until it passed. He struggled to his feet, knowing he was growing weaker but could not stop. In the distance there were other lights—streetlights! And another fence . . . ! Freedom, *freedom.*

Straining every muscle, grip by grip, he scaled the fence, only to confront coiled barbed wire at the top. It did not matter. With what seemed like his last vestige of strength, he propelled himself over, shredding his clothes and his flesh as he dropped to the ground. He lay there breathing deeply, alternately holding his stomach and his chest. Go *on! Now!*

He reached the road; it was one of those unkempt narrow thoroughfares that frequently surround airports, no real estate development because of the noise. Still, cars sped by, shortcuts known to natives. Awkwardly, unsteadily, he walked onto it, holding up his arms at an approaching automobile. The driver, however, was having no part of him. He swung to the left and raced by. Moments later a second car approached from his right; he stood as straight as he could and raised one hand, a civilized signal of distress. The car slowed down; it stopped as the Czech reached into his holster for his gun.

"What's the problem?" asked the man in a naval uniform behind the wheel. The gold wings signified that he was a pilot.

"I'm afraid I've had an accident," replied Varak. "I drove off the road a mile or so back and no one has stopped to help me."

"You're pretty smashed up, pal. . . . Climb in and I'll get you to the hospital. *Jesus,* you're a *mess*! Come on, I'll give you a hand."

"Don't bother, I can manage," said Varak, walking around the hood. He opened the door and climbed in. "If I soil your car I'll gladly pay—"

"Let's worry about that in a month of Tuesdays." The naval officer shifted into gear and raced off as the Czech replaced his unseen automatic in the holster.

"You're very kind," said Milos, digging a scrap of paper out of his pocket and removing his pen, writing brief words and numbers in the darkness.

"You're very hurt, pal. Hang on."

"Please, I must find a *telephone. Please!*"

"The fucking insurance can wait, buddy."

"No, not insurance," stammered Varak. "My wife. She expected me hours ago. . . . She has psychological problems."

"Don't they all?" said the pilot. "Do you want me to make the call?"

"No, thank you very much. She would interpret that as a crisis far worse than it is." The Czech arched back in the seat, grimacing.

"There's a fruit stand about a mile down the road. I know the owner and they have a phone."

"I can't thank you enough."

"Take me to dinner when you get out of the hospital."

The perplexed owner of the fruit store handed Varak the phone as the naval officer watched, concerned for his damaged passenger. Milos dialed the Westlake Hotel. "Room Fifty-one, if you please?"

"Hello, *hello*?" cried Khalehla from out of a deep sleep.

"Do you have an answer for me?"

"Milos?"

"Yes."

"What's wrong?"

"I'm not terribly well, Miss Rashad. Do you have an *answer*?"

"You're hurt!"

"Your *answer*!"

"Green light. Payton will back off. If Evan can get the nomination, it's his. The race is on."

"He's needed more than you'll ever know."

"I don't know that he'll agree."

"He *has* to! Keep your line free. I'll call you right back."

"You *are* hurt!"

The Czech depressed the bar on the phone and immediately redialed.

"Yes?"

"Sound Man?"

"Prague?"

"How are things progressing?"

"We'll be done in a couple of hours. The typist's got the earphones on and is pounding away. . . . She's rough on all-night overtime."

"Whatever the cost, it's . . . covered."

"What's wrong with you? I can barely hear you."

"A slight cold. . . . You'll find ten thousand in your studio mailbox."

"Yes, come on, I'm not a thief."

"I roll high, remember?"

"You *really* don't sound right, Prague."

"In the morning, take everything to the Westlake, Room Fifty-one. The name of the woman is Rashad. Give it only to her."

"Rashad. Room Fifty-one. I've got it."

"Thank you."

"Listen, if you're in trouble, let me know about it, okay? I mean if there's anything I can do—"

"Your car's at the airport, somewhere in Section C," said the Czech, hanging up. He lifted the phone for the last time and dialed again. "Room Fifty-one," he repeated.

"Hello?"

"You will receive . . . everything in the morning."

"Where *are* you? Let me send help!"

"In the . . . morning. Get it to Mr. *B*!"

"*Goddamn* you, Milos, where *are* you?"

"It doesn't matter. . . . Reach Kendrick. He may know."

"Know *what*?"

"Photographs. . . . The Vanvlanderen woman . . . Lausanne, the Leman Marina. The Beau-Rivage—the gardens. Then Amsterdam, the Rozengracht. In the hotel . . . her study. *Tell* him! The man is a *Saudi* and things happened to him . . . millions,

millions!" Milos could hardly talk; he had so little breath. Go on . . . go *on*! "Escape . . . millions!"

"What the hell are you *talking* about?"

"He may be the *key*! Don't let anyone remove the photographs. . . . Reach *Kendrick*. He may remember!" The Czech lost control of his movements; he swung the telephone back onto the counter missing the cradle, then fell to the ground in front of the fruit stand on a backcountry road beyond the airport in San Diego. Milos Varak was dead.

38

The morning's headlines and related articles obscured all other news. The Secretary of State and his entire delegation had been brutally killed in a hotel on Cyprus. The Sixth Fleet was heading toward the island, all weapons and aircraft at the ready. The nation was transfixed, furious, and not a little frightened. The horror of some uncontrollable force of evil seemed to loom on the horizon, edging the country toward the brink of wholesale confrontation, provoking the government to respond with equal horror and brutality. But in a stroke of rare intuitive geopolitical brillance, President Langford Jennings controlled the storm. He reached Moscow, and the result of those communications had brought forth dual condemnations from the two superpowers. The monstrous event on Cyprus was labeled an isolated act of terrorism that enraged the entire world. Words of praise and sorrow for a great man came from all the capitals of the globe, allies and adversaries alike.

And on pages 2, 7 and 45, respectively, in the *San Diego Union,* and pages 4, 50 and 51 in the *Los Angeles Times,* were the following far less important wire service reports.

San Diego, Dec. 22—Mrs. Ardis Vanvlanderen, chief of staff for Vice President Orson Bollinger, whose husband, Andrew Vanvlanderen, died yesterday of a cerebral hemorrhage, took her own life early this morning in apparent grief. Her body washed up on the beach in Coronado, death attributed to drowning. On his way to the airport, her attorney, Mr. Crayton Grinell, of La Jolla, had dropped her off at the funeral home for a last viewing of her husband.

According to sources at the home, the widow was under severe strain and barely coherent. Although a limousine waited for her, she slipped out a side door and apparently took a taxi to the Coronado beach. . . .

Mexico City, Dec. 22—Eric Sundstrom, one of America's leading scientists and creators of highly complex space technology, died of a cerebral hemorrhage while on vacation in Puerto Vallarta. Few details are available at this time. A full report of his life and work will appear in tomorrow's editions.

San Diego, Dec. 22—An unidentified man without papers, but carrying a gun, died of gunshot wounds on a back road south of the International Airport. Lt. Commander John Demartin, a U.S. Navy fighter pilot, picked him up, telling the police the man claimed to have been in an automobile accident. Due to the proximity of the private field adjacent to the airport, authorities suspect that the death may have been drug-oriented. . . .

Evan flew to San Diego on the first morning flight from Denver. He had insisted on seeing Manny at 6:00 A.M. and would not be denied. "You're going to be fine," he had lied. "And you're a horseshit artist," Weingrass had shot back. "Where are you going?" ". . . Khalehla. San Diego. She needs me." ". . . Then get the hell out of here! I don't want to see your ugly face another second. Go to her, help her. Get those bastards!"

The taxi from the airport to the hotel in the early traffic seemed interminable, the situation hardly relieved by the driver, who recognized him and kept up a flow of inane chatter laced with invective directed at all Arabs and all things Arabic.

"Every fuckin' one of 'em should be taken out and shot, right?"

"Women and children, too, of course."

"*Right!* The brats grow up and the broads make more brats!"

"That's quite a solution. You might even call it final."

"It's the only way, *right*?"

"Wrong. When you consider the numbers and the price of ammunition, the cost would be too high. Taxes would go up."

"No *kiddin'*? Shit, I pay enough. There's gotta be another way."

"I'm sure you'll come up with one. . . . Now, if you'll forgive me, I have some reading to do." Kendrick returned to his copy of the *Denver Post* and the terrible news from Cyprus. And, either miffed or feeling he had been put down, the driver turned on the radio. Again, as in the newspapers, the coverage was almost exclusively about the abominable act of terrorism in the Mediterranean, on-site recordings and repeated interviews from world figures in various translated languages condemning the barbaric act. And as if death had to follow death, a stunned Evan heard the newscaster's words:

"Here in San Diego there was another tragedy. Mrs. Ardis Vanvlanderen, Vice President Bollinger's chief of staff, was found dead early this morning when her body washed up on the beach in Coronado, an apparent suicide. . . ."

Kendrick shot forward on the seat. . . . *Ardis?* Ardis *Vanvlanderen* . . . ? Ardis *Montreaux*! The Bahamas . . . a dissolute minor player from Off Shore Investments of years ago said Ardis Montreaux had married a wealthy Californian! Good *Christ*! That was why Khalehla had flown to San Diego. Mitchell Payton had found the "money whore"—Bollinger's chief of staff! The announcer went on to speculate on the new widow's grief, a speculation Kendrick thought suspect.

He walked across the hotel lobby and took the elevator to the fifth floor. Studying the numbered arrows, he started down the hall toward Khalehla's room both anxious and depressed—anxious to see her and hold her, depressed about Manny, about the wholesale slaughter on Cyprus, about *so* much, but mainly Emmanuel Weingrass, scheduled victim of murder. He reached the door and rapped four times, hearing the racing footsteps inside before he removed his hand. The door swung back and she was in his arms.

"My God, I love you," he whispered into her dark hair, the words rushed. "And everything's so rotten, so goddamned *rotten*!"

"Quickly. Inside." Khalehla closed the door and returned to him, holding his face in her hands. "Manny?"

"He's got somewhere between three and six months to live," replied Evan, his voice flat. "He's dying of a virus he couldn't possibly have gotten except through injection."

"The nonexistent Dr. Lyons," said Rashad, making a statement.

"I'll find him if it takes me twenty years."

"You'll have all the help Washington can give you."

"The news is rotten everywhere. Cyprus, the best man in the administration blown to bits—"

"It's tied in here, Evan. Here in San Diego."

"What?"

Khalehla backed away and took his hand, leading him across the room to where there were two chairs, a small round table between them. "Sit down, darling. I've got a lot to tell you that I couldn't tell you before. Then there's something you have to do . . . it's why I asked you to fly out here."

"I think I know one of the things you're going to tell me," said Kendrick, sitting down. "Ardis Montreaux, the widow Vanvlanderen. I heard it on the radio; they say she committed suicide."

"She did that when she married her late husband."

"You came to see her, didn't you."

"Yes." Rashad nodded as she sat down at the table. "You'll hear and read everything. There are tapes and transcripts of all of it; they were delivered to me an hour ago."

"What about Cyprus?"

"The order came from here. A man named Grinell."

"Never heard of him."

"Few people have. . . . Evan, it's worse than anything we could imagine."

"You learned that from Ardis? . . . Yes, she was Ardis and I was Evan."

"I know that. No, not from her; with her we only glimpsed the outline and that was frightening enough. Our main source is a man who was killed last night out by the airport."

"For God's sake, *who*?"

"The blond European, darling."

"*What?*" Kendrick fell back in the seat, his face flushed.

"He taped not only *my* interview but a subsequent conversation that blew the lid off the top. Except for Grinell, we don't have names, but we can piece together a picture, as in a puzzle with blurred figures, and it's terrifying."

"A government within the government," said Evan quietly. "Those were Manny's words. 'The servants running the master's house.' "

"As usual, Manny's right."

Kendrick got up from the chair and walked to a window, leaning against the sill and staring outside. "The blond man, who was he?"

"We never learned, but whoever he was he died delivering us the information."

"The Oman file. How did he *get* it?"

"He wouldn't tell me other than to say that his source was a good person who supported you for higher political office."

"That doesn't tell me *anything*!" shouted Evan, whipping around from the window. "There has to be *more*!"

"There isn't."

"Did he have any idea what they've *done*? The lives that were lost, the *butchering*!"

"He said he'd grieve over the errors of judgment more than anyone else. He didn't know that his grief would only last a couple of hours."

"Goddamnit!" roared Kendrick at the walls of the room. "What about this Grinell? Have they got him?"

"He's disappeared. His plane left San Diego for Tucson. No one knew about it until morning. It was on the ground for about an hour, then took off without filing a flight plan—that's how we found out."

"Planes can collide that way."

"Not if they patch into Mexican air traffic across the border. MJ has an idea that Grinell's security may have spotted the federal vehicles waiting for him near his house in La Jolla."

Evan returned to the table and sat down, a man exhausted, beaten. "Where do we go from here?"

"Downstairs to the Vanvlanderen suite. Our European wanted you to look at something—photographs, actually. I don't *know* why, but he said the man was a Saudi and you might remember. Something about millions and an escape. We've secured the apartment. No one goes in or out under the national security statutes insofar as she was Bollinger's chief of staff and there could be confidential papers."

"All right, let's go."

They took the elevator down to the third floor and approached the doors of the Vanvlanderen apartment. The two armed, uniformed police officers in front nodded as the man on the left turned. He inserted the key and opened the door.

"It's an honor to meet you, Congressman," said the officer on the right, impetuously extending his hand.

"A pleasure to meet you," said Kendrick, shaking the hand and going inside.

"How does it feel being such a celebrity?" asked Khalehla, closing the door.

"Neither comfortable nor gratifying," replied Evan as they walked across the marble foyer and down into the sunken living room. "Where are the photographs?"

"He wasn't specific—only that they were in her office, and you should find ones taken in Lausanne, Switzerland, and in Amsterdam."

"Over there," said Kendrick, seeing a lighted desk lamp in a room to the left. "Come on."

They walked across the carpeted room into the study. Evan adjusted his eyes to the shadowed interior, then crossed to another lamp across the room and turned it on. The crisscrossing arrangement of photographs sprang into light.

"Good Lord, how do we start?" said Khalehla.

"Slowly and carefully," answered Kendrick, quickly dismissing the panel on the left and concentrating on the right wall. "This is Europe," he said, his eyes roaming. "That's Lausanne," he added, focusing on two people in an enlarged snapshot with the Leman Marina in the background. "It's Ardis and . . . no, it couldn't be."

"What couldn't be?"

"Wait a minute." Evan followed the pattern to the lower right, concentrating on another framed enlargement, the faces clearer. "Lausanne, again. This is in the gardens of the Beau-Rivage. . . . Is it *possible*?"

"Is what? . . . He mentioned the Beau-Rivage, the blond man, I mean. Also Amsterdam, the rose something-or-other."

"The Rozengracht. Here it is." Kendrick pointed at a photograph in which the two subjects' faces were even sharper, more distinct. "My God, it's him!"

"*Who?*"

"Abdel Hamendi. I knew him years ago in Riyadh. He was a minister for the Saudis until the family caught him working on his own, making millions with false leases and ersatz contracts. He was to be publicly executed, but he got out of the country. . . . They say he built a fortress for himself somewhere in the Alps near Divonne and went into brokering a new business. Armaments. I was told he's become the most powerful arms merchant in the world with the lowest profile."

"Ardis Vanvlanderen mentioned Divonne on the second tape. It was a quick reference, but now it makes sense."

Evan stepped back and looked at Khalehla. "Our dead European's instincts were right. He didn't remember the details, but he saw the blood on Hamendi as surely as if it were coming out of that photograph. . . . A government within the government dealing with a global brokerage house for all the illicit weapons in the world." Kendrick suddenly frowned, his expression startled. "Is it all tied in with *Bollinger*?"

"The European said there was no way to tell. What does he know or what doesn't he know? There's only one thing that's certain. He's the rallying point for the heaviest political contributors in the country."

"My God, they're entrenched—"

"There's something else you should know. Ardis Vanvlanderen's husband was the one who made contact with the terrorists. He arranged for the attacks on your homes."

"*Jesus!*" roared Evan. "*Why?*"

"You," answered Khalehla softly. "You were the target; he wanted you killed. He acted alone—it's why his wife was murdered when the others found out; to cut off any ties to them—but they're all afraid of you. Starting next week there's going to begin a nationwide campaign to put you on the ticket replacing Bollinger as the new Vice President."

"The blond European's people?"

"Yes. And the men around Bollinger can't tolerate that. They think you'll squeeze them out, reduce their influence to nothing."

"I'm going to do more than that," said Evan. "I'm not going to squeeze them out, I'm going to rip them out. . . . Cyprus, Fairfax, Mesa Verde—*bastards*! Who are they? Is there a list?"

"We can compile one with a great many names, but we don't know who's involved and who isn't."

"Let's find out."

"How?"

"I'm going inside Bollinger's camp. They're going to see another Congressman Kendrick—one who can be bought off a national ticket."

Mitchell Jarvis Payton stared out the window from his desk in Langley, Virginia. There was so much to think about he could not think about Christmas, which was a minor blessing. He had no regrets about the life he had chosen, but Christmas was a bit trying. He had two married sisters in the Midwest and assorted nieces and nephews to whom he had sent the usual presents appropriately purchased by his secretary of many years, but he had no desire to join them for the holidays. There was simply nothing much to talk about; he had been too long on the other side of the world for conversations about a lumberyard and an insurance firm, and, of course, he could say nothing about his own work. Too, the children, most of them grown, were an unremarkable lot, not a scholar among them, and adamant in their collective pursuit of parental decrees for the good, stolid life of financial security. It was all better left alone. It was probably why he gravitated to his fictional niece, Adrienne Rashad—he had better get used to calling her Khalehla, he reflected. She was part of his world, hardly by any choice of his, but part of it, and outstanding. Payton wished for a moment that they were all back in Cairo when the Rashads insisted he come over for their yearly Christmas dinners, complete with a brilliantly decorated tree and recordings of the Mormon Tabernacle Choir singing carols.

"Really, MJ," Rashad's wife would exclaim. "I'm from California, remember? I'm the light-skinned one!"

Where had those days gone? Would they ever come back? Of course not. He ate alone at Christmas.

Payton's red phone rang. His hand shot out, picking it up. "Yes?"

"He's *crazy,*" yelled Adrienne-Khalehla. "I mean he's *nuts,* MJ!"

"He's turned you down?"

"Get off it. He wants to go see *Bollinger*!"

"On what grounds?"

"To play a fink! Can you *believe* it?"

"I might if you'll be somewhat clearer—"

There was an obvious tugging at the telephone as several obscenities were hurled back and forth. "Mitch, this is Evan."

"I gathered that."

"I'm going inside."

"Bollinger's?"

"It's logical. I did the same thing in Masqat."

"You can win one and then lose one, young man. Once successful, twice burned. Those people play hardball."

"So do I. I *want* them. I'll get them."

"We'll monitor you—"

"*No,* it's got to be solo. They have what you people call equipment—eyes all over the place. I've got to play it out by myself, the point being that I can be persuaded to fade from politics."

"That's too big a contradiction from what they've seen of you, heard of you. It wouldn't work, Kendrick."

"It will if I tell them part of the truth—a very essential part."

"What's that, Evan?"

"That I did what I did in Oman strictly out of self-interest. I was heading back to pick up the pieces, to make all that money I left behind. It's something they'd understand, they'd damn *well* understand."

"Not good enough. They'll ask too many questions and want to confirm your answers."

"None I *can't* answer," broke in Kendrick. "All part of the truth, all easily confirmed. I was convinced I knew who was behind the Palestinians and why—he'd used the same tactics on my company: the truth. I had connections with the most powerful men in the Sultanate and full government protection. Let them check with young Ahmat, he'd love to get that straightened out; his nose is still out of joint. Again, the truth, even when I was in the prisoner compound, where I was watched every minute by the police. . . . My objective throughout was merely to get the information I knew existed to nail a maniac who called himself the Mahdi. The *truth*."

"I'm sure there are gaps that can trip you up," said Payton, writing notes he would later shred.

"Not one I can think of, and that's all that matters. I've heard the European's tape; they've got billions riding on the next five years and can't afford to weaken their status quo by one iota. It doesn't matter that they're wrong, but they see me as a threat to them, which under different circumstances I damn well would be—"

"What might those circumstances be, Evan?" interrupted the older man in Langley.

"What . . . ? If I stayed in Washington, I imagine. I'd ride herd on every son of a bitch who plays loose with the government's coffers and figures out ways to get around the laws for a few million here and a few million there."

"A veritable Savonarola."

"No fanaticism, MJ, just a goddamned angry taxpayer who's sick and tired of all those screaming scare tactics designed to bleed the taxpayers for excessive profits. . . . Where was I?"

"A threat to them."

"Right. They want me out of the way and I'll convince them I'm ready to go, that I want nothing to do with this campaign to put me on the ticket . . . but I have a problem."

"This, I assume, is the kicker?"

"I'm first and foremost a businessman, a construction engineer by training and profession, and the office of Vice President would provide me with a global posture I could never enjoy without it. I'm relatively young; in five years I'll still be in my forties and as a former Vice President I'll have financial backing and influence available to me all over the world. That's a very tempting prospect for an international builder who intends to return to the private sector. . . . What do you think would be the reaction of Bollinger and his advisers, MJ?"

"What else?" said the director of Special Projects. "You're emulating their own voices with just the right amount of ooze. They'll offer you a five-year shortcut with all the financial resources you need."

"That's what I thought you'd say; that's what I think they'll say. But again, like any decent negotiator who's made a fair share of money in his day, I have another problem."

"I can't wait to hear it, young man."

"I need proof and I need it quickly so I can firmly reject the political committee out of Denver that's priming Chicago for next week. Reject it before it gets off the ground and possibly out of control."

"And the proof you require is a general commitment of sorts?"

"I'm a businessman."

"So are they. They won't put anything in writing."

"That's negotiable among men of goodwill. I want a meeting of intent with the principals. I'll set forth my plans, vague as they are, and they can respond. If they can convince me that they're trustworthy, I'll act accordingly. . . . And I think they'll be very convincing, but by then it won't matter."

"Because you'll have the nucleus," agreed Payton, smiling. "You'll know who they are. I must say, Evan, it all sounds feasible, even remarkably so."

"Just sound business practice, MJ."

"However, *I* have a problem. At the outset, they'll never believe that you're going back over there. They'll think you're lying. The whole Middle East is too unstable."

"I didn't say I was going back next week; I said 'one day,' and God knows I wouldn't mention the Mediterranean. But I will talk about the Emirates and Bahrain, Kuwait and Qatar, even Oman and Saudi Arabia, all the places in the gulfs where the Kendrick Group operated. They're as normal as they'll ever be, and as OPEC gets its act together it'll be business and profits as usual. Like every West European construction outfit, I want part of the action and I want to be ready for it. I'm back in the private sector."

"Good heavens, you're persuasive."

"Businesswise, I'm not far off the mark, either. . . . I've got the marbles, Mitch. I'm going in."

"When?"

"I'm calling Bollinger in a few minutes. I don't think he'll refuse my call."

"Not likely. Langford Jennings would burn his ass."

"I want to give him several hours to gather his flock, at least the few he counts on. I'll ask for a meeting late this afternoon."

"Make it in the evening," corrected the CIA executive. "After business hours, and be explicit. Say you want a private entrance away from his personnel and the press. It'll convey your message."

"That's very good, MJ."

"Sound business practice, Congressman."

Lieutenant Commander John Demartin, U.S. Navy, was in jeans and a T-shirt, applying generous portions of cleaning fluid over the upholstery of his car's front seat, trying with minimal success to remove the bloodstains. It was going to take a professional job, he concluded, and until it was done he would tell the kids he had spilled some cherry soda on the way home from the field. Still, the more he reduced the stains, the less it would cost—he hoped.

Demartin had read the report in the morning's *Union* identifying him by name and stating that the authorities believed the wounded hitchhiker he had picked up was a drug death; the pilot, however, was not convinced. He was not on speaking terms with any drug dealers that he knew of, yet he could not imagine that too many of them were so polite as to offer to pay for soiling a seat. He assumed that such men, if wounded, would be in panic, not so controlled, so courteous.

Pressing down, Demartin scrubbed the rear of the seat again. His exposed knuckles touched something, something sharp yet instantly flexible. It was a note. He pulled it out and read it, reading beneath the bloodstains.

Urgt. Mx s'c'ty. Relay contct 3016211133 S-term

The last letters drifted off as if there had been no strength left to write them. The naval officer dragged himself out of the seat and stood in the driveway studying the note, then walked up the flagstone path to his front door. He went inside, proceeded into the living room and picked up the phone; he knew whom to call. Moments later a WAVE secretary put him through to the base's chief of intelligence.

"Jim, it's John Demartin—"

"Hey, I read about that crazy episode last night. What some fly-boys won't do for a little grass. . . . You're taking me up on the fishing Saturday?"

"No, I'm calling you about last night."

"Oh? How come?"

"Jim, I don't know who or what that guy was, but I don't think he had anything to do with drugs. Then a few minutes ago I found a note creased into the seat where he was sitting. It's kind of bloody but let me read it to you."

"Go ahead, I've got a pencil."

The naval officer read the awkwardly printed words, letters and numbers. "Does it make any sense?" he asked when he had finished.

"It . . . may," said the intelligence chief slowly, obviously rereading what he had written. "John, describe what happened last night, will you? The article in the paper was pretty sketchy."

Demartin did so, beginning with the observation that although the blond man spoke excellent English, he had a foreign accent. He ended with the hitchhiker's collapse in front of the fruit stand. "That's it."

"Do you think he knew how severely he was wounded?"

"If he didn't, I did. I tried not to stop for the telephone but he insisted—I mean, he *pleaded,* Jim. Not so much in words but with his eyes. . . . I won't forget them for a long time."

"But there was no question in your mind that he was coming back to the car."

"None. I think he wanted to make a last call; even as he fell he reached up for the phone on the counter, but he was coming back."

"Stay where you are. I'll call you right back."

The pilot hung up and walked to a rear window overlooking the small pool and outside patio. His two children were splashing about and yelling at each other while his wife reclined in a lounge chair reading the *Wall Street Journal,* a practice for which he was grateful. Thanks to her, they were able to live somewhat beyond his salary. The phone rang; he returned to it. "Jim?"

"Yes. . . . John, I'll be as clear as I can and that's not going to be too clear. There's a fellow here on loan to us from Washington who's more familiar with these things than I am, and this is what he wants you to do. . . . Oh, boy."

"What is it? Tell me?"

"Burn the note and forget about it."

The CIA officer in the rumpled suit reached for the small yellow package of M&M's, the telephone held to his left ear. "You got all that?" asked Shapoff, otherwise known as Gingerbread.

"Yes," replied MJ Payton, the word drawn out as if the information was both bewildering and startling.

"The way I read it, this guy, whoever he was, combined 'urgent' with 'maximum security' figuring that if he didn't make it this navy officer would have enough sense to call Base Security rather than the cops."

"Which is exactly what he did," agreed MJ.

"Then Security would reach the 'relay contact' and deliver the message, thinking it'd be channeled to the right people."

"The message being that someone called code name *S* had been terminated."

"We got an operation with a code-*S*?"

"No."

"Maybe it's the Bureau of Treasury."

"I doubt it," said Payton.

"Why?"

"Because in this case the relay is the last stop. The message wouldn't have gone any further."

"How do you know that?"

"Area code three-zero-one is Maryland, and unfortunately I recognize the number. It's unlisted and very private."

Payton leaned back in his chair, briefly understanding how alcoholics felt thinking they could not get through the next hour without a drink, which meant a step away from reality. How ludicrously, illogically *logical*! The voice heard by the ears of presidents, a man the nation's leaders knew had the nation's interests always in the forefront of his profound thinking, without fear, without favor, objectivity a constant. . . . He had chosen the future. He had selected a little-known but outstanding congressman with a story to tell that would mesmerize the country. He had guided his anointed prince through the political labyrinth until the designated tyro emerged into the media sunlight, no longer a fledgling but a practitioner to be reckoned with. Then with the suddenness and audacity of a bolt of lightning, the *story* was told and the nation, indeed a large part of the world, was transfixed. A giant wave had been set in motion, carrying the prince to a land he had never considered, a land of power, a royal house of awesome responsibility. The White House. Samuel Winters had broken the rules and, far worse, at an enormous loss of life. Mr. A had not dropped from the sky in a crisis. The blond European had worked solely for the august Samuel Winters.

The director of Special Projects picked up his phone and gently touched the numbers on his console. "Dr. Winters," he said in response to the single word Yes. "This is Payton."

"It's been a terrible day, hasn't it, Doctor?"

"That's not a title I use anymore. I haven't for years."

"A shame. You were a fine scholar."

"Have you heard from Mr. A since last evening?"

"No. . . . Although his information was tragically prophetic, there'd be no reason for him to call me. As I told you, Mitchell, the man who employs him—a far more distant acquaintance than you—suggested he reach me . . . very much as you did. My reputation exceeds my presumed influence."

"Through you I saw the President," said Payton, closing his eyes at the old man's lies.

"Well, yes. The news you brought me was devastating, as was Mr. A's. In his case I naturally thought of you. I wasn't sure Langford or his people had the expertise that you did—"

"I obviously didn't have it," interrupted MJ.

"I'm certain you did all you could."

"Back to Mr. A, Dr. Winters."

"Yes?"

"He's dead."

The gasp of breath was like an electric shock over the line. It was several seconds before Winters spoke, and when he did his voice was hollow. "What are you *saying*?"

"He's dead. And someone known to you as code name *S* has been killed."

"Oh, my *God,*" whispered the spokesman of Inver Brass, the whisper a tremulous echo of itself. "How do you come by this . . . information?"

"I'm afraid that's privileged, even from you."

"*Damn* you, I gave you *Jennings*! The President of the United States!"

"But you didn't tell me why, Doctor. You never explained to me that your overriding concern—your consummate concern—was the man you had chosen. Evan Kendrick."

"*No!*" protested Winters, as close to a scream of denial as he could manage. "You must not delve into such matters, they're not your business! No laws have been broken."

"I'd like to think you believe that, but if you do, I'm afraid you're terribly wrong. When you contract the talents of someone like your European, you can't divorce yourself from his methods. . . . As we've pieced it together they include political extortion through blackmail, the corruption of the legislative process, the theft of maximum-classified documents and indirectly causing the death and maiming of numerous government personnel—and finally murder. Code name *S* was terminated."

"Oh, dear *God* . . . !"

"That's who you were playing—"

"You don't understand, Mitchell, that's not the way things *happened*!"

"On the contrary, it's exactly the way they happened."

"I know nothing about such things, you *must* believe that."

"I do because you employed a skilled professional for results, not for giving you explanations."

" 'Employed' is too simplistic a term! He was a dedicated man who had his own mission in life."

"So I was told," interrupted Payton. "He came from a country whose government had been stolen from its people."

"What do you think is happening *here*?" said the leader of Inver Brass, his words now controlled but the depth of their meaning clear.

It was several moments before MJ replied, again with his eyes closed. "I know," he said softly. "We're putting that together, too."

"They killed the Secretary of State and the entire delegation on Cyprus. They have no conscience, no allegiance to anything but their own ever-expanding wealth and power. . . . I want nothing, *we* want nothing!"

"I understand. You wouldn't get it if you wanted it."

"That's why he was chosen, Mitchell. We found the extraordinary man. He's too perceptive to be fooled and too decent to be bought. In addition, he has the personal requisites to command attention."

"I can't fault your choice, Dr. Winters."

"So where are we?"

"In a dilemma," said Payton. "But for the moment it's mine, not yours."

7:25 P.M. San Diego. They held each other; Khalehla leaned back, touching his hair as she looked at him. "Darling, can you do it?"

"You forget, *ya anisa,* I've spent most of my profitable life dealing with the Arabic propensity for negotiation."

"That was negotiating—exaggeration, of course—not *lying,* not sustaining a lie in front of people who'll be suspicious of everything you say."

"They'll desperately want to believe me; that's two points for our side. Besides, once I see them and meet them, I don't really give a damn what they believe."

"I wouldn't advise you to think that way, Evan," said Rashad, lowering her hand and stepping away. "Until we have them, which includes degrees of traceable evidence, they'll operate as usual—down and dirty. If they think for a moment that it's a trap, you could be found washed up on the beach, or maybe just not found at all, just out there somewhere in the Pacific."

"As in the shark-infested shoals of Qatar." Kendrick nodded, remembering Bahrain and the Mahdi. "I see what you mean. Then I'll make it plain that my office knows where I am tonight."

"It wouldn't happen tonight, darling. Down and dirty doesn't mean stupid. There'll be a mix in there—some legitimate staffers and probably a smattering of Bollinger's kitchen cabinet. Old friends who act as advisers—they're the ones you want to zero in on. Use that well-recognized cool of yours and be convincing. Don't let anything throw you."

The telephone rang and Evan started toward it. "That's the limousine," he said. "Gray with tinted windows, as befits the Vice President's residence in the hills."

8:07 P.M. San Diego. The slender man walked rapidly through the terminal at San Diego's international airport, a garment two-suiter slung over his right shoulder, a black medical bag in his left hand. The automatic glass doors to the taxi area snapped back as he passed through onto the concrete pavement. He stood for a moment, then headed for the first cab in the line of taxis queued up for passengers. He opened the door as the driver lowered a tabloid newspaper.

"I assume you're available," said the new fare curtly as he climbed in, throwing the carryon across the seat and lowering his medical bag to the floor.

"No trips over an hour, mister. That's when I pack it in for the night."

"You'll make it."

"Where to?"

"Up in the hills. I know the way. I'll direct you."

"Gotta have an address, mister. It's the law."

"How about the California residence of the Vice President of the United States?" asked the passenger testily.

"It's an address," replied the driver, unimpressed.

The taxi started off with a planned mean-spirited jolt, and the man known briefly in southwest Colorado as Dr. Eugene Lyons was slapped back into the seat. He was unaware of the insult, however, his anger clouding all normal perceptions. He was a man who was *owed,* a man who had been cheated!

39

The introductions were brief and Kendrick had the distinct impression that not all the names or titles were entirely accurate. As a result, he studied each face as if he were about to commit it to a canvas he was incapable of painting. Khalehla had been right, the seven-man council *was* a mix but not as difficult to discern as she thought. A staffer making thirty to forty thousand dollars a year did not dress or behave like someone who spent such sums on a weekend visit to Paris . . . or Divonne. He judged that the staff was in the minority: three official aides versus four outside advisers—the kitchen cabinet from California.

Vice President Orson Bollinger was a man of medium height, medium build, medium middle age, and afflicted with a medium high voice that fell between the narrow parameters of being dismissable and convincing. He was . . . well, medium, the ideal second in command as long as Number One was in eminent good health and vigor. He was vaguely perceived as a toady who might just possibly rise to the occasion, but only possibly. He was neither a threat nor a stupid man. He was a political survivor because he understood the unwritten rules of the also-ran. He greeted Congressman Evan Kendrick warmly and led him into his impressive private library, where his "people" were assembled, sitting in various leather armchairs and dark leather couches.

"We've canceled our Christmas festivities here," said Bollinger, sitting in the most prominent chair and indicating that Evan should sit beside him, "in deference to dear Ardis and Andrew. Such a terrible tragedy, two such magnificently patriotic people. She simply couldn't live without him, you know. You'd have to have seen them together to understand."

Nods and impatient grunts of agreement came from around the room. "I understand, Mr. Vice President," interjected Kendrick sadly. "As you may know, I met Mrs. Vanvlanderen a number of years ago in Saudi Arabia. She was a remarkable woman and so very sensitive."

"No, Congressman, I *didn't* know that."

"It's immaterial, but of course not to me. I'll never forget her. She was remarkable."

"As, indeed, is your request for a meeting this evening," said one of the two official aides sitting on the couch. "We're all aware of the Chicago movement to challenge the Vice President, and we understand that it may not have your endorsement. Is that true, Congressman?"

"As I explained to the Vice President this afternoon, I didn't hear about it until a week ago. . . . No, it doesn't have my endorsement. I've considered other plans that do not concern further political pursuits."

"Then why not simply declare your noncandidacy?" asked a second aide from the same couch.

"Well, I guess things are never as simple as we'd like them to be, are they? I'd be less than candid if I said I wasn't flattered by the proposal, and during the past five days my staff did some fairly extensive polling, both regionally and among the party leadership. They've concluded that my candidacy is a viable prospect."

"But you just said you had other plans," interrupted a heavyset man in gray flannels and a gold-buttoned navy blue blazer . . . not an aide.

"I believe I said that I've *considered* other plans, other pursuits. Nothing's finalized."

"What's your point, Congressman?" asked the same staffer who had suggested that Evan declare his noncandidacy.

"That could be between the Vice President and me, couldn't it?"

"These are my people," offered Bollinger unctuously, smiling benignly.

"I understand that, sir, but my people are not here . . . perhaps to guide me."

"You don't look or sound like someone who needs a hell of a lot of guidance," said a short, compact adviser-contributor from a leather chair unflatteringly large for his small frame. "I've seen you on television. You've got some pretty strong opinions."

"I couldn't change those any more than a zebra could change his stripes, but there may be mitigating circumstances why they should remain privately held beliefs rather than publicly expressed ones."

"Are you trading horses?" asked a third contributor, this a tall, lanky man in an open shirt and deeply tanned features.

"I'm not trading anything," objected Kendrick firmly. "I'm attempting to explain a situation that hasn't been clarified and I think it damn well should be."

"No need to get upset, young fella," said Bollinger earnestly, frowning at his large suntanned adviser. "It's not a demeaning choice of words, you know. 'Trading' is intrinsic to our great democratic contract. Now, what's this situation that should be clarified?"

"The Oman crisis. . . . Masqat and Bahrain. The basic reason why I've been singled out for higher political office." Suddenly it was apparent that the Vice President's people all thought they were going to be given information that might wash away the Oman myth, vitiate the potential candidate's strongest appeal. All eyes were riveted on the Congressman. "I went to Masqat," continued Evan, "because I knew who was behind the Palestinian terrorists. He used the same tactics on me, driving my company out of business and robbing me of *millions.*"

"You wanted revenge, then?" suggested the heavyset adviser in the gold-buttoned blazer.

"Revenge, *hell,* I wanted my company back—I still want it. The time will come fairly soon now and I want to head back to pick up the pieces, to make up for all those profits I left behind."

The fourth contributor, a florid-faced man with a distinct Boston accent, leaned forward. "You goin' back t' the Middle East?"

"No, to the Persian Gulf states—there's a difference. The Emirates, Bahrain, Qatar, Dubai, they're not Lebanon or Syria or Qaddafi's Libya. The word out of Europe is that construction's starting up all over again and I intend to be there."

"You sold your company," said the tall, suntanned contributor with the open shirt, his speech laconic but precise.

"At a *forced sale.* It was worth five times what I was paid. But that's not too large a problem for me. Up against West German, French and Japanese capital, I may have a few problems at the beginning, but my contacts are as extensive as anyone else's. Also . . ." Kendrick played out his scenario with understated conviction, touching on his relationships with the royal houses and ministers of Oman, Bahrain, Abu Dhabi and Dubai, mentioning the protection and the assistance, including private transportation, provided him by the governments of Oman and Bahrain during the Masqat crisis. Then, as abruptly as he began, he stopped. He had drawn the impending picture sufficiently for their imaginations; more might be too much.

The men in the library looked at one another, and with an almost imperceptible nod from the Vice President, the heavyset man in the navy blue blazer spoke. "It strikes me that your plans are pretty well solidified. What would you want with a job that pays a hundred and fifty thou a year and too many chicken dinners? You're not a politician."

"Considering my age, the time factor could be attractive. Five years from now I'll still be in my forties, and the way I read things, even if I started tomorrow over there it would take me two, perhaps three, years to be in full operation, and I could be shy a year there—there are no guarantees. But if I go the other way and actively seek the nomination, I might actually get it—that's no reflection on you, Mr. Vice President. It's merely the result of the media treatment that I've been given."

When several others began speaking at once, Bollinger held up his hand, barely inches above the arm of his chair. It was enough to quiet them. "*And,* Congressman?"

"Well, I think it's pretty obvious. There's no question in anyone's mind that Jennings will win the election, although he may have problems with the Senate. If I were fortunate enough to be on the ticket, I'd go from the House to the vice presidency, spend my time and come out with more international influence—and, quite frankly, resources—than I could ever hope to have otherwise."

"*That,* Congressman," cried an angry young third aide from a straight-backed chair next to his colleagues on the couch, "is blatantly using the trust of public office for personal profit!"

There was a mass lowering and straying of the contributors'

eyes. "If I didn't think you impetuously misspoke yourself because you don't understand," said Evan calmly, "I'd be extremely offended. I'm stating an obvious fact because I want to be completely open with Vice President Bollinger, a man I deeply respect. What I mentioned is the truth; it goes with the office. But in *no* way does that truth take away from the energy or the commitment I'd give to that office while serving it and the nation. Whatever rewards might come from such a position, whether in the form of publishing, corporate boardrooms or golf tournaments, they wouldn't be given to a man who took his responsibilities lightly. Like Vice President Bollinger, I couldn't operate that way."

"Well said, Evan," commented the Vice President softly while looking harshly at the impulsive aide. "You're owed an apology."

"I apologize," said the young man. "You're right, of course. It all goes with the office."

"Don't be too apologetic," admonished Kendrick, smiling. "Loyalty to one's boss isn't anything to be sorry about." Evan turned to Bollinger. "If he's a black belt, I'm getting out of here fast," he added, breaking the momentary tension with laughter.

"He plays a mean game of Ping-Pong," said the older aide on the left of the couch.

"He's very creative keeping score," said the oldest staffer on the right. "He cheats."

"At any rate," continued Evan, waiting until the grins—mostly forced—had left the assembled faces. "I meant it when I said I wanted to be completely frank with you, Mr. Vice President. These are the things I have to think about. I've lost four, almost five years, of a career—a business—I worked extremely hard to develop. I was short-circuited by a mad killer and forced to sell because people were afraid to work for me. He's dead and things have changed; they're getting back to normal, but the European competition is heavy. Can I do it by myself or should I actively campaign for the ticket and, if I succeed, have certain guarantees that result from holding the office? On the other hand, do I really want to spend the additional years and the enormous amounts of time and energy that go with the job? . . . These are questions only I can answer, sir. I hope you understand."

And then Kendrick heard the words he had hoped beyond hope to hear—hope in this case far more meaningful than in his statement to Bollinger.

"I know it's late for your staff, Orson," said the tall, lanky man in the open shirt that set off his suntanned flesh, "but I'd like to talk a little further."

"Yes, certainly," agreed the Vice President, turning to his aides. "These poor fellas have been up since dawn, what with the dreadful news about Ardis and all. Go home, boys, and have Christmas with your families—I brought all the wives and kids out here on Air Force Two, Evan, so they could be together."

"Very thoughtful, sir."

"Thoughtful, hell. Maybe they *all* have black belts. . . . You're dismissed, troops. Tomorrow's Christmas Eve, and if I remember correctly, the next day's Christmas. So unless the Ruskies blow up Washington, I'll see you in three days."

"Thank you, Mr. Vice President."

"You're very kind, sir."

"We can stay, if you wish," said the oldest, as each successively got out of his chair.

"And have you mauled by your two associates?" asked Bollinger, grinning at the expressions of the others. "I wouldn't hear of it. On your way out, send in the butler. We might as well have a brandy while we solve all the world's problems."

See-No-Evil, Speak-No-Evil, and Hear-No-Evil left the room, programmed robots reacting to a familiar marching tune. The man in the gold-button navy blue blazer leaned forward in his chair, his stomach making it difficult for him. "You want to talk frankly, Congressman? Real frank and real honest? Well, we're going to do that."

"I don't understand, Mr. . . . I'm sorry, I didn't get your name."

"Cut the hoss-shit!" exclaimed the florid Bostonian. "I've heard better crap from the ward heelers in Southie."

"You may fool the pols in D.C.," said the small man in the too-large chair, "but we're businessmen, too, Kendrick. You've got something to offer and maybe—just *maybe*—we've got something to offer."

"*How* do you enjoy southern California, Congressman?" The tall man with the open shirt and the outstretched legs spoke loudly as a butler entered the room.

"Nothing, *nothing,*" exclaimed Bollinger, addressing the tuxedoed servant. "Never mind. Leave us."

"I'm sorry, sir, I have a message for you," said the butler, handing the Vice President a note.

Bollinger read it; his face at first grew red, then rapidly paled.

"Tell him to wait," he ordered. The butler left the room. "Where were we?"

"At a price," said the man from Boston. "That's what we're talkin' about, isn't it, Congressman?"

"That's a little blunt," answered Evan. "But the term is in the realm of possibility."

"You should understand," said the small man with the pinched face, "that you passed through two separate powerful detectors. You may get sick from the X rays, but you don't have any recording machines on you."

"They'd be the last things I'd want."

"Good," said the tall man, getting out of the chair as if solely to impress the others with his formidable height and his image as the tanned, rugged yachtsman or whatever he was; strength was the message. He sauntered to the fireplace mantel—High Noon in the Town of Corruption, thought Kendrick. "We caught your leeward drift about German, French and Japanese capital. How steep are the waves in open water?"

"I'm afraid I'm not a sailor. You'll have to be clearer."

"What are you up against?"

"Financially?" asked Evan, pausing, then shaking his head in dismissal. "Nothing I can't handle. I can commit seven to ten million, if I have to, and my lines of credit are extensive . . . but, of course, so are the interest rates."

"Suppose lines of credit were established without those kinda burdens?" said the man familiar with the ward heelers of South Boston.

"Gentlemen," interrupted Bollinger sharply, getting out of his chair as those seated did also in deference to his obviously imminent departure. "I understand that I have an urgent matter to attend to. If you need anything, feel free to ask for it."

"We won't be long, Mr. Vice President," said Kendrick, knowing why Bollinger had to distance himself from whatever ensuing conversation took place; deniability was the byword. "As I mentioned, this is a problem that only I can properly resolve. I just wanted to be open with you."

"It's greatly appreciated, Evan. Stop in and see me before you leave. I'll be in my office."

The Vice President of the United States left the book-lined room, and like jackals descending on their prey, the contributors turned to the congressman from Colorado. "We level now, son," said the six-foot-five yachtsman, his arm on the mantel like a leaning, angry weed.

"I'm not a relative of yours, thank you, and I resent the familiarity."

"Big Tom always talks like that," chimed in the Bostonian. "He don't mean no harm by it."

"The harm is in his presumption with a member of the House of Representatives."

"Oh, come on, Congressman!" interjected the obese man in the navy blue blazer.

"Let's all relax," said the small-framed, pinched-faced man sitting down in the overlarge armchair. "We're all here for the same purpose, and courtesies aside, let's get on with it. . . . We want you out, Kendrick. Do we have to be clearer?"

"Since you're so adamant, I think you'd better be."

"All right," continued the short contributor, his legs barely touching the carpeted floor. "As someone said, let's be honest—doesn't cost a damn thing. . . . We represent a political philosophy every bit as legitimate as you think yours is, but because it's ours we naturally feel it's more realistic for the times. Basically, we believe in a far stronger defense-oriented system of priorities than you do for the country."

"I believe in a strong defense, too," broke in Evan. "But not in budget-crippling, excessively *offensive* systems where forty percent of the expenditures result in waste and ineffectiveness."

"Good point," agreed Kendrick's undersized opponent from the large chair. "And these areas of procurement will be rectified by the marketplace."

"But not until billions are spent."

"Naturally. If it were otherwise, you're talking about another system of government that doesn't permit the Malthusian law of economic failure. The forces of the free market will correct those excesses. Competition, Congressman Kendrick. Competition."

"Not if they're rigged in the Pentagon or in those boardrooms where there are too many alumni from the Defense Department."

"*Hell!*" exclaimed the yachtsman from the fireplace mantel. "If they're that fucking obvious, let 'em hang!"

"Big Tom's right," said the florid-faced Bostonian. "There's plenty to go around, and those nickel-and-dime colonels and generals are just lubrication, anyway. Get rid of them if you like, but don't stop the treadmill, for Christ's sake!"

"Do you hear that?" asked the gold-buttoned blue blazer. "Don't *stop* until we're so strong no Soviet leader would even *think* about a strike."

"Why do you think any of them *would* consider it, consider blowing up a large part of the civilized world?"

"Because they're Marxist fanatics!" roared the yachtsman, standing erect in front of the mantel, his arms akimbo.

"Because they're stupid," corrected the short man from his chair calmly. "Stupidity is the basic road to global tragedy, which means the strongest and the smartest will survive. . . . We can handle our critics in the Senate and the House, Congressman, but *not* in the administration. *That* we can't tolerate. Am I clear?"

"You really think I'm a threat to you?"

"Of course you are. You get on your soapbox and people listen, and what you say—very effectively, I might add—is not in our interests."

"I thought you had such respect for the marketplace."

"I do in the long run, but in the short run excessive oversight and regulation can cripple the country's defense with delays. This is no time to throw the baby out with the bath water."

"Which means throwing away profits."

"They go with the job, as you so rightly explained regarding the office of Vice President. . . . Go your way, Congressman. Rebuild your aborted career in Southwest Asia."

"With what?" asked Evan.

"Let's start with a credit line of fifty million dollars at the Gemeinschaft Bank in Zurich, Switzerland."

"That's very convincing, but they're only words. Who's putting up the collateral?"

"The Gemeinschaft knows. You don't have to."

It was all Kendrick had to hear. The full weight of the United States government bearing down on a Zurich bank with known connections to men who dealt with terrorists from the Baaka Valley to Cyprus would be enough to break the Swiss codes of secrecy and silence. "I'll confirm the line of credit in Zurich in thirty-six hours," he said, getting up. "Will that give you sufficient time?"

"More than sufficient," replied the small man in the large chair. "And when you have confirmation, you'll do Vice President Bollinger the courtesy of sending him a copy of your telegram to Chicago irrevocably withdrawing your name for consideration on the national ticket."

Kendrick nodded, glancing briefly at the three other contributors. "Good evening, gentlemen," he said quietly and then headed for the library door.

Out in the hallway a black-haired, muscular man with sharp, clean-cut features and the green dot of the Secret Service in his lapel rose from a chair beside a pair of thick double doors. "Good evening, Congressman," he said pleasantly, taking a step forward. "It'd be an honor to shake your hand, sir."

"My pleasure."

"I know we're not to say who comes and goes around here," continued the member of the Treasury Department detail, gripping Evan's hand, "but I may break that rule for my mother in New York. Perhaps it sounds crazy, but she thinks you should be Pope."

"The Curia might find me lacking. . . . The Vice President asked me to see him before I left. He said he'd be in his office."

"Certainly. It's right here, and let me tell you he'd welcome the interruption. He's got an irritated man in there with such a short fuse I didn't trust the machines and nearly strip-searched him. I wouldn't let him take his bag of paraphernalia inside."

For the first time, Kendrick saw the garment carryon draped across the chair at the left of the double doors. Beneath it, on the floor, was a bulky black case commonly referred to as a medical bag. Evan stared at it; he had seen it before. The inner screen of his mind was jolted, fragments of images replacing one another like successive explosions! Stone walls in another hallway, another door; a tall, slender man with a ready smile—too ready, too ingratiating for a stranger in a strange house—a *doctor* casually, amusingly stating that he would merely thump a chest and take a sample of blood for analysis.

"If you don't mind," said Kendrick, somehow through the mists, realizing that he could barely be heard, "please open the door."

"I've got to knock first, Congressman—"

"No, *please*! . . . Please do as I say."

"The Vipe—the Vice President—won't appreciate that, sir. We're always to knock first."

"Open that door," ordered Evan, his rasping voice a whisper, his eyes wide, fixed briefly on the Secret Service man. "I'll take full responsibility."

"Sure, sure. If anyone's entitled I guess you are."

The heavy door on the right swung silently back, the words hissed by a tight-throated Bollinger clearly heard. "What you're saying is preposterous, *insane*! . . . Yes, what *is* it?"

Kendrick walked through the terrible space and stared at the shocked, panic-stricken face of "Dr. Eugene Lyons."

"*You!*" screamed Evan, the isolated world inside his head going mad as he lunged, racing across the room, his two hands the claws of a maniacal animal intent only on the kill—the *kill*! "He's going to *die* because of you—because of *all* of you!"

In a blur of violence, arms gripped him; hands chopped into his head, and knees crashed up into his groin and his stomach, his eyes bruised by experienced fingers. Despite the agonizing pain, he heard the muted screams—one after another.

"I've got him! He's not going to move."

"Close the door!"

"Get me my bag!"

"Keep everyone *out*!"

"Oh, Jesus, he knows *everything*!"

"What do we *do*?"

". . . I know people who can handle this."

"Who the hell are *you*?"

"Someone who should introduce himself . . . *Viper.*"

"I've *heard* that name. It's an insult! Who *are* you?"

"For the moment I'm in charge, that's who I am."

"Oh, *Christ* . . . !"

Darkness—the oblivion that comes with the deepest shock. All was black; nothing.

40

He felt the wind and the spray first, then the motion of the sea, and finally the wide cloth straps that constricted him, binding him to the metal chair bolted into the deck of the pitching boat. He opened his eyes in the moving darkness; he was in the stern, the foaming wake receding in front of him, and was suddenly aware of cabin lights behind him. He turned, craning his neck to see, to understand. Abruptly, he was face-to-face with the dark-haired, swarthy Secret Service guard whose mother in New York thought he should be Pope . . . and whose voice he had heard proclaiming himself to be in charge. The man sat in an adjacent deep-sea fighting chair, a single strap across his waist.

"Waking up, Congressman?" he asked politely.

"What the hell have you *done*?" roared Kendrick, struggling against the restricting straps.

"Sorry about those, but we didn't want you falling over the side. The water's a little rough; we were just protecting you while you got some air."

" 'Protecting . . . ?' *Goddamn* you, you bastards *drugged* me and carried me out of there against my will! You've kidnapped me! My office knows where I went tonight . . . you're going to draw twenty years for this, all of you! And that son of a bitch Bollinger will be impeached and spend—"

"Hold it, *hold* it," broke in the man, raising his hands, calmly protesting. "You've got it all wrong, Congressman. Nobody drugged you, you were *sedated.* You went crazy back there. You attacked a guest of the Vice President; you might have *killed* him—"

"I would have, I *will* kill him! Where's that doctor, where *is* he?"

"What doctor?"

"You lying *shit*!" yelled Kendrick into the wind, straining at the cloth straps. Then he was struck by a thought. "My limousine, the *driver*! He knows I didn't leave."

"But you did. You weren't feeling too well, so you didn't say much and you wore your tinted glasses, but you were very generous with your tip."

As the boat lurked in the water, Evan suddenly looked down at the clothes he was wearing, squinting in the dim wash of light coming from the cabin behind him. The trousers were a thick corduroy and the shirt a coarse black denim . . . not his clothes. "*Bastards!*" he roared again, and again another thought. "Then they saw me get out at the hotel!"

"Sorry, but you didn't go to the hotel. About the only thing you said to the driver was to drop you off at Balboa Park, that you had to meet someone and you'd take a cab home."

"You covered yourselves right down to my clothes. You're all garbage, you hired *killers*!"

"You keep getting it wrong, Congressman. We were covering for *you,* not anybody else. We didn't know what you'd been snorting or shooting into your veins, but as my excitable grandfather would say, we saw you go *pazzo,* crazy, you know what I mean?"

"I know exactly what you mean."

"So naturally we couldn't let you be seen in public, you can understand that, can't you?"

"*Va bene,* you Mafia prick. I heard you—'I'm in charge,' you said. 'I know people who can handle this,' you said that, too."

"You know, Congressman, although I admire you a great deal, I'm very offended by anti-Italian generalizations."

"Tell that to the federal prosecutor in New York," replied Kendrick as the boat dipped sharply, then rose with a heavy wave. "Giuliani's been putting you away by the truckload."

"Yes, well, talking about things that go bump in the night, which we weren't but we could have been in this water, a number of people in Balboa Park saw a man who could easily fit your description—I mean dressed like you when you left the hotel and then in the limo—going into the Balthazar."

"The what?"

"It's a coffeehouse in Balboa. You know we've got a lot of students down here; they come from all over, and there's a large contingent from the Mediterranean. You know, kids from families who lived in Iran and Saudi Arabia and Egypt . . . even what some still call Palestine, I guess. Sometimes the coffee gets out of hand—politically, that is—and the police have to quiet things and confiscate items like guns and knives. Those people are very emotional."

"And I was seen going inside, and naturally there'll be those *inside* who'll confirm *I* was there."

"Your bravery has never been questioned, Congressman. You go into the most dangerous places looking for solutions, don't you? Oman, Bahrain . . . even the house of the Vice President of the United States."

"Add bribery to your list, garbageman."

"Now just a minute! I haven't anything to do with whatever you came to see Viper about, get that straight. I'm just providing a service beyond my official duties, that's all."

"Because you '*know* people who can handle this,' like someone wearing my clothes and using my car and walking in Balboa Park. And maybe a couple of others who were able to get me out of Bollinger's place with no one recognizing me."

"A private ambulance service is very convenient and discreet when guests become ill or overindulge."

"And, no doubt, one or two others to divert whatever press or maintenance people might be around."

"My nongovernment associates are on call for emergencies, sir. We're happy to provide assistance wherever we can."

"For a price, of course."

"Definitely. . . . They *pay,* Congressman. They pay in lots of ways, now more than ever."

"For also including a fast boat and an experienced captain?"

"Oh, we can't take credit where it isn't due," protested the man from the Mafia, enjoying himself. "This is their equipment, their skipper. There are just some things people do better for themselves, especially if one of them is going into the heavily patrolled waters between the U.S. and Mexico. There's clout and then again there's different clout, if you know what I'm saying."

Kendrick felt a third presence but, turning in the chair, saw no one else on the deck of the pleasure yacht. Then he raised his eyes to the aft railing of the fly bridge. A figure stepped back into the shadows but not quickly enough. It was the excessively tall, deeply tanned contributor from Bollinger's library, and from what could be seen of his face, it was contorted in hatred. "Are all of the Vice President's guests on board?" he asked, seeing that the mafioso had followed his gaze.

"What guests?"

"You're cute, Luigi."

"There's a captain and one crew. I've never seen either of them before."

"Where are we going?"

"On a cruise."

The boat slowed down as the beam of a powerful searchlight shot out from the bridge. The Mafia soldier unstrapped himself and got up; he walked across the deck and down into the lower cabin. Evan could hear him on an intercom, but with the wind and the slapping waves was unable to make out the words. Moments later the man returned; in his hand was a gun, a standard issue, Colt .45 automatic. Suppressing the panic he felt, Kendrick thought of the sharks of Qatar and wondered if another Mahdi across the world was about to carry out the sentence of death pronounced in Bahrain. If it was to be, Evan made the same decision he had made in Bahrain: he would fight. Better a quick, expeditious bullet in the head than the prospect of drowning or being torn apart by man-eaters of the Pacific.

"We're here, Congressman," said the mafioso courteously.

"Where is here?"

"Damned if I know. It's some kind of island."

Kendrick closed his eyes, giving thanks to whoever cared to accept them, and began to breathe without trembling again. The hero of Oman was a fraud, he reflected. He simply did not care to die and, fear aside, there was Khalehla. The love that had eluded him all his life was his, and every additional minute he was permitted to live was a minute of hope. "From the looks of you I don't think you really need that," he said, nodding his head at the weapon.

"Not from your press," replied the Secret Service guard positioned by the upper ranks of the underworld. "I'm going to unbuckle you, but if you make any sudden moves you won't step foot on land, *capisce?*"

"*Molto bene.*"

"Don't blame me, I've been given my instructions. When you provide a service, you accept reasonable orders."

Evan heard the snaps and felt the wide cloth straps loosening around his arms and legs. "Has it occurred to you that if you carried out those orders, you might never get back to San Diego?" he asked.

"Certainly," answered the mafioso casually. "That's why we've got the Viper in a vise. 'Viper in a vise.' Acceptable alliteration, wouldn't you say?"

"I wouldn't know. I'm a construction engineer, not a poet."

"And I've got a gun in my hand, which means I'm not a poet either. So behave, Congressman."

"I assume 'Viper' is the Vice President."

"Yes, and he said he'd heard the name and it was an insult. Can you imagine? Those fuckers had the moral turpitude to bug our unit?"

"I'm appalled," replied Kendrick, rising awkwardly from the metal chair and shaking his arms and legs, restoring circulation.

"*Easy!*" cried the Secret Service man, leaping back, his .45 leveled at Evan's head.

"You try sitting in that damned thing for as long as I did the way I did and think you're going to walk a straight line!"

"Okay, okay. Then walk a crooked line over there to the side of this fancy tug, to the steps. That's where you're getting off."

The yacht circled in what appeared to be a cove, then in fits and starts—with sputtering forward and reverse screws—banked into a dock perhaps a hundred feet in length, with three additional boats, each smaller, faster, more powerful, bobbing on the other side. Shaded wire-meshed lights illuminated the watery berth as two figures raced out of darkness from the base of dry ground, stationing themselves beside the appointed pylons. As the boat was expertly maneuvered into its tire-protected resting place, lines were thrown fore and aft, the stern line whipped over by the mafioso, the weapon in his left hand, the bow line by the lone crewman. "*Off!*" he yelled at Kendrick as the yacht bounced gently into the dock.

"I'd like to personally thank the captain for a safe and pleasant trip—"

"Very funny," said the Secret Service man, "but save it for the movies and get the hell off. You're not going to see anybody."

"You want to bet, Luigi?"

"You want your balls on the deck? And the name's not Luigi."

"How about 'Reginald'?"

"Off!"

Evan walked down the island pier toward the sloping ground and an ascending stone path, the mafioso behind him. He passed between two signs, both hand-painted: white lettering on stained brown wood, each done tastefully, professionally. The sign on the left was in Spanish, the one on the right in English.

PASAJE A CHINA
PROPIEDAD PRIVADA
ALARMAS

PASSAGE TO CHINA
PRIVATE PROPERTY
ALARMS

"Hold it there," ordered the Secret Service man. "Don't turn around. Look straight ahead." Kendrick heard the sound of running feet on the dock, then quiet voices, the distinguishable words spoken in English but with Hispanic accents. Instructions were being given. "Okay," continued the mafioso. "Go up the path and take the first right. . . . Don't turn around!"

Evan obeyed, although he walked with difficulty up the sharp incline; the long constricting trip on the yacht had severely numbed his legs. He tried to study the surroundings in the semidarkness, the shaded lights from the dock only barely compensated by small amber lamps lining the stone path. The foliage was lush and thick and damp; trees everywhere rose to heights of twenty, perhaps thirty, feet, with heavy vines that appeared to spring from one trunk to another, arms enveloping arms and bodies. Clusters of bushes and overgrowth had been cut back and down with precision, forming identical waist-high walls on both sides of the path. Order had been imposed on the wild. Then his vision was sharply reduced by the steep ascent and the growing darkness away from the pier, and sounds became the focus. What assaulted his ears were not unlike the sounds of the incessant staccato eruptions of the rapids during his runs in the white water, but these had a beat of their own, a pulse that controlled their own particular thunder. . . . *Waves,* of course. Waves crashing against rocks and never very far away, or perhaps amplified by echoes bouncing up from stone and reverberating through the wild greenery.

The ground-level amber lights divided into two sets of parallel lines, one heading straight ahead and up, the other to the right; Kendrick turned into the latter. Heading across, the path leveled off, a ridge cut out of the hill, when suddenly there was an alarming increase in visibility. Black shafts and swelling shadows became dark trunks and spotted palms and tangled blue-green underbrush. Directly ahead was a cabin, lights shining through two windows flanking a central door. It was not, however, an ordinary cabin, and at first Evan did not know why he thought so. Then as he drew closer he understood. It was the windows; he had never seen any like them, and they accounted for the burst of light when the source appeared to be minimal. The beveled glass was at least four inches thick, like two huge rectangular prisms magnifying the interior light many times its candlepower. And there was something else that accompanied this imaginative feat of design. The windows were impenetrable . . . from both sides.

"That's your suite, Congressman," said the Secret Service man who provided extraofficial services. " 'Your own villa' describes it better, doesn't it?"

"I really couldn't accept such generous accommodations. Why don't you find me something a little less pretentious?"

"You're a regular comedian. . . . Go on over and open the door, there's no key."

"No *key*?"

"Surprises you, doesn't it?" laughed the mafioso. "Me, too, until that guard explained. Everything's *electronica.* I've got a little widget, like a garage opener, and when I press a button a couple of steel bars slide out of the frame and back into the door. They work inside, too."

"With time I might have figured that out for myself."

"You're cool, Congressman."

"Not as cool as I should have been," said Kendrick, walking down the path to the door and opening it. His eyes were greeted by the rustic splendor of a well-appointed New England mountain retreat, in no way reminiscent of southern California or northern Mexico. The walls consisted of bulging logs cemented together, two thick windows on each of the four walls, a break in the center of the rear wall obviously for a bathroom. Every convenience had been considered: a kitchen area was located at the far right, complete with a mirrored bar; on the far left was a king-sized bed and, in front of it, seating quarters with a large television set and several quilted armchairs. The builder in Evan concluded that the small house belonged more properly in a snow-laden Vermont than in the waters somewhere south and west of Tijuana. Still, it was bucolically charming and he had no doubt that many guests on the island enjoyed it. But it had another purpose. It was also a prison cell.

"Very pleasant," said Bollinger's guard, walking into the large single room, his weapon constantly but unobtrusively leveled at Kendrick. "How about a drink, Congressman?" he asked, heading for the recessed mirrored bar. "I don't know about you, but I could use one."

"Why not?" replied Evan, looking around the room designed for a northern climate.

"What's your pleasure?"

"Canadian and ice, that's all," said Kendrick, moving slowly from area to area, examining the interior construction of the cabin, his practiced eye seeking flaws that might lead to a way out. There were none; the place was airtight, escape-proof. The window sashes were secured, not with recessed magnesium nails but with bolts concealed by laycred plaster; the front door had internal hinges, impossible to reach without a powerful drill, and finally, walking into the bathroom, he saw that it was windowless, the two vents small grilled apertures four inches wide.

"Great little hideaway, isn't it?" said the mafioso, greeting Evan with his drink as he emerged from the bathroom.

"As long as you don't miss sightseeing," replied Kendrick, his eyes aimlessly straying over to the kitchen area. Something was odd, he considered, but again nothing specific came to him. Aware of the guard's weapon, he passed the mirrored bar and went to a dark-stained oval oak table, where presumably meals were served. It was perhaps six or seven feet in front of a long counter in the center of which a stove had been inserted beneath a line of cabinets. The sink and the refrigerator, separated by another counter, were against the right wall. What was it that bothered him? Then he saw a small microwave oven built in below the last cabinet on the left; he looked back at the stove. That was it.

Electric. Everything was *electric,* that was the oddity. In the vast majority of rustic cabins, propane gas was piped in from portable tanks outside to eliminate the need for electricity for such appliances as stoves and ovens. The maxim was to keep the amperage as low as possible, not so much because of expense but for convenience, in case of electrical malfunctions. Then he thought of the lamps on the pier and the amber ground lights along the paths. Electricity. An abundance of *electricity* on an island at least twenty, if not fifty, miles away from the mainland. He was not sure what it all meant, but it was something to think about.

He walked out of the designated kitchen zone and over to the living room area. He looked down at the large television set and wondered what kind of antenna was required to pull signals across so many miles of open water. He sat down, now only barely aware of his armed escort, his mind on so many other things, including—painfully—Khalehla back at the hotel. She had expected him hours ago. What was she doing? What *could* she do? Evan raised his glass and drank several swallows of the whisky, grateful for the warming sensation that spread quickly through him. He looked over at Bollinger's guard, who stood casually by the stained oak table, his weapon confidently on top of it, but on the edge, near his free right hand.

"Your health," said the man from the Mafia, raising the glass in his left hand.

"Why not?" Without returning the courtesy, Kendrick drank, again feeling the quick, warming effects of the whisky. . . . *No!* It was too quick, too harsh, not warming but *burning*! Objects in the room suddenly pulsed in and out of focus; he tried to get up from the chair, but he could not control his legs or his arms! He stared at the obscenely grinning mafioso and started to shout but no sound came. He heard the glass shattering on the hard wood floor and felt a terrible weight pressing down on him. For the second time that night the darkness came as he kept falling, falling into an infinite void of black space.

The Secret Service man crossed to an intercom console built into the wall next to the mirrored bar. Frowning in thought, he pressed the three numbers he had been given on the boat.

"Yes, Cottage?" answered a soft male voice.

"Your boy's asleep again."

"Good, we're ready for him."

"I've got to inquire," said the well-spoken *capo.* "Why did we bring him to in the first place?"

"Medical procedure, not that it's any of your business."

"I wouldn't take that attitude, if I were you. We are owed and you're the debtors."

"All right. Without a medical history there are acceptable and unacceptable limits of dosage."

"Two moderate applications rather than a single excessive one?"

"Something like that. Our doctor is very experienced in these things."

"If he's the same one, keep him out of sight. He's on Kendrick's death list. . . . And send down your Hispanics, I'm not contracted for hauling bodies."

"Certainly. And don't concern yourself about that doctor. He was on another list."

"MJ, he's still not back and it's three-fifteen in the morning!" cried Khalehla into the phone. "Have you *learned* anything?"

"Nothing that makes sense," replied the director of Special Projects, his voice thin and weary. "I haven't called you because I thought you were getting some rest."

"Don't lie to me, Uncle Mitch. You've never had a problem telling me to work all night. That's *Evan* out there!"

"I know, I know. . . . Did he mention anything to you about meeting someone in Balboa Park?"

"No, I don't think he knows what it is or where it is."

"Do you?"

"Of course. My grandparents live here, remember?"

"Do you know a place called the Balthazar?"

"It's a coffeehouse for hotheads, Arab hotheads to be exact, students mostly. I was there once and never went back. Why do you ask?"

"Let me explain," said Payton. "After your call several hours ago, we reached Bollinger's house—as Kendrick's office, of course—saying we had an urgent message for him. We were told he'd left around nine o'clock, which contradicted your information that he hadn't returned by eleven; at best it's a thirty-minute drive from the Vice President's home to your hotel. So I contacted Gingerbread—Shapoff—who's terribly good in these situations. He tracked everything down, including the driver of Evan's limousine. . . . Our congressman asked to be let off at Balboa Park, so Gingerbread did his thing and 'rustled up the neighborhood,' as he phrased it. What he learned can be put in two enigmatic conclusions. One: a man fitting Evan's description was seen walking in Balboa Park. Two: a number of people inside the Balthazar have stated that this same man wearing dark glasses entered the establishment and stood for a long time by the cardamom-coffee machines before going to a table."

"*Mitch,*" screamed Khalehla. "I'm looking at his dark glasses now! They're on the bureau. He sometimes wears them during the day so he won't be recognized, but never at night. He says they draw attention at night and he's right about that. That man *wasn't* Evan. It's a setup. They're holding him somewhere!"

"Hardball," said Payton quietly. "We'll have to get into the game."

Kendrick opened his eyes as a person does who is unsure of where he is or what condition he is in or even whether he is awake or still asleep. There was only bewilderment, clouds of confusion swirling about in his head, and a numbness caused by frightening uncertainty. A lamp was on somewhere, its glow washing the beamed ceiling. He moved his hand, lifting his right arm off the unfamiliar bed in the unfamiliar room. He studied both hand and arm, then suddenly, swiftly he raised his left arm. What had *happened*? He swung his legs off the bed and unsteadily stood up, equal parts of terror and curiosity gripping him. Gone were the thick corduroy trousers and the coarse black denim shirt. He was dressed in his own clothes! In his navy blue suit, his congressional suit, as he frequently and humorously referred to it, the suit he had worn to Bollinger's house! And his white oxford broadcloth shirt and his striped regimental tie, all freshly cleaned and laundered. What had happened? Where *was* he? Where was the well-appointed rustic cabin with the all-electric appliances and the recessed mirrored bar? This was a large bedroom he had never seen before.

Slowly, regaining balance, he moved about the strange surroundings, a part of him wondering if he was living a dream or had just lived one previously. He saw a pair of tall, narrow French doors; he walked rapidly over and opened them. They led out to a small balcony large enough for a couple to have coffee on but no more than that—a miniature round table and two wrought-iron chairs had been placed for such a ritual. He stood in front of the waist-high railing and looked out over the darkened grounds, dark except for a practically nonexistent moon and the parallel lines of amber lights that branched off in various directions . . . and something else. Far in the distance, lit up by the dim wash of floodlights, was a fenced area not unlike an immense wire cage. Within it there appeared to be blocks of massive machinery, some of it jet-black and glistening, others chrome or silver, equally shimmering in the dull, cloud-covered moonlight. Evan concentrated on the sight, then turned his head to listen; there was a steady uninterrupted hum, and he knew he had found the answer to a question that had confused him. He did not have to see the signs that read, *DANGER High Voltage;* they were there. The wire-enclosed machinery were components of a huge generator undoubtedly fed by giant underground tanks of fuel, and fields of photovoltaic cells to alternately capture the solar energy of the tropical sun.

Below the balcony was a sunken brick patio, the drop twenty-five feet or more, which meant a twisted ankle or a broken leg if a person tried to leave that way. Kendrick studied the exterior walls; the nearest drainpipe was at the corner of the structure, far out of reach, and there were no vines that could be scaled, only sheer stucco. . . . Blankets? *Sheets!* Tied firmly together, he could handle a drop of eight to ten feet! If he *hurried* . . . He suddenly stopped all movement, ended all thoughts of racing into the room and to the bed, as a figure appeared walking down an amber-lighted path on the right, a rifle strapped over his shoulder. He raised his arm, a signal. Evan looked to the left; a second man was signaling back, patrols acknowledging each other. Kendrick pulled his watch up to his eyes, trying to read the second hand in the dull night light. If he could time the sentries' coordinates, have everything *prepared*... Again he was forced to stop what plans his desperation created. The bedroom door opened, and the reality that was, was now confirmed.

"I thought I heard you moving around," said the Secret Service man from the ranks of the Mafia.

"And I should have realized the room was bugged," said Evan, coming in from the balcony.

"You keep getting things wrong, Congressman. This is a guest room in the main house. You think these people would listen in on their guests' private conversations or their perfectly natural indulgences together?"

"I think they'd do anything. Otherwise, how did you know I was up?"

"Easy," answered the mafioso, crossing to the bureau against the far right wall and picking up a small flat object from the top. "One of these. They're provided for people with infants. My sister in New Jersey won't go anywhere without them—they come in pairs. Plug it in one room, then plug it in another room and you can hear the child screaming. Let me tell you, her children scream a lot. You can hear them in Manhattan."

"Very enlightening. When did I get my clothes back?"

"I don't know. The Hispanics took care of you, not me. Perhaps you were raped and don't know it."

"Again, enlightening. . . . Have you any idea what you've done, what you're involved in? You've abducted a not-unknown holder of government office, a member of the House of Representatives."

"Good Lord, you make it sound like snatching the maître d' at Vinnie's Pasta Palace."

"You're not amusing—"

"*You* are," interrupted the guard, removing his automatic from a shoulder holster. "You're also on call, Congressman. You're wanted downstairs."

"Suppose I refuse the invitation?"

"Then I blow a hole through your stomach and kick a corpse down the stairs. Whichever, I really don't care. I'm being paid for a service, not a guaranteed delivery. Take your choice, hero."

The room was a naturalist's nightmare. The heads of slain animals hung from the white stucco walls, their false eyes, eagerly inserted, reflecting the panic of impending death. Skins of leopard, tiger and elephant were the upholstery, neatly stretched and brass-tacked over chairs and couches. If nothing else, it was an assertion of the power of man's bullet over unsuspecting wildlife, and not so much imposing as sad, as sad as the hollow triumphs of the victors.

The Secret Service guard had opened the door, gestured to Kendrick to go inside, and then closed it, remaining in the hallway. Once the initial effect of the room wore off, Evan realized that a man was seated at a large desk, only the back of his head visible. Several moments after the door closed, as if to make certain they were alone, the man turned around in the swivel chair.

"We've never met, Congressman," said Crayton Grinell in his soft, pleasant lawyer's cadence, "and as discourteous as it may appear, I prefer to remain nameless. . . . Please, sit down. There's no reason to be more uncomfortable than necessary. It's why your clothes were returned to you."

"I gather they served their purpose in a place called Balboa

Park." Kendrick sat down in a captain's chair in front of the desk; the seat was covered with leopard skin.

"Providing us with options, yes," agreed Grinell.

"I see." Evan suddenly recognized the distinctive voice he knew he had heard before. It was on the blond European's tape recording. The man in front of him was the vanished Crayton Grinell, the attorney responsible for wholesale death on Cyprus, killer of the Secretary of State. "But since you don't want me to know who you are, am I to infer that one of those options might find me back in San Diego?"

"Quite possibly, but I must emphasize the questionable part. I'm being frank with you."

"So were your friends at Bollinger's house."

"I'm sure they were and so were you."

"Did you have to do it?"

"Do what?"

"Kill an old man."

"We had nothing to do with that! Besides, he's not dead."

"He will be."

"So will we all one day. . . . It was a gratuitously stupid act, as stupid as her husband's incredible manipulations through Zurich. We may be many things, Congressman, but we're not stupid. However, we're wasting time. The Vanvlanderens are gone, and whatever happened is buried with them. The erstwhile 'Dr. Lyons' will never be seen again—"

"I *want* him!" Kendrick broke in.

"But we got him and *he* got the maximum penalty a court can impose."

"How can I be sure of that?"

"How can you doubt it? Could the Vice President, could any of us, tolerate the association? . . . We deeply regret what's happened to Mr. Weingrass, but we had absolutely nothing to do with it. I repeat, the doctor and the Vanvlanderens are gone. It's all a closed book, can you accept that?"

"Was it necessary to drug me and bring me out here to convince me?"

"We couldn't very well leave you in San Diego saying the things you were saying."

"Then what are we talking about now?"

"Another book," replied Grinell, leaning forward in the chair. "We want it back, and in exchange you're free. You'll be returned to your hotel in your own clothes and nothing's changed.

It's morning in Zurich; a line of credit in the amount of fifty million dollars has been established in your name."

Stunned, Evan tried not to show his astonishment. "Another book? . . . I'm not sure I follow you."

"Varak stole it."

"Who?"

"Milos Varak!"

"The European . . . ?" His sudden recognition of the name unconsciously slipped out. It was the Milos.

"Inver Brass's very professional, very dead lackey!"

"Inver *who*?"

"Your would-be promoters, Congressman. You don't think you got where you are by yourself, do you?"

"I knew someone was pushing me—"

"*Pushing?* 'Catapulting' is more like it. . . . Meddling lunatics! They didn't realize that one of them was also one of us."

"What makes you think the European . . . that this Varak's dead?" asked Evan, if only to gain moments to adjust to revelations that were coming too fast.

"It was in the paper—not listing him by name, of course, but unmistakable. But before he died, he was somewhere else, *with* someone else who worked for *us.* He *had* to be or he never would have come to the airport. . . . He *stole* it."

"This other book?" said Kendrick hesitantly.

"An industrially coded ledger, meaningless to any but a selected few."

"And you think I have it." A statement.

"I think you know where it is."

"Why?"

"Because in his zeal Varak would have mistakenly believed it should be in your hands. He couldn't trust Inver Brass any longer."

"Because he learned that one of them was also one of you."

"Essentially, yes," said Grinell. "I'm hypothesizing, of course. It's a professional habit, but it's served me well over the years."

"Not this time. I don't know anything about it."

"I wouldn't lie if I were you, Congressman. It would be futile in any event. There are so many ways of loosening minds and mouths these days."

He couldn't allow drugs! Under them he would reveal everything, signing Khalehla's death warrant as well as giving the contributors all the information they needed to mount their indi-

vidual smoke screens and in other cases disappear. The dying Manny deserved better than that! If ever he needed credibility it was now. He was back in another compound, not in Masqat but on an island in the waters of Mexico. He had to be every bit as convincing as he was among the terrorists, for these men, these killers from the boardrooms, were no less than terrorists themselves.

"Listen to me," said Evan firmly, leaning back and crossing his legs, his eyes leveled on Grinell. "You can think whatever the hell you care to think, but I don't want the vice presidency, I want a fifty-million-dollar line of credit in Zurich. Do I make myself clear?"

"Clear and recorded, naturally."

"Good, *fine*! Run a full scam on me and put it on videotape—"

"But you see, it is," interrupted the attorney.

"Excellent! Then we're both in the same hot tub, aren't we?"

"Same tub, Congressman. So where's the ledger?"

"I haven't the vaguest idea, but if this Varak sent it to me, I know how you can get it. . . . I'll call my office in Washington and tell my secretary, Annie O'Reilly, to express it out overnight to wherever you like."

The two negotiators stared at each other, neither wavering for an instant. "That's a fair solution," said Grinell, finally.

"If you can think of a better one, use it."

"That's even fairer."

"Am I on board?"

"On board and on your way to Zurich," replied Grinell, smiling. "Once you settle certain items on our agenda, like Chicago."

"The telegram will go out in the morning. I'll have O'Reilly send it from the office."

"With a copy to our esteemed Vice President, of course."

"Of course."

The chairman of the contributors' board of directors sighed audibly, pleasantly. "Oh, how venal we all are," he said. "You, for instance, Congressman, you're a bundle of contradictions. Your public persona would never accept our accommodation."

"If this is for the benefit of your videotape, let me make a statement. I was burned and did my best to put out the fires in Oman because they had burned *me,* killing a great many friends. I see no contradiction of issues."

"So recorded, Representative Kendrick."

Suddenly, without any indication whatsoever, the quiet conference was broken apart by a combination of signals. A bright red light started flashing from the console of the radio telephone on the desk, and a muted siren came from somewhere in the stuccoed walls, probably from the mouth of a dead animal. The door crashed open and the tall figure of the deeply tanned captain of the boat, the laconic angry weed from the Town of Corruption, burst into the room.

"What are you *doing*?" roared Grinell.

"Get that fart *out* of here," the yachtsman yelled. "I thought he was a trap from the beginning and I was right! There are government people dispatched by Washington all over Bollinger's place looking for him, questioning everyone as if they were in a police lineup."

"*What?*"

"We're handling that, but we've got a bigger problem. The ledger! Bollinger got a call. It's with the bitch's own *lawyer*!"

"Shut *up*!" commanded Grinell.

"He's talking ten million, which she told him her Andy-boy promised her. Now *he* wants it!"

"I told you to shut *up*! . . . What did you mean that the federal men were questioning everyone?"

"Just what I said. They're not only grilling them, they got search warrants. They won't find anything, but not for lack of trying."

"In the *Vice President's* house? It's *unheard* of!"

"They're playing it smart. They're telling Bollinger that they're protecting him from his subordinates. But no one's going to convince me." The yachtsman turned on Evan. "That son of a bitch was sent in to trap us. The hero's word against everybody else's!"

Grinell stared at Kendrick. "There can't be a hero's word if there's no hero. . . . *Adiós,* Congressman." Grinell touched a button on the side of his desk and the door to the huge room of dead animals opened once again. The mafioso's automatic waved back and forth as he entered cautiously. "Take him out," ordered the attorney. "The Mexicans will tell you where. . . . You really fooled me, Congressman. I'll remember the lesson. Beware the persuasive philosophical turncoat."

The sound of the waves crashing against the island's rock-bound coastline below grew louder as they walked down the amber-lit path. Up ahead the ground lights came to an end, and a white barrier was starkly in place between the final domed lamps, the amber wash illuminating the letters of the two signs on the white obstruction. The left was again in Spanish, the right in English.

¡Peligro! . . . Danger!

Beyond the barrier was a promontory overlooking the sea, the angry waters churning in the erratic moonlight, the sound of the crashing waves now deafening. Kendrick was being led to his execution.

41

Pockets of swirling vapor spewed up from the rocks of the promontory above the Pacific. Evan suppressed his panic, remembering his covenant with himself: he would not die passively; he would not be killed without a struggle, no matter how futile. Yet even last-ditch efforts presumed the outside possibility of survival, and he had spent his adult life studying the complexities of specifics. There were tropical vines all around him, thick and strong from the moisture and the winds constantly assaulting their trunks. There was lush overgrowth on both sides of the string of amber bulbs and loose wet dirt within that twisted foliage, mud that never knew a dry moment. The Mexican who had directed the mafioso to the killing ground was a reluctant partner to murder. His voice grew fainter as they approached the final steps toward the white barrier.

"*¡Al frente, al frente!*" he cried nervously. "*¡Adelante!*"

"Go over it or around it, Congressman," said the Secret Service man, his tone cold, a professional doing his professional job, someone for whom life and death meant nothing.

"I can't," answered Kendrick. "It's too high to step over and there's some kind of barbed wire spreading out from the sides."

"Where?"

"Here." Kendrick pointed down into the dark overgrowth.

"I don't see—"

Now! screamed the silent voice inside Evan's throat as he whipped around, both hands surging for the large ugly weapon, gripping it and pushing it away as he bent the mafioso's wrist back and crashed his shoulder into the guard's chest, pulling the arm forward, and desperately, with all the strength that was in him, heaving the man off-balance and into the brush and the wet dirt. The gun fired, the explosion melding with the sounds of the crashing waves below. Kendrick shoved the weapon into the soft earth and, freeing his right hand, grabbed a fistful of mud and slapped it into the mafioso's face, grinding it into his eyes.

The guard shouted garbled words of fury, trying simultaneously to wipe his eyes and yank the gun out of the earth and himself from Evan's grip. Kendrick remained on top of the writhing, thrashing killer, repeatedly crashing his knee up into the man's groin as his right hand continuously scooped up mud, crushing it into the mafioso's eyes and mouth. His knuckles struck a hard, jagged object . . . a *rock*! It was almost too large for the panicked spread of his fingers, but nothing could, nothing *would,* stop him. Straining muscles he had not exerted in months, years, holding off the convulsive assaults beneath him, he pulled the heavy, jagged rock out of the mud, raised it, and crashed it down into the head of his would-be executioner. The killer-guard went limp as the man's body sank into the wet brush and the soft ground.

Evan grabbed the gun and snapped his eyes up toward the Mexican. The Hispanic, waiting to see who would live and who would die yards away in the mist-laden, shadowed foliage, crouched, backing into an amber lamp, smashing it with his foot. Seeing the survivor, he spun around, digging his feet into the path to run.

"*Stop!*" yelled Kendrick breathlessly, leaping up and lurching out of the bordering overgrowth. "Stop or I'll kill you! You understand me well enough for that."

The Mexican stopped, turning slowly in the wash of light to face Evan. "I am no part of these things, señor," he said in surprisingly clear English.

"You mean you don't pull the trigger, you just tell them where *they* can pull it!"

"I am no part," repeated the man. "I am a fisherman but there is no decent pay on the boats these days. I make my pesos and go home to my family in El Descanso."

"Do you want to see your family again?"

"*Sí,* very much," replied the Hispanic, his lips and hands trembling. "If this is what happens, I will not come back."

"Are you telling me it's never happened before?"

"Never, señor."

"Then how did you know the *way*!" shouted Kendrick against the sound of the wind and the crashing waves. He was regaining his breath, gradually aware of the mud that covered him and the pain everywhere inside him.

"We are brought here and given maps of the island, which we must know completely in two days or we are sent home."

"Why? For multiple executions?"

"I told you no, señor. These are drug waters—*narcóticos*—and very dangerous. Mexican and American patrols can be summoned quickly, but still the island must be guarded."

"Summoned quickly?"

"The owner is a powerful man."

"Is his name Grinell?"

"I do not know, señor. All I know is the island itself."

"You speak fluent English. Why didn't you speak English before?" Even gestured toward the dead mafioso. "To *him*!"

"I say it again, I wanted no part. I was told where to take you, and as we grew closer I began to understand. . . . No part, señor. But I have my family back in El Descanso, and the men who come here are powerful men."

Evan stared at the man in indecision. It would be easy, *so* easy, to end his life and eliminate a risk, yet there was a glimmer of opportunity as well if the frightened Mexican was not a liar. Kendrick knew he was negotiating for his life, but there was another life involved, too, and it made the negotiation easier. "You understand," he said, drawing closer to the man, raising his voice to be heard clearly, "that if you go back down to the house without *him* and he doesn't appear or they find his dead body up here or washed up on the rocks, you'll be killed. You *do* understand that, don't you?"

The Mexican nodded twice. "*Sí.*"

"But if *I* don't kill you, you've got a chance, don't you?" asked Evan, raising the mafioso's gun. The member of the staff closed his eyes and nodded once. "So, it's in the best interests of you and your family back in El Descanso to join me, isn't it?"

"*Sí.*" The Mexican opened his eyes. "Join you in *what*?"

"Getting out of here—*away* from here. There's a boat down at that dock next to a gas tank. It's large enough to handle the trip."

"They have other boats," interrupted the executioner's guide. "They go faster than the government drug boats and there is a helicopter with powerful searchlights."

"*What?* Where?"

"Down near the beach on the other side of the island. There is a cement landing ground. . . . Are you a pilot, señor?"

"I wish I were. What's your name?"

"Emilio."

"Are you coming with me?"

"I have no choice. I want to leave here and go home to my family and move to a town in the mountains. Otherwise I die and they will go hungry."

"I warn you, if you give me any reason to think you're lying, you'll never see El Descanso *or* your family."

"It is understood."

"Stay at my side. . . . First I want to check out my hangman."

"Your what, señor?"

"My friendly executioner. Let's *go*! We've got a lot to do and not much time to do it."

"To the boat?"

"Not yet," said Kendrick, a vague, fragmented plan coming into abstract focus. "We're going to disrupt this goddamned island. Not just for you and me but for everybody. *Everybody.* . . . Is there a toolshed—a place where they keep things like shovels, picks, hedge clippers, those kinds of things?"

"The *mantenimiento,*" answered Emilio. "For the gardeners, although we are often required to assist them."

"We'll make a stop first, then take me there," continued Evan, awkwardly and in pain rushing back to the dead mafioso. "Come on!"

"We must be careful, señor!"

"I know, the guards. How many are there?"

"Two on each of the four passable beach areas and the pier. Ten for each shift. All carry radio alarms that set off *sirenas*—very loud sirens."

"How long are the shifts?" asked Kendrick, bending over the corpse of the Secret Service man.

"Twelve hours. Twenty *guardas* and four *jardineros*—gardeners. Those not on duty are in what they call the 'barracks.' It is a long building north of the main house."

"Where are the tools?"

"In a metal garage fifty meters south of the *generador.*"

"The generator?"

"*Sí.*"

"Good." Evan removed the mafioso's wallet and black plastic identification case, then went through the mud-soaked pockets, finding upward of a thousand dollars, undoubtedly not from a federal payroll. Finally, he took out the small electronic "key" that released the bolts and opened the door of the cabin-cell in the woods. "Let's go," he repeated, rising with difficulty from the soft, wet earth and the underbrush.

They started down the path of amber ground lamps. "*¡Uno momento!*" whispered Emilio. "The lights. Kick them out, señor. The more darkness, the better we are."

"Good thinking," agreed Kendrick, heading back with the Mexican to the white barrier, where they proceeded to crush each domed bulb on both sides. They reached the main island path that on the left led down to the boats and the dock, on the right up to the manor house on the top of the hill, with an offshoot leading to the escape-proof rustic cabin. Evan and the Mexican raced from one lamp to another, demolishing each until they came to the cabin path. "That way!" ordered Kendrick, rushing ahead to the right. "Forget the lights. We'll take them out on our way back."

"*¿La cabaña?*"

"Hurry up!" Once again the startling magnified wash of light from the thick beveled windows illuminated the clearing in front of the small, solid house. Evan approached the door and pressed a green button on the electronic key. He heard the bolts slap back into the frame; he turned the knob and went inside. "Get in here," he called to Emilio. The Mexican did as he was told and Kendrick closed the door, pressing the red button, locking it.

He ran to the kitchen area, opened drawers and cabinets one after another, selecting items that struck him as useful: a flashlight, a large carving knife and several smaller knives, a meat cleaver, three small cans of Sterno, a box of hunters' matches—coated with paraffin, strikable on any hard surface—and a stack of folded dish towels. With everything on the oval oak table, he glanced over at Emilio, who was watching him. He picked up one of the knives, the handle extended, and held it out for the Mexican. "I hope you don't have to use this, but if you do, don't miss."

"There are men I could not kill without reasoning with them first, for they are as desperate as myself for employment. But there are others, the ones who have been here longest, I would have no such problems."

"*Goddamn* you, you can't have *any* problems! If one alarm is raised—"

"*No* alarms will be raised by my friends, señor, not if they know it is I, Emilio. Besides, most of them are in the barracks asleep. They use the *veteranos* for the night patrols; they fear the boats at night."

"You'd better be right."

"I wish to go home, believe that."

"Take some towels, a can of Sterno and a handful of matches. Hurry!" Picking up the remaining items and putting them in his pockets, Kendrick left the meat cleaver until last. He gripped it, went to the intercom console on the wall and, standing sideways, sliced the heavy blade into the back of the equipment, prying it off the wall and out of its recess. "Get the two lamps over there," he said to the Mexican. "Smash them. I'll get the stove lights and the lamp on the other side of the room."

Less than a minute later the two desperate men were out on the path, the previously brightly lighted clearing in front of the cabin now eerily dark. "The *tools*—the gardeners' tools. Take me to them."

"*¡Con mucho cuidado!* We must be careful going around the big house. We will put out the path lights only up to where I say. From the second level those in the house can see they are not on, and there will be alarms. If there are patrols, let me study them first."

"Let's go. They've got problems up there, but pretty soon someone's going to wonder where my executioner is. Hurry *up*!"

They smashed the amber lamps up to a ridge that preceded the level ground of the huge manor house—great house, thought Evan, thinking of the tropic zone and the great houses of the Caribbean. The Mexican suddenly grabbed Kendrick's arm and pulled him through the bordering foliage of the path, then pushed his shoulder down, gripping the flesh; the message was clear: Crouch and be still. A guard, his rifle strapped over his shoulder, passed them on the path going in the opposite direction. "Now quickly, señor! There is no one until the back *galeria* where they drink wine and smoke fish!"

A large patio with a barbecue pit, thought Evan, following Emilio through the thick greenery, wishing he had a machete to cut through the vines but grateful for the strangely ever-present sound of the wind and the crashing waves. They circled down and around the house, when another sound intruded. It was the massive generator, its hum constant, bass-toned, awesome. The engineer in Kendrick tried to calculate the power it produced and the fuel it consumed and the auxiliary input of the necessary field of photovoltaic cells—it was mind-blowing. He had installed generators from Bahrain to the west deserts of Saudi Arabia, but they were temporary, to be used only until electricity could be cabled in; nothing like this.

Again the Mexican gripped Evan's shoulder, now more fiercely, his hand trembling, and again they crouched in the underbrush behind the long clipped wall of shrubbery. Kendrick looked up and with sudden fear understood. Ahead, to the left, above the hedgelike border of the path, a guard had heard something or seen something. His upper body was clearly visible in the glow of the amber lights; he moved forward rapidly, snapping the rifle off his shoulder and leveling it in front of him. He walked directly toward them, then only feet away he poked the barrel of the weapon into the brush.

"*¿Quién es?*" shouted the patrol.

Suddenly, lashing out and pouncing like an angry cat, Emilio shot up, grabbing the rifle and pulling the guard through the foliage. There was an abrupt expunging of air that cut off the start of a scream; the man fell into the greenery, the base of his throat a mass of blood. The knife was in Emilio's right hand.

"Good *God*!" whispered Evan as he and the Mexican dragged the body farther into the brush.

"I had no problem with this *perro*!" said Emilio. "This dog smashed the head of a boy, a young gardener who would not accommodate him, if you understand, señor."

"I understand, and I also understand that you just saved our lives. . . . Wait a minute! The rifle, his cap. We can save time! There are no uniforms here, just work clothes—the weapon *is* the uniform. Put on the cap and strap the rifle over your shoulder. Then walk out there and I'll stay as close to you as I can over here. If it's quicker for me to go on the path myself, you can make sure it's clear!"

"*Bueno,*" said the Mexican, reaching for the cap and the weapon. "If I am stopped I will say that this *perro* forced me to replace him for an hour or so. They will laugh but no one will doubt it. . . . I go. Stay close, and when I tell you, come through the bushes and walk at my side. Not in front and not in back, but at my side. Do you speak Spanish?"

"Not well enough to talk to anyone."

"Then say nothing. Stay close!" Emilio broke through the bordering hedge, the rifle over his shoulder, and started down the path. Thrashing against the dark tangled greenery, Kendrick did his best to keep pace, every now and then whispering to the

Mexican to slow down. Once at a particularly thick area, Evan removed the meat cleaver from his belt and hacked at a webbed mass of tropical vines, only to hear Emilio cry out under his breath. "*¡Silencio!*" . . . Then he heard another command: "Now, señor! Come out and walk with me. *Quickly!*"

Kendrick did so, forcing his way through the bushes to join the Mexican, who suddenly, emphatically, began accelerating his strides down the sloping path. "Is going this fast such a good idea?" asked Evan breathlessly. "If we're seen, someone might think we were running while on duty."

"We have come to the back of the main house," answered Emilio, rushing forward. "There is no one here at this hour but two guards on different paths who meet at the stone *galeria,* then go back over the hill and down to the beaches. It takes them many minutes and they have just left. We can run across the *galeria* and up the far path, then through the woods to the *mantenimiento*—the tools, señor."

They reached a sunken brick patio, the same patio Kendrick had studied from the small balcony of the guest room above. He remembered the two guards signaling each other from the bases of the opposing paths. The Mexican, who was now very much in charge, grabbed Evan's arm and nodded to his left, breaking into a run. They raced down into the sunken patio, which was far larger than Kendrick had realized; it extended the length of the house itself, and white wrought-iron furniture had been placed around the central area in front of a large brick barbecue pit. They ran by the side of the house under the balconies, then sprinted across and up the south path of amber lights to a flat area bordered by tall grass, a knoll overlooking the ocean and two beaches separated by a rock-filled coastline perhaps six hundred feet below. The amber lights were now behind them, nothing in front but a narrow descending dirt road.

From this vantage point, a great deal of the back island could be seen in the sporadic moonlight. Directly on the right, no more than three hundred yards away and washed in floodlights, was the enormous generator. Beyond the fenced enclosure were the blurred outlines of a long, low building, Emilio's "barracks," assumed Evan. Then far below, just above the beach on the right, its white concrete standing out like a huge flat beacon was the helipad, with a large military helicopter resting in place—painted in civilian colors and with Mexican identification but unmistakably United States military.

"*Come!*" whispered Emilio. "And say nothing, for voices are heard on this side of the island." The Mexican started down a dark, unlighted path cut out of the woods, a forest alleyway used only in daylight. And then, thinking about Emilio's words, Kendrick realized what was missing. The sound of the wind and the crashing waves had all but vanished—voices *would* carry across the calm of these acres, and a helicopter could maneuver into its threshold with minimum difficulty.

The metal "garage" Emilio had referred to was an apt description, but it was far larger than any garage Evan had ever seen except for those outsized, sterilized padded structures housing an Arabian royal family's various limousines. Conversely, this was an ugly mass of corrugated aluminum with several tractors, assorted gas-operated lawn mowers, chain saws and clipping machines, none useful because of the noise they would make. On the side wall and the floor below, however, were more practical objects. They included a row of gasoline cans, and above, on hooks and suspended between nails, axes, hatchets, scythes, long-handled wire cutters, machetes and telescoped rubber-handled tree clippers—all the tools required to hold back the tropical foliage from its incredibly swift takeover.

The decisions were minor, instinctive and simple. The meat cleaver went in favor of a hatchet and a machete—for both himself and Emilio. Added to these were the wire cutters, one full can of gasoline and one ten-foot-extension tree clipper. Everything else from the cabin remained in their pockets.

"The helicopter!" said Kendrick.

"There is a path joining the north and south roads below the *generador.* Hurry! The guards have reached the beaches by now and will soon start back." They ran out of the gardeners' warehouse and over to the first dirt road, their tools precariously held by belts, in their hands and under their clenched arms. With Emilio leading, they darted across into the border of high grass and worked their way down to the narrow path heading across the sloping hill. "*¡Cigarrillo!*" whispered the Mexican, shoving Evan back into the still reeds of grass. A bobbing lighted cigarette glowed as the guard trudged up the hill and passed them less than eight feet away. "Come!" cried Emilio softly as the guard reached the knoll above. Crouching, they raced to the north road; there was no sign of the second patrol, so they walked out and began their descent to the concrete helicopter pad.

The huge repainted military aircraft stood like a silent behemoth about to strike out at an enemy only it could see in the night. Taut heavy chains were looped around the landing mounts and anchored in cement; no sudden storms from the sea would move the chopper unless they were strong enough to tear it apart. Kendrick approached the enormous machine as Emilio stayed in the grass by the road watching for the return of the guard, prepared to warn his American companion. Evan studied the aircraft with only one thought in mind: Immobilize it and do so without making a sound loud enough to be carried up the quiet island slope. Neither could he use his flashlight; in the darkness the beam would be spotted. . . . *Cables.* On top under the rotor blades and in the tail assembly. Gripping first a door handle, then the frame of a window, he pulled himself up in front of the flight deck, the long-handled wire cutters protruding from his trousers. In seconds he had crawled over the pilot's curving windshield to the top of the fuselage; unsteadily, cautiously, he made his way on his hands and knees to the base of the rotor machinery. He pulled out the wire cutters, stood up, and three minutes later had severed those cables he could see in the dark night light.

The whistle was sharp and brief! It was Emilio's signal. The guard had come over the crest of the hill and would reach the helicopter pad above the beach in barely minutes. The engineer in Kendrick was not satisfied. Had he immobilized the aircraft or merely wounded it? He had to reach the tail assembly; it was his backup in this mechanical age where every machine that went airborne had backups after backups in case of in-flight malfunctions. He crawled down the fuselage as rapidly as possible without risking his balance and sliding off, plummeting twenty feet to the white concrete. He reached the sloping tail and could see nothing; everything was encased in metal . . . no, *not* everything! Straddling the sleek body while holding on to the rising tail, he leaned over and spotted two thick ropelike cables that branched off into the right aileron. Working furiously, his sweat dripping and rolling down the shiny metal, he could feel the wire cutters doing their work as succeeding strands of the top cable sprang loose. Suddenly there was a loud snap—*too* loud, a massive *crack* in the still night—as a whole louvered section of the aileron thumped down into a vertical position. He had done it; his backup was secure.

Running feet! Shouts from below. "*¿Qúe cosa? ¡Quédese!*" Beneath the tail assembly the guard stood on the concrete, his rifle angled up in his right arm aimed at Evan while his left hand reached for the radio alarm clipped to his belt.

42

It could not happen! As if he had suddenly lost all balance, all control, Kendrick raised his arms as he slid off the fuselage, crashing the wire cutters down into the stock of the rifle. The guard started to cry out in pain as the weapon was whipped out of his arm to the ground, but before the scream could reach a crescendo Emilio was on him, crashing the blunt end of his hatchet into the man's skull.

"Can you *move*?" the Mexican asked Evan, whispering. "We must leave here! *Quickly!* The other guard will run over to this side."

Writhing on the concrete, Evan nodded his head and struggled to his feet, picking up the wire cutters and the rifle as he rose. "Get him out of here," he said, instantly realizing that he did not have to give the order; Emilio was dragging the unconscious man across the helipad into the tall grass. Limping, his left ankle and his right knee burning with pain, Kendrick followed.

"I have made a mistake," said the Mexican, shaking his head and still whispering. "We have only one chance. . . . I watched you as you walked. We can never reach the dock and the boats without being seen before the other guard will understand he has no *compañero.*" Emilio pointed to his oblivious countryman. "In the darkness I must *be* him, and get close enough before the other one realizes I am not."

"He'll shout first, ask you what happened. What'll you say?"

"I stepped into the grass to relieve myself and struck a large sharp rock in my haste. I will limp as you are limping and offer to show him where I bleed."

"Can you get away with it?"

"Pray to the Virgin that I can. Otherwise we both die." The Mexican rose and slung the rifle over his shoulder. "One request, please," he added. "This *guarda* is not a bad man, and he has family in El Suazal, where there is no work at all. Bind his legs and his arms and stuff his mouth with his own clothes. I cannot kill him."

"Do you know who the other guard is?" asked Evan harshly.

"No."

"Suppose you can't kill *him,* either?"

"Why is it a problem? I am a strong fisherman from El Descanso when there are boats that will hire me. I can bind him myself—or bring back another *compañero* for us."

The second option was not to be. No sooner had the limping Emilio reached the dirt road at the side of the helipad than the south guard came running down. As they drew closer there was a brief exchange in Spanish, then suddenly a vocal eruption from one of the two men and it was not the fisherman from El Descanso. Silence instantly followed and moments later Emilio returned.

"No *compañero,*" said Kendrick, not asking a question.

"That snarling *rata* would claim his mother is a whore if the *policía* paid him enough!"

" 'Would,' as in the past tense?"

"*No comprende.*"

"He's dead?"

"Dead, señor, and in the grass. Also, we have less than thirty minutes before the light comes up in the east."

"Then let's go . . . your friend is bound."

"To the dock? To the boats?"

"Not yet, *amigo.* We have something else to do before we get there."

"I tell you it will be *light* soon!"

"If I do things right, there'll be a lot more light sooner than that. Get the gasoline and pick up the tree clippers. I can't manage much more than what I've got."

Step by agonizing step, Evan climbed the narrow dirt road behind the Mexican until they reached the island's immense fence-enclosed generator, the bass-toned hum assaulting their ears to the point of painful vibrations. Signs of *¡Peligro! . . . Danger!* were everywhere, and the single gate to the interior was secured by two huge plate locks that apparently took simultaneous insertions of keys to open. Limping around into the darkest shadows of the floodlights, Kendrick gave the order while handing Emilio the wire cutters. "Start here, and I hope you're as strong as you say you are. This is heavy-gauge fence. Slice an opening, three feet's enough."

"And *you,* señor?"

"I have to look around."

He *found* them! Three iron disks screwed into concrete thirty feet apart, three enormous tanks, cisterns for fuel, supplemented by banks of photovoltaic cells somewhere, which no longer concerned him. Opening a disk required a T-squared sexagonal wrench, its upper bars long enough for two strong men on each bar. But there was another way, and he knew it well from the desert tanks in Saudi Arabia—an emergency procedure in the event the caravans of fuel trucks forgot the implement, not uncommon in the Jabal deserts. Each supposedly impenetrable disk had fourteen ridges across the top, not much different from the manhole covers in most American cities, although much smaller. Hammered slowly counterclockwise, the circular vaults would loosen until hands and fingers could reach the sides and unscrew them.

Kendrick walked back to Emilio and the near-deafening island generator. The Mexican had cut through two parallel vertical lines and was starting at the ground-level base. "Come with me!" said Evan, shouting into Emilio's ear. "Have you got your hatchet?"

"*Pues sí.*"

"So do I."

Kendrick led the Mexican back to the first iron disk and instructed him how to use the dish towels from the electronic cabin to muffle the blows from the blunt ends of their hatchets. "*Slowly,*" he yelled. "A spark can set off the fumes, *comprende*?"

"No, señor."

"It's better that you don't. *Easy,* now! One tap at a time. Not so hard! . . . It's *moving*!"

"Now harder?"

"Christ, no! Easy, *amigo.* Like you were cracking a diamond."

"It has not been my pleasure—"

"It will be if we get out of here. . . . *There!* It's *free*! Unscrew it to the top and leave it there. Give me your towels."

"For *what,* señor?"

"I'll explain as soon as you get me through that door you're cutting in the fence."

"That will take time—"

"You've got about two minutes, *amigo*!"

"*Madre de Dios!*"

"Where did you put the gasoline?" Kendrick moved closer to be heard.

"*There!*" replied the Mexican, pointing to the left of the "door" he was cutting.

Crouching painfully in the shadows, Evan tied the towels together, tugging at each knot to make sure it was secure until he had a single ten-foot length of cloth. His body aching with each twisting movement, he unscrewed the top of the gasoline can and drenched the string of towels, squeezing each as if it were a dish cloth. In minutes he had a ten-foot fuse. His knee now boiling, his ankle swelling rapidly, he crawled back to the fuel tank dragging the towels at his side. Straining, he pried up the iron cover, inserted three feet of fuse and moved the heavy disk off center so that a flow of air would circulate throughout the black tank below. Backtracking, he pressed each towel, each leg of his fuse, firmly in the ground, sprinkling dirt over each, but only "dusting" them so as to retard the speed of the flame from base to gaseous contact.

The last towel in place, he stood—wondering briefly how long he could stand—and limped back to Emilio. The Mexican was pulling the heavy-gauged cut-out section of the fence toward him, bending it up to permit access into massive, glistening machinery that through the dynamoelectrical process converted mechanical energy into electricity.

"That's enough," said Kendrick, bending over to speak close to Emilio's ear. "Now listen to me carefully, and if you don't understand, stop me. From here on everything is timing—something happens and we do something else. *Comprende?*"

"*Sí.* We move to other places."

"That's about it." Evan reached into the pocket of his mud-encrusted suit coat and withdrew the flashlight. "Take this," he continued, nodding his head at the hole in the fence. "I'm going in there and I hope to hell I know what I'm doing—these things have changed since I installed them—but if nothing else, I can shut it down. There may be a lot of noise and big sparks—"

"*¿Cómo?*"

"Like short bolts of lightning and . . . and sounds like very loud static on the radio, do you understand?"

"It is enough—"

"*Not* enough. Don't get near the fence—don't *touch* it and at the first crack, turn away and shut your eyes. . . . With any luck, all the lights will go out and when they do, shine the flashlight on the opening in the fence, okay?"

"Okay."

"As soon as I get through to this side, swing the light over there." Kendrick pointed at the last of his knotted towels protruding out of the ground. "Have your rifle over your shoulder and hold out one for me—have you got the cap you took from the first guard? If you do, give it to me."

"*Sí.* Here." Emilio took the cap out of his pocket and handed it to Evan, who put it on.

"When I'm clear of the fence, I'll go over there and strike a match, setting the towels on fire. The second I do that we get out of here to the other side of the road, *comprende?*"

"I understand, señor. Into the grass at the other side of the road. We hide."

"We hide; we work our way up the hill in the grass, and when everyone starts running around, we *join* them!"

"*¿Cómo?*"

"Twenty-odd personnel," said Kendrick, checking his pockets and removing the two cans of Sterno, replacing them in his trousers, then ripping the coat off his back and and the tie off his neck. "We're only two of them in the dark, but we'll be making our way over the hill and down to the dock. With two rifles and a Colt forty-five."

"I understand."

"Here we go," said Evan as he awkwardly, painfully bent down and picked up the rubber-based tree clipper and a machete.

He crawled through Emilio's opening and rose to his feet, studying the whirring, life-threatening machinery. Some things had not changed, they never would. Above on the left, bolted into a fifteen-foot-high tar-covered pole was the main transformer, the shunt wires carrying the major load of power to the various offshoots, the cables encased in rubber conduit at least two inches in diameter to prohibit seepage from water—rain and humidity—which would short-circuit the load. Ten feet away on the ground and diagonally opposed above the two black squat main dynamos were the grid plates, whirling maniacally on flywheels on top of the machinery, changing one field of energy into another, protected by a heavy latticework of wire and cooled by the air that had open access. He would study them further but not now.

First things *first,* he thought, moving to his left and extending the telescoped tree clipper to its full height. Above in the floodlights the saw-toothed jaws of the long instrument gripped the upper shunt cable, and as he had done with the wire cutters on the tail assembly of the helicopter, he worked furiously up and down until his professional instincts told him he was within millimeters of the first layer of coiled copper. He gently leaned the extended metal pole against the fence and turned to the first of the two main dynamos.

If it were merely a question of shorting out the island's electrical power, he would simply continue slicing into the transformer's conduit while gripping the nonconductive rubber handles and let the short take place by angling the metal clipper into the metal fence when he struck cable. There would be a brief electrical explosion and all the power terminated. However, more was at stake; he had to face the probability that neither he nor Emilio would survive, and a damaged transformer cable could be repaired in a matter of minutes. He had to inflict more than damage; he had to cripple the system. He could not know what was happening in San Diego, he could only give Payton's forces time by disabling the machinery to the point where it would take days to *replace,* not repair. This island compound, this headquarters of a government within a government, had to be immobilized, isolated, without means of communication or departure. The transformer was, in actuality, his backup, his far less desirable option, but it had to be there and ready to execute. Time was *everything* now!

He approached the dynamo, cautiously peering into the enormous wire-encased flywheel. There was a horizontal space, no more than a half inch wide, separating the upper and lower screens of thick latticework that kept objects of any size from penetrating the whirring interior. That space or something similar was what he had hoped to find, the reason for the machete. Sections of all generators, needing air, had openings of extremely limited dimensions, vertically and horizontally; this was his. It was either his or he was its in death; one slip meant instant electrocution, and even if he avoided death by millecounts of high voltage, he could be blinded by the exploding streaks of white electric light if he did not turn away in time, keeping his eyes tightly closed. But if he could do it, the island's generator would be shut down for major replacement. Time . . . *time* might well be the last gift he had to give.

He pulled the machete out of his belt, sweat pouring down his face despite the wind from the flywheel, and inched the blade toward the horizontal space. . . . Trembling, he yanked the machete back; he had to steady his hands! He could not *touch* either edge of the narrow space! He tried again, inserting one inch, then two, and three . . . he rammed the heavy blade inside, snapping back both hands before the blade made contact and lurched to the ground behind him, his face and eyes buried under his arms. The self-contained electrical detonations were ear-shattering, and despite his tightly closed eyes, white blinding light was everywhere in the darkness. The flywheel would not stop! It kept chewing up the primitive metal of the machete while spewing out bolts of Frankenstein electrical charges, spitting jaggedly, violently into the fence.

Kendrick leaped up, shielding his eyes, and, step by cautious step, crossed back to the tree clipper, its saw-toothed jaws embedded in the transformer's conduit. He gripped the rubber handles, and in desperation crashed them back and forth until the jolt threw him off his feet. He had struck the cable proper and the telescoped metal clippers fell into the metal fence. The whole generator complex went mad, as if its electrical inhabitants were infuriated by mere man's interference with his superior inventions. Lights went out everywhere, but there was still blinding, erratic, jagged streaks of electrical lightning within the lethal fenced enclosure. He had to get *out*!

Scrambling on his stomach, his arms and legs propelling him like a racing spider's, he reached the hole in the fence, the beam of the flashlight guiding him through. When he got to his feet, the rifle was thrust into his hands by Emilio.

"*Matches!*" yelled Evan, unable to reach his own; the Mexican gave him a handful while angling the flashlight over to the last towel. Kendrick ran, limping to his fuse, lurching to the ground and striking a half-dozen matches on a rock. As they flared he threw them on the last towel; the flame caught and started its deadly journey slowly, relentlessly, no more than a glow in the dirt.

"Hurry!" cried Emilio, helping Evan to his feet and leading him, not to the path back to the dirt road but instead into the high grass below. "Many have come out of the house and are running down! *Pronto,* señor!"

They raced, literally diving into the grass as a swarm of panicked men, most with rifles, approached the blinding, erupting generator, shielding their eyes and shouting at one another. During the chaos Kendrick and his Mexican companion crawled through the grass below the terror-stricken crowd. They reached the road as another equally stupefied stream of men came rushing out of the long, low building that was the staff's barracks. Most were only half dressed, many in undershorts, and not a few showing the effects of too much alcohol.

"*Listen* to me," whispered Evan into Emilio's ear. "We'll get out there carrying our rifles and start up the road. . . . Keep shouting in Spanish as though we were following someone's orders. *Now!*"

"*¡Traenos agua!*" roared the Mexican as both men sprang out of the grass and joined the stunned, screaming crowd from the barracks. "*¡Agua! . . . ¡Traenos agua!*" They broke through the mass of excited bodies, only to be confronted by the panicked contingent from the main house, half of whom had cautiously moved down the path to the dying, smoking, spitting machinery that had been the island's source of power. The darkness was awesome, made eerie by the maniacal voices shouting everywhere in the dim, intermittent moonlight. Then beams of flashlights shot out from the house above.

"The *path*!" cried Kendrick. "Head for the main path down to the dock. For God's sake, *hurry*! That tank will blow any second and there'll be a stampede for the boats!"

"It is ahead. We must pass through the *galeria.*"

"*Christ,* they'll be at the windows, on the balconies!"

"There is no other way, no quicker way."

"Let's go!"

The dirt road stopped, replaced by the narrow path that only minutes ago had been bordered by the parallel rows of domed amber lights. They ran, Kendrick lurching in agony, down into the sunken patio, racing across the bricks to the steps that led to the main path.

"*Stop!*" roared a deep voice as the beam of a powerful flashlight swung down on them. "Where are you. . . . *Jesus Christ,* it's *you!*" Evan looked up. Directly above, standing on the short balcony he had stood on barely an hour ago was the outsized yachtsman. In his hand was a gun; it was being raised, aimed at Kendrick. Evan fired his rifle at the same instant the yachtsman's weapon exploded. He felt the searing hot bullet slice into his left shoulder, hurling him back off his feet. He fired again and again as the giant above held his stomach, screaming at the top of his lungs. "It's *him*! It's *Kendrick*! . . . Stop the son of a bitch, *stop* him! He's going down to the *boats*!"

Kendrick took closer aim and fired a last shot. High Noon in the Town of Corruption grabbed his throat, arched his neck, then fell forward over the railing and down into the brick patio. Evan's eyes began to close, the mists swirling about his head.

"*No,* señor! You must run! Get to your feet!" Kendrick felt his arms being pulled out of their sockets and his face being repeatedly, harshly slapped. "You will come with me or you will die, and I will *not* die with you! I have loved ones in El Descanso—"

"*What?*" shouted Evan, saying nothing, agreeing to nothing, but answering everything as part of the mists cleared. His shoulder on fire, the blood drenching his shirt, he rose and lurched for the steps, somehow in the far reaches of his mind remembering the Colt .45 he had taken from the mafioso, ripping it out of his back pocket, tearing the stretched cloth to remove the weapon too large for its recess. "I'm with you!" he cried out to Emilio.

"I know," replied the Mexican, slowing his pace and turning around. "Who pulled you up the steps, señor? . . . You are hurt and the path is dark, so I must use the *linterna*—the flashlight."

Suddenly the earth exploded, shaking the ground with the impact of a block-sized meteor, smashing windows throughout the manor house on top of the hill and sending fire up into the night sky. The generator's fuel tank erupted into the heavens as the two fugitives raced down the path, Kendrick staggering, trying desperately to focus on the wavering beam of the flashlight ahead, his knee and ankle searing in pain.

Shots. Gunfire! Bullets snapped above them, around them, digging up the earth in front of them. Emilio switched off the flashlight and grabbed Evan's hand. "It is not much longer now. I know the way and I will not let go of you."

"If we ever get away from here, you're going to have the biggest fishing boat in El Descanso!"

"No, señor, I will move my family to the hills. These men will come after me, after my *niños.*"

"How about a ranch?" The moon abruptly emerged from beyond the rushing low-flying clouds, revealing the island's dock barely two hundred feet away. The gunfire had ceased; it started up again, but again the earth seemingly blew apart, an isolated galactic mass in frenzy. "It *happened*!" shouted Kendrick as they neared the base of the dock.

"*Señor?*" cried the Mexican, terrified at the ear-shattering, unexpected detonation, panicked by the ball of smoke and the branches of fire that rose beyond the house on the hill. "This island will go into the sea! *What* happened?"

"The second tank blew! I couldn't predict, I could only hope."

A single gunshot. From the dock. Emilio was *hit*! He doubled over, grabbing his upper thigh as the blood spread through his trousers. A man with a rifle moved out of the moonlight shadows fifty feet away, raising a hand-held intercom to his face.

Evan crouched, his whole body now a festering boil, and raised his left hand to steady his right and the Colt automatic. He fired twice, one or both of his shots hitting the target. The guard reeled, dropping both the rifle and the radio; he fell on the thick wood planks and was still.

"Come on, *amigo*!" cried Kendrick, gripping Emilio's shoulder.

"I cannot *move*! I have no *leg*!"

"Well, I'm not going to die with *you,* you bastard! I've got a couple of loved ones, too, over there. Get off your ass or swim back to El Descanso and your *niños*!"

"*¿Cómo?*" shouted the Mexican furiously as he struggled to rise.

"That's better. Get angry! We've both got a lot to be angry about." His arm around Emilio's waist, his barely functioning shoulder and legs supporting the Mexican, the two men walked out on the dark dock. "The big boat on the right!" yelled Evan, grateful that the moon had gone back behind the clouds. "You know about boats, *amigo*?"

"I am a fisherman!"

"Boats like this?" asked Kendrick, propelling Emilio over the side onto the deck, laying the .45 on the gunwale.

"You don't catch fish on these boats, you catch *turistas.*"

"There's another definition—"

"*Es igual.* . . . Still, I have run many boats. I can try. . . . The *other* boats, señor! They will come out and find us, for they are much faster than this beautiful one."

"Could any of them make it to the mainland?"

"Never. They cannot take heavy swells, and burn fuel too quickly. Thirty, forty kilometers and they must come back. This is the *barca* for us."

"Give me your Sterno!" yelled Evan, hearing shouts up on the main path. The Mexican yanked the small can out of his right pocket as Kendrick removed his two and pried up the lids with the carving knife. "Open yours, if you can!"

"I have. Here, señor. I go up to the bridge."

"Can you make it?"

"I have to. . . . El Descanso."

"Oh, *Christ*! A key! For the *engine*!"

"In these private docks it is customary to leave the key on board in case storms or heavy winds make it necessary to move—"

"Suppose they didn't?"

"All fishermen go out with many drunken captains. There are panels to open and wires to cross. Get the lines, señor!"

"Two ranches," said Evan as Emilio hobbled to the fly bridge ladder.

Kendrick turned, grabbing the Colt automatic from the gunwale, and digging out the solid fuel of the Sterno with his fingers. He ran down the dock throwing handfuls over the Bimini canvas of each huge speedboat, heaving each empty can into each boat. At the last boat he reached into his pocket and pulled out a fistful of hunters' matches, crouching in pain and frantically striking one after another on the wooden planks of the dock and lobbing them into the globs of scattered jelly until the flames leaped up from all the coverings. With each speedboat he fired the automatic into the hulls near the water lines, the powerful weapon blowing large holes in whatever the light alloy was that permitted the boats their excessive speed.

Emilio had *done* it! The deep-throated roar of the fishing yacht's engines broke through the water. . . . *Shouts!* Men were racing down the steep path from the manor house on the hill, the fires beyond it now a steady glow.

"*Señor!* Quickly . . . the *lines*!"

The ropes on the pylons! Kendrick ran to the thick pole on the right and struggled with the knotted line; it pulled free and slipped into the water. He lurched, barely able to stay on his feet, and reached the second pylon, yanking in panic until it, too, came loose.

"*Stop them! Kill them!*" It was the frenzied voice of Crayton Grinell, chairman of the board of a government within the government. Men swarmed onto the base of the island dock, their weapons suddenly on open fire, the fusillades shattering. Evan dove off the pier and into the stern of the yacht as Emilio swung the boat to the left, engines at full power, and curved out of the cove into the darkness of the sea.

A third and final immense detonation burst over the hill beyond the manor house. The distant night sky became a yellow cloud, then jagged streaks of white and red intruded; the last tank had blown apart. The island of the murderous government within a government was immobilized, isolated, incommunicado. No one could leave. They had done it!

"*Señor!*" screamed Emilio from the fly bridge.

"*What?*" yelled Kendrick, rolling on the deck, trying but unable to rise, his body jolting everywhere in torment, the blood from his wound forming bulges of floating liquid inside his shirt.

"You must come up here!"

"I can't!"

"You *must*! I am *shot.* The *pecho*—the chest!"

"It's your *leg*!"

"No! . . . From the *dock.* I am falling, señor. I cannot handle the *wheel.*"

"Hold *on*!" Evan yanked his shirt out of his trousers; pools of blood poured onto the deck. He crawled over to the shellacked ladder and, calling upon reservoirs of strength he could not believe existed, pulled himself up rung by rung to the bridge. He breached the upper deck and looked over at the Mexican. Emilio was holding on to the wheel, but his body had sunk below the bridge's windows. Kendrick grabbed the railing and got to his feet, barely able to steady himself. He lurched over to the wheel, appalled by the darkness and the swell of the waves that rocked the boat. Emilio fell to the floor, his hand springing away from the circular rudder. "What can I *do*?" yelled Evan.

"The . . . *radio,*" choked the Mexican. "I haul nets and I am not a captain, but I have heard them in bad weather. . . . There is a channel for *urgencia, numero dieciséis*!"

"What?"

"Sixteen!"

"Where's the *radio*?"

"On the right of the wheel. The switch is on the left. *Pronto!*"

"How do I *call* them?"

"Take out the *micrófono* and press the button. Say you are *primero de mayo*!"

"May Day?"

"¡Sí! . . . Madre de Dios . . ." Emilio collapsed on the flybridge deck, unconscious or dead.

Kendrick lifted the plastic-coiled microphone out of its cradle, snapped on the radio and studied the digital readout below the console. Unable to think, the boat battered by swells he could not see, he kept tapping the keyboard until the number *16* appeared and then pressed the button.

"This is Congressman Evan *Kendrick*!" he screamed. "Am I *reaching* anyone?" He released the button.

"This is Coast Guard, San Diego," came the flat reply.

"Can you patch me into a telephone line at the Westlake Hotel? It's an *emergency*!"

"Anybody can say anything, sir. We're not a phone service."

"I *repeat.* I'm Congressman Evan Kendrick from the Ninth District of Colorado and this is an emergency. I'm lost at sea somewhere west or south of Tijuana!"

"Those are Mexican waters—"

"Call the *White House*! Repeat what I've just told you . . . Kendrick of Colorado!"

"You're the guy who went to that *Oman* . . . ?"

"Get your orders from the White House!"

"Keep your radio open, I'll take your coordinates for the RDF—"

"I don't have *time* and I don't know what you're talking about."

"It's the radio directional finder—"

"For Christ's *sake,* Coast Guard, patch me through to the *Westlake* and get your orders! I have to reach that hotel."

"Yes, *sir,* Commando Kendrick!"

"Whatever works," mumbled Evan to himself as the sounds from the console speaker erupted in different tones until there was the hum of a telephone ringing. The switchboard answered. "Room Fifty-one! Hurry, please."

"*Yes?*" cried the strained voice of Khalehla.

"*It's me!*" shouted Kendrick, pressing the button for transmission, then instantly releasing it.

"For God's sake, where *are* you?"

"In the ocean somewhere, *forget* it! There's an attorney, a lawyer Ardis used for herself and he's got a ledger that spells out *everything*! Find him! *Get* it!"

"Yes, of course, I'll reach MJ right away. But what about *you*? Are you—"

Another voice intruded, the deep commanding tones unmistakable. "This is the President of the United States. Find that boat, find that *man,* or all your asses are in a sling!"

The swells tossed the boat like an insignificant bauble in a furious sea. Evan could no longer hold on to the wheel. The mists returned and he collapsed over the body of the fisherman from El Descanso.

43

He was aware of violently swaying weightlessness, then of hands grabbing him and a harsh wind buffeting him, finally of a deafening roar above him. He opened his eyes to blurred figures frantically moving around him, unbuckling straps . . . then a sharp puncture in his flesh, on his arm. He tried to rise but was restrained as men carried him to a flat, padded surface inside a huge, vibrating metal cage.

"*Easy,* Congressman!" shouted a man in a white navy uniform that gradually came into focus. "I'm a doctor and you're pretty bashed up. Don't make things more difficult for me because the President himself will officiate at my court-martial if I don't do my job."

Another puncture. He could not take any more *pain.* "Where am I?"

"A logical question," replied the medical officer, emptying a syringe into Kendrick's shoulder. "You're in a big whirlybird ninety miles off the coast of Mexico. You were on your way to *China,* man, and those seas are rugged."

"That's *it*!" Evan tried to raise his voice, but could barely hear himself.

"What's 'it'?" The doctor leaned down as a corpsman above him held a bottle of plasma.

"Passage to China—an *island* called Passage to China! Seal it *off*!"

"I'm a doctor, not a member of the Seals—"

"Do as I *tell* you! . . . Radio San Diego, get planes out there, boats out there! Take *everyone*!"

"Hey, man, I'm no expert, but these are Mexican waters—"

"Goddamnit, call the *White House*! . . . *No!* Reach a man named Payton at the CIA. . . . Mitchell Payton, *CIA*! Tell him what I just told you. Say the name Grinell!"

"Wow, this is heavy," said the young doctor, looking up at a third man at the foot of Kendrick's padded resting place. "You heard the Congressman, Ensign. Go up to the pilot. An island called Passage to China, and a man named Payton at Langley, and someone else called Grinell! Hop to it, guy, this is the

President's *boy*! . . . Hey, is this anything like what you did to the Arabs?"

"*Emilio?*" asked Evan, dismissing the question. "How is he?"

"The Mex?"

"My friend . . . the man who saved my life."

"He's here right beside you; we just got him up."

"How *is* he?"

"Worse off than you—much worse. At best it's sixty-forty against him, Congressman. We're flying back to the base hospital as fast as we can."

Kendrick elbowed himself up and looked at the prone, unconscious figure of Emilio, barely two feet away behind the doctor. The Mexican's arm was on the deck of the helicopter, his face ashen, close to a mask of death. "Give me his hand," ordered Evan. "*Give* it to me!"

"Yes, sir," said the doctor, reaching over and pulling Emilio's hand up so Kendrick could grasp it.

"*El Descanso!*" roared Evan. "*El Descanso* and your family—your *wife* and the *niños*! You goddamned son of a bitch, don't *die* on me! You fucking know-nothing fisherman, put some *juice* in your stomach!"

"*¿Cómo?*" The Mexican's head thrashed back and forth as Kendrick tightened his grip.

"That's better, *amigo.* Remember, we're angry! We *stay* angry. You hang in there, you *bastard,* or I'll kill you myself. *Comprende?*"

His head turned toward Evan, Emilio partially opened his eyes, a smile creasing his lips. "You think you could kill this strong fisherman?"

"*Try* me! . . . Well, maybe I couldn't, but I can get you a big boat."

"You are *loco,* señor," coughed the Mexican. ". . . Still, there is El Descanso."

"Three ranches," said Kendrick, his hand falling away under the effect of the navy doctor's hypodermic needle.

One by one the graceful limousines drove through the dark streets of Cynwid Hollow to the estate on Chesapeake Bay. Where on previous occasions there had been four such vehicles, on this night there were but three. One was missing; it belonged to a company founded by Eric Sundstrom, traitor of Inver Brass.

The members sat around the large circular table in the extraordinary library, a brass lamp in front of each. All the lamps on the table were lit but one, and that was the one in front of a fifth empty chair. Four pools of light shone down on the polished wood; the fifth source was extinguished, implying no honor in death—instead, perhaps, a reminder of human frailty in an all too human world. On this night there was no humorous small talk, no badinage to remind them that they were mortal and not above the common touch despite their awesome wealth and influence. The empty chair was enough.

"You have the facts," said Samuel Winters, his aquiline features in the flow of light. "Now I ask you for your comments."

"I have only one," Gideon Logan stated firmly, his large black head in shadows. "We can't stop, the alternative is too devastating. The unleashed wolves will take over the government—what they haven't usurped already."

"But there's nothing to *stop,* Gid," corrected Margaret Lowell. "Poor Milos set everything in motion in Chicago."

"He hadn't finished, Margaret," said Jacob Mandel, his gaunt face and frame in his accustomed chair next to Winters. "There's Kendrick himself. He must accept the nomination, be convinced that he should take it. If you recall, the subject was brought up by Eric, and now I wonder why he did. He might have left well enough alone, for it could be our Achilles' heel."

"Sundstrom was consumed, as always, by his insatiable curiosity," said Winters sadly. "The same curiosity that, when applied to space technology, made him betray us. Having said that, however, it doesn't answer Jacob's question. Our congressman could walk away."

"I'm not sure Milos thought it was that serious a problem, Jacob," reflected Attorney Lowell, leaning forward, her elbow on the table, her extended fingers against her right temple. "Whether he actually said it or not is immaterial, but he certainly implied that Kendrick was an intensely, if unfashionably, moral man. He loathed corruption, so he went into politics to replace a corrupter."

"And he went to Oman," added Gideon Logan, "because he believed that with his expertise he could help with no thought of reward for himself—that was proven to us."

"And *that* was what convinced all of us to accept him," said Mandel, nodding. "Everything dovetailed. The extraordinary man in a very ordinary field of political candidates. But is it enough? Will he agree even if there's the national ground swell that Milos had so well orchestrated."

"The assumption was that if genuinely summoned, he would

respond to the call," said Winters flatly. "But is it an accurate assumption?"

"I think it is," replied Margaret Lowell.

"I do, too." Logan nodded his large head and moved forward into the reflected pool of light from the table. "Still, Jacob has a point. We can't be *sure,* and if we're wrong, it's Bollinger and business as usual, and the wolves take over next January."

"Suppose Kendrick was confronted with the alternative of your wolves, with proof of their venality, their entrenched behind-the-scenes power that's permeated the entire Washington structure?" asked Winters, his voice no longer a monotone but very much alive. "Under those circumstances, do you think he *will* answer the call?"

The huge black entrepreneur leaned back into the shadows, his large eyes squinting. "From everything we know . . . Yes, yes, I do."

"And you, Margaret?"

"I agree with Gid. He *is* a remarkable man—with a political conscience, I believe."

"Jacob?"

"Of course, Samuel, but how is it to be done? We have no documentation, no official records—good heavens, we burn our own notes. So beyond the fact that he'd have no reason to believe us, we can't reveal ourselves and Varak's *gone.*"

"I have another to take his place. A man who, if necessary, can make certain Evan Kendrick is given the truth. The whole truth if he doesn't know it already."

Stunned, all eyes were on the spokesman for Inver Brass. "What the hell are you *saying,* Sam?" cried Margaret Lowell.

"Varak left instructions in the event of his death, and I gave him my word not to open them unless he was killed. I kept my word because in all honesty I didn't care to know the things he might tell me. . . . I opened them last night after Mitchell Payton's call."

"How will you handle Payton?" asked Lowell suddenly, anxiously.

"We're meeting tomorrow. None of you have anything to fear; he knows nothing about you. We'll either reach an accommodation or we won't. If we don't, I've lived a long and productive life—it will be no sacrifice."

"Forgive me, Samuel," said Gideon Logan impatiently, "but we all face those decisions—we wouldn't be at this table if we didn't. What were Varak's instructions?"

"To reach the one man who can keep us—or conceivably the collective *you*—completely and officially informed. The man who was Varak's informer from the beginning, the one without whom Milos could never have done what he did. When our Czech uncovered the discrepancy in the State Department's logs sixteen months ago, the omission that had Kendrick listed as entering State but with no record of his departure, Varak knew where to look. What he found was not only a willing informer but a dedicated one. . . . Milos is, of course, irreplaceable, but in this day of high technology our new coordinator is among the most rapidly rising young officials in government. There isn't a major department or agency in Washington that's not vying for his services, and the private sector has offered him contracts reserved for former presidents and secretaries of state at least twice his age."

"He must be a hell of a lawyer or the youngest foreign service expert on record," interjected Margaret Lowell.

"He's neither," countered the white-haired spokesman of Inver Brass. "He's considered the foremost technologist of computer science in the country, perhaps in the West. Fortunately for us, he comes from considerable wealth and isn't tempted by private industry. In his way he's as committed as Milos Varak in pursuit of the nation's excellence. . . . In essence, he was one of us when he understood his gifts." Winters leaned forward over the table and pressed an ivory button. "Will you come in, please?"

The heavy door of the extraordinary library opened and in the frame stood a young man still in his twenties. What set him apart from most others of his age were his striking looks; it was as though he had walked out of a glossy advertisement for men's fashions in an expensive magazine. Yet his clothes were subdued, neither tailored nor cheap—just ordinarily neat. It was the chiseled, nearly ideal Grecian face that was startling.

"He should forget computers," said Jacob Mandel quietly. "I have friends at the William Morris Agency. They'll get him a television series."

"Do come in, please," interrupted Winters, placing his hand over Mandel's arm. "And, if you will, introduce yourself."

The young man walked confidently but without arrogance to the west end of the table below the black cylinder that when lowered was a screen. He stood for a moment looking down at the pools of light on the table.

"It's a particular honor for me to be here," he said pleasantly.

"My name is Gerald Bryce, and I am currently director of GCO, Department of State."

"GCO?" asked Mandel. "Another alphabet?"

"Global Computer Operations, sir."

The California sun streamed through the windows of the hospital room as Khalehla, her arms around Evan, gradually released him. She sat back on the bed above him and smiled wanly, her eyes glistening from the residue of tears, her light olive skin so pale. "Welcome to the land of the living," she said, gripping his hand.

"Glad to be here," whispered Kendrick weakly, staring at her. "When I opened my eyes, I wasn't sure it was you or whether I was . . . whether they were playing more tricks on me."

"Tricks?"

"They took my clothes . . . I was in some old blue jeans and a corduroy—then I was back in my suit—my blue—"

"Your 'congressional threads,' I believe you called them," interrupted Khalehla gently. "You'll have to get another suit, my darling. What was left of your trousers after they cut them away was beyond a tailor."

"Extravagant girl. . . . *Christ,* do you know how good it is to *see* you? I never thought I'd see you again—it made me so goddamned angry."

"I know how good it is to see *you.* That hotel carpet has been worn through. . . . Rest now; we'll talk later. You just woke up and the doctors said—"

"*No.* . . .To hell with the doctors, I want to know what's happened. How's Emilio?"

"He'll make it, but one lung is gone and his hip is shattered. He'll never walk properly again, but he's alive."

"He doesn't have to walk, just sit in a captain's chair."

"What?"

"Forget it. . . . The *island.* It's called Passage to China—"

"We know," broke in Khalehla firmly. "Since you're so rotten stubborn, let *me* do the talking. . . . What you and Carallo did was incredible—"

"Carallo? . . . Emilio?"

"Yes. I've seen the photographs—my God, what a mess! The fire spread everywhere, especially over the east side of the island. The house, the grounds, even the dock where the other boats exploded—it's gone; it's all gone. By the time the navy choppers arrived with marine assault troops, everyone on the place was frightened to death and waiting on the west beaches. They greeted our people as if we were liberators."

"Then they got *Grinell.*"

Khalehla looked down at Evan; she paused, then shook her head. "No. I'm sorry, darling."

"*How . . . ?*" Kendrick started to rise, wincing at the pain in his bandaged sutured shoulder. Again gently, Rashad held him, lowering him down on the pillow. "He *couldn't* have gotten away! They didn't *look*!"

"They didn't have to. The Mexicans told them."

"What? *How?*"

"A seaplane flew out and picked up the *patrón.*"

"I don't understand. All communications were out!"

"Not all. What you didn't know—couldn't know—was that Grinell had small auxiliary generators in the cellar of the main house with enough power to reach his people at an airfield in San Felipe—we've learned that much from the Mexican transmission authorities; not who but where. He can run and even disappear, but he can't hide forever; we've got the tail of a trail."

"Very alliterative, as my executioner might say."

"What?"

"Forget it—"

"I wish you'd stop saying that."

"Sorry, I mean it. What about Ardis's lawyer and the ledger I told you about?"

"Again, we're closing in but we're not there yet. He's taken a hike somewhere, but where no one knows. All his phones are monitored and sooner or later he'll have to reach one of them. When he does, we'll have him."

"Could he have any idea that you're after him?"

"It's the big question. Grinell was able to reach the mainland, and through San Felipe he could have sent word to Ardis's lawyer. We simply don't know."

"Manny?" asked Evan hesitantly. "Then again you didn't have time—"

"Wrong, I had nothing *but* time, desperation time, to be exact. I called the hospital in Denver last night, but all the floor nurse could tell me was that he was stable . . . and, I gather, something of a nuisance."

"The understatement of the week." Kendrick closed his eyes, shaking his head slowly. "He's dying, Khalehla. He's dying and there's nothing anyone can do about it."

"We're all dying, Evan. Every day is one day less of life.

That's not much help, but Manny's over eighty and the verdict's not in until it's in."

"I know," said Kendrick, looking at their entwined hands, then up at her face. "You're a beautiful lady, aren't you?"

"It's not something I dwell on, but I suppose I'll pass for okay-plus. You're not exactly Quasimodo yourself."

"No, I just walk like him. . . . It's not very modest, but our kids have a fair chance of being decent-looking little bastards."

"I'm all for the first part but somewhat dubious about the second."

"You understand that you just agreed to marry me, don't you?"

"Try getting away from me and you'll find out how really good I am with a gun."

"That's nice. '. . . Oh, Mrs. Jones, have you met my wife, the gunslinger? If anyone's crashed your party, she'll nail him right between the eyes.' "

"I'm also black belt, first class, in case a weapon makes too much noise."

"Hey, terrific. Nobody's going to push me around anymore. Pick a fight with me, I'll let her off the leash."

"*Grrrr,*" growled Khalehla, baring her bright lovely teeth, then composing her face, looking down as if studying him, her dark eyes soft, floating. "I *do* love you. God knows what we two misfits think we're doing, but I guess we're going to give it a try."

"No, not a try," said Evan, reaching for her with his right hand. "A lifetime," he added. She bent down and they kissed, holding each other like two people who had nearly lost each other. And the telephone rang.

"*Damn!*" cried Khalehla, springing up.

"Am I that irresistible?"

"Hell, no, not *you.* It's not supposed to ring in here, those were my instructions!" She picked up the phone and spoke harshly. "*Yes,* and whoever you are I'd like an explanation. How did you get through to this room?"

"The explanation, Officer Rashad," said Mitchell Payton in Langley, Virginia, "is comparatively simple. I countermanded a subordinate's order."

"MJ, you haven't *seen* this man! He looks like a nuked Godzilla!"

"For a grown-up woman, Adrienne, one who has admitted in my presence that she's over thirty, you have an untidy habit of frequently talking like an adolescent. . . . *And* I've also spoken to the doctors. Evan needs some rest and must keep his ankle strapped and his leg quiet for a day or so and his shoulder wound periodically checked, but beyond these minor inconveniences, he could go right back into the field."

"You are one frozen *fish,* Uncle Mitch! He can barely talk."

"Then why have you been talking to him?"

"How did you know . . . ?"

"I didn't. You just told me. . . . May we please deal with realities, my dear?"

"What's Evan? *Unreal?*"

"Give me that phone," said Kendrick, awkwardly taking the instrument from Khalehla's hand. "It's me, Mitch. What's happening?"

"How are you, Evan? . . . I suppose that's a foolish question."

"Very. Answer mine."

"Ardis Vanvlanderen's lawyer is at his summer house in the San Jacinto Mountains. He called his office for messages and we got an area fix. A unit is on its way there now to evaluate. They should be there in a matter of minutes."

"Evaluate? What the hell is there to evaluate? He's got the book! Go in and get it! It obviously spells out their whole global structure, every rotten arms merchant they've used in the world! Grinell can run to any of them and be hidden. *Grab* it!"

"You're forgetting about Grinell's own sense of survival. I assume Adrienne . . . Khalehla told you."

"Yes, a seaplane picked him up. So what?"

"He wants that ledger as much as we do, and he's no doubt reached Mrs. Vanvlanderen's man by now. Grinell won't risk coming up himself, but he'll send someone he can trust to retrieve it. If he knows we're closing in, and all it would take is another pair of eyes on the lawyer's house, what do you suppose the instructions will be to his trusted courier, who must, after all, get that book into Mexico?"

"Where he could be stopped at the border or in an airport—"

"With us in attendance. What do you think he'll tell that person?"

"To burn the damn thing," said Kendrick quietly.

"Precisely."

"I hope your men are good at what they do."

"Two men, and one is just about the best we have. His name is Gingerbread; ask your friend about him."

"Gingerbread? What kind of dumb name is that?"

"Later, Evan," interrupted Payton. "I've got something to tell you. I'm flying out to San Diego this afternoon and we have to talk. I hope you'll be up to it because it's urgent."

"I'll be up to it, but why can't we talk now?"

"Because I wouldn't know what to say . . . I'm not sure I will later, but at least I'll have learned more. You see, I'm meeting with a man in an hour from now, an influential man who's intensely interested in you—has been for the past year."

Kendrick closed his eyes, feeling weak as he sank back into the pillows. "He's with a group or a committee that calls itself . . . Inver Brass."

"You *know*?"

"Only that much. I've no idea who they are or what they are, just that they've screwed up my life."

The tan sedan, its codified government plates signifying the Central Intelligence Agency, drove through the imposing gates of the estate on Chesapeake Bay and up the circular drive to the smooth stone steps of the entrance. The tall man in an open raincoat that revealed a rumpled suit and shirt—evidence of nearly seventy-two hours of continuous wear—got out of the backseat and walked wearily up the steps toward the large stately front door. He shivered briefly in the cold morning air of the overcast day that promised snow—snow for Christmas, reflected Payton. It was Christmas Eve, simply another day for the director of Special Projects, yet a day he dreaded, the impending meeting one he would trade several years of his life not to have insisted upon. Throughout his long career he had done many things that caused the bile to erupt in his stomach, but none more so than the destruction of good and moral men. He would destroy such a man this morning and he loathed himself for it, yet there was no alternative. For there was a higher good, a higher morality, and it was found in the reasonable laws of a nation of decent people. To abuse those laws was to deny the decency; accountability was the constant. He rang the bell.

A maid preceded Payton through an enormous sitting room overlooking the Chesapeake to another stately door. She opened it and the director walked inside the extraordinary library, trying to absorb everything that struck his eyes. The huge console that took up the entire wall on the left with its panoply of television monitors and dials and projection equipment; the lowered silver screen on the right and the burning Franklin stove in the near corner; the cathedral windows directly across and the large circular table in front of him. Samuel Winters got up from the chair beneath the wall of sophisticated technology and came forward, his hand extended.

"It's been too long, MJ—may I call you that?" said the world-renowned historian. "As I recall, everyone called you MJ."

"Certainly, Dr. Winters." They shook hands and the septuagenarian scholar waved his arm, encompassing the room.

"I wanted you to see it all. To know that we have our fingers on the pulse of the world—but not for personal gain; you must understand that."

"I do. Who are the others?"

"Please sit down," said Winters, gesturing at the chair facing his own, on the opposite side of the circular table. "Take off your coat, by all means. When one reaches my age, all the rooms are much too warm."

"If you don't mind, I'll keep it on. This will not be a long conference."

"You're certain of that?"

"Very," replied Payton, sitting down.

"*Well,*" said Winters softly but emphatically as he went to his chair, "it's the unusual intellect that chooses its position without regard to the parameters of discussion. And you *do* have an intellect, MJ."

"Thank you for your generous, if somewhat condescending, compliment."

"That's rather hostile, isn't it?"

"No more so than your deciding for the country who should run and be elected to national office."

"He's the right man at the right time for all the right reasons."

"I couldn't agree with you more. It's the way you did it. When one lets loose a rogue force to achieve an objective, he can't know the consequences."

"*Others* do it. They're doing it *now.*"

"That doesn't give you the right. Expose them if you can, and with your resources I'm sure you can, but don't imitate them."

"That's sophistry! We live in an animal world, a politically oriented world dominated by *predators*!"

"We don't have to become predators to fight them. . . . Exposure, not imitation."

"By the time the word gets out, by the time even the few understand what's happened, the brutal herds have stampeded, trampling us. They change the rules, alter the laws. They're untouchable."

"I respectfully disagree, Dr. Winters."

"Look at the Third Reich!"

"Look what happened to it. Look at Runnymede and the Magna Carta, look at the tyrannies of the French court of Louis, look at the brutalities of the czars—for *Christ's* sake, look at Philadelphia in 1787! The *Constitution,* Doctor! The people react goddamned quickly to oppression and malfeasance!"

"Tell that to the citizens of the Soviet Union."

"Checkmate. But don't try to explain that to the refuseniks and the dissidents who every day make the world more aware of the dark corners of Kremlin policy. They *are* making a difference, Doctor."

"*Excesses!*" cried Winters. "Everywhere on this poor doomed planet there is excess. It will blow us apart."

"Not if reasonable people expose excess and do not join it in hysteria. Your cause may have been right, but in *your* excess you violated laws—written and unwritten—and caused the deaths of innocent men and women because you considered yourself above the laws of the land. Rather than telling the country what you knew, you decided to manipulate it."

"That is your determination?"

"It is. Who are the others in this Inver Brass?"

"You *know* that name?"

"I just said it. Who *are* they?"

"You'll never learn from me."

"We'll find them . . . ultimately. But for my own curiosity, where did this organization start? If you don't care to answer, it doesn't matter."

"Oh, but I *do* care to answer," said the old historian, his thin hands trembling to the point where he gripped them together on the table. "Decades ago Inver Brass was born in chaos, when the nation was being torn apart, on the edge of self-destruction. It was the height of the great depression; the country had come to a stop and violence was erupting everywhere. Hungry people care little about empty slogans and emptier promises, and productive people who've lost their pride through no fault of their own are reduced to fury. . . . Inver Brass was formed by a small group of immensely wealthy, influential men who had followed the advice of the likes of Baruch and were unscathed by the economic collapse. They were also men of social conscience and they put their resources to work in practical ways, stemming riots and violence not only by massive infusions of capital and supplies into inflamed areas, but by silently ushering laws through Congress that helped to bring about measures of relief. It is in that tradition that we follow."

"Is it?" asked Payton quietly, his eyes cold, studying the old man.

"*Yes,*" answered Winters emphatically.

"Inver Brass. . . . What does it mean?"

"It's the name of a marshland lake in the Highlands that's not on any map. It was coined by the first spokesman, a banker of Scot descent, who understood that the group had to act in secrecy."

"Therefore without accountability?"

"I repeat. We seek *nothing* for ourselves!"

"Then why the secrecy?"

"It's necessary, for although our decisions are arrived at dispassionately for the good of the country, they're not always pleasant or, in the eyes of many, even defensible. Yet they *were* for the good of the nation."

" 'Even defensible'?" repeated Payton, astonished at what he was hearing.

"I'll give you an example. Years ago our immediate predecessors were faced with a government tyrant who had visions of reshaping the laws of the country. A man named John Edgar Hoover, a giant who became obsessed in his old age, who had gone beyond the bounds of rationality, blackmailing presidents and senators—decent men—with his raw files, which were rampant with gossip and innuendo. Inver Brass had him eliminated before he brought the executive and the legislative, in essence the government, to its knees. And then a young writer named Peter Chancellor surfaced and came too close to the truth. It was he and his intolerable manuscript that caused the demise of Inver Brass then—but could not prevent its resurrection."

"Oh, my *God*!" exclaimed the director of Special Projects softly. "Good and evil, decided solely by you, sentences pronounced *only* by you. A legend of arrogance."

"That's unfair! There was no other solution. You're wrong!"

"It's the truth." Payton stood up, pushing the chair behind him. "I've nothing more to say, Dr. Winters. I'll leave now."

"What are you going to do?"

"What has to be done. I'm filing a report for the President, the Attorney General and the congressional oversight committees. That's the *law*. . . . You're out of business, Doctor. And don't bother to see me to the door, I'll find my way."

Payton walked out into the cold gray morning air. He

breathed deeply, trying to fill his lungs but was unable to do so. There was too much weariness, too much that was sad and offensive—on Christmas Eve. He reached the steps and started down to his car when suddenly, shattering the grounds, was a loud report—a *gunshot.* Payton's driver lunged out of the car, crouching in the drive, his weapon steadied by both hands.

MJ slowly shook his head and continued toward the back door of the vehicle. He was drained. There were no reservoirs of strength to draw from; his exhaustion was complete. Neither was there now the urgency to fly out to California. Inver Brass was finished, its leader dead by his own hand. Without the stature and authority of Samuel Winters, it was in shambles and the manner of his death would send the message of collapse to those who remained. . . . Evan Kendrick? He had to be told the whole story, all sides of it, and make up his own mind. But it could wait—a day at least. All MJ could think of as the driver opened the door for him was to get home, have several more drinks than were good for him, and sleep.

"Mr. Payton," said the driver, "you had a radio Code Five, sir."

"What was the message?"

" 'Reach San Jacinto. Urgent.' "

"Return to Langley, please."

"Yes, sir."

"Oh, in case I forget. Have a Merry Christmas."

"Thank you, sir."

44

"We'll look in on him at least once an hour, Miss Rashad," said the middle-aged navy nurse behind the counter. "Rest assured of it. . . . Did you know the President himself called the Congressman this afternoon?"

"Yes, I was there. And speaking of phones, there are to be no calls put through to his room."

"We understand. Here's the note; it's a copy of the one each operator has at the switchboard. All calls are to be referred to you at the Westlake Hotel."

"That's correct. Thank you very much."

"It's a pity, isn't it? Here it is Christmas Eve, and instead of being with friends and singing carols or whatever, he's bandaged up in a hospital and you're stuck by yourself in a hotel room."

"I'll tell you something, Nurse. The fact that he's here and alive makes it the best Christmas I could ever hope to have."

"I know, dear. I've seen you two together."

"Take care of him. If I don't get some sleep, he won't consider me much of a present in the morning."

"He's our number one patient. And you rest, young lady. You look a mite haggard and that's a medical opinion."

"I'm a mess is what I am."

"In my best days I should be such a mess."

"You're sweet," said Khalehla, putting her hand on the nurse's arm and squeezing it. "Good night. See you tomorrow."

"Merry Christmas, dear."

"It *is*. And have a merry one yourself." Rashad walked down the white corridor to the bank of elevators and pressed the lower button. She had meant it about needing sleep; except for a brief twenty minutes when both she and Evan dozed off, she had not closed her eyes in nearly forty-eight hours. A hot shower, a warm room-service meal, and bed was the order of the night. In the morning she would shop in one of those stores that stayed open for the benefit of errant people who had forgotten someone and buy a few silly presents for her . . . intended? My God, she thought. For my *fiancé*. Too much.

It was funny, though, how Christmas undeniably brought out the gentler, kinder aspects of human nature—regardless of race, creed, or lack of both. The nurse, for instance. She *was* sweet, and probably a rather lonely woman with too large a body and a pudgy face unlikely to be chosen for a Wave poster. Yet she had tried to be warm and kind. She had said that she knew how the Congressman's lady felt because she had seen them together. She had not. Khalehla remembered every person who had come into Evan's room and the nurse was not one of them. Kindness . . . reaching out, whatever one cared to call it, it was Christmas. And her man was safe. The elevator doors parted and she walked into the descending cage feeling secure and warm and kind.

Kendrick opened his eyes to the darkness. Something had awakened him . . . what was it? The door to his room? . . . Yes, of course, it was the door. Khalehla had told him he was going to be checked and rechecked all night long. Where did she think he would go? Out dancing? He sank back into the pillow, breathing deeply, no strength in him, all energy elusive. . . . *No.* It was not the door. It was a presence. Someone was there in the room!

Slowly he moved his head, inch by inch on the pillow. There was a blurred splash of white in the dark, no upper or lower extensions, just a dull space of white in the darkness.

"Who is it?" he said, finding his barely audible voice. "Who's there?"

Silence.

"Who the hell *are* you? What do you *want*?"

Then, like a rushing onslaught, the white mass came toward him out of the dark and crashed into his face. A *pillow.* He could not *breathe*! He swung his right hand up, pushing against a muscular arm, then sliding off the flesh into a face, a soft face, then into the scalp of . . . *woman's* hair! He yanked the strands in his grip with all the strength he could summon, rolling to the right on the narrow hospital bed, pulling his predator down to the floor beneath him. He released the hair and hammered the face under him, his shoulder in torment, the sutures broken, blood spreading through the bandages. He tried to yell, but all that emerged was a throated cry. The heavy woman clawed at his neck, her fingers sharp, heard points breaking his skin . . . then up into his eyes, tearing his lids and scraping his forehead. He surged up, spinning out of her grip, beyond her reach, crashing into the wall. The pain was intolerable. He lurched toward the door, but she was on him, hurling him into the side of the bed. His hand struck the carafe of water on the table; he grabbed it, and, spinning again, swung it up into the head, into the maniacal face above him. The woman was stunned; he rushed forward, throwing his right shoulder into her heavy body, smashing her into the wall, then lunged for the door and yanked it open. The white antiseptic hall was bathed in dim gray light except for a bright lamp behind the floor counter halfway down the corridor. He tried again to scream.

"*Someone . . . ! Help* me!" The words were lost; only guttural, muted cries came out of his mouth. He limped, his swollen ankle and damaged leg barely able to support him. Where *was* everybody? No one was there . . . no one behind the counter! Then two nurses came casually through a door at the far end of the hallway, and he raised his right hand, waving it frantically as the words finally came. "*Help me . . . !*"

"Oh, my *God*!" screamed one of the women as both rushed forward. Simultaneously, Kendrick heard another set of racing feet. He spun around only to watch helplessly as the heavy, muscular nurse ran out of his room and down the hall to a door beneath a red-lettered EXIT sign. She crashed it open and disappeared.

"Call the doctor down in emergency!" cried the navy nurse who reached him first. "*Hurry.* He's bleeding all over the place!"

"Then I'd better reach the Rashad girl," said the second nurse, heading for the counter. "She's to be called with any change of status, and, *Jesus,* this is certainly that!"

"*No!*" yelled Evan, his voice at last a clear, if breathless, roar. "Leave her alone!"

"But Congressman—"

"Please do as I say. *Don't call her!* She hasn't slept in two or three days. Just get the doctor and help me back to my room. . . . Then I have to use the phone."

Forty-five minutes later, his shoulder resutured and his face and neck cleaned up, Kendrick sat in bed, the telephone in his lap, and dialed the number in Washington he had committed to memory. Against strenuous objections, he had ordered the doctor and the nurses not to call the military police or even the hospital's security. It had been established that no one on the floor knew the heavyset woman other than a name, obviously false, through transfer papers; which had been presented that afternoon from the base hospital in Pensacola, Florida. Ranking officer nurses were coveted additions to any staff; no one questioned her arrival and no one would stop her in her swift departure. And until the whole picture was clearer, there could be no official investigations triggering new stories in the media. The blackout was still in effect.

"Sorry to wake you, Mitch—"

"*Evan?*"

"You'd better know what happened." Kendrick described the all too real nightmare he had lived through, including his decision to avoid the police, civilian and military. "Maybe I was wrong, but I figured the moment she reached that exit door there wasn't much chance of getting her and every chance of hitting the papers if they tried."

"You were right," agreed Payton, speaking rapidly. "She was a hired gun—"

"Pillow," corrected Evan.

"Every bit as lethal if you hadn't woken up. The point is, hired killers plan ahead, usually with several different exits and an equal number of changes of clothes. You did the right thing."

"Who hired her, Mitch?"

"I'd say it's pretty obvious. Grinell did. He's been a malignantly busy man since he got off that island."

"What do you mean? Khalehla didn't tell me."

"Khalehla, as you call her, doesn't know. She has enough stress with you on her hands. How is she taking tonight?"

"She hasn't been told. I wouldn't let them call her."

"She'll be furious."

"At least she'll get some sleep. What about Grinell?"

"Ardis Vanvlanderen's lawyer is dead and the ledger is nowhere to be found. Grinell's people got to San Jacinto first."

"*Goddamnit!*" shouted Kendrick hoarsely. "We've lost it!"

"It would appear so, but there's something that doesn't quite add up. . . . Do you recall my telling you that all Grinell needed in order to know we were closing in was someone watching the attorney's house?"

"Certainly."

"Gingerbread found him."

"*And?*"

"If they did get that book, why station a lookout after the fact? Indeed, why risk it?"

"Force the lookout to tell you! Drug him up, you've done it before."

"Gingerbread thinks not."

"*Why* not?"

"Two reasons. The man may be a low-scale watchman who knows absolutely nothing, and second, Gingerbread wants to follow him."

"You mean this Gingerbread found the lookout but the lookout doesn't know it?"

"I told you he was good. Grinell's man doesn't even know we found the dead lawyer. All he saw was a company truck and two gardeners in Green Thumb coveralls who proceeded to mow the lawns."

"But if the lookout's so low-scale, what will Gingerbread—Christ, that's a dumb name—what will he learn by following him?"

"I said he *may* be low-scale with only a relay telephone number to call periodically that wouldn't tell us anything. On the other hand, he may *not* be. If he's upscale he could lead us to others."

"For God's sake, Mitch, drug him and find out!"

"You're not following me, Evan. A relay phone is called *periodically* . . . at specific times. If the schedule's broken, we send Grinell the wrong message."

"You're all convoluted fruitcakes," said a weakened, exasperated Kendrick.

"It's not much of a living, either. . . . I'll have a couple of shore patrols placed at your door. Try to get some rest."

"What about you? I know you said you couldn't fly out here and now I understand why, but you're still at the office, aren't you?"

"Yes, I'm waiting to hear from Gingerbread. I can work faster from here."

"You don't want to talk about yesterday morning—about your meeting with the honcho from that Inver Brass?"

"Perhaps tomorrow. It's no longer urgent. Without him there is no Inver Brass."

"Without him?"

"He killed himself. . . . Merry Christmas, Congressman."

Khalehla Rashad dropped the packages in her arms and screamed. "What *happened*?" she cried, rushing to the bed.

"Medicare's a bunch of bullshit," replied Evan.

"That's not *funny*! . . . The SPs at your door and the way they looked at my ID downstairs when I said I was coming to see you—what *happened*?"

He told her, omitting the parts about the replaced stitches and the blood in the hallway. "Mitch agrees with what I did."

"I'll have his *head*!" yelled Khalehla. "He should have *called* me!"

"Then you wouldn't look as lovely as you do. The shadows around your eyes are only half black. You slept."

"Twelve hours," she admitted, sitting on the edge of the bed. "That *sweet* pudgy *nurse*? I can't believe it!"

"I could have used some of your black belt, first class, training. I don't make a point of fighting very often, and hardly ever with women—except hookers who overcharge."

"Remind me never to let you pay. . . . Oh, *God,* Evan, I knew I should have insisted on a larger room with two beds and *stayed* with you!"

"Don't carry this protective routine too far, kid. I *am* the man, remember?"

"And you remember that if we're ever mugged, let *me* make the moves, all right?"

"There goeth all my masculine pride. . . . Be my guest, just feed me bonbons and champagne while you beat the hell out of the bastards."

"Only a man could even joke like that," said Rashad, bending down and kissing him. "I *love* you so, that's my problem."

"Not mine." They kissed again and quite naturally the telephone rang. "Don't yell!" he insisted. "It's probably Mitch." It was.

"*Breakthrough!*" exclaimed the director of Special Projects from Langley, Virginia. "Has Evan told you? About Grinell?"

"No, nothing."

"Put him on, he can explain things to you—"

"Why didn't you *call* me last night—this morning?"

"*Put* him on!"

"Yes, sir."

"What is it, Mitch?"

"The break we've needed—we've got it!"

"Gingerbread?"

"Oddly enough, no. From an entirely different source. You look for crazy things in this business and sometimes you find them. On an outside chance we sent a man to the offices of Mrs. Vanvlanderen's attorney with a mocked-up document permitting him access to the files of the Vice President's late chief of staff. In her employer's absence the secretary wasn't about to let anyone prowl around the files, so she called the San Jacinto house. Knowing she wouldn't get an answer, our man hung in there for a couple of hours playing the angry Washington official with orders from the National Security Council while she kept trying to reach the lawyer. Apparently she was genuinely upset; he was supposed to be in an all-day conference out there with important clients. . . . Whether it was frustration or self-defense that made her say it, we don't know and don't care, but she blurted out the fact that our man probably wanted all those confidential pages she'd Xeroxed, but he couldn't get them anyway because they were all in a safety box down in a bank vault."

"*Bingo,*" said Evan quietly, inwardly shouting.

"Unquestionably. She even described the ledger. . . . Our astute attorney was perfectly willing to sell Grinell the book, then proceed to blackmail him with the copy. Grinell's lookout was in San Jacinto for simple curiosity, nothing more, and the ledger will be ours within the hour."

"Get it, Mitch, and break it down! Look for a man named Hamendi, Abdel Hamendi."

"The arms dealer," said Payton, confirming the information. "Adrienne told me. The photographs in Vanvlanderen's apartment—Lausanne, Amsterdam."

"That's the one. They'll use a code name for him, of course, but trace the money, the transfers in Geneva and Zurich—the Gemeinschaft Bank in Zurich."

"Naturally."

"There's something else, Mitch. Let's clean house as much as we can. A man like Hamendi supplies arms to all the fanatic splinter groups he can find, each side killing the other with what he sells them. Then he looks for other killers, the ones in thousand-dollar suits and sitting in plush offices whose only cause is money, and he brings them into his network. . . . Production increases ten times what it was, then twenty, and there's more killing, more causes to sell to, more fanatics to fuel. . . . Let's take him out, Mitch. Let's give a part of this screwed-up world a chance to breathe—without his supplies."

"It's a tall order, Evan."

"Give me a few weeks to get patched together, then send me back to Oman."

"*What?*"

"I'm going to make the biggest purchase of weapons Hamendi ever dreamed of."

Sixteen days passed, Christmas a painful memory, the New Year greeted cautiously, with suspicion. On the fourth day Evan had visited Emilio Carallo and given him a photograph of a fine new fishing boat, along with its ownership papers, a prepaid course for his captain's license, a bankbook, and a guarantee that no one from the island of Passage to China would ever bother him in El Descanso. It was the truth; of the selected brethren of the inner government who had conferred on that insidious government's island, none cared to acknowledge it. Instead, they huddled with their batteries of lawyers, and several had fled the country. They were not concerned with a crippled fisherman in El Descanso. They were concerned with saving their lives and their fortunes.

On the eighth day the ground swell came out of Chicago and rolled through the Middle West. It started with four independent newspapers within a sixty-mile radius editorially proposing the candidacy of Congressman Evan Kendrick for the vice presidential nomination. Within seventy-two hours three more were added, in addition to six television stations owned by five of the papers. Proposals became endorsements and the voices of the journalistic turtles were heard in the land. From New York to Los Angeles, Bismarck to Houston, Boston to Miami, the brotherhood of media giants began studying the concept, and the editors of *Time* and *Newsweek* called emergency meetings. Kendrick was moved to an isolated wing of the base hospital and his name removed from the roster of patients. In Washington, Annie Mulcahy O'Reilly and the staff informed hundreds of callers that the representative from Colorado was out of the country and not available for comment.

On the eleventh day the Congressman and his lady returned to Mesa Verde, where to their astonishment they found Emmanuel Weingrass, a small cylinder of oxygen strapped to his side in case of a respiratory emergency, overseeing an army of carpenters repairing the house. Manny's pace was slower and he sat down a great deal, but his illness had no effect on his ever present irascibility. It was a constant; the only time he lowered his voice even a decibel was when he spoke with Khalehla—his "lovely new daughter, worth much more than the bum who is always hanging around."

On the fifteenth day Mitchell Payton, working with a young computer genius he had borrowed from Frank Swann at State, broke the codes of Grinell's ledger, the bible according to the inner government. Working through the night with Gerald Bryce at the keyboard, the two men compiled a report for President Langford Jennings, who told them exactly how many printouts were to be made. One additional report rolled out of the word processor before the disk was destroyed, but MJ was not aware of it.

One by one the limousines arrived at night, not at a darkened estate on Chesapeake Bay but instead at the south portico of the White House. The passengers were escorted by marine guards to the Oval Office of the President of the United States. Langford Jennings sat behind his desk, his feet on a favorite ottoman to the left of his chair, acknowledging with a nod everyone who came—all but one. Vice President Orson Bollinger was simply stared at, no greeting extended, only contempt. The chairs were arranged in a semicircle in front of the desk and the awesome man behind it. Included in the entourage, each carrying a single manila envelope, were the majority and minority leaders of both houses of Congress, the Acting Secretary of State and the Secretary of Defense, the directors of the Central Intelligence and the

National Security agencies, the members of the Joint Chiefs of Staff, the Attorney General and Mitchell Jarvis Payton, Special Projects, CIA. All sat down and waited in silence. The waiting was not long.

"We're in a pile of deep shit," said the President of the United States. "How it happened I'll be damned if I know, but I'd better get some answers tonight or I'll see a number of people in this town spending twenty years on a rock pile. Do I make myself clear?"

There was a scattered nodding of heads, but more than a few objected, angry faces and voices resenting the President's implications.

"*Hold* on!" continued Jennings, quieting the dissenters. "I want the ground rules thoroughly understood. Each of you has received and presumably read the report prepared by Mr. Payton. You've all brought it with you and again presumably, as ordered, none of you has made copies. Are these statements accurate? . . . Please answer individually, starting on my left with the Attorney General."

Each of the assembled group repeated the action and the words of the nation's chief law enforcement officer. Each held up the manila envelope and said, "No copies, Mr. President."

"Good." Jennings removed his feet from the ottoman and leaned forward, his forearms on the desk. "The envelopes are numbered, gentlemen, and limited to the number of people in this room. Furthermore, they will remain in this room when you leave. Again, understood?" The nods and the mutterings were affirmative. "Good. . . . I don't have to tell you that the information contained in these pages is as devastating as it is incredible. A network of thieves and killers and human garbage who hired killers and paid for the services of *terrorists.* Wholesale slaughter in Fairfax, in Colorado—and, oh my God—on Cyprus, where a man worth any five of you bastards was blown up with his whole delegation. . . . It's a litany of horrors; of boardrooms across the country in constant collusion, of setting prices for outrageous margins of profit, buying influence in all sectors of the government, turning the nation's defense industry into a grab bag of riches. It's also a litany of deceptions, of illegal transactions with arms merchants all over the world, lying to armaments control committees, buying licenses for export, rerouting shipments where they're disallowed. *Christ,* it's a fucking mess! . . . And there's not one of you here that isn't touched by it. Now, did I hear a few objections?"

"*Mr.* President—"

"Mr. *President*—"

"I've spent thirty years in the *Corps* and no one has ever *dared*—"

"*I* dare!" roared Jennings. "And who the hell are you to tell me I can't? Anyone *else*?"

"Yes, Mr. President," replied the Secretary of Defense. "To indulge in your language, I don't know what the *fuck* you're specifically alluding to and I object to your innuendos."

"Specifics? *Innuendos?* Screw you, Mac, read the figures! Three million dollars for a tank that's estimated to cost roughly one million five to produce? *Thirty* million for fighter aircraft that's been so overloaded with Pentagon goodies it can't perform, then goes back to the drawing board and another *ten* million per machine? Forget the toilet seats and the goddamned wrenches, you've got much bigger problems."

"They're all minor expenditures compared to the totality, Mr. President."

"As a friend of mine said on television, tell that to the poor son of a bitch who has to balance a checkbook. Maybe you're in the wrong job, Mr. Secretary. We keep telling the country that the Soviet economy is in shambles, its technology light-years behind ours, and yet every year when you produce a budget, you tell us we're up shit's creek because Russia's outperforming *us* economically and technologically. There's a slight contradiction there, wouldn't you say?"

"You don't understand the complexities—"

"I don't have to. I understand the contradictions. . . . And what about you, you four glorious stalwarts from the House and Senate—members of my party and the loyal opposition? You never *smelled* anything?"

"You're an extremely popular President," said the leader of the opposition. "It's politically difficult to oppose your positions."

"Even when the fish is rotten?"

"Even when the fish is rotten, sir."

"Then you should get out, too. . . . And our astute military elite, our Olympian Joint Chiefs of Staff. Who's watching the goddamned store, or are you so rarefied you forgot the address of the Pentagon? Colonels, generals, admirals, marching in lockstep out of Arlington into the ranks of defense contractors and selling the taxpayers down the drain."

"I *object*!" shouted the chairman of the JCS, spitting through his capped teeth. "It's not our job, Mr. President, to keep tabs on every officer's employment in the private sector."

"Perhaps not, but your approval of recommendations makes damned sure who gets the rank that *makes* it possible. . . . And how about the country's superspies, the CIA and the NSA? Mr. Payton here excluded—and if any of you try to railroad him to Siberia, you'll answer to me for the next five years—where the hell were *you*? Arms sent all over the Mediterranean and the Persian Gulf—to ports the Congress and I said were off *limits*! You couldn't trace the *traffic*? Who the hell was on the *switch*?"

"In a number of cases, Mr. President," said the director of the Central Intelligence Agency, "when we had reason to question certain activities, we assumed they were being carried out with your authority, for they reflected your policy positions. Where the laws were involved we believed you were being advised by the Attorney General, as is the accepted procedure."

"So you shut your eyes and said 'Let Joe Blow handle the pot of hot potatoes.' Very commendable for saving your ass, but why didn't you check with *me*?"

"Speaking for the NSA," broke in the director of the National Security Agency, "we spoke several times with both your chief of staff and your National Security adviser about several unorthodox developments that came across our desks. Your NSC adviser insisted that he knew nothing about what he termed 'vicious rumors,' and Mr. Dennison claimed they were—and I quote him accurately, Mr. President—'a bunch of shit spread by ultraliberal wimps taking cheap shots at you.' Those were his words, sir."

"You'll notice," remarked Jennings coldly, "that neither of those men is in this room. My NSC adviser has retired, and my chief of staff is on leave tending to personal business. In Herb Dennison's defense, he may have run a tight, pretty autocratic ship, but his navigation wasn't always accurate. . . . Now we come to our chief law enforcement officer, the guardian of our nation's legal system. Considering the laws that were broken, bent and circumvented, I have the idea that you went out to lunch three years ago and never came back. What are you running over at Justice? Bingo games or jai alai? Why are we paying several hundred lawyers over there to look into criminal activities against the government and not *one* of the goddamned crimes listed in this report was ever uncovered?"

"They were not in our purview, Mr. President. We've concentrated on—"

"What the hell is a *purview*? Corporate price-fixing and outrageous overruns aren't in your *purview*? Let me tell you something, whack-a-doo, they damn well *better* be! . . . To hell with you, let's turn to my esteemed running mate—the last is by far not the least in terms of vital importance. Our groveling, sniveling tool of *very* special interests is the big man on the *campus*! They're all your *boys,* Orson! How could you *do* it?"

"Mr. President, they're *your* men, too! They raised the money for your first campaign. They raised millions more than your opposition, virtually assuring your election. You espoused their causes, supported their cries for the unencumbered expansion of business and industry—"

"Reasonably unencumbered, *yes,*" said Jennings, the veins in his forehead pronounced, "but not *manipulated.* Not *corrupted* by dealings with arms merchants all over Europe and the Mediterranean, and, *goddamn* you, not by collusion, extortion and terrorists for *hire*!"

"I knew *nothing* about such things!" screamed Bollinger, leaping to his feet.

"No, you probably didn't, Mr. Vice President, because you were an all too easy mark peddling influence for them to risk their losing you through panic. But you sure as hell knew there was a lot more fat in the fire than there was smoke in the kitchen. You just didn't want to know what was burning and smelling so rotten. Sit *down*!" Bollinger sat, and Jennings continued. "But get this clear, Orson. You're not on the ticket and I don't want you near the convention. You're out, *finished,* and if I ever learn that you're peddling again or sitting on a board other than for charity . . . well, just don't."

"*Mr.* President!" said the leather-faced chairman of the Joint Chiefs as he stood up. "In light of your remarks and all too obvious disposition, I tender my resignation, effective immediately!"

The declaration was followed by half a dozen others, all standing and emphatic. Langford Jennings leaned back in his chair and spoke calmly, his voice chilling. "Oh, no, you're not getting off that easy, any of you. There's not going to be a reverse Saturday-night massacre in this administration, no crawling off the ship and into the hills. You're going to stay right where you are and make damned sure we get back on course. . . . Understand me clearly, I don't care what people think of me or you or the house I'm temporarily occupying, but I do care about the country, I care about it deeply. So deeply, in fact, that this preliminary report—preliminary because it isn't finished by a long shot—is going to remain the sole property of this President under the statutes of executive nondisclosure until I think the time is right to release it . . . which it *will* be. To release it now would cripple the strongest presidency this nation has had in forty years and do irreparable damage to the country, but I repeat, it *will* be released. . . . Let me explain something to you. When a man, and I trust someday a woman, reaches this office, there's only one thing left, and that's his mark on history. Well, I'm taking myself out of that race for immortality within the next five years of my life, because during that time this *completed* report, with all its horrors, will be made public. . . . But not until every wrong committed on my watch has been righted, every crime paid for. If that means working night and day, then that's what you're all going to do—all but my pandering, sycophantic Vice President, who's going to fade away and with any luck will have the grace to blow his brains out. . . . A final word, gentlemen. Should any of you be tempted to jump this rotten ship we've all created by omission *and* commission, please remember that I'm the President of the United States with incredible powers. In the broadest sense they include life and death—that's merely a statement of fact, but if you care to take it as a threat . . . well, that's your privilege. Now, get out of here and start thinking. Payton, you stay."

"Yes, Mr. President."

"Did they get the message, Mitch?" asked Jennings, pouring himself and Payton a drink from a bar recessed in the left wall of the Oval Office.

"Let's put it this way," replied the director of Special Projects. "If I don't have that whisky in a matter of seconds, I'm going to start shaking again."

The President grinned his famous grin as he brought Payton's drink to him at the window. "Not bad for a guy who's supposedly got the IQ of a telephone pole, huh?"

"It was an extraordinary performance, sir."

"That's what this office has been largely reduced to, I'm afraid."

"I didn't mean it that way, Mr. President."

"Of course you did and you're right. It's why the king, with all his clothes on or naked, needs a strong prime minister who, in turn, creates his own royal family—from both parties, incidentally."

"I beg your pardon?"

"Kendrick. I want him on the ticket."

"Then you'll have to convince him, I'm afraid. According to my niece—I call her my niece but she's not really—"

"I know all about it, all about her," interrupted Jennings. "What does she say?"

"That Evan's perfectly aware of what's happened—what's happening—but hasn't made up his mind. His closest friend, Emmanuel Weingrass, is extremely ill and not expected to live."

"I'm aware of that, too. You didn't use his name but it's in your report, remember?"

"Oh, sorry. I haven't had much sleep lately. I forget things. . . . At any rate, Kendrick insists on going back to Oman, and I can't dissuade him. He's obsessed with the arms merchant Abdel Hamendi. He quite rightly believes that Hamendi's selling at least eighty percent of all the firepower used in the Middle East and Southwest Asia, destroying his beloved Arab countries. In his way, he's like a modern-day Lawrence, trying to rescue his friends from international contempt and ultimate oblivion."

"What exactly does he think he can accomplish?"

"From what he's told me, it's basically a sting operation. I don't think it's clear to him yet, but the objective is. That's to expose Hamendi for what he is, a man who makes millions upon millions by selling death to anyone who'll buy it."

"What makes Evan believe Hamendi gives a damn what his buyers think of him? He's in the arms business, not evangelism."

"He might if more than half the weapons he's sold do not function, if the explosives don't explode, and the guns don't fire."

"Good *God,*" whispered the President, turning slowly and walking back to his desk. He sat down and placed his glass on the blotter, staring in silence at the far wall. Finally, he turned in his chair and looked up at Payton by the window. "Let him go, Mitch. He'd never forgive either one of us if we stopped him. Give him everything he needs, but make goddamned sure he comes back. . . . I want him back. The country needs him back."

Across the world, pockets of mist drifted in from the Persian Gulf, blanketing Bahrain's Tujjar Road, causing inverted halos beneath the street-lamps and obscuring the night sky above. It was precisely four-thirty in the morning as a black limousine intruded upon this deserted waterfront section of the sleeping city. It came to a stop in front of the glass doors of the building known as the Sahalhuddin, until sixteen months ago the princely high chambers of the man-monster who called himself the Mahdi. Two robed Arabs emerged from rear doors of the imposing vehicle and walked into the wash of dull neon lights that illuminated the entrance; the limousine quietly drove away. The taller man tapped softly on the glass; inside, the guard at the reception desk glanced at his wristwatch, got out of his chair and walked rapidly to the door. He unlocked it and bowed to the odd-hour visitors.

"All is prepared, great sirs," he said, his voice at first barely above a whisper. "The outside guards have been granted early dismissal; the morning shift arrives at six o'clock."

"We'll need less than half that time," said the younger, shorter visitor, obviously the leader. "Has your well-paid preparedness included an unlocked door upstairs?"

"Most assuredly, great sir."

"And only one elevator is in use?" asked the older, taller Arab.

"Yes, sir."

"We'll lock it above." The shorter man started toward the bank of elevators on the right, his companion instantly catching up with him. "If I'm correct," he continued, speaking loudly, "we walk up the final flight of stairs, is that so?"

"Yes, great sir. All the alarms have been disengaged and the room restored exactly as it was . . . before that terrible morning. Also, as instructed, the item you requested has been brought up; it was in the cellars. You may be aware, sir, that the authorities tore the room apart, then sealed it for many months. We could not understand, great sir."

"It wasn't necessary that you did. . . . You will alert us if anyone seeks entrance into the building or even approaches the doors."

"With the eyes of a hawk, great sir!"

"Try the telephone, please." The two men reached the elevators and the taller subordinate pressed the button; a panel opened immediately. They walked inside and the door closed. "Is that man competent?" asked the shorter Arab as the machinery whirred and the elevator began its ascent.

"He does what he is told to do and what he has been told is not complicated. . . . Why was the Mahdi's office sealed for so many months?"

"Because the authorities were looking for men like us, waiting for men like us."

"They tore the room apart . . . ?" said the subordinate hesitantly, questioningly.

"As with us, they did not know where to look." The elevator slowed down, then stopped and the panel opened. With quickening steps the two visitors walked to the staircase that led to the Mahdi's floor and former "temple." They reached the office door and the shorter man stopped, his hand on the knob. "I've waited over a year for this moment," he said, breathing deeply. "Now that it's arrived, I'm trembling."

Inside the huge, strange mosquelike room with its high domed ceiling filled with brilliantly colored mosaic tiles, the two intruders stood in silence, as if in the presence of some awesome spirit. The sparse furniture of dark burnished wood was in place like ancient statues of ferocious soldiers guarding the inner tomb of a great pharaoh; the outsized desk was symbolic of the sarcophagus of a dead revered ruler. And standing against the far right wall, in clashing contradiction, was a modern metal scaffold rising to a height of eight feet, side bars permitting access to the top. The taller Arab spoke.

"This could be Allah's resting place—may His will be done."

"You didn't know the Mahdi, my innocent friend, on both counts," replied the associate's superior. "Try the Phrygian Midas. . . . Quickly now, we waste time. Move the scaffold to where I tell you, then climb above." The subordinate walked rapidly to the raised platform and looked back at his companion. "To the left," continued the leader. "Just beyond the second slit of the window."

"I don't understand you," said the tall man, stepping on the slip clamps and climbing to the top of the scaffold.

"There are many things you don't understand and there's no reason why you should. . . . Now, count to the left, six tiles from the window seam, and then five above."

"Yes, *yes* . . . it is a stretch for me and I am not short."

"The Mahdi was far taller, far more impressive—but not without his faults."

"I beg your pardon?"

"No matter. . . . Press the four corners of the tile at the very edges, then force the palm of your hand with all your strength into the center. *Now!*"

The mosaic tile literally burst from its recess; it was all the tall Arab could do to hold on to it without falling. "Beloved *Allah*!" he exclaimed.

"Simple suction balanced by weights," said the shorter man

below without elaboration. "Now reach inside and withdraw the papers; they should all be together." The subordinate did as he was told, pulling out layered sheets of an extensive computer printout held together by two rubber bands. "Drop them to me," continued the leader, "and replace the tile exactly as you removed it, starting first with pressure in the center."

The tall Arab awkwardly carried out his orders, then climbed down the scaffold's crossbars onto the floor. He approached his superior, who had unfolded several sheets of the printout and was scanning them intensely. "This was the treasure you spoke of?" he asked softly.

"From the Persian Gulf to the western shores of the Mediterranean, there is no greater," answered the younger man, his eyes racing across the papers. "They executed the Mahdi, but they could not destroy what he created. Retreat was necessary, retrenchment demanded—but not dismemberment. The myriad branches of the enterprise were neither crushed nor even exposed. They merely fell away and returned to the earth, ready to sprout trunks of their own one day."

"Those odd-looking pages tell you that?" The superior nodded, still reading. "What in Allah's name do they say?"

The shorter man looked curiously up at his taller companion. "Why not?" he said, smiling. "These are the lists of every man, every woman, every firm, company and corporation, every contact and conduit to the terrorists ever reached by the Mahdi. It will take months, perhaps several years, to put everything back together again, but it will be done. You see, they're waiting. For ultimately the Mahdi was right: this is *our* world. We will surrender it to no one."

"The word will *spread,* my friend!" cried the older, taller subordinate. "It will, will it *not*?"

"Very carefully," replied the young leader. "We live in different times," he added enigmatically. "Last week's equipment is obsolete."

"I cannot pretend to understand you."

"Again it's not necessary."

"Where do you *come* from?" asked the bewildered subordinate. "We are told to obey you, that you know things that men like me are not privileged to know. But *how,* from *where*?"

"From thousands of miles away, preparing for years for this moment. . . . Leave me now. Quickly. Go downstairs and tell the guard to have the scaffold removed to the cellars, then flag the car as it circles the street. The driver will take you home; we'll meet tomorrow. Same time, same place."

"May Allah and the Mahdi be with you," said the tall Arab, bowing and rushing out the door, closing it behind him.

The young man watched his companion leave, then reached under his robes and pulled out a small hand-held radio. He pressed a button and spoke. "He'll be outside in two or three minutes. Pick him up and drive to the rocks of the south coast. Kill him, strip him, and throw the gun into the sea."

"So ordered," replied the limousine's driver several streets away.

The youthful leader replaced the radio inside his robes and crossed solemnly toward the huge ebony desk. He removed his ghotra, dropping it on the floor as he walked to the thronelike chair and sat down. He opened a tall wide drawer on his lower left and lifted out the jewel-encrusted headdress of the Mahdi. He placed it on his head and spoke softly to the mosaic ceiling.

"I thank you, my Father," said the inheritor with a doctorate in computer sciences from the University of Chicago. "To be chosen among all your sons is both an honor and a challenge. My weak white mother will never understand, but as you incessantly made clear to me, she was merely a vessel. . . . However, I must tell you, Father, that things are different now. Subtlety and long-range objectives are the order of the times. We will employ your methods where they are called for—killing is no problem for us—but it is a far larger part of the globe that we seek than you ever sought. We will have cells in all of Europe and the Mediterranean, and we will communicate in ways you never thought of—secretly, by satellite, interception impossible. You see, my Father, the world no longer belongs to one race or another. It belongs to the young and the strong and the brilliant, and we are they."

The new Mahdi stopped whispering and lowered his eyes to the top of the desk. Soon what he needed would be there. The greater son of the great Mahdi would continue the march.

We must *control.*

Everywhere!

BOOK THREE

45

It was the thirty-second day since the wild departure from the island of Passage to China, and Emmanuel Weingrass walked slowly into the enclosed veranda in Mesa Verde; his words, however, were rushed. "Where's the bum?" he asked.

"Jogging in the south forty," replied Khalehla on the couch, having her morning coffee and reading the newspaper. "Or up in the mountains by now, who knows?"

"It's two o'clock in the afternoon in Jerusalem," said Manny.

"And four o'clock in Masqat," added Rashad. "They're all so clever over there."

"My daughter, the smart-mouth."

"Sit down, child," said Khalehla, patting the cushion beside her.

"Smarter-mouth infant," mumbled Weingrass, walking over and removing his short cylinder of oxygen to lower himself to the couch. "The bum looks good," continued Manny, leaning back and breathing heavily.

"You'd think he was training for the Olympics."

"Speaking of which, you got a cigarette?"

"You're not supposed to have one."

"So give."

"You're impossible." Khalehla reached into her bathrobe pocket, withdrew a pack of cigarettes and shook one up while reaching for a ceramic lighter on the coffee table. She lit Weingrass's cigarette and repeated, "You *are* impossible."

"And you're my Arab Mother Superior," said Manny, inhaling as though he were a child wallowing in a forbidden third dessert. "How are things in Oman?"

"My old friend the sultan is a little confused, but my younger friend his wife will straighten him out. . . . Incidentally, Ahmat sends you his best."

"He should. He owes me for his grades at Harvard, and he never paid me for the broads I got him in Los Angeles."

"Somehow you always get to the heart of things. . . . How is everyone in Jerusalem?"

"Speaking of sending regards, Ben-Ami sends you his."

"*Benny?*" cried Rashad, sitting forward. "Good Lord, I haven't thought of him in years! Does he still wear those silly designer blue jeans and strap his weapon back over his tail?"

"He probably always will and charge the Mossad double for both."

"He's a good guy and one of the best control agents Israel's ever had. We worked together in Damascus; he's small and a little cynical, but a good man to have on your side. Tough as nails, actually."

"As your bum would say, 'Tell me about it.' We were closing in on the hotel in Bahrain and all he did was give me lectures over the radio."

"He'll join us in Masqat?"

"He'll join *you,* you not-very-nice person who has shut me out."

"Come on, Manny—"

"I know, I know. I'm a burden."

"What do *you* think?"

"All right, I'm a burden, but even burdens are kept informed."

"At least twice a day. Where's Ben-Ami going to meet us? And how? I can't imagine that the Mossad wants any part of this."

"After the Iranian mess the moon's too close, especially with CIA input and banks in Switzerland. Ben will leave a telephone number at the palace switchboard for a Miss Adrienne—my idea. . . . Also, someone's coming with him."

"Who?"

"A lunatic."

"That helps. Does he have a name?"

"Only one I knew was code Blue."

"*Azra!*"

"No, that was the other one."

"I know, but the Israeli killed Azra the Arabic Blue. Evan told me it sickened him, two kids with such hatred."

"With the kids it's all sickening. Instead of baseball bats, they carry repeating rifles and grenades. . . . Has Payton straightened out your transportation?"

"He worked it out with us yesterday. Air Force cargo to Frankfurt and on to Cairo, where we go under cover in small craft to Kuwait and Dubai, with the last leg by helicopter. We'll reach Oman at night, landing in the Jabal Sham, where one of Ahmat's unmarked cars will meet us and drive us to the palace."

"That's really underground," said Weingrass, nodding, impressed.

"It has to be. Evan's got to disappear while stories are planted that he was seen in Hawaii and is supposedly holed up at an estate on Maui. Graphics is working up some photos showing him over there and they'll hit the newspapers."

"Mitchell's imagination is improving."

"There's none better, Manny."

"Maybe he should run the Agency."

"No, he hates administrative work and he's a terrible politician. If he doesn't like someone or something, everybody knows it. He's better off where he is."

The sound of the front door opening and closing had an immediate effect on Weingrass. *"Oy!"* he cried, shoving his cigarette into the startled Khalehla's mouth and blowing away the smoke above him, waving his hands to move the incriminating evidence toward Rashad. "Naughty *shiksa*!" he whispered. "Smoking in my presence!"

"Impossible," said Khalehla softly, removing the cigarette and crushing it in an ashtray as Kendrick walked through the living room and onto the porch.

"She'd *never* smoke that close to you," admonished Evan, dressed in a blue sweat suit, perspiration rolling down his face.

"Now you've got the ears of a Doberman?"

"And you've got the brains of a hooked snapper."

"Very smart fish."

"Sorry," said Rashad calmly. "He can be terribly demanding."

"Tell me about it."

"What did I just say?" shouted Weingrass. "He says that all the time. It's the sign of a highly developed, misplaced superiority complex and very irritating to really superior intellects. . . . Have a good workout, dummy?"

Kendrick smiled and walked to the bar, where there was a pitcher of orange juice. "I'm up to thirty minutes, heavy pace," he answered, pouring himself a glass of juice.

"That's very nice if you're a cowboy's quarter horse on a roundup."

"He says things like that all the time," protested Kendrick. "It's aggravating."

"Tell me about it," Khalehla replied, drinking her coffee.

"Any calls?" asked Evan.

"It's barely past seven, darling."

"Not in Zurich. It's past one in the afternoon over there. I was talking to them before I went out."

"Talking to whom?" asked Rashad.

"Mainly to the director of the Gemeinschaft Bank. Mitch scared his bladder dry with the information we have and he's trying to cooperate. . . . Wait a minute. Did anyone check the telex in the study?"

"No, but I heard the damn thing clacking away about twenty minutes ago," said Weingrass.

Kendrick put down his glass and walked rapidly out of the porch and across the living room to a door beyond the stone hallway. Khalehla and Manny watched him, then looked at each and shrugged. Within moments the Congressman returned, gripping a telex sheet in his hand, his expression conveying his excitement. "They *did* it!" he exclaimed.

"Who did what?" asked Weingrass.

"The bank. You remember the fifty-million line of credit Grinell and his consortium of thieves in California set up for my buy-out?"

"My *God,*" exclaimed Khalehla. "They couldn't have left it *standing*!"

"Of course not. It was canceled the moment Grinell got off the island."

"*So?*" said Manny.

"In this age of complicated telecommunications, computer errors crop up now and then and a beaut was just made. There's no record of the cancellation having been received. The credit's *on;* only, it's been transferred to a sister bank in Bern with a new, coded account number. It's all there."

"They'll never pay!" Weingrass was emphatic.

"It'll be charged against their reserves, which are ten times fifty million."

"They'll *fight* it, Evan," insisted Khalehla, as emphatic as the old man.

"And parade themselves in the Swiss courts? Somehow I doubt it."

The Cobra helicopter without markings stuttered across the desert at an altitude of less than five hundred feet. Evan and Khalehla, exhausted from nearly twenty-six hours in the air and racing to covert connections on the ground, sat next to each other, Rashad's head on Kendrick's shoulder, his own slumped down into his chest; both were asleep. A man in belted khaki coveralls with no insignia walked out of the flight deck and down the fuselage. He shook Evan's arm in the dim light.

"We'll be there in about fifteen minutes, sir."

"Oh?" Kendrick snapped up his head, blinking his eyes and opening them wide to rid them of sleep. "Thanks. I'll wake my friend here; they always do things before arriving anywhere, don't they?"

"Not this 'they,' " said Khalehla out loud without moving. "I sleep to the very last minute."

"Well, forgive me, but I don't. I can't. Necessity calls."

"Men," remarked the agent from Cairo, removing her head from his shoulder and shifting to the other side of the seat and into the bulkhead. "No control," she added, her eyes still closed.

"We'll keep you posted," said the Air Force flight officer, laughing quietly and returning to the deck.

Sixteen minutes passed and the pilot spoke over the intercom. "Flare spotted directly ahead. Buckle up for touchdown, please." The helicopter decelerated and hovered over the ground, where the headlights of two automobiles facing each other had replaced the flare. Slowly, the chopper was lowered into its threshold. "Depart the aircraft as quickly as possible, please," continued the pilot. "We have to get out of here *fast,* if you catch my drift."

No sooner had they stepped down the metal ladder to the ground than the Cobra, its rotors thundering, rose in the night sky; it turned, stuttering in the desert moonlight, kicking up what sand there was, and headed north, accelerating rapidly, the noise receding in the darkness above. Walking into the beams of a car's headlights was the young sultan of Oman. He was in slacks, an open white shirt replacing the New England Patriots jersey he had worn that first night he had met with Evan in the desert sixteen months ago.

"Let me talk first, okay?" he said as Kendrick and Rashad approached.

"Okay," replied Kendrick.

"First reactions can be not too smart, agreed?"

"Agreed," agreed Evan.

"But I'm supposed to be smart, right?"

"Right."

"Still, consistency is the product of small minds, isn't that so?"

"Within reasonable boundaries."

"Don't qualify."

"Don't you play lawyer. The only bar you ever passed was with Manny in Los Angeles."

"Why, that hypocritical Israeli nut—"

"At least you didn't say Jew."

"I wouldn't. I don't like the sound of it any more than I like the sound of 'dirty Arab.' . . . Anyway, Manny and I didn't pass too many bars in L.A. that we didn't go into."

"What's your point, Ahmat?"

The young ruler breathed deeply and spoke quickly. "I know the whole story now and I feel like a damned idiot."

"The *whole* story?"

"Everything. That Inver Brass crowd, Bollinger's munitions bandits, that bastard Hamendi, who my royal Saudi brothers in Riyadh should have executed the moment they caught him . . . the whole ball of wax. And I should have known you wouldn't do what I thought you did. 'Commando Kendrick' versus the rotten Arab isn't you, it never *was* you. . . . I'm sorry, Evan." Ahmat walked forward and embraced the congressman from Colorado's Ninth District.

"You're going to make me cry," said Khalehla, smiling at the sight in front of her.

"*You,* you Cairo tigress!" cried the sultan, releasing Kendrick and taking Rashad in his arms. "We had a girl, you know. Half American, half Omani. Sound familiar?"

"I know. I wasn't permitted to contact you—"

"We understood."

"But I was so touched. Her name's Khalehla."

"If it weren't for you, Khalehla One, there'd be no Khalehla Two. . . . Come on, let's go." As they started for Ahmat's limousine the sultan turned to Evan. "You look pretty fit for a guy who's been through so much."

"I heal rapidly for an old man," said Kendrick. "Tell me something, Ahmat. Who told you the whole story, the whole 'ball of wax'?"

"A man named Payton, Mitchell Payton, CIA. Your President Jennings phoned me and said I was to expect a call from this Payton and would I please accept it, it was urgent. Hey, that Jennings is one charming character, isn't he? . . . Although I'm not sure he knew everything that Payton told me."

"Why do you say that?"

"I don't know, it was just a feeling." The young sultan stood by the car door and looked at Evan. "If you can pull this off, my friend, you'll do more for the Middle East and us on the Gulf than all the diplomats in ten United Nations."

"We're going to pull it off. But only with your help."

"You've got it."

Ben-Ami and code Blue walked down the narrow street into the Al Kabir bazaar looking for the outdoor café that served evening coffee. They were dressed in neat dark business suits, as befitted their Bahrainian visas, which stated that they were executives with the Bank of England in Manamah. They saw the sidewalk café, threaded their way through the crowds and the stalls, and sat at the empty table nearest the street as instructed. Three minutes later a tall man in white robes and Arab headdress joined them.

"Have you ordered coffee?" asked Kendrick.

"Nobody's come around," replied Ben-Ami. "It's a busy night. How are you, Congressman?"

"Let's try 'Evan,' or better yet, 'Amal.' I'm here, which in a way answers your question."

"And Weingrass?"

"Not very well, I'm afraid. . . . Hello, Blue?"

"Hello," said the young man, staring at Kendrick.

"You look very businesslike, very unmilitary in those clothes. I'm not sure I'd recognize you if I didn't know you were going to be here."

"I'm not military any longer. I had to leave the Brigade."

"It'll miss you."

"I miss it, but my wounds didn't heal properly—various tendons, they tell me. Azra was a good fighter, a good commando."

"Still the hatred?"

"There's no hatred in my voice. Anger, of course, over many things, but not hatred for the man I had to kill."

"What are you doing now?"

"I work for the government."

"He works for us," interrupted Ben-Ami. "For the Mossad."

"Speaking of which, Ahmat apologizes for not having you to the palace—"

"Is he *crazy*? All he needs is members of the Mossad in his house. It wouldn't do us much good if anyone found out, either."

"How much did Manny tell you?"

"With his big mouth, what didn't he tell me? He also called

after you left the States with more information that Blue was able to use."

"How, Blue? . . . Incidentally, do you have another name?"

"With respect, sir, not for an American. In consideration of us both."

"All right, I accept that. What did Weingrass say that you could use, and how?"

The young man leaned over the table; all their heads were closer. "He gave us the figure of fifty million—"

"A *brilliant* manipulation!" broke in Ben-Ami. "And I don't believe for a minute that it was Manny's idea."

"What . . . ? Well, it could have been. Actually, the bank had no choice. Washington leaned hard on it. What about the fifty million?"

"South Yemen," answered Blue.

"I don't understand."

"Fifty million is a very large amount," said the former leader of the Masada Brigade, "but there are larger amounts, especially in the cumulative sense. Iran, Iraq, et cetera. So we must match the people with purse. Therefore, South Yemen. It is terrorist and poor, but its distant, almost inaccessible location, sandwiched between the Gulf of Aden and the Red Sea, makes it strategically important to other terrorist organizations supported by far wealthier sources. They constantly seek out land, secret training grounds to develop their forces and spread their poison. The Baaka is constantly infiltrated, and no one cares to deal with Qaddafi. He's mad and can't be trusted and any week may be overthrown."

"I should tell you," interrupted Ben-Ami again," "that Blue has emerged as one of our more knowledgeable experts on counterterrorism."

"I'm beginning to see that. Go on, young man."

"You are not so much older than me."

"Try twenty years, or close to it. Go ahead."

"Your idea, as I understand it, is to have air shipments of munitions from Hamendi's suppliers all over Europe and America pass through Masqat, where supposedly corrupted officials close their eyes and let them fly on to Lebanon and the Baaka Valley. Correct?"

"Yes, and as each cargo plane comes in the damage is done by the sultan's guards posing as Palestinians checking the supplies for which they've paid Hamendi while the crews are in quarantine. Each plane holds, say, sixty to seventy crates, which will be pried open by teams of ten men per plane and saturated with corroding acid. The process won't take more than fifteen to twenty minutes an aircraft; the timing's acceptable and we're in total control. The Masqat garrison will cordon off the area and no one but our people will be allowed inside."

"Commendable," said Blue, "but I suggest that the process would also be too rushed and too risk-prone. Pilots object to leaving their planes in this part of the world, and the crews, by and large hoodlums with strong backs and no minds, will cause trouble when pushed around by strangers; they smell officialdom, believe me. . . . Instead, why not convince the most prominent leaders in the Baaka Valley to go to South Yemen with their veteran troops. Call it a new provisional movement financed by the enemies of Israel, of which there are quite a few around. Tell them there is an initial fifty million in arms and equipment for advanced training as well as for sending their assault forces up to Gaza and the Golan Heights—more to be supplied as needed. It will be irresistible to those maniacs. . . . And instead of many air-cargo shipments, one *ship,* loaded out of Bahrain, rounding the Gulf here, and proceeding south along the coast on its way to the port of Nishtun in South Yemen."

"Where something will happen?" suggested Kendrick.

"I'd say in the waters west of Ra's al Hadd."

"*What* happens?"

"Pirates," answered Blue, a slight smile creasing his lips. "Once in control of the ship, they would have two days at sea to accomplish what they must far more subtly and thoroughly than they would racing around an airport's cargo area where, indeed, Hamendi might station his own people."

A harried waiter arrived, whining his apologies and cursing the crowds. Ben-Ami ordered cardamom coffee as Kendrick studied the young Israeli counterterrorist. "You say 'once in control,' " said Evan, "but suppose it doesn't happen? Suppose something goes wrong . . . say, our hijackers can't take the ship, or just one message is radioed back to Bahrain—only a word, 'Pirates.' Then there's *no* control. The undamaged weapons get through and Hamendi walks away free, more millions in his pocket. We'd be risking too much for too little."

"You risk far more at the airport in Masqat," argued Blue, his whisper emphatic. "You *must* listen to me. You came back here for only a few days a year and a half ago. You haven't been here in years; you don't know what airports have become. They are zoos of corruption! . . . Who is bringing in what? Who has been bribed and how do I blackmail him? Why is there a change in procedures? *Tell* me, my Arab *astiga,* or my good Hebrew *freund*! They are *zoos*! Nothing escapes the eyes of the jackals looking for money, and money is *paid* for such information. . . . Taking a ship at sea is the lesser risk with the greater benefit, *believe* me."

"You're convincing."

"He's right," said Ben-Ami as their coffee arrived. "*Shukren,*" said the Mossad control agent, thanking and paying the waiter as the man raced to another table. "It must, of course, be your decision, Amal Bahrudi."

"Where do we find these pirates?" asked Evan. "*If* they can be found and *if* they are acceptable?"

"Being convinced of my projections," replied Blue, his eyes rigid on Kendrick's face, which went in and out of the shadows created by the passing crowds, "I broached the possibility of such an assignment to my former comrades in the Masada. I had more volunteers than I could count. As you loathed the Mahdi we loathe Abdel Hamendi, who supplies the bullets that kill our people. I chose six men."

"Only *six*?"

"This must not be solely an Israeli operation. I reached six others I knew on the West Bank. . . . Palestinians who are as sickened by the Hamendis of this world as I am. Together we will form a unit, but it is still not enough. We need six others."

"From *where*?"

"From the host Arab country that willingly, knowingly breaks the back of Abdel Hamendi. Can your sultan provide them from his personal guards?"

"Most are his relatives—cousins, I think."

"That helps."

The illegal purchase of armaments on the international market is a relatively simple procedure, which accounts for the fact that relatively simple people from Washington to Beirut can master it. There are basically three prerequisites. The first is immediate access to undisclosed and undisclosable funds. The second is the name of an intermediary, usually supplied over lunch—not over the telephone—by any senior executive of an arms-producing company or a bribable member of an intelligence organization. This intermediary must be capable of reaching the primary middleman, who will put the package together and coordinate the processing of end-users certificates. This aspect in the United States simply means that export licenses are granted for armaments on their way to friendly nations; they are rerouted en route. The third prerequisite should be the easiest but is usually the most difficult because of the extraordinary variety and complexity of the merchandise. It is the preparation of the list of weapons and auxiliary equipment desired for purchase. Apparently no five buyers can agree on the lethal capabilities and effectiveness of an arms inventory, and not a few lives have been lost during heated debates over these decisions, the buyers frequently given to outbursts of hysteria.

Which was why young code Blue's management talents were most welcome in terms of time and specificity. The Mossad's agents in the Baaka Valley forwarded a list of the currently most favored merchandise, including the usual crates of repeating weapons, hand grenades, time-fused explosives, black PVC landing craft, long-range underwater tank and demolitions accoutrements, and assorted training and assault equipment, such as grappling hooks, heavy ropes and rope ladders, infrared binoculars, electronic mortars, flamethrowers, and antiaircraft rocket missiles. It was an impressive inventory that chewed up approximately eighteen million of the estimated twenty-six million one could buy from an arms merchant for fifty million American dollars—the fluctuating rates of exchange always in favor of the merchant. Therefore, Blue added three small Chinese tanks under the technical umbrella of "location defense" and the list was complete—not only complete but entirely believable.

The unknown, unrecorded, never-to-be-acknowledged agent of control, namely, one Ben-Ami, now dressed in his favored Ralph Lauren blue jeans, operated out of the Mossad safe house next to the Portuguese cemetery in the Jabal Sa'ali. To his fury, the intermediary for Abdel Hamendi was an Israeli in Bet Shemesh. He concealed his contempt and negotiated the huge purchase, in the forefront of his mind knowing that there would be a death in Bet Shemesh if and when they all survived.

The two units of six commandos arrived, one after another, at night in the desert of Jabal Sham above flares that directed the two helicopters into their thresholds. The sultan of Oman greeted the volunteers and introduced them to their comrades, six highly skilled personal guards from the Masqat garrison. Eighteen men—Palestinians, Israeli and Omani—gripped hands in their common objective. Death to the merchant of death.

The training began the next morning beyond the shoals of Al Ashkarah in the Arabian Sea.

Death to the merchant of death.

Adrienne Khalehla Rashad walked into Ahmat's office cradling the infant named Khalehla in her arms. Beside her was the child's mother, Roberta Yamenni, from New Bedford, Massachusetts, among the elite of Oman known as Bobbie. "She's so *beautiful*!" exclaimed the agent from Cairo.

"She had to be," said the father behind the desk, Evan Kendrick in a chair beside him. "She has a name to live up to."

"Oh, nonsense."

"Not from where I'm sitting," said the American congressman.

"You're an oversexed bear."

"I'm also leaving tonight."

"And so am I," added the sultan of Oman.

"You can't—"

"You *can't*!" The high female voices were in concert. "What the hell do you think you're *doing*?" yelled the sultan's wife.

"What I wish to do," replied Ahmat calmly. "In these areas of royal prerogative, I don't have to consult with anyone."

"That's *bullshit*!" cried the wife and mother.

"I know, but it works."

The training was over in seven days, and on the eighth day twenty-two passengers climbed into a trawler off the coast of Ra's al Hadd, their equipment stowed below the gunwales. On the ninth day, at sundown in the Arabian Sea, the cargo ship from Bahrain was picked up on the radar. When darkness came the trawler headed south to the intercept-coordinates.

Death to the merchant of death.

46

The cargo ship was a bobbing hulk on the swells of the dark sea, its bow rising and falling like an angry predator intent on feeding. The trawler from Ra's al Hadd stopped in the water a half mile to starboard of the approaching vessel. Two large PVC lifeboats were lowered over the side, the first holding twelve men, the other ten and one woman. Khalehla Rashad was between Evan Kendrick and the young sultan of Oman.

All were encased in wet suits, their darkened faces barely visible within the folds of the form-fitting black rubber. In addition to canvas knapsacks across their backs and the bound waterproofed weapons clipped to their belts, each wore large circular suction cups strapped to his knees and forearms. The two boats pitched and rolled beside each other in the dark sea as the cargo ship plowed forward. Then, as the great black wall of the vessel rose above them, the lifeboats pulled alongside, their quiet motors drowned out by the slapping waves. One by one the "pirates" clamped their cups on to the hull, each checking his companion on the left to make certain he was secure. All were.

Slowly, like a cluster of ants crawling up a filthy garbage can, the force from Oman made its way to the top of the hull, to the gunwales, where the suction cups were released and dropped back into the sea.

"Are you all right?" whispered Khalehla beside Evan.

"All *right*?" protested Kendrick. "My arms are killing me, and I think my legs are somewhere in the water down there, which I don't intend to look at!"

"Good, you're all right."

"You do things like this for a living?"

"Not very often," said the agent from Cairo. "On the other hand, I've done worse."

"You're all maniacs."

"*I* didn't go into a compound filled with terrorists. I mean, *that's* crazy!"

"*Shhh!*" ordered Ahmat Yamenni, sultan of Oman, on Rashad's right. "The teams are going over. Be quiet."

The Palestinians took out the barely awake men on watch at the bow, midships and stern while the Israelis raced up the gangways to an upper deck and captured five seamen who were sitting against a bulkhead drinking wine. By design, as they were in the waters of the Gulf of Oman, the Omanis ran up to the bridge to formally instruct the captain that the ship was under their control by royal decree and its present course was to be maintained. The crew was rounded up and checked for weapons, all their knives and guns removed. They were confined to quarters with an Omani, a Palestinian and an Israeli, in rotating units of three, standing guard. The captain, a gaunt fatalist with a stubble of a beard, accepted the circumstances with a shrug of his shoulders and offered neither resistance nor objection. He stayed at the wheel, asking only that his first and second mates relieve him at the proper times. The request was granted and his subsequent comment summed up his philosophical reaction:

"Arabs and Jews together are now the pirates of the high seas. The world is a little madder than I thought."

The radioman, however, was the most startling surprise. The communications room was approached cautiously, Khalehla leading two members of the Masada Brigade and Evan Kendrick. At her signal the door was crashed open and their weapons leveled at the operator. The radioman pulled a small Israeli flag out of his pocket and grinned. "How's Manny Weingrass?" he asked.

"Good *God*!" was the only response the congressman from Colorado could manage.

"It was to be expected," said Khalehla.

For two days on the water toward the port of Nishtun, the force from Oman worked in shifts around the clock in the hold of the cargo ship. They were thorough, as each man knew the merchandise he was dealing with, knew it and effectively destroyed it. Crates were resealed, leaving no marks of sabotage in evidence; there were only neatly repacked weapons and equipment precisely as if they had come off assembly lines all over the world and gathered together by Abdel Hamendi, seller of death. At dawn on the third day the ship sailed into the harbor of Nishtun, South Yemen. The "pirates" from the West Bank, Oman and the Masada Brigade, as well as the female agent from Cairo and the American congressman, had all changed into the clothes packed in their knapsacks. Half Arab, half Western, they wore the disheveled garments of erratically employed merchant seamen scratching for survival in an unfair world. Five Palestinians, posing as Bahrainian off-loaders, stood by the gangplank that in moments would be lowered. The rest watched impassively from the lower deck as the crowds gathered at the one enormous pier in the center of the harbor complex. Hysteria was in the air; it was everywhere. The ship was a symbol of deliverance, for rich and powerful people somewhere thought the proud, suffering fighters of South Yemen were *important.* It was a carnival of vengeance, over what they might not collectively agree upon but wild mouths below wild eyes screamed screams of violence. The vessel docked and the frenzy on the pier was ear-shattering.

Selected members of the ship's crew, under the watchful eyes and guns of the Omani force, were put to work at their familiar machinery and the massive unloading process began. As skids of crates were lifted out of the hold by cranes and swung over the side down to the cargo area, rabid cheers greeted each delivery. Two hours after the unloading started, it ended with the emergence of the three small Chinese tanks, and if the crates sent the crowds into frenzy, the tanks took them up into orbit. Raggedly uniformed soldiers had to hold back their countrymen from swarming over the armor-plated vehicles; again they were symbols of great importance, of immense recognition—from somewhere.

"Jesus Christ!" said Kendrick, gripping Ahmat's arm, staring down at the base of the pier. "*Look!*"

"Where?"

"I see!" broke in Khalehla, in trousers, her hair swept up under a Greek fisherman's hat. "My God, I don't *believe* it! It's *him,* isn't it?"

"Who?" demanded the young sultan angrily.

"*Hamendi!*" answered Evan, pointing at a man in a white silk suit surrounded by other men in uniforms and robes. The procession continued onto the pier, the soldiers in front clearing the way.

"He's wearing the same white suit he wore in one of the photographs in the Vanvlanderens' apartment," added Rashad.

"I'm sure he's got dozens," explained Kendrick. "I'm also sure he thinks they make him look pure and godlike. . . . I'll say this for him—he's got balls leaving his armed camp in the Alps and coming here only a few hours by air from Riyadh."

"Why?" said Ahmat. "He's protected; the Saudis wouldn't dare inflame these crazies by taking any action across the border."

"Besides," interrupted Khalehla, "Hamendi smells millions more where this ship came from. He's securing his turf and that's worth a minor risk."

"I *know* what he's doing," said Evan, speaking to Khalehla but looking at the young sultan. " 'The Saudis wouldn't dare,' " continued Kendrick, repeating Ahmat's words. "The *Omanis* wouldn't dare . . ."

"There are perfectly sound reasons to leave well enough alone where fanatics are concerned and let them sink in their own quagmires," responded the sultan defensively.

"That's not the point."

"What is?"

"We're counting on the fact that when all these people, especially the leaders from the Baaka Valley, find out that most of what they paid for is a bunch of crap, Hamendi will be called a fifty-million-dollar thief. He's a pariah, an Arab who betrays Arabs for money."

"The word will spread like falcons in the wind, as my people would have said only a couple of decades ago," agreed the sultan. "From what I know of the Baaka, hit teams will be sent out by the dozens to kill him, not simply because of the money but because he's made fools of them."

"That's the optimum," said Kendrick. "That's what we're hoping for, but he's got millions all over the world and there are thousands of places to hide."

"What *is* your point, Evan?" asked Khalehla.

"Maybe we can move up the timetable and with any luck *ensure* the optimum."

"Speak English, not Latin," insisted the agent from Cairo.

"That's a circus down there. The soldiers can barely hold back the crowds. All that's needed is for a movement to get started, people shouting in unison, *chanting* until their voices shake the damn city. . . . *Farjunna! Farjunna! Farjunna!*"

"*Show* us!" translated Ahmat.

"One or two crates pried open, rifles held up in triumph . . . then ammunition's found and handed over."

"And shot off by lunatics into the sky," completed Khalehla, "but they don't *fire.*"

"Then *other* crates are opened," went on the sultan, catching the shared enthusiasm. "Equipment ruined, life rafts slashed, flamethrowers fizzling. And Hamendi's right there! . . . How can *we* get down there?"

"You can't, either one of you," said Kendrick firmly, signaling a member of the Masada team. The man ran over and Evan continued rapidly, not giving Ahmat or Rashad a chance to speak as they stared at him, stunned. "You know who I am, don't you?" he asked the Israeli.

"I'm not supposed to, but, of course, I do."

"I am considered the leader of this entire unit, aren't I?"

"Yes, but I'm grateful that there are others—"

"Irrelevant! I *am* the leader."

"All right, you're the leader."

"I want these two people placed under cabin arrest immediately."

The sultan's and Khalehla's protests were drowned out by the

Israeli's own reaction. "Are you out of your *mind*? *That* man is—"

"I don't care if he's Muhammad himself and she's *Cleopatra.* Lock them *up*!" Evan raced away toward the gangplank and the hysterical crowds below on the pier.

Kendrick found the first of the five Palestinian "off-loaders" and pulled him away from a group of soldiers and screaming awed civilians surrounding one of the Chinese tanks. He spoke quickly into the man's ear; the Arab responded by nodding his head and pointing to one of his companions in the crowd, gesturing that he would reach the others.

Each man ran along the pier from one frenzied group to another, shrieking at the top of his lungs, repeating the message over and over until the feverish cry was picked up for the command it was. Like an enormous rolling wave pounding across a human sea, the shouting erupted, a thousand disparate voices slowly coming into concert.

"*Farjunna! Farjunna! Farjunna! Farjunna . . . !*" The crowds converged en masse onto the cargo area, and the small elite procession in which Abdel Hamendi was the center of attraction was literally swept aside, *inside* the huge doors of the run-down warehouse near the end of the pier. Apologies were shouted to and accepted with false grace by the arms merchant, who looked as though he had come to the wrong part of town and could not wait to get out and would have if it were not for the rewards that could be his by staying.

"*This* way!" yelled a voice Evan knew only too well. It was Khalehla! And beside her was Ahmat, both barely holding their own within the tumultuous, frantic crowds.

"What the hell are you *doing* here?" roared Kendrick, joining them, bodies pushing and shoving all around them.

"*Mister* Congressman," said the sultan of Oman imperiously, "you may be the leader of the unit, which is entirely debatable, but *I* command the ship! My damned troops *took* it!"

"Do you know what'll happen if she loses her hat or her shirt and these lunatics see she's a woman? And have you any idea of the reception *you'll* get if anyone has the slightest clue who you—"

"Will you two *stop* it!" cried Rashad, giving an order, not asking a question. "Hurry up! The soldiers could lose control any minute, and we've got to make sure it happens our way."

"How?" shouted Evan.

"The *crates*!" answered Khalehla. "The stacks on the left with the red markings. Go ahead of me, I'll never get through by myself. I'll hold your arm."

"That's quite a concession. Come *on*!" The three of them crashed sideways through the dense, constantly moving, jostling crowds, pummeling their way to a double-stack of crates at least ten feet high held together by wide jet-black metal straps. A cordon of nearly panicked soldiers, too few to lock arms but gripping hands, formed a circle around the lethal merchandise, holding back the increasingly impatient, increasingly angry throngs who now demanded, *Farjunna, Farjunna!*—to be shown the supplies that signified their own importance. "These are the guns and everyone knows it!" yelled Kendrick into Rashad's ear. "They're going *crazy*!"

"Of course they know it and of course they're going crazy. Look at the markings." All over the wooden crates were stenciled dozens of the same insignia: three red circles, two progressively smaller ones within the largest. "Bull's-eyes, the universal symbol of a target," explained Khalehla. "And bull's-eyes mean weapons. It was Blue's idea; he figured that terrorists live by guns, so they'd flock to them."

"He knows his new business—"

"Where's the *ammunition*?" asked Ahmat, pulling two small pronged instruments from his pockets.

"The West Bankers are taking care of it," replied Rashad, crouching under the assault of thrashing arms around her. "The crates are unmarked, but they know which ones they are and will break them open. They're waiting for us!"

"Let's go, then," cried the young sultan, handing Evan one of the instruments he had removed from his pockets.

"What . . . ?"

"Pliers! We have to snap as many of the crate straps as we can to make sure they all fall apart."

"Oh? They would have, anyway—never mind! We have to rush this bunch of maniacs forward and break the ring. Move back, Ahmat, and you get behind us," said Kendrick to the agent from Cairo, fending off the furious arms and fists, knees and feet that kept hammering at them from all directions. "When I nod," continued Evan, shouting at the sultan of Oman as they smashed through the frenzied bodies all trying to reach the crates. "Hit the line like you just got signed by the Patriots!"

"No, *ya Shaikh,*" yelled Ahmat. "Like I just got signed by

Oman—under fire, as it should be. These are the enemies of my *people*!"

"*Now!*" roared Kendrick as he and the muscular young ruler crashed forward into the figures in front of them, shoulders and extended arms propelling the screaming terrorists into the circle of soldiers. The line broke! The assault on the ten-foot-high double sacks of heavy crates was total, and Evan and Ahmat surged through balloon-trousered legs and flailing arms to the wood and the wide metal straps, their pliers working furiously. The bindings snapped and the crates tumbled down as if exploded from within, the weight and strength of a hundred assaulters precipitating their violent descents. Wooden slats everywhere came apart, and where they did not, maniacal hands pried them apart. Then, like starving locusts attacking the sweet leaves of trees, the terrorists of South Yemen and the Baaka Valley crawled over the crates, yanking out weapons from their plastic casements and throwing them to their brothers while shrieking and straddling the large cartons that took on the grotesque images of coffins.

Simultaneously, the Palestinian team from the West Bank heaved boxes of ammunition all around and over the collapsed wooden mountain of death, supplied by the seller of death, Abdel Hamendi. The guns were varied, all types and all sizes, ripped with abandon from their soft recesses. Many did not know what shells went into which weapons, but many others, mainly from the Baaka, did, and they instructed their less sophisticated brothers from South Yemen.

The first repeating machine gun that was fired in triumph from atop the ersatz pyramid of death blew off the face of the one who pulled the trigger. In the midst of staccato sounds everywhere, others were fired; there were several hundred fruitless clicks, but also dozens of explosions where heads and arms and hands were blown away. *Blown away!*

Hysteria fed upon hysteria. Terrorists threw down their guns in terror, while others used their hands and whatever implements they could find to pry open the unmarked crates everywhere. It was as the young sultan of Oman had predicted. Items of equipment were dragged out all over the pier, yanked from boxes and unfolded or pulled apart or ripped from their plastic casings—and displayed for all to see. As each piece was examined the crowds went wilder and wilder, but no longer in triumph, instead in animal fury. Among the items were infrared binoculars with smashed lenses, rope ladders with their rungs severed, grappling hooks without points, underwater oxygen tanks with holes drilled in the cylinders; flamethrowers, their nozzles crushed together, guaranteeing instant incineration to whoever operated them and anyone within thirty yards; rocket missile launchers without detonating caps, and again, as Ahmat had projected, landing craft held up to show where the seams had been split, all of which threw the manic crowd into paroxysms of rage over the betrayal.

In the chaos, Evan weaved through the hysterical bodies to the warehouse at the midpoint of the huge pier; he pressed his back against the wall and sidestepped to within three feet of the massive open doors. The white-suited Hamendi was shouting in Arabic that everything would be replaced; his and *their* enemies in the Bahrain depots who did this would be killed, every *one killed*! His protestations drew looks of narrowed-eyed suspicion from those he addressed.

And then a man in a dark conservative pin-striped suit appeared, rounding the corner of the warehouse, and Kendrick froze. It was Crayton Grinell, attorney and chairman of the board for the government within the government. After his initial shock, Evan wondered why he was astonished, even surprised. Where else could Grinell go but to the core of the international network of arms merchants? It was his last and only secure refuge. The lawyer spoke briefly to Hamendi, who instantly translated Grinell's words, explaining that his associate had already reached Bahrain and learned what had happened. It was *Jews*! he exclaimed. Israeli terrorists had assaulted an off-island depot, killed all the men on watch, and had done these terrible things.

"How could that be?" asked a stocky man in the only pressed revolutionary uniform replete with at least a dozen medals. "All these supplies were in the original crates, even boxes within cartons, the casings unbroken. How could it *be*?"

"The Jews can be ingenious!" screamed Hamendi. "You know that as well as I do. I shall fly back immediately, replace the entire order, and learn the truth!"

"What do we do in the meantime?" asked the obvious leader of South Yemen's revolutionary regime. "What do I tell our brothers from the Baaka Valley? We are all, all of us, *disgraced*!"

"You will have your vengeance as well as your weapons, be assured." Grinell spoke again to the arms merchant, and once more Hamendi translated. "I am informed by my associate that our radar clearances are only in effect for the next three hours—at an extraordinary expense to me personally, I might add—and we must leave at once."

"Restore us our dignity, fellow Arab, or we will find you and you will lose your life."

"You have my guarantee that the first will happen, and there will be no necessity for the second. I leave."

They were going to get away! thought Kendrick. Goddamnit, they were going to get *away*! Grinell had given Hamendi the unctuous words, and both of them were going to fly out of this hub of insanity and go on doing their insane, obscene business-as-usual! He had to *stop* them. He had to *move*!

As the two arms merchants walked rapidly out the doors of the warehouse and around the corner of the building, Evan raced across the opening—as one more hysterical terrorist—and thrashed his way toward the two well-dressed men through the excited crowds on the pier. He was within feet of Crayton Grinell, then inches. He pulled his long-bladed knife out of its scabbard on his belt and lunged, circling his left arm around the American attorney's neck and forcing him to pivot, to confront him face-to-face, inches one from the other.

"*You!*" screamed Grinell.

"This is for an old man who's dying and thousands of others you've killed!" The knife plunged into the lawyer's stomach, and then Kendrick ripped it up through the chest. Grinell fell to the planks on the pier amid a multitude of rushing paranoid terrorists who had no idea that another terrorist had been killed and lay beneath them.

Hamendi! He had raced ahead, oblivious of his associate, determined only to reach the vehicle that would take him to his radar-cleared plane out of South Yemen across hostile borders. He must not *reach* it! The merchant of death could not be allowed to deal in death *anymore*! Evan literally sledgehammered a path through the onslaught of running, screaming figures to the base of the pier. There was a wide ascending stretch of concrete that led up to a dirt road, where a Russian Zia limousine waited, the exhaust fumes indicating that the engine was roaring, waiting for the car's escaping passengers. Hamendi, his white silk jacket billowing behind him, was within yards of his escape! Kendrick called upon strengths within him that defied the outer regions of his imagination and raced up the concrete incline, his legs about to collapse, and then they did collapse twenty feet from the Zia as Hamendi approached the door. From his prone position, his weapon barely steadied by both trembling hands, he fired again and again and again.

Abdel Hamendi, the king of the court of international arms merchants, reached for his throat as he fell to the ground.

It was not *over*! screamed a voice in Kendrick's mind. There was something else to do! He crawled down the concrete incline, reaching into his pocket for a map code Blue had provided everyone in the event of separation and possible escape. He tore off a fragment, taking a small blunt pencil from another pocket, and wrote the following in Arabic:

Hamendi the liar is dead. Soon all the merchants will die, for everywhere the treachery has begun, as you have seen for yourself this day. Everywhere they have been paid by Israel and the Great Satan America to sell us defective weapons. Everywhere. Reach our brothers everywhere and tell them what I have told you and what you have witnessed this day. No weapons from this day on can be trusted. Signed by a silent friend who knows.

Painfully, as though the wounds from the island off Mexico had returned, Evan got to his feet and ran as fast as he could back into the angry, still-shrieking crowds toward the doors of the warehouse. Feigning hysterical pleas to Allah over the death of a brother, he fell prostrate in front of the small group of leaders, which now included those from the Baaka Valley in Lebanon. As hands came down to offer comfort he shoved the paper toward them, rose suddenly to his feet screaming, and raced out of the warehouse doors, disappearing into the now wailing, grieving crowds kneeling beside mutilated corpses everywhere. In panic he heard the bass-toned whistles from the cargo ship—signals of departure! He pummeled his way to the far side of the pier, where he saw Khalehla and Ahmat standing by the gangplank, shouting up to the men on deck, if possible more panicked than himself.

"Where the hell have you *been*!" screamed Rashad, her eyes furious.

"They were lying their way out!" yelled Kendrick as Ahmat shoved both of them onto the gangplank, which, at his signal, began its retreat into the ship.

"Hamendi?" asked Khelehla.

"And Grinell—"

"Grinell?" shouted the agent from Cairo as the three of them staggered forward. "Of *course* Grinell," added Rashad. "Where *else*—"

"You're a goddamned fool, Congressman!" roared the young

sultan of Oman, still shoving his charges, now onto the deck of the ship, which had already floated away from the pier. "Another thirty seconds and you would have stayed back there. Any minute that crowd could have turned on us, and I couldn't risk the lives of these men!"

"Christ, you've really grown up."

"We all do our thing when it's our turn. . . . What about Hamendi and this whoever-he-is?"

"I killed them."

"Just like that," said Ahmat breathlessly, but calmly.

"We all do our thing when it's our turn, Your Highness."

Gerald Bryce walked into the computerized study of his house in Georgetown and went directly to his processor. He sat down in front of it and turned on the switch; as the screen lit up he typed in a code. Instantly the green letters responded.

Ultra Maximum Secure
No Existing Intercepts
Proceed

The young, strikingly handsome expert smiled and continued to type.

I have now read all the max confidential printouts reaching the CIA and coded for only M. J. Payton's modem. In a word, the entire report is incredible and already the effects of the operation are seen. To date, barely two weeks after the events in South Yemen, seven of the most prominent arms merchants have been assassinated, and it is estimated that the flow of weapons to the Middle East has been cut by 60 percent. Our man is invincible. More to the point, however, combined with the previous information we possess, the White House must—repeat must—listen to us in the event we care to have our voice heard. We will, of course, exercise this prerogative with the utmost circumspection, but it is, nevertheless, ours to exercise. For regardless of outcome, positive or negative, national and international laws have been broken, the administration directly and indirectly associated with murder, terrorism, corruption, and, indeed, approached the edge of that all-inclusive condemnation, crimes against humanity. As we agree, there must always be a benevolent, selfless power above the White House to give it direction, and the means to that power is to know the innermost secrets of any administration. In this regard we are succeeding in ways undreamed of by those who came before us. If there is a God, may He grant that we and our successors be truthful to our beliefs. Penultimately, it strikes me that the sound and the partial cadence of Inver Brass is not far distant from a medical term: intravenous. It's quite appropriate, I believe. Finally, I am working on several other projects and will keep you informed.

In a boat off Glorious Cay in the Bahamas a large black man sat in the opulent cabin of his Bertram yacht studying the computer screen in front of him. He smiled at the words he read. Inver Brass was in good hands, young capable hands, immense intelligence coupled with decency and a desire for excellence. Gideon Logan, who had spent much of his wealthy adult life for the betterment of his people—even to the point of disappearing for three years as the silent, unseen ombudsman of Rhodesia during its transition to Zimbabwe—felt the relief that came with principled, outstanding succession. Time was winding down for him as it was for Margaret Lowell and old Jacob Mandel. Mortality mandated that they would be replaced; and this young man, this attractive honorable young genius, would choose their successors. The nation and the world would be better for them.

Time was winding down.

Gerald Bryce sipped his glass of Madeira and returned to his equipment. He was elated for many reasons, not the least of which was what he termed their "fraternity of brilliance." What was so extraordinary was the ordinariness of its inevitability. Their brotherhood was preordained, inescapable, its origins found in the most common of occurrences: the coming together of people with similar interests, the advanced regions of those interests demanding superior intellects—and, to be realistic, little patience with a society governed by mediocrity. One thing always led to another, always obliquely, but nevertheless inevitably.

When time permitted, Bryce lectured and held seminars, a sought-after leader in the field of computer science who was careful not to publicly explore the outer limits of his expertise. But every now and then there was that extraordinary person who grasped where he was heading. In London, Stockholm, Paris, Los Angeles and Chicago—the University of Chicago.

Those few people were scrutinized beyond anything their imaginations could conceive of and, to date, four had been reached again—and again. A new Inver Brass was a faint but definite outline on the horizon. The most extraordinary of those four would be reached now.

Bryce entered his code, punched the keys for *Addendum,* and read the letters on the screen.

Satellite transmission. Mod-Sahalhuddin. Bahrain.
Proceed.

47

Emmanuel Weingrass confounded the medical specialists, especially those at the Centers for Disease Control in Atlanta. Not that he was recovering, for he was not, and there was no change in the terminal status of the virus infection. However, he was not getting evidently much worse; his rate of decline was far slower than had been anticipated. The doctors would not by any means pronounce the disease arrested; they were simply confused. As the pathologist in Denver phrased it, "Let's say on a scale of one to minus ten—minus ten being check-out time—the old guy's hovering around minus six and won't move down."

"But the virus is still there," said Kendrick as he and Khalehla walked with the doctor on the grounds of the Colorado house out of Manny's earshot.

"It's rampant. It's just not incapacitating him to the degree that it should."

"It's probably the cigarettes he cons and all the whisky he steals," stated Rashad.

"He *doesn't,*" said the pathologist, surprised and even more bewildered.

Evan and Khalehla nodded their heads in resigned confirmation. "He's a bellicose survivor," explained Kendrick, "with more wisdom and larceny in his head than anyone I've ever met. Also, since the prognosis was severe in terms of time, we haven't exactly kept our eyes wide open every minute we've been around him."

"Please understand, Congressman, I don't want to give you any false hope. He's a terribly ill eighty-six-year-old man—"

"Eighty-*six*?" exclaimed Evan.

"Didn't you know?"

"No. He said he was *eighty-one*!"

"I'm sure he believes it, or at least has convinced himself. He's the sort who when they turn sixty, the next birthday's fifty-five. Nothing wrong with that at all, by the way, but we wanted a complete medical history, so we went back to his days in New York City. Did you know he had three wives by the time he was thirty-two?"

"I'm sure they're still looking for him."

"Oh, no, they've all passed away. Atlanta wanted their histories, too—possible latent sexually related complications, that sort of thing."

"Did they check Los Angeles, Paris, Rome, Tel Aviv, Riyadh, and all of the Emirates?" asked Khalehla dryly.

"*Remarkable,*" said the pathologist softly, but with emphasis, a medical mind apparently pondering, perhaps envying. "Well, I should be leaving, I'm due back in Denver by noon. And, Congressman, thank you for the private jet. It saved me a great deal of time."

"I couldn't do anything less, Doctor. I appreciate everything you're doing, everything you've done."

The pathologist paused, looking at Evan. "I just said 'Congressman,' Mr. Kendrick. Perhaps I should say 'Mr. Vice President,' as I and, indeed, most of the country believe you should be. In truth, if you're not in the running, I don't intend to vote, and I can tell you I speak for the majority of my friends and associates."

"That's not a viable position, Doctor. Besides, the issue hasn't been resolved. . . . Come on, I'll walk you to the car. Khalehla, check on our sybaritic adolescent and make sure he's not taking a bath in sour mash, will you?"

"If he is, do you think *I'm* going to walk in there? . . . Sure, I will." Rashad shook hands with the pathologist from Denver. "Thank you for everything," she said.

"I'll know you mean it if you convince this young man he really must be our next Vice President."

"I repeat," said Kendrick, leading the physician across the lawn to the circular drive. "That issue is far from resolved, Doctor."

"The issue *should* be resolved!" shouted Emmanuel Weingrass from his recliner on the enclosed porch, the Congressman and

Khalehla sitting in their accustomed positions on the couch so that the old architect could glower at them. "What do you think? It's all *finished*? So Bollinger and his fascist thieves are out and there's no one to take their *places*? You're that *stupid*?"

"Cut it out, Manny," said Evan. "There are too many areas where Langford Jennings and I differ for a President to be comfortable with someone like me who might possibly succeed him—and the thought of *that* scares the hell out of me."

"Lang knows all that!" cried Weingrass.

"Lang?"

The architect shrugged. "Well, you'll learn soon enough—"

"Learn *what* soon enough?"

"Jennings kind of invited himself out to lunch here a few weeks ago, when you and my lovely daughter were winding things up in Washington. . . . So what could I do? Tell the President of the United States he couldn't nosh a little?"

"Oh, shit!" said Kendrick.

"Hold it, darling," interrupted Khalehla. "I'm fascinated, really *fascinated.*"

"Go *on,* Manny!" yelled Evan.

"Well, we discussed many things—he's not an intellectual, I grant you, but he has smarts and he understands the larger picture, that's what he's good at, you know."

"I *don't* know, and how *dare* you intercede for me?"

"Because I'm your *father,* you ungrateful idiot. The only father you've ever *known*! Without me you'd still be hustling a few buildings with the Saudis and wondering if you could cover your costs. Don't talk about my daring—you were lucky I dared—talk about your obligations to others. . . . All right, all right, we couldn't have done what we did without your balls, without your strength, but I was *there,* so listen to me."

In exasperation, Kendrick closed his eyes and leaned back on the couch. Suddenly, Khalehla realized that Weingrass was unobtrusively signaling her, his lips in exaggerated movement; the silent words were easily read. *It's an act. I know what I'm doing.* She could only respond by looking at the old man, bewildered. "Okay, Manny," said Evan, opening his eyes and staring at the ceiling. "You can cut it out. I'm listening."

"That's better." Weingrass winked at the agent from Cairo and continued. "You can walk away and nobody's got the right to say or think a bad word because you're owed, and you don't owe anybody anything. But I know you, my friend, and the man I know has a streak of outrage in him that he keeps running away from yet never can because it's part of him. In short words, you don't happen to like rotten people—present older company excepted—and it's a good thing for this meshugenah world that guys like you are around; there are too many of the other type. . . . Still, I see a problem, and to put it in an eggshell, it's that not too many of your kind can do a hell of a lot because no one listens to them. Why should anyone? Who *are* they? Troublemakers? Whistle-blowers? Insignificant agitators? . . . They're easily disposed of, anyway. Jobs are lost, promotions withheld, and if they're really serious they wind up in the courts where their whole lives are soiled—dirt dug up on them that's got nothing to do with what they're there for by expensive lawyers who've got more tricks than Houdini—and if all they end up with is a Chapter Eleven and usually no wife and kids, maybe it could be worse. Maybe they could be found under a truck or down in the tracks of a subway at an inappropriate time. . . . Now, you, on the other hand, everybody listens to you—look at the polls; you're the top cardinal of the country, granting the fact that Langford Jennings is Pope—and there's not a shyster in or out of sight who'd take you on in the courts, much less the Congress. As I see it, you've got the chance to speak from the top for a hell of a lot of people down below who can't get a hearing. Lang will bring you in on everything—"

"Lang, again," muttered Kendrick, interrupting.

"Not *my* doing!" exclaimed Weingrass, palms outstretched. "I started right off the right way with a 'Mr. President,' ask the nurses who all had to go to the bathroom the minute he came inside—he's some mensch, I tell you. Anyway, after a drink, which he himself got for me from the bar when the girls were out, he said I was refreshing and why didn't I call him Lang and forget the formal stuff."

"Manny," broke in Khalehla, "why did the President say you were 'refreshing'?"

"Well, in small talk I mentioned that the new building they're putting up on some avenue or other—it was in the *New York Times*—wasn't so hotsy-totsy, and he shouldn't have congratulated that asshole architect on television. The goddamned renderings looked like Neoclassic Art Deco, and believe me, the combination doesn't work. Also, what the hell did *he,* a President, know about square-foot construction costs that came in at about one third of what they're going to be. Lang's looking into it."

"Oh, *shit,*" repeated Evan, defeat in his voice.

"Back to the point I'm trying to make," said Weingrass, his face suddenly very serious as he stared at Kendrick while pausing for several long intakes of breath. "Maybe you've done enough, maybe you should walk away and live happily ever after with my Arab daughter here making lots more money. The respect of the country, even much of the world, is already yours. But maybe also you've got to think. You can do what not too many others can do. Rather than going *after* the rotten people, by which time there's so much corruption and loss of life, maybe you can stop them before they play dirty—at least some of them, perhaps more than some—from the top of the mountain. All I ask is that you listen to Jennings. Listen to what he has to say to you."

Their eyes locked, father and son acknowledged each other on the deepest level of their relationship. "I'll call him and ask him for a meeting, all right?"

"That's not necessary," replied Manny. "It's all set up."

"What?"

"He'll be in Los Angeles tomorrow at the Century Plaza for a dinner raising scholarship funds in honor of his late Secretary of State. He's cleared some time before then and expects you at the hotel at seven o'clock. You, too, my dear; he insists."

The two Secret Service men in the hallway outside the Presidential Suite acknowledged the Congressman by sight. They nodded at him and Khalehla as the man on the right turned and rang the bell. Moments later Langford Jennings opened the door, his face pale and haggard with dark circles of exhaustion below his eyes. He made a brief attempt at his famous grin but could not sustain it. Instead, he smiled gently, extending his hand.

"Hello, Miss Rashad. It's a pleasure and a privilege to meet you. Please, come in."

"Thank you, Mr. President."

"Evan, it's good to see you again."

"It's good to see you, sir," said Kendrick, thinking as he walked inside that Jennings looked older than he had ever seen him.

"Please sit down." The President preceded his guests into the living room of the suite, toward two opposing couches, a large round glass coffee table linking them. "Please," he repeated, gesturing at the couch on the right as he headed for the one on the left. "I like to look at attractive people," he added as they all sat down. "I suppose my detractors would say it's another sign of my superficiality, but Harry Truman once said, 'I'd rather look at a horse's head than his ass,' so I rest my case. . . . Forgive the language, young lady."

"I didn't hear anything to forgive, sir."

"How's Manny?"

"He's not going to win, but he's putting up a fight," answered Evan. "I understand you visited him several weeks ago."

"Was that wicked of me?"

"Not at all, but it was a little wicked of him not to tell me."

"That was my idea. I wanted to give us—you and me—both time to think, and in my case I had to learn more about you than what was written in several hundred pages of government jargon. So I went to the one source that made sense to me. I asked him to be quiet until the other day. I apologize."

"No need to, sir."

"Weingrass is a brave man. He knows he's dying—his diagnosis is wrong but he knows he's dying—and he pretends to treat his impending death like a statistic on a construction proposal. I don't expect to see eighty-one, but if I do, I hope I have his courage."

"Eighty-six," said Kendrick flatly. "I thought he was eighty-one, too, but we found out yesterday he's eighty-six." Langford Jennings looked hard at Evan, then, as if the Congressman had just told an extraordinarily amusing joke, he leaned back on the couch, his neck arched, and laughed quietly but wholeheartedly. "Why is that so funny?" asked Kendrick. "I've known him for twenty years and he never told the truth about his age, even on passports."

"It dovetails with something he said to me," explained the President, speaking through his soft, subsiding laughter. "I won't bore you with the details, but he pointed out something to me—and he was *damned* right—so I offered him an appointment. He said to me, 'Sorry, Lang, I can't accept. I couldn't burden you with my graft.' "

"He's an original, Mr. President," offered Khalehla.

"They broke the mold. . . ." Jennings's voice trailed off as his expression became serious. He looked at Rashad. "Your Uncle Mitch sends you his love."

"Oh?"

"Payton left an hour ago. I'm sorry to say he had to get back to Washington, but I spoke with him yesterday and he insisted on flying out to see me before I met with Congressman Kendrick."

"Why?" asked Evan, disturbed.

"He finally told me the whole story of Inver Brass. Well, not everything, of course, because we don't know everything. With Winters and Varak gone, we'll probably never learn who broke open the Oman file, but it doesn't matter now. The holy Inver Brass is finished."

"He hadn't told you *before*?" Kendrick was astonished, yet he remembered Ahmat saying that he was not sure Jennings knew everything Payton had told *him*.

"He was honest about it while offering his resignation, which I promptly rejected. . . . He said that if I knew the entire story I might have squashed the bid being made in your name for you to be my running mate. I don't know, I might have, I certainly would have been furious. But that's irrelevant now. I've learned what I wanted to learn and you're not only out of the starting gate, you've got a national mandate, Congressman."

"Mr. President," protested Evan. "It's an artificial—"

"What the *hell* did Sam Winters think he was *doing*?" interrupted Jennings, firmly cutting off Kendrick. "I don't give a damn how pristine their motives were; he forgot a lesson of history that he above all men should have remembered. Whenever a select group of benevolent elitists consider themselves above the will of the people and proceed to manipulate that will in the dark, without accountability, they've set in motion a hell of a dangerous machine. Because all it takes is one or two of those superior beings with very different, *unpristine* ideas to convince the others or replace the others or survive the others, and a republic is down the drain. Sam Winters's high-sounding Inver Brass was no better than Bollinger's tribe of boardroom thugs. Both wanted things done only one way. Their way."

Evan shot forward. "It's precisely for those reasons—"

The doorbell of the Presidential Suite rang, four short rings lasting no more than a half-second each. Jennings held up his hand and looked at Khalehla. "You'd appreciate this, Miss Rashad. What you just heard is a code."

"A *what*?"

"Well, it's not terribly sophisticated, but it works. It tells me who's at the door, and the 'who' in this case is one of the more valuable aides in the White House. . . . Come *in*!"

The door opened and Gerald Bryce walked inside, closing it firmly behind him. "I'm sorry to intrude, Mr. President, but I've just gotten word from Beijing and I knew you'd want to know."

"It can wait, Gerry. Let me introduce you—"

"*Joe . . . ?*" The name slipped out of Kendrick's mouth as the memory of a military jet to Sardinia and a handsome young specialist from the State Department came into focus.

"Hello, Congressman," said Bryce, walking to the couch and shaking hands with Evan while nodding to Khalehla. "Miss Rashad."

"That's *right,*" interjected Jennings. "Gerry told me he briefed you on the plane when you flew to Oman. . . . I won't blow his horn in front of him, but Mitch Payton stole him from Frank Swann at the State Department and I stole him from Mitch. He's positively terrifying when it comes to computer communications and how to keep them secret. Now, if someone will restrain the secretaries, he may have a future."

"You're embarrassingly kind, sir," said Bryce, the efficient professional. "But as to Beijing, Mr. President, their answer is affirmative. Shall I reconfirm your offer?"

"That's another code," explained Jennings, grinning. "I said I'd jawbone our leading bankers on the QT not to get too greedy in Hong Kong and make it rough for the Chinese banks when the '97 transition occurs. Of course, in return for—"

"Mr. *President,*" interrupted Bryce with all due courtesy but not without a tone of caution.

"Oh, sorry, Gerry. I know it's top secret and eyes-only and all that other stuff, but I hope that pretty soon nothing will be withheld from the Congressman."

"Speaking of which, sir," continued the White House communications expert, glancing at Kendrick and briefly smiling, "in the absence of your political staff here in Los Angeles, I've approved Vice President Bollinger's statement of withdrawal tonight. It's in line with your thinking."

"You mean he's going to shoot himself on television?"

"Not quite, Mr. President. He does say, however, that he intends to devote his life to improving the lot of the world's hungry."

"If I find that mother stealing a chocolate bar, he's in Leavenworth for the *rest* of his life."

"Beijing, sir. Shall I reconfirm?"

"You certainly may, and add my gratitude, the thieves." Bryce nodded to Kendrick and Khalehla and left, again closing the door firmly behind him. "Where were we?"

"Inver Brass," replied Evan. "They created me and artificially put me before the public as someone I'm not. Under those conditions my nomination could hardly be called the will of the people. It's a charade."

"*You're* a charade?" asked Jennings.

"You know what I'm talking about. I neither sought it nor wanted it. As you put it so well, I was manipulated into the race and shoved down everyone's throat. I didn't win it or earn it in the political process."

Langford Jennings studied Kendrick; the silence was both pensive and electric. "You're wrong, Evan," said the President finally. "You did win it and you did earn it. I'm not talking about Oman and Bahrain, or even the still-underwraps South Yemen—those events are simply acts of personal courage and sacrifice that have been used to initially call attention to you. It's no different from a man having been a war hero or an astronaut, and a perfectly legitimate handle to propel you into the limelight. I object to the way it was done as much as you do because it was done secretly, by men who broke laws and unconsciously wasted lives and hid behind a curtain of influence. But that wasn't you, *they* weren't you. . . . You earned it in this town because you said things that had to be said and the country heard you. Nobody mocked up those television tapes and nobody put the words in your mouth. And what you did behind the scenes in those closed intelligence hearings had the Beltway choking in its fumes. You asked questions for which there were no legitimate answers, and a hell of a lot of entrenched bureaucrats used to having their own way still don't know what hit them, except that they'd better get their acts together. Lastly, and this is from me, Lang Jennings of Idaho. You saved the nation from my most zealous contributors, and I do mean zealous, like in zealots. They would have taken us down a road I don't even want to think about."

"You would have found them yourself. Sometime, somewhere, one of them would have pushed you too far and you would have pushed back and found them all. I saw a man try to lean on you in the Oval Office, and he knew when a tree was about to fall on him."

"Oh, Herb Dennison and that Medal of Freedom." The President's world-famous grin momentarily came back to him as he laughed. "Herb was tough but harmless and did a lot of things I don't like doing myself. He's gone now; the Oval Office did it for him. He got a call from one of those old firms on Wall Street, the kind where everyone's a member of some exclusive club no one can get into and you and I wouldn't want to, so he's heading back to the money boys. Herb finally got the colonel's rank he always wanted."

"I beg your pardon?" said Kendrick.

"Nothing, forget it. National security, state secret, and all that other stuff."

"Then let me make clear what we both know, Mr. President. I'm not qualified."

"*Qualified?* Who in heaven or hell is qualified for *my* job? No one, that's who!"

"I'm not talking about your job—"

"You could be," interrupted Jennings.

"Then I'm light-years away from being ready for that. I never could be."

"You are already."

"*What?*"

"Listen to me, Evan. I don't fool myself. I'm well aware that I have neither the imagination nor the intellectual capacities of a Jefferson, either of the Adamses, a Madison, a Lincoln, a Wilson, a Hoover—yes, I said Hoover, that brilliant, much maligned man—or an FDR, a Truman, a Nixon—yes, Nixon, whose flaw was in his character, not in his geopolitical overview—or a Kennedy, or even the brilliant Carter, who had too many brain cells for his own good politically. But we've come into a different age now. Drop Aquarius and insert *Telerius*—that's the full-grown age of television; instant, immediate communication. What I have is the trust of the people because they see and hear the *man.* I saw a nation wallowing in self-pity and defeat and I got angry. Churchill once said that democracy may have a lot of flaws but it was the best system man ever devised. I *believe* that, and I believe all those bromides about America being the greatest, the strongest, the most benevolent country on the face of the earth. Call me Mr. Simplistic, but I *do* believe. That's what the people see and hear and we're not so bad off for it. . . . We all recognize reflections of ourselves in others and I've watched you, listened to you, read everything there is to say about you, and talked at length with my friend Emmanuel Weingrass. In my very skeptical judgment, this is the job you must take—almost whether you want it or not."

"Mr. President," broke in Kendrick softly, "I appreciate everything you've done for the nation, but in all honesty there are differences between us. You've espoused certain policies I can't support."

"Good *Christ,* I don't *ask* you to! . . . Well, on the surface, I'd appreciate your shutting up until you talked to me about the issues. I trust you, Evan, and I won't close you out. *Convince* me. Tell me where I'm wrong—without fear or favor—that's what this goddamned office needs! I can get carried away on some things and know I should be pulled back. Ask my wife. After the last press conference two months ago, I walked into our kitchen upstairs in the White House and expected some kind of congratulations, I guess. Instead I got hit with 'Who the hell do you think you are? Louis the Fourteenth with regal decrees? You made as much sense as Bugs Bunny!' And my daughter, who was visiting us, said something about giving me a book on grammar for my birthday. . . . I know my limitations, Evan, but I also know what I can do when I have the *best* people to advise me. *You* got rid of the garbage! Now step in."

"I repeat, I'm not equipped."

"The people think you are, *I* think you are. It's why the nomination is yours for the taking. Don't kid yourself, you may have been forced on the ticket, but to deny you would be an affront to millions of voters, the PR people made that clear."

"PR? Public Relations? Is that what it's all about?"

"Far more than either of us would like, but, yes, it's a large part of what *everything's* about these days. To say otherwise would be to deny reality. Better it's people like you and me than a Genghis Khan or an Adolf Hitler. Beneath our differences, we want to save, not destroy."

It was Kendrick's turn to study the President of the United States. "Good Lord, you *are* a charmer."

"It's my stock-in-trade, Mr. Vice President," said Jennings, grinning, "That and a few honestly held beliefs."

"I don't know. I just don't know."

"I do," interrupted Khalehla, reaching for Evan's hand. "I think Field Officer Rashad should really resign."

"Also something else," said President Langford Jennings, his eyebrows arched. "You *should* get married. It would be most unseemly for my running mate to be living in sin. I mean, can you imagine what all those evangelicals who deliver so many votes would do if your current status was revealed? It's simply not part of my *image.*"

"Mr. President, sir?"

"Yes, Mr. Vice President?"

"Shut up."

"Gladly, sir. But I should like to add a note of clarification for the record—for God's sake, don't tell my wife I told you. After both our divorces we lived together for twelve years and had two children. We tied the proverbial knot in Mexico three weeks before the convention and predated the marriage. Now, that's really a state secret."

"I'll never tell, Mr. President."

"I know you won't. I trust you and I need you. And our nation will be better off for the both of us—quite conceivably because of you."

"I doubt that, sir," said Evan Kendrick.

"I don't. . . . Mr. President."

The bell of the Presidential Suite rang once again. Four short, sharp half-second bursts.

ABOUT THE AUTHOR

ROBERT LUDLUM is the author of twenty-one novels published in thirty-two languages and forty countries, with worldwide sales in excess of 200 million copies. His works include *The Scarlatti Inheritance, The Osterman Weekend, The Matlock Paper, The Rhinemann Exchange, The Gemini Contenders, The Chancellor Manuscript, The Road to Gandolfo, The Holcroft Covenant, The Matarese Circle, The Bourne Identity, The Parsifal Mosaic, The Aquitaine Progression, The Bourne Supremacy, The Icarus Agenda, Trevayne, The Bourne Ultimatum, The Road to Omaha, The Scorpio Illusion, The Apocalypse Watch, The Cry of the Halidon*, and *The Matarese Countdown.* He lives in Florida.